STEPHEN JONES lives in London, England. He is the winner of two World Fantasy Awards, three Horror Writers Association Bram Stoker Awards and two International Horror Guild Awards as well as being a thirteen-time recipient of the British Fantasy Award and a Hugo Award nominee. A former television producer/director, and genre movie publicist and consultant (the first three *Hellraiser* movies, *Night Life*, *Nightbreed*, *Split Second*, *Mind Ripper*, *Last Gasp* etc.), he is the co-editor of *Horror: 100 Best Books*, *The Best Horror from Fantasy Tales*, *Gaslight & Ghosts*, *Now We Are Sick*, *H.P. Lovecraft's Book of Horror*, *The Anthology of Fantasy & the Supernatural*, *Secret City: Strange Tales of London* and *The Mammoth Book of Best New Horror*, *Dark Terrors*, *Dark Voices* and *Fantasy Tales* series. He has written *Creepshows: The Illustrated Stephen King Movie Guide*, *The Essential Monster Movie Guide*, *The Illustrated Vampire Movie Guide*, *The Illustrated Dinosaur Movie Guide*, *The Illustrated Frankenstein Movie Guide* and *The Illustrated Werewolf Movie Guide*, and compiled *The Mammoth Book of Terror*, *The Mammoth Book of Vampires*, *The Mammoth Book of Zombies*, *The Mammoth Book of Werewolves*, *The Mammoth Book of Frankenstein*, *The Mammoth Book of Dracula*, *The Mammoth Book of Vampire Stories by Women*, *Shadows Over Innsmouth*, *Dancing With the Dark*, *Dark of the Night*, *Dark Detectives*, *White of the Moon*, *Exorcisms and Ecstasies* by Karl Edward Wagner, *The Vampire Stories of R.Chetwynd-Hayes* and *Phantoms and Friends* by R. Chetwynd-Hayes, *James Herbert: By Horror Haunted*, *The Conan Chronicles* by Robert E. Howard (two volumes), *Clive Barker's A-Z of Horror*, *Clive Barker's Shadows in Eden*, *Clive Barker's The Nightbreed Chronicles* and the *Hellraiser Chronicles*. You can visit his web site at www.herebedragons.co.uk/jones.

Also available

THE MAMMOTH BOOK OF

BEST NEW HORROR

VOLUME TWELVE

Edited and with an Introduction by
STEPHEN JONES

CARROLL & GRAF PUBLISHERS
New York

Carroll & Graf Publishers
An imprint of Avalon Publishing Group, Inc.
161 William Street
16th Floor
NY 10038–2607
www.carrollandgraf.com

First published in the UK by Robinson,
an imprint of Constable & Robinson Ltd. 2001

First Carroll & Graf edition 2001

ISBN 0–7867–0919–7

Printed and bound in the EU

CONTENTS

ACKNOWLEDGMENTS

I would like to thank Mandy Slater, David Barraclough, Nicholas Royle, Bill Congreve, Douglas E. Winter, Sara Broecker, Andrew I. Porter, Jo Fletcher, Gordon Van Gelder, William K. Schafer, Robert Morgan, Barbara Roden, David Pringle, the late Frederick S. Clarke, Andy Cox, Peter Crowther, Janet L. Hetherington, Richard Dalby, Robert T. Garcia, Jay Broecker, Andrew Smith, Frank Eisgruber, Hugh Lamb and Val and Les Edwards for all their help and support. Special thanks are also due to *Locus*, *Interzone*, *Science Fiction Chronicle*, *Variety* and all the other sources that were used for reference in the Introduction and the Necrology.

published in *The Third Alternative*, Issue 23. Reprinted by permission of the author.

AT EVENTIDE copyright © Kathe Koja 2000. Originally published in *Graven Images*. Reprinted by permission of the author.

PAREIDOLIA copyright © Steve Rasnic Tem 2000. Originally published in *City Fishing*. Reprinted by permission of the author.

I HAVE A SPECIAL PLAN FOR THIS WORLD copyright © Thomas Ligotti 2000. Originally published in *Horror Garage*, Issue #2. Reprinted by permission of the author.

THE HANDOVER copyright © Michael Marshall Smith 2000. Originally published in *Dark Terrors 5: The Gollancz Book of Horror*. Reprinted by permission of the author.

THE OTHER SIDE OF MIDNIGHT copyright © Kim Newman 2000. Originally published in *Vampire Sextette*. Reprinted by permission of the author.

NECROLOGY: 2000 copyright © Stephen Jones and Kim Newman 2001.

USEFUL ADDRESSES copyright © Stephen Jones 2001.

INTRODUCTION

Horror in 2000

WHILE THE GENERAL DECLINE IN THE NUMBER OF horror books published by the mass-market in North America continued, there was an astonishing increase in print-on-demand titles and, to a lesser extent, e-books, alongside the usually supportive small presses.

While it remains to be seen if the on-demand boom will be financially viable (the trade paperbacks are usually less attractive and slightly more expensive than regular books), it does mean that many out-of-print titles are again available through the Internet.

In America, Leisure Books editor Don D'Auria published on average two horror titles a month, while Kensington/Pinnacle began reprinting a number of titles from the old Zebra imprint as well as also releasing several new horror novels.

Carol Publishing Group, which filed for bankruptcy in November 1999, sold off its assets to Kensington Publishing Corp. for $2.5 million. The deal included a backlist of more than 1,500 titles and 130 unpublished projects.

In Britain, the number of reprint genre titles was up, mostly due to Orion/Gollancz's classic fantasy and science fiction series. And while there was an increase in the total number of mass-market genre books published in the UK, horror was down to the lowest number of titles to appear since the late 1980s, although it still accounted for a bigger share of the market than in America.

James Middlehurst, CEO of British publisher Dorling Kindersley, resigned after admitting that the company had "seriously misjudged" the number of *Star Wars* books they published. Although they printed thirteen million copies of two *Star Wars: Episode 1: The Phantom Menace* tie-ins, only three million copies sold and the company announced a pre-tax loss of £28 million. Subsequently, founder and chairman Peter Kindersley agreed to sell his shares in the company to the Pearson corporation, owner of the Penguin Group, for more than £3 million.

In December 2000, an Ontario teenager whose favourite writer is Stephen King was arrested and jailed by Canadian police after reading his story aloud to a drama class at Tagwi Secondary School in Avonmore.

The story was entitled "Twisted", and it ended with the implied bombing of a high school as an act of revenge by a bullied student. After the boy was suspended and then permanently expelled by the high school's principal, concerned parents also complained to the police. Despite the lack of proof that the story was anything but a piece of fiction, the sixteen-year-old was arrested and spent more than a month in jail charged with making death threats. The case sparked a national debate about freedom of expression and various Ottawa authors, including Charles de Lint, organized a support group for the youngster.

Originally announced as *Harry Potter and the Doomspell Tournament*, J.K. Rowling's *Harry Potter and The Goblet of Fire*, the fourth book in the phenomenally successful children's series, was already top of the Amazon.com bestseller list more than two months prior to publication because of pre-orders. With an initial 3.8 million hardcover run in the US, it was selling out just days after its record-breaking July 8th release.

Barnes & Noble had its biggest weekend in history, having sold 502,000 copies (including around 100,000 through its Web site) by the close of business on the Sunday night. Amazon.com had pre-orders of nearly 350,000 copies, and FedEx delivered 250,000 copies for Amazon on the Saturday, with ninety-five per cent of the orders arriving at customers' homes before 4:00p.m. With more than 50,000 extra orders being placed over the weekend, US publisher Scholastic decided to print another two million copies of the book. Scholastic also set a 3.2 million printing for the paperback edition.

A twenty-hour audio version of *The Goblet of Fire* from Listening Library went out with a first issue of 180,000 copies, the largest ever for a children's audiobook. Booksellers report that it was the fastest selling audiobook ever – children's or adult. Listening Library subsequently went back to press three times for an additional 110,000 copies.

In Britain, with a first print run of one million copies, the *Harry Potter* title broke UK publishing records by selling 372,775 copies on its first day. In fact, books by J.K. Rowling accounted for nineteen per cent of the total value of the entire British book market during the launch week.

Helped by the *Harry Potter* phenomenon, which accounted for nearly ten per cent of the company's total income, Scholastic's revenues were up ninety-nine per cent for the first fiscal quarter of 2000 in the US, while UK publisher Bloomsbury benefited from an increase of sales of seventy-eight per cent and profits almost doubled.

In March, author Nancy Stouffer filed suit in a US District Court against Scholastic, J.K. Rowling, Time Warner, Mattel and Hasbro, claiming eight counts of trademark infringement and unfair competition for the use of the Muggles characters in the *Harry Potter* books. In 1984 Stouffer wrote a book entitled *The Legend of Rah and the Muggles*, which also included a character named Larry Potter. A spokesperson for Scholastic described the suit "completely meritless". Neil Gaiman was also dragged reluctantly into the controversy when newspaper articles cited the bespectacled boy wizard hero of his 1990 graphic novel *The Books of Magic* as another influence. However, Rowling's childhood friend Ian Potter claimed that *he* provided the inspiration for her character.

Not that author J.K. Rowling probably cared all that much. Along with receiving an O.B.E. in the Queen's birthday honours on June 17th, she entered the annual *Forbes* survey of the world's richest entertainers with estimated 1999 earnings of $42 million. It was still some way behind Stephen King ($65 million) and George Lucas, who topped the list with an incredible $400 million.

In March, the headteacher of a Church of England Primary School in Kent, England, banned the *Potter* books because their elements of magic supposedly contradict Biblical teachings and the school's own "church ethos" and suggested that parents take similar action at home.

Meanwhile, a school superintendent in Michigan bowed to pressure from local groups and an advisory committee and withdrew most of the restrictions he placed on the *Harry Potter* books in 1999.

In early August, the Pagan Federation announced that TV shows such as *Buffy the Vampire Slayer* and *Sabrina the Teenage Witch* and the success of the *Harry Potter* books had resulted in a rapid growth of interest in witchcraft amongst children. The organization revealed that it was receiving around 100 inquiries a month from youngsters who wanted to be witches. Predictably, the editor of the Christian young people's magazine *Youthwork* said he had no doubt that such stories could "fuel a fascination" in the occult, leading to "psychological and spiritual damage."

A list of 100 titles adults most wanted taken off US library shelves in the 1990s was released to mark the American Library Association's 20th annual Banned Books Week in September. Out of 20,000 complaints over the past decade, the most unwelcome books were Alvin Schwartz's popular young adult collections of *Scary Stories*, while J.K. Rowling's *Harry Potter* titles made the list at No.48. Muggles for Harry Potter was a nationwide organization created by a school teacher and a parent to stop libraries banning the books. Also in the top ten banned titles were J.D. Salinger's *The Catcher in the Rye* and Mark Twain's *Huckleberry Finn*.

In early 2000, Stephen King signed a new three-book deal with Simon and Schuster in the US and Hodder & Stoughton in the UK worth, according to some press reports, a record-breaking $40 million. The deal covered two novels and a collection of stories.

King's non-fiction book, *On Writing: A Memoir of the Craft* was a slight but extremely entertaining volume split into three distinct sections relating to the author's memories of his early career, his advice on how to write, and his thoughts following his near-fatal encounter with a van in June 1999. The British edition from New English Library also included a short story competition, with the winner to be published in the paperback edition. It was won by Garrett Addams (aka Adam Howe), after King selected his story "Jumper" from among 3,000 submissions.

A follow-up volume, *Secret Windows: Essays and Fiction on the Craft of Writing*, was only available to members of the US Book-of-the-Month Club and included obscure fiction, essays and juvenilia by King with an introduction by Peter Straub.

With worldwide sales of 200 million copies, Dean Koontz's latest No.1 novel, *From the Corner of His Eye*, weighed in at a hefty 600-plus pages and had a first printing in America of 500,000 copies. It was about Bartholomew Lampion, whose eyes were removed by surgeons at the age of three but who mysteriously regained his sight a decade later. *Three Complete Novels* was an omnibus reprint of three of Koontz's horror novels: the pseudonymous *The Key to Midnight* (1979), *Cold Fire* and *Hideaway*.

With an American first printing of 750,000 copies from Knopf, Anne Rice's *Merrick* was a cross-over novel in which a descendant of the author's Mayfair Witches encountered some of her vampire characters.

Ramsey Campbell's latest novel, the psychological thriller *Silent Children*, was published in America by Tor's Forge imprint. It concerned a mother whose children were taken by a deranged killer who wanted to make them "perfect".

The Ghosts of Sleath/'48 was an omnibus edition of two recent novels by James Herbert, published by Encore.

Peter James' thirteenth novel, *Faith*, was aimed at the mainstream thriller audience as the eponymous heroine was menaced by her abusive plastic surgeon husband.

A Shadow on the Wall was a new ghost novel in the M.R. James tradition by Jonathan Aycliffe (aka Denis McEoin/Daniel Easterman), published by Severn House. It involved a Cambridge medievalist haunted by an entity accidentally freed from an opened tomb in the early 1890s. Under his Easterman byline, the author also published *The Jaguar Mask*, in which a series of ritual murders in France was connected to the discovery of a lost city.

Rain, *Lightning Strikes* and *Eye of the Storm* were the first three volumes in a new Gothic horror series published under the late V.C. Andrews® byline, but still probably written by Andrew Niederman. *Orphans* was an omnibus edition of the first four volumes in the author's 1998 series.

More family secrets were revealed in John Saul's *Nightshade*.

* * *

For pulp fans, *Shadows Bend: A Novel of the Fantastic and Unspeakable* by David Barbour and Richard Raleigh featured *Weird Tales* authors H.P. Lovecraft, Robert E. Howard and Clark Ashton Smith joining forces in the mid-1930s to save the world from the eldritch evils of the Cthulhu Mythos.

He may be in his nineties, but pulp legend Hugh B. Cave proved he was still going strong with the paperback original *The Dawning*, in which a polluted Earth took revenge on mankind.

A haunted prep school resulted in *Mischief*, a new novel by Douglas Clegg published simultaneously in mass-market paperback by Leisure and a 750-copy hardcover from CD Publications. The author announced that he was also donating all the paperback royalties of his original e-novel *Naomi* to the National Down's Syndrome Society.

A woman who sold spells was blamed for a miser's death in Andrew Neiderman's *Curse*, and a private detective investigated a series of strange deaths and a town of witches in Bentley Little's *The Walking*.

In Ed Gorman's *The Poker Club*, a simple suburban card game resulted in murder and included references to cannibalism and vampires, while Craig Spector's *To Bury the Dead* involved a firefighter investigating the murder of his daughter and was a "super-release" from HarperCollins.

Nicholas Royle's fourth novel, *The Director's Cut*, featured movies, murder and madness as a body wrapped in celluloid was discovered on the site of a suicide filmed fifteen years earlier. Jesus (aka "Joe Panther") was alive and well and tracking down serial killers in modern-day Melbourne in *The Second Coming*, the second book in the series by Andrew Masterson. In *Blood*, Joseph Glass' second novel featuring psychic Susan Shader, the police psychologist was on the trail of a serial killer. Mary Higgins Clark's *Before I Say Good-Bye* also involved a woman with psychic powers, and Yvonne Navarro's *That's Not My Name* was another psychological chiller.

Tom Piccirilli's *The Deceased* involved a writer haunted by the ghosts of his murdered family, and a painter encountered the ghost of a girl in Lisa Carey's *In the Country of the Young*.

Josephine Boyle's *The Spirit of the Family* involved a woman whose London flat was haunted by the spirits of previous occupants, and Nancy Atherton's character Lori and her ghostly

Aunt Dimity teamed up for the sixth time to solve a mystery dating back to the First World War in the amusing *Aunt Dimity Beats the Devil*.

Jeffrey E. Barlough's *Dark Sleeper* was a Victorian dark fantasy in which a series of supernatural portents heralded the raising of a demon by an ancient immortal, while Kim Wilkins' *The Resurrectionists*, set in a small Yorkshire village with a dark secret, came with a guarantee from HarperCollins Australia that it was "better than Anne Rice or your money back"!

Anne Bishop's *Queen of the Darkness* was the final volume in "The Black Jewels" trilogy, in which a witch's adoptive father Saetan (*sic*) and his sons Lucivar and Daemon were the heroes. *The Demon Circle* by Dan Schmidt involved a former Oklahoma policeman battling a Satanic cult.

A 4,000-year-old Peruvian mummy was the carrier of a deadly plague in *Excavation* by James Rollins (aka James Clemens). *The Summoning God* was the second volume in Kathleen O'Neal Gear and W. Michael Gear's "Anasazi Mysteries" anthropological horror series, and unfrozen prehistoric cats roamed the foothills of Southern California in Jeff Rovin's *Fatalis*.

Rick R. Reed's *A Face Without a Heart* was a contemporary retelling of *The Picture of Dorian Gray*, while Brent Monahan's *The Jekyl Island Club* was an historical mystery. William M. Valtos' *The Authenticator* drew on Edgar Allan Poe's "The Facts in the Case of M. Valdemar" when an investigator discovered a woman kept in a near-death condition.

Even excluding the *Buffy* and *Angel* tie-ins, the number of original vampire novels increased more than twenty-five per cent over the previous year, with the number of reprints also up.

Necroscope: Defilers (aka *E-Branch: Defilers*) was the second volume in Brian Lumley's third and final *Necroscope* trilogy. This time reluctant hero Jake Cutter was defending the Earth from an attack by the Vampire World while seeking personal revenge against the Italian mobsters who killed the woman he loved.

Hunting Ground was the fourth volume in Charles Grant's *Black Oak* series and involved the leader of Black Oak Security, Ethan Proctor, taking a much-needed vacation in Atlantic City, where he encountered vampires.

Chelsea Quinn Yarbro's *Come Twilight* featured Csimenae, a

beautiful vampire created by the undead Saint-Germain in Spain, and P.N. Elrod's undead private detective Jack Fleming returned in a new hardcover, *The Vampire Files: Lady Crymsyn*, the ninth in the series.

First published in the UK by Headline, Richard Laymon's *The Travelling Vampire Show* strayed into Ray Bradbury country with its tale of the eponymous attraction arriving in a sleepy summer town during the early 1960s.

Published by Canada's Baskerville Books, *Bloodlover* was the fourth volume in Nancy Kilpatrick's "Powers of the Blood" sequence and involved a clash of wills between the undead Comte Julien de Villier and his victim Jeanette Price.

Lois Tilton's *Darkspawn*, about a vampire prince released from his tomb, was the first original work of fiction from Hawk Publishing. Karen Taylor's *Blood of My Blood* was the fourth in the *Vampire Legacy* series, in which the undead Diedre Griffin searched New Orleans for her missing detective husband.

Laurell K. Hamilton's *Obsidian Butterfly* was the ninth in the series featuring Anita Blake, vampire hunter. This time, the tough heroine teamed up with a bounty-hunter who specialised in the preternatural to investigate a monstrous killer terrorizing the American Southwest. The paperback original also included an eight-page preview of the author's next book.

In Mick Farren's *Darklost*, a sequel to *The Time of Feasting*, a colony of Los Angeles vampires discovered that someone was trying to raise Lovecraft's Cthulhu!

The Silence in Heaven by Peter Lord-Wolff was the first in a trilogy about how vampires were created by a fallen angel, while travel writer Jade MacGregor was followed back from Scotland by the undead in *When Darkness Falls*, the second volume in Shannon Drake's paperback vampire trilogy.

Kyle Marffin's *Gothique*, published by Design Image Group, involved a group of urban Goths encountering the real undead in contemporary Chicago. *Lusts of the Forbidden* was another entry in the erotic vampire series by Valentina Cilescu, and Thomas M. Sipos' *Vampire Nation* was a first novel set in Communist Transylvania. It was available as a print-on-demand title from Xlibris.

Laws of the Blood: Partners was the second volume in Susan Sizemore's series about vampire Enforcers, and *Daughters of the*

Moon was a first novel by Joseph Curtin and featured Countess Erzsebet Bathory in the mid-twentieth century. Mary Ann Mitchell's *Quenched* was a sequel to the author's *Sips of Blood*, involving a vampiric Marquis de Sade in San Francisco.

Elaine Bergstrom's *Blood to Blood: The Dracula Story Continues* was a sequel to the author's *Mina* and again featured the characters of Mina and Jonathan Harker from Bram Stoker's novel, this time menaced by Dracula's sister, Joanna Tepes. Victoria Ann Roberts' *Moon Rising* involved Stoker in a fictional love affair in the nineteenth century Yorkshire town of Whitby.

Kim Newman's 1998 novel *Judgment of Tears: Anno Dracula 1959*, the third in the author's revisionist vampire series, was finally published in the UK under its original title *Dracula Cha Cha Cha*, and *Vlad Tapes* was an omnibus paperback containing Fred Saberhagen's novels *An Old Friend of the Family* (1979) and *Thorn* (1980).

Argentine psychotherapist Federico Andahazi's 1998 novel *The Merciful Woman* (*Las Piadosas*) was translated from the Spanish by Alberto Manguel and involved Doctor Polidori entering into a Faustian pact with a mysterious woman who agreed to produce for him the most compelling vampire story ever written.

In P.D. Cacek's *Canyons*, a rookie tabloid reporter uncovered a secret society of werewolves living in urban Denver. *Murcheston: The Wolf's Tale* by David Holland was written as a journal by a Victorian aristocrat cursed with lycanthropy, and Kij Johnson's *The Fox Woman* was a reworking of the popular Japanese folk tale about shape-changing foxes.

The political thriller *War of the Werewolf* was an on-demand title by Gary Greenberg and Jerome Tuccile, about a schizophrenic lycanthrope, while in Fredrick Bloxham's *Lycanthropia*, a group of Los Angeles werewolves hunted shape-changing killers to protect their own existence.

Douglas E. Winter's hardboiled first novel *Run* arrived boasting quotes from Peter Straub and Elmore Leonard. A "missing" chapter from the book turned up in *Criminal Minded*, a collection of short fiction from Canongate Crime presented by Ian Rankin.

Newcomer Jim Butcher's *Storm Front* was the first novel in "The Dresden Files", in which Chicago wizard Harry Dresden investigated a gory murder case and found himself suspected of the crime.

A woman's psychic powers linked her to a Civil War mystery in *By Blood Possessed*, a first novel by Elena Santangelo. In Alvin Lu's *The Hell Screens*, a Chinese American investigated a series of murders linked by an evil spirit, and Sarah Blake's *Grange House* was a literary debut novel with ghosts.

Mark Z. Danielewski's *House of Leaves* was a literary first novel about a building that was bigger on the inside than it was on the outside. With an introduction and notes by Johnny Truant, various editions of the Pantheon trade paperback and signed limited hardcover apparently had selected text printed in different colours and/or Braille.

First published in Canada, Andrew Pyper's debut novel *Lost Girls* involved a teacher accused of murdering two teenage girls near a haunted lake, while a student at Harvard discovered his dorm was haunted in *Adam's Fall* by newcomer Sean Desmond.

Will Self's satirical literary novel *How the Dead Live* was an after-death memoir by a woman who died of cancer. *From a Past Life* by Penny Faith was a ghost story about two women who shared a supernatural link, and Barabara Erskine's *Whispers in the Sand* was a supernatural romance set in Egypt.

In Arthur Rosenfeld's *A Cure for Gravity*, a motorcyclist attempted to escape a ghost and encountered the daughter he did not know he had, while Alice Hoffman's *The River King* also included ghosts and was set in a strange school.

Michael Faber's *Under the Skin* involved a woman who picked up hitch-hikers in Scotland for her own psychotic needs.

Mark Hazard Osmun's *Marley's Ghost* was a prequel to Charles Dickens' *A Christmas Carol*, telling the story of Jacob Marley, while Marcel Mario Salas' *Frankenstein: The Dawning and the Passing* was a literary sequel to Mary Shelley's classic with framing sequences set in 2351 AD.

Mary Shelley's original 1818 novel was reissued with a new foreword by Walter James Miller and a previously published afterword by Harold Bloom, along with a revised and updated bibliography.

William Beckford's 1816 decadent novel *Vathek* was reprinted by Creation Press with a new introduction by Jeremy Reed and illustrations by Odilon Redon. The same publisher issued the original *Lippincott's* magazine version of Oscar Wilde's *The Picture of Dorian Gray*, along with the preface and chapter XVI from the 1891 edition.

Tales of Soldiers and Civilians and Other Stories collected thirty-six stories and two articles by Ambrose Bierce, including ten supernatural tales from *Can Such Things Be?* (1893), with an introduction and notes by Tom Quirk. The complete weird fiction of Bierce's contemporary, Robert W. Chambers, was collected in Chaosium's *The Yellow Sign and Other Tales*, in which editor S.T. Joshi selected stories from several collections along with the novel *In Search of the Unknown*, and four chapters from *The Tracer of Lost Persons*.

M.P. Shiel's revised 1929 post-holocaust novel *The Purple Cloud* was reissued by the University of Nebraska Press with an introduction by John Clute.

The Conan Chronicles Volume 1: The People of the Black Circle was the first of two volumes collecting all of Robert E. Howard's original stories and fragments featuring his barbarian warrior from the pulps. Edited with an historical afterword by Stephen Jones, it was the eighth volume in Orion/Millennium's excellent new series of classic *Fantasy Masterworks* reprints.

Shirley Jackson's 1949 collection of twenty-five superior tales, *The Lottery and Other Stories*, was reissued with a new introduction by Patrick McGrath.

In Britain, Anthony Burgess' 1962 novel *A Clockwork Orange* was reissued as part of a boxed set with a widescreen video version of Stanley Kubrick's controversial 1971 movie.

Jonathan Carroll's stunning 1980 debut novel *The Land of Laughs* was the ninth volume in Orion/Millennium's *Fantasy Masterworks* series, while editor Douglas E. Winter's 1988 anthology *Night Visions 5*, featuring three stories each from Stephen King and Dan Simmons, and a novella by George R.R. Martin, was reprinted by Orion's classy Indigo imprint under the British title *Dark Visions*.

Nancy A. Collins' first Sonja Blue novel, *Sunglasses After Dark*, was reissued by White Wolf in a slightly revised tenth anniversary trade paperback, illustrated by a number of comic book artists.

Witch Hill, the late Marion Zimmer Bradley's 1990 novel about witchcraft and romance, appeared in trade paperback from Tor Books. Although originally published in 1993, the late Robert Bloch's anthology *Monsters in Our Midst*, co-edited with Martin H. Greenberg, finally received a paperback edition from Tor.

Veteran film producer Jack H. Harris sued the publishers of the *Goosebumps* books in the Los Angeles federal district court. Harris, creator of the 1958 cult SF movie *The Blob* starring Steve McQueen, claimed that the book *The Blob That Ate Everyone* was a breach of his copyright and that publication should cease and initial damages of $100,000 should be paid.

Jane Mendelsohn's *Innocence* was an offbeat literary vampire story about a series of apparent suicide pacts at a private Manhattan school which *The Village Voice* described as "a kind of *Rosemary's Baby* channeled through J.D. Salinger".

Dreamtime was a new six-part young adult series by different authors linked by The Shadowman, a mythic figure who manipulated the dreams and reality of children in an attempt to break into the real word. Contributing authors included Stephen Bowkett, Jenny Jones and Colin Greenland.

In the new series *The Saga of Darren Shan* by Darren Shan (actually author Darren O'Shaughnessy) the young half-vampire protagonist who travelled with the Cirque du Freak became involved with an agent of death and encountered a werewolf.

Legacy of Lies was the first volume in the "Dark Secrets" series by Elizabeth Chandler (aka Mary Claire Helldorfer), while Jenny Carroll's *The Mediator: Shadowland* was the first in a series of novels about a girl who could talk with the dead.

Witches' Night Out by the unlikely-named Silver RavenWolf was the first volume in the "Witches Chillers" series about a coven of five teenage friends using magic to investigate a murder.

A teen witch had to save her mother from witch-hunters and a murder charge in *Magic Can Be Murder* by Vivian Vande Velde, and a cursed pompom turned cheerleaders into monsters in Sarah J. Jett's aptly-titled *Night of the Pompom*.

In Amelia Atwater-Rhodes' *Demon in My View*, a teenaged author encountered a boy who was just like the villain in her vampire novel.

Don't Open Your Eyes was a new horror novel by Ann Halam (aka Gwyneth Jones) in which a teenage girl's boyfriend returned from the grave as a ghoul.

Something Wicked's in Those Woods was a first novel by Marisa Montes in which a pair of orphans encountered ghosts in their new home, and there were more spectres to be found in *The Ghost of Fossil Glen* by Cynthia DeFelice.

James A. Moore's *Under the Overtree*, published by Meisha Merlin, featured a race of evil woodland creatures who granted the wishes of a bullied teenager, and a mysterious ghost-hunter named John Crowley.

Beast by Jo Donna Napoli told the eponymous character's side of the story from *Beauty and the Beast*.

A young boy time-travelled back to the Irish potato famine in *The Grave* by James Heneghan, while in Claudio Apone's *My Grandfather Jack the Ripper* (originally published in Italy in 1998 as *Mio Nono Jack Lo Squartatore*) a teenager discovered he was living in the house of the Ripper's last murder and used his psychic powers to travel back in time.

Samantha Lee's *Amy* was expanded from the author's novella originally scheduled to appear in the 1999 mosaic novel *Horror at Halloween*, while the author's *The Bogle* was another volume in Scholastic's "Point Horror Unleashed" series that also included *Lowlake* by Roger Davenport and *In Spirit* by Nick Turnball. *Scissorman* was the bogeyman used to ensure children behaved in the novel by John Brindley.

The Cunning Man by Celia Rees was about the eponymous wrecker of ships, while the new *Mutant* series included *Ortho's Brood* by Roger Davenport, *Carnival of the Dead* by Laurence Staig, and *Dissolvers* and *Night of the Toxic Slime* both by Anthony Masters.

4 Fantastic Novels was an omnibus of Daniel Pinkwater's books *Yobgorgle: Mystery Monster of Lake Ontario*, *The Worms of Kukumlima*, *The Snarkout Boys & The Baconburg Horror* and *Borgel*, with a foreword by Scott Silmon.

Neal Shusterman's *MindBenders: Stories to Warp Your Brain* collected nine stories and an afterword by the author, while *Ghosts of the Southern Belle* was a picture book about a sea ghost, written by Odds Bodkin and illustrated by Bernie Fuchs.

Edo van Belkom selected fifteen tales of horror for Tundra

Books' superior young adult anthology *Be Afraid!*, including new
fiction by Steve Rasnic Tem, Nancy Kilpatrick, Ed Gorman, Scott
Nicholson and Paul Finch, plus reprints from Richard Laymon,
Joe R. Lansdale and Nancy Etchemendy. Only Robert J. Sawyer's
story seemed out of place, and this was a rare case where the
contribution by the editor turned out to be one of the best in the
book.

In *That's Ghosts for You: 13 Scary Stories*, editor Marianne
Carus collected a baker's dozen young adult stories (four originals) by Josepha Sherman, Nancy Etchemendy and others, most
of which first appeared in *Cricket* magazine.

From Hodder & Stoughton Australia, *Tales from the Waste-
land* was an apocalyptic horror anthology with stories by Robert
Hood, Lucy Sussex, Pamela Freeman, Jenny Pausacker and
others.

With *Top Ten: Horror Stories* from Scholastic's Hippo imprint, Michael Cox and illustrator Michael Tickner used such
classics as *Dracula, Frankenstein, Dr. Jekyll and Mr. Hyde, The
Hound of the Baskervilles* and "The Monkey's Paw" to create
jokes and cartoons around.

Peter Straub's *Magic Terror* collected seven stories, only two of
which were overtly fantastic but all were disturbing and engross-
ing.

Kim Newman had two new mass-market collections published:
Seven Stars collected five short stories plus the multi-part novel of
the title with an introduction by Stephen Jones, while Eugene
Byrne introduced *Unforgivable Stories*, which featured thirteen
stories, including two individual collaborations with Byrne and
Paul J. McAuley.

Richard Laymon's *Dreadful Tales* was a world first edition
hardcover from Headline, containing twenty-five stories (one
original) which were mostly unfamiliar to UK readers. The author
also included a brief preface in which explained why he didn't
read prefaces.

Edited by Stephen Jones, R. Chetwynd-Hayes' *Phantoms and
Fiends* was a hardcover volume of twenty-one previously un-
collected stories (two original) with an affectionate foreword by
Charles Grant.

Graham Masterton's *Feelings of Fear* contained twelve stories (three original), Bill Pronzini's paperback original *Night Freight* collected twenty-six stories (one original), and J.N. Williamson's *Frights of Fancy* contained sixteen stories (three original) with an introduction by Ed Gorman.

Boasting blurbs by Iain Sinclair and Harlan Ellison, *Time's Hammer: The Collected Short Fiction of James Sallis* was a welcome compilation of twenty-seven SF and fantasy stories by the one-time editor of *New Worlds*, published in paperback by Birmingham's Toxic imprint.

M. John Harrison's *Travel Arrangements* contained fourteen previously published stories, including an expansion of a story that originally appeared in Dennis Etchison's *MetaHorror* anthology.

Published as an attractive trade paperback by Australia's Eidolon Books, Terry Dowling's *Blackwater Days* was a series of seven linked stories (three reprint) based around Shaun Tan's cover and the patients and staff at the Blackwater Psychiatric Hospital in Everton, Australia.

From Canada's Mosaic Press came the trade paperback *The Vampire Stories of Nancy Kilpatrick*, a collection of nineteen previously published tales with an introduction by Chelsea Quinn Yarbro and a foreword by the author.

Dark Terrors 5: The Gollancz Book of Horror was the first bi-annual edition of the non-themed horror anthology edited by Stephen Jones and David Sutton. It included thirty new stories by Christopher Fowler, Chaz Brenchley, David J. Schow, Ramsey Campbell, Graham Masterton, Tanith Lee, Michael Marshall Smith, Roberta Lannes, Kim Newman, Lisa Tuttle, Dennis Etchison, Mick Garris, Peter Straub, Gahan Wilson and many others, plus a major novella by David Case.

Expertly edited by Nancy Kilpatrick and Thomas S. Roche, *Graven Images* featured fifteen tales of myth and magic by Storm Constantine, Kathryn Ptacek, Gene Wolfe, Esther Friesner, Yvonne Navarro, Nina Kiriki Hoffman, Chelsea Quinn Yarbro, Kathe Koja, Tanith Lee and others, including reprints from Robert Silverberg, Brian McNaughton, and a collaboration between Jack Ketchum and Edward Lee.

Kilpatrick was also one of the contributors to editor Michael Rowe's *Queer Fear*, somewhat unnecessarily subtitled *Gay Hor-*

ror Fiction and published by Vancouver's Arsenal Pulp Press as a trade paperback. It contained eighteen new stories by such authors as Douglas Clegg, Michael Marano, Gemma Files, Brian Hodge, Caitlín R. Kiernan and Ron Oliver.

Edited by Peter Haining, *The Mammoth Book of Haunted House Stories* featured thirty-five ghost stories by Joan Aiken, Robert Bloch, Ramsey Campbell, James Herbert, M.R. James, Nigel Kneale, Ruth Rendell, Ian Watson and many others, including an original poetic collaboration by eight-year-old Elizabeth Albright and Ray Bradbury.

Peter Crowther's *Foursight* collected four novellas in hardcover by Graham Joyce, James Lovegrove, Kim Newman and Michael Marshall Smith which were first published individually under the editor's small press imprint, PS Publishing. The stories were subsequently paperbacked together as two *Binary* "doubles" without Crowther's introduction.

Whispered from the Grave was an anthology of fourteen ghost stories (one reprint) compiled by The Design Image Group and featuring such authors as Nancy Kilpatrick, Rick R. Reed, Barry Hoffman, Don D'Ammassa, Edo van Belkom and P.D. Cacek.

From the same publisher and edited by Cacek, *Bell, Book & Beyond* was an anthology of twenty-one "Witchy Tales" by affiliate members of the Horror Writers Association, with an introduction by S.P. Somtow. Contributors included Michael Oliveri, John R. Platt and the team of L.H. Maynard and M.P.N. Sims.

Although subtitled "A Science Fiction Anthology", Ellen Datlow's superior *Vanishing Acts*, which featured stories about endangered species, included Suzy McKee Charnas, Paul J. McAuley, Ian McDowell, Brian Stableford, David J. Schow and Michael Cadnum amongst its sixteen contributors (four with reprints). Ostensibly a collection of fairy tale fantasies for adults, *Black Heart, Ivory Bones* co-edited by Datlow and Terri Dowling also contained some darker tales from among its twenty contributors, who included Tanith Lee, Neil Gaiman, Jane Yolen, Brian Stableford, Michael Cadnum, Joyce Carol Oates and Howard Waldrop. The editors' young adult anthology, *A Wolf at the Door and Other Retold Fairy Tales*, covered much the same ground with some of the same authors.

Martin H. Greenberg rescued the late Mike Baker's anthology

My Favorite Horror Story, in which such authors as Stephen King, F. Paul Wilson, Ramsey Campbell, Peter Atkins, Peter Straub, Poppy Z. Brite, Dennis Etchison, Harlan Ellison and seven others chose their favorite horror story by the likes of Robert Bloch, Richard Matheson, M.R. James, Arthur Machen, H.P. Lovecraft, Robert Aickman and Edgar Allan Poe.

In collaboration with Russell Davis, Greenberg also edited *Mardi Gras Madness: Tales of Terror and Mayhem in New Orleans* featuring eleven original stories by Charles de Lint, Nancy Holder, Peter Crowther and others.

Published by Thunder's Mouth/Adrenaline, *Dark: Stories of Madness, Murder and the Supernatural* was an anthology of twenty-one stories (including six novel excerpts) edited by Clint Willis and featuring Iain Banks, Shirley Jackson, Edgar Allan Poe and Rudyard Kipling. *One Dark Night: 13 Masterpieces of the Macabre*, edited by Kathleen Blease, included classic work by Bram Stoker, F. Marion Crawford, H.G. Wells and Mark Twain.

From Invisible Cities Press, *Ghost Writing: Haunted Tales by Contemporary Writers* was a literary anthology of twenty-one spook stories (four reprints) edited by Roger Weingarten and featuring John Updike, Peter Straub and others.

Edited by Nicholas Royle, the second volume of *The Time Out Book of London Short Stories* included fine work by such genre names as Christopher Fowler, Kim Newman, Toby Litt, Iain Sinclair, Paul J. McAuley, Conrad Williams, Rhonda Carrier, Chris Petit, Geoff Nicholson, Christopher Kenworthy and Michael Moorcock, although only some of the twenty-nine stories were fantastical. *The New English Library Book of Internet Stories* edited by Maxim Jakubowski contained twenty-four stories by such familiar contributors as Pat Cadigan, Kim Newman, Ian Watson and China Miéville.

Editor Paula Guran's *Embraces: Dark Erotica* was an anthology of twenty stories (two reprints) from Venus or Vixen Press featuring stories by Poppy Z. Brite, Nancy Holder, Jay Russell, David J. Schow and, predictably, John Shirley, while *A Taste of Midnight* was an anthology of eleven erotic vampire tales (two reprints) edited by Cecilia Tan for Circlet Press.

Marvin Kaye's anthology *The Vampire Sextette* was produced exclusively for Doubleday's GuildAmerica Books club. It contained six new vampire novellas with an erotic spin by Kim

Newman, Chelsea Quinn Yarbro, Brian Stableford, Nancy A. Collins, S.P. Somtow and Tanith Lee.

Published by Forge, the first annual collection of *The World's Finest Mystery and Crime Stories* edited by Ed Gorman and Martin H. Greenberg included fiction by David Morrell, Peter Crowther, Peter Tremayne, Edward Bryant, Joyce Carol Oates, Bill Pronzini and many others.

Ellen Datlow and Terri Windling's *The Year's Best Fantasy and Horror Thirteenth Annual Collection* boasted the usual fine cover painting by Tom Canty and included thirty-seven stories, ten poems and an essay by Douglas E. Winter, along with two summations, three separate round-ups and the usual list of "Honorable Mentions" which were not good enough to include in the book. *The Mammoth Book of Best New Horror Volume Eleven* edited by Stephen Jones contained twenty-one stories and novellas, along with the usual annual summary, extensive Necrology and list of useful addresses. Both volumes overlapped with an unprecedented six stories, by Steve Rasnic Tem, Gemma Files, Neil Gaiman, Tim Lebbon, Paul J. McAuley and Michael Marshall Smith. Four were picked by Datlow, with the remaining pair chosen by Windling.

After seeing nearly twenty per cent wiped off its stock market value in June, online retailer Amazon.com announced losses of $480 million for the final three months of 2000, a rise of $198 million on the same period in 1999. Although sales nearly doubled for the year, so did losses, with the result that 1,300 jobs (almost a sixth of the workforce) were made redundant in early 2001. The company predicted it would be operating profitably by the fourth quarter of 2001.

Barnesandnoble.com also laid off 350 employees (sixteen per cent of the workforce) after a larger-than-predicted net loss during its fourth quarter (up more than 260 per cent over the previous year, despite a rise in sales) and an overall loss of $275.7 million for the year.

Meanwhile, German media company Bertelsmann abandoned plans to float its online book and music site bol.com on the stock market in May because of "unfavourable market conditions".

Stephen King released his new 16,000-word supernatural novella, "Riding the Bullet", exclusively on the Internet in March.

The initial demand was phenomenal, with 400,000 downloads in the first twenty-four hours. The author estimated that he would make as much as $450,000 for the story (he would have received around $10,000 if he had sold it to *The New Yorker* or a similar magazine).

In late July, King stirred up plenty of publicity by offering an episodic horror novel at $1.00 per download through his Philtrum Press website. "In the 1980s, I started an epistolary novel called *The Plant*," he explained. "I published limited editions of the first three short volumes, giving them out to friends and relatives (folks who are usually but not always the same) as funky Christmas cards. I gave *The Plant* up not because I thought it was bad, but because other projects intervened.

"I was intrigued by the success of 'Riding the Bullet' (stunned would probably be a more accurate word), and since then have been anxious to try something similar."

There were more than 152,000 downloads of the first 5,000-word instalment of *The Plant* during the first week, with over seventy-six per cent paying the fee under an honour system. "We've proved that the guy who shops for entertainment on the Net can be as honest as the one in a retail bricks-and-mortar store," said King.

However, after the author increased the price to $2.00 and the number of downloads dropped below forty-six per cent, King announced in November that *The Plant* was "Going back into hibernation" after the sixth chapter and continuation of the story would be postponed indefinitely.

At least one commentator pointed out that by making his pledge over the Internet, King may have created a series of separate contracts with individual readers who, if he stopped publishing more instalments and they continued to make the due payments, could theoretically have grounds to sue him for breach of contract.

Meanwhile, it was estimated that the serial novel earned King more than $700,000, and the author's own publishing imprint, Philtrum Press, offered all six instalments as an e-book, *The Plant: Book One: The Rise of Zenith*, for $7.00.

Beginning in July, Douglas Clegg's free e-mail serial novel, *Nightmare House*, was distributed as a chapter a week to his mailing list, sponsored by Cemetery Dance. The haunted house posting also featured horror trivia quizzes with prizes including limited edition hardcovers and subscriptions to *Cemetery Dance* magazine. Meanwhile, Clegg's novella "Purity" was available on Internet-enabled cell phones as a free "m-book" download and attracted more than 10,000 readers in less than three weeks.

The online magazine *SciFi.com* edited by Ellen Datlow went on line in May with stories by Robert A. Heinlein, Pat Cadigan, James P. Blaylock, Howard Waldrop and others. It later posted such new fiction as "Castle in the Desert: Anno Dracula 1977" by Kim Newman, "A Cold Dish" by Lisa Tuttle, and "The Origin of Truth" by Tim Lebbon.

Darren McKeeman's *Gothic.net* was one of the most popular and successful electronic markets for horror, but amongst the other numerous online magazines and websites that featured fiction, poetry and articles were *Horrorfind.com*, Brett Savory's *The Chiaroscuro*, *Imaginary Worlds*, *Sinister Element*, Paul Kane and John Ford's *Terror Tales*, *Would That it Were*, Kim Guilbeau's *The Haunted* and Simon Clark's *Nailed By the Heart*.

Despite only being sold on diskette, CD-ROM or as a file download, editor Steve Eller's original electronic anthology *Brainbox: The Real Horror* featured a surprisingly strong line-up of fifteen contributors that included P.D. Cacek, Gerard Daniel Houarner, Charlee Jacob, Scott Nicholson, Brian A. Hopkins, Karen E. Taylor and Gary Braunbeck.

Interest in online publishing was given a boost when Random House Ventures, an investment subsidiary of the mass-market publisher, bought a "significant" minority share (reputedly forty-nine per cent) in e-book and print-on-demand publisher Xlibris Corporation. The company also created its own online imprint, AtRandom, and launched Nancy A. Collins' on-demand imprint Scrapple Press in June with the author's new collection, *Avenue X and Other Dark Streets*.

Stealth Press was a new imprint set up by Craig Spector and a venture catalyst company to sell books directly through the Internet and not through bookstores. The premier release in November was a beautifully designed edition of screenwriter Peter Atkins' 1992 vampire/serial killer novel, *Morningstar*. It was also the first American hardcover of the book. From the same publisher came *The Light at the End*, a reprint of the debut "'splatterpunk" serial killer novel by John Skipp and Craig Spector.

Meanwhile, Dave Hinchberger's Overlook Connection Press launched its own on-demand line entitled Infinity. One of the first titles was a reprint of Edward Lee's 1997 novel *Bighead* in the author's preferred version, which included extra material, illustrated by Erik Wilson.

Alan Rodgers' Lovecraftian novella *Her Misbegotten Son* appeared as a print-on-demand trade paperback from New Jersey's Wildside Press, which reported its sales more than doubled during the second half of the year. From the same imprint came revised editions of the author's *Bone Music* and *Fire*, plus *Ghost Who Cannot Sleep*, a collection of Rodgers' stories and poems with an introduction by Dean Wesley Smith.

Rodgers also contributed the introduction to Bruce Holland Rogers' collection of ten stories, *Wind Over Heaven and Other Dark Tales*, while Keith R.A. DeCandido introduced Adam-Troy Castro's collection *A Desperate, Decaying Darkness*, which contained thirteen stories (three original) and was published by Wildside, who also issued the author's collection *An Alien Darkness*.

Stephen Mark Rainey's *The Last Trumpet* collected thirteen loosely-connected stories in the author's Lovecraftian "The Fugue Devil Cycle", several featuring the mysterious Asberry family and the haunted town of Beckham. Rainey's *Balak*, also from Wildside, was a Lovecraft-inspired novel involving missing children and the monstrous entity Golgolith.

Darrell Schweitzer's *Nightscapes: Tales of the Ominous and Magical* was a print-on-demand collection of seventeen reprint stories from Wildside Press, and *Necromancies and Netherworlds* was a collection of ten uncanny stories, some with a touch of Lovecraft about them, by Schweitzer and Jason Van Hollander. Also from Wildside, *Tripping the Dark Fantastic* contained eight dark fantasy stories (three original) by David Bischoff with an introduction by Charles Sheffield.

DarkTales Publications and Internet company Bookface teamed up to offer readers the opportunity to preview publications online and then make print-on-demand downloads.

Sephera Giron's novel of contemporary witches and vampires, *Eternal Sunset*, was an online title available from DarkTales.

From the same imprint came Mort Castle's *Moon on the Water*, a collection of eighteen horror stories; *Clickers*, a giant crab novel by J.F. Gonzalez and Mark Williams; and *DeadTimes*, Yvonne Navarro's tale about a woman who sold her soul in return for nine lives. Steve Savile's *Secret Life of Colours* involved a former cop tracking down a supernatural serial killer, while *Tribulations* by Michael J. Straczynski was another demonic serial killer novel set in Los Angeles.

David J. Schow's 1990 collection *Lost Angels* was reissued by Babbage Press as an on-demand title. The new edition replaced one of the five stories with an original tale and added an afterword by the author.

The Snake Woman of Ipanema, Lucille Belluci's novel about supernatural revenge, was published as a print-on-demand title by iUniverse.com

One of the most disappointing books of the year was *Arkham's Masters of Horror*, grandly subtitled *A 60th Anniversary Anthology Retrospective of the First 30 Years of Arkham House*. Despite including mostly unfamiliar or previously unpublished stories by Clark Ashton Smith, Donald Wandrei, Robert E. Howard, Robert Bloch, Carl Jacobi, E. Hoffman Price, Ray Douglas (*sic*) Bradbury, John (*sic*) Ramsey Campbell, Seabury Quinn and eleven others, and a fannish but fascinating introduction by editor Peter Ruber, this collection of classic authors was marred by numerous typos, poor writing and some of the most mean-spirited author notes ever to grace a small press anthology. If ever there was a book that would have benefited considerably from the sure editorial hand of Arkham's late founder, August Derleth, this was it.

From the same publisher, *In the Stone House* was a collection of twenty-four of his own favourite stories from the past two decades by Barry N. Malzberg.

In February, Fedogan & Bremer announced a new distribution deal with Arkham House, the imprint it was set up to emulate in 1989. Along with the first of a planned two-volume collection of Donald Wandrei's eponymous pulp criminologist, *Frost*, F&B celebrated Hugh B. Cave's ninetieth birthday with the publication of *Bottled in Blonde* under its "Mystery" imprint. Containing a short foreword by the author and an introduction by Don

Hutchison, the hardcover also collected all nine of Cave's hard-boiled Peter Kane stories originally published in the *Dime Detective* pulp magazine from the mid-1930s until the early '40s. It was also available in a signed edition limited to 100 copies.

Cave also supplied the introduction to *The Vampire Master and Other Tales of Terror*, a handsome hardcover collection of nine pulp stories by Edmond Hamilton, published by Haffner Press. A 100-copy slipcased edition was signed by Cave and dustjacket artist Jon Arfstrom.

As part of its ongoing deal with the author, Subterranean Press reissued Joe R. Lansdale's early 1980s weird-ish Western *Blood Dance* as volume three in the hardcover "Lost Lansdale" series. It was available in a signed edition "limited" to 1,000 copies.

Lansdale's Edgar Award-winning *The Bottoms* was a new novel based on the author's Bram Stoker Award-winning novella "Mad Dog Summer" (from *999: New Stories of Horror and Suspense*), published in a signed and slipcased edition of 400 numbered and twenty-six lettered copies by Subterranean and a mass-market hardcover by Mysterious Press containing slightly more text. The author's killer hurricane novella, *The Big Blow* (originally published in Douglas E. Winter's 1997 *Revelations* aka *Millennium* anthology), also appeared in expanded form as a limited edition hardcover.

Tim Powers' ambitious historical thriller *Declare* combined spying and the supernatural in 1963, with appearances by T.E. Lawrence, Kim Philby and a touch of a Thousand and One Nights. It appeared in a special signed edition of 474 copies and a twenty-six copy lettered edition traycased with an original illustration by the author. Limited to 1,500 signed copies, *Night Moves and Other Stories* collected nine of Powers' stories (including a collaboration with James P. Blaylock, who also contributed an introduction), plus notes by the author.

Plastic Jesus was an alternate history novella written and illustrated by Poppy Z. Brite, about gay politics and British popular music. It was available in a trade hardcover edition and also in 600 copies signed by the author.

A Touch of the Creature was the long-awaited new collection from Charles Beaumont, the late author's first new book since 1968. Unfortunately, despite an introduction by Richard Matheson and an attractive supernatural-themed dustjacket illustration by Phil Parks, most of the fourteen previously unpublished stories were neither fantasy nor horror.

Once again ably edited by David J. Schow (with a little help from Stefan Dziemianowicz), *Hell on Earth: The Lost Bloch Volume II* contained four rarely-reprinted novellas from the pulps by Robert Bloch with an introduction by Douglas E. Winter and a transcription of a 1990 radio interview with the late author. It was limited to 1,250 signed and numbered copies and a twenty-six copy lettered edition.

Subterranean's *Taps and Sighs* edited by Peter Crowther was one of the year's best original anthologies. Squeezed between another introduction by Winter and a very brief afterword by veteran Richard Matheson were eighteen mostly excellent tales of ghosts and hauntings by a stellar line-up of authors that included Richard Christian Matheson, Michael Marshall Smith, Brian Stableford, Ramsey Campbell, Charles de Lint, Graham Joyce, Poppy Z. Brite, Ian McDonald, Mark Morris, Terry Lamsley, Gene Wolfe, Chaz Brenchley and others. The book also boasted a dustjacket illustration by J.K. Potter and was available as a trade hardcover, a signed limited edition and a signed lettered edition.

James P. Blaylock's first collection, *Thirteen Phantoms and Other Stories*, contained sixteen previously published stories (including the World Fantasy Award-winner of the title and two co-written with Tim Powers) in a hardcover edition from Edgewood Press.

Despite the death in 1999 of founder James Turner, his Golden Gryphon Press imprint was continued by his brother Gary with *Beluthahatchie and Other Stories*, a first-rate collection of eleven tales (two original) by Andy Duncan, with a foreword by Michael Bishop and an afterword by John Kessel. The same was true for *High Cotton: Selected Stories of Joe R. Lansdale*, an outstanding collection of twenty-one of the author's favourite own stories.

From Florida's Necro Publications, *The Long Ones* collected four novellas (one original) and an afterword by Lansdale, illustrated by Robert Copley. It was published in a signed 400-copy hardcover edition and a deluxe traycase edition of twenty-six copies.

Douglas Clegg's new novels *Mischief* and *You Come When I Call You* appeared from Cemetery Dance Publications. CD also published F. Paul Wilson's series of *Sims* novellas, set in a world in which most simple manual labour was done by genetically-altered chimps created by SimGen. *Sims Book One: La Causa* was published in a hardcover trade edition and a traycased edition of twenty-six signed and lettered copies, bound in leather, with satin ribbon page marker and additional artwork.

Originally published in paperback a decade ago, William F. Nolan's serial killer novel *Helltracks* was reissued in a revised version by CD with a new introduction by Richard Matheson, a new preface by the author, and the inclusion of Nolan's "Lonely Train a Comin", the original short story that inspired the book. It was limited to 500 hardcover copies signed by both Nolan and Matheson, and a traycased deluxe edition of twenty-six signed and lettered copies.

Thomas Tessier's *Ghost Music and Other Tales* was a collection of stories and novellas (including two originals), limited to 600 signed hardcover copies and a traycased edition of twenty-six signed and lettered copies.

Richard Laymon's novel *Once Upon a Halloween* was a fun series of tricks and treats, featuring Satanic cults, a haunted house and a cast of terrified teens, available in a signed edition of 2,000 hardcover copies. Cemetery Dance also published the first American edition of the author's *The Traveling Vampire Show* in hardcover.

Laymon's horror anthology *Bad News* appeared from Cemetery Dance in time for Halloween and featured fiction from the editor, plus Simon Clark, Jack Ketchum, Lucy Taylor, Rick Hautala, Gary Brandner, Bentley Little, Ed Gorman, Tom Piccirilli, Bill Pronzini, Edward Lee, John Pelan, Nancy Holder, Richard Chizmar, F. Paul Wilson and others. It was also available in a traycased lettered edition of fifty-two signed copies.

Edited by Richard Chizmar and Robert Morrish, *October Dreams: A Celebration of Halloween* was a grab-bag of twenty-two stories (eleven reprints), thirty "Favorite Halloween Memories", a poem and three essays. Contributors included Ray Bradbury, Poppy Z. Brite, Richard Laymon, Michael Marshall Smith, Caitlín R. Kiernan and John Shirley. A slipcased leather-bound edition of 400 signed and numbered copies included a special Halloween Art Section, containing full-colour paintings created exclusively for the book.

Nicely designed to look like the author's previous three hardcover collections from Scream/Press, DreamHaven's *The Death Artist* collected twelve superior short stories (one original) from Dennis Etchison, suitably illustrated with J.K. Potter's bizarre photo-montages.

Published by Gauntlet Press, *All the Rage* by F. Paul Wilson was another Repairman Jack novel in which mythology was made real by a new designer drug. Gauntlet also reissued Caitlín R. Kiernan's 1998 debut novel *Silk* in a 450-copy signed hardcover with a new introduction by the author and an afterword by Poppy Z. Brite. A deluxe limited edition was also available, and both versions featured artwork by Clive Barker.

From the same publisher came Kiernan's excellent collection entitled *Tales of Pain and Wonder*, illustrated by Richard A. Kirk. The hardcover contained twenty-one stories (two previously unpublished), an original poem, an amusing introduction by Douglas E. Winter, an incomprehensible afterword by Peter Straub, and a preface by the author. It was also available in a signed and numbered edition of 500 copies.

Dystopia was a hefty 500-plus page collection containing sixty memorable short-short horror stories by Richard Christian Matheson, beautifully illustrated with Harry O. Morris' disturbing colour photo-images. Introduced by the author's father, the legendary Richard Matheson, and with a sensible afterword this time by Peter Straub, the book also boasted guest pieces by Clive Barker, Ray Bradbury, Poppy Z. Brite, Ramsey Campbell, Ellen Datlow, Dennis Etchison, Mick Garris, George Clayton Johnson, Stephen Jones, Stephen King, Dean R. Koontz, Joe R. Lansdale, Michael Marshall Smith, F. Paul Wilson, Douglas E. Winter and several others. The special lettered edition was signed by most of the contributors (including King) and came with a video of the author's thirteen-minute directorial debut *Arousal* and a CD of him reading six of his stories plus music from his band The Existers.

Limited to a 350-copy edition from Gauntlet, David B. Silva's collection *Through Shattered Glass* contained seventeen short stories with an introduction by Dean Koontz, while *A Life in the Cinema* was an impressive debut collection of eight stories (two original) and an unpublished screenplay "written and directed" by film and miniseries-maker Mick Garris, with a little help from his friends Stephen King (introduction), Tobe Hooper (afterword) and Clive Barker (cover and bookmark).

The Ushers was a collection of nineteen extreme horror stories (seven original) by Edward Lee, published by Obsidian Press in a signed, limited hardcover. At least the author admitted in his foreword that he was "not trying to be the Proust of horror". Lee also introduced Overlook Connection's *Graven Images*, a downbeat novella by Gary Raisor available in a signed trade paperback, signed hardcover or signed leather edition.

Tom Piccirilli's *The Night Class*, from ShadowLands Press, was a murder mystery involving stigmata.

Edited by Edward E. Kramer and published by Bereshith/ShadowLands Press in a signed limited edition of 400 copies and a 100-copy gilt-edged deluxe edition with limited sculpture, *Strange Attraction: Turns of the Midnight Carnival Wheel* was an anthology of twenty-four stories and a poem inspired by the kinetic sculptures of Lisa Snellings. Contributors included Ray Bradbury, Gene Wolfe, Michael Bishop, Charles de Lint, Caitlín R. Kiernan, S.P. Somtow, Nancy A. Collins, Peter Crowther and Neil Gaiman, while Harlan Ellison supplied an introduction.

Unfortunately, HWA vice-president Kramer was subsequently arrested in August for allegedly molesting a thirteen-year-old boy and his fifteen-year-old brother. Prompted by an anonymous complaint, the editor and author was charged with aggravated child molestation and denied bail in a September hearing in Atlanta, Georgia. After being released on a bond of $75,000 in November, he was returned to jail after apparently breaking his bail conditions. Kramer pleaded not guilty to all the charges.

City Fishing by Steve Rasnic Tem was a superb, career-spanning collection of thirty-eight stories (four original) by a master of the form. Published by Silver Salamander Press in an edition of fifty deluxe numbered, 300 limited numbered, and 500 trade copies, the volume would have been even better had the author revealed a little about each of the stories contained therein.

Britain's RazorBlade Press issued Tim Lebbon and Gavin Williams' novel *Hush* in trade paperback. It involved an animal-rights activist who discovered an even more gruesome conspiracy behind closed doors. From the same publisher, *Hideous Progeny* was an anthology of twenty Frankenstein stories with an introduction by Kim Newman.

Co-published by The Alchemy Press/Airgedlámh Publications in a hardcover edition of 500 signed and numbered copies, Newman's *Where the Bodies Are Buried* reprinted four inter-connected horror novellas with a new introduction by Peter Atkins and interior illustrations by Randy Broecker.

Also from The Alchemy Press/Saladoth Publications came *Swords Against the Millennium*, editor Mike Chinn's anthology of eleven heroic fantasy stories (two reprints) by Ramsey Campbell, Adrian Cole, Simon R. Green, Joel Lane, Stan Nicholls and others. Featuring artwork by Bob Covington, David Bezzina, Alan Hunter and Jim Pitts, it was available as both a trade paperback and in a signed, limited hardcover edition.

Shane Ryan Staley's Delirium Books published Jeffrey Thomas' *Terror Incognita*, a collection of thirteen stories (five original) introduced by Mark McLaughlin and illustrated by Jamie Oberschlake. *Up, Out of Cities That Blow Hot and Cold* from the same imprint was a collection of fifteen stories (five original) by Charlee Jacob, with an introduction by Tom Piccirilli and interior artwork by Gak. Piccirilli also introduced Barbara Malenky's *Human Oddities*, a collection of six stories. P.D. Cacek contributed the introduction to *Cage of Bones & Other Deadly Obsessions*, a collection of twenty stories (eight original) by John Everson, illustrated by Andrew Shorrock. Each Delirium title was published in a limited hardcover edition.

Available in an edition of just fifty signed presentation copies for friends and colleagues, Jeff VanderMeer's *The Book of Winter* collected three reprint stories and was supposedly published by the author's fictional Hoegbottom Press. Out from VanderMeer's The Ministry of Whimsy Press and boasting a cover quote by Ramsey Campbell, Jeffrey Thomas' *Punktown* collected nine inter-related stories (two reprints) set on a planet where a hundred sentient species collided.

Dark Highway's Press published the original anthology *Skull Full of Spurs*, a "roundup" of thirteen weird Western stories edited by Jason Bovberg and Kirk Whitham, available in a 1,000-copy numbered edition with an introduction by Norman Patridge. Despite an excellent dustjacket illustration by Allen G. Douglas, the fiction by Brian Hodge, Jack Ketchum, Richard Lee Byers, Edward Lee, Yvonne Navarro, Rick Hautala, Nancy

A. Collins, Richard Laymon, Robert Devereaux and others was mostly disappointing.

Brian A. Hopkins' Martin Zolotow continued the occult detective tradition in *The Licking Valley Coon Hunters Club*, a novel originally serialised on e-mail and published in trade paperback by Yard Dog Press.

Thank You for the Flowers: Stories of Suspense & Imagination was a collection of thirteen tales (two apparently original) by L. Ron Hubbard Writers of the Future winner Scott Nicholson, published in trade paperback by North Carolina's Parkway Publishers.

E.P. Berglund's *Shards of Darkness* reprinted eleven Lovecraftian stories in an attractive paperback from Mythos Books and was the second volume in editor Robert M. Price's "Fan Mythos Series".

From Time Bomb Publishing came two new novels by Paul Pinn: in *The Horizontal Split* a young schizophrenic mother searched for her stolen baby in India, while *The Pariah* involved a psychotic who could infiltrate the minds of others.

Oklahoma's Hawk Publishing issued John Wooley's wish-fulfilment novel *Dark Within*, while the ubiquitous D.F. Lewis collaborated with his father, Gordon, on "ten honestly strange and mostly ghostly tales" in *Only Connect*, published by Cartref.

Wondrous Strange: Tales of the Uncanny was a collection of twenty-five stories (nine reprints) by Robin Spriggs from Circle Myth Press.

Dark Matters was the third Ash-Tree Press collection from Terry Lamsley. Limited to 600 copies and boasting another excellent Douglas Walters dustjacket, it contained eleven recent stories (two original), plus an introduction by the author about where he *doesn't* get his ideas from.

Limited to 500 copies, *We've Been Waiting For You* was a welcome collection from Ash-Tree of twenty-two (one original) of John Burke's "tales of unease", with an introduction by Nicholas Royle.

A.F. Kidd's *Summoning Knells and Other Inventions* collected forty-six ghost stories in an edition of 500 copies. *Shadows and Silence*, Ash-Tree Press' second original anthology edited by Barbara and Christopher Roden, was also the first book from the publisher to boast a full-colour dustjacket (by Jason van

Hollander). Limited to a 600-copy edition, the twenty-five ghostly new stories included work by Steve Duffy, Jessica Amanda Salmonson, Steve Rasnic Tem, John Pelan, Ramsey Campbell, Paul Finch, John Whitbourn, Hugh B. Cave and Stephen Volk.

Reunion at Dawn and Other Uncollected Ghost Stories was an unpublished Arkham House collection of seventeen stories by H.R. Wakefield, edited by Peter Ruber with an afterword by Barbara Roden. The volume finally completed Ash-Tree's "Collected Wakefield" series.

Expertly edited and introduced by Mike Ashley, *Phantom Perfumes and Other Shades: Memories of Ghost Stories Magazine* collected seventeen of the best stories to appear in the rare pulp publication between 1926 and 1931, while *The Horror on the Stair and Other Weird Tales* collected twenty-six stories by Sir Arthur Quiller-Couch, edited by S.T. Joshi.

The Haunted Grange of Goresthorpe by Arthur Conan Doyle was a "lost" 1870s story from *Blackwood's Magazine* published for the first time as a slim hardcover by Ash-Tree Press on behalf of The Arthur Conan Doyle Society.

Ash-Tree's companion imprint, Calabash Press, issued Ron Weighell's *The Irregular Casebook of Sherlock Holmes*, which collected five new stories by Dr Watson, three of which involved the supernatural and included appearances by M.R. James, Aleister Crowley, Arthur Machen and even Elizabethan Dr. John Dee.

Jane Rubino's *Knight Errant: The Singular Adventures of Sherlock Holmes* contained three adventures that Watson only tantalizingly hinted of, but never mentioned. Also published by Calabash, John Warwick Montgomery's *The Transcendent Holmes* featured a number of essays exploring various long-debated problems in the Holmes canon, plus a "dialogue" between the consulting detective and Watson.

Robert Morgan's Sarob Press published *Echoes of Darkness: Supernatural Tales*, a new hardcover collection of nine stories (two original) by L.H. Maynard and M.P.N. Sims, illustrated by Iain Maynard. From the same imprint came William I.I. Read's *Degrees of Fear: Tales from Usher College*, a collection of eight humorous "Dennistoun" stories (five original), illustrated by Nick Maloret. Both titles were published in editions of 250 numbered copies.

Richard Dalby's impressive "Mistresses of the Macabre" series continued with *"Number Ninety" and Other Ghost Stories*, a collection of fifteen macabre tales by B. (Bithia) M. (Mary) Croker, and *Not for the Night-Time*, an 1889 collection of four ghost stories and a poem by children's writer Theo Gift (aka Dorothy Henrietta Havers), both edited and introduced by Dalby, illustrated by Paul Lowe and limited to 250 and 300 numbered copies, respectively.

The publisher also inaugurated a new Sarob Science Fiction & Fantasy imprint with Brian Stableford's *Year Zero*, a satirical millennial novel illustrated by Tim Denton and limited to 300 hardcover copies. *Parallax View* collected six collaborative stories by Keith Brooke and Eric Brown plus one by each author. Limited to 250 copies, it included a foreword by Stephen Baxter.

From North Yorkshire's Tartarus Press, Rhys R. Hughes' *The Smell of Telescopes* was a hardcover collection of twenty-five often comic horror stories, published in an edition of 250 copies.

A separate edition of Arthur Machen's 1906 novella *A Fragment of Life* added an original fourth chapter and a new introduction, while a reprinting of Machen's 1933 novel *The Green Round* included an extensive introduction by Mark Valentine.

Valentine also contributed the introduction to John Meade Falkner's *The Lost Stradivarius & 2 Previously Uncollected Short Stories*, the title story of which involved a nineteenth-century student possessed by an eighteenth-century necromancer through a Stradiavarius violin hidden in an Oxford college. This 300-copy edition also included the tales "A Midsummer's Night Marriage" and "Charalampia".

Algernon Blackwood's 1912 collection *Pan's Garden* contained fifteen stories and a new introduction by Mike Ashley and was available in an edition of 300 copies. *Shapes in the Fire* was a reprint of M.P. Shiel's 1896 collection of five decadent stories, a poem and an essay. With a new introduction by Brian Stableford, it was published in an edition of 300 copies.

The Salutation was a reprint of the 1932 collection by the late Sylvia Townsend Warner, containing fifteen stories and a new introduction by Claire Harman. *Ringstones and Other Curious Tales* reprinted the 1951 collection of six stories by Sarban (aka John William Well) and added another recently discovered tale to the 350-copy edition from Tartarus.

From Runa Raven Press, Hanns Heinz Ewers' *Strange Tales* collected ten occult stories along with a foreword by Don Webb and a bio/bibliography by Stephen Flowers.

Edited with a preface by Mike Ashley, *A Haunting Beauty* from Seattle's Midnight House collected the best psychological horror stories by Sir Charles Birkin, limited to 450 numbered copies. For the same imprint, John Pelan edited an expanded edition of Clive Pemberton's rare 1906 collection *The Weird O'It*, and Pelan and Steve Savile compiled *The Black Gondolier*, the first of two volumes collecting the best of Fritz Leiber's horror stories.

With *Sesta & Other Strange Stories*, editor Lee Weinstein compiled a previously unpublished/uncollected volume of stories by Edward Lucas White. Also from Midnight House, and limited to 460 copies, came Dick Donovan's 1899 collection of fourteen stories, *The Corpse Light and Other Tales of Terror*, with an introduction by Richard Dalby.

Expertly edited and introduced by John Pelan but disappointingly illustrated by Kenneth Waters, *The Third Cry to Legba and Other Invocations* was the first in a proposed five-volume hardcover series of "The Selected Stories of Manly Wade Wellman" from San Francisco's Night Shade Books, containing all sixteen John Thunstone stories and five Lee Cobbett stories by the legendary pulp author.

From the same publisher, *As the Sun Goes Down* was a handsome hardcover collection containing sixteen stories (half of them original) by Tim Lebbon with an introduction by Ramsey Campbell, while S.P Somtow's *Tagging the Moon: Fairy Stories from L.A.* contained ten stories (one original), interior illustrations by Gak and photographs by the author.

New Genre was the first volume of a new bi-annual anthology series which declared its intention to "legitimize" the horror and science fiction genres. Editors Jeff Paris and Adam Golaski chose stories by Paul Walther, Charlee Jacob, A.R. Morlan, Mark Rich and Jan Wildt for their debut softcover.

Peter Crowther's PS Publishing continued to produce some of the most attractive and collectable chapbooks around with new titles by Stephen Baxter, Peter F. Hamilton and Ian McDonald. Tim Lebbon's carefully-observed zombie novella *Naming of Parts* was published in signed and numbered editions of 300 paperbacks and 200 hardcovers by PS, with an introduction by Steve Rasnic Tem.

Meanwhile, Crowther's own urban fantasy novella *Gandalph Cohen and The Land at the End of the Working Day* appeared as a chapbook from Subterranean Press in a signed edition of 250 numbered copies and twenty-six lettered copies, with an introduction by Ian McDonald.

James P. Blaylock's *Home Before Dark* was an original short story in Subterranean's new deluxe chapbook series, limited to 350 signed and numbered copies and featuring two colour printing throughout. It went out of print upon publication.

Garcia Publishing Services released Steve Rasnic Tem and Melanie Tem's semi-autobiographical short story *The Man on the Ceiling* as the first chapbook from the American Fantasy imprint. The 500-copy edition featured a cover illustration by J.K. Potter.

Len Maynard and Mick Sims' prolific Enigmatic Press published *The Dark Satanic . . .* which contained two terror tales from the North of England by Paul Finch. *A Letter to Lovecraft*, a special presentation by Enigmatic Press reprinting Peter Tennant's eponymous winner of The Enigmatic Story of the Year 1998-99, was illustrated by Iain Maynard. Maynard also supplied the artwork for *Millennium Macabre*, the sixth volume in the "Enigmatic Novellas" series, which collected three Scottish horror stories (one previously published online) by William Meikle, including a collaboration with Graeme Hurry.

As part of the series of "Enigmatic Variations" chapbooks, Derek M. Fox's *Treading on the Past* contained four new supernatural stories, including the title tale, introduced by Mark Chadbourn and illustrated by Frank Mafrici. In the same series, *Ballymoon* by Alastair G. Gunn collected three debut stories in the Jamesian tradition, illustrated by Cathy Buburuz, while Paul Finch's *The Shadow Beneath* contained three stories (one reprint), illustrated by Gerald Gaubert.

Enigmatic Press and The British Fantasy Society teamed up to publish *F20*, the first in a proposed series of annual chapbooks edited by Len Maynard, Mick Sims and David J. Howe and featuring fiction by Derek M. Fox, Steve Savile (a reprint), Paul Finch, Steve Lockley and Paul Lewis, and Tim Lebbon. Bob Covington and David Bezzina contributed the illustrations.

The British Fantasy Society also published *The Spiral Garden*, a collection of five stories by Louise Cooper (one original). It was edited by Jan Edwards with an introduction by Diana Wynne Jones.

From Shadow Publishing came David Sutton's fascinating seven-part memoir *On the Fringe for Thirty Years: A History of Horror in the British Small Press* with an introduction from Stan Nicholls and cover art by Stephen Jones.

Billed as "A Creative Tribute to Jack Finney's Novel *The Body Snatchers*", Day Off Publications' *Poddities* featured nine stories by such writers as Brian Keene, D.F. Lewis, Tim Lebbon, Dan Keohane and editor Suzanne Donahue, along with brief reminiscences and tributes from Michael Marshall Smith, Ed Gorman, Nicholas Royle, Thomas F. Monteleone, Stanley Wiater, Jack Williamson, Christopher Fowler, David B. Silva, Jack Ketchum, Christopher Golden and Ramsey Campbell.

Texas-based Gargadillo Publications published John Pelan's haunted house novelette *An Antique Vintage*, limited to 150 copies with an introduction by Simon Clark and illustrations by Gak and Allen Koszowski. Gak also illustrated Gerard Houarner's *Dead Cat Bounce: A Fable to Horrify the Inner Child*, about a dead cat's journey to Hell and back, published by Space and Time.

Chicago's Twilight Tales/11th Hour Productions continued its chunky chapbook series edited by Tina L. Jens with *Daughter of Dangerous Dames*, which included new and reprint fiction and poetry by a number of women writers, including Jody Lynn Nye, Karen E. Taylor, Nancy Kilpatrick, Carol Anne Davis, Chelsea Quinn Yarbro, Yvonne Navarro, Sephera Giron, Lois Tilton and Jo Fletcher. Also edited by Jens, *Cthulhu and the Coeds/Kids & Squids* contained mostly new comedy Cthulhu stories and poems from Charles Stross, Mark McLaughlin, Bryce Stevens, Jo Fletcher, Stephen Dedman, Esther M. Friesner and others. Andrea Dubnick edited *Tales from the Red Lion*, based around readings at the eponymous Chicago pub. It included ten stories and an interview and, like the other two volumes, was limited to 250 copies. Dubnick was also one of the featured authors in Tina Jens' *Sort-of Scary Stories: Tales of Make-Believe for Children*, which appeared in an edition of just fifty copies, featuring eleven stories by Bruce Holland Rogers, Robert Weinberg, Lois Tilton and others.

Haunted Dreams #3: Desecration Day was a chapbook from Paul Bradshaw's Dream Zone Publications that included two tales of crime and horror by Paul Finch and a "special bonus novella" by Simon Logan, illustrated by Desmond Knight. The busy Bradshaw was also behind Haunted Dreams Press, publisher of Peter Tennant's novella *Confession of a Hollow Man*, which featured an introduction by Andrew Busby and impressive cover artwork by Mitch Phillips.

Paul Bradshaw's own fiction was collected in *The Reservoir of Dreams* from John B. Ford's BJM Press. It featured ten new stories illustrated by Iain Maynard, Gerald Gaubert and others. Also published by BJM, illustrator Steve Lines' *Dreams of a Diseased Mind* was a collection of Lovecraftian sonnets purportedly written by the fictional mad author Haydon Atwood Prescott.

Paul Finch's *By the Flame Gas Flickering* featured four stories plus an introduction by Paul Kane, whose own collection from BJM Press, *Alone (In the Dark)*, contained twelve stories and a song.

From Nashville House, *Gothic Fevers* collected six stories by Gary William Crawford, selected by Bruce Boston and illustrated by Margaret Ballif Simon. Cullen Bunn's Undaunted Press published Octavio Ramos, Jr's *The Folio of Edicts*, a new story also illustrated by Margaret Simon, and *Pig Tales: Stories from the Trough*, a collection of seven porcine poems and stories by Mark McLaughlin and others.

McLaughlin was everywhere in the small press. Arizona's Eraserhead Press published his chapbook *I Gave at the Orifice*, a collection of seven previously-published stories and one original, while *Shoggoth Cacciatore and Other Eldritch Entrees* from Delirium Books contained ten comedic Cthulhu Mythos-inspired stories (four reprints), with an introduction by Simon Clark and artwork from Colleen Crary.

Simon Clark: A Working Bibliography & A Trip Out for Mr. Harrison appeared in an edition of 250 signed and numbered chapbooks and twenty-six lettered hardcovers. Compiled by Paul Miller and published by Earthling Publications, the booklet contained introductions by Tim Lebbon and Clark, and the first publication of the eponymous 1978 radio story.

Michael Marshall Smith: A Primary and Secondary Bibliogra-

phy was available in a special signed and numbered edition compiled and introduced by Lavie Tidhar and published in an edition of just forty copies from Last Call Publishing.

The thirteenth issue of Michael Malefica Pendragon's *Penny Dreadful* was a bumper 168-page collection of tales and poems of fantastic terror by Mark McLaughlin, Scott Thomas, James S. Dorr, Brian Keene, John B. Ford and others. Featured artist Eric York's work was excellent and should have been used on the front cover.

Isis Rising: The Goddess in the New Aeon was a massive collection of mostly new poetry and art featuring Mark McLaughlin, Steve Sneyd, Scott E. Green and Charlee Jacob, amongst others, edited by Denise Dumars for Temple of Isis Los Angeles. Published by California's Anamnesis Press, *The Weird Sonneteers* collected 123 Lovecraftian poems by editor Keith Allen Daniels, Jerry H. Jenkins and Ann K. Schwader.

Editor Scott Urban's Skull Job Productions published *A Student in Hell*, a signed chapbook collection of thirty-five poems by Tom Piccirilli with an introduction by Charlee Jacob and illustrations by five artists. From Louisiana's Gothic Press, *Yellow Rider and Other Fantasy Poems* was a collection of thirty-four poems by Steve Eng, selected by Gary William Crawford and illustrated by Charles Vess, S. Scott Sate, Hannes Bok, Jim Garrison and Mel White.

In mid-August, Wizards of the Coast Group announced the suspension of the latest incarnation of the venerable SF magazine *Amazing Stories* with the Summer 2000 edition. It was subsequently announced that the title had been purchased by Internet company GalaxyOnline (itself facing financial problems), which revealed plans to produce the periodical in quarterly electronic formats. However, after the resignation of GalaxyOnline publisher Ben Bova and fiction editor Rick Wilber, the deal fell through. *Amazing* had been published in various different formats since 1926.

Following the death of its namesake and founder in 1999, *Marion Zimmer Bradley's Fantasy Magazine* ceased publishing with its 50th issue in December.

Sovereign Media/Homestead Publications cancelled its fiction title *Science Fiction Age* with the May issue because of falling circulation, resulting in the resignation of editor Scott Edelman. The magazine, which started in 1992, published forty-six issues. A few months later, Edelman was appointed editor-in-chief of *Science Fiction Weekly*, an online magazine sponsored by the Sci-Fi Channel.

Meanwhile, *Science Fiction Age*'s sister magazine *Realms of Fantasy*, edited by literary agent Shawna McCarthy, continued to appear bi-monthly and included Gahan Wilson's regular book reviews, plus a Frankenstein story by Bruce Glassco and an article on movie vampires by Marty Baumann.

It was joined on the stands by the first issue of editor John O'Neil's quarterly *Black Gate: Adventures in Fantasy Literature* (cover dated Spring, 2001) which included new fiction by Charles de Lint, Jeffrey Ford and Richard Parks, a reprint from the late Karl Edward Wagner, and an excerpt from a new Elric novel by Michael Moorcock.

Gordon Van Gelder liked *The Magazine of Fantasy & Science Fiction* so much that he bought it. Editor of the fiction digest since 1996, he purchased the magazine in October from Mercury Press, Inc. and its publisher and owner Edward L. Ferman. Van Gelder then left his twelve-year editorial position at St Martin's Press to devote himself full-time to the title, which began publishing in 1949.

During the year, *F&SF* published stories and novellas by John Whitbourn, S.N. Dyer, Tanith Lee, Bradley Denton, M. John Harrison, Joyce Carol Oates, Gary W. Shockley, Brian Stableford, Tananarive Due, Jack Dann, Nina Kiriki Hoffman, Jack Cady, Dale Bailey, Michael Blumlein, Scott Bradfield and Ray Bradbury, plus non-fiction from Daniel Keyes, Paul J. McAuley, Mike Ashley and David Langford, and the usual book review columns by Charles de Lint, Robert K.J. Killheffer, Elizabeth Hand, Michelle West and James Sallis.

Knowledgeably edited by Paula Guran, *Horror Garage* published its first two issues with fiction by the prerequisite John Shirley, Brian Hodge, Kathe Koja, Dennis Etchison, Norman Partridge, Thomas S. Roche, Caitlín R. Kiernan, Ed Gorman, David J. Schow, Steve Rasnic Tem, Thomas Tessier, Elizabeth Engstrom, Thomas Ligotti and others, along with interviews with Julie Strain, Alice Cooper and Craig Spector, essays on Wes Craven and (of course) John Shirley, plus music-themed articles and book and video/DVD reviews. The first issue also included a free "Shocking Sounds of Horror" CD featuring Alice Cooper. Once the untidy design is sorted out, the magazine could become a major market for new horror fiction.

Editor and publisher David Pringle's *Interzone* featured some fine horror stories by Liz Williams, Richard Calder's "Lord Soho" historical fantasy series, and fiction from Don Webb, Tanith Lee and Yvonne Navarro, amongst others. There was also a guest editorial by Bruce Sterling; interviews with Guy Gavriel Kay, Paul Di Filippo, Harlan Ellison, Alastair Reynolds, John Meaney, Tricia Sullivan, Ben Jeapes, Steven Gould and Laura J. Mixon, Philip Pullman, Walter Jon Williams, Juliet McKenna, and Charles de Lint; the customary lively letters and controversial columns, plus film and book reviews.

Despite contributions from Keith Roberts, Stephen Baxter, Eric Brown, John Christopher, Garry Kilworth, Charles Stross, Jack Deighton, Barrington J. Bayley and others, *Spectrum SF*, a new British paperback-format magazine from editor Paul Fraser, still had a very long way to go before it could come close to matching the quality of *Interzone*.

Richard T. Chizmar's *Cemetery Dance* managed just a single issue which featured fiction from Graham Masterton, Tim Lebbon and Charles Beaumont, plus interviews with Christopher Golden and Leisure Books editor Don D'Auria.

As usual, editor Andy Cox produced four impressive-looking issues of *The Third Alternative* featuring cutting-edge fiction from M. John Harrison, Charles M. Saplak, Graham Joyce, Mark Morris, Rhys Hughes, Paul J. McAuley, Christopher Kenworthy, Charlee Jacob, Conrad Williams and others, along with regular columns by Peter Crowther and Allen Ashley, interviews with William Gibson and Peter Straub, features on Ed Wood, Dennis Potter, Federico Fellini and Jan Svankmajer, and numerous book reviews.

Also from TTA Press and editor Cox, the perfect-bound *Crimewave 3: Bringing Down the House* included fiction from Chaz Brenchley, James Lovegrove, Peter Crowther and Tom Piccirilli, while *4: Mood Indigo* featured contributions from Sean Doolittle, Marion Arnott, Brian Hodge and Brenchley again. Another TTA publication was *Zene*, a nicely-produced market guide to the independent press with reviews and short features.

Edited by George Scithers and Darrell Schweitzer and now in its "77th year", DNA Publications' *Weird Tales* produced four quarterly issues of the much-diminished pulp magazine featuring fiction from William F. Nolan, Stephen Dedman, Ian Watson, Brian Stableford, Tanith Lee, Richard A. Lupoff, Don Webb and Brian A. Hopkins, plus an interview with Neil Gaiman.

Angela Kessler's vampire magazine *Dreams of Decadence* was also published by DNA, and the three issues which appeared included a novel excerpt by Laurell K. Hamilton and short fiction from Josepha Sherman, Lawrence Watt-Evans, Lois Tilton, Don Webb and Laura Anne Gilman.

After a hiatus of more than three years, the "quarterly" *Century*, edited by Robert K.J. Killheffer and Jenna A. Felice, managed two issues and included some fine fiction by Michael Bishop, Ian R. MacLeod, Kathe Koja and Terri Windling.

Patrick and Honna Swenson's attractive digest *Talebones* produced three issues featuring science fiction and dark fantasy stories and poetry by James Van Pelt, Mark McLaughlin, Bruce Boston, Steve Beai and others, along with interviews with Greg Bear and Amy Thomson and the usual review columns by Ed Bryant, Janna Silverstein and others.

Sherry Decker's "Wondrously Weird & Offbeat" *Indigenous Fiction* published three issues of fiction and poetry by Mark McLaughlin, Charlee Jacob, Gerard Daniel Houarner and others, plus an interview with Frederik Pohl.

The two issues of Gordon Linzner's *Space and Time* included stories and poetry from James Van Pelt, Charlee Jacob, Joey Froehlich, Del Stone Jr. and others, along with a colour cover by Allen Koszowski.

Edited by Daniel Conrad and Benoît Domis, the attractive French trade paperback magazine *Ténèbres* featured fiction from Richard Matheson, Richard Christian Matheson, Roberta Lannes, Norman Patridge, Brian A. Hopkins and numerous French writers, plus interviews with both Mathesons and artist Alan M. Clark.

Wine Dark Sea was a new Australian magazine, edited by Adrian Tan.

The July/August issue of *Firsts: The Book Collector's Magazine* featured an excellent article on collecting Robert E. Howard books by Don Herron. The same issue also included pieces on remembering Charles Beaumont by William F. Nolan, Davis Grubb's *The Night of the Hunter*, and restoring an early edition of Jules Verne's *Twenty Thousand Leagues Under the Sea*. The October issue was a "SciFi & Fantasy" special with features on collecting Clark Ashton Smith with a checklist by Herron, an overview of "The Best of 1999" (which gave short shrift to horror), a conversation with Jonathan Lethem and a look at Curt Siodmak's *Donovan's Brain*.

The July *Paperback Parade* was a special H.P. Lovecraft issue with articles on collecting HPL paperbacks and the illustrated Cthulhu Mythos, and an appreciation of the author by Gary Lovisi.

The September/October issue of *Book* featured articles and interviews with both Anne Rice and Ursula K. Le Guin.

The founder of *Famous Monsters of Filmland*, Forrest J Ackerman, was awarded more than $720,000 in compensatory and punitive damages by a Los Angeles court in his case against former business associate Ray Ferry, the current owner of the magazine title. Ackerman's suit charged his former business partner with fraud, deceit, breach of contract and trademark violation for using the pseudonym "Dr Acula". Amongst those who testified on Ackerman's behalf were Ray Bradbury (who turned eighty on August 22nd) and John Landis. Ferry's counter-suit, in which he claimed that the eighty-three-year-old Ackerman was stalking him and sending threatening faxes, was thrown out by the jury.

Frederick S. Clarke's excellent *Cinefantastique*, "The Magazine with a Sense of Wonder", continued its bi-monthly schedule with cover features on *The Green Mile*, *The World is Not Enough*, *Star Trek: Voyager*, *Babylon 5* (a double issue), *X-Men*, *The X Files* and *Star Trek: Deep Space Nine* (another double issue).

David Miller's monthly *Shivers*, Britain's definitive "Magazine of Horror Entertainment" from Visual Imagination, looked at *The League of Gentlemen*, *A Nightmare on Elm Street*, *Buffy the Vampire Slayer*, *The Evil Dead*, *Lost Souls*, *Nightbreed*, *The Cell*, *The People Under the Stairs*, Tigon productions, and Italian director Mario Bava (by Joe Dante!). It also included interviews with Sean Cunningham, Alyson Hannigan (from *Buffy*), Robert

Zemeckis, Harrison Ford, Chuck Russell, Dario Argento, Brian Clemens, Brian Yuzna and Don Sharp, tributes to Peter Cushing and Michael Ripper, regular columns by Ingrid Pitt, Kim Newman and Josephine Botting, and the usual film, video, TV and book reviews.

Its companion title, *Starburst*, included the opinion piece "Whatever Happened to Horror?" by book publicist Nicola Sinclair.

Tim and Donna Lucas' always fascinating *Video Watchdog* featured such contributors as Kim Newman, Douglas E. Winter, Max Allan Collins, Ken Hanke and M.J. Simpson writing about *The Blair Witch Project*, James Bond, Stanley Kubrick, Stephen Weeks, Poverty Row Horror, Dr. Mabuse, Eurociné, Hercules, Donald Cammell, Universal Monsters and Paul Naschy. There were also interviews with Richard Gordon, Bert I. Gordon and Herschell Gordon Lewis, and the usual detailed video, DVD and audio reviews.

Michael Stein and James J.J. Wilson's enjoyable *Filmfax: The Magazine of Unusual Film & Television* included interviews with veteran actors Christopher Lee, Carla Laemmle, Turhan Bey, Francine York, Gordon Mitchell and Douglas Fairbanks Jr, writer Earl Hammer Jr, directors Jim Clark and Paul Landres, plus many others, along with a tribute to Sir Alec Guinness and AIP producer Louis M. "Deke" Heyward's ongoing reminiscences.

Following his resignation from the company, editor Scott Edelman was replaced by Dan Perez on Sovereign Media's *Sci-Fi Entertainment: The Official Magazine of the Sci-Fi Channel*. The multi-media news and reviews title got a new design and went to a bi-monthly schedule. Issues included features on *Sleepy Hollow*, *Pitch Black*, *The Hollow Man*, *X-Men*, *Blair Witch 2*, make-up artist Tom Savini, and such TV shows as *Angel*, *Harsh Realm*, *The Others*, *Lexx* and *The Invisible Man*.

Titan Magazines continued to turn out monthly titles dedicated to *Buffy the Vampire Slayer*, *Xena Warrior Princess*, *The X Files* and other TV tie-ins.

Empire's *The Greatest Horror Movies Ever: The Definitive Guide*, was a special glossy collectors' edition that covered such topics as Creature Features, Nightmare Movies, Hauntings, Slasher Movies, Diabolic, Psychomania and Comedy Horror.

Profiling forty-six films, from *An American Werewolf in London* to *Witchfinder General*, contributors included Kim Newman.

Locus, the newspaper of the science fiction field, reached its thirty-third year of publication with interviews with artists Leo and Diane Dillon, and authors Brian Aldiss, Laurell K. Hamilton, Terry Bisson and George R.R. Martin, amongst many others.

Editor/publisher Andrew I. Porter managed to get out two more issues of his newszine *Science Fiction Chronicle* (founded in 1979) before he sold the title to Warren Lapine's DNA Publications, the publishers of *Weird Tales*, *Dreams of Decadence* and several other periodicals. Porter remained with the magazine as news editor, and DNA announced plans to eventually increase the title's schedule back to monthly. Under its new publisher, *SFC* managed a further two issues during the year, but these suffered from poor design and numerous typographical errors (recurring problems with DNA-published titles). Along with the usual news and reviews from Jeff Rovin and Don D'Ammassa, the magazine also featured interviews with Nalo Hopkinson, Robert J. Sawyer, George Zebrowski and Bradley Denton, plus articles by Frederik Pohl, John Betancourt, Cecilia Tan and Allen M. Steele.

Building upon its success as the UK's major small press magazine of supernatural fiction, *Enigmatic Tales* under the tireless editorship of L.H. Maynard and M.P.N. Sims expanded into a hefty perfect-bound paperback featuring fiction from Tim Lebbon, Peter Tennant, Alec Worley, D.F. Lewis and his father Gordon, John Pelan, James S. Dorr, Iain Maynard and many others, along with Hugh Lamb's fascinating rediscovery series "Tales from the Grave".

However, in August, Maynard and Sims announced that Enigmatic Press was suspending its operations due to a withdrawal of funds from the Eastern Arts Board, which constituted more than sixty per cent of their revenue support. Despite attempts to find alternative sources of funding, the 80,000-word *Enigmatic Tales* No.10 was the final issue, while Enigmatic Variations and the Enigmatic Electronic web-zine ceased publication immediately. "This is entirely due to the withdrawal of support from Eastern Arts Board," revealed Sims, "who consider the project was not viewed a priority in relation to other demands." The editors added that they would try to resurrect an imprint in the future, and that Enigmatic Press "will be kept in a state of suspended animation".

Ghosts & Scholars from Haunted Library Publications contained the usual M.R. James-inspired fiction, reviews and letters. Edited by Barbara and Christopher Roden, *All Hallows*, the journal of The Ghost Story Society, published excellent perfect-bound editions featuring fascinating articles by Steve Duffy, David G. Rowlands, Andy Sawyer, Hugh Lamb and Richard Dalby; M.R. Jamesian fiction from Geoffrey Warburton, Paul Finch, John Whitbourn, Michael Chislett, Tim Waggoner, David G. Rowlands, Tina Rath and others, along with all the usual news, reviews, letters and queries.

Graeme Hurry's dependable *Kimota* featured fiction by Paul Finch, Peter Tennant, Hugh Cook and others, plus some impressive artwork by the mysteriously named "T23".

Although it had published nothing new since Summer 1999, owner Marc Michaud denied that Necronomicon Press was in financial troubles or going out of business. However, Robert M. Price's long-running *Crypt of Cthulhu* magazine moved to Mythos Books with two delayed issues featuring Lovecraftian fan fiction and articles by Will Murray, T.G.L. Cockcroft, Kenneth W. Faig, Jr, Darrell Schweitzer and others.

After its launch in 1999, Cullen Bunn's magazine of horror and dark fantasy, *Whispers from a Shattered Forum*, continued with new issues featuring fiction and poetry by Suzanne Donahue, Scott E. Green, Sandy DeLuca, Thomas Zimmerman and D.F. Lewis, amongst others.

Paul J. Lockley's *Unhinged*, subtitled "A Magazine of Disturbing Fiction", also entered its second year with two new issues, a new design, and fiction and artwork by D.F. Lewis, Peter Tennant, Gerald Gaubert and others. It subsequently changed to an electronic format.

The eighth issue of editor Paul Bradshaw's *The Dream Zone* included stories by D.F. Lewis, Paul Lockey, Paul Finch, Peter Tennant, John B. Ford and others, plus small press reviews, a letters column and artwork by Iain Maynard, Gerald Gaubert and Desmond Knight.

The first issue of Sandy DeLuca's *Something Wicked: A Tapestry of Darkness* featured fiction by Trey R. Barker, Gerard

Daniel Houarner, Scott H. Urban, the ever-busy Mark McLaughlin, and others.

Dark Regions & Horror Magazine published an "All Fantasy Issue" featuring stories and poetry by Ardath Mayhar, Ken Wisman, Mary Soon Lee, Lois Tilton, Bruce Boston, Mark McLaughlin and others, plus an interview with Raymond Feist.

Prism UK, the British Fantasy Society's bi-monthly news and reviews magazine, expanded under editor Jane Prior but was burdened for most of the year with dull clip-art covers. The six perfect-bound issues featured regular columns by Chaz Brenchley and Tom Arden, articles from Mark McLaughlin, Jane Yolen, Guy N. Smith and others, interviews with Peter Cannon, Stephen Bowkett and David Gemmell, plus numerous book and media reviews.

With the May issue, author Kathryn Ptacek took over as editor of *The Official Newsletter of the Horror Writers Association*, following the resignation of previous editor Vincent M. Harper. The quality, content and frequency of the monthly magazine immediately improved under Ptacek's guidance, and it featured interviews with Tor Books editor Melissa Ann Singer (a reprint) and UK author D.F. Lewis, along with plenty of news, articles, convention reports and market reports. Only Brian Keene's somewhat selfish and mean-spirited advice about how horror authors should promote themselves at the expense of other writers and bookstore staff gave the wrong impression. He should perhaps have taken notice of fellow columnist Steve Beai's rules on how to behave professionally and courteously to fellow writers and editors.

For fans of Harlan Ellison, *Rabbit Hole* was the newsletter of The Harlan Ellison Recording Collection. Edited by the author's wife Susan, for $10 per year members received four issues of the magazine containing news and views by and about Ellison, along with exclusive offers of signed books.

With a useful foreword by Ramsey Campbell, The British Library's *Shadows in the Attic: A Guide to British Supernatural Fiction 1820–1950* was a hefty 550-plus page bibliographic tome compiled by professional librarian Neil Wilson, which catalogued the work of 200 writers of supernatural fiction in alphabetical order with bibliographic and biographical information given on each author.

Published by McFarland, Jean-Marc Lofficier and Randy Lofficier's 800-page *French Science Fiction, Fantasy, Horror and Pulp Fiction: A Guide to Cinema, Television, Radio, Animation, Comic Books and Literature* contained exactly what the title said it did, along with an introduction by Stephen R. Bissette. From the same publisher, James R. Keller's *Anne Rice and Sexual Politics: The Early Novels* looked at the author's vampire novels and pseudonymous erotica.

Edo Van Belkom's *Writing Horror* was part of the Self-Counsel Press' "Writing Series". Despite containing some basic information for those just starting out and useful commentary from Nancy Kilpatrick, Stanley Wiater, Richard Laymon, Douglas Clegg and others, it was difficult to take seriously a volume that recommended such authors as Gary Brander, Jack Ketchum, Edward Lee and Andrew Neiderman, but somehow forgot to include Robert Aickman, William Hope Hodgson, M.R. James or Fritz Leiber!

The Fear Codex: The Australian Encyclopedia of Horror and Dark Fantasy was an electronic publication by Bryce Stevens that needed more work before it became a definitive reference source.

Published by the Southern Illinois University Press, Philip L. Simpson's *Psycho Paths: Tracking the Serial Killer Through Contemporary American Film and Fiction* looked at serial killers as part of the same Gothic mythology that gave rise to vampires and werewolves.

Gothic Radicalism: Literature, Philosophy, and Psychoanalysis in the Nineteenth Century by Andrew Smith was a critical study of such seminal novels as *Frankenstein*, *Dracula*, etc.

In Desert Island Books' *Dracula: Sense & Nonsense*, Elizabeth Miller explored the often erroneous mythology that has built up around the character and the book.

From Greenwood Press, David A. Oakes' *Science and Destabilization in the Modern American Gothic: Lovecraft, Matheson and King* explored at pre-1900 American Gothic literature and was also a critical study of the three authors. From the same imprint came *Ray Bradbury: A Critical Companion* by Robin Anne Reid.

Editors David E. Schulz and S.T. Joshi charted H.P. Lovecraft's life through extracts from his prolific correspondence in *Lord of a Visible World: An Autobiography in Letters*, published by Ohio University Press. Joshi was also responsible for *The Annotated*

Supernatural Horror in Literature, a detailed critical study of Lovecraft's 1927 essay, published in trade paperback by New York's Hippocampus Press.

Published by Subterranean Press in a signed edition of 500 numbered copies and a lettered edition of twenty-six copies, Bill Sheehan's *At the Foot of the Story Tree: An Inquiry into the Fiction of Peter Straub* looked at each of the author's books and included an interview with Straub and a primary bibliography. Michael Collings' *Hauntings: The Official Peter Straub Bibliography* was the first in a new series of biographies from Overlook Connection Press. It included a guide to all the author's work (including liner notes written for jazz recordings!), plus an interview with Straub by Stanley Wiater.

Former agent and editor Julius Schwartz has had one of the most eclectic and influential careers, as he detailed with the help of Brian M. Thomsen in his autobiography *Man of Two Worlds: My Life in Science Fiction and Comics*, which included a distinctive afterword by Harlan Ellison.

Richard Matheson's *Mediums Rare* from CD Publications looked at the history of psychic research.

Movie tie-ins by well-known authors included *Pitch Black* by Frank Lauria, *The 6th Day* by Terry Bisson and *X-Men* by Kristine Kathryn Rusch and Dean Wesley Smith.

Peter Lerangis' *The Sixth Sense* was an unlikely young adult novelization of the film, which included eight pages of colour stills and an interview with director M. Night Shyamalan.

D.A. Stern's books *Blair Witch: The Secret Confession of Rustin Parr* and *Blair Witch: Book of Shadows* were original novelizations based around the movie mythology, while *The Blair Witch Files: The Witch's Daughter*, *The Dark Room* and *The Drowning* were three young adult novels by Cade Merrill in the "Case File" series loosely based on the two movies.

The Crow: Wicked Prayer was an original novel by Norman Partridge, inspired by the comics and movie series created by James O'Barr.

Based on the classic creatures, David Jacobs' novel *The Devil's Brood* was subtitled *The New Adventures of Dracula, Frankenstein & the Universal Monsters*.

Once again, *Buffy the Vampire Slayer* was top of the TV tie-ins.

Amongst the numerous adult and young adult *Buffy* titles published throughout the year were *Deep Water* by Laura Anne Gilman and Josepha Sherman, *Prime Evil* and *Doomsday Deck* by Diana G. Gallagher, *The Xander Years, Vol.2* by Jeff Mariotte, *Here Be Monsters* by Cameron Dokey, *The Evil That Men Do* by Nancy Holder, *Paleo* by Yvonne Navarro, *Ghoul Trouble* by John Passarella and *Revenant* by Mel Odom. The first in a spin-off series, *Spike and Dru: Pretty Maids All in a Row* by Christopher Golden, was set in the 1940s and also published as a book club hardcover.

The *Buffy* anthology *How I Survived My Summer Vacation, Vol.1* included six stories by Nancy Holder, Yvonne Navarro, Michelle West, Cameron Dokey and Paul Ruditis.

Buffy's undead former boyfriend *Angel* also spawned his own series of novelisations by many of the same authors, including *Not Forgotten* by Nancy Holder, *Close to the Ground* and *Hollywood Noir* by Jeff Mariotte, *Redemption* by Mel Odom and *Shakedown* by Don DeBrandt.

Maelstrom by Matthew Costello and *The Shadows Between* by L.A. Liverakos were the second and third volumes in the series of books based on the TV show *Poltergeist The Legacy*.

Graeme Grant and Andy Lane, respectively, novelized the disappointing new *Randall & Hopkirk {Deceased}* series with *Ghosts from the Past* and *Ghost in the Machine*.

The young adult *The X Files* series continued with *Quarantine* by Les Martin, *Haunted* by Ellen Steiber and *Miracle Man* by Terry Bisson.

Based on the Archie Comics character and popular TV show, there were more than thirty *Sabrina the Teenage Witch* novelizations available, the latest being *Switcheroo* by Margot Batrae, *Mummy Dearest* by Mel Odom, *Reality Check* by Diana G. Gallagher, *Knock on Wood* by John Vornholt and *It's a Miserable Life* by Cathy Dubowski.

More witches were to be found in *Charmed: Kiss of Darkness* by Brandon Alexander, the second young-adult novelisation based on the TV series about the three Halliwell sisters. It was followed by *The Crimson Spell* by F. Goldsborough, *Whispers from the Past* by Rosalind Noonan, *Voodoo Man* by Wendy Corsi Staub and *Haunted by Desire* by Cameron Dokey.

At least the *Quantum Leap* series of novelizations finally came to an end with the eighteenth volume, *Mirror's Edge* by Carol Davis and Esther D. Reese. *Merlin Part 3: The End of Magic* was the final volume in the trilogy based on the magical mini-series, written by James Mallory.

The 10th Kingdom and *Arabian Nights*, both by Kathryn Wesley (an obvious pseudonym of Kristine Kathryn Rusch and Dean Wesley Smith) featured sixteen pages of colour photos and an introduction by producer Robert Halmi, Sr.

Hasbro-owned gaming manufacturer Wizards of the Coast was downsized in December with around 150 people let go. A downturn in Pokémon revenues and disappointing results from the previous year's *Star Wars* movie were blamed. Former CEO Peter Adkinson, who founded the company in 1990, was one of several executives who resigned.

White Wolf's *World of Darkness* series based on the role-playing game *Clan* continued with the novels *Ravnos* by Kathleen Ryan, *Giovanni* by Justin Achilli, *Malkavian* by Stewart Wieck, *Brujah* and *Nosferatu* by Gherbod Fleming and *Tremere* by Eric Griffin, plus *Clan Novel Anthology*, a compilation of thirteen stories edited by Stewart Wieck.

World of Darkness: Predator & Prey: Vampire by Carl Bowen launched a new six-part cross-over series based on White Wolf's role-playing games *Vampire: The Masquerade* and *Hunter: The Reckoning*.

S.D. Perry's *Resident Evil 5: Nemesis* was a novelization of the shoot 'em up zombie video games.

Written by Andrew Migliore and John Strysik and published by Seattle's Armitage House, *The Lurker in the Lobby: A Guide to the Cinema of H.P. Lovecraft* was a well-researched and profusely illustrated look at films inspired by the late author's work. Along with a preface by S.T. Joshi, it included brief interviews with Roger Corman, Daniel Haller, John Carpenter, Stuart Gordon, Jeffrey Combs, Brian Yuzna, Dan O'Bannon and Bernie Wrightson, amongst others.

Published by Titan Books, Bill Warren's long-awaited *The Evil Dead Companion* contained everything you ever needed to know about Sam Raimi's cult trilogy.

New film and entertainment imprint Reynolds & Hearn launched in March with Jonathan Rigby's comprehensive study

English Gothic: A Century of Horror Cinema with a foreword by Richard Gordon, and Roy Ward Baker's biography *The Director's Cut: A Memoir of 60 Years in Film and Television* with a foreword by Roger Moore C.B.E. The publisher's subsequent volumes included *The Peter Cushing Companion* by David Miller, an in-depth look at the stage and screen career of the late Hammer Films star, including previously unpublished interviews and a foreword by Veronica Carlson.

From McFarland came *Uneasy Dreams: The Golden Age of British Horror Films, 1956–1976* by American author Gary A. Smith with a foreword by Hammer composer James Bernard; *Screen Sirens Scream! Interviews with 20 Actresses from Science Fiction, Horror, Film Noir and Mystery Movies, 1930s to 1960s* by Paul Parla and Charles P. Mitchell; *The Films of John Carpenter* by John Kenneth Muir; *Herschell Gordon Lewis, Godfather of Gore: The Films* by Randy Palmer with forewords by the cult movie director himself and David E. Friedman, and *Pop Lit, Pop Cult and The X Files: A Critical Exploration* by Denver English professor Jan Delasara.

Scream: The Unofficial Guide to the Scream Trilogy was John Brosnan's look at Wes Craven's slasher series, from Boxtree. *Inside The Wicker Man* by Allan Brown explored every aspect of the cult supernatural movie, including interviews with cast and crew members. The 1978 novelisation of *The Wicker Man: A Novel* by Robin Hardy and Anthony Shaffer was also reissued with a new introduction by Brown.

The Monster Club.Com Guide to Horror included a foreword by Ben Chapman, who played the Gill Man on land in *Creature from the Black Lagoon*. Berkley published yet another updated paperback edition of John Stanley's *Creature Features* guide, this time in a larger but still unillustrated format.

In Chronicle Books' *It Came from Bob's Basement*, movie memorabilia collector Bob Burns and John Michlig presented a visual trip through Burns' incredible archive of film artifacts, from King Kong's metallic armature to a life-size Alien Queen.

Pocket Essentials, edited by Paul Duncan, were small inexpensive paperback reference guides by various authors on such topics as *Buffy the Vampire Slayer*, *Doctor Who*, *Alfred Hitchcock*, *David Lynch*, *Stanley Kubrick* and *Film Noir*.

* * *

There was no denying that Robert Weinberg's *Horror of the 20th Century: An Illustrated History* from Collector's Press was an extremely handsome-looking volume, but that made its faults all the more obvious: despite containing some marvellous full-colour images (particularly the chapters devoted to the pulps), the use of contemporary reprints instead of original covers, a film section predominantly lifted from Ronald V. Borst's *Graven Images*, and a "history" of the genre that consisted of gaping holes and glaring omissions revealed an unusually indolent approach by its knowledgeable compiler. The volume was also not helped by an incompetent index and the mis-spelling of Edgar Allan Poe's name on the dustjacket.

From the same publisher, Ron Goulart's *Comic Book Culture: An Illustrated History* did the same thing for the Golden Age of American comics, but with more satisfying results.

The Classic Era of American Pulp Magazines by Peter Haining was a handsome-looking hardcover from Prion Books, featuring a personal history of the field along with black and white illustrations and full-colour reproductions of numerous pulp magazine covers throughout. Equally as impressive was *The Adventure House Guide to the Pulps*, an attempt by historians Doug Ellis, John Locke and John Gunnison to produce a complete index to the pulp magazines, with cover reproductions of most of the 900 individual titles listed.

Spectrum 7: The Best in Contemporary Fantastic Art was as usual edited by Cathy and Arnie Fenner. It contained an expanded 200 pages of full colour art and appeared in both hardcover and paperback editions from Underwood Books.

Vertigo Visions: Artwork from the Cutting Edge of Comics was a stunning compilation of covers, trading cards and gallery art from DC Comics' "adult" Vertigo imprint (launched in 1993). With text by Alisa Kwitney and full-colour illustrations from Simon Bisley, Dave McKean, Gahan Wilson, Clive Barker, Michael Wm. Kaluta, Tom Canty, Brian Bolland, Bill Sienkiewicz, John Bolton, Phil Hale, Phil Winslade, Glenn Fabry and many others, it was a volume that should be required reading for every art director in horror publishing.

British artist Glenn Fabry's often striking work was also showcased in *Preacher: Dead or Alive*, a full-colour compilation of covers from the DC Comics/Vertigo series that included the artist's preliminary sketches and designs.

Following on from his definitive volumes on Batman and Superman, Les Daniels' *Wonder Woman: The Life and Times of the Amazon Princess* was a complete history of the comics character created by the unconventional Dr William Moulton Marston, beautifully designed by Chip Kidd and with an introduction by actress Lynda Carter (who portrayed the character on TV).

Greetings from Earth: The Art of Bob Eggleton was another of Paper Tiger's excellent softback collections, with text by Nigel Suckling and numerous paintings and sketches by the multiple award-winning artist.

The Strange Case of Edward Gorey featured a biographical essay by the late artist's long-time friend and neighbour Alexander Theroux along with numerous illustrations by Gorey. Finally published in a trade edition, Gorey's *The Iron Tonic: or, A Winter Afternoon in Lonely Valley* was only previously available in a limited edition of 226 copies in 1969.

Robert D. San Souci's macabre fairy tale, *Cinderella Skeleton*, was aimed at pre-teen readers and beautifully illustrated by David Catrow.

The 2001 Cthulhu Calendar from Armitage House/Pagan Publishing featured Alan Moore's examination of Lovecraft's Mythos from a Cabbalistic perspective, with illustrations by John Coulthart and important Lovecraftian dates compiled by Cthulhu chronologist Guy Bock.

For would-be collectors with plenty of cash to spare, the second edition of *The Original Comic Art Price Guide* by Jerry Weist contained the latest prices for original SF art, pulps, monster magazines, fanzines and comics.

Chicago-based Moonstone Books acquired the comic book rights to the White Wolf role-playing games *Vampire: The Masquerade* and *Werewolf: The Apocalypse*, along with the *Kolchak: The Night Stalker* TV series, Lee Falk's *The Phantom* newspaper strip and the Kenneth Robeson pulp hero *The Avenger*. Each title was planned as a perfect-bound quarterly.

William Hope Hodgson's classic 1908 novel *The House on the Borderland* was adapted for DC Comics/Vertigo by Simon Revelstroke and artist Richard Corben, with an introduction by Alan Moore.

Written by Alan Moore and illustrated by Kevin O'Neill, the first volume of America's Best Comics' *The League of Extraordinary Gentlemen* was a Victorian romp featuring the team of Allan Quatermain, Captain Nemo, the invisible Hawley Griffin, Dr Henry Jekyll and Mr Edward Hyde, and Mina Murray (from *Dracula*), who were recruited by the enigmatic Campion Bond to save the world from the nefarious "Doctor" (Fu Manchu) and others. The handsome hardcover compilation also included an illustrated Lovecraftian prose story by Moore.

The Night Terrors was a new black and white horror comic created by Bernie Wrightson and Joseph M. Monks and published by Chanting Monks Studios. The first issue also included work by Wm. Stout, Ronn Sutton, Quinton Hoover and Randy Zimmerman.

Savoy's *Lord Horror* series of graphic magazines continued with *Reverbstorm 7* written as usual by David Britton and illustrated and designed by John Coulthart.

Wolff & Byrd, Counselors of the Macabre, returned in Batton Lash's latest graphic novel, *Sonovawitch! and Other Tales of Supernatural Law*, in which the two attorneys encountered more creatures of the night (courts). Lash also contributed an introduction to *Eternally Yours*, a collection of Canadian writer/ illustrator Janet L. Hetherington's black and white romance horror strips, published by Best Destiny.

In February, Hammer Films once again announced that it was about to make a comeback. Now owned by a consortium of media tycoons (including advertising executive Charles Saatchi), who purchased the company for £2.25 million, the predictable plans included a new TV series, remakes of various classic Hammer movies and a number of new media tie-ins such as computer games, magazines and other merchandising.

Following its defeat in a test case in July, the British Board of Film Classification changed its rules and announced that it planned to make fewer cuts to "18"-rated movies, but would reduce the amount of violence found in lower classifications.

Proving that you can't go back into the woods again, a handful of devotees of the original legend emerged from the trees unable to account for five hours in the $10 million flop follow-up *Book of Shadows: Blair Witch 2*, which could only manage a measly $26.4 million at the US boxoffice. Perhaps the problem was because director Joe Berlinger didn't consider his film a horror movie, but instead described it as a "disturbing psychological thriller". Yeah, right.

The (hopefully) final episode of Wes Craven's franchise, *Scream 3* was based around the making of a Hollywood slasher film but failed to match the boxoffice success of the previous two entries. However, Keenen Ivory Wayans' infantile *Scary Movie*, a hit-and-miss spoof of such post-modern horror films as the *Scream* series, along with *The Sixth Sense* and *Shakespeare in Love*, was a surprise hit on both sides of the Atlantic. Carmen Electra's cameo probably helped.

A knife-wielding maniac was slicing and dicing the local virgins in Geoffrey Wright's wittily-titled *Cherry Falls*, while John Ottman's redundant sequel *Urban Legends Final Cut* involved a group of film students being stalked by yet another crazed killer. It briefly topped the American boxoffice chart before stalling at $21.5 million.

A serial slasher was preying on teens in Robert Lee King's spoof *Psycho Beach Party*, written by cult New York playwright Charles Busch (who also turned up in drag as a policewoman).

Probably the best teen horror film of the year was *Final Destination* from the former *X Files* and *Millennium* team of Glen Morgan and James Wong. When several students missed a doomed flight to Paris, Death set out to reclaim them in bizarrely complicated ways, heralded by John Denver songs! There were some surprise shocks, and Tony Todd turned up as a creepy undertaker.

Norio Tsuruta's *Ring O: Birthday* was an unnecessary prequel to the successful Japanese *Ring* franchise about a cursed video tape, and you could guess the "surprise" twist from the trailer for Robert Zemeckis' ghost story *What Lies Beneath*, which starred Harrison Ford and Michelle Pfeiffer as the "perfect" couple haunted by a body in the bathtub.

Meg Ryan co-produced cinematographer Janusz Kaminski's irritating directorial debut *Lost Souls*, a troubled updating of *The Omen* in which a clearly disturbed part-time exorcist (Winona Ryder) believed that an atheist author (Ben Chaplin) would become the new Antichrist on his thirty-third birthday. In fact, she was right. But despite a re-shot ending, it still flopped, taking just $16.8 million at the US boxoffice.

Poor Kim Basinger had to protect her niece from a cult of mad Satanists in *Bless the Child*, Chuck Russell's silly reworking of *The Omen*, and Johnny Depp was a book dealer in search of a Satanic tome in Roman Polanski's *The Ninth Gate*, based on the novel by Arturo Perez-Reverte.

Elizabeth Hurley's sexy Satan granted tech-support nerd Elliot Richards (Brendan Fraser) seven wishes designed to win him the affections of his work colleague (Frances O'Connor) in Harold Ramis' disappointing remake of the 1967 Peter Cook and Dudley Moore comedy, *Bedazzled*. Even worse was Adam Sandler's irritating spawn of the Devil, who went to New York to take his brothers back to Hell and fell for the charms of design student Patricia Arquette in the boxoffice flop *Little Nicky*. It cost a reported $80 million and struggled to take half that in nine weeks. Quentin Tarantino turned up in a cameo as a blind preacher.

Based on the controversial novel by Bret Easton Ellis, *American Psycho* starred Christian Bale as the sartorial serial killer Patrick Bateman, ably supported by Reese Witherspoon, Willem Dafoe and Chloe Sevigny. Despite taking just $15.1 million at the US boxoffice, a sequel was quickly announced.

Music video and commercials director Tarsem Singh made his feature debut with *The Cell*, a laughable serial killer/SF thriller in which an empathic psychologist (miscast singer Jennifer Lopez) entered the twisted psyche of a psycho (a hysterical Vincent D'Onofrio) to discover the location of his latest kidnap victim. A 1997 episode of the TV series *Sleepwalkers* had an almost identical plot.

After sitting on the shelf for a year or so, Stephan Elliott's psycho drama *Eye of the Beholder*, starring Ewan McGregor and Ashley Judd, finally received a belated release. Keanu Reeves was the homicidal maniac pursued by James Spader's FBI agent in Joe Charbanic's feature debut *The Watcher*.

In Patrick Lussier's *Wes Craven Presents Dracula 2000* (re-titled *Dracula 2001* for its delayed release in the UK) Joel Soisson's pulpy script made a case for Dracula (a dull Gerard Butler) being the Biblical Judas. However, the film was ruined by gratuitous product placement for Virgin Stores. E. Elias Merhige's revisionist *Shadow of the Vampire* featured an Oscar-nominated Willem Dafoe as real vampire/actor Max Shreck, hired in 1922 by German film director F.W. Murnau (John Malkovich) to lend some authenticity to his *Nosferatu*.

Asia Argento starred in Guillaume Canet's *Les Morsures de L'Aube* (aka *Bites of the Dawn*), a look at the vampire world of Paris. The animated *Vampire Hunter D* was a semi-remake of the 1985 *anime*, also from Japan, while in the Italian comedy *Zora the Vampire*, Dracula (Toni Bertorelli) was a Romanian immigrant living in poverty in Rome.

Based on the series of young adult novels by Angela Sommer-Bodenburg, Uli Edel's *The Little Vampire* featured Jonathan Lipnicki as a resourceful young boy who aided a dysfunctional Scottish vampire family (which included Richard E. Grant and Alice Krige).

Bryan Singer's *X-Men* was a surprisingly dark and adult version of the hit Marvel comic book series, set in a near-future where mutants were seen as a threat by humans.

TV Highlander Adrian Paul teamed up with movie Highlander Christopher Lambert in the fourth film in the immortal series, *Highlander Endgame*. The children's time travel adventure *Merlin: The Return* featured a bearded Rik Mayall as the Arthurian wizard and Craig Sheffer as the evil Mordred.

Scripted by an unlikely David E. Kelley (TV's *Ally McBeal*), Steve Miner's fun *Lake Placid* had Bill Pullman, Bridget Fonda and Oliver Platt menaced by a thirty-foot CGI crocodile. After Hollywood's pathetic 1998 revamp, the original jolly green giant was back battling a prehistoric UFO in Takao Okawara's *Godzilla 2000*.

Scientist Sebastian Caine (Kevin Bacon) tested an invisibility serum on himself and became obsessed with his power in Paul Verhoeven's *Hollow Man*, which pretended to have nothing to do with H.G. Wells' original, while Eddie Murphy played an entire dysfunctional family in the Jekyll and Hyde comedy sequel *Nutty Professor II: The Klumps*.

An uncredited rewrite by John Sayles couldn't save *The 6th Day*, Roger Spottiswoode's big budget SF thriller in which Arnold Schwarzenegger's near future family man discovered that he had been replaced with an illegal human clone by a ruthless business corporation. It grossed a pathetic $34.5 million in the US.

David Twohy's delayed *Pitch Black* featured a group of space survivors menaced by creatures of the night on a barren planet. John Travolta was laughed off the screen when he co-produced and starred as a nine-foot tall alien in director Roger Christian's overblown version of L. Ron Hubbard's *Battlefield Earth: A Saga of the Year 3000*. US critics called it "the worst movie of the century".

Gregory Hoblit's *Frequency* was a *Twilight Zone*-ish time-travel serial killer story, while Bruce Willis played the sole survivor of a train wreck who encountered Samuel L. Jackson's mysterious comics fan suffering from a degenerative bone disease in *Unbreakable*, M. Night Shyamalan's much-anticipated follow-up to *The Sixth Sense* (which grossed nearly $700 million worldwide).

John Cusack and an almost unrecognizable Cameron Diaz got inside John Malkovich's head – literally – in Spike Jonz's fascinating fantasy *Being John Malkovich*.

Frank Darabont's adaptation of *The Green Mile* featured a terrific ensemble cast headed by Tom Hanks and was based on Stephen King's 1996 serial novel.

Warner Bros.' reissue of the "Director's Cut" of *The Exorcist* (1973) contained an extra eleven minutes of footage, including Regan's "spider walk" down the stairs and a new ending. It grossed more than $34.8 million domestically, making it the highest-earning reissue outside the *Star Wars* trilogy.

The most successful film of 2000 was *Dr. Seuss' How the Grinch Stole Christmas*, which grossed more than $250 million at the domestic boxoffice. In the American Top 20 it was followed by such other genre titles as *X-Men* (6), *Scary Movie* (7), *What Lies Beneath* (8), *Dinosaur* (11), *Nutty Professor II: The Klumps* (13) and *Unbreakable* (20). Other big earners were *Space Cowboys*, *Scream 3* (which failed to crack the $100 million mark) and *Hollow Man*. Further down the chart were *The Cell*, *Mission to Mars* (which still managed just over $60 million), *Fantasia 2000* and *Final Destination*.

As usual, genre films picked up many of the technical prizes at the 2000 Academy Awards in Los Angeles: *Sleepy Hollow* was presented with Best Art Direction, while Phil Collins' "You'll Be in My Heart' from Disney's animated *Tarzan* was voted Best Original Song. However, the big winner was *The Matrix*, which won in the Film Editing, Sound, Sound Effects Editing and Visual Effects categories.

At The Orange British Academy Film Awards in April, Charlie Kaufman's script for *Being John Malkovich* was awarded Best Adapted Screenplay, *Sleepy Hollow* won Best Costume and Best Production Design, and *The Matrix* again picked up Best Sound and Best Achievement in Special Effects. The late Stanley Kubrick was awarded an Academy Fellowship, collected by his widow Christiana.

In a landmark statement in May, the British Board of Film Classification announced that it would allow hardcore videos to be sold in licensed sex shops after it lost a High Court bid to block the distribution of seven films.

Craig Sheffer, the star of Clive Barker's *Nightbreed*, found himself on the end of the Cenobites' hooked chains in Scott Derrickson's *Hellraiser: Inferno*, the fifth entry in Barker's ever-diminishing direct-to-video franchise.

Richard Clabaugh's fun, low budget monster movie *Python* involved a group of bike-riding twenty-somethings battling a giant CGI mutant hybrid snake. The slumming cast included Wil Wheaton, John Franklin, a bizarrely-accented Casper van Dien, Robert Englund (proving himself a worthy successor to Donald Pleasence), and victim cameos from Jenny McCarthy, Ed Lauter and Marc McClure.

John Eyres' *Octopus* featured a tentacled monster enlarged by a sunken super toxin, while Tobe Hooper's career hit rock bottom with *Crocodile*. Jack Sholder's giant alien spider film *Arachnid* was shot in Spain, as was Brian Yuzna's *Faust*, based on the comic book by David Quinn and Tim Vigil and starring Jeffrey Combs and Andrew Divoff.

In *The Nest*, a swarm of insects on a remote island laid waste to a cast of B-movie actors that included Dean Stockwell. David DeCoteau's *Ancient Evil: Scream of the Mummy* involved an Aztec mummy menacing students in an old dark house during a storm, while *Jack Frost 2* was more comedy than horror.

Ted V. Mikels decided that the world was finally ready for *Corpse Grinders 2*, and the masked killer from the *Scream* movies made a surprise appearance in the low budget Hong Kong slasher movie, *Resort Massacre*.

In the sleazy video category, Darian Caine starred as a softcore S&M monster in Seduction Cinema's *Mistress Frankenstein*. The DVD "Collectors Edition" included an uncut version of the film, behind-the-scenes out-takes, and the producers' home video out-takes. Gregory Cabot's *Date With a Vampire* involved the undead taking lots of nude showers.

The Shock-O-Rama Cinema label released "Uncut" versions of *Vamps Deadly Dreamgirls*, *Psycho Sisters* and John Russo's *Santa Claws*, the latter starring the awful Debbie Rochon and reuniting original *Night of the Living Dead* cast members Karl Hardman, Maryilyn Eastman and Bill Hinzman.

From Video Outlaw came the low budget vampire videos *Blood Kiss* and *At Dawn They Sleep*.

Alvin and the Chipmunks Meet the Wolf Man was a cartoon feature released directly to video and initially supported by a national sweepstakes promotion with Sun-Maid Raisins. Based on the new TV series, video cassettes of *Archie's Weird Mysteries: Archie and the Riverdale Vampires* included a free exclusive *Archie's Weird Mysteries Comic Book*, while *Scooby-Doo and the Alien Invaders* was a new feature-length animated adventure released in time for Halloween.

To tie-in with the special edition of Tim Burton's *The Nightmare Before Christmas* on video and DVD, which included the director's short *Vincent* and the full-length version of *Frankenweenie*, two American video chains offered a series of exclusive figures and toys based on the movie around Halloween time. Burton's *Edward Scissorhands* also made its debut on DVD, celebrating its 10th anniversary with plenty of extras.

The two-disc, 25th anniversary DVD of *The Rocky Horror Picture Show* added a making-of documentary, commentary by Richard O'Brien and Patricia Quinn and numerous other extras, including great sing-a-long subtitles.

The DVD of *Nosferatu: Special Edition* contained the original 1922 vampire film with two Dolby Digital scores for orchestra and organ, plus commentary by German film historian Lokke Heiss.

Boris Karloff: Horror's Gentleman was a value-for-money two hour video compilation from VideoSteve Productions that included "Fantastic Film Trailers: 1931–1968" and "Boris Karloff in Television-Land". At just over an hour in length, *Vincent Price:*

A Master of Horror followed a similar format, while *Monsterland Matinee* featured Hammer's 1958 TV pilot *Tales of Frankenstein*, trailers for all seven Hammer *Frankenstein* movies, and the English-dubbed version of *Aztec Mummy vs. The Robot* (1959).

Billy Zane and Gloria Reuben starred in the four-hour Fox miniseries *Dean Koontz's Sole Survivor*, about a mysterious plane crash.

Joe Chappelle's low budget cable TV movie *Dark Prince: The True Story of Dracula* starred the uncharismatic Rudolf Martin as ruthless fifteenth-century Romanian ruler Prince Vlad. Despite using the trappings of the vampire genre, only the final sequence of this historical drama actually involved the supernatural.

Timothy Dalton and Christopher Plummer starred in the Showtime movie *The Possessed*, Steven E. deSouza's dramatization of the real-life case that inspired *The Exorcist*.

In the Disney Channel's comedy *Mom's Got a Date with a Vampire*, single mother Caroline Rhea met her unsuitable suitor via the Internet, while Disney's *Phantom of the Megaplex* was about a trio of children who investigated several strange happenings prior to a movie preview.

Matt Frewer played an eccentric Sherlock Holmes for the Odyssey Channel in yet another version of *Hound of the Baskervilles*. Much better was writer David Pirie's gruesome two-hour BBC-TV movie *Murder Rooms: The Dark Beginnings of Sherlock Holmes*, in which young medical student Arthur Conan Doyle (Robin Laing) assisted his tutor, pioneering forensic pathologist Dr Joseph Bell (Ian Richardson), as they found themselves on the trail of a serial killer (possibly even Jack the Ripper) in 1878 Edinburgh.

Unfortunately, Pirie's two-hour adaptation of J.S Le Fanu's Gothic melodrama *The Wyvern Mystery* was less successful, despite featuring menacing housekeepers, a wardrobe full of cockroaches and a disfigured mad woman.

Based on the novel by Gillian White, director Stuart Orme's *The Sleeper* was an excellent made-for-TV chiller, with Anna Massey and George Cole in fine form as two pensioners who suspected something bad had happened to their friend.

Andrew McCarthy's American architect arrived in London to renovate an old hotel and soon started seeing dead people in *The*

Sight, Paul W.S. Anderson's two-hour pilot movie on the Fox Network and British Sky Broadcasting that did not contain a single original idea.

Yancy Butler was the New York City policewoman who used the powers of an ancient gauntlet to battle evil in the TNT movie *Witchblade*, based on the Top Cow comic book series.

Armand Assante, Rachel Ward and Bryan Brown survived a nuclear apocalypse in Russell Mulcahy's Showtime remake of Nevil Shute's novel *On the Beach*, while Richard Dreyfuss, Harvey Keitel, Noah Wyle, Brian Dennehy, George Clooney, James Cromwell and Sam Elliott attempted to avert the end of the world in a *live* remake of the 1964 film *Fail Safe* for CBS-TV.

The first two books in Mervyn Peake's "unfilmable" *Gormenghast* trilogy were turned into a lavish but uneven four-hour BBC mini-series set in the eponymous castle-state. A fine ensemble cast of UK actors and comedians, including Stephen Fry, Richard Griffiths, Christopher Lee, Warren Mitchell, Ian Richardson, John Sessions, Fiona Shaw, Zoë Wanamaker, Eric Sykes, Windsor Davies, Martin Clunes and Spike Milligan, portrayed the eccentric and often bizarre characters.

From the ever-busy Hallmark Entertainment, Steve Barron's *Arabian Nights* was a stylish mini-series that included a pair of stunning CGI dragons created by Jim Henson's Creature Shop. Henson was also responsible for the computer-created deaths-head harpies in Hallmark's erratic mini-series *Jason and the Argonauts*, which was not a patch on the 1963 Ray Harryhausen version.

With Kathleen Turner as the wicked stepmother and Jane Birkin as the magical Mab, Channel Four's *Cinderella* was a bizarre contemporary reworking of the classic fairy tale, filmed in the Isle of Man.

Wisconsin Death Trip was James Marsh's award-winning docudrama made for the BBC's *Arena* series. Adapted from the book by Michael Lesy and narrated by Ian Holm, it was based on real events of murder, madness, myths and mayhem that took place in the state of Wisconsin between 1890 and 1900 as published in the newspaper of the town of Black River Falls.

Gahan Wilson's The Kid was a cartoon comedy on Showtime about a boy with an overactive imagination voiced by Edward Asner, William Shatner and Jennifer Tilly.

*   *   *

In September, NBC-TV decided to ban a Nike commercial which was screened during the network's coverage of the Australian Olympics. It depicted runner Suzy Favor Hamilton in Nike trainers escaping from a masked assailant wielding a chainsaw in the woods. In an echo of the hysteria that had earlier greeted the *Harry Potter* books, outraged American viewers and commentators branded the advertising as "stupid, ill-conceived and repellant" and "disgusting and misogynistic". In fact, it was simply a clever spoof on slasher films.

In *The X Files*, FBI agents Fox Mulder (David Duchovny) and Dana Scully (Gillian Anderson) investigated an apparent werewolf attack in Los Angeles in a shot-on-video spoof of the Fox Network's *Cops* show. Mulder also travelled to the town of Bethany, Vermont, to investigate ravens, broken mirrors and murder, and discovered a "perfect" housewife transformed into a clawed monster. A smart-mouthed female genie (Paula Sorge) resulted in Mulder and Scully becoming involved in a variation on "The Monkey's Paw", while in one of the series' best-ever episodes, written and directed by Duchovny, the duo found themselves being portrayed in a movie by a pair of unlikely actors (Garry Shandling and Duchovny's wife Tea Leoni) battling sniper zombies. An audaciously poetic coda had the dancing dead rise from their graves on a Hollywood soundstage.

After coming to a settlement with the Fox Network and creator Chris Carter over his lawsuit claiming loss of potential profits, David Duchovny agreed to return for half of *The X Files* episodes in the 2000–2001 season. So with his character Mulder abducted by aliens in the previous season's finale, the show immediately picked up with the introduction of Scully's new partner, John Doggett (Robert Patrick), as the new team investigated a decades-old mystery involving a mutant man-bat monster seeking revenge.

Following the destruction of Sunnydale High School, the eponymous heroine (Sarah Michelle Gellar) went to college in *Buffy the Vampire Slayer*, where werewolf Oz (Seth Green) discovered that his former girlfriend Willow (Alyson Hannigan) was now in a romantic relationship with good witch Tara (Amber Benson), and Buffy's super-soldier boyfriend Riley (Marc Blucas) had an unhealthy addiction to vampires.

The fifth season opened with "Buffy vs. Dracula", in which

Buffy was bitten and fell under the spell of the legendary Dracula (Rudolf Martin, who also played an historical Vlad in the TV movie *Dark Prince: The True Story of Dracula*). Meanwhile, Buffy mysteriously acquired a younger sister, Dawn (Michelle Trachtenberg), who was not all she seemed to be; Giles (Anthony Stewart Head) became the proprietor of Sunnydale's magic shop; vampire Spike (James Marsters) fell in love with the Slayer, and Buffy's mother Joyce (Kristine Sutherland) shockingly died of a brain haemorrhage.

There were also big changes over at spin-off series *Angel* when Irish demon Doyle (Glenn Quinn) was heroically killed off and replaced by Wesley Wyndam-Pryce (Alexis Denisof), while J. August Richards joined the regular cast as street gang member Charles Gunn. Told he may one day be human again, vampire-with-a-soul Angel (David Boreanaz) moved back into a Los Angeles hotel, and his obsessive crusade against the firm of attorneys Wolfram & Hart brought him into contact with re-negade Slayer Faith (Eliza Dushku) and his old undead flame Darla (Julie Benz).

Urban Gothic was a clichéd, cheap-looking half-hour anthol-ogy series created for Britain's Channel 5 by Tom de Ville and co-executive producer Steve Matthews. Among the slightly better episodes were those about a bitter, chain-smoking vampire who allowed a documentary film crew to follow him around London's Soho for a night (where he encountered actress Ingrid Pitt, playing herself); four college students used a necromancy spell to raise the corpse of a wizard they discovered in an old house; a pair of young heroin addicts found themselves prisoners in a bizarre psychiatric hospital beyond death, and a young news-paper reporter investigating a series of mysterious disappearances in London discovered that the heart of the City harboured a secret evil between the cracks of its façade as he encountered its rotting zombie slaves.

Other episodes dealt with a ruthless young villain who joined a very different kind of underworld club; five upwardly mobile friends whose lives were destroyed by a demonic stranger who used their secret desires against them; a group of teenagers in school detention who realized that they were living out a slasher movie, and two doctors who discovered a feral man and were soon behaving like animals. Despite the series' low quality and lack of imagination, a second season was announced.

In the four half-hour episodes of BBC Scotland's *Ghost Stories for Christmas*, Christopher Lee portrayed provost Montague Rhodes James, recounting the classic ghost stories "The Stalls of Barchester", "The Ash Tree", "Number 13" and "A Warning to the Curious" to students at Kings College, Cambridge, on Christmas Eve.

The BBC's short-lived *The Mrs Bradley Mysteries*, based on the detective/mystery novels by Gladys Mitchell, had high society sleuth Adela Bradley (Diana Rigg) and her faithful chauffeur George Moody (Neil Dudgeon) investigating sightings of a ghostly soldier and also discovering that the murderous disciple of a Satanic cult leader was recurring character Inspector Christmas (Peter Davison).

Another unjustly short-lived series was NBC-TV's *The Others*, executive produced (and often scripted) by the team of James Wong and Glen Morgan. College junior Marian Kitt's (Julianne Nicholson) special ability to see into the afterlife brought her to the attention of a small and mysterious group of misfits known as The Others. Directors included supervising producer Mick Garris, Tobe Hooper, Bill Condon and Tom McLoughlin, while an almost unrecognizable Clive Barker turned up in a cameo in the prerequisite Jack the Ripper episode.

The Fearing Mind was an offbeat comedy on the Fox Family channel about the darkness inside the mind of horror author Bill Fearing (Harry van Gorkum). The Fox Network quickly cancelled the *Blair Witch*-inspired *Freakylinks*, in which Ethan Embry investigated the supernatural for the eponymous paranormal web site while trying to solve the murder of his twin brother.

Over on NBC and Pax, Adrian Pasdar and Rae Dawn Chong teamed up to investigate paranormal activity in *Mysterious Ways*, while the third season of Disney's *So Weird* introduced a new character played by Alexzandra Johnson, who took over the investigation into unexplained phenomena.

Too much comedy and Vic Reeves' mugging performance as the ghostly Marty Hopkirk spoiled *Randall & Hopkirk {Deceased}*, the BBC's six-part, fifty-minute revival of the 1960s TV series. The impressive list of guest stars included Tom Baker as

Marty's ghostly mentor Wyvern, Steven Berkoff, Peter Bowles, Martin Clunes, Charles Dance, Anthony Daniels, Alexis Denisof, Hugh Laurie, Hugh Lloyd, Phyllis Logan, Simon Pegg, Gareth Thomas, Richard Todd, Wanda Ventham, Arabella Weir and even original star, the late Mike Pratt (as a ghost!).

After averting the apocalypse, the three witchy Halliwell sisters, Prue (Shannen Doherty), Piper (Holly Marie Combs) and Phoebe (Alyssa Milano), discovered that an evil organization of warlocks was behind the past two seasons of magical attacks in *Charmed*.

The fourth season of *Sabrina the Teenage Witch* ended with rival boyfriends Josh (David Lascher) and Harvey (Nate Richert) competing for Sabrina's heart. For the fifth season, the show moved from ABC-TV to The WB channel. Sabrina (Melissa Joan Hart) broke up with Harvey, who could not handle the fact that his girlfriend was a witch, and she finally attended college where she met new characters Roxie (Soleil Moon Frye), Miles (Trevor Lissauer) and Morgan (Elisa Donovan).

Inspired by the novel by H.G. Wells and the classic 1933 movie, Universal's *The Invisible Man* was a smart, funny and stylish series in which burglar Darien Fawkes (the likeable Vincent Ventresca) had a synthetic gland implanted in his brain which, when it released the "Quicksilver" hormone, made him invisible. Unfortunately, using his power for more than thirty minutes had the side-effect of turning him insane unless he was given the counter-agent.

Co-created by James Cameron, *Dark Angel* was a series set in a dystopian Seattle of 2019 where bar-coded messenger Max (Jessica Alba) discovered she was one of twelve genetically-created super-warriors who escaped as a child from a secret military organization.

Indiana Jones-type adventurer Professor Sydney Fox (Tia Carrere) and her British assistant Nigel Bailey (Christien Anholt) searched for Zeus' sundial and encountered a cult of female vampires in an episode of ABC-TV's Canadian-French series *Relic Hunter*. The aspiring French writer (Chris Demetral) teamed up with inventor Phileas Fogg (Michael Praed) to confront a Carpathian vampire king (Patrick Duffy) in an episode of the Canadian series *The Secret Adventures of Jules Verne*.

Lorenzo Lamas' sword-wielding hero had been sending demons back to Hell for 400 years after they killed his wife and kidnapped their child in the syndicated series *The Immortal*. Created by Terry Marcel and Harley Cokeliss, *Dark Knight* was a cheap-looking series filmed in New Zealand that blatantly ripped off *Dungeons & Dragons*. In an episode from the final season of *Xena Warrior Princess*, the eponymous warrior woman had a confrontation with Lucifer (Alex Mendoza).

Gena Lee Nolin was the shape-changing jungle heroine of UPN's *Sheena*, based on the classic comics character.

Loosely inspired by the uncredited classic movie, in *Kong The Animated Series* eighteen-year-old Jason Jenkins could merge his DNA codes with the friendly giant ape, recreated on the hidden prehistoric world of Kong Island by his scientist grandmother.

The bizarre adventures of Archie Andrews and his friends in the town of Riverdale was the basis for the cartoon series *Archie's Weird Mysteries*, featuring characters appearing in Archie Comics.

The Baskervilles was a young children's cartoon series about the adventures of the eponymous family in Underworld: The Theme Park (aka Hell) run by "The Boss" (aka Satan).

Max Steel was a stunning-looking CGI cartoon series about a college student whose body was transformed after becoming infected with Max Probes. In one episode, the super-powered secret agent and Team Steel were sent to Egypt where they discovered a robotic giant mummy and other ancient death gods.

The Simpsons Halloween Special XI opened with a great black and white spoof of *The Munsters*, then a dead Homer had to do one good deed to get into Heaven, Bart and Lisa encountered an evil witch and other Grimm characters, and humans were banished to the sea by vengeance-seeking dolphins. Also created by Matt Groenig, *Futurama* was set the year 3001. In "The Honking", which opened the third season, the alcoholic robot Bender was attacked on the moors and subsequently transformed into a murderous werecar each midnight.

The Christmas special of the BBC's cult comedy series *The League of Gentlemen* was supposedly inspired by the old Amicus anthology movies. On Christmas Eve, three parishioners of Royston Vasey visited the church and told the misanthropic vicar a trio of spooky stories. These involved a masked witchcraft coven, a church choir of vampires and a nineteenth-century vet who fell prey to a bloody Monkey's Paw-type curse. Genre veteran Freddie Jones had a cameo.

In a bizarre story strand of the thirty-year-old soap opera *Days of Our Lives*, a pregnant woman (Kristian Alfonso) was being held captive. In a dream she was rescued by arch-villain Stefano DiMera (Joseph Mascolo) and they were menaced by a giant spider crawling up a castle wall!

Writer/director Adam Simon's *The American Nightmare* was an ambitious documentary for The Independent Film Channel that attempted (not always successfully) to draw comparisons between horror films and social events in America from the late 1960s onwards. It featured interviews with George Romero, John Carpenter, Tom Savini, David Cronenberg, Wes Craven, Tobe Hopper, John Landis and various academics.

To launch *Monsterfest 2000: The Classics Come Alive*, a Halloween tribute to the monster movies, AMC kicked off with the documentary *Bride of Monstermania*, a salute to the female stars of horror films.

For Turner Classic Movies, Kevin Brownlow's impressive feature-length documentary *Lon Chaney: A Thousand Faces* included rare home movies, still photographs, behind-the-scenes footage and clips of the silent film star along with interviews with Ray Bradbury, Forrest Ackerman, Orson Welles, Michael F. Blake, Ron Chaney, Lon Chaney Jr, Jackie Coogan, Patsy Ruth Miller, Sara Karloff and the voice of Loretta Young. Nicely narrated by Kenneth Branagh, Hugh M. Hefner was executive producer.

Shadow of the Blair Witch was a *faux*-documentary on the Sci-Fi Channel to promote the disappointing *Book of Shadows: Blair Witch 2*, while *A Taste of the Vampire* was a half-hour documentary for Channel Four about the one-day Vampyria II gathering in London that featured actors Eileen Daily, Madeleine and Mary Collinson, Damien Thomas (dressed as Count Karnstein) and interviews with various fetish fans who like to dress up in rubber and pretend to be members of the undead.

Finally, Chicago attorney Marvin Rosenblum, who owns the film and television rights to George Orwell's *Nineteen Eighty-Four*, filed a lawsuit in August against CBS-parent company Viacon and Orwell Productions claiming that the companies intentionally misled viewers to believe that their hit reality TV show *Big Brother* was connected with Orwell's classic novel.

Gilles Maheu's Europop musical *Notre Dame de Paris* was based on the novel by Victor Hugo and universally panned by the UK critics in May.

A musical stage production of *The Witches of Eastwick* opened in London two months later. Based on the novel by John Updike and the 1987 movie, Ian McShane starred as the Devilish Darryl Van Horne, with Lucie Arnaz, Maria Friedman and Joanna Riding as the women whose fantasies he made come true.

On the toy shelves, H.P. Lovecraft fans could get themselves a cute and cuddly Cthulhu plush doll with poseable wire wings and floppy tentacles.

Sideshow Toys continued its eight-inch Universal Monsters series with the Metaluna Mutant from *This Island Earth*; The Invisible Man with interchangeable heads; Lon Chaney, Sr's Hunchback of Notre Dame with removable crown and sceptre; Henry Hull complete with scarf, coat and cap as the WereWolf of London; Boris Karloff as the Son of Frankenstein, and one of the Mole People. Sideshow also released an articulated version of Karloff as the Frankenstein Monster, complete with shackles, daises and a brain in a jar, plus a two-foot caricature of the Monster with a wire armature, and a four-foot Little Big Head version limited to only 250 individually numbered fibreglass figures for a cool $1,000 apiece.

Sideshow also continued its series of Little Big Heads with Classic Monster Wrestlers (Big Frankie, Mad Mummy, Freaky Phantom, Crazy Creature and Dangerous Drac) and Glow-in-the-Dark versions of Frankenstein's Monster, The Mummy, The Wolf Man, Bride of Frankenstein, Dracula, The Invisible Man, The Phantom of the Opera and The Creature from the Black Lagoon.

On a somewhat taller scale, there was the Universal Studios Classic Monster Bobble Heads (Frankenstein's Monster, The Wolf Man, The Mummy and Dracula), while The Munsters Bobble Heads featured nodding-head figures of TV's Herman Munster and Grandpa.

The twenty-one-inch *Bela Lugosi as Count Dracula* vinyl model kit was sculpted by Tony McVey and authorized by Bela Lugosi, Jr.

The latest in the Movie Maniacs series of collectible figures included detailed versions of King Kong, Edward Scissorhands, David Cronenberg's The Fly, John Carpenter's The Thing, Kurt Russell in *Escape from L.A.* and Bruce Campbell from *Army of Darkness*.

The first series of Silent Screamers from Art Asylum included figures from such classic silent films as Graf Orlok and Knock Renfield from *Nosferatu*, and Dr. Caligari and Cesare from *The Cabinet of Dr Caligari*.

X-Plus Toys of Japan offered resin statues in various sizes and poses of such classic Ray Harryhausen creations as the Cyclops and Skeleton Warrior from *The 7th Voyage of Sinbad*, the Ymir from *20 Million Miles to Earth*, and Talos the bronze giant from *Jason and the Argonauts*.

For fans of TV's *Buffy the Vampire Slayer*, Moore Action Collectibles released six-inch figures of Buffy, Angel, Willow and the undead Master from season one.

Playmates' *The Simpsons Treehouse of Horror* boxed playset was released exclusively to Toys 'Я' Us in time for Halloween and included Bart as The Fly, Ned Flanders as the Devil, Homer as King Kong and Mr Burns as Dracula.

World Horror Convention 2000, the tenth annual gathering, was held in Denver, Colorado, over May 11–14th. Chaired by Edward Bryant, the impressive line-up of returning past guests of honour featured Peter Straub, Harlan Ellison, Steve Rasnic Tem, Melanie Tem, J. Michael Straczynski, artist Rick Lieder, Ellen Datlow and toastmaster Dan Simmons. International Horror Guild Awards for recognition of achievement in the field of horror during 1999 were presented to Stephen King's *The Storm of the Century* for Best Television Show and the Richard Matheson adaptation *Stir of Echoes* for Best Film. Paula Guran's electronic newsletter *DarkEcho* won for Publication, the Artist award went to Charles Burns, and DC/Vertigo's *Flinch* #1-7 won in the Graphic Story category. Editor Neil Barron's massive *Fantasy and Horror: A Critical and Historical Guide to Literature, Illustration, Film, TV, Radio, and the Internet* won Best Nonfiction, *Subterranean Gallery* edited by Richard Chizmar and William Schafer was voted Best Anthology, and Douglas Clegg's

The Nightmare Chronicles received the award for Collection. Gemma Files' "The Emperor's Old Bones" (from *Northern Frights 5*) was Best Short Fiction, Lucius Shepard's "Crocodile Rock" (from *The Magazine of Fantasy & Science Fiction*) was Best Long Fiction, and Michael Cisco's *The Divinity Student* was voted Best First Novel. *A Prayer for the Dying* by Stewart O'Nan won in the Novel category, and the Living Legend Award went to Richard Matheson. In an example of blatant nepotism, the IHG judges also voted a Special Award to editor Don D'Auria for Leisure Books' fledgling mass-market horror series.

A whole raft of The Horror Writer's Association Bram Stoker Awards for Superior Achievement were also presented during a banquet at the same convention on the Saturday. The Specialty Press Award (presented by the Board of Trustees) went to Christopher and Barbara Roden's Ash-Tree Press, and the Lifetime Achievement Awards were presented to past HWA president Charles Grant and the late Edward Gorey. Harlan Ellison's audio version of *I Have No Mouth and I Must Scream* won the Other Media award, J.K. Rowling's *Harry Potter and the Prisoner of Azkaban* picked up the award in Work for Young Readers, and M. Night Shyamalan's *The Sixth Sense* received the Screenplay award. Neil Gaiman's *Sandman: The Dream Hunters* won Illustrated Narrative, the Nonfiction award went to Paula Guran's newsletter *DarkEcho*, and *999: New Stories of Horror and Suspense* edited by Al Sarrantonio was top Anthology. *The Nightmare Chronicles* by Douglas Clegg won Fiction Collection, F. Paul Wilson's "Aftershock" (from *Realms of Fantasy*) won for Short Fiction, and there was a tie in the Long Fiction category between "Five Days in April" by Brian A. Hopkins (from *The Chiaroscuro*) and "Mad Dog Summer" by Joe R. Lansdale (from *999*). *Wither* by J.G. Passarella (Jack Passarella and Joe Gangemi) collected First Novel, and Peter Straub's *Mr. X* won the Novel category.

Due to a loss of revenue and the problems of presenting the Stokers under the banner of another organisation's convention, it seems unlikely that the two events will be combined again.

Held in its usual location of Rhode Island, the informal Necon celebrated its twentieth anniversary with a 300-plus page trade paperback featuring a history of the horror convention and stories and articles by Les Daniels, Peter Straub, Douglas E. Winter, Kathryn Ptacek, F. Paul Wilson, Ramsey Campbell, Brian

Lumley, Joe R. Lansdale, Neil Gaiman, Jack Ketchum, Kim Newman, Thomas Tessier and many others, including a previously unpublished collaboration between Stephen King and Edgar Allan Poe, written in the early 1970s. The instant collectible, limited to just 333 copies, also featured artwork by, amongst others, Don Maitz, Jill Bauman, Jeff Jones, Bob Eggleton, Rick Lieder and Rick Berry.

The winners of the British Fantasy Awards were announced at Fantasycon 2000, held over September 8–10th, in Birmingham, England, with guests of honour Stephen Lawhead, Storm Constantine, Stan Nicholls and actor Doug Bradley. British Fantasy Society members voted RazorBlade Press the Best Small Press, and Peter Crowther's *Lonesome Roads*, from the same publisher, was awarded Best Collection. Best Artist was Les Edwards, while *The Mammoth Book of Best New Horror Volume Ten* edited by Stephen Jones picked up the award for Best Anthology. Tim Lebbon's novella *White* was voted the Best Short Fiction, and Graham Joyce was presented with the August Derleth Award for his novel *Indigo*. The special Karl Edward Wagner Award went to Anne McCaffrey, who paid tribute to the late author.

The 2000 World Fantasy Awards were presented on October 29th at a banquet at the World Fantasy Convention in Corpus Christi, Texas. The British Fantasy Society won the Special Award: Non-Professional, and Gordon Van Gelder picked up the Special Award: Professional for his editing at St. Martin's Press and *The Magazine of Fantasy & Science Fiction*. Best Artist was Jason Van Hollander, Best Collection was a tie between *Moonlight and Vines* by Charles de Lint and *Reave the Just and Other Tales* by Stephen R. Donaldson, and Best Anthology went to *Silver Birch, Blood Moon* edited by Ellen Datlow and Terri Windling. Ian R. MacLeod's "The Chop Girl" (from *Asimov's*) was voted Best Short Fiction, there was another tie in Best Novella between Laurel Winter's "Sky Eyes" (from *F&SF*) and Jeff VanderMeer's "The Transformation of Martin Lake" (from *Palace Corbie 8*), while Martin Scott's (aka Martin Millar) obscure *Thraxas* was considered Best Novel by the five judges. Lifetime Achievement Awards were announced for Michael Moorcock and the late Marion Zimmer Bradley.

The WFC softcover souvenir book was dedicated to the convention's theme – *El Dia de los Muertos*/The Day of the Dead –

and featured profiles of guests of honour K.W. Jeter and John Crowley, toastmaster Joe R. Lansdale and artist guest Charles Vess, along with fiction and articles by Jeter, Terri Windling, Charles de Lint and Bradley Denton (a new "Blackburn" story).

Not surprisingly, California dealer Barry R. Levin's Annual Collector's Award for Most Collectable Author of the Year went to J.K. Rowling. The lettered authorial presentation binding state of *Pegasus in Space* earned Anne McCaffrey the Most Collectable Book of the Year award (as publisher), and the Lifetime Collectors Award went to Erle Melvin Korshak for his pioneering efforts as an early science fiction publisher and bookseller.

When I announced the line-up of authors and stories for this particular volume of *Best New Horror*, there were apparently some complaints on the Internet from members of the horror community that I was once again using "the same British novelists" in the book.

Partly as a result of these criticisms, I decided that this would be as good a time as any to explain how I determine which stories are selected for *Best New Horror*.

If those who complained had bothered to look carefully at the contents of this volume and previous editions, they would have noted that while it is true that two-thirds of this year's contributors happen to be British, that is not always the case. Not only would they see that I try to take a representative amount of fiction from the so-called small presses, but that I also endeavour to include new or upcoming writers in each and every volume. However, I do not adopt a quota policy, and I will only publish a new writer if – in my opinion as the book's editor – I think that their story merits inclusion.

I also have an obligation to my publishers and my readers to deliver a commercial and entertaining work that will appeal to as wide a readership as possible – not just a handful of vocal horror "fans".

Each year I read many hundreds of stories from a wide variety of sources for *Best New Horror* – which let us not forget is a genuine book, not an e-book, not a print-on-demand title, not a limited edition, but an actual book that pays appropriate advances and royalties and is available in printings of *thousands* of copies in bona fide bookstores on both sides of the Atlantic.

I always select the stories for each volume on the basis of the quality of the writing – not which country (or which sex, or which ethnic background) the author comes from. Although the majority of writers in this year's edition happen to be British, it should be pointed out that many of their stories herein were first published in the United States.

Best New Horror is a genuinely open market. Submission guidelines are regularly published online and in the major genre magazines, as well as being available on my web site, and I always make myself available to talk to people at conventions and signings.

So far as this particular volume is concerned, I have never published two of the writers anywhere before. It is only the second time I have worked with five of the authors, eight of the stories are reprinted from small press or electronic formats, and only six tales originally appeared in so-called "mainstream" publishing projects. That is not a bad spread, even if I do say so myself. And for a book that is intended to reflect the current trends in horror and dark fantasy publishing, the list of authors included in this edition ably showcases some of the most talented people writing in the field today. However, it falls to reason that much of the best work to be collected in a volume such as this is going to come from the established (and therefore the more experienced and most widely published) authors associated with the genre.

As for those new and upcoming writers who, in my personal judgment, have not quite made the grade yet, then I try to draw your attention to as many of their names and as much of their work as I can through my annual overview of the horror field. Hopefully you will eventually recognise some of them on the contents pages of future editions of this series. However, I would never be as disingenuous as to list purported honourable mentions of stories which, to put it bluntly, were just *not good enough* to be included in the final selection. If I think a story is worthwhile, then I will publish it.

After all, that's what the title of the book says.

The Editor
July, 2001

KIM NEWMAN

Castle in the Desert

KIM NEWMAN LIVES IN LONDON. His recent books include the novels *Life's Lottery*, *An English Ghost Story* and *The Matter of Britain* (with Eugene Byrne), the collections *Seven Stars*, *Unforgivable Stories* and *Where the Bodies Are Buried*, and the non-fiction volumes *Millennium Movies: End of the World Cinema* and *BFI Classics: Cat People*.

This is the first of two stories in this volume which will eventually form part of the next book in Newman's award-winning *Anno Dracula* sequence. You do not necessarily have to be a movie buff or a vampire fan to enjoy the following, but, as the author explains later on, it will certainly help . . .

Anno Dracula 1977

The man who had married my wife cried when he told me how she died. Junior – Smith Ohlrig Jr, of the oil and copper Ohlrigs – hadn't held on to Linda much longer than I had, but their marriage had gone one better than ours by producing a daughter.

Whatever relation you are to a person who was once married to one of your parents, Racquel Loring Ohlrig was to me. In Southern California, it's such a common family tie you'd think there'd be a neat little name for it, pre-father or potential-parent. The last time I'd seen her was at the Poodle Springs bungalow her mother had given me in lieu of alimony. Thirteen or fourteen

going on a hundred and eight, with a micro-halter top and frayed
jean-shorts, stretch of still-chubby tummy in between, honey-
coloured hair past the small of her back, an underlip that couldn't
stop pouting without surgery, binary star sunglasses and a leather
headband with Aztec symbols. She looked like a pre-schooler
dressed up as a squaw for a costume party, but had the voca-
bulary of a sailor in Tijuana and the glittery eyes of a magpie with
three convictions for aggravated burglary. She'd asked for
money, to gas up her boyfriend's "sickle", and took my television
(no great loss) while I was in the atrium telephoning her mother.
In parting, she scrawled "fuck you, piggy-dad" in red lipstick on a
Spanish mirror. Piggy-Dad, that was me. She still had prep school
penmanship, with curly-tails on her 'ys' and a star over the 'i'.

Last I'd heard, the boyfriend was gone with the rest of the Wild
Angels and Racquel was back with Linda, taking penicillin shots
and going with someone in a rock band.

Now, things were serious.

"My little girl," Junior kept repeating, "my little girl . . ."

He meant Racquel.

"They took her away from me," he said. "The vipers."

All our lives, we've known about the vampires, if only from books
and movies. Los Angeles was the last place they were likely to
settle. After all, California is famous for sunshine. Vipers would
frazzle like burgers on a grill. Now, it was changing. And not just
because of affordable prescription sunglasses.

The dam broke in 1959, about the time Linda was serving
me papers, when someone in Europe finally destroyed Dracula.
Apparently, all vipers remembered who they were biting when
they heard the news. It was down to the Count that so many
of them lived openly in the world, but his continued unlife –
and acknowledged position as King of the Cats – kept them in
the coffin, confined to joyless regions of the old world like
Transylvania and England. With the wicked old witch dead,
they didn't have to stay on the plantation any longer. They
spread.

The first vipers in California were elegant European predators,
flush with centuried fortunes and keen with red thirsts. In the
early '60s, they bought up real estate, movie studios, talent
agencies (cue lots of gags), orange groves, restaurant franchises,

ocean-front properties, parent companies. Then their get began to appear: American vampires, new-borns with wild streaks. Just as I quit the private detective business for the second time, bled-dry bodies turned up all over town as turf wars erupted and were settled out of court. For some reason, drained corpses were often dumped on golf courses. Vipers made more vipers, but they also made viper-killers – including such noted humanitarians as Charles Manson – and created new segments of the entertainment and produce industry.

As the Vietnam War escalated, things went quiet on the viper front. Word was that the elders of the community began ruthless policing of their own kind. Besides, the cops were more worried about draft-dodgers and peace-freak protesters. Now, vampires were just another variety of Los Angeles fruitcake. Hundred-coffin mausolea were opening up along the Strip, peddling shelter from the sun at five bucks a day. A swathe of Bay City, boundaried by dried-up canals, was starting to be called Little Carpathia, a ghetto for the poor suckers who didn't make it up to castles and estates in Beverly Hills. I had nothing real against vipers, apart from a deep-in-the-gut crawly distrust it was impossible for anyone of my generation – the Second World War guys – to quell entirely. Linda's death, though, hit me harder than I thought I could be hit, a full-force ulcer-bursting right to the gut. Ten years into my latest retirement, I was at war.

To celebrate the Bicentennial Year, I'd moved from Poodle Springs, back into my old Los Angeles apartment. I was nearer the bartenders and medical practitioners to whom I was sole support. These days, I knocked about, boring youngsters in the profession with the Sternwood case or the Lady in the Lake, doing light sub-contract work for Lew Archer – digging up family records at county courthouses – or Jim Rockford. All the cops I knew were retired, dead or purged by Chief Exley, and I hadn't had any pull with the D.A.'s office since Bernie Ohls's final stroke. I admitted I was a relic, but so long as my lungs and liver behaved at least eight hours a day I was determined not to be a shambling relic.

I was seriously trying to cut down on the Camels, but the damage was done back in the puff-happy '40s when no one outside the cigarette industry knew nicotine was worse for you than heroin. I told people I was drinking less, but never really kept score. There were times, like now, when Scotch was the only soldier that could complete the mission.

Junior, as he talked, drank faster than I did. His light tan suit was the worse for a soaking, and had been worn until dry, wrinkling and staining around the saggy shape of its owner. His shirtfront had ragged tears where he had caught on something.

Since his remarriage to a woman nearer Racquel's age than Linda's, Junior had been a fading presence in the lives of his ex-wife and daughter (ex-daughter?). I couldn't tell how much of his story was from experience and how much filtered through what others had told him. It was no news that Racquel was running with another bad crowd, the Anti-Life Equation. They weren't all vipers, Junior said, but some, the ringleaders, were. Racquel, it appears, got off on being bitten. Not something I wanted to know, it hardly came as a surprise. With the motorcycle boy, who went by the name of Heavenly Blues but liked his friends to address him as "Mr President", she had been sporting a selection of bruises that didn't look like they'd come from taking a bad spill off the pillion of his hog. For tax purposes, the Anti-Life Equation was somewhere between religious and political. I had never heard of them, but it's impossible to keep up with all the latest cults.

Two days ago, at his office – Junior made a pretence of still running the company, though he had to clear every paper-clip purchase with Riyadh and Tokyo – he'd taken a phone call from his daughter. Racquel sounded agitated and terrified, and claimed she'd made a break with the ALE, who wanted to sacrifice her to some elder vampire. She needed money – that same old refrain, haunting me again – to make a dash for Hawaii or, oddly, the Philippines (she thought she'd be safe in a Catholic country, which suggested she'd never been to one). Junior, tower of flab, had written a cheque, but his new wife, smart doll, talked him out of sending it. Last night, at home, he had gotten another call from Racquel, hysterical this time, with screaming and other background effects. They were coming for her, she said. The call was cut off.

To his credit, Junior ignored his lawfully-married flight attendant and drove over to Linda's place in Poodle Springs, the big house where I'd been uncomfortable. He found the doors open, the house extensively trashed and no sign of Racquel. Linda was at the bottom of the kidney-shaped swimming pool, bitten all over, eyes white. To set a seal on the killing, someone had driven an iron spike through her forehead. A croquet mallet floated above her. I realized he had gone into the pool fully-dressed and hauled Linda out. Strictly speaking, that was violating the crime scene but I would be the last person to complain.

He had called the cops, who were very concerned. Then, he'd driven to the city to see me. It's not up to me to say whether that qualified as a smart move or not.

"This Anti-Life Equation?" I asked Junior, feeling like a shamus again. "Did it come with any names?"

"I'm not even sure it's called that. Racquel mostly used just the initials, ALE. I think it was Anti-Life Element once. Or Anti-Love. Their guru or nabob or whatever he calls himself is some kind of hippie Rasputin. He's one of them, a viper. His name is Khorda. Someone over at one of the studios – Traeger or Mill or one of those kids, maybe Bruckheimer – fed this Khorda some money on an option, but it was never-never stuff. So far as I know, they never killed anyone before."

Junior cried again and put his arms around me. I smelled chlorine on his ragged shirt. I felt all his weight bearing me down, and was afraid I'd break, be no use to him at all. My bones are brittle these days. I patted his back, which made neither of us feel any better. At last, he let me go and wiped his face on a wet handkerchief.

"The police are fine people," he said. He got no argument from me. "Poodle Springs has the lowest crime rate in the state. Every contact I've had with the PSPD has been cordial, and I've always been impressed with their efficiency and courtesy."

The Poodle Springs Police Department were real tigers when it came to finding lost kittens and discreetly removing drunken ex-spouses from floodlit front lawns. You can trust me on this.

"But they aren't good with murder," I said. "Or vipers."

Junior nodded. "That's just it. They aren't. I know you're retired. God, you must be I don't know how old. But you used to be connected. Linda told me how you met, about the Wade-Lennox case. I can't even begin to imagine how you could figure out that tangle. For her, you've got to help. Racquel is still alive. They didn't kill her when they killed her mother. They just took her. I want my little girl back safe and sound. The police don't know Racquel. Well, they do . . . and that's the problem. They said they were taking the kidnap seriously, but I saw in their eyes that they knew about Racquel and the bikers and the hippies. They think she's run off with another bunch of freaks. It's only my word that Racquel was even at the house. I keep thinking of my little girl, of sands running out. Desert sands. You've got to help us. You've just got to."

I didn't make promises, but I asked questions.

"Racquel said the ALE wanted to sacrifice her? As in tossed into a volcano to appease the Gods?"

"She used a bunch of words. 'Elevate', was one. They all meant 'kill'. Blood sacrifice, that's what she was afraid of. Those vipers want my little girl's blood."

"Junior, I have to ask, so don't explode. You're sure Racquel isn't a part of this?"

Junior made fists, like a big boy about to get whipped by someone half his size. Then it got through to the back of his brain. I wasn't making assumptions like the PSPD, I was asking an important question, forcing him to prove himself to me.

"If you'd heard her on the phone, you'd know. She was terrified. Remember when she wanted to be an actress? Set her heart on it, nagged for lessons and screen tests. She was – what? – eleven or twelve? Cute as a bug, but froze under the lights. She's no actress. She can't fake anything. She can't tell a lie without it being written all over her. You know that as well as anyone else. My daughter isn't a perfect person, but she's a kid. She'll straighten out. She's got her Mom's iron in her."

I followed his reasoning. It made sense. The only person Racquel had ever fooled was her father, and him only because he let himself be fooled out of guilt. She'd never have come to me for gas money if Junior were still giving in to his princess's every whim. And he was right – I'd seen Racquel Ohlrig (who had wanted to call herself Amber Valentine) act, and she was on the Sonny Tufts side of plain rotten.

"Khorda," I said, more to myself than Junior. "That's a start. I'll do what I can."

Mojave Wells could hardly claim to come to life after dark, but when the blonde viper slid out of the desert dusk, all four living people in the diner – Mom and Pop behind the counter, a trucker and me on stools – turned to look. She smiled as if used to the attention but deeming herself unworthy of it, and walked between the empty tables.

The girl wore a white silk minidress belted on her hips with interlocking steel rings, a blue scarf that kept her hair out of the way, and square black sunglasses. Passing from purple twilight to fizzing blue-white neon, her skin was white to the point of colourlessness, her lips naturally scarlet, her hair pale blonde. She might have been Racquel's age or God's.

I had come to the desert to find vampires. Here was one.

She sat at the end of the counter, by herself. I sneaked a look. She was framed against the "No Vipers" sign lettered on the window. Mom and Pop – probably younger than me, I admit – made no move to throw her out on her behind, but also didn't ask for her order.

"Get the little lady whatever she wants and put it on my check," said the trucker. The few square inches of his face not covered by salt-and-pepper beard were worn leather, the texture and colour of his cowboy hat.

"Thank you very much, but I'll pay for myself."

Her voice was soft and clear, with a long-ago ghost of an accent. Italian or Spanish or French.

"R.D., you know we don't accommodate vipers," said Mom. "No offence, ma'am, you look nice enough, but we've had bad ones through here. And out at the castle."

Mom nodded at the sign and the girl swivelled on her stool. She genuinely noticed it for the first time and the tiniest flush came to her cheeks.

Almost apologetically, she suggested. "You probably don't have the fare I need?"

"No, ma'am, we don't."

She slipped off her stool and stood up. Relief poured out of Mom like sweat.

R.D., the trucker, reached out for the viper's slender, bare arm, for a reason I doubt he could explain. He was a big man, not slow on the draw. However, when his fingers got to where the girl had been when his brain sparked the impulse to touch, she was somewhere else.

"Touchy," commented R.D.

"No offence," she said.

"I've got the *fare* you need," said the trucker, standing up. He scratched his throat through beard.

"I'm not that thirsty."

"A man might take that unkindly."

"If you know such a man, give him my condolences."

"R.D.," said Mom. "Take this outside. I don't want my place busted up."

"I'm leaving," said R.D., dropping dollars by his coffee cup and cleaned plate. "I'll be honoured to see you in the parking lot, Missy Touchy."

"My name is Geneviève," she said, "accent acute on the third e."

R.D. put on his cowboy hat. The viper darted close to him and lightning-touched his forehead. The effect was something like the Vulcan nerve pinch. The light in his eyes went out. She deftly sat him down at a table, like a floppy rag-doll. A yellow toy duck squirted out of the top pocket of his denim jacket and thumped against a plastic ketchup tomato in an unheard-of mating ritual.

"I am sorry," she said to the room. "I have been driving for a long time and could not face having to cripple this man. I hope you will explain this to him when he wakes up. He'll ache for a few days, but an icepack will help."

Mom nodded. Pop had his hands out of sight, presumably on a shotgun or a baseball bat.

"For whatever offence my kind has given you in the past, you have my apologies. One thing, though: your sign – the word 'viper'. I hear it more and more as I travel West, and it strikes me as insulting. 'No Vampire Fare on Offer' will convey your message, without provoking less gentle *vipers* than myself."

She looked mock-sternly at the couple, with a hint of fang. Pop pulled his hold-out pacifier and I tensed, expecting fireworks. He raised a gaudy Day of the Dead crucifix on a lamp-flex, a glowing-eyed Christ crowned by thorny lightbulbs.

"Hello, Jesus," said Geneviève, then added, to Pop: "Sorry, sir, but I'm not that kind of girl."

She did the fast-flit thing again and was at the door.

"Aren't you going to take your trophy?" I asked.

She turned, looked at me for the first time, and lowered her glasses. Green-red eyes like neons. I could see why she kept on the lens caps. Otherwise, she'd pick up a train of mesmerised conquests.

I held up the toy and squeezed. It gave a quack.

"Rubber Duck," said Mom, with reverence. "That's his CB handle."

"He'll need new initials," I said.

I flew the duck across the room and Geneviève took it out of the air, an angel in the outfield. She made it quack, experimentally. When she laughed, she looked the way Racquel ought to have looked. Not just innocent, but solemn and funny at the same time.

R.D. began moaning in his sleep.

"May I walk you to your car?" I asked.

She thought a moment, sizing me up as a potential geriatric Duckman, and made a snap decision in my favour, the most encouragement I'd had since Kennedy was in the White House.

I made it across the diner to her without collapsing.

I had never had a conversation with a vampire before. She told me straight off she was over five hundred and fifty years old. She had lived in the human world for hundreds of years before Dracula changed the rules. From her face, I'd have believed her if she said she was born under the shadow of Sputnik and that her ambition was to become one of Roger Vadim's ex-wives.

We stood on Main Street, where her fire-engine red Plymouth Fury was parked by my Chrysler. The few stores and homes in sight were shuttered up tight, as if an air raid was due. The only place to go in town was the diner and that seemed on the point of closing. I noticed more of those ornamental crucifixes, attached above every door as if it were a religious holiday. Mojave Wells was wary of its new neighbours.

Geneviève was coming from the East and going to the West. Meagre as it was, this was the first place she'd hit in hours that wasn't a government proving ground. She knew nothing about the Anti-Life Equation, Manderley Castle or a viper named Khorda, let alone Racquel Ohlrig.

But she was a vampire and this was all about vampires.

"Why all the questions?" she asked.

I told her I was a detective. I showed my licence, kept up so I could at least do the sub-contract work, and she asked to see my gun. I opened my jacket to show the shoulder-holster. It was the

first time I'd worn it in years, and the weight of the Smith &
Wesson .38 special had pulled an ache in my shoulder.

"You are a private eye? Like in the movies."

Everyone said that. She was no different.

"We have movies in Europe, you know," she said. The desert
wind was trying to get under her scarf, and she was doing things
about it with her hands. "You can't tell me why you're asking
questions because you have a client. Is that not so?"

"Not so," I said. "I have a man who might think he's a client,
but I'm doing this for myself. And a woman who's dead. Really
dead."

I told the whole story, including me and Linda. It was almost
confessional. She listened well, asking only the smart questions.

"Why are you here? In . . . what is the name of this village?"

"Mojave Wells. It calls itself a town."

We looked up and down the street and laughed. Even the
tumbleweeds were taking it easy.

"Out there in the desert," I explained, "is Manderley Castle,
brought over stone by stone from England. Would you believe it's
the wrong house? Back in the '20s, a robber baron named Noah
Cross wanted to buy the famous Manderley – the one that later
burned down – and sent agents over to Europe to do the deal.
They came home with Manderley Castle, another place entirely.
Cross still put the jigsaw together, but went into a sulk and sold it
back to the original owners, who emigrated to stay out of the
War. There was a murder case there in the '40s, nothing to do
with me. It was one of those locked-room things, with Borgia
poisons and disputed wills. A funny little Chinaman from Hawaii
solved it by gathering all the suspects in the library. The place was
abandoned until a cult of moon-worshippers squatted in it in the
'60s, founded a lunatic commune. Now, it's where you go if you
want to find the Anti-Life Equation."

"I don't believe anyone would call themselves that."

I liked this girl. She had the right attitude. I was also surprised
to find myself admitting that. She was a bloodsucking viper,
right? Wasn't Racquel worried that she was to be sacrificed to a
vampire elder? Someone born in 1416 presumably fit the description. I wanted to trust her, but that could be part of her trick. I've
been had before. Ask anyone.

"I've been digging up dirt on the ALE for a few days," I said, "and they aren't that much weirder than the rest of the local kooks. If they have a philosophy, this Khorda makes it all up as he goes along. He cut a folk rock album, *Deathmaster*. I found a copy for 99 cents and feel rooked. 'Drinking blood/Feels so good', that sort of thing. People say he's from Europe, but no one knows exactly where. The merry band at the ALE includes a Dragon Lady called Diane LeFanu, who may actually own the castle, and L. Keith Winton, who used to be a pulp writer for *Astounding Stories* but has founded a new religion that involves the faithful giving him all their money."

"That's not a *new* religion."

I believed her.

"What will you do now?" she asked.

"This town's dead as far as leads go. Dead as far as anything else, for that matter. I guess I'll have to fall back on the dull old business of going out to the castle and knocking on the front door, asking if they happen to have my wife's daughter in the dungeon. My guess is they'll be long gone. With a body left back in Poodle Springs, they have to figure the law will snoop for them in the end."

"But we might find something that'll tell us where they are. A clue?"

" 'We'?"

"I'm a detective, too. Or have been. Maybe a detective's assistant. I'm in no hurry to get to the Pacific. And you need someone who knows about vampires. You may need someone who knows about other things."

"Are you offering to be my muscle? I'm not that ancient I can't look after myself."

"I *am* that ancient, remember. It's no reflection on you, but a new-born vampire could take you to pieces. And a new-born is more likely to be stupid enough to want to. They're mostly like that Rubber Duck fellow, bursting with impulses and high on their new ability to get what they want. I was like that once myself, but now I'm a wise old lady."

She quacked the duck at me.

"We take your car," I said.

Manderley Castle was just what it sounded like. Crenellated turrets, arrow-slit windows, broken battlements, a drawbridge, even a stagnant artificial moat. It was sinking slowly into the sands and the tower was noticeably several degrees out of the vertical. Noah Cross had skimped on foundation concrete. I wouldn't be surprised if the minion who mistook this pile for the real Manderley was down there somewhere, with a divot out of his skull.

We drove across the bridge into the courtyard, home to a VW bus painted with glow-in-the-dark fanged devils, a couple of pick-up trucks with rifle racks, the inevitable Harley-Davidsons and a fleet of customized dune buggies with batwing trimmings and big red eye lamps.

There was music playing. I recognised Khorda's composition, "Big Black Bat in a Tall Dark Hat".

The Anti-Life Equation was home.

I tried to get out of the Plymouth. Geneviève was out of her driver's side door and around (over?) the car in a flash, opening the door for me as if I were her great-grandmama.

"There's a trick to the handle," she said, making me feel no better.

"If you try and help me out, I'll shoot you."

She stood back, hands up. Just then, my lungs complained. I coughed a while and red lights went off behind my eyes. I hawked up something glistening and spat it at the ground. There was blood in it.

I looked at Geneviève. Her face was flat, all emotion contained.

It wasn't pity. It was the blood. The smell did things to her personality.

I wiped off my mouth, did my best to shrug, and got out of the car like a champion. I even shut the door behind me, trick-handle or no.

To show how fearless I was, how unafraid of hideous death, I lit a Camel and punished my lungs for showing me up in front of a girl. I filled them with the smoke I'd been fanning their way since I was a kid.

Coffin nails, they called them then.

We fought our aesthetic impulses and went towards the music. I felt I should have brought a mob of Mojave Wells villagers with flaming torches, sharpened stakes and silvered scythes.

"'What a magnificent pair of knockers,'" said Geneviève, nodding at a large square door.

"There's only one," I said.

"Didn't you see *Young Frankenstein*?"

Though she'd said they had movies in Europe, somehow I didn't believe vipers – vampires, I'd have to get used to calling them if I didn't want Geneviève ripping my throat out one fine night – concerned themselves with dates at the local passion pit. Obviously, the undead read magazines, bought underwear, grumbled about taxes and did crossword puzzles like everyone else. I wondered if she played chess.

She took the knocker and hammered to wake the dead.

Eventually the door was opened by a skinny old bird dressed as an English butler. His hands were knots of arthritis and he could do with a shave.

The music was mercifully interrupted.

"Who is it, George?" boomed a voice from inside the castle.

"Visitors," croaked George the butler. "You are visitors, aren't you?"

I shrugged. Geneviève radiated a smile.

The butler was smitten. He trembled with awe.

"Yes," she said, "I'm a vampire. And I'm very, very old and very, very thirsty. Now, aren't you going to invite me in? Can't cross the threshold unless you do."

I didn't know if she was spoofing him.

George creaked his neck, indicating a sandy mat inside the doorway. It was lettered with the word WELCOME.

"That counts," she admitted. "More people should have those."

She stepped inside. I didn't need the invite to follow.

George showed us into the big hall. Like all decent cults, the ALE had an altar and thrones for the bigwigs and cold flagstones with the occasional mercy rug for the devoted suckers.

In the blockiest throne sat Khorda, a vampire with curly fangs, the full long-hair-and-tangled-beard hippie look and an electric guitar. He wore a violent purple and orange kaftan, and his chest was covered by bead-necklaces hung with diamond-eyed skulls, plastic novelty bats, Austro-Hungarian military medals, inverted crucifixes, a "Nixon in '72" button, gold marijuana leaves and a dried human finger. By his side was a wraith-thin vision in velvet I assumed to be Diane LeFanu, who claimed – like a lot of vipers –

to be California's earliest vampire settler. I noticed she wore discreet little ruby earplugs.

At the feet of these divines was a crowd of kids, of both varieties, all with long hair and fangs. Some wore white shifts, while others were naked. Some wore joke-shop plastic fangs, while others had real ones. I scanned the congregation, and spotted Racquel at once, eyes a red daze, kneeling on stone with her shift tucked under her, swaying her ripe upper body in time to the music Khorda had stopped playing.

I admitted this was too easy. I started looking at the case again, taking it apart in my mind and jamming the pieces together in new ways. Nothing made sense, but that was hardly breaking news at this end of the century.

Hovering like the Wizard of Oz between the throne-dais and the worshipper-space was a fat living man in a 1950s suit and golf hat. I recognized L. Keith Winton, author of "Robot Rangers of the Gamma Nebula" (1946) and other works of serious literature, including *Plasmatics: The New Communion* (1950), founding text of the Church of Immortology. If ever there were a power-behind-the-throne bird, this was he.

"We've come for Racquel Loring Ohlrig," announced Geneviève. I should probably have said that.

"No one of that name dwells among us," boomed Khorda. He had a big voice.

"I see her there," I said, pointing.

"Sister Red Rose," said Khorda.

He stuck out his arm and gestured. Racquel stood. She did not move like herself. Her teeth were not a joke. She had real fangs. They fit badly in her mouth, making it look like an ill-healed red wound. Her red eyes were puffy.

"You turned her," I said, anger in my gut.

"Sister Red Rose has been elevated to the eternal."

Geneviève's hand was on my shoulder.

I thought of Linda, bled empty in her pool, a spike in her head. I wanted to burn this castle down, and sew the ground with garlic.

"I am Geneviève Dieudonné," she announced, formally.

"Welcome, Lady Elder," said the LeFanu woman. Her eyes held no welcome for Geneviève. She made a gesture, which unfolded membrane-like velvet sleeves. "I am Diane LeFanu. And this is Khorda, the Deathmaster."

Geneviève looked at the guru viper.

"General Iorga, is it not? Late of the Carpathian Guard. We met in 1888, at the palace of Prince Consort Dracula. Do you remember?"

Khorda/Iorga was not happy.

I realized he was wearing a wig and a false beard. He might have immortality, but was well past youth. I saw him as a tubby, ridiculous fraud. He was one of those elders who had been among Dracula's toadies, but was lost in a world without a King Vampire. Even for California, he was a sad soul.

"Racquel," I said. "It's me. Your father wants . . ."

She spat hissing red froth.

"It would be best if this new-born were allowed to leave with us," Geneviève said, not to Khorda but Winton. "There's the small matter of a murder charge."

Winton's plump, bland, pink face wobbled. He looked anger at Khorda. The guru trembled on his throne, and boomed without words.

"Murder, Khorda?" asked Winton. "Murder? Who told you we could afford murder?"

"None was done," said Khorda/Iorga.

I wanted to skewer him with something. But I went beyond anger. He was too afraid of Winton – not a person you'd immediately take as a threat, but clearly the top dog at the ALE – to lie.

"Take the girl," Winton said to me.

Racquel howled in rage and despair. I didn't know if she was the same person we had come for. As I understood it, some vampires changed entirely when they turned, burned out their previous memories and became sad blanks, reborn with dreadful thirsts and the beginnings of a mad cunning.

"If she's a killer, we don't want her," said Winton. "Not yet."

I approached Racquel. The other cultists shrank away from her. Her face shifted, bloating and smoothing as if flatworms were passing just under her skin. Her teeth were ridiculously expanded, fat pebbles of sharp bone. Her lips were torn and split.

She hissed as I reached out to touch her.

Had this girl, in the throes of turning, battened on her mother, on Linda, and gone too far, taken more than her human mind had intended, glutting herself until her viper thirst was assuaged?

I saw the picture only too well. I tried to fit it with what Junior had told me.

He had sworn Racquel was innocent.

But his daughter had never been innocent, not as a warm person and not now as a new-born vampire.

Geneviève stepped close to Racquel and managed to slip an arm round her. She cooed in the girl's ear, coaxing her to come, replacing the deathmaster in her mind.

Racquel took her first steps. Geneviève encouraged her. Then Racquel stopped as if she'd hit an invisible wall. She looked to Khorda/Iorga, hurt and betrayal in her eyes, and to Winton, with that pleading moué I knew well. Racquel was still herself, still trying to wheedle love from unworthy men, still desperate to survive through her developing wiles.

Her attention was caught by a noise. Her nose wrinkled, quizzically.

Geneviève had taken out her rubber duck and quacked it.

"Come on, Racquel," she said, as if to a happy dog. "Nice quacky-quacky. Do you want it?"

She quacked again.

Racquel attempted a horrendous smile. A baby-tear of blood showed on her cheek.

We took our leave of the Anti-Life Equation.

Junior was afraid of his daughter. And who wouldn't be?

I was back in Poodle Springs, not a place I much cared to be. Junior's wife had stormed out, enraged that this latest drama didn't revolve around her. Their house was decorated in the expensive-but-ugly mock Spanish manner, and called itself ranch-style though there were no cattle or crops on the grounds.

Geneviève sat calmly on Junior's long grey couch. She fit in like a piece of Carrera marble at a Tobacco Road yard sale. I was helping myself to Scotch.

Father and daughter looked at each other.

Racquel wasn't such a fright now. Geneviève had driven her here, following my lead. Somehow, on the journey, the elder vampire had imparted grooming tips to the new-born, helping her through the shock of turning. Racquel had regular-sized fangs, and the red in her eyes was just a tint. Outside, she had been experimenting with her newfound speed, moving her hands so fast they seemed not to be there.

But Junior was terrified. I had to break the spell.

"It's like this," I said, setting it out. "You both killed Linda. The difference is that one of you brought her back."

Junior covered his face and fell to his knees.

Racquel stood over him.

"Racquel has been turning for weeks, joining up with that crowd in the desert. She felt them taking her mind away, making her part of a harem or a slave army. She needed someone strong in her corner, and Daddy didn't cut it. So she went to the strongest person in her life, and made her stronger. She just didn't get to finish the job before the Anti-Life Equation came to her house. She called you, Junior, just before she went under, became part of their family. When you got to the house, it was just as you said. Linda was at the bottom of the swimming pool. She'd gone there to turn. You didn't even lie to me. She was dead. You took a mallet and a spike – what was it from, the tennis net? – and made her truly dead. Did you tell yourself you did it for her, so she could be at peace? Or was it because you didn't want to be in a town – a world – with a *stronger* Linda Loring? She was a fighter. I bet she fought you."

There were deep scratches on his wrists, like the rips in his shirt I had noticed that night. If I were a gather-the-suspects-in-the-library type of dick, I would have spotted that as a clue straight off.

Junior sobbed a while. Then, when nobody killed him, he uncurled and looked about, with the beginnings of an unattractive slyness.

"It's legal, you know," he said. "Linda was dead."

Geneviève's face was cold. I knew California law did not recognise the state of undeath. Yet. There were enough vampire lawyers on the case to get that changed soon.

"That's for the cops," I said. "Fine people. You've always been impressed with their efficiency and courtesy."

Junior was white under the tear-streaks. He might not take a murder fall on this, but Tokyo and Riyadh weren't going to like the attention the story would get. That was going to have a transformative effect on his position in Ohlrig Oil and Copper. And the PSPD would find something to nail him with: making false or incomplete statements, mutilating a corpse for profit (no more alimony), contemptible gutlessness.

Another private eye might have left him with Racquel.

She stood over her father, fists swollen by the sharp new nails extruding inside, dripping her own blood – the blood that she had made her mother drink – onto the mock-mission-style carpet.

Geneviève was beside her, with the duck.

"Come with me, Racquel," she said. "Away from the dark red places."

Days later, in a bar on Cahuenga just across from the building where my office used to be, I was coughing over a shot and a Camel.

They found me.

Racquel was her new self, flitting everywhere, flirting with men of all ages, sharp eyes fixed on the pulses in their necks and the blue lines in their wrists.

Geneviève ordered bull's blood.

She made a face.

"I'm used to fresh from the bull," she said. "This is rancid."

"We're getting live piglets from next week," said the bartender. "The straps are already fitted, and we have the neck-spigots on order."

"See," Geneviève told me. "We're here to stay. We're a market."

I coughed some more.

"You could get something done about that," she said, softly.

I knew what she meant. I could become a vampire. Who knows: if Linda had made it, I might have been tempted. As it was, I was too old to change.

"You remind me of someone," she said. "Another detective. In another country, a century ago."

"Did he catch the killer and save the girl?"

An unreadable look passed over her face. "Yes," she said, "that's exactly what he did."

"Good for him."

I drank. The Scotch tasted of blood. I could never get used to drinking that.

According to the newspapers, there'd been a raid on the castle in the desert. General Iorga and Diane LeFanu were up on a raft of abduction, exploitation and murder charges; with most of the murder victims undead enough to recite testimony in favour of their killers, they would stay in court forever. No mention was made of L. Keith Winton, though I had noticed a storefront on Hollywood Boulevard displaying nothing but a stack of Immortology tracts. Outside, fresh-faced new-born vampires smiled under black parasols and invited passersby in for "a blood test'. Picture thus: followers who are going to give you all their money *and* live forever. And they said Dracula was dead.

"Racquel will be all right," Geneviève assured me. "She's so good at this that she frightens me. She won't make get again in a hurry."

I looked at the girl, surrounded by eager warm bodies. She'd use them up by the dozen. I saw the last of Linda in her, and regretted that there was none of me.

"What about you?" I asked Geneviève.

"I've seen the Pacific. Can't drive much further. I'll stay around for a while, maybe get a job. I used to know a lot about being a doctor. Perhaps I'll try to get into med school, and requalify. I'm tired of jokes about leeches. Then again, I have to unlearn so much. Mediaeval knowledge is a handicap, you know."

I put my licence on the bar.

"You could get one like it," I said.

She took off her glasses. Her eyes were still startling.

"This was my last case, Geneviève. I got the killer and I saved the girl. It's been a long goodbye and it's over. I've met my own killers, in bottles and soft-packs of twenty. Soon, they'll finish me and I'll be sleeping the big sleep. There's not much more I can do for people. There are going to be a lot more like Racquel. Those kids at the castle in the desert. The customers our bartender is expecting next week. The suckers drawn into Winton's nets. Some are going to need you. And some are going to be real vipers, which means other folk are going to need you to protect them from the worst they can do. You're good, sweetheart. You could do good. There, that's my speech over."

She dipped a finger-tip in her glass of congealing blood and licked it clean, thinking.

"You might have an idea there, gumshoe."

I drank to her.

IAIN SINCLAIR

The Keeper of the Rothenstein Tomb

IAIN SINCLAIR LIVES, WORKS AND WALKS IN LONDON. His acclaimed books include *White Chappell Scarlet Tracings*, the award-winning *Downriver*, *Radon Daughters*, *Slow Chocolate Autopsy* (with artist Dave McKean) and *Lights Out for the Territory*.

His latest novel, *Landor's Tower*, although employing his standard transgeneric, paranoid/visionary style, is unusual in being set outside London. It is a return to the country of his birth, Wales; an investigation and celebration of the borderland (Machen quests and Utopian communities). A second branch of this post-Powys Mabinogion grows out along the other bank of the River Severn (unexplained suicides in the defence industry, a political conspiracy). The now-defunct Aust service station, overlooking the Severn Bridge, is seen as the hinge of the whole affair; a Hitchcockian location where the importunate dead encounter night travellers and stoic comedians.

" 'The Keeper of the Rothenstein Tomb' is the underside of an earlier investigation," explains the author, "undertaken with the artist Rachel Lichtenstein (and published as 'Rodinsky's Room'). A Spitalfields hermit disappears, leaving behind him a garret stuffed with clothes, records, books, cabbalistic transcriptions. Lichtenstein teases out the truth of this sorry episode, and then, in subsequent researches, learns of a man who is paid to live in a Jewish graveyard, as the keeper of a single tomb . . ."

M EN WERE SICK, WOMEN PREGNANT; Norton kept on walking. This was the form his mania took, hammering for hours at a time, out there beyond the traces of the Roman wall. He could no longer enter the city, the density of surveillance undid him, leeched his energies. Instead, he played the canary, fluttering around the rim of the affected area, interested to discover at what point he would go down. Norton was stone crazy, written out. If he stopped moving, so he believed, the treadmill would grind to a halt, buildings would topple, ancient streams would rise to the surface, the Walbrook, the Fleet, the Tyburn; the Wall would crumble back into dust and the demons of greed, paranoia, corruption would escape.

Hoxton hurt. Clerkenwell was a reservoir of self-images, a lake of shimmering paper reflections. Through dusty picture-windows, he drank the deep blues of photographed water. He found a surrogate calm in secondhand greenery, private parks and landscaped gardens reproduced on stiff white card. Idylls no thicker than a spray of varnish. Cabinets of naked strangers stared back at him.

Poetry was accessed from boards outside newsagents' shops, the ones that summarised what was happening in a tactful arrangement of uppercase lettering: BLIND BEGGAR SOLD. He loved these messages, covert dispatches produced for his eyes only. They were like transcripts taken down, hot, from a psychic wire service. In the towers of Hawksmoor churches and derelict end-of-terrace houses, waiting for demolition, were spies and watchers who tapped in their reports. BLIND BEGGAR SOLD. This was all that was left of pure information; lean, spare, pertinent. Norton aspired to, but never achieved, the style of these anonymous masters with their calligraphic half-haikus. BLIND BEGGAR SOLD.

His spirits lifted. The oasis of Bunhill Fields, the effigy of John Bunyan with grass growing from his sockets, hadn't lost its resonance; the stone-cistern monument of the woman was tap'd for the dropsy. He looked forward, literally – previewing streetscapes in a rush of single-frame images – to his breakfast with the only woman in London who would still commission a story. The only one generous enough to humour his affliction, his curse, this compulsion to repeat himself, do the police and all other citizens in the *same* voice; to tell it and keep telling it, beyond the point where he required listeners, a single listener, anyone.

An off-duty academic, down from Cambridge on a jolly, moonlighting as a tour guide, one of three jobs he needed to keep himself in Walter Benjamin reissues, told Norton about a set of examination papers he'd been called on to assess. A student from the Middle East, offering his response to the usual sneaky stuff about Beowulf, *The Pardoner's Tale*, Jane Austen, racial stereotypes in Conrad, Harry Potter, came up with precisely the same essay, copied out five times. The stratagem had been discovered by accident. The man was sailing through quite nicely. "Very respectable upper 2/1," breezed the don, taking a refill, one for the road, before the dash to King's Cross. "He'd hit on the perfect form. Content doesn't matter. A smooth passage between relevant bullet points."

Early light in Fortune Street soothed him, soothed Norton; leaf-patterns carpeting the grey tarmac, fish-shadows, movement. The voices of girls singing behind the fence of the primary school, singing as they skipped. Like a newsreel from the lost Fifties.

> *Ring-a-bell, Ring-a-bell,*
> *Mamma's belly's going to swell.*

"It's a privilege to be here, at all, don't you think?" the young woman, Katie Harwood, asked. "Before it disappears." Give her credit, she could put away a decent plate of meat, two kinds of sausage, a couple of kidneys, liver black as treacle, nestling on a bed of refried potato, a bright wink of egg. She passed on the stout, the whisky chaser Norton offered – to collect from the bar. Katie was – paying, picking up the tab for her employers to process.

Norton liked her warmth, the moist heat of a woman who enjoyed a good walk, knocking off twenty miles every weekend. She was in bloom, hair shining, catching the best of the neon strips, the fluctuating interference in that fan-cooled dungeon beneath Smithfield meat-market. A pale-gold moustache added distinction to the modelling of that interesting area above the upper lip. What do they call it? Not labium. You could use the term for the lip itself, but it might give the wrong impression. Good word though. Evocative, but inaccurate.

John Major – remember him? – horribly misnamed, was a man defined by this apparently insignificant area of his physiognomy.

Major had a swelling beneath the vertical trench that runs from lip to nose. It looked like a gumshield that had slipped, a moustache growing on the inside. The way the ridge bounced artificial light was his undoing. Nobody listened to what he had to say, the Librium drone of a peevish man keeping his rage in check, vanity in a solemn disguise. You could see them at cabinet meetings, the Lamonts and Lawsons, leonine Heseltine, baggy Ken, pantingly ambitious Portillo, sniggering behind their hands. The PM has a prow like the *Titanic*, so who cares what he wants us not to do? Better fix up something in the city, sketch out the slimming books, before the whole mess goes public; before the punters get another chance to check out that inflexible philtrum.

That's the word, one of the best. Pure music. Philtrum with philtral ridge. Katie's was a beauty. Especially when she talked, flicked her hair back, told Norton what she had in mind: a follow-up to a book he'd managed to get his name on, years before, a Jewish girl's research into a Whitechapel cabbalist who had disappeared from a cluttered room. Except that he hadn't and he wasn't: magician or golem or golem-maker. Just a sad survivor, the last of his family, swept away by social reform. Plenty of stuff had been liberated from the garret, the weavers' attic, books and manuscripts, real and fraudulent and really fraudulent, surfacing now with boring frequency in rare book-dealers' catalogues. The synagogue itself was so well-preserved nobody had set foot in it for years, except for kosher artists, names who did things with installations and pretty lights.

"Rodinsky's mirror has been traced. It was photographed aeons ago in some book we're still trying to locate," said Katie. "But it seems to have acquired, in the years of its disappearance, a rather sinister reputation. Stare into it long enough and you see his room. As it was. What *really* happened. The mirror never learnt to lie. It's fixed in a perpetually present tense, the moment when the room was sealed, the window boarded over, and the light died."

"Fine," said Norton, disguising a yawn in a swipe of eggy bread. He'd heard it all before and was weary of these Gothic retrievals, now that they'd run with the tide to Chelsea, Fulham, Putney and points west. The whole business had been heritaged, art-streamed, given a provisional blessing by lottery sponsors with a sharp eye for the way a good yarn can underwrite development; tents on swamps, fairground rides rebranded as futurist architecture and operated by airlines looking for a way to get out of hardware. What better than wingless modules attached to a bicycle wheel, a journey that never leaves the terminal? Great views, plenty of point-of-sale merchandising, minimal upkeep. We were back, all unknowingly, to those two quid flights around the bay. A glimpse of the pier, a quick chuck in the brown bag, and home for tea.

Norton blamed himself. He couldn't keep shtum, didn't know when to leave well alone. He had to worry at, tease out, secrets that were better left untold: vanishing caretakers, patterns of malign energy that linked eighteenth-century churches, labyrinths, temples, plague pits. Now they were far too loudly on the map, or trashed by attention. All he ever wanted was to write himself out, to fade into the masonry, become one of the revenants someone else would track. But there wasn't enough of him to interest even the most desperate bounty hunter. Biography? The guy had never done anything, been anywhere, said anything memorable. He was a material ghost. An addict of the city, not of smack or booze, women or whips. He couldn't even offer family interest, a monster father or a mum who put it about.

"Men were buried with their weapons, women with mirrors. Polished copper ovals – like ping-pong bats with a touch of mange. Super examples in the museum at Heraklion," Katie gushed. "Been to Crete lately?"

"I had a kebab once," Norton replied. "Didn't care for it. Like gnawing your way through a mummified arm."

"It's just that I was thinking of, you know, the famous Phaistos Disk. The patterns of dust in Rodinsky's mirror, silvered flakes, where the backing has chipped away, seem to make up, if you want to see it, a sort of serpentine path. With mysterious figures or letters from an alphabet nobody has cracked."

I've cracked it, Norton thought. I know what I am: a set of Scottish teeth. That is to say, an absence that nags; phantom pains, aching gums to remind you that something was once there. It was like sex. He'd been dreaming lately of pleasures he hadn't experienced in thirty years. The taste of good food. Being able to bite back in a friendly domestic tussle. He relished nightmares involving an underground bunker, passages opening from passages, an earthy chill. And how, as his flickering candle failed, spilling hot wax on his trembling hand, he located the magic box, arm at full stretch, in a spidery aperture. Opening it, his fingers traced the solid tines of a Celtic comb, king brooch or miniature diadem. Before the light failed, leaving him disorientated, prematurely incarcerated in a vacant tomb, he saw what he'd found: some hermit's upper set, a denture put aside against the lucky day when meat would be back on the menu.

"Why I suggested the Cock for our meeting," said Katie, discreetly sliding an envelope across the wreckage of the table, "was that the market porters drink here when they've finished their shift. What with the new Euro regulations and all the silly fuss about beef on the bone, Smithfield's a shrunken operation. Clean as a whistle, no blood in the sawdust, no trolleys of cows' heads . . ."

"Talking of which," Norton suggested, "they do a very nice bubble and squeak, if you could go another round. And a Guinness to wash it down."

"Look over there, but discreetly," she whispered, as Norton, feigning interest, was up on his toes. "The two old boys in that booth. Know who they are? Last of the bummarees. They still haul *fantastic* weights. Some of those carts weigh five-hundred pounds, empty. George is nearly seventy years old, ex-boxer, friend of all the villains. But he's sweet as pie. Keeps going, so they say, on alcohol."

Norton expected creatures from the lower depths (not unlike himself), but in greasy leather aprons. And discovered instead two elderly gentlemen in business suits and wing collars being served with enormous tact and deference by the guv'nor. Two or three bone-helmet lads, with tattoos and prominent veins, stood back from the table, showing off their cross of St George T-shirts as if auditioning for entry to a Templar Lodge.

"It's what they call their 'Parliament'. They meet here every morning after they've punched their cards," Katie said. "The bummarees, a few of the security chaps – ex-military police – and skinhead footsoldiers from Dagenham, BNP, putting the world to rights. Old George is married to a tax lawyer, has a flat in the Barbican."

"Mosley was a prince," George was telling them. "Toffs don't move like the rest of us. Brought up with horses, born in the saddle, so to speak. And dancing lessons . . ."

"Buggered rigid in all them schools," his friend chipped in, approvingly.

"Discipline. Top-drawer personal hygiene. You've seen the films of Cable Street, Ned, rank and file like a load of bleedin' ants, rushing and jerky, with old Nick still as a statue. Hand on hip. He always put me in mind of Robert Donat, or Cary Grant, white tie and tails, stuck with the Keystone Kops."

Katie led Norton over to George's table. This parliament, the hack thought, isn't much different from the one in Westminster. They all talk as if they've got too much tongue in the mouth. They yawn and scratch like monkeys. The old boys, it's true, have better manners, less ego. They don't have to disguise their opinions and they've put in a proper morning's graft before they let their prejudices out for an airing.

"Please don't get up, no, really, George," Katie fluttered, laying a cool hand on the pinstriped sleeve. "We don't want to interrupt your meal. It's just that my friend is trying to get in touch with your friend, the one who works in the burial ground."

"Who's she on about?" Ned wanted to know. Women weren't welcome on the wrong side of the bar, unless plates needed shifting, or an ashtray was beginning to spill.

"You know, the lovely old chap who hurt his back and had to find a less demanding occupation. I don't know *how* you pull those weights. Carts are so unstable on cobbles and slippery floors. You're both so frightfully fit."

"Bent Les," Ned shouted. "The bint means Bent Les. He's only gone and got 'isself webbed up with a Jew Boy. Whossit? Marks? Spencer? Lew Grade?"

"Sorry, Miss," George said. "We've lost touch with Leslie since he transferred east. I believe he's found employment taking care of the tomb of one of them banking families. Usurers, money grubbing scum, but they take care of their own. Respect for the dead. And beautifully polished shoes."

"Could you tell us *which* burial ground?"

"It's a foreign country down there now, Miss. I couldn't say. Try Brady Street. There was a few nice little boozers round that way, before they sent the Twins down."

"Thanks so much," Katie said. "So helpful." And she signalled the guv'nor to bring another round. The parliament went back to giving the single European currency, regulations governing the transportation of livestock, a bit of a going over.

Restored to their table, Katie showed her delight by squeezing Norton's hand. He caught a nostalgic whiff of coconut butter. It seemed that Katie's hunch was confirmed, the whispers that her researcher (a man called Kaporal) was trying to punt: Bent Les, the supposed keeper of Rodinsky's mirror, was hiding out in a Jewish Burial Ground, just off the Whitechapel Road, within a stone's throw of the Royal London Hospital. You'd catch a great view of the stone slabs, lined up on an east/west orientation, and hidden among scraggy trees, as they choppered you in after a major road accident. Norton, in his wanderings, had often paused, near the new Sainsbury's, to watch the latest Glasgow wet-brain being elbowed by security guards. Despite the Dalgleish-impenetrable curses and the waving arms, these demented Jocks never spilled a drop of their industrial-strength Tennents. Then there was the noise. You didn't see the red helicopters making for the hospital roof, you saw trees sway, windows rattle in the flats. The uncut grass of the burial ground, behind walls, glimpsed through a locked gate, was woven into crop circles. Weed-trees, sycamore and London plane, lost bark, felt their root-anchors give: as if the Day of Judgement had come early, the Whitechapel Apocalypse when the parched ground gives up its dead.

". . . have to fly, late for my appointment at the clinic."

Norton had drifted off on his East London heritage trail; decommissioned synagogues, chirpy Marxists disputing the pavement, old Jack conducting his experiment in social engineering, a premature National Health gynaecologist. The word "clinic" brought him up sharp. He wasn't a fastidious man, but he broke off his attempt to spear Katie's leftover rind.

"Anything . . . serious?"

"I'm pregnant. We, I, both of us . . . absolutely chuffed. Due on Midsummer's Day. My first."

Useless at noticing these things, or knowing what to say, Norton chewed his fingers. He'd read some stuff about the Transit of Venus, a shift in the cosmological gears that was having a devastating effect. Women, in Norton's experience, conceived to ward off bad karma. One of his wives hadn't been able to go within five miles of Glastonbury without getting knocked up. "An evil place," she'd mutter, as he embarked on his circumnavigation of the Tor. She couldn't read John Cowper Powys without breaking out in hives. "I'm not pregnant," she would reply to impertinent questions. "I'm having a baby."

"Go down there. See if you can persuade this man, Leslie, to show you the mirror. Keep it under 2,000 words. We're not the *LRB*. No digressions, nothing heavy. Bit of a mystery, blah-de-blah. Like opening a Pharaonic tomb or the Palace of King Midas. Facilitate him, if you have to. And we'll arrange to send a photographer. That's *important*. The story has to be picture led."

On the street, abandoned, left to a fractured narrative of self, Norton searched out potential parentheses. He was being paid in millennial increments: grave-robber, mirror, morbid frisson wasn't much to be going on with. He'd never been able to sculpt a page with dialogue (it came out like Pinter slumming). He couldn't work out where to leave those lovely white spaces the Sexton Blake gang exploited to polyfill their 30,000 word novellas.

He got out of the sun and into a medieval church, strolled the crescent, the shady stone forest, as if he had a perfect right to the cloisters. He admired the stills from *Shakespeare in Love*, read verses dedicated to men whose lives were reduced to polished heads, ruffed and chill, in wall safes with a bit of text.

Then he retraced his steps through laneways with perfect Elizabeth proportions, wine bars that serviced futures traders, victims who had signed up to the Net – and, consequently, weren't there, not really. You saw them walking with things clamped to their heads like battery chargers. Their lips never rested, driving, eating, lounging al fresco, chatting to their mates. They talked while they were talking, talked over themselves, contributed to the universal babble that formed a permanent electronic cloud over the city. Norton had been in bars and heard them yelp, "Where are you?" to someone sitting at the next table. And still they were happy to carry a spit-stick against the cheek. Like an electric-razor that chats back.

The last time Katie had called him, caught him in his favourite grease caff, Norton thought she was on the job. She was panting so much he could barely hear what she had to say. It turned out she was running for a bus.

Nothing in the slog through Clerkenwell, Shoreditch, Tower

Hamlets, took Norton's eye. If he'd had a camera, he would have left it in the bag. London was a book with no surprises. It knew itself too well. When self-consciousness turns into art, art into fashion, fashion into property, it's time to pull the plug. If that were an option. London, for Norton, was like life: unremittingly grim, until you considered the alternative.

They were putting up a fresh poster outside a newsagent's shop on Bethnal Green Road: CHERIE, IT'S A BOY! Didn't she know?

For a week or more, Norton hung around Mocatta House, ducking into the Bangladeshi minimart to buy a bottle of milk and a packet of brightly coloured dust that looked like broken biscuits and burnt a hole in his tongue. He'd been all round the Brady Street burial ground and hadn't found a way in. Most of the original doors had been bricked up. Norton didn't want to lurk in such a way that the CCTV cameras picked him up. He waited and he watched.

A child, male, one of the dusky ones, a local, had a key. Either that or he knew how to pick a lock. Early, every third day, he would heft a clinking carrier bag, leaning heavily against the bias of its weight, into the burial ground. Norton positioned himself to track where the lad went, when he passed through the gate. But that didn't help. He saw the blackened memorial slabs, the shell of a gatehouse, several grassy mounds and an unnecessary profusion of trees. The place was half wilderness. It had been let go, sealed, willed towards erasure. As if someone wanted to wipe the slate, overdraw the memory bank: the stones here were mute. The sounds of the city ran around the perimeter wall, cracking bricks, but didn't penetrate the ash-garden within. Norton refuted Bishop Berkeley: here was a tree in the forest that fell unseen, and still experienced a profound existence. An otherness. The places, people, buildings that weren't there, were the ones that affected Norton most. Chain the doors, cover hospitals with plastic sheeting, plant a crop of screening bushes and the ghosts must sing. It was the bits you couldn't see, black holes on the map, unlisted bunkers and disregarded lives that made most noise. When an old tin street sign was chucked in the skip, Norton withered, felt the wind from the steppes creep into his bones.

The boy with the bag walked up to a black marble monument

and vanished. Maybe it was the shock of finding one memorial in perfect nick, ready for inspection at any time. Norton stayed on watch until he reappeared, bag empty, rolled into a truncheon with which he swiped the heads from dandelions.

Outside Tyler House (Masonic implications noted), Norton tried to suborn the lad. "Oi, baldy. Fuck off, you. Pervert," shouted a squad of his older mates, mobhanded but slender. They saw enough in Norton's eye, the way he ignored them, to appreciate that the designer vagrant was still capable of inflicting collateral damage. "Oi, wanker. Oi oi oi," they taunted, moving off in search of better turf; reverting to the old language, bird-swift, choral, provoking laughter. Neat as knives.

For the price of a couple of dozen Pokémon figures from a machine outside the minimart, a deal was struck. Bad habits dying hard, the pedant Norton worried about the plural of Pokémon (obviously, in his jellied brain-computer, he was writing this as he went along, translating life into language). Pokémons? Pokémen? Or the one that sounds like an Afro-Caribbean menu, "Poké, mon. Poké and beans."

Next time up, when the kid delivered his groceries to the man in the burial ground, the one who might be Bent Les, Norton would shadow him; make his play.

Norton was waiting outside Mocatta House at dawn, looking at the lion. And it was worth the trouble. There was a plaque set into the wall above the bit that said: "Erected 1905. Modernised 1980." The plaque had been dosed so heavily with emulsion that it was almost drowned, but you could still make out the Lion of St Mark, the wreaths forming the inner rim of a mandala, a botched labyrinth. Jewish mysticism of some kind, Norton supposed. He owed a lot, more than he cared to admit, to Jewish patrons who emerged from time to time to underwrite some of his crazier projects, like publishing books. Through these relationships, practical wisdom that ran deep, he had defined himself, found out who he was: a void, a man without family, tribe or allegiance. An outsider to outsiders.

The kid plucked at his shirt-tails, rattled the keys. He moved fast, effortlessly, barely seeming to touch the ground. They were through the gate and locked inside this secret garden before

Norton had time to register the drop in temperature, the coldness of his hands.

The black marble tomb was a magnificent thing, belonging to various Rothensteins. "Vessels of Wrath", Norton punned. Someone had been busy with the weedkiller and the polish. What made his grandiloquent sepulchre stand out, like a Rodin dropped amongst bits of coloured string and beanbags in the Tate Modern, was the unloved bleakness that surrounded it. Dead stones. Half-eradicated histories. An angry form of black pollution, part crustose lichen, part soot, crept from the ground like a living shadow to swallow memory.

"Come on, mate. Hurry up then," the kid called. Norton couldn't see him. He'd done his trick again and disappeared into thin air. Norton tapped the Rothenstein tomb till his knuckles bled: solid as an investment portfolio. He was glad that, in respect, he'd covered his head – by cutting the peak from a baseball – cap. He felt exposed, watched. He'd been turfed out of graveyards too many times; asked what he wanted, who he was looking for, if he knew where he was: the difficult ones.

There were glass snails on the stone slabs, eyes without pupils, oval shapes you might find in Italy or Greece with photographs of the officially dead. Such things, Norton reckoned, didn't belong in a Jewish burial ground. He was niggling at this anomaly when a hand tugged his trouser cuff. The kid was in a hole in the ground.

Les had done the crypt out quite nicely. Nobody knew who he was. Nobody knew he was there. Money was paid to an associate by an unknown intermediary for the upkeep of a single tomb. Les was bareheaded, silvery-pale with a black mouth. Like a burnt-out light bulb. He was shifty, rocking his shoulders in a constant sparring action, dry-popping his lips.

He'd got a mattress, a table, a couple of chairs, a paraffin lamp and a battery-driven TV set that flickered and faded as a constant irritant in the shadowy depths of the chamber. There was also a cat, an albino that looked as if it had never seen the light of day.

"My brother," Les said, "was in the demolition. Had first call on every fucking church in the East End. He done Princelet Street. Fetched out this mirror. Old, he reckoned. What you call it, Gregorian, Georgian. The business, John. I told him to run it up Camden Passage of a Wednesday."

Down here, under Whitechapel, under poignant earth, Norton was in no hurry. The kid left his carrier bag and skipped. Norton had waited through sixty lifetimes to broach this dark reservoir of time, he wasn't going to jeopardise the possibility of shifting dimensions, accessing a parallel world, by arguing the toss with a pensioned member of Mosley's legions. He let Les drag out cases of gas masks, bundles of newspapers, boots with brown labels, ceremonial robes. The longer this went on, the more time would coalesce overhead. There might, at last, be a way out of his fix. A way of quitting London, definitively, without taking another step. The crypt, Norton imagined, ran into other crypts, other passageways. His dream of the dripping candle and the treasure hidden in an alcove began to seem prophetic. A bad sign.

Rustling the cashmoney from Katie Harwood's envelope under Les' nose was like belling one of Pavlov's dogs. Les was keen to be shot of this inopportune intruder, keen to return to silence and the oracle of the TV monitor (so old it played programmes that had decayed *before* they could be repeated).

"A oncer in the hand. Give me a receipt and I'll take it away," Norton grunted. And, muttering, Les shuffled off into the darkness, the inner sanctum; where he scratched about, searching for a pen.

Picking up the mirror, the terrible thing that once hung on the wall of the hermit Rodinsky's attic, Norton lost his breath. There wasn't, as promised, a room frozen in time, but a face! Vague, dolorous, tragic. Shaped from pain. Hair gone, mouth creased; toothless, with sunken cheeks. Norton. He was staring at himself. His first emotion was relief. He balanced the mirror against a stack of books and stepped back like a connoisseur. The face stayed where it was. An X-ray of the Turin shroud, a flash of white heat. A negative. That made sense. Fear projected into the silver surface like elective alchemy.

This wasn't Norton. This was the *back* of the mirror. Sacking and wood with the vague imprint of a man who had turned the mirror, long ago, to face the wall.

You could scam Norton once, scam him again, as often as you liked if you were female, but this contract smelt iffy. With Les still cursing and stumbling, Norton pulled back the oilcloth and looked under the table: a dozen mirrors, wreckers' plunder picked up for a couple of bob in Club Row. Naughty Les was pulling a flanker, raising funds for the party and the bummarees; an irony they would appreciate as they gummed a hunk of bull. An immigrant myth was being exploited to fund stiffer immigration laws, alien expulsions, detention camps. Les was punting his final solution to the Princelet Street mystery wholesale.

Very neat. Norton called Les out to congratulate him, before he smashed his ribs. But Les was gone. The TV had stuck on mob footage, face after face, accusing Norton, screaming their approval in a silent paroxysm of hero worship.

He was alone. He sat at Les' table. He thought he heard the cat once, then nothing for hours. Days. He reversed the mirror. And there *was* a room. Like this. *Exactly* like this: mattress, table, lamp. With one minor difference: no Norton. An empty room with darkening shadows. A mortality Polaroid quietly transmuting into oil. Darkness that lapped around his ankles, threatening to rise.

Some time later, when Norton realized, and accepted, that he would never leave this place, he brought out the other mirrors. Each one contained a different room, a crypt. Unfurnished chambers with slabs for beds. Frames of film from a bureaucratic catalogue, a monumental library of the dead. Beneath London was an untenanted necropolis. While up above, pale sunlight glinted on the glass snails, those small oval frames that had attached themselves with sticky secretions to the gravestones. In each frame now was a face, one of the sleepers from limbo, involuntary zombies; one of those who had to know how the story turned out.

MICK GARRIS

Forever Gramma

AWARD-WINNING FILM-MAKER MICK GARRIS began writing fiction at the age of twelve. By the time he was in high school, he was writing music and film journalism for various local and national publications.

His first movie business job was as a receptionist for George Lucas' Star Wars Corporation, where he worked his way up to running the remote-controlled R2-D2 robot at personal appearances, including that year's Academy Awards ceremony. After working in film publicity at Avco Embassy and Universal Pictures, Steven Spielberg hired him as story editor on the *Amazing Stories* series for NBC-TV, where he wrote or co-wrote ten of the forty-four episodes.

Since then, he has written or co-authored several feature films (**Batteries Not Included*, *The Fly II*, *Hocus Pocus*, *Critters 2*) and teleplays (*Quicksilver Highway*, *Virtual Obsession*, *The Others*), as well as directing and producing for cable TV (Showtime's *Psycho IV: The Beginning*), features (*Critters 2*, *Sleepwalkers*), television films (*Quicksilver Highway*, *Virtual Obsession*), series pilot (*The Others*), and network mini-series (*The Stand*, *The Shining*). His latest film is the four-hour mini-series based on author Steve Martini's novel, *The Judge*.

The recent collection *A Life in the Cinema* is his first book, although he has had stories published in several magazines and anthologies, including *Dark Terrors 5*, *Hot Blood*, *Silver Scream*, *Splatterpunks*, *Midnight Graffiti* and *Carpe Noctem*.

"'Forever Gramma' was the story that almost wasn't," Garris

reveals. "After my story 'A Life in the Cinema' was published in David J. Schow's anthology *Silver Scream*, John Skipp and Craig Spector asked me to contribute a story to the follow-up volume to their *Book of the Dead*, stories that take place in the world of George Romero's *Night of the Living Dead*. Well, when Skipp and Spector rejected the story, my confidence in it was diminished, to say the least. So diminished, in fact, that I came very close to not including it in my first book.

"However, the collection was a bit underweight without the story, so I decided to add it for the calories. Imagine my surprise when it was cited as a favourite story in several reviews (which may say more about the other stories than this one), and included in this very volume you hold in your hands. I guess Gramma lives, after all."

F olks think that what I saw happen to Gramma when she died when I was little might mess me up for the rest of my life, but I'm almost a teenager now, and that's a long time since I was nine, and I'm okay. Nobody ever believed me, of course, because I was just a little kid – except for one guy, and he ain't telling nobody nothing . . . least so far as I know about it. So I just stopped telling it. I mean, what's the point of telling if everybody thinks you're a liar? I ain't no liar, no matter what you hear. Anyhow, they always get all het up about the gooshy dead and dying stuff – if they knew about the sex, they'd right have a hissy.

It takes a while for word to get to Juniper Hill, and that suits the folks around here just fine. There ain't many of us in the first place, and they like that, too. Juniper Hill is mostly a bunch of houses the folks made for themselves, or their great-grandfolks did, anyway, and kind of handed them down to their kids, and to their kids, and like that. I guess I like it being so pretty and natural and all – and there ain't even a church or nothing, except for the Baptists, so I like that – but I sure wish we had the cable. Old Mr Cootie Man – I mean, Mr Cooperman down to the General Store's got one of them satellite things, but it got knocked down in the big storm when I was really little, so we ain't got no TV at all. He keeps meaning to fix it up, but for close to five years now it's just been playing pigeon pond.

When I think about Gramma, I don't think about the gooshy stuff, anyway. I think about peach cobbler. Mom and Dad got their own memories about her, but to me – and I bet to most people who knew her – it's that thick glass deep dish, with juicy yellow peach parts with the heat bubbles you can see coming up through the sweet crumbly stuff on the top. When Gramma was making cobbler, you could smell it far as the eye can see. Once I even smelled it from in the underground fort all the way out in the field, and I came running.

I love my mom and dad, but they got their problems, like most folks, and they get to fighting. There's a lot of what they call cabin fever on the Hill, especially when it's snowing, and folks kind of get their backs up, and you really can't blame them. Being cooped up kind of gets you antsy, particularly if you ain't got moving pictures or the TV or even a library to keep your mind off it. Dad kind of takes any excuse to make the thirty-mile trip to the post office to check the mail, even though all that's ever in there are coupons for stuff you can't even get at the Cootie Man's.

Gramma's the only person, male or female, that I never seen get cranky. She's just like the Gramma they got in that Dick and Jane book, you know, with them appley cheeks, kind of plump and old-fashioned like, with salt-and-pepper hair pulled back in what you call a bun, and always in her flour-dusty apron. When you see a picture of a grandmother, that's my Gramma. I think she looks that way on purpose. Anyway, she's always got something cooking, or she did, and was always smiling and happy and seeing the silver lining in every cloud, and looking for the silk purse in every sow's ear. Everybody liked Gramma, but I think I was her special favorite. She always had something special for me around the house, like warm chocolate chip cookies, and a bottle of Dr Pepper, or a not-too-old issue of *The X-Men* that she got from some mysterious place, and she never told me that comic books would rot my mind. When Mom would bitch at me, Gramma would just tell her, "At least he's *reading*," and give me a crinkly old Santa Claus wink. Kind of like we were spies on the same side.

Gramma didn't shop at the Cootie Man's too much, because she had a pretty good garden of her own. She had all them fruit trees and vines and vegetables, and she didn't mind the neighbors picking them if they wanted to just help themselves. And that drove the old Cootie crazy. She said store-bought stuff was all full of chemicals, and she liked her food the way God grew it. So the only time she went to the Cootie Man's store was for them police magazines she liked so much. It's kind of funny how an old lady could get so much pleasure reading about silk stocking murders and shotgun killings and stuff, but that was Gramma.

But what kind of cracked me up about the Cootie was that he had this big crush on Gramma. He was an old guy, but, as he told Gramma, "not a stranger to romance". So she called him Stranger, but always with a little twinkle in her eye so she didn't hurt his feelings. So here's this old guy who's just crazy about this old lady, and she never buys his groceries, and only goes into his store once a month. Not long before she died, whenever them magazines come in, he'd close up the store and come out himself, all personal like, and bring them to her.

Everybody on the Hill knew the Cootie had a crush on my Gramma, and they all thought it was real cute. It just cracked me up, because he was this crabby old guy, always yelling at you if you wanted to see if you'd already read one of the dusty old books on his rack, and grouching if you didn't have the right change or nothing. He was just a lonely unhappy old guy who took it out on kids, because the grown-ups wouldn't take any of his guff. But when he was within spitting distance of Gramma, he turned into Mr Google, all sweet and nervous and fumbly, with a bobbing Adam's apple and a voice that cracked more than the Pembertons' teenage son Mackie, who's got the Down's Syndrome, which means he's retarded.

When Gramma died, I cried a whole lot, but remember, I was just a little kid back then. Even still, I still felt embarrassed to soak my pillow. I didn't know how hard it hurt to love somebody and lose them. It was kind of like there was a piece of her in me, and some crazy doctor came in and took a slice of Gramma offa me without any of that anesthetic stuff. It may have been my heart that was hurting, but my whole body felt the pain. Nobody'd ever died on the Hill since I was born, and I didn't know much about the system.

Did you know that when you die, they take out your blood and your guts, and all your insides, and sew you up and pump you full of stuff called formaldehyde before they buried you?

It's true. Well, you might guess that they don't have no

mortuaries in a place as little as Juniper Hill to do that gruesome stuff, so they was just about to make arrangements to send her off to Steepleton before the Cootie raised his hand to volunteer.

Back when he was a young man, which I don't believe was *ever*, seems he was an animal doctor. Fact is, when Grampa died, and this was before I was even born, the Cootie was the guy who got him ready for the Big Sleep. It turns out that most of the folks that passed away on the Hill in the last twenty years or so got put to rest at the hands of the Cootie. So somehow it seemed natural that if he took care of Grampa, he should take care of his widow, too.

So he did, even though I hated the idea of his hands on and inside my Gramma. But they didn't consult me on this matter, so the dirty deed was done. It made me sick to my stomach – not a good sick like too much of Gramma's bread pudding, but an ugly kind of sick, devil sick, like something mean and ugly's tugging at your innards.

They had the funeral at Gramma's house. The Baptists said we could have it their place, but Gramma always said if she had a drop of Baptist blood in her veins, she'd cut her wrists and let it all run out. I know that don't sound like the sweet old granny I been telling you about, but that's what she said, anyway.

Everybody on the Hill showed up, and even some folks from Steepleton. It was a grand affair, and I think it was so crowded not only because everybody loved Gramma so much, but also because there was nothing much to do around here anyhow. Everybody made one heck of a hissy, and there was lots of big love words and tear-wet shirts and dresses. Even my Daddy cried, and that kind of scared me, because I never saw him do that before. Once when he was chopping wood, I seen the head come flying off the hatchet and stick with a bone chop plunk into the cradle of his arm, and all it made him do was yell a bunch of F-words and their cousins. He even watched the doctor in town sew it up so's you couldn't see the raw meat inside no more, and his eyes never ever even got watery.

I try not to let nobody ever see it, but there's something wrong with my eye plumbing, cause it's real easy to get the river to flow. Sometimes just stubbing my toe will set them to stinging and they'll get all wet and shiny, and I'll act like it's my allergy or something, but it ain't. One time I remember just seeing a hawk way up there in the top of the old spruce feeding her baby hawks, and the sky was so blue it was almost purple, and the clouds were like cotton balls, and it was all so darn pretty that it started again. I feel like a baby when it happens, but there ain't nothing I can do about it, the Lord just built me a little off-kilter. It don't make me queer or nothing, just a little wet-eyed sometimes. Some folks is like that.

So I hated that old funeral. There was people everywhere, and Gramma looking like a wax dummy in a wood box, and it didn't even look like her. But they was baking Gramma's recipes for all the folks, and I guess that's what really did me in. I smelled that peach cobbler, and it just made my belly do jumping jacks. I felt all yucky and queasy, and my eyes just started running. No way I was gonna eat no imitation cobbler some old lady thought she could make like Gramma. She could copy the spices and the recipe, but nobody could put in that little pinch of Gramma.

I pretended to start sneezing, even though lots of other folks – mostly the ladies – was bawling their hearts out. I just wandered outside and sat under a tree by myself. There was a big crowd up by the casket, and I watched them through the doorway. Like I said, everybody loved Gramma, and they all wanted to pay their respects. I don't think it was so respectful to be eating at her funeral, and trying to copycat Gramma's food, but adults got different ideas from kids, and they run stuff, so I just sat and missed her.

It was kinda creepy how they all kept walking up and saying how natural she looked. It seemed kinda ghoulish to me, all of them talking about her corpse like it was some kinda pretty new wallpaper or something. And the Cootie Man was there, soaking it all up like he was the Leonardo daVinci of dead folks. They was telling him what a genius he was, and ain't it awful how the Lord called her home, and he was just all puffed up and not looking sad for real at all.

When everybody else was jawing over the cookies and coffee, I saw the Cootie Man look real close at Gramma, kind of a gooey romance movie kind of look, and then he stroked her face real gentle with the back of his hand. Then he leaned down, and – I couldn't really tell for sure from my place outside – he either whispered some private secret to her or kissed her on the ear.

Either way, it gave me the willies, and if she was alive, she'd have smacked him a good one right across the face. He turned around real sneaky like to make sure that no one was looking, and he saw me looking back at him, and turned the color of his bow tie: bright ugly red, with pink spots. I looked away, wanting to throw up. I didn't want to feel such a – what do you call it . . . *intimate*? – moment with that old crabapple. But it was too late. I glanced back, and his eyes were burning holes in my head, and we was both embarrassed. Then he brushed at her face like there was a smudge or something, and that he was doing business, not swiping a kiss off my dead grandmother. But he didn't fool me. I hated him, and I bet he felt the same about me.

Gramma always wanted to be buried out under God's eye, so everybody got together to make the trip out to the meadow where they buried Grampa. Mr Cooperman had a van because of the store, so he loaded the casket inside, and took off to meet everybody at the field for the burial. We all waited a long time before he finally showed up. He said he had to get gas, and so everybody else had been waiting there, wiping their shoes on their pantlegs, and talking about what a perfect day it was, and how happy Gramma would be about it. I hated how they talked about how Gramma used to be. She still lived in my heart – I mean I was just talking with her a few days before, and she told me a joke and gave me a Pepper Free – and to all these people she was like Abraham Lincoln and Marilyn Monroe and John F. Kennedy and all them other dead history people. Grownups got weird ways to handle their problems; they push them away and put them in a box with something like their problems, but not exactly the same, and not painful, so that what hurts them don't hurt them no more. If you know what I mean, and I bet you don't.

Well, that was the longest day of my life, even up to now, and I was glad when it got dark and I didn't have to look at the masks everybody wore on their faces. It took me a long time to get to sleep that night, I remember, because I kept thinking of Gramma, and the Cootie kissing her gave me a real nervous headache.

It was a long time later that the creepy stuff started happening. It must have been the end of summer, maybe a month or two after the funeral, because I remember it was a real hot dry day, and the evening was still kind of what Gramma would have called sultry. Mom and Dad just declared war for the eighth time that week, and I was just outside walking and hiding my leaking eyes. My chest was hurting, but I knew little kids didn't have heart attacks so I wasn't going to die. But my heart sure did give me pain.

I just wanted to get lost, but that was easier said than done on the Hill. I spent my life roaming the area, mostly because there wasn't nothing else to do. I'd been out for hours, and never even had my dinner. My stomach was howling like a coyote, but I didn't pay it no mind.

I started thinking of Gramma, and just plain missing her. I never knew how close we were until she died, and now she just left a big chunk out of me. That old lady took up a lot of space in my heart, and now that Mom and Dad were at it again, I had no place to take it but the woods. I thought about the way she sang to me when I was a baby, and those big red cheeks, and the little veins on her nose, and the dark blue dresses with white polka dots, and stopped and sat under the tree, my heart weighing a million tons.

All of a sudden I knew why I started thinking about Gramma, I mean more than the missing her, and my folks' fighting. My nostrils started doing a dance . . . Gramma's peach cobbler was in the air! I kind of shook off the jacket of walk-around I was wearing, and found myself on the dirt road that circles the old Cootie's place. I never would have come there on my own, but somehow some secret autopilot in my brain hooked into the cobbler scent and brought me here.

There was no mistaking it: there was a pinch of nutmeg, and just a whiff of ripeness that Gramma waited for to make her cobbler the juiciest. Nobody made cobbler like Gramma, even when they tried to like at the funeral. But I smelled Gramma's cobbler now. And it was coming out of the Cootie's window, and that just didn't seem right.

Well, I ain't no peeping Tommy, but I hiked up onto my tippytoes, and Indian-walked quiet as I could through the crackly leaves and up to the window. The scent of the cobbler was so strong now you could almost *see* it hang in that summer air.

Now, I never been inside the Cootie's before, and I didn't right know what to expect. I couldn't see a whole lot, because the windows were real crusty, you know, old man bachelor dirty, and there was some girly looking lace curtains hanging kind of half-assed in the way. The whole place just seemed kind of dark and messy, a *lot* cruddier than my room at its very *worst*. There was junk all around that I couldn't really see, and a stuffed duck-billed platypus on the mantle by the stove.

The Cootie was even creepier at home than in his store, and I guess he was some kind of animal lover, because the platypus wasn't the only stuffed animal I saw there. There was a pile of old-fashioned teddy bears lying all over the floor, and over by the front door, I swear to God, there was a big stuffed black bear, full-sized, standing up and posing like he was a ballet dancer. If it weren't so goose-bumpy, it might have been funny.

Now that I'm remembering it, it seems like I saw more than I thought I did at the time, because of the windows and the curtain. But the main thing I remember was seeing Mr Cooperman himself sitting at the table, a big old poop-eating grin on his face, eating a dish of what looked to me like Gramma's cobbler. He didn't have a shirt on, and he was all red and pink-dotty in the face, all sweaty like he'd been cutting wood or something. He might have been naked, I couldn't see past the table, and didn't want to. It was bad enough seeing that he had titties, almost like a lady. It was disgusting.

Anyhow, he was just talking and laughing, and acting all happy and weird. I couldn't see if there was anybody else there that he was talking to, or if he was just crazy and talking to his own self. I suspected the latter.

Well, by now, as you might guess, I was getting mighty creeped out. I couldn't see nothing more, so I just kind of hauled ass. Even home seemed better than Mr Cooperman's nut house at that point, so I ran home and climbed in the bedroom window so's I wouldn't have to interrupt the parental argument that was still happening in the front room.

Well, the old creep that I tried to steer real clear of was now becoming a center of intrigue. I just kind of lay in my bed, turning it over in my head, wondering what any of this meant. The Cootie ain't no cook, that much was sure. And that cobbler was Gramma's, no doubt about it. Maybe he had some in the freezer, and popped it in the microwave. I doubted that Gramma would have encouraged him by baking him cobbler. That was her special dish, and she just didn't give out her special dish to Cooties, least not to my knowledge.

But the thing that kept sticking in my mind like a ghost story was his face, all blotchy and purple and sweaty, with a big, cobbler-choked smile, and his hair all oily and mussed up, and them big man-titties shaking when he laughed.

Yuck.

I knew I had to go back to the Cootie's, and the next time I did, I was as sorry as much as I was glad. Maybe sorrier.

It got real cold real fast; I thought it was gonna be sultry like that other night, so I didn't wear a jacket. It turned real cold after dark, and I was shivering when I got there. It looked like nobody was home at first, and I remember saying a dirty word or two to myself. But the van was in the driveway, so even though there weren't any lights on that I could see, it was obvious that he must be home. Where else could he be on Juniper Hill?

I stalked the place, real sneaky like, and went back to the same window I stood at a few nights before. Nothing. Just moonlight making scary shadows on the stuffed animals. But everything was real still, not even a breeze to lift the dying leaves off their branches. It felt like a ghost town. A *cold* ghost town.

There was really nothing much to see, though it looked creepier in the dark than it did the other night, so I started to make a circle around the place. It was real secluded there, just a bunch of grandfather trees and a wagon wheel fence around the house, and that was no big deal to step over. He didn't have no living animals, which seemed kind of weird for a guy who used to be an animal doctor. But what about the Cootie *wasn't* weird? But it got weirder, just the same.

The next window I came to was the bathroom. I guess when you don't live next to nobody, they don't put that ripply knobbly glass in so folks can't see you pooping. The Cootie just had plain old glass there, and I could see right inside. I couldn't see nothing happening in there, and it was so cold I was getting ready to go home without a story, until I saw the yellow light.

Way down at the far end of the hall, there was just a flicker, a little sunburst of firelight coming from under the door. He was home after all.

I finished the circle around the house, and ended up at the bedroom window. Even before I got there, I could see the light peeking out into the night through the crusty window . . . I sneaked over there, stretched up on my toes, and played spy vs. spy.

My eyes had to adjust, because the moon was real full and

bright that night. All I could see at first was silhouettes, because
the fireplace was at the other side of the room, with a big, hot fire
crackling. I saw it all through the lace curtain, which ticked me
off; and my breath in the cold night air kept fogging up the glass.
At first, it was just shapes kind of squiggling on the bed, but
before long, I could kind of bring it all into focus.

It's kind of hard for me to make my brain remember this stuff,
because it really don't want to. But I think I'm gonna feel a whole
lot better if I get it all out, every bit of it, because not a whole lot of
it made sense to me. The stomach-ache that always comes with
the memory always goes away, anyhow.

The first thing was seeing that old Mr Cooperman was lying
naked on his belly on top of the bed. That was almost enough to
set my gorge to rise, and once again, I almost turned around and
headed home. He was kind of moving and humping, sort of like
doing the Bottom Ups, but not in the bathtub. It was like he was
trying to drill into the bed with his middle section.

It was kind of half-disgusting and half-fascinating and educa-
tional watching them two big white moons of his butt moving up
and down, clenching and jiggling like Jell-O molds with a muscle
inside. He was all hot and bothered, and because I was just a little
kid then, I didn't know what the heck was going on. I just thought
he was rubbing his tummy on a pile of pillows, like some weird
grown-up hobby or something, but you probably guessed that he
was sexing.

Well, it weren't pillows he was sexing with, and this is the hard
part. He was grunting and puffing like the 9:15 through Steepleton before he rolled over and fell onto his back. He had that
same purple sweaty smile on his face I told you about when he
was eating that cobbler, and that's the first thing I noticed. That
and his little wet and gummy pecker hiding under his big fat belly.

But my brain made my eyes move across the bed to the white
puffy pile that he rolled off of. It took a while for me to make it
out through the grime and the curtains, but that was a body he
was humping. He had himself a woman, and I never seen a naked
woman before, so I looked.

She wasn't moving, it seemed like, and certainly not heaving
and out of breath like Mr Cooperman. She had a big old tummy,
kind of stretched tight looking, like a water balloon, and real
yellow, though that could have been from the firelight. And then,

I saw my first naked boobies . . . leastwise the first ones since when I was a nursing baby, but I don't remember them. These was real big and kind of saggy, and fell onto the bed on both sides of her as she lay on her back, with big long stretchy creases on them. They just kind of hung there and settled into bowls of titty under her arms. She had long hair down around her shoulders, salt-and-pepper grey, just like Gramma's, except not in a bun. And candy-apple cheeks just like Gramma's.

My soul got caught in my throat, and I felt my body scream like a little girl . . . Old Mr Cooperman was sexing with my dead grandmother!

I could see juices running out between her chubby thighs, making her grey hair down there get all sticky and shiny in the firelight, and I thought she was peeing in her sleep, like little kids sometimes do. But somehow I knew, even at age nine, that he had been poking his wiener in there, and he got his wet in her.

And then, that old horse-crap pig that invaded my Gramma looked up at the window, right into my eyes, and I saw the fear of God move in.

Well, the thing inside me that set me to screaming took hold of me and threw me on the ground, and wouldn't let me move. I suddenly felt the cold get a million times colder, and I finally started to shiver so hard it wouldn't stop. My body was shaking, and my eyes were running, and my mouth just wouldn't stay shut. I know I screamed some more, and couldn't stop screaming. The old Cootie came running out of the house, buck naked in the night, his baggy old skin turning into baggy old gooseflesh, and he picked me up by the scruff of the neck and shook me real hard to try to shut me up. It was like he had to tell me excuses, make me think he was a good guy, instead of a creepy old pig that fouled my Gramma.

He was yelling at me, but scared like, not mad, but I was too messed up back then to understand what he was saying. "I brought her back!" he kept yelling, like it made any difference to me. "It was the seed! The seed!"

Well, a nine-year-old kid don't know dick about no seed, I'm here to tell you, but he went on about how potent his seed was, and the power of the reproductive organ, and how much his love for my Gramma brought her back to life. I couldn't look at him, my eyes just dropped and fixated on his shriveled up little pee-pee, all sticky and matted and ugly. I didn't want to see it, but it was right in my face.

The Cootie tried to pull me up, but I just yanked away; I didn't want the son-of-a-bitch to touch me. He smelled all sour and filthy, and I just wanted to upchuck all over him and his darned house. And he just kept trying to "explain" to me. I didn't want to hear it. I know now that he was even crazier than I thought, with all his talk about his "seed", but to a little kid, he was just a big, weird, scary grown-up.

He looked like a big old bald-headed polar bear out in the moonlight, and without his glasses his face looked all beady and dim-witted. The goosebumps made him look like a plucked turkey from some angles, and my brain must have thought it was real funny-looking, because it made my mouth start to laugh and wouldn't let it stop. My body was still shaking from the cold, and my breath was steam, there was tears running like rivers down my face, and he's trying to tell me his side of the story.

Finally I got myself together enough to pull away from his fat guy hands that couldn't get a tight grip anyway, and turned and ran . . .

Right into Gramma!

It right scared the cider out of me. My dead grandmother was standing in my way, naked as a newborn, her boobies swinging side to side, her eyes staring holes through me. I waited for her to say something, or do something, or help in some way, but she just stood there, her mouth falling open and a long string of saliva dribbling out across her lip. Her eyes were kind of half-mast, somehow stupid, and it looked to me like there was nobody home. Her body was all swollen up, ripe looking like a melon, but dry as summer dirt. It's funny how even though I knew right away that it was Gramma's body, it only seemed just barely related to her with her spark extinguished.

She was dee-ee-double-dee dead, without any doubt. And she smelled real bad, and I knew where the Cootie had gotten sour. She smelled like something the dog dug up, and in a way I guess she was. The look on her face told me she didn't know much of what was going on, but as she watched me, I saw something flicker in her head, and her jaw started to rock from side to side. Her lips, all dried up in a roadmap of wrinkles, were working, moving. She was trying to talk.

Her words were as dusty and corroded as she was, and it took a while for me to figure them out. It was more the rhythm I recognized than the actual words; it was a familiar, singsong refrain I'd heard many times at her house . . .

"All I've got is diet."

Not all of Gramma's lights were out, but they sure had gotten dim. She stared at me from under leaded lids, but there was no connection. This wasn't the way I wanted to remember Gramma. I blinked, and the tears blurred her, and for just a flash I saw her at the oven, dusted with flour, a polka dot apron with peach juice on it, carving me out a big hunk of cobbler.

But old Mr Cooperman's voice brought me back home. His voice was real high and girly now, and it was like some kind of monster was talking through him. "She's still with us, boy, don't you see? Stay here, she'll make cobbler! Won't you, Emily?"

I felt like I was going crazy with him, standing between these bulging, naked old bodies, one sweaty and drooping, the other dry and swollen, rotting. I tried to run, and Gramma turned to look at me in an empty, vacant-barn stare. I ran into a tree, and it was like somebody took a flash picture in my face. I fell again, and Gramma was coming after me, like maybe to put a Band-Aid on the boo-boo. The Cootie freaked and grabbed at her, afraid she was leaving him. His hand caught onto her titty, and it just kind of burst with a little pop, and slid off her body into his hand. I saw a bunch of little worms and crawly stuff wiggling out of the hole on her chest and in the flesh soup in his hand.

My head hurt, and the ground started to tilt and spin, and I could hear laughing from far away, kind of like from people who lived here a long time ago in history. I was real dizzy, and I saw Mr Cooperman start to cry.

Naked Gramma turned to face him, cocking her head from side to side like a curious puppy as she stared at him. The Cootie called out her name real soft and romantic like, and reached for her hand. She took his hand in both of hers, and brought it up next to her lips, just staring at it for the longest time before sticking it into her mouth.

The Cootie was smiling until the bite, which I could hear real loud from the garden. Her dentures crushed the bones in two of his fingers, and she sucked on them, ignoring his screams. I think she was eating the marrow out of them. Then she pulled away, and I saw the skin from his fingers in her mouth stretch like rubber bands and snap with a final tug.

Blood was spurting from his finger holes, and she looked like she was wearing old-time lipstick as she chewed his fingers like Fritos. Old Cootie Man couldn't move; the blood was gushing and his eyes was bugging out like they was like to pop out of his head and into the garden. But they didn't till later.

Gramma just kind of swooned and fell on top of him, and their bare bodies chafed together like fingers on a chalkboard, making my skin crawl. My head hurt too much to move, and my eyes wouldn't look away as Gramma's hands worked their way down the Cootie's flesh, just like an old lady checking for the ripest peaches in the store.

She found what she was looking for; both her hands wrapped around his sticky little wienie and balls. He stopped screaming for a minute, and her red lips kind of gaped apart real slow, like a wound that wasn't quite healed splitting open, with blood getting thick in strings across the opening of her lips. She took his peter and balls into her mouth like a fifty-fifty bar, and started to chew.

Gramma didn't even open her mouth when she looked up at me, and the hairy skin around his peter just tore and spurted like a butchered buck. The ground was still spinning when our eyes locked, and she stared at me with a mouthful of Mr Cooperman. His screams went real far away as I threw up and passed out.

It wasn't till right after sunup the next day that I woke up to my Dad picking me up and carrying me to the pickup. I saw what was left of the old Cootie on the ground, big rib bones sticking out of the chewed-up skin, a big chunk of his head missing. Dad kept turning my head away, but I had to keep looking back to see. There was no sign of Gramma anywhere.

I couldn't talk much for a while after that, and I was scared that I was gonna be in trouble because nobody'd believe me about my Gramma coming back. But I was nine and the Cootie man was mauled up pretty good. Folks figured I saw *something*, but I was little and they wanted to protect me or something. Everybody was scared there was some kind of crazy killer or renegade bear for a while, and after a while I just let it go. Nobody ever even thought twice about Gramma. Far as they knew, she was at rest in the field next to Grampa. I wanted to think so too.

But every now and then, when the nights go all sultry and we pop open the Dr Peppers, I think about the Gramma who loved me, and made me stuff to eat, and saved me the best parts of the chicken, and my eyes go all wet and girly. But I have had occasion – more than once – to make my way past the Cootie Man's house, still abandoned after all these years. And I swear on all I hold holy that I've smelled peach cobbler cooling just inside the window. But I ain't had the guts to go up close and look.

Now I never knew you could come back after you die, and folks say you can't. Even real smart teacher-type folks.

But I know different, and I know true. I don't know what brought her back: the Cootie Man's seed or her own will. But I do know that if she came back, it wouldn't be to go sexing around with him. And I also know one other thing . . . wherever she is, part of her has a little house in a chamber in my heart, where she is forever.

I love you, Gramma.

CHRISTOPHER FOWLER

At Home in the Pubs of Old London

CHRISTOPHER FOWLER IS THE DIRECTOR OF London's The Creative Partnership, which markets films like *Hannibal* and *American Psycho*. His novels include *Roofworld*, *Rune*, *Red Bride*, *Darkest Day*, *Spanky*, *Psychoville*, *Disturbia*, *Soho Black* and *Calabash*. His short fiction has been collected in *City Jitters*, *The Bureau of Lost Souls*, *Flesh Wounds*, *Sharper Knives* and *Uncut*, and he was the 1998 recipient of the British Fantasy Award for his short story "Wageslaves".

His story "The Master Builder" became a CBS-TV movie starring Tippi Hedren, while another, "Left Hand Drive", won Best British Short Film. He also scripted the 1997 graphic novel *Menz Insana*, illustrated by John Bolton.

"I think the English treat London in the same way that they treat their language," says Fowler, "with a certain amount of healthy disrespect. We like new words and new buildings, and see no reason why they should not co-exist with the old.

"I was commissioned to produce a spoken-word piece for those good chaps at Filthy McNasty's bar, and decided to write something that would use locations as characters. I also wanted to try a story where the payoff is the result of denying the reader a piece of information.

"I'm always making lists, and like exploring cities. I limited myself to thirteen sites in one city, as I had with an earlier story called 'Thirteen Places of Interest in Kentish Town'. Naturally, I had to visit all of the sites mentioned in the story . . ."

The Museum Tavern, Museum Street, Bloomsbury

Despite its location diagonally opposite the British Museum, its steady turnover of listless Australian barstaff and its passing appraisal by tourists on quests for the British pub experience (comprising two sips from half a pint of bitter and one Salt 'n' Vinegar flavoured crisp, nibbled and returned to its packet in horror), this drinking establishment retains the authentically seedy bookishness of Bloomsbury because its corners are usually occupied by half-cut proofreaders from nearby publishing houses. I love pubs like this one because so much about them remains constant in a sliding world; the smell of hops, the ebb of background conversation, muted light through coloured glass, china tap handles, mirrored walls, bars of oak and brass. Even the pieces of fake Victoriana, modelled on increasingly obsolete pub ornaments, become objects of curiosity in themselves.

At this time I was working in a comic shop, vending tales of fantastic kingdoms to whey-faced netheads who were incapable of saving a sandwich in a serviette, let alone an alien planet, and it was in this pub that I met Leslie. She was sitting with a group of glum-looking Gothic Gormenghast offcuts who were on their way to a book launch at the new-age smells 'n' bells shop around the corner, and she was clearly unenchanted with the idea of joining them for a session of warm Liebfraumilch and crystal-gazing, because as each member of the group drifted off she found an excuse to stay on, and we ended up sitting together by ourselves. As she refolded her jacket a rhinestone pin dropped from the lapel, and I picked it up for her. The badge formed her initials – L,L – which made me think of Superman, because he had a history of falling for women with those initials, but I reminded myself that I was no superman, just a man who liked making friends in pubs. I asked her if she'd had a good Christmas, she said no, I said I hadn't either and we just chatted from there. I told Leslie that I was something of an artist and would love to sketch her, and she tentatively agreed to sit for me at some point in the future.

The World's End, High Street, Camden Town

It's a funny pub, this one, because the interior brickwork makes it look sort of inside out, and there's a steady through-traffic of punters wherever you stand, so you're always in the way. It's not my kind of place, more a network of bars and clubs than a proper boozer. It used to be called the Mother Red Cap, after a witch who lived in Camden. There are still a few of her pals inhabiting the place if black eyeliner, purple lipstick and pointed boots make you a likely candidate for cauldron-stirring. A white stone statue of Britannia protrudes from the first floor of the building opposite, above a shoe shop, but I don't think anyone notices it, just as they don't know about the witch. Yet if you step inside the foyer of the Black Cap, a few doors further down, you can see the witch herself, painted on a tiled wall. It's funny how people miss so much of what's going on around them. I was beginning to think Sophie wouldn't show up, then I became convinced she had, and I had missed her.

Anyway, she finally appeared and we hit it off beautifully. She had tied back her long auburn hair so that it was out of her eyes, and I couldn't stop looking at her. It's never difficult to find new models; women are flattered by the thought of someone admiring their features. She half-smiled all the time, which was disconcerting at first, but after a while I enjoyed it because she looked like she was in on a secret that no one else shared. I had met her two days earlier in the coffee shop in Bermondsey where she was working, and she had suggested going for a drink, describing our meeting place to me as "that pub in Camden near the shoe shop". The one thing Camden has, more than any other place in London, is shoe shops, hundreds of the bastards, so you can understand why I was worried.

It was quite crowded and we had to stand, but after a while Sophie felt tired and wanted to sit down, so we found a corner and wedged ourselves in behind a pile of coats. The relentless music was giving me a headache, so I was eventually forced to take my leave.

The King's Head, Upper Street, Islington

The back of this pub operates a tiny theatre, so the bar suddenly fills up with the gin-and-tonic brigade at seven each evening, but the front room is very nice in a battered, nicotine-scoured way. It continued to operate on the old monetary system of pounds, shillings and pence for years, long after they brought in decimal currency. I'm sure the management just did it to confuse non regulars who weren't in the habit of being asked to stump up nineteen and elevenpence halfpenny for a libation. Emma was late, having been forced to stay behind at her office, a property company in Essex Road. The choice of territory was mine. Although it was within walking distance of her office she hadn't been here before, and loved hearing this mad trilling coming from a door at the back of the pub. I'd forgotten to explain about the theatre. They were staging a revival of a twenties musical, and there were a lot of songs about croquet and how ghastly foreigners were. I remember Emma as being very pale and thin, with cropped blonde hair; she could easily have passed for a jazz-age flapper. I told her she should have auditioned for the show, but she explained that she was far too fond of a drink to ever remember anything as complicated as a dance step. At the intermission, a girl dressed as a giant sequinned jellyfish popped out to order a gin and French; apparently she had a big number in the second act. We taxed the barman's patience by getting him to make up strange cocktails, and spent most of the evening laughing so loudly they probably heard us on stage. Emma agreed to sit for me at some point in the future, and although there was never a suggestion that our session would develop into anything more, I could tell that it probably would. I was about to kiss her when she suddenly thought something had bitten her, and I was forced to explain that my coat had picked up several fleas from my cat. She went off me after this, and grew silent, so I left.

The Pineapple, Leverton Street, Kentish Town

This tucked-away pub can't have changed much in a hundred years, apart from the removal of the wooden partitions that separated the snug from the saloon. A mild spring morning, the Sunday papers spread out before us, an ancient smelly labrador flatulating in front of the fire, a couple of pints of decent bitter and two packets of pork scratchings. Sarah kept reading out snippets from the *News of the World*, and I did the same with the *Observer*, but mine were more worthy than hers, and therefore not as funny. There was a strange man with an enormous nose sitting near the gents' toilet who kept telling people that they looked Russian. Perhaps he was, too, and needed to find someone from his own country. It's that kind of pub; it makes you think of home.

I noticed that one of Sarah's little habits was rubbing her wrists together when she was thinking. Every woman has some kind of private signature like this. Such a gesture marks her out to a lover, or an old friend. I watched her closely scanning the pages – she had forgotten her glasses – and felt a great inner calm. Only once did she disturb the peace between us by asking if I had been out with many women. I lied, of course, as you do, but the question remained in the back of my head, picking and scratching at my brain, right up until I said goodbye to her. It was warm in the pub and she had grown sleepy; she actually fell asleep at one point, so I decided to leave quietly.

The Anchor, Park Street, Southwark

It's pleasant here on rainy days. In the summer, tourists visiting the nearby Globe fill up the bars and pack the riverside tables. Did you know that pub signs were originally provided so that the illiterate could locate them? The Anchor was built after the Southwark fire, which in 1676 razed the South bank just as the Great Fire had attacked the North side ten years earlier. As I entered the pub, I noticed that the tide was unusually high, and the Thames was so dense and pinguid that it looked like a setting jelly. It wasn't a good start to the evening.

I had several pints of strong bitter and grew more talkative as our session progressed. We ate toad-in-the-hole, smothered in elastic gravy. I was excited about the idea of Carol and I going out together. I think she was, too, although she warned me that she had some loose ends to tie up, a former boyfriend to get out of her system, and suggested that perhaps we shouldn't rush at things. Out of the blue, she told me to stop watching her so much, as if she was frightened that she couldn't take the scrutiny. But she can. I love seeing the familiar gestures of women, the half smiles, the rubbing together of their hands, the sudden light in their eyes when they remember something they have to tell you. I can't remember what they say, only how they look. I would never take pictures of them, like some men I've read about. I never look back, you understand. It's too upsetting. Far more important to concentrate on who you're with, and making them happy. I'd like to think I made Carol feel special. She told me she'd never had much luck with men, and I believe it's true that some women just attract the wrong sort. We sat side by side watching the rain on the water, and I felt her head lower gently onto my shoulder, where it remained until I moved – a special moment, and one that I shall always remember.

The Lamb & Flag, Rose Street, Covent Garden

You could tell summer was coming because people were drinking on the street, searching for spaces on the windowsills of the pub to balance their beerglasses. This building looks like an old coaching inn, and stands beside an arch over an alleyway, like the Pillars of Hercules in Greek Street. It's very old, with lots of knotted wood, and I don't suppose there's a straight angle in the place. The smoky bar is awkward to negotiate when you're carrying a drink in either hand – as I so often am!

This evening Kathy asked why I had not invited her to meet any of my friends. I could tell by the look on her face that she was wondering if I thought she wasn't good enough, and so I was forced to admit that I didn't really have any friends to whom I could introduce her. She was more reticent than most of the girls I had met until then, more private. She acted as though there was something on her mind that she didn't want to share with me. When I asked her to specify the problem, she either wouldn't or couldn't. To be honest, I think the problem was me, and that was why it didn't work out between us. Something about my behaviour made her uneasy, right from the start. There was no trust between us, which in itself was unusual, because most women are quick to confide in me. They sense my innate decency, my underlying respect for them. I look at the other drinkers standing around me, and witness the contempt they hold for women. My God, a blind man could feel their disdain. That's probably why I have no mates – I don't like my own sex. I'm ashamed of the whole alpha male syndrome. It only leads to trouble.

I made the effort of asking Kathy if she would sit for me, but knew in advance what the answer would be. She said she would prefer it if we didn't meet again, and yelped in alarm when I brushed against her hip, so I had to beat a hasty retreat.

The King William IV, High Street, Hampstead

Paula chose this rather paradoxical pub. It's in the middle of Hampstead, therefore traditional and okay, with a beer garden that was packed on a hot summer night, yet the place caters to a raucous gay clientele. Apparently, Paula's sister brought her here once before, an attractive girl judging from the photograph Paula showed me and such a waste, I feel, when she could be making a man happy. I wondered if, after finishing with Paula, I should give her sister a call, but decided that it would be playing a little too close to home. We sat in the garden on plastic chairs, beside sickly flowerbeds of nursery-forced plants, but it was pleasant, and the pub had given me an idea. I resolved to try someone of the same gender next time, just to see what a difference it made. I picked up one of the gay newspapers lying in stacks at the back of the pub, and made a note of other venues in central London. I explained my interest in the newspaper by saying that I wanted to learn more about the lifestyles of others. Paula squeezed my hand and said how much she enjoyed being with someone who had a liberal outlook. I told her that my policy was live and let live, which is a laugh for a start. I am often shocked by the wide-eyed belief I inspire in women, and wonder what they see in me that makes them so trusting. When I pressed myself close against her she didn't flinch once under my gaze, and remained staring into my eyes while I drained my beerglass. A special girl, a special evening, for both of us.

The Admiral Duncan, Old Compton Street, Soho

Formerly decorated as a cabin aboard an old naval vessel, with lead-light bay windows and a curved wood ceiling, this venue was revamped to suit the street's new status as a home to the city's homosexuals, and painted a garish purple. It was restored again following the nail-bomb blast that killed and maimed so many of its customers. Owing to the tunnel-like shape of the bar, the explosive force had nowhere to escape but through the glass front, and caused horrific injuries. A monument to the tragedy is inset into the ceiling of the pub, but no atmosphere of tragedy lingers, for the patrons, it seems, have bravely moved on in their lives.

In here I met Graham, a small-boned young man with a gentle West Country burr that seemed at odds with his spiky haircut. We became instant drinking pals, buying each other rounds in order to escape the evening heat of the mobbed street beyond. After what had occurred in the pub I found it astonishing that someone could be so incautious as to befriend a total stranger such as myself, but that is the beauty of the English boozer; once you cross the threshold, barriers of race, class and gender can be dropped. Oh, it doesn't happen everywhere, I know, but you're more likely to make a friend in this city than in most others. That's why I find it so useful in fulfilling my needs. However, the experiment with Graham was not a success. Boys don't work for me, no matter how youthful or attractive they appear to be. We were standing in a corner, raising our voices over the incessant thump of the jukebox, when I realized it wasn't working. Graham had drunk so much that he was starting to slide down the wall, but there were several others in the vicinity who were one step away from being paralytic, so he didn't stick out, and I could leave unnoticed.

The Black Friar, Queen Victoria Street, Blackfriars

This strange little pub, stranded alone by the roundabout on the North side of the river at Blackfriars, has an Arts and Crafts style interior, complete with friezes, bas-reliefs and mottos running over its arches. Polished black monks traipse about the room, punctuating the place with moral messages. It stands as a memorial to a vanished London, a world of brown Trilbys and woollen overcoats, of rooms suffused with pipe smoke and the tang of Brilliantine. In the snug bar at the rear I met Danielle, a solidly-built Belgian au pair who looked so lonely, lumpen and forlorn that I could not help but offer her a drink, and she was soon pouring out her troubles in broken English. Her employers wanted her to leave because she was pregnant, and she couldn't afford to go back to Antwerp.

To be honest I wasn't listening to everything she was saying, because someone else had caught my eye. Seated a few stools away was a ginger-haired man who appeared to be following our conversation intently. He was uncomfortably overweight, and undergoing some kind of perspiration crisis. The pub was virtually deserted, most of the customers drinking outside on the pavement, and Danielle was talking loudly, so it was possible that she might have been overheard. I began to wonder if she was lying to me about her problems; if, perhaps they were more serious than she made them sound, serious enough for someone to be following her. I know it was selfish, but I didn't want to spend any more time with a girl who was in that kind of trouble, so I told her I needed to use the toilet, then slipped out across the back of the bar.

The Angel, Rotherhithe

Another old riverside inn – I seem to be drawn to them, anxious to trace the city's sluggish artery site by site, as though marking a pathway to the heart. The interesting thing about places like The Angel is how little they change across the decades, because they retain the same bleary swell of customers through all economic climates. Workmen and stockbrokers, estate agents, secretaries, van-drivers and tarts, they just rub along together with flirtatious smiles, laughs, belches and the odd sour word. The best feature of this pub is reached by the side entrance, an old wooden balcony built out over the shoreline, where mudlarks once rooted in the filth for treasure trove, and where you can sit and watch the sun settling between the pillars of Tower Bridge.

As the light faded we become aware of the sky brushing the water, making chilly ripples. Further along the terrace I thought I saw the red-haired man watching, but when I looked again, he had gone. Growing cold, we pulled our coats tighter, then moved inside. Stella was Greek, delicate and attractive, rather too young for me, but I found her so easy to be with that we remained together for the whole evening. Shortly before closing time she told me she should be going home soon because her brother was expecting her. I was just massaging some warmth back into her arms – we were seated by an open window and it had suddenly turned nippy – when she said she felt sick, and went off to the Ladies. After she failed to reappear I went to check on her, just to make sure she was all right. I found her in one of the cubicles, passed out.

The Ship, Greenwich

The dingy interior of this pub is unremarkable, with bare-board floors and tables cut from blackened barrels, but the exterior is another matter entirely. I can imagine the building, or one very like it, existing on the same site for centuries, at a reach of the river where it is possible to see for miles in either direction. I am moving out toward the mouth of the Thames, being taken by the tide to ever-widening spaces in my search for absolution. There was something grotesquely Victorian about the weeds thrusting out of ancient brickwork, tumbledown fences and the stink of the mud. It was unusually mild for the time of year, and we sat on the wall with our legs dangling over the water, beers propped at our crotches.

Melanie was loud and common, coarse-featured and thick-legged. She took up room in the world, and didn't mind who knew it. She wore a lot of make-up, and had frothed her hair into a mad dry nest, but I was intrigued by the shape of her mouth, the crimson wetness of her lips, her cynical laugh, her seen-it-all-before eyes. She touched me as though expecting me to walk out on her at any moment, digging nails on my arm, nudging an elbow in my ribs, running fingers up my thigh. Still, I wondered if she would present a challenge, because I felt sure that my offer to sketch her would be rebuffed. She clearly had no interest in art, so I appealed to her earthier side and suggested something of a less salubrious nature.

To my surprise she quoted me a price list, which ruined everything. I swore at her, and pushed her away, disgusted. She, in turn, began calling me every filthy name under the sun, which attracted unwanted attention to both of us. It was then that I saw the ginger-headed man again, standing to the left of me, speaking into his chubby fist.

The Trafalgar Tavern, Greenwich

I ran. Tore myself free of her and ran off along the towpath, through the corrugated iron alley beside the scrap-yard and past the defunct factory smoke-stacks, keeping the river to my right. On past The Yacht, too low-ceilinged and cosy to lose myself inside, to the doors of The Trafalgar, a huge gloomy building of polished brown interiors, as depressing as a church. Inside, the windows of the connecting rooms were dominated by the gleaming grey waters beyond. Nobody moved. Even the bar staff were still. It felt like a funeral parlour. I pushed between elderly drinkers whose movements were as slow as the shifting of tectonic plates, and slipped behind a table where I could turn my seat to face the river. I thought that if I didn't move, I could remain unnoticed. In the left pocket of my jacket I still had my sketchbook. I knew it would be best to get rid of it, but didn't have the heart to throw it away, not after all the work I had done.

When I heard the muttered command behind me, I knew that my sanctuary had been invaded and that it was the beginning of the end. I sat very still as I watched the red-headed man approaching from the corner of my eye, and caught the crackle of radio headsets echoing each other around the room. I slowly raised my head, and for the first time saw how different it all was now. A bare saloon bar filled with tourists, no warmth, no familiarity, no comfort.

When I was young I sat on the step – every pub seemed to have a step – with a bag of crisps and a lemonade, and sometimes I was allowed to sit inside with my dad, sipping his bitter and listening to his beery laughter, the demands for fresh drinks, the dirty jokes, the outraged giggles of the girls at his table. They would tousle my hair, pinch my skinny arms and tell me that I was adorable. Different pubs, different women, night after night, that was my real home, the home I remember. Different pubs but always the same warmth, the same smells, the same songs, the same women. Everything about them was filled with smoky mysteries and hidden pleasures, even their names, The World Turned Upside Down, The Queen's Head and Artichoke, The Rose and Crown, The Greyhound, The White Hart, all of them had secret meanings.

People go to clubs for a night out now, chrome and steel, neon lights, bottled beers, drum and bass, bouncers with headsets. The bars sport names like The Lounge and The Living Room, hoping to evoke a sense of belonging, but they cater to an alienated world, squandering noise and light on people so blinded by work that their leisure-time must be spent in aggression, screaming at each other, shovelling drugs, pushing for fights. As the red-haired man moved closer, I told myself that all I wanted to do was make people feel at home. Is that so very wrong? My real home was nothing, the memory of a damp council flat with a stinking disconnected fridge and dogshit on the floor. It's the old pubs of London that hold my childhood; the smells, the sounds, the company. There is a moment before the last bell is called when it seems it could all go on forever. It is that moment I try to capture and hold in my palm. I suppose you could call it the land before Time.

The Load Of Hay, Havistock Hill, Belsize Park

The red-haired officer wiped at his pink brow with a Kleenex until the tissue started to come apart. Another winter was approaching, and the night air was bitter. His wife used to make him wear a scarf when he was working late, and it always started him sweating. She had eventually divorced him. He dressed alone now and ate takeaway food in a tiny flat. But he wore the scarf out of habit. He looked in through the window of the pub at the laughing drinkers at the bar, and the girl sitting alone beside the slot-machine. Several of his men were in there celebrating a colleague's birthday, but he didn't feel like facing them tonight.

How the hell had they let him get away? He had drifted from them like bonfire smoke in changing wind. The Trafalgar had too many places where you could hide, he saw that now. His men had been overconfident and undertrained. They hadn't been taught how to handle anyone so devious, or if they had, they had forgotten what they had learned.

He kept one of the clear plastic ampoules in his pocket, just to remind himself of what he had faced that night. New technology had created new hospital injection techniques. You could scratch yourself with the micro-needle and barely feel a thing, if the person wielding it knew how to avoid any major nerve-endings. Then it was simply a matter of squeezing the little bulb, and any liquid contained in the ampoule was delivered through a coat, a dress, a shirt, into the flesh. Most of his victims were drunk at the time, so he had been able to connect into their bloodstreams without them noticing more than a pinprick. A deadly mixture of RoHypnol, Zimovane and some kind of coca-derivative. It numbed and relaxed them, then sent them to sleep. But the sleep deepened and stilled their hearts, as a dreamless caul slipped over their brains, shutting the senses one by one until there was nothing left alive inside.

No motives, no links, just dead strangers in the most public places in the city, watched by roving cameras, filled with witnesses. That was the trouble; you expected to see people getting legless in pubs.

His attention was drawn back to the girl sitting alone. What was she doing there? Didn't she realize the danger? No one heeded the warnings they issued. There were too many other things to worry about.

He had been on the loose for a year now, and had probably moved on to another city, where he could continue his work without harassment. He would stop as suddenly as he had begun. He'd dropped a sketchbook, but it was filled with hazy pencil drawings of pub interiors, all exactly the same, and had told them nothing. The only people who would ever really know him were the victims – and perhaps even they couldn't see behind their killer's eyes. As the urban landscape grew crazier, people's motives were harder to discern. An uprooted population, on the make and on the move. Fast, faster, fastest.

And for the briefest of moments he held the answer in his hand. He saw a glimmer of the truth – a constancy shining like a shaft through all the change, the woman alone in the smoky saloon, smiling and interested, her attention caught by just one man; this intimacy unfolding against a background warmth, the pulling of pints, the blanket of conversation, the huddle of friendship – but then it was gone, all gone, and the terrible sense of unbelonging filled his heart once more.

CAITLÍN R. KIERNAN

In the Water Works (Birmingham, Alabama 1888)

CAITLÍN R. KIERNAN'S SHORT FICTION HAS APPEARED in many anthologies since 1995, and has been collected in three volumes: *Candles for Elizabeth* (1998), *Tales of Pain and Wonder* (2000) and *From Weird and Distant Shores* (2001). She has also written graphic novels for the DC Comics/Vertigo line, including *The Dreaming* and *The Girl Who Would Be Death*.

Her first novel, *Silk*, received the Barnes & Noble and International Horror Guild awards for best first novel, and her second full-length work, *Threshold: A Novel of Deep Time*, was recently published by Roc.

" 'In the Water Works' is a prequel of sorts to my new novel, *Threshold* (formerly *Trilobite*)," explains Kiernan. "It was a very difficult novel for me to get started, or to finish, for that matter, and doing this story first helped me begin to get a feel for the book's parameters.

"The water works tunnel is real and it has always fascinated and frightened me. There's a very old stone blockhouse at the entrance on Red Mountain, with a rusty wrought-iron gate to keep people out. But the gate is only held shut by a padlock and a length of chain, and occasionally kids cut the lock off and break in. You can tell how long it's been since a break-in by how rusty the chain and padlock are. If you stand at the entrance with your face to the bars you can make out the huge pipes snaking away into the darkness, like intestines, something from a Giger painting. On hot summer days there's always a stream of cool, damp air flowing from the water works tunnel, but it smells terrible, dank, fetid, like mould and mushrooms, mud and bat guano. There are weathered limestone boulders near the entrance, left from the excavations, and you can still find fossils on them.

"In *Threshold*, the water works tunnel is a nexus, a point of origin and departure both real and metaphoric."

R ed Mountain, weathered tip-end of Appalachia's long and scabby spine, this last ambitious foothill before the land slumps finally down to black belt prairies so flat they've never imagined even these humble altitudes. And as if Nature hasn't done her best already, as if wind and rain and frost haven't whittled aeons away to expose the limestone and iron ore bones, Modern Industry has joined in the effort, scraping away the stingy soil and so whenever it rains, the falling sky turns the ground to sea slime again, primordial mire the color of a butchery to give this place its name, rustdark mud that sticks stubborn to Henry Matthews' hobnail boots as he wanders over and between the spoil piles heaped outside the opening to the Water Works tunnel.

Scarecrow tall and thin, young Mr Henry S. Matthews, lately of some place far enough north to do nothing to better the reputation of a man who is neither married nor church-going, who teaches geography and math at the new Powell School on Sixth Avenue North and spends the remainder of his time with an assortment of books and rocks and pickled bugs. The sudden rumble of thunder somewhere down in the valley, then, and he moves too fast, careless as he turns to see, almost losing his footing as the wet stones slip and tilt beneath his feet.

"You best watch yourself up there, Professor," one of the workmen shouts and there's laughter from the black hole in the mountain's side. Henry offers a perfunctory nod in the general direction of the tunnel, squints through the haze of light October rain and dust and coal smoke at the rough grid of the little city laid out north of the mountain; barely seventeen years since John

Morris and the Elyton Land Company put pen to ink, ink to paper, and incorporated Birmingham, drawing a city from a hasty scatter of ironworks and mining camps. Seventeen years, and he wonders for a moment what this place was like before white men and their machines, before axes and the dividing paths of railroad tracks.

The thunder rolls and echoes no answer he can understand and Henry looks back to the jumbled ground, the split and broken slabs of shale at his feet. The rain has washed away the thick dust of the excavations, making it easier for him to spot the shells and tracks of sea creatures preserved in the stone. Only a few weeks since he sent a large crate of fossils south to the State Geological Survey in Tuscaloosa and already a small museum's worth of new specimens line the walls of his cramped room, sit beneath his bed and compete with his clothing for closet space, with his books for the shelves. An antediluvian seashore in hardened bits and pieces, and just last week he found the perfectly preserved carapace of a trilobite almost the length of his hand.

A whistle blows, shrill steam blast, and a few more men file out of the tunnel to eat their lunches in the listless rain. Henry reaches into a pocket of his waistcoat for the silver watch his mother gave him the year he left for college, wondering how a Saturday morning could slip by so fast; the clockblack hands at one and twelve and he's suddenly aware of the tugging weight of his knapsack, the emptiness in his belly, hours now since breakfast but there's a boiled egg wrapped in waxed paper and a tin of sardines in his overcoat. The autumn sky growls again and he snaps his watch closed and begins to pick his way cautiously down the spoil toward the other men.

Henry Matthews taps the brown shell of his hard-boiled egg against a piece of limestone, crack, crack, crack, soft white insides exposed and he glances up at the steelgrey sky overhead; the rain has stopped, stopped again, stopped for now, and crystalwet drops cling to the browngoldred leaves of the few hickory and hackberry trees still standing near the entrance of the tunnel. He sits with the miners, the foreman, the hard men who spend dawn to dusk in the shaft, shadowy days breaking stone and hauling it back into the sunlight. Henry suspects that the men tolerate his presence as a sort of diversion, a curiosity to interrupt the monotony of their days. This thin Yankee dude, this odd bird who picks about the spoil like there might be gold or silver when everyone knows there isn't anything worth beans going to come out of the mountain except the purplered ore and that's more like something you have to be careful not to trip over than try to find.

Sometimes they joke, and sometimes they ask questions, their interest or suspicion piqued by his diligence, perhaps; "What you lookin' for anyways, Mister?" and he'll open his knapsack and show them a particularly clear imprint of a snail's whorled shell or the mineralized honeycomb of a coral head. Raised eyebrows and heads nodding and maybe then someone will ask, "So, them's things what got buried in Noah's flood?" and Henry doubts any of these men have even heard of Lyell or Darwin or Cuvier, have any grasp of the marvelous progress that science has made the last hundred years, concerning the meaning of fossils and the progression of geological epochs. So always politic, aware that the wrong answer might get him exiled from the diggings, and genuinely wishing that he had time to explain the wonders of his artefacts to these men, Henry only shrugs and smiles for them; "Well, actually, some of them are even a bit older than that," or a simple and noncommittal "Mmmmm" and usually that's enough to satisfy.

But today is different and the men are quiet, each one eating his cold potatoes or dried meat, staring silent at muddy boots and lunch pails, the mining car track leading back inside the tunnel and no one asks him anything. Henry looks up once from his sardines and catches one of the men watching him, smiles and the man frowns and looks quickly away. When the whistle blows again, the men rise slow, moving with a reluctance that's plain enough to see, back toward the waiting tunnel. Henry wipes his fingers on his handkerchief, fishoil stains on white linen, is shouldering his knapsack, retrieving his geologist's hammer, when someone says his name, "Mr Matthews?," voice low, almost whispered and he looks up into the foreman's hazelbrown eyes.

"Yes, Mr Wallace? Is there something I can do for you today?" and Warren Wallace looks away, nervous glance to his men for a moment that seems a lot longer to Henry who's anxious to get back to his collecting.

"You know all this geology business pretty good, don't you,

Mr Matthews? All about these rocks and such?" and Henry shrugs, nods his head, "Yes sir, I suppose that I do. I had a course or two . . ."

"Then maybe you could take a look at somethin' for me sometime," the foreman says, interrupting, looking back at Henry and there are deep lines around his eyes, worry or lack of sleep, both maybe. The foreman spits a shitbrown streak of tobacco at the ground and shakes his head. "It probably ain't nothing, but I might want you to take a look at it sometime."

"Yes. Certainly," Henry says, "Anytime you'd like," and already Warren Wallace is walking away from him, following his men toward the entrance of the tunnel, shouting orders and, "Be careful up there, Mr Matthews," he says, spoken without turning around and Henry replies that he always is, but thanks for the concern anyway and he goes back to the spoil piles.

Fifteen minutes later it's raining again, harder now, a cold and stinging rain from the north and wind that gusts and swirls dead leaves like drifting ash.

May 1887 when the Birmingham Water Works Company entered into a contract with Judge A.O. Lane, Mayor and Alderman, and plans were drawn to bring water from the distant Cahaba River north across Shades Valley to the thirsty citizens of the city. But Red Mountain standing in the way, standing guard or simply unable to move and its slopes too steep for gravity to carry the water over the top, so the long tunnel dreamed up by engineers, the particular brainchild of one Mr W.A. Merkel, first chief engineer of the Cahaba Station. A two thousand, two hundred foot bore straight through the sedimentary heart of the obstacle, tons of stone blasted free with gelignite and nitro, pickaxes and sledge hammers and the sweat of men and mules. The promise of not less than five million gallons of fresh water a day, and in this bright age of invention and innovation it's a small job for determined men, moving mountains, coring them like ripe and crimson apples.

A week later and Henry Matthews is again picking over the spoil heaps, a cool and sunny October day crisp as cider, autumnsoft breeze that smells of dry and burning leaves, and his spirits are high, three or four exceptional trilobites from the hard limestone

already and a single, disc-shaped test of some species of echino-
dermia he's never encountered before, almost as big as a silver
dollar. He stoops to get a better look at a promising slab when
someone calls his name and he looks up, mildly annoyed at the
intrusion; foreman Wallace is standing nearby, scratching at his
thick, black beard and he points at Henry with one finger.

"How's the fishin', Professor?" he asks and it takes Henry a
moment to get the joke; he doesn't laugh, but a belated smile,
finally, and then the foreman is crossing the uneven stones toward
him.

"No complaints," Henry says and produces the largest of the
trilobites for the foreman's inspection. Warren Wallace holds the
oystergrey chunk of limestone close and squints at the small, dark
Cryptolithus outstretched on the rock.

"Well," the foreman says and rubs at his beard again, wrinkles
his thick eyebrows and stares back at Henry Matthews. "Ain't
that some pumpkins. And this little bug used to be alive? Crawlin'
around in the ocean?"

"Yes," Henry replies and he points to the trilobite's bulbous
glabellum, the pair of large, compound eyes to either side and,
"This end was its head," he says. "And this was the tail," as his
fingertip moves to the fan-shaped lobe at the other end of the
creature. Warren Wallace glances back at the fossil once more
before he returns it to Henry.

"Now, Professor, you tell me if you ever seen anything like this
here," and the foreman produces a small bottle from his shirt
pocket, apothecary bottle Henry thinks at first and then no, not
medicine, nitroglycerine. Warren Wallace passes the stoppered
bottle to the schoolteacher and for a moment Henry Matthews
stares silently at the black thing trapped inside.

"Where did this come from?" he asks, trying not to show his
surprise but wide eyes still on the bottle, unable to look away
from the thing coiling and uncoiling in its eight ounce glass
prison.

"From the tunnel," the foreman replies, spits tobacco juice, and
glances over his shoulder at the gaping hole in the mountain.
"About five hundred feet in, just a little ways past where the
limestone turns to sandstone. That's where we hit the fissure."

Henry Matthews turns the bottle in his hand and the thing
inside uncoils, stretches chitinous segments, an inch, two inches,

almost three before it snaps back into a legless ball that glimmers iridescent in the afternoon sun.

"Ugly little bastard, ain't it?" the foreman says and spits again. "But you *ain't* never seen nothin' like it before, have you?" And Henry shakes his head, no, never, and now he wants to look away, doesn't like the way the thing in the bottle is making him feel, but it's stretched itself out again and he can see tiny fibers like hairs or minute spines protruding between the segments.

"Can you show me?" he asks, realizes that he's almost whispering now, library or classroom whisper like maybe he's afraid someone will overhear, like this should be secret. "Where it came from, will you take me there?"

"Yeah. I was hopin' you'd ask," the foreman says, rubs his beard. "But let me tell you, Professor, you ain't seen nothin' yet." And after Warren Wallace has taken the bottle back, returned it to his shirt pocket so that Henry doesn't have to look at the black thing anymore, the two men begin the climb down the spoil piles to the entrance of the tunnel.

A few feet past the entrance, fifteen, twenty, and the foreman stops, stands talking to a fat man with a pry bar while Henry looks back at the bright day framed in raw limestone and bracing timbers, blinking as his eyes slowly adjust to the gloom. "Yeah," the fat man says, "Yeah," and Warren Wallace asks him another question. It's cooler in the tunnel, in the dark, and the air smells like rock dust and burning carbide and another smell tucked somewhere underneath, unhealthy smell like a wet cellar or rotting vegetables that makes Henry wrinkle his nose. "Yeah, I seen him before," the fat man with the pry bar says, wary reply to the foreman's question and a distrustful glance toward Henry Matthews.

"I want him to have a look at your arm, Jake, that's all," and Henry turns his back on the light, turns to face the foreman and the fat man. "He ain't no doctor," the fat man says. "And I already seen Doc Joe, anyways."

"He's right," Henry says, confused now, no idea what this man's arm and the thing in the jar might have to do with one another, blinking at Wallace through the dancing, whiteyellow afterimages of the sunlight outside. "I haven't had any medical training to speak of, certainly nothing formal."

"Yeah?" the foreman says and he sighs loud, exasperation or disappointment, spits on the tunnel floor, tobacco juice on rusted steel rails. "C'mon then, Professor," and he hands a miner's helmet to Henry, lifts a lantern off an iron hook set into the rock wall. "Follow me and don't touch anything. Some of these beams ain't as sturdy as they look."

The fat man watches them, massages his left forearm protectively when the schoolteacher steps past him, and now Henry can hear the sounds of digging somewhere in the darkness far ahead of them. Relentless clank and clatter of steel against stone, and the lantern throws long shadows across the rough lime stone walls; fresh wound, these walls, this abscess hollowed into the world's thin skin. And such morbid thoughts as alien to Henry Matthews as the perpetual night of this place and so he tells himself it's just the sight of the odd and squirming thing in the bottle, that and the natural uneasiness of someone who's never been underground before.

"You're wonderin' what Jake Isabell's arm has to do with that damned worm, ain't you?" the foreman asks, his voice too loud in the narrow tunnel even though he's almost whispering. And "Yes," Henry replies, "Yes, I was, as a matter of fact."

"It bit him a couple of days ago. Jesus, made him sick as a dyin' dog, too. But that's all. It bit him."

And "Oh," Henry says, unsure what else he should say and beginning to wish he was back out in the sun looking for his trilobites and mollusks with the high, Octoberblue sky hung far, far overhead. "How deep are we now?" he asks and the foreman stops and looks up at the low ceiling of the tunnel, rubs his beard.

"Not very, not yet . . . hundred and twenty, maybe hundred and thirty feet." And then he reaches up and touches the rock ceiling a couple of inches above his head. "You know how old these rocks are, Professor?" and Henry nods his head, tries too hard to sound calm when he answers the foreman.

"These layers of limestone here . . . well, they're probably part of the Lower Silurian system, some of the oldest with traces of living creatures found in them," and he pauses, realizes that he's sweating despite the cool and damp of the tunnel, wishes again he'd declined the foreman's invitation into the mountain. "But surely hundreds of thousands, perhaps *millions* of years old," he says.

"Damn," the foreman says and spits again. "Now that's somethin' to think about, ain't it, Professor? I mean, these rocks sittin' here all that time, not seein' the light of day all that time, and then *we* come along with our picks and dynamite . . ."

"Yes sir," Henry Matthews says and wipes the sweat from his face with his handkerchief. "It is indeed," but Warren Wallace is moving again, dragging the little pool of lantern light along with him and Henry has to hurry to catch up, almost smacks his forehead on the low, uneven ceiling. Another three hundred feet or so and they've reached the point where the grey limestone is overlain by beds of punky, reddish sand stone, the bottom of the Red Mountain formation; lifeblood of the city locked away in these strata, clotthick veins of hematite for the coke ovens and blast furnaces dotting the valley below and "Not much farther," the foreman says. "We're almost there."

The wet, rotten smell stronger now and glistening rivulets meander down the walls, runoff seeping down through the rocks above them, rain filtered through dead leaves and soil, through a hundred or a thousand cracks in the stone. Henry imagines patches of pale and rubbery mushrooms, perhaps more exotic fungi, growing in the dark. He wipes his face again and this time keeps the handkerchief to his nose, but the thick and rotten smell seeps up his nostrils anyway. *If an odor alone could drown a man*, he thinks, is about to say something about the stench to Warren Wallace when the foreman stops, holds his lantern close to the wall and Henry can see the big sheets of corrugated tin propped against the west side of the tunnel.

"At first I thought we'd hit an old mine shaft," he says, motions toward the tin with the lantern, causing their shadows to sway and contort along the damp tunnel. "Folks been diggin' holes in this mountain since the forties to get at the ore. So that's what I thought, at first."

"But you've changed your mind?" Henry asks, words muffled by the useless handkerchief pressed to his face.

"Right now, Professor, I'm a whole lot more interested in what *you* think," and then Wallace pulls back a big section of the tin, lets it fall loud to the floor, tin clamor against the steel rails at his feet. Henry gags, bilehot rush from his gut and the distant taste of breakfast in the back of his mouth; "Jesus," he hisses, not wanting to be sick in front of the foreman, and the schoolteacher leans against the tunnel wall for support, presses his left palm against moss slick stone, stone gone soft as the damprough hide of some vast amphibian.

"Sorry. Guess I should'a warned you about the stink," and Warren Wallace frowns, grim face like Greek tragedy and takes a step back from the hole in the wall of the tunnel, hole within a hole, and Henry's eyes are watering so badly he can hardly see. "Merkel had us plowin' through here full chisel until we hit that thing. Now it's all I can do to keep my men workin'."

"Can't exactly blame them," Henry wheezes and gags again, spits at the tunnel floor but the taste of the smell clings to his tongue, coats it like a mouthful of cold bacon grease. The foreman gestures for him to come closer, close enough he can peer down into the gap in the rock and Henry knows that's the last thing he wants to do. But he loathes that irrational fear, fear of the unknown that keeps men ignorant, keeps men down, and all his life gone to the purging of that instinctual dread, first from himself and then his students. And so Henry Matthews holds his breath against the stench and steps over the mining car tracks, glances once at Warren Wallace and to see a strong man so afraid and hardly any effort into hiding it is enough to get him to the crumbling edge of the hole.

And that's the best word, hole, a wide crevice in the wall of the tunnel maybe four feet across and dropping suddenly away into darkness past the reach of the lantern, running west into more blackness but pinching closed near the tunnel's ceiling. A natural fault, he thinks at first, evidence of the great and ancient forces that must have raised these mountains up, and the smell could be almost anything. Perhaps this shaft opens somewhere on the surface, a treacherous, unnoticed pit in the woods overhead, and from time to time an unfortunate animal might fall, might lie broken and rotting in the murk below, food for devouring mold and insects. And the thing in the jar probably nothing more or less than the larvae of some large beetle new to entomology or perhaps only the hitherto unknown pupa of a familiar species . . .

"Take the lantern," Warren Wallace says, then, handing the kerosene lamp to the schoolteacher. "Hold it right inside there, but don't lean too far in, mind you," and Henry feels the foreman's hand on his shoulder, weight and strength meant to be reassuring.

"Hold it out over the hole," he says, "and look down."

Henry Matthews does as he's told, already half-convinced of his clever induction and preparing himself for the unpleasant (but perfectly ordinary) sight of a badly decomposed raccoon or opossum, maybe even a deer carcass at the bottom and the maggots, maybe more of the big black things that supposedly bit Mr Isabell's arm. He exhales, a little dizzy from holding his breath, gasps in another lungful of the rancid air rising up from the pit. One hand braced against the tunnel wall and he leans as far out as he dares, a foot, maybe two, the flickering yellow light washing down and down, and he almost cries out at the un-expected sight of his own reflection staring back up at him from the surface of a narrow, subterranean pool.

"It's flooded," he says, half to himself, half to the foreman, and Warren Wallace murmurs a reply, yeah, it's flooded and some-thing else that Henry doesn't quite catch. He's watching the water, ten feet down to the surface at the most, water as smooth and black as polished obsidian.

"Now look at the *walls*, Professor, where they meet the water," and he does, positions the lantern for a better view and maybe just a little braver now, a little more curious so he's leaning a little farther out, the foreman's hand still holding him back.

At first he doesn't see anything, angle a little less than ninety degrees where black rock meets blacker water, at first, and then he does see something and thinks it must be the roots of some plant growing in the pool, or, more likely, running down from the forest above to find this hidden moisture. Gnarled roots as big around as his arm, twisted wood knotted back upon itself.

But one of them moves, then, abrupt twitch as it rolls away from the others, and Henry Matthews realizes that they're *all* moving now, each tendril creeping slow across the slick face of the crevice like blind and roaming fingers, searching, and "My God," he whispers, "My God in Heaven," starts to pull away from the hole but the foreman's hand holds him fast; "No. Not yet," Warren Wallace says calmly, and, "Watch them for just another second, Professor."

And one of the tendrils has pulled free of the rest, rises silent from the water like a charmed cobra; Henry can see that it's turning toward him, already six or seven feet of it suspended above the dark water but it's still coming. The water dripping off it very, very loud, impossible drip, drip, drip like a drumbeat in his ears, like his own racing heart, and then he notices the constant movement on the underside of the thing and knows at once what he's seeing. The worm thing in Wallace's bottle, coiling and uncoiling, and here are a thousand of them, restless polyps sprouting from this greater appendage, row upon writhing row, and now it's risen high enough that the thing is right in front of him, shimmering in the lantern light, a living question mark scant feet from Henry Matthew's face.

And later, lying awake in his room or walking at night along 20th Street, or broad daylight and staring up toward the mountain from the windows of his classroom, this is the part that he'll struggle to recall: Warren Wallace pulling him suddenly backwards, away from the hole as the tendril struck, the lantern falling from his hand, tumbling into the hole, and maybe he heard it hit the water, heard it splash at the same moment he tumbled backwards into the dark, tripped on the rails and landed hard on his ass. And the foreman cursing, the sounds of him hastily working to cover the hole in the tunnel wall again, and lastly, the dullwet *thunk*, meatmallet thud again and again from the other side of the tin barrier.

Minutes later that seem like days and the schoolteacher and the foreman sit alone together in the small and crooked shed near the tunnel, sloppy excuse for an office, a table and two stools, blueprints and a rusty stovepipe winding up toward the ceiling. Coal soot and the sicklysweet smell of Wallace's chewing tobacco. Henry Matthews sits on one of the stools, a hot cup of coffee in his hand, black coffee with a dash of whiskey from a bottle the foreman keeps in a box of tools under the table. And Warren Wallace sits across from him, staring down at his own cup, watching the steam rising from the coffee.

"I won't even try," Henry starts, stops, stares at the dirt floor and then begins again. "I *can't* tell you what that was, what it is. I don't think anyone could, Mr Wallace."

"Yeah," the foreman says, shakes his head slow and sips at his coffee. Then, "I just wanted you to see it, Professor, before we bring in a fellow to brick up that hole next week. I wanted someone with some education to see it, so someone besides me and my men would know what was down there."

And for a while neither of them says anything else and there's only the rattle and clatter of a locomotive passing by a little farther up the mountain, hauling its load of ore along the loop of the L.& N. Mineral Railroad. In the quiet left when the train has gone, the foreman clears his throat and, "You know what 'hematite' means?"

"From the Latin," Henry answers. "It means 'blood stone,'" and he takes a bitter, bourbon-tainted sip of his own coffee.

"Yeah," the foreman says. "I looked that up in a dictionary. Blood stone." And "Why?" Henry asks, watching the foreman, and Wallace looks a lot older than he ever realized before, deep lines and wrinkles, patches of grey in his dark beard. And the foreman reaches beneath the table, lifts something wrapped in burlap and sets it in front of Henry Matthews. "Just that maybe we ain't the only thing in the world that's got a use for that iron ore," he says and pulls the burlap back, reveals a large chunk of hematite. Granular rock the exact color of dried blood and the foreman doesn't have to point out the deep pockmarks in the surface of the rock, row after row, each no bigger around than a man's finger, no bigger around than the writhing black thing in Warren Wallace's nitroglycerine bottle.

The chill and tinderdry end of November: Mr W.A. Merkel's tunnel finished on schedule and the Water Works began laying the two big pipes, forty-two and thirty inches round, that would eventually bring clean drinking water all the way from the new Cahaba Pumping Station. Henry Matthews never went back to the spoil heaps outside the tunnel, never saw Warren Wallace again; the last crate of his Silurian specimens shipped away to Tuscaloosa and his attentions, his curiosity, shifted instead to the great Warrior coal field north of Birmingham, the smokegrey shales and cinnamon sandstones laid down in steamy Carboniferous swamps uncounted ages after the silt and mud, the ancient reefs and tropical lagoons that finally became the strata of Red Mountain, were buried deep and pressed into stone.

But the foreman's pitted chunk of hematite kept in a locked strongbox in one undusted corner of Henry's room, and wrapped in cheesecloth and Excelsior, nestled next to the stone and floating in cloudy, preserving alcohol, the thing in the nitroglycerine bottle. Kept like an unlucky souvenir or memento of a nightmare, and late nights when he awoke coldsweating and mouth too dry to speak, these were things to take out, to hold, something undeniable to look at by candle or kerosene light. A proof against madness, or a distraction from other memories, blurred, uncertain recollection of what he saw in that last moment before he fell, as the lantern tumbled toward the oilblack water and the darker shape moving just beneath its mirror surface.

> "All would be well.
> All would be heavenly —
> If the damned would only stay damned."
>   – Charles Fort

PAUL J. McAULEY

Bone Orchards

PAUL J. McAULEY'S FIRST NOVEL, *Four Hundred Billion Stars*, won the Philip K. Dick Memorial Award. Since then he has been awarded the 1995 Arthur C. Clarke Award for best SF novel published in Britain, the John W. Campbell Award for best novel, the British Fantasy Award for Best Short Story, and the Sidewise Award for Best Long Form Alternate History fiction.

His other novels include *Fairyland*, *The Secret of Life* and *Whole Wide World*, while his acclaimed "The Book of Confluence" trilogy is actually a single novel comprising *Child of the River*, *Ancients of Days* and *Shrine of Stars*. The story which follows is a sequel to his tale "Naming the Dead" (published in the previous volume of *Best New Horror*), which also featured the mysterious Mr Carlyle.

"If you're in London," the author recommends, "Abney Park is well worth a visit (the 73 bus will take you to Church Street in Stoke Newington, which has a good selection of bookshops, too). Like most Victorian burial grounds in the city, it was built on a pyramid scheme; fees for new burials were the only income to pay for upkeep of the place. When no more graves could be squeezed in, the money ran out, and it soon became like an engraving from Richard Jeffries' *After London* – a little patch of wilderness guarded by the dead."

C emeteries are fine, private, quiet places, for it is the living, not the dead, who make ghosts. It is the living who slough shells of anger or terror, shed shivers of joy or ooze sullen residues of hate, sticky as spilled crude oil. Only the living, at the crucial moment of transition, cast off yearning or puzzled phantoms, and because most ghosts do not know they are dead, they do not often stray into the gardens of the dead. And so it is that I go to cemeteries to find respite from the blooming, buzzing confusion of the city.

Usually my clients must seek me out, and I make sure that I am not easy to find because I am their last hope, not their first. But, rarely, I discover someone I can help, and this was one such affair, begun in the peace of a bone orchard.

It was in the spring of 199—. Collective manias and delusions at the end of that dreadful century had set loose a host of strange and wild things. I had taken to walking about the city, trying to understand the redrawn maps of influence. It was a transformation as slow but sure as the yielding of winter to spring, but more profound, more permanent. It was as if the climate was changing. My walks were not entirely random. I made a point of stopping for an hour or two of peaceful contemplation in the sanctuary of one or another of the city's cemeteries. The secret garden of the Moravian cemetery, entered by an unmarked door next to a public house off the King's Road. Kensal Green Cemetery, with its great Doric arch and gravelled roads wide enough for horse-drawn carriages. The ordered plots of Brompton Cemetery, radiating from the central octagonal chapel. The City of London Cemetery, its drained lake now a valley of catacombs. Even Bunhill Cemetery, its weathered tombs protected by prissy green municipal railings, could afford a little tranquillity as long as one avoided the lunchtime crowds of office workers.

That day, I had walked north up the Kingsland Road, past the new mosque (although my family has a long and honourable tradition in the matter of the dead, I am not a religious man, but any sign of communal faith gives me hope), through the brawl and tacky commerciality of Dalston (the Santería shop was closed down; I wondered if that had been caused by a minor fluctuation of the new climate), to Stoke Newington and Abney Park Cemetery.

Abney Park:

Beyond the modest entrance off Church Street, hard by the fire station, beyond the imposing graves of Salvation Army generals, paths divide and divide again, leading you away from city noise. The place is thick with trees, and saplings push up between close-set graves or are even rooted in the graves themselves, as if the dead are sprouting at skull or ribs or thigh. There are angels and pyramids and obelisks and hundreds of ordinary headstones. There is a lion. There are anchors cast on a rough boulder. Many graves are tilted, as if the dead, restless for Judgement Day, have been pounding on the roofs of their tombs. At the centre is the derelict chapel of rest, a Gothic ruin surprisingly free of graffiti, its windows boarded up or covered in bright new corrugated iron, every bit of glass smashed from the rose at the apex of the square tower. Boards have been prised away from one window; the scraps of the trespassers' spent lust curl within like exhausted snakes.

That day, yellow daffodils nodded in the mild breeze above some graves – the last land our lives leave, our final plot, is a garden the size of our bodies – and others were bright with rainwashed silk flowers. I wandered the paths, munching chocolate bourbons from the packet I had purchased at a Turkish corner shop. The blue sky was netted by a web of bare branches. Birds sang, defining their territories. A man in a grubby T-shirt and a wrinkled leather jacket led an eager mongrel on a string and carried a can of strong beer; imps hid from me in the tangled rat-tails of his hair. An art student in black was hunched on a bench, sketching one of the angels (its left arm had been broken off at the elbow; fresh stone showed as shockingly white as bone against its weathered grey skin). A man and a woman in identical shell suits sat at another bench, talking quietly. A young woman pushed her baby in an old-fashioned perambulator.

And an old woman in a shabby grey anorak knelt like a penitent at a grave. Something about her made me stop and sit at a bench nearby. I took out my book (a badly foxed copy of Abellio's *La Fin de l'ésotérisme*), and pretended to ruffle through its pages while raking her with covert glances. She was bathed in sunlight that fell at an angle between close-laced branches, like a saint in a medieval woodcut. A quite unremarkable woman in her late sixties, with a pinched, exhausted face devoid of make up, coarse grey hair caught under a flowery scarf. Her anorak, her rayon trousers and her cheap flat shoes had all been bought in the same high street emporium. She was tidying the grave with slow, painful care, raking its green gravel, straightening the silk roses in their brass pot, washing city dirt from the white headstone. She did not see me; nor did she see what seemed to be a small child running about the old graves in the distance.

No one could see it but me.

At last, the woman pulled a shiny black purse from the pocket of her anorak, opened it, and took out a piece of paper. She lifted up a smooth beach pebble, removed something, and tucked the paper underneath. Then she labouriously got to her feet, one hand on the small of her back, dusted her hands, and hobbled away down the path.

I shut my book and went to the grave and retrieved the paper. It was a sheet torn from a cheap, lined writing pad, as soft as newspulp, folded twice into a square. I was about to unfold it when something said, "That's mine."

It presented as a girl of ten or eleven, thin, determined, petulant, in a pale dress fifty years out of date. A scarf was knotted at her skinny neck. Eyes that were no more than dark smudges were half-hidden by tangled hair that stirred in a breeze I could not feel. It stamped ineffectively and said again, "That's mine."

I held out the folded sheet of paper.

"I don't want it now, not now you've touched it, you smelly old thing."

"I will read it for you, if you like."

"Smelly old fat thing," it said spitefully, and turned and took a few steps along the path the old woman had taken before stopping and looking at me over its shoulder, hesitant, unsure.

"I can read it for you," I said again. "I am not like the others. I speak for people like you."

The pale child ran up to me and swiped at the paper with fingers crooked into talons. It failed to take it, of course, and was suddenly dancing in fury. "Fat fucker! Smelly fat fucking fucker!"

The sun seemed to darken, and the child grew in definition, as a candle flame steadies after it has been lit. Branches moved overhead like bony fingers rubbing together.

"You fucking fat smelly fuck!"

Stuff like drool slicked the child's chin, dripped onto the path.

I waited, holding out the paper. When the child was quiet again, I said, "I can read it for you. I do not think you can."

"Fuck you."

Quieter now.

"Is she your mother?"

"She's mine. She's always been mine. You can't have her."

And then the child was chasing away through the trees after the old woman like smoke blown from a gun. There was a wetness on the path, frothy as the mucus shed by a salted slug.

I unfolded the sheet of paper, read the few lines written in painstaking copperplate, then looked at the headstone of the grave.

Jennifer Burton
28th November 1933 – 28th November 1944
Taken from us, she sleeps in peace

I had thought the grave only a few years old. It had been faithfully tended for over fifty years.

I wrote down the particulars in the flyleaf of my book, copied the lines on the sheet of paper, and tucked it back under the pebble.

"Jennifer Burton was murdered," Detective-Superintendent Rawles told me. "Strangled by the scarf her mother gave her for her birthday. Murdered, but not sexually assaulted. Her sister was found wandering the streets nearby, with scratches on her arms and face. She had been attacked too, but she must have managed to get away when her sister was strangled, and she couldn't remember anything. It's funny to think of ordinary crimes being committed then, while the war was going on, but there it is. The case is still open."

"Like a wound," I said, remembering the scarf around the little girl's neck.

We were sitting in the snug of The Seven Stars, the comfortable old pub just around the corner from Lincoln's Inn Fields. Rawles was due to give evidence at a murder trial in an hour. He was uncharacteristically nervous, and kept stealing glances at his watch as I described my encounter and worked my way through a steak and kidney pie. Around us, sleek lawyers in dark suits talked loudly about chambers' gossip and old and forthcoming cases. The sad quiet shade of a pot boy drifted about a dark corner of the bar; out of courtesy, we pretended to ignore each other.

Rawles passed a hand over his close-cropped white hair and sighed. My old friend and ally looked worn out. There were deep lines either side of his mouth, and nests of hair in his ears. The skin on the backs of his hands was as loose as a lizard's, and crazed with a diamond pattern. He said, "Do you really think you should be prying into this, Carlyle?"

"How long is it until you retire, Robert?"

"Three months, as you know very well. I'm dreading it."

"The bungalow in Essex? Your roses?"

"I can't wait to get out of the city. What I dread is the party they're going to give me."

"I will be there in spirit."

Rawles drained his pint glass and said, "The bungalow is brand new. No ghosts at all."

"There are ghosts everywhere, Rawles. I can look at your bungalow, if you like. You might be surprised."

"I'd rather live in ignorant bliss. That's going to be my motto from now on. See nothing, hear nothing. What about you, Carlyle? Why the interest in this?"

"Think of it as spring cleaning. It is the time of year when you do all those little jobs that in the depths of winter you always meant to get around to but never quite did. Now the world wakes, and you do too."

"I've seen your place," Rawles said. "I don't think you've ever dusted in your life."

"It is merely a metaphor. In these strange times, a small bit of work like this will do me some good. Think of it as a charitable case."

Rawles said. "I'm going to be out of it soon, thank Christ," and pushed the brown folder across the table. It was tied with faded green string. "I'll want this back. And if the animal that killed her is still alive, I suppose I'll have to do something about it."

Jennifer Burton had been murdered a few streets from where she lived, on a bombsite where, according to the police report, the local kids had made a kind of camp or den. She had been found amidst candle stubs and broken bits of furniture, strangled by her birthday scarf.

It was amongst the anonymous streets just to the east of the British Museum and Bloomsbury, where cheap tourist hotels, student hostels, council blocks, red brick mansions blocks and university offices crowd together along treeless streets where the sun never quite reaches. There was a block of flats – white concrete and metal-framed windows – where the bombsite had been. I rang bells at random. When at last someone answered, I said, "It's me," and shouldered aside the door when it was buzzed open.

I found a stair down to the basement, and stood a while in the dim light that seeped from a pavement grill, amongst bicycles and boxes of discarded belongings, under pipes that snaked across the ceiling. There was nothing there, but I had not expected anything. The ghost of the murdered girl had fled with her sister, I thought, and she had carried that burden ever since.

My Darling Jennifer, the old woman had written. *It is a lovely spring day and so I came to visit you, and see that you were nice and tidy. It will soon be the next century, the new millennium, and I wonder how it is that I am still alive. I carry you with me always, my darling.*

The fierce deep anguish that burned through these banal sentiments!

I had learned little from the old police files. Jennifer Burton had been eleven when she had died, older by a half hour than her twin, Joan. The police had interviewed known sex offenders and every soldier arrested in London for drunkenness or desertion in the weeks following the murder, but with no result. Joan had been interviewed three times, but remembered nothing of that day. The case had gone cold.

I left that quiet basement and found the address where the two girls had been living with their mother. They had only recently returned from the village in Devon to which they had been evacuated at the beginning of the Blitz. The building had been made over into offices, with a stark modern foyer behind big plate glass windows. A security guard sat behind a bleached oak desk. I could have worked up some plausible bluff, but someone who could help me was nearby, and I went to find him instead.

Coram's Fields, in the middle of the parish of St. Pancras, is one of the happiest places I know. There is a playground to which adults are admitted only in the company of children, and there is an adjoining park, St. George's Gardens, where I sometimes sit for a while. The playground is built on the site of the Foundling Hospital; the gardens are laid out on what was once a cemetery. I know only too well how much of London is built on her dead.

That the park and playground are unmarked by darkness is due in large part to its unofficial and unacknowledged guardian. Harry Wright was a pacifist who became a volunteer fireman during the war. He was killed at the height of the Blitz, when the front of a burning house collapsed on him as he went in to rescue three children trapped inside. I sat on a bench amongst clipped, mulched rose beds in cold sunlight. The shrieks and laughter of children at play was clear and sharp. Presently Harry drifted over, tentative and curious.

"It's you, Mr Carlyle," he said, smiling with relief. "For a moment, I thought it might be trouble."

"I am afraid that I have brought a little trouble, Harry. Sit down, and I will tell you about it."

"I'll keep watch if you don't mind, Mr Carlyle, and I do it better standing."

He was a small, tough, bantam-rooster of a man in his mid thirties, in shirt and braces, his honest face smudged and indistinct, like a half-erased sketch. He drifted around the bench, head cocked for any trouble, as I explained my encounter at Abney Park Cemetery.

"Oh, I couldn't go all the way up there," he said, when I had finished. "I have enough of a job here."

"I understand. What I have in mind is much closer to home."

"I don't know if I could, Mr Carlyle."

"There is a child to be helped, Harry, and it will take only a little of your time."

"Still," he said doubtfully, "things are difficult at the moment. It all seems so hopeless sometimes, as if the whole world is bearing down on me and my little patch."

"Things are changing, Harry. We all feel it."

"I saw that librarian chap a while ago," Harry said. He was still patrolling my bench, keeping watch on the perimeters of the park. "Was it last week? Anyway, he felt the same thing."

Like many of his kind, Harry was vague about time. I knew it must have been at least several months ago, for that was when the librarian had been devoured. It had been my fault. I had sent him against something whose strength I had underestimated. I still carried the guilt, like an ink stain on my soul.

I said, "I am afraid that he has passed on."

"That's a shame. Him and me, we had some interesting talks. Very well educated, he was, and polite as anyone I've met. Perhaps it was for the best, Mr Carlyle. I don't suppose he would have liked the changes to his place."

The old Reading Room of the British Library was closed; its books had been transferred to the new red brick building on Euston Road. When I had last been there, I had stood a while in the wood-panelled room where autograph manuscripts had once been on view, and where display boards and glass-cased models of the new extension now stood, mantled with a fine layer of concrete dust from the building works, disturbed only by the occasional tourist who had taken a wrong turning. I had waited a long time, but he had not come.

I told Harry Wright's restlessly circling ghost, "You are quite right. He would have hated it."

"He was a man of his time, Mr Carlyle. Now, I think I can help you, but I'll have to be quick. Even the day isn't safe any more."

I was glad that I did not have to compel him. I waited outside the office building while Harry made his search. I waited more than an hour, pretending to read my book under the gaze of a security cameras, and I grew so anxious that I almost cried out in amazement when at last Harry appeared with his burden.

"We'll take the poor mite to my place," he said, brisk and matter-of-fact. "Safer that way."

I lost him when I had to wait for a gap in the traffic shuddering angrily down Judd Street, but he was waiting for me in the rose garden. He was still holding the child he had rescued. Her face was pressed against his shoulder. There was a scarf around her neck, and she wore the same dress as the venomously angry thing I had confronted in Abney Park.

"She's scared," Harry said. "She was hiding in a cupboard. It's all right now, darling," he added, speaking softly to the child. "You're safe here."

It took a while to coax her round. At last, Harry set her on her feet and resumed his patrol while she scampered about, stopping every minute to look up at the sky. I waited until she drifted back to me, shy and sidelong.

"You're a funny man," she said.

She stood on one foot, twisting the other behind her calf. A breeze could have blown her away.

"I know I am," I said.

A woman walking her dog glanced at me as she went past; I suppose she would have seen an overweight man in a black raincoat, hunched over and talking to himself. Hardly an uncommon sight in these troubled times.

The girl said, "So many people came at first, and they were making such a fuss, that I hid. But then they went away and after that I couldn't make anyone hear me. I thought Joan would find me. I waited and waited. Will you take me to her?"

"I cannot do that. But I can help you, if you will help me. I want to know what happened to you. Do you understand?"

She nodded. She said, "It was like being filled with black boxes. The dark came flying in, and it had corners. It filled me up."

"Did you see who brought the dark, Jennifer?"

The child's hands had gone to her throat, plucking at the knotted scarf. She said, "I don't want to cause trouble."

"None of that matters, not any more."

"That's what the nice man told me," the child said, and added, "He said that he was a fireman."

"So he is. And a very good one. We both want to help you, Jennifer. I think that I know what happened, but I need to be sure. Will you tell me?"

"Joan was cross. She wanted my scarf because she said that it was nicer than hers. She said I always got nicer things because I was older. She wanted it, and I wouldn't give it to her because it was mine!"

She ran then. I did not try to follow her, and at last Harry brought her back. She would not talk, but it did not matter, because I knew now how wrong I had been. I told the little girl that she could rest. That she could sleep. And then I sent her away.

Harry said, "Is it like that, Mr Carlyle? Like going to sleep?"

"I do not know," I said. "But that is what everyone wants to believe."

Harry brushed his hands together. "There's no rest for the

wicked, as my gran used to say. I'll be back to work. It's getting dark, and there can be trouble, after dark."

A week later, I was sitting on the bench in Abney Park Cemetery, near Jennifer Burton's grave. I had been coming here every day, waiting for Jennifer's sister, and her burden. Every day, at dusk, when I knew that the old woman would not come, I passed by her mean little basement flat in Albion Road on my way home. I once saw her coming up the steps in her grey coat and her neat scarf, moving slowly and painfully, bowed under the weight of her burden, which hissed like a cat when it spied me across the street.

It was another sunny day. The buds were beginning to break on the trees, so that the stark outlines of their branches were blurred by a ghostly scantling of green. The old woman came just after noon, and her burden came with her, circling us both at a distance, hardly more than broken shadow and sunlight. At last, the old woman finished tidying her sister's grave. She took out a piece of folded paper and tucked it under the pebble, and crumpled up the note I had carefully replaced.

The ghost circled through the trees as the old woman went away down the path. I called its name and told it to come to me and it did, glaring at me through the tangle of its hair.

"You fat old fucker," it said. "You don't scare me."

"I know why you did it, Joan. You wanted the scarf. You did not realize that you had hurt your sister so badly."

"She messed her knickers," the thing said, with a vicious smile. "She made a funny sound and messed her knickers, the smelly silly."

It was the ghost Joan Burton had cast off in a moment of sudden and intense anger. It was the memory that she could never acknowledge, the memory of murdering her own sister. She had been imprisoned by it ever since, a longer sentence than any court would have imposed.

It glared at me through its tangled hair and hissed, "Keep away from me, you fat fucker. I'll hurt you. I will."

"Enough," I said, and gathered it to me. It was like lifting up an armful of icy briars, but only for a moment.

"So you found nothing," Detective-Superintendent Rawles said. "That's not like you, Carlyle. You usually like to see things through to the end."

Once again, we had met in The Seven Stars. Once again, Rawles was stealing glances at his watch. The jury in his case was expected to announce its verdict that afternoon.

I said, "Times are changing."

"Times change, Carlyle, but you don't. You're more or less the same as when I met you back in '64."

"Ah, but I was already old then."

"You do have a bit of a spring in your step today," Rawles said. "I noticed when I came in."

"I did? I suppose it is the season. Everything seems hopeful at this time of year."

I had passed Joan Burton on the way out of the cemetery. She was still stooped, but I think it was out of habit, not necessity. I said, "A nice day, is it not?"

She glanced at me and smiled, and I saw in that smile the pretty girl she had once been. "I hadn't noticed," she said, "but yes, you're right. Isn't it beautiful?"

RAMSEY CAMPBELL

No Strings

RAMSEY CAMPBELL HAS RECEIVED MORE AWARDS for horror fiction than any other writer. He has been named Grand Master by the World Horror Convention and received a Lifetime Achievement Award from the Horrors Writers Association.

His latest novel is *Pact of the Fathers*, and a film of the book is already in development in Spain. He has also recently completed a new supernatural novel, *The Darkest Part of the Woods*. Campbell's M.R. Jamesian anthology *Meddling With Ghosts* is published by The British Library, and he has co-edited *Gathering the Bones* with Jack Dann and Dennis Etchison. S.T. Joshi's study *Ramsey Campbell and Modern Horror Fiction* is available from Liverpool University Press.

" 'No Strings' was written at the behest of Michele Slung for an anthology about strangers," the author reveals. "Sadly, she decided it wasn't strange enough. I bear no resentment: without Michele the story wouldn't exist, and I'm grateful.

"It was written in the mornings of most of a fortnight of August 1998 in an apartment, or rather on the balcony thereof, west of Tavronitis in Crete. Just shows how much darker it tends to be inside my head."

"**G**ood night till tomorrow," Phil Linford said, having faded the signature tune of *Linford Till Midnight* up under his voice, "and a special good night to anyone I've been alone with." As he removed his headphones, imitated by the reverse of himself in the dark beyond the inner window, he felt as if he was unburdening himself of all the voices he'd talked to during the previous two hours. They'd been discussing the homeless, whom most of the callers had insisted on describing as beggars or worse, until Linford had declared that he respected anyone who did their best to earn their keep, to feed themselves and their dependants. He hadn't intended to condemn those who only begged, if they were capable of nothing else, but several of his listeners did with increasing viciousness. After all that, the very last caller had hoped aloud that nobody homeless had been listening. Maybe Linford oughtn't to have responded that if they were homeless they wouldn't have anywhere to plug in a radio, but he always tried to end with a joke.

There was no point in leaving listeners depressed: that wasn't the responsibility he was paid for. If he'd given them a chance to have their say and something to carry on chewing over, he'd done what was expected of him. If he wasn't doing a good job he wouldn't still be on the air. At least it wasn't television – at least he wasn't making people do no more than sit and gawk. As the second hand of the clock above the console fingered midnight he faded out his tune and gave up the station to the national network.

The news paced him as he walked through the station, killing lights. This year's second war, another famine, a seaboard devastated by a hurricane, a town buried by a volcano – no room for anything local, not even the people who'd been missing for weeks or months. In the deserted newsroom computer terminals presented their blank bulging profiles to him. Beyond the unstaffed reception desk a solitary call was flashing like a warning on the switchboard. Its glow and its insect clicking died as he padded across the plump carpet of the reception area. He was reaching for the electronic latch to let himself into the street when he faltered. Beyond the glass door, on the second of the three concrete steps to the pavement, a man was seated with his back to him.

Had he fallen asleep over the contents of his lap? He wore a black suit a size too large, above which peeked an inch of collar gleaming white as a vicar's beneath the neon streetlights, not an ensemble that benefited from being topped by a dark green baseball cap pulled as low as it would stretch on the bald neck. If he was waiting for anyone it surely couldn't be Linford, who nonetheless felt as if he had attracted the other somehow, perhaps by having left all the lights on while he was alone in the station. The news brought itself to an end with a droll anecdote about a music student who had almost managed to sell a forged manuscript before the buyer had noticed the composer's name was spelled Beathoven, and Linford eased the door open. He was on the way to opening enough of a gap to sidle through, into the stagnant July heat beneath the heavy clouds, when *Early Morning Moods* commenced with a rush of jaunty flourishes on a violin. At once the figure on the steps jerked to his feet as though tugged by invisible strings and joined in.

So he was a busker, and the contents of his lap had been a violin and its bow, but the discovery wasn't the only reason why Linford pulled the door wide. The violinist wasn't merely imitating the baroque solo from the radio, he was copying every nuance and intonation, an exact echo no more than a fraction of a second late. Linford felt as though he'd been selected to judge a talent show. "Hey, that's good," he said. "You ought —"

He had barely started speaking when the violinist dodged away with a movement that, whether intentionally or from inability, was less a dance than a series of head-to-toe wriggles that imparted a gypsy swaying to the violin and bow. Perhaps to blot out the interference Linford's voice represented, he began to play louder, though as sweetly as ever. He halted in the middle of the pedestrianised road, between the radio station and a department store lit up for the night. Linford stayed in the doorway until the broadcast melody gave way to the presenter's voice, then closed the door behind him, feeling it lock. "Well done," he called. "Listen, I wonder —"

He could only assume the musician was unable to hear him for playing. No sooner had the melody ended than it recommenced as the player moved away as though guided by his bunch of faint shadows that gave him the appearance of not quite owning up to the possession of several extra limbs. Linford was growing frustrated with the behaviour of someone he only wanted to help. "Excuse me," he said, loud enough for the plate glass across the street to fling his voice back at him. "If it's an audition you need I can get you one. No strings. No commission."

The repetition of the melody didn't falter, but the violinist halted in front of a window scattered with wire skeletons sporting flimsy clothes. When the player didn't turn to face him, Linford followed. He knew talent when he heard it, and local talent was meant to be the point of local radio, but he also didn't mind feeling like the newsman he'd been until he'd found he was better at chatting between his choices of music too old to be broadcast by anyone except him. Years of that had landed him the late-night phone-in, where he sometimes felt he made less of a difference than he had in him. Now here was his chance to make one, and he wasn't about to object if putting the violinist on the air helped his reputation too, not when his contract was due for renewal. He was almost alongside the violinist – close enough to glimpse a twitching of the pale smooth cheek, apparently in time with a mouthing that accompanied the music – when the other danced, if it could be called a dance, away from him.

Unless he was mute – no, even if he was – Linford was determined to extract some sense from him. He supposed it was possible that the musician wasn't quite right in some way, but then it occurred to him that the man might already be employed and so not in need of being discovered. "Do you play with anyone?" he called at the top of his voice.

That seemed to earn him a response. The violinist gestured ahead with his bow, so tersely that Linford heard no break in the music. If the gesture hadn't demonstrated that the player was going Linford's way, he might have sought clarification of whatever he was meant to have understood. Instead he went after the musician, not running or even trotting, since he would have felt absurd, and so not managing to come within arm's length.

The green glow of a window display – clothed dummies exhibiting price tags or challenging the passer-by to guess their worth, their blank-eyed faces immobile and rudimentary as death-masks moulded by a trainee – settled on the baseball cap as the player turned along the side street that led to the car park, and the cap appeared to glisten like moss. A quarter of a mile away down the main road, Linford saw a police car crested with lights speed across a junction, the closest that traffic was allowed to approach. Of course the police could drive anywhere they liked, and their cameras were perched on roofs: one of his late-night partners in conversation had declared that these days the cameras were the nearest thing to God. While Linford felt no immediate need of them, there was surely nothing wrong with knowing you were watched. Waving a hand in front of his face to ward off a raw smell the side street had enclosed, he strode after the musician.

The street led directly into the car park, a patch of waste ground about two hundred yards square, strewn with minor chunks of rubble, empty bottles, squashed cans. Only the exit barrier and the solitary presence of Linford's Peugeot indicated that the square did any work. Department stores backed onto its near side, and to its right were restaurants whose bins must be responsible for the wafts of a raw smell. To the left a chain fence crowned with barbed wire protected a building site, while the far side was overlooked by three storeys of derelict offices. The musician was prancing straight for these beneath arc-lights that set his intensified shadows scuttling around him.

He reached the building as Linford came abreast of the car. Without omitting so much as a quaver from the rapid eager melody, the violinist lifted one foot in a movement that suggested the climax of a dance and shoved the back door open. The long brownish stick of the bow jerked up as though to beckon Linford. Before he had time to call out, if indeed he felt obliged to, he saw the player vanish into a narrow oblong, black as turned earth.

He rested a hand on the tepid roof of the car and told himself he'd done enough. If the musician was using the disused offices as a squat he was unlikely to be alone, and perhaps his thinness was a symptom of addiction. The prospect of encountering a roomful of drug addicts fell short of appealing to Linford. He was fishing out his keys when an abrupt silence filled the car park. The music, rendered hollow by the dark interior, had ceased in the midst of a phrase, but it hadn't entirely obscured a shrill cry from within – a cry, Linford was too sure to be able to ignore it, for help.

Five minutes – less if he surprised himself by proving to be in a condition to run – would take him back to the radio station to call the police. There might even be a phone booth in the main street that accepted coins rather than cards. Less than five minutes might be far too long for whoever needed help, and so Linford stalked across the car park, waving his arms at the offices as he raised his face to mouth for help at the featureless slate sky. He was hoping some policeman was observing him and would send reinforcements – he was hoping to hear a police car raise its voice on its way to him. He'd heard nothing but his own dwarfed isolated footsteps by the time he reached the ajar door.

Perhaps someone had planned to repaint it and given up early in the process. Those patches of old paint that weren't flaking were blistered. The largest blister had split open, and he saw an insect writhe into hiding inside the charred bulge as he dealt the door a slow kick to shove it wide. A short hall with two doors on each side led to a staircase that turned its back on itself halfway up. The widening glare from the car park pressed the darkness back towards the stairs, but only to thicken it on them and within the doorways. Since all the doors were open, he ventured as far as the nearest pair and peered quickly to either side of him.

Random shapes of light were stranded near the windows, all of which were broken. The floorboards of both rooms weren't much less rubbly than the car park. In the room to his left two rusty filing cabinets had been pulled fully open, though surely there could have been nothing to remove from them, let alone to put in. To his right a single office desk was leaning on a broken leg and grimacing with both the black rectangles that used to contain drawers. Perhaps it was his tension that rendered these sights unpleasant, or perhaps it was the raw smell. His will to intervene was failing as he began to wonder if he had really heard any sound except music – and then the cry was repeated above him. It could be a woman's voice or a man's grown shrill with terror, but there was no mistaking its words. "Help," it pleaded. "Oh God."

No more than a couple of streets away a nightclub emitted music and loud voices, followed by an outburst of the slamming of car doors. The noises made Linford feel less alone: there must be at least one bouncer outside the nightclub, within earshot of a yell. Perhaps that wasn't as reassuring as he allowed it to seem, but it let him advance to the foot of the stairs and shout into the dimness that was after all not quite dark. "Hello? What's happening up there? What's wrong?"

His first word brought the others out with it. The more of them there were, the less sure he was how advisable they might be. They were met by utter silence except for a creak of the lowest stair, on which he'd tentatively stepped. He hadn't betrayed his presence, he told himself fiercely: whoever was above him had already been aware of him, or there would have been no point to the cry for help. Nevertheless once he seized the splintered banister it was on tiptoe that he ran upstairs. He was turning the bend when an object almost tripped him – the musician's baseball cap.

The banister emitted a groan not far short of vocal as he leaned on it to steady himself. The sound was answered by another cry of "Help", or most of it before the voice was muffled by a hand over the mouth. It came from a room at the far end of the corridor ahead. He was intensely aware of the moment, of scraps of light that clung like pale bats to the ceiling of the corridor, the rat's tails of the flexes that had held sockets for light bulbs, the blackness of the doorways that put him in mind of holes in the ground, the knowledge that this was his last chance to retreat. Instead he ran almost soundlessly up the stairs and past two rooms that a glance into each appeared to show were empty save for rubble and broken glass. Before he came abreast of the further left-hand room he knew it was where he had to go. For a moment he thought someone had hung a sign on the door.

It was a tattered office calendar dangling from a nail. Dates some weeks apart on it – the most recent almost a fortnight ago – were marked with ovals that in daytime might have looked more reddish. He was thinking that the marks couldn't be fingerprints, since they contained no lines, as he took a step into the room.

A shape lay on the area of the floor least visited by daylight, under the window amid shards of glass. A ragged curtain tied at the neck covered all of it except the head, which was so large and bald and swollen it reminded him of the moon. The features appeared to be sinking into it: the unreadably shadowed eyes and gaping whitish lips could have passed for craters, and its nostrils were doing without a nose. Despite its baldness, it was a woman's head, since Linford distinguished the outline of breasts under the curtain – indeed, enough bulk for an extra pair. The head wobbled upright to greet him, its scalp springing alight with the glare from the car park, and large hands whose white flesh was loose as oversized gloves groped out from beneath the curtain. He could see no nails on them. The foot he wasn't conscious of holding in mid-air trod on a fragile object he'd failed to notice – a violinist's bow. It snapped and pitched him forward to see more of the room.

Four desk drawers had been brought into it, one to a corner.

Each drawer contained a nest of newspapers and office scrap. Around the drawers were strewn crumpled sheets of music, stained dark as though – Linford thought and then tried not to – they had been employed to wipe mouths. Whatever had occurred had apparently involved the scattering about the bare floor of enough spare bows to equip a small string orchestra. By no means anxious to understand any of the contents of the room until he was well clear of it, Linford was backing away when the violin recommenced its dance behind him.

He swung around and at once saw far too much. The violinist was as bald as the figure under the window, but despite the oddly temporary nature of the bland smooth face, particularly around the nose, it was plain that the musician was female too. The long brown stick she was passing back and forth over the instrument had never been a bow – not that one would have made a difference, since the cracked violin was stringless. The perfect imitation of the broadcast melody was streaming out of her wide toothless mouth, the interior of which was at least as white as the rest of her face. Despite her task she managed a smile, though he sensed it wasn't for him but about him. She was blocking the doorway, and the idea of going closer to her – to the smell of rawness, some of which was certainly emerging from her mouth – almost crushed his mind to nothing. He had to entice her away from the doorway, and he was struggling to will himself to retreat into the room – struggling to keep his back to it – when a voice cried "Help."

It was the cry he'd come to find: exactly the cry, and it was behind him in the room. He twisted half round and saw the shape under the window begin to cover her mouth, then let her hand fall. She must have decided there was no longer any reason to cut the repetition short. "Oh God," she added, precisely as she had before, and rubbed her curtained stomach.

It wasn't just a trick, it was as much of an imitation as the music had been. He had to make more of an effort than he could remember ever having used to swallow the sound the realization almost forced out of his mouth. For years he'd earned his living by not letting there be more than a second of silence, but could staying absolutely quiet now save him? He was unable to think what else to do, not that he was anything like sure of being capable of silence. "Help, oh God," the curtained shape repeated, more of a demand now, and rubbed her stomach harder. The player dropped the violin and the other item, and before their clatter faded she came at Linford with a writhing movement that might have been a jubilant dance – came just far enough to continue to block his escape.

His lips trembled, his teeth chattered, and he couldn't suppress his words, however idiotic they might be. "My mistake. I only —"

"My mistake. I only." Several voices took up his protest at once, but he could see no mouths uttering it, only an agitation of the lower half of the curtain. Then two small forms crawled out from underneath, immediately followed by two more, all undisguised by any kind of covering. Their plump white bodies seemed all the more wormlike for the incompleteness of the faces on the bald heads – no more than nostrils and greedily dilated mouths. Just the same they wriggled straight to him, grabbing pointed fragments of glass. He saw the violinist press her hands over her ears, and thought that she felt some sympathy for him until he grasped that she was ensuring she didn't have to imitate whatever sound he made. The window was his only chance now: if the creature beneath it was as helpless as she seemed, if he could bear to step over or on her so as to scream from the window for somebody out there to hear — But when he screamed it was from the floor where, having expertly tripped him, the young were swarming up his legs, and he found he had no interest in the words he was screaming, especially when they were repeated in chorus to him.

KATHRYN PTACEK

The Grotto

KATHRYN PTACEK HAS SOLD OVER two hundred short stories, reviews, essays, and interviews in her two-decade career. Her recent publication credits include *Canadian Fiction Magazine*, *Northern Horror*, *The Mammoth Book of Vampire Stories by Women* and two stories in *100 Crafty Little Cat Stories* (Barnes & Noble). The editor of *The Official Newsletter of the Horror Writers Association* and compiler of *The Gila Queen's Guide to Markets*, Ptacek's company Little Bird Editorial Services looks at fiction and non-fiction manuscripts.

"I had to write a story with images of old gods in it for a themed anthology," the author explains, "and for the longest time, I couldn't pin down what I wanted. Then I thought of those 'grotesques' that decorate some buildings. But where to set the story? For a long time now I've wanted to visit Tuscany, and once I started doing the research, I realized how well the ark gods of the Etruscans fit."

C eil Uccello Wallace had always wanted to visit Tuscany. It was a shame that she had returned to her ancestral home only now, when she was dying.

Ceil slowed her pace, then detached herself from the tour group that she'd been following all morning; and wandered down a narrow cobblestone street, so angled and steep that she thought if she fell she'd just bounce, much like a pinball, off the thick stucco walls all the way down to the vineyard below the walled town. She chuckled.

The tour group was out of sight now, heading toward the town's unassuming church; otherwise she was the only one out and about this close to one. Overhead the sky was a stark cerulean, and a faint spicy smell wafted from the profusion of bright flowers blooming in windowboxes. A black and white cat sitting in a doorway yawned as she passed by.

San Damonio, northwest above Florence, had been her family's home for more generations than anyone could count. Local tradition held that her family, the Uccellos, and a handful of others were Etruscan farmers who had migrated to this valley some three thousand years ago.

Ceil thought that was a fanciful story, fabricated to satisfy historyhungry tourists.

Tourists, like herself, she thought ruefully. In a single day she'd played the role: checking the handful of shops – none with the usual tourist knickknacks, which she found refreshing – as well as visiting the church, a most unpretentious structure with nothing of value to offer: not a single marble statue, lofty bell tower, stunning mosaic or fresco, or even a worthy *cappella* or chapel. In fact, she had never seen such a boring church. It was almost as if the place were unused, and yet she had seen some townspeople going inside. Hadn't she spotted a priest earlier . . . ?

Actually, as she thought about it, there was very little in San Damonio of interest to visitors. On her map the town appeared as just a tiny dot, and when she'd tried to find out more about it, she'd met with a dead-end.

San Damonio wasn't famous for its nondescript church, nor was it known for the wine from its vineyards – in fact, what she had glimpsed of those on her way into town seemed sadly insignificant to the vast and renowned vineyards she had seen in Chianti, south of Florence. Surely, though, the town must have *something* of note.

As she reached *La Rondine*, the town's one and only inn, a flock of birds wheeled overhead. She shielded her eyes with one hand and peered upward into the bright sky. The flock dipped, barreling straight toward the street, then abruptly changed direction and flew out of sight.

Were they swallows? she wondered, or just common sparrows?

She didn't know if there had actually ever been swallows in the area to give the inn its name.

Still, for all that, it was a pleasant place, and the staff seemed quite friendly.

She headed straight for the dining-room. It was close enough to lunchtime, if the slight rumbling in her stomach was to be believed. Besides, she'd had only a cup of tea before leaving that morning.

"*Buon giorno*, and how did the *signorina* sleep last night?" Arturo Ventaglio, the owner of *La Rondine*, asked in English. He was an older man, with hair dusted with grey. Marco, the teenaged morning desk clerk who also served as the dining-room waiter, smiled widely, revealing a few gaps in that handsome expression.

"Quite well, thank you. It's so restful here." Ceil thought Signore Ventaglio was being quite diplomatic, referring to her as a young woman. She wasn't old at forty-one, but then she guessed she didn't fall in the young woman category, either . . . not any more. Still, it was flattering.

Ventaglio bobbed his head. "Very soothing, *si*?"

Marco nodded, too. "Very very, healthy, too!"

"Yes, so I understand," she said with some irony. "The climate is certainly ideal."

She was grateful both men spoke English, because her Italian was rusty. Her parents had fled the village during the ravages of World War Two and settled in New York City and then later, as the family grew, across the Hudson to Kearny, New Jersey. But always when they spoke of "home" it was the Tuscan village. Once Ceil started school, her parents insisted that they speak only English. Sometimes, though, her father and mother reverted, and Ceil and her brother and sister picked up the language that way.

Her parents had died before they could return, and so Ceil had taken it upon herself to go to San Damonio. Year after year, though, she cancelled her plans, with one decade dissolving into another. Her sister and brother were to accompany her, but early in the year Michael had died in an army training mission, while Lucy had been killed by a drunk driver at 2 o'clock in the afternoon. Shortly after that, Ceil and her husband of two years separated, and it was the following month that she had had the wakeup call of cancer. In that moment she knew she had to go "home."

She'd told no one of her coming; she wasn't even sure any family remained. If that were so, then that made her journey even more poignant – she was the last of the Uccellos.

"More sightseeing today?" Signore Ventaglio asked, escorting her into the dining room. He drew out the highbacked chair with a flourish, and she smiled.

"Yes." He did tend to fuss a bit over her, but as she scanned the dining-room she didn't see many other guests – a retired couple by their appearance, and a man about her age. Perhaps Signore Ventaglio just felt the need to hone his hospitality skills.

"Ah, good. There are many ruins north of town. Very old. Who knows how old, *si*? And you must visit the vineyard – tell them that Arturo Ventaglio sent you, and they will give you a bottle of their best *vino*."

"And the *grotta*," Marco called as he headed toward the kitchen to get her tea. She noticed that he walked with a marked limp.

Signore Ventaglio scowled at Marco. "*Si*, the *grotta*, although that is a difficult climb for most. Straight up." He gestured with both hands. "Much better for a *capra*." He saw her confusion. "A goat."

Interesting, but her guidebook hadn't mentioned a grotto, not here in this outoftheway village. "Tell me more, *signore*."

The man shrugged. "The *grotta*. It isn't very spectacular. Damp. Dirty. Not a place for a lady such as yourself."

"No, no, no," Marco said, shaking his head. He was back with her pot of tea. "Not a place for a lady."

She smiled. "I'm hardly a lady – I'm a historian who's been on many archaeological digs. I've gotten dirty with the best of them."

The innkeeper's frown deepened. "It is not a place for a lady such as yourself," he repeated, then took Marco by the shoulder and shoved him back into the kitchen. The door swung shut behind them as Ventaglio's voice rose, loud and angry. She heard the word *imbecille*. She felt sorry that Marco was in trouble because of her.

But, she told herself, she'd done nothing. The boy had volunteered the information. She read the menu, forcing herself to ignore the shouting. A few minutes later Marco returned, a chastised expression on his face. He stood by her chair, waiting for her to make up her mind.

"Just an *antipasti*," she said. He nodded and shuffled back to the kitchen. Her appetite had decreased over the past few weeks; she knew she should eat more; it was just that nothing tasted or smelled good. When her doctor told her of the cancer, she panicked – she wanted to run from the exam room, as if she could escape her fate. She stayed, though, and listened to him, noted his recommendation for an oncologist. The next few days remained a blur – the cancer specialist saw her; then he gave her the prognosis. Yes, he could fill her body with chemicals and radiation, but it wouldn't matter; nothing would help at this late stage. She was dying. It was just a matter of time.

Curiously Ceil remained somewhat aloof from all this; it was as if it was happening to someone else. The specialist said he would sign her into the hospital that afternoon to start the therapy, but she said no; she thanked him, then dressed and returned to the university where she taught for the past decade. She typed out her resignation, handed it to her bewildered department chairman – summer classes were in session – waved to her fellow history lecturers, packed up the few personal items in her office, and went home.

There, she unplugged the phone and crawled into bed fully dressed, burrowing under the covers. She lay there for nearly twenty hours before finally emerging. She hadn't slept much, just dozing here and there. All the time she did little but think. Mentally she felt like a mouse in a maze . . . her mind running down first one corridor, then another, and all of them dead-ends; there had to be some way out, some corridor that didn't dead-end. She did know, however, she didn't have enough time left to lay around the house and feel sorry for herself. She showered, dressed in her favorite pair of jeans and shirt, and called a travel agent. Then she called a real estate agent who was a friend and had the house put up for sale; funds from that sale – she would take the first offer, she said – were to be wired to her. Of her belongings she took only what she would need for a prolonged visit. Everything else she donated to charities.

Four days later she was on her way to Italy.

Any time, the specialist had said; she could die any time. It could be a week from now, a month . . . a year; it could even be longer . . . or not. She had medicine for the pain that the doctor said would come later. Mostly, though, she just felt tired.

As she poked at a pepper on the *antipasti* plate, she realized that she still hadn't cried about it. Of course, what good would that do? Crying wouldn't cure her. Besides, she had too much to do yet, so much to see. Better for her to focus on that.

For the past month she toured Venice, Rome, Naples, and Milan, leaving Florence and the surrounding Tuscany country-side to the last.

And now that she was here . . . she didn't know. She didn't feel like she'd come home; she didn't feel much of anything, besides a certain curiosity.

She speared an olive as she gazed out the window. The same black and white cat she had seen earlier lounged on a bench opposite the inn. He yawned and rolled over, exposing a white belly to the summer sunshine. A shadow spread across the dozing cat, and the animal leaped up and darted into a shop. She peered up, saw nothing. An eagle or a hawk, perhaps. Did they have eagles here? she wondered and reminded herself to search for a book on the local flora and fauna; the guidebook was certainly useless in that respect.

"Excuse me," said a smooth baritone voice.

Startled, Ceil dropped her fork onto the plate.

"I'm sorry to have frightened you." It was the man from the other side of the dining-room.

"You didn't," she replied somewhat crossly. She picked up her fork, then set it down. "I'm sorry. That was bad manners. Please, sit down and join me."

"I could not help but overhear your conversation. You expressed interest in the *grotta*."

"Yes."

"I could take you there, Signorina . . ."

"Uccello. Ceil Uccello." Until this moment she had been going by her husband's last name. It was time to change, she thought; time . . . and how much longer of that did she have? Would she stand up after this meal and simply drop dead? Would she simply not wake up one morning? She forced herself to concentrate on what the man was saying.

"Ah. Did you know that your last name means 'bird'?"

She nodded. "My parents told me when I was small."

"Ah. But yes, about the grotto . . . it's close to the villa up the hill."

"I see." Ceil wasn't sure about this. The man spoke with a slight accent, almost English.

"I am sorry again. My name is Laurence San Damonio."

She arched a brow. "The same as the town?"

The corners of his thin mouth lifted ever so slightly. "The very same. My family has been here for a long time – but as to whether we were named after the town, or it after us, no one can say. My mother, though, was English; as a child I lived in Kent; when I was old enough I came home."

"I see." She was repeating herself. What a dunce he must think her. "And you're a tour guide now?" she asked lightly.

He laughed, a rich sound. "Hardly. A businessman. A little of this, a little of that."

Oh swell, she thought, a ne'er-do-well, and yet he hardly looked the part. His clothes, while casual, seemed expensive, and he was well groomed. Maybe, one part of her said, he was a mass murderer – a local one – and he was waiting to get her alone before he stabbed her seven thousand times. Go ahead, another part of her said; who cares.

Who cares, indeed? Ceil wondered, and realized she did.

"Okay. When?"

"Tomorrow?"

"Fine." If she lived that long. Ceil, Ceil, stop it, she told herself. Stop, stop, stop.

"I'll meet you here around noon then." He stood and bowed ever so perceptibly, then returned to his table.

Ceil finished her *antipasti* and set down her fork, Signore Ventaglio approached, as if he had timed his entrance to that very moment.

"Signore San Damonio is quite a gentleman," Ventaglio said as he whisked her plate away. "Very charming, indeed?"

"Indeed," Ceil said, trying hard not to smile. "Very continental."

"*Si!*" He beamed at her. "And would there be anything else for you?"

Yes, a new life. Aloud: "Not today, *grazie*." As she started to leave the dining room, she noticed for the first time a terracotta medallion to one side of the door. The bas-relief appeared quite worn in places as though many fingers had rubbed it. "What's that?"

"Janus, the God of the Sun and of all portals, doorways, and thresholds," the innkeeper said.

A grotesque, she knew, was an architectural decoration, a fanciful creature or representation of a person . . . commonly found on old architecture. Did this date from some ancient temple? "Oh, yes, of course – Janus, the Roman God!"

"The *Etruscan* God," Signore Ventaglio corrected politely.

Of course. Rome's authority lessened the farther north she went. Here, the Etruscan influence remained strong.

Interesting. Perhaps there was a book about the Etruscan gods . . . if she could find a bookshop. All these books she was buying . . . when would she have time to read them? She had the rest of her life, and she nearly laughed aloud at the idea.

She could have gone to her room for a nap, but she wasn't tired, at least not yet; and besides, wouldn't she have time enough later on to rest . . .

It was close to 3:30 now and the shops were just beginning to reopen. Ceil nodded to an elderly woman sweeping the stoop in front of a grocer's. Several times she thought she was being watched, but when she turned around she saw no one – only another black and white cat. Or was that the same one? Always a magnet for animals, she wouldn't be surprised if this one adopted her. She'd seen few animals in the village, which was odd because in other towns she'd visited she'd seen dozens of roaming dogs and cats.

At a fruit vendor's, she selected several oranges. A few steps away she discovered a store filled with antiques. Much of the contents, she realized after she had stepped inside and greeted the owner, weren't much older than a few decades. But still . . . there might be something she just couldn't live without.

She paused, an ironic smile on her lips. Sometimes . . . for a moment or two . . . she forgot. Briefly tears threatened to sting her eyes; she bit her lower lip and moved away so that the owner couldn't see her.

"What is this?" she asked, holding up a bronze object, one of many on a table. It was shaped almost like a bowl, the center a sun face, with an outer circle of moons.

"Etruscan lamp," the proprietor answered, her dark eyes solemn. "Very, very old. From two thousand years ago. It comes from the tombs. A sepulchral lamp. Very famous."

Ceil studied the lamp. Olive oil had filled the vessel, the wick floating. The lamp might well date from the time of Christ; yet if the lamp were a copy it was well done. She ran her fingers along it, the bronze cool against her skin.

"I'll take it." She paid for the lamp, tucked it into her oversized purse, then stopped at the threshold – another terracotta medallion hung by the door. This one depicted a youth wearing a cape and helmet, his right hand holding a lance. The carving was so lifelike that she reached up to touch the rounded cheeks. "Mars?" she guessed.

"Laran."

"The Etruscan version, I see."

By the time she arrived at the vineyard, she was hot, dusty, and extremely thirsty. She traipsed into the winery's restaurant and ordered a glass of wine. "On the house", the man said, proffering a glass of Chianti. She thanked him and asked if it were all right to wander through the vineyard. He nodded toward another door.

Outside again, she strolled up and down the orderly rows. She wasn't sure why she wanted to do that – she scarcely knew anything about wine. Some wines were white, some red, some sweet, some dry, French, Italian, Californian, New York. That was the sum total of her *vino* knowledge.

Here and there olive trees intermingled with the vines. The trees were gnarled, old, perhaps even ancient. How many decades – centuries – had they grown? she wondered. These trees would be here long after she was dead. She marveled at the age of everything in this town; Americans, with a history of only a few centuries, could not comprehend something a thousand years or older.

Insects buzzed around the fruit – the only sound. She paused under the shade of an olive tree. A dusty haze hung over one end of the vineyard; perhaps, she thought, someone was working there. With the heat of the sun and the droning of the insects, she felt drowsy now.

Suddenly something moved a few rows away from her; she'd caught a glimpse of it out of the corner of her eye. She stepped back into the sun and peered around a fat bunch of grapes.

Nothing. Her skin prickled, and again she sensed being watched. Surely there were workers – pickers? harvesters? – out here. As she glanced around she saw no one.

She returned the glass to the man and thanked him. She checked for a terracotta medallion – surely the winery had one. In the tasting room she found it: a man in middle years, his smiling face surrounded by grapes and grapeleaves.

"Bacchus?" she said, pointing.

The man shook his head. "Fufluns, the God of wine. Of vitality." He winked.

"Ah." So, it would seem, at least in the townspeople's versions that the Roman gods could all be traced to the Etruscan Gods. That made sense; the Etruscans were the first to settle this area, and it was the tongue of Tuscany, after all, the basis of the language of the country.

She wondered if any of the shops sold the medallions. She would ask Signore Ventaglio about it; he would know. The lamp, the medallion . . . what would she do with all these things she was suddenly adding to her life? She could always send them to her husband . . . her soon to be ex-husband; the divorce proceedings hadn't started yet. Perhaps he would be curious as to why she wasn't there. Perhaps not. And she wished with all her heart that she could turn back the clock, return to when she'd met her husband and change that chance encounter – she'd find someone who would truly love her for the time she had left.

She shook her head sharply. Enough.

"You are sad," the man said. She shrugged. "You are so young yet, you must live."

"I wish," she said bitterly and left the winery. She took her time returning to the inn; it was all uphill now and sometimes quite steep. Exhausted, she paused only to wave to Signore Ventaglio and climbed the stairs to her room.

She wanted a bath badly. The minute she reached her room she started stripping clothes off. She ran hot water until the tub was half filled, then eased into the warmth, and almost immediately the aches of the day began to fade. She closed her eyes. She would rest for a moment or so.

When she awoke, the bath water was cold. She finished bathing, toweled herself dry, then slipped into a long T-shirt that served as her nightgown. Checking her watch, she was shocked to see that it was after nine. She had been in the tub over an hour. She should go downstairs for dinner, but just the thought of talking to someone right now seemed too much of a strain.

She had her oranges; she'd dine on those. And perhaps if she got ravenous later, she'd ask if a tray could be delivered to the room.

She sat on the bed, peeling her first orange carefully, and flipped through the guidebook reading about all the places she hadn't visited yet. She finished the orange, then selected another, but when she realized she was doing more yawning than peeling, she put the orange down, and washed her hands. She wobbled back across the room, turned out the light, and fell into bed.

Almost instantly she drifted off to sleep.

It seemed like only a moment later that she opened her eyes, but she knew she'd been asleep for some time. Was that a noise that had awakened her? She listened hard, but heard nothing. As she moved her legs she touched something furry, and she yelped, leaped up and switched on the light. The black and white cat lay curled on the mattress. It blinked at her, then yawned.

She laughed nervously. "Just how did you get in here?" The window – wide open. She had forgotten to latch it. "I suppose you can stay!" She flicked the light off and crawled back into bed. The cat shifted, its head resting on her shin. She closed her eyes.

And woke again much later. She reached out to touch the cat, but it must have shifted. The air seemed thick, almost like velvet, and she could scarcely breathe. Sitting up, she shivered. The room was pitch dark, but outside there seemed to be a faint light. She rose and crossed to the window and saw a full moon in the inky sky.

Faint lights, like the flames of candles, dotted the slope above the town. In the street below a flame bobbed along. It paused beneath her window, and she saw a face – horribly disfigured – and then she realized it was a mask, one of a grinning youth, whose nose was so long and sharp that it nearly met with its equally pointed chin.

Whoever was behind the mask stared up at her. Quickly she stepped away from the window; surely she couldn't be seen. Her heart pounding, she waited until she thought it was safe, then sneaked a glance out the window. The man in the mask now stood farther up the street, but he had turned and was watching her even now.

She gasped, stepped back and latched the window, then drew the curtain across the rod. She fled to the bed, pulling the sheet up over her head. She was shaking, and she lay, too fearful to lower the sheet. After all, what if she peeked out and saw the masked man inside her room? Don't be ridiculous, Ceil, one part of her said.

She was being silly. It had probably just been a trick of light; that person couldn't see her. But still . . .

She closed her eyes, but all she could see was that hateful mask and the way it had looked at her.

When she finally did awake in the morning, she ached all over. The cat, seeing she was up, started purring and rubbing its head against her. The purring intensified as she scrinched it behind the ears. She didn't want to move, didn't want to get up and bathe and dress. She didn't care. She would stay in bed all day. She wasn't even hungry. She closed her eyes. Was this how it was to be? No, she wouldn't give up, not yet at least. She peered at her wristwatch. Almost 11:30.

Suddenly she leaped from the bed, startling the cat, who hissed. She was meeting that man at noon! She had almost forgotten! She jumped into the tub, scrubbed briskly, washed her hair, threw on her make-up and clothes, peered into the mirror at her pale face and the dark circles beneath her eyes, sighed, then grabbed the cat and left the room.

She arrived in the dining room just as San Damonio sat down. Breathlessly she rushed to the table.

"You've brought me a cat?" he asked, his tone droll. "How kind."

"It slipped into my room last night." She set the cat down, and immediately, purring loudly, it began threading its way around her legs.

"You have a friend."

"And I haven't even fed it. But perhaps someone in the kitchen could."

"Perhaps. Are you ready?"

"Yes."

"Do you want me to drive or do you want to walk?" he asked.

This was a test, she figured . . . let's see the lazy American in action. "Walk. It's not really that far, is it?"

"A few miles. Uphill."

"I'll manage." And she hoped she would.

"Good. I'll point out some sights along the way."

San Damonio set off briskly; Ceil hurried to catch up.

They encountered no one else on the rugged road, lined with tall cypress, and as for interesting sights, there were few. Once, he stopped by a ruin, only tumbled blocks now.

"This was the abbey," he explained. "It was abandoned several centuries ago." He kicked one of the blocks, knocking a sizable chunk off. It rolled down the slope a few yards, then stopped when it hit a tuft of grass.

"And the Church didn't rebuild?"

"The Church never cared about San Damonio."

"Oh." They started walking again. "I saw lights last night – up here, I think. Was there a festival or something?"

"Lights?" He shrugged.

That gesture could mean anything. He hadn't said no, there weren't lights; but he hadn't said there were. He seemed far less friendly than the day before, and for the first time she wondered at her eagerness to follow a man she didn't know to an isolated spot.

This is Italy, Ceil reminded herself, not the United States. But still . . . she wasn't being very careful.

And once more she had the sense of being watched. Pausing, she scanned the hills. Nothing. But of course it would be so easy for someone to hide from sight. She glanced back and saw a small black and white object.

"Oh oh."

"What?" San Damonio asked.

"The cat from the inn is following me."

He glanced back at the animal. "Ridiculous beast."

A curious way of putting it, she thought, and more and more she felt uneasy. Yet they weren't that far away now; she saw the villa pressed up hard against the hill, almost as if the earth had tried to swallow it.

Overhead birds, dark against the sky, wheeled in lazy patterns. She wondered what kind they were, and when she glanced back at the cat, she saw it had flattened itself against the ground, as if it feared being attacked.

They reached the villa – once grand, it had obviously not been maintained for years now. Here and there Ceil saw missing roof tiles, and the windows all looked curiously blank. Like dead eyes, she thought with a slight shiver.

Instead of escorting her up to the double front doors, San Damonio led her around the side to a huge stone arch, under that and into a modest-sized courtyard, paved with slabs of volcanic rock. A marble fountain, long unused, sat in the center. Blue wildflowers grew now where water had once splashed.

"This is lovely. It's too bad it's fallen into disrepair. Is this yours?" Ceil asked.

San Damonio nodded. "I live here."

"Oh. I'm sorry, I didn't mean—"

He cut her off. "It's all right. The family has fallen onto hard times, as you Americans say. I've closed off most of the villa, and this is one part we haven't repaired yet. We'll get to it. Soon."

She studied the walls for the first time. Dozens and dozens of medallions – like those she seen in the town below, but of bronzewere set into the courtyard's walls.

"They're beautiful! The workmanship is marvelous! These must be worth a fortune."

"Or two," he said wryly. "There," he said, gesturing to one high up on the left. "That's Horta, the Goddess of Agriculture. That one is Losna, the Etruscan Moon goddess."

Losna's medallion reminded her of the sepulchral lamp, only the inner face was of the goddess, the outer ring showing the moon in its different phases.

"Who's this naked fellow?" she asked, indicating a bearded figure over San Damonio's shoulder.

"The God of Fresh Water – Nethuns." In quick succession he rattled off a dozen names that swirled in her head: Juventus, Menrva, Mlukukh, Picus, Summamus, Zirna, and more. Gods and goddesses . . . some of them long forgotten, some evolved into familiar Roman deities: Minerva and Diana, among others.

"And this?" she asked. This medallion had caught her eye even more than the others, for the goddess depicted was part animal, part human, part bird, with snakes entwined in her hair and along her arms. There was something about the fierce stare of the goddess that alarmed her, and she took a step back, bumping with San Damonio.

"Tuchulcha. The Goddess of Death. There is no other Goddess

like her anywhere in the world . . . even the Romans, who took so much from us, did not corrupt her. She's partly of the sky, partly of the earth . . ." Running his fingers across the medallion now, San Damonio traced the outline of Tuchulcha's visage, caressed the stone snakes.

Shivering, Ceil edged away. She rubbed her hands along her bare arms. It was hot today, but suddenly she was cold.

"The grotto?" she asked.

"Come this way." He led her through another arch, smaller than the first, and down a flight of crumbling steps. As she peered back toward the fountain she thought she saw something move. She was getting creeped out; perhaps they should postpone seeing the grotto. And yet they were almost there . . . and it *was* a long hike, one that she didn't want to repeat. She was so tired now.

Down and down the couple went until finally they reached an old wooden door. San Damonio pulled the door open, and they stepped inside.

The blackness swallowed the light from the doorway. It was indeed damp, as Signore Ventaglio had claimed. Again the skin on her arms prickled, and she rubbed the flesh hard, trying to warm up.

Abruptly San Damonio stopped. She couldn't see his face now. "What's wrong?" she whispered.

"You must go on by yourself now."

"I don't understand."

He pressed something in her hand. A sepulchral lamp, just like the one she bought. Or was it the same? Firmly San Damonio gripped her by the shoulder and pushed her past him. "Go on. You must go alone."

Inside her chest her heart fluttered like a panicked bird. "No, I think I want to go back now. Take me back to the inn!"

"It's too late."

"What?"

Ceil struggled to get away, but he held her easily, though not unkindly, and suddenly over his shoulder she saw the doorway crowded with other people now, all of them silent. She could never push past them.

She realized that they wore masks – or were they? There was so little light, and yet wasn't that Veive, the God of Revenge? Cautha, Janus, Summamus . . . all that she had seen in the village and out in the courtyard.

Who were they? The villagers? Something more? Wasn't that Signore Ventaglio with the Janus mask? And that had to be Marco, limping, under the Laran face? What were they doing here? Why had they followed her?

One of the watchers held the black and white cat which, seeing Ceil, leaped to the ground and ran to her. She scooped the animal up with one arm, and retreated as San Damonio and the others silently pressed forward.

She realized now that the lamp was burning – she nearly dropped it. She glanced back, saw those staring faces in the flickering light, and stumbled away.

The blackness pressed down on her, threatening to swallow her, and she tried not to whimper. She had never been afraid of the dark . . . until now. She prayed that the flame of her lamp would not be extinguished.

Deeper into the grotto she went, and it seemed that the walls, so confining here, were carved with strange animals and figures, all of them grotesque. They seemed to stare at her, to watch her, and she ducked her head.

From time to time Ceil glanced back, afraid the others were still behind her, but she was alone. She didn't understand what the villagers wanted . . . didn't know why they were acting so strangely. Perhaps there was another way out here. She'd find it, and she'd leave – with the cat, of course – and she'd run back to the village, and in no time at all she'd be back in Florence. She almost laughed aloud at the thought – it was so easy!

Overhead the grotesque faces acquired identity, and as she walked on, Ceil saw her father's face, her mother's, that of her sister and her brother. There was her friend from the third grade, Amy, who had died from a burst appendix. Peering over Amy's shoulder was Danny, Ceil's boyfriend from high school who had died during the first Tet offensive. Her grandparents were there, her great-aunt, the young man she had dated during college, students from classes she had taught, and ringing them all were the pets of her childhood: the abandoned birds she'd brought home to nurse tenderly, only to have them die unexpectedly; the stray cats and dogs . . . all of them dying after only a few years.

Dying . . . as everyone in her life had. Dying . . . as did everything – everyone – she touched. She wondered that her husband had survived; perhaps it had only been a matter of time for him.

The walls fanned out now, and above her she saw still more faces, more and more fanciful, some part animal. The cat jumped to the ground and trotted after her.

Ahead Ceil heard rushing water. The tunnel widened into an immense cavern with a fast and wide river. The grotto proper. On this side of the waterway a man in a boat waited; cautiously she approached him.

Charon. Or Charun, as the Etruscans knew him.

Wordlessly Charun beckoned to her and not knowing what else to do, she climbed into the boat and handed him the lamp. He blew out the flame, and yet Ceil could still see. The cat jumped in beside her, and Charun pushed away from the riverbank. From the tunnel the grotesque faces watched.

Ceil didn't speak to Charun, nor he to her. The cat, trembling, crawled into her lap; she tried to calm it by petting it, but her own hand was shaking. Silently they floated across the river, and there on the other side, Ceil saw a woman waiting . . . no, something more. A Goddess.

Tuchulcha, she recognized with a stab of cold fear. The Goddess of death. Tuchulcha was part human, bird, and animal, with snakes in her hair and curled around her arms. The Goddess looked at her, and Ceil felt the ice grow inside her. Above them the dark birds circled, their cries echoing in the grotto's greatness.

Ceil wanted to cry out; she wasn't ready; not yet, not yet. But would she ever be ready for death? Would she? She who had brought so much death in her life.

She hadn't meant to! she wanted to cry aloud. She hadn't wanted any of them dead. But they had all died, had left her . . . left her to die alone in this cold cavern.

Somehow Ceil found herself standing on the shore, still clutching the cat. Already Charun was halfway across the river. She tried to call to him, but the cold of the underground stole the words from her.

She faced the Goddess, who reached out to her with her long fingers.

Ceil squeezed her eyes shut as the fingers and snakes spiraled around her arms, drawing her and the cat closer. The animal struggled, and she murmured words of comfort to it. She shivered, feeling both hot and cold. Once more she saw her parents, her sister, her brother, Danny, all the others of her life, one face after another, their features melting to reveal the masks beneath . . . all grotesque.

It had been a long journey, she thought, but she had come home. Home to this underground grotto. And all of them here had known, had waited for her. A feather brushed her cheek.

Then abruptly the exhaustion she'd fought for so long was gone. She was no longer cold. She opened her bright bird eyes. She gazed down at the snakes curling and writhing around her arms, at the soft black and white fur stretched across her abdomen. And she finally cried, grief mixed with joy.

GEOFFREY WARBURTON

Merry Roderick

GEOFFREY WARBURTON STARTED WRITING in the early 1990s, since when his short fiction has appeared in *All Hallows* and other small press magazines. He has also written a number of novels which, to date, are still trying to find a publisher.

"'Merry Roderick' sprouted from an episode of Michael Aspel's spooky TV show," recalls the author, "which featured an old house with a portrait like the one I describe. A friend's wife, a picture restorer, had told me about working at Calke Abbey, which gave me the idea for Hayshott. After that, I had the fun of writing it."

L aura told herself the dizziness was due to the heat, which was close enough to the truth to pass for it. She waited until the tour guide turned, then slipped away from the press of tourists about her. The world grew dark around the edges, and she felt herself heel to port as she walked; into the alcove, a cooler space, lighter than the tight pressing corridor they'd shuffled down, battered by the beehive drone of the man's voice.

A red rope hung knee high from brass tipped stands, tassels limp in the tired air. She cocked one leg, awkward in the pencil skirt; slid it over, then tottered to a chair. She sat, closed her eyes and listened to the meadow buzz grow small. The red haze behind her eyelids dimmed, as clouds crossed the sun. Her forehead cooled, and the nausea passed. Just a warning; feed me, or face the consequences. She hadn't skipped breakfast, but lunch was overdue. If she had something to eat soon, she'd be okay.

When she felt able, Laura stood and looked about her, then clutched the waistband of her skirt and wiggled. She tugged at her shirt collar to let in cool air. The alcove, when she looked around, was deeper than she'd thought; there was a turn at the end, a few feet away. After a moment's hesitation, she walked down there to take a look; something she'd done all her life in places like this. She pulled back her hair, thick blonde skeins heavy in her hand; turned the corner and came to a halt. Eyes pierced hers like darts. Darkness pressed close, and she retreated until the wall slammed into her back as if repaying an injury.

It's a painting.

A very good one. A full length portrait of a man against a dark background; sixteenth century, going by the costume. While her breathing slowed, she took the time to wonder who would have put a portrait like this in such a situation. She would speak with Harrison about it when she returned the next week with her working hat on. Laura took a deep breath, and decided she could face the world again. Even the guided tour was preferable to this corner with only the portrait of the jester for company. That was what he was, in his cap and bells; rather, what he had been. A squat bull of a man, with a heavy jowled face that looked ill-placed above the ermine collar, the jewelled doublet.

"You don't look so funny to me," she told him. She stayed a moment longer to prove she hadn't been afraid, then quick stepped to catch up to the tour group. Her back tingled every lonely yard of the way.

I can't believe they pay me for doing this.

Laura smiled to herself. She was back at Hayshott, roughing it there while she helped explore the disused rooms, crammed to the coving with ancient junk; untouched by damp or rot.

She'd spent the week preparing for her visit to the house, where she camped out with other academics in the west wing, already cleared; they worked by day here in the east wing, emptied each room and arranged for whatever they found to be taken down for storage and restoration. She'd had one bad night in the wake of the portrait encounter, a dream which ended with the drawing of the dark curtain behind the jester to reveal just what small shape held back the lower corner. Laura woke, bolt upright in her single bed, teeth clenched tight to hold in what would have been a scream if she'd woken a second later.

That seemed to put an end to the matter. She was too level headed to worry, and if she thought about the portrait at odd times in the days that followed – recalling details she could barely remember seeing – then that was because it was a very good painting. In fine condition too, where many paintings of the period had been restored by blind house painters with palsy, if some of the wrecks she'd seen were anything to go by.

She had her own speciality to worry about. Laura looked for Jacobean furniture, abandoned by that previous owner who ruined a perfectly good manor house by tacking on wings in the eighteenth century. When family fortunes altered the wings were used as storage space. The father of the present owner hit on the idea of opening house and grounds. Now his son, a cheerfully plebeian scion of the rebuilder, (whom Laura had taken for a farm hand on being introduced), had opened the wings to the local university. If his intentions were less to do with the pursuit of knowledge than with the chirp and hum of cash registers when the contents had been renovated and put on display, Laura didn't mind. She would have paid for the privilege of being where she stood, delighted at the prospect of rummaging through rooms crammed with the junk of three centuries.

Solitary but happy, Laura tugged on a pair of overalls. She dragged a mouldering tarpaulin from a pile of boxes and set to work. The first thing she laid her hands on was the cedar chest. It was lunchtime when she went to a neighbouring room to fetch Dave Ellis, and they carried it between them down to a store room on the ground floor. That was when she saw Clive Weston, and the day, which had started so well, slid sideways into a pile of excrement so high she couldn't see the top of it.

The rest of the day passed slowly; the happy exertions of the morning turned to a grey grind by Laura's mood, which only lifted when she climbed out of her overalls. She walked the darkening corridors back to the west wing, dumped her gear in her room, and headed straight for the bathroom, where she showered for half an hour.

You can't wash him away.

Maybe not, but she'd keep trying.

They had been students on the same course; Weston in the year above. Tall, fair haired, easy to look at. For a time, she had considered going out with him. There had been stories, but she chose to forget them when she ended up alone with him one night, after the group they'd been drinking with had slipped away one by one. Looking back, what happened could have been a sight worse. She'd fought him off in the end; Laura stood five feet ten in her bare feet, and was built to match. Clive realized he wouldn't get what he wanted without killing her. He gave up and strode away, leaving her to gather her torn clothes about her and stumble home alone. In her hall of residence room, she had counted bruises and scratches while she snivelled into a Kleenex.

That won't stop him next time.

There won't be a next time.

The part of her that knew better just smirked from the dark inside her head, and her brow furrowed. Laura tightened the belt of her towelling robe with one hard jerk and stepped out of the bathroom.

The figure didn't register until she'd turned away from the corner where it stood; grey, hooded, short, familiar. By the time she swivelled around he was close enough to grab her, and would have done but for her instinctive swing of the bag she held. It clipped the side of his head; raised dust from the faded cloth hood.

A gloved hand grabbed for her throat, and she felt one single red line of pain at the back of her neck, sharp and bright. She caught the other hand, and felt it slip from her grasp like wet raw meat held loose. Laura swung an elbow and felt it connect.

A scream locked in her throat like a jammed piston. She ran and her bare feet pounded the aged carpet, kicking up dust when that ended and she sprinted on bare boards. Laura reached the corner before she realized there was no pursuit. She turned and saw blank corridor behind her; stopped, at the intersection. Off to her right, men leaned out of doorways. Clive Weston was among them. When she tried to carry on walking, he blocked her way. Laura glared at him. There was a half smile on his face, dark glee beneath it.

"Don't you come near me," she said. He made a production number of standing back to let the little woman through, complete with courtly bow. If he'd had a cape, he would have laid it down. She walked past him and the doorway audience, aiming at dignity and willing to settle for not being thought mad. She wondered if she should tell them what had happened; decided not to. She managed to twitch her lips into what might have passed for a smile when she walked past Dave Ellis, his pale, round face a quizzical balloon in the soft yellow light from the forty watt bulb in the room behind him. The words were in her throat, but then she had walked past. Laura walked to her room and switched on all the lights; dressed in a hurry, which was when she noticed that the cross and chain were gone from around her neck. She sat on her bed for all of five minutes. The night stretched out in front of her; nerves pulled tight as bridge hawsers. No. She pulled on a jacket, mostly because its bulk gave her a sense of security she knew was as false as Clive Weston's look of concern.

She walked back the way she had come, all the way back to the bathroom, alone. The lights were off in that stretch of corridor. She flicked the switch, and nothing happened. Laura pulled out her torch, and swung the beam around. She walked to the spot where the man had stood, waiting. The air was cool, and a fungal hint of damp rode on it. She played the beam over an ancient radiator, saw the glove on the floor below, and picked it up. The leather was grey with age and damp, and felt as welcome as a leper's handshake.

Sleep didn't so much come as shuffle in and refuse to settle. Laura slipped in and out of dream tatters, never sure whether she was awake or not. At some point, a man stalked around her bed; dark, never wholly visible, angry because he couldn't reach her. She spent a while wondering how he could have entered, given that she'd piled empty bottles against the door and arranged a trip wire between that and the bed with a length of string and two chairs. When the window let in the first hint of grey light, he was gone; Laura stirred, and gave up on sleep.

Half the morning passed, and she almost managed to forget the attack, happy in her work. Her thoughts turned to the cedar chest, and she kept an eye open for a likely key. She wandered over to the section where the men worked, telling herself it was because she wanted company. When she walked into the long gallery and saw Clive Weston, it was too late to turn and sneak out. He watched her approach, then turned to the rest of the men there and muttered something that brought one incontinent bray amid general laughter. Some of them failed to appreciate the joke. One or two looked embarrassed and walked off when she joined the group, as if it were her fault.

Collectively, they looked younger than their years, with all the physical oddities of teenagers. Laura felt herself threatened by hooked noses, Adam's apples. She started counting cold sores, and made herself stop. White skylight gleamed at her, blanking the spectacle lenses it reflected from; she was the focus of silver insect eyes. Clive Weston stared at her as if she were a piece of tired fruit with an unsightly bruise.

"I was attacked last night, when I came out of the bathroom," she said. The men froze. Only Weston seemed relaxed, sitting on a crate, long legs swinging. He watched her with a gaze she felt on the side of her face. A couple of the men had this rabbit in the headlights look. She almost felt sorry for them.

"I know it wasn't anyone here; you were all in your rooms when I went past. I'm telling you because I hope you'll think about it and help me work out who it might have been."

Weston grinned at her, an exposure of perfect white teeth like the flicker of a camera shutter.

"Wishful thinking, Laura?"

She carried on as if he hadn't spoken.

"He wore a grey hooded top. His face was covered. He was quite short, but broad and strong. That's all I can tell you. Can anyone think who it might have been?"

Turning to watch them all. Few could meet her eye and hold it. Dave Ellis shrugged, and said no. She felt the creeping ingress of guilt, and for the life of her couldn't rationalize it away. Weston's smart remark was the irritant it grew around. She looked him in the eye, until he turned casually aside; he didn't look so much discomforted as bored. Weakness rose in her like tepid water poured into a pitcher.

"There's something I want to ask you, Dave, if you've got a minute," she said. Her voice was steady, but she knew that if she spoke to the others again it would slide out of her control. The change of subject felt like a U-turn at speed in a shopping street, but there was no way around it she could see. Dave Ellis looked up, eyes big and brown behind his spectacles. She walked him away from the group of men, and felt the backwash of their relief; gritted her teeth at the silence behind her, gravid with their need to talk about the mad woman.

"I was here last week, taking a look around. I went into an alcove in the main house for a breather, and I found a full length portrait of a man in jester's costume. I wondered what you knew about it."

He stared at the floor, bottom lip sticking out.

"Can't bring it to mind, Laura."

He pushed his glasses up the bridge of his nose with a fore-finger, and permitted himself one sweeping glance at her face.

"It'll be time for lunch soon. I could come back then, take you over there and show you if you like," she said.

Dave nodded, happy puppy. Everything was going to cock; half the men thought she was deranged, and if she gave this one the slightest encouragement he'd follow her home.

What can't be cured must be endured.

Mother's wisdom, gentle mockery echoing in her head. She risked a smile at Dave and walked out.

Later, the lunchtime crowds had shuffled down to the refectory or gardens, either to make a down payment on a cream tea or sit in the shade and throw warm, flat sandwiches to the birds. They had the corridor to themselves, stale air and all. Laura strode to the spot where she had rested on her first visit. Then she glanced up and down the corridor before walking a little further. She came to a startled halt when she turned what she took for a corner and found herself in a shallow alcove, nose tip an inch from the wainscot.

"What's wrong?" Dave asked.

"I can't find it," she said; she turned and inspected the other wall.

"The painting?"

"The alcove it was in. There was a short corridor, lit by concealed windows. The painting was around a corner at the far end of it."

"Laura, is this a joke?" Dave Ellis's benign ball head had a frown on it now.

"Nooo. Listen, maybe I've got the wrong part of the building."

She went on to describe the painting in detail, surprising herself by how much she recalled. Dave Ellis frowned, and nodded sometimes. As she came to a close, and her words petered out to be replaced by hand gestures she had to make herself stop doing, his face brightened a little.

"Laura, there was a painting exactly like the one you described," he said. "It was destroyed when the place was bombed, back in '44. A single Heinkel came by, lost, looking for somewhere to park its payload before the long haul home. The plane dropped a stick of bombs across the grounds; the last one landed just outside the house and brought part of the wall down. If we asked the owner, I bet a month's salary he'd tell us it took out the alcove you claimed to have sat in last week."

"So I'm making up a ghost story for the fun of it?" she asked him, and wondered why he still smiled.

"No. But I know where you've seen the painting. Come with me."

She followed him to the library, where he hauled down a large volume from a shelf beside the door.

"Should be here somewhere . . . yep. This your bloke?"

She made herself look over his shoulder. She knew what was coming, but it still came as a jolt. A full page black and white photograph of the portrait she had seen; eyes like knife points. The curtain, rendered as solid darkness by the printing, lifted slightly at the bottom left corner. A smudge of lighter grey – a monkey's paw? – tugged her eye there. Then she roamed over the costume, checking details; the quilted doublet, studded with jewels. The ermine collar. The sulking, heavy jowled face. Her chest froze when she looked down at the hands. The gloves; he wore one, and held the other.

"Roderick the merry, which is a bit like saying Hitler the reasonable. Date of birth unknown, died 1532. Stabbed through the eye and serve the bugger right, by all accounts. A favourite of the man who built Hayshott, though God alone knows why. He's known to have raped a girl from the village, and he was involved in at least one murder. All round bad lot. He your man, Laura?"

She gritted her teeth so hard her jaw hurt, and nodded. When she dared open her eyes, the world was still there. She felt Dave stare at her, and knew that if she turned she'd see a saintly, caring look on his face. There was nothing to be said that wouldn't make things worse. Laura walked out.

*　　　*　　　*

She woke at four and held her breath, tense as a cocked gun. She could feel him; she could *smell* him.

Laura whipped back the duvet and slid out of bed. She turned on the table lamp; blinked at the light and relaxed. She was alone. The feeling that someone else had been there ebbed away, leaving her weak and cross. Her new security measures were still in place; soft drink cans piled in a stumpy pyramid in front of the door, a trip wire sagging unimpressively. She sat in the chair at the side of the bed, and reached out to pick up the key she'd found before she knocked off for the day. She played with the heavy iron key, and felt herself soothed. Laura wondered if it would fit the cedar chest. She planned to find out in the morning.

It's connected to him. Roderick the merry. Roddy the rapist. Hot Rod.

She tried to remember if she had seen the cedar chest in the portrait; then reminded herself she couldn't even have seen the portrait, if what Dave had said was true. She felt herself on shifting ground. She trusted her memory, but the facts undermined her. Laura asked herself if Dave could be right.

Not very likely, Davey boy. Until yesterday, I'd never been in the library. And I'd bet two month's wages I've never seen another copy of the book. What I saw was the portrait of the man himself. And if I stood in a place that disappeared fifty years ago to do it, well, you'll have to accept that. Or choke on it. Your choice.

Sorted. She grinned into the dim room, but there wasn't much mirth in it. Laura sat and waited for the dawn to come.

"No time like the present, Dave."

"I can't see why you want me here in the first place," he said, trailing after her like a child stumbling to school. The house was flooded with dawn light. It was going to be a good day.

"Bodyguard, Dave. For when I find Roderick Random in the big box."

He managed to grin and look baffled at the same time. Laura smiled back, then walked into the room where the cedar chest was stored. Other stuff was piled around it now; they negotiated furniture, and edged warily around indifferent landscape paintings. She stood over the box, and felt disinclined to go any further. For a couple of seconds the worst of her tried to supply a halfway decent reason for turning around and walking away. She squatted down to try the lock with the huge key. It slipped in, noiselessly; she looked up at Dave Ellis, whose expression was carefully neutral.

He thinks I'm losing it. My last ally.

What can't be cured. She turned the key as smoothly as if the lock had been oiled the day before. Laura grasped the front of the lid, and paused; then pushed upwards, smooth and strong. A bitter scent prickled in her nostrils, then faded. She looked down at crumpled linen, white shading into yellow around the edges. She reached gently in, and folded back the material. More sheets, and a small paper package she took out and put in her lap, appropriating the thing before Dave could even mention it.

"Nothing else?" he asked. She shook her head, and slipped the package into her overall pocket, then took the hand he offered to help her to her feet.

"Happy now?" he asked her.

"Ask me later," she said, and walked away.

At the far end of the east wing, in a room they hadn't reached yet, she found what she'd been looking for. Laura walked across the dim room, DMs loud on the wooden boards. Paintings stood around the walls, daylight prickling through mouldering canvas where they hid the windows. The edges of the room were piled with junk, while the middle of the floor was clear but for the second box. It was bigger than the cedar chest, more of a size for what she thought might be inside.

They wouldn't bury you. And they dared not dump you away from here. When you died but kept hanging around, they'd do whatever it took to appease you.

Laura fingered the package she'd taken from the cedar chest. She tore the paper with her thumbnail, and slowly unwrapped what lay within. When the second key lay in her hand, she smiled. She walked to the box, and slipped the key into the lock. It turned, and she gripped the lid and raised it without hesitation; looked down at browned bones, bedded in a mess of dust and scraps of finery. A pearl drop ear ring gleamed dully next to the skull. Her gold chain and crucifix looped tidily about a hand like a bunch of dry twigs. Laura looked up, where the window light had darkened. The hooded man stood there; hard to see. She recognised the grey clothes, the short, bent legs. One gloved hand.

Don't do this. Don't do it.

Not even words in her head; just mute appeal from the figure, fading even as it stood in alien daylight. She stood, and tipped the contents of the box across the floor. Kicked aside bones and dust. Picked up a femur and swung it against the door frame until it shattered. Laura stomped the ribs until they broke, by ones and twos. She kicked fragments to ruin across the room. She lashed the spine against the floor until there was nothing left to swing. When she finally stopped, she shook; sweat coated her flanks, and her breath came hard and ragged. There wasn't an intact bone among the scattered pile on the floor. She found a burlap sack, and gathered the pieces together.

Around lunchtime, she walked down through the grounds to the river. She sat in a quiet spot, and tossed the bone fragments, one by one, into the dark, fast waters. Returning, she met Clive Weston, who said something unpleasant. Laura dropped him with a straight right to the side of his face. He landed on the grass in a tangle of arms and legs, and had to be helped away. She carried on into the house, and never looked back.

TERRY LAMSLEY

Climbing Down from Heaven

TERRY LAMSLEY ADMITS THAT HIS writing has been going through a "quiet period". However, his short fiction has recently appeared in Peter Crowther's *Taps and Sighs*, Ramsey Campbell's *Meddling With Ghosts*, and two German anthologies, *Psycho-Express* and *Dead Ends*. His third collection from Ash-Tree Press is entitled *Dark Matters*.

"Climbing Down from Heaven" comes from the latter volume and, as the author explains, it "was one of those stories that got up and started running without much effort on my part. At the time I thought I might be writing a tragedy. I suspect now, though, that it's a somewhat perverse and decadent tale, but I don't suppose it's any the worse for that."

> It's all this smell of cooped-up angels
> Worries me.
> — Christopher Fry,
> *A Sleep of Prisoners.*

I

While she was up in her room making her bed Millie noticed she had not replaced the cover on the lens of her telescope the previous night. The sky had been particularly clear and God alone knew what time it had been when she had finally managed to turn away from her contemplation of the heavens. She must have been exhausted or in some kind of star-struck trance when she had finally gone to bed, as she had no recollection of climbing in between the sheets. She flicked, with the tip of a tissue, the few motes of dust she imagined might have settled on the lens during the few hours it had been exposed, took up the lens cover, and carefully screwed it in place. Normally, when not in use, she kept the telescope shrouded under a silky black sheet, but the forecast was for clear skies for the night to come, and she hoped to be able to take advantage of this dark window of opportunity.

Also, it pleased her, occasionally, to leave the thing uncovered. The matt-black metal tube set on its grey tripod had sculptural qualities that appealed to her and that aroused welcome, if somewhat melancholy, thoughts of her father. The telescope, along with a half dozen star-charts he had drawn for her when she had been very little, were all she had to remember him by: indeed, these items, along with a couple of monochromatic snap shots of the man, now in the possession of Millie's sister, and taken by the unsteady hand of their mother on a cheap camera, were pretty much all that remained to prove he had existed. He had died alone and abroad a long time ago.

"It brings the stars down very close, Millie," he had explained, when he had first allowed her to use the telescope. She had been so tiny at the time she had to stand on tiptoe to see through the eyepiece. As her father showed her how to focus, he said, "When you've had a good look at whatever star interests you most, and you've seen enough, it goes back up into its place in the sky again as soon as you take your eye away from the lens." When she witnessed the effects of magnification this appeared to be true and made sense to Millie, and for years she was under the impression that she could tamper with the fabric of the universe, pluck the stars down out of the heavens at will, trap them in the tube of the instrument for inspection, and send them back to their rightful place in the vault of heaven as soon as she got bored with them. Sometimes, in those far off days, as she gazed up through the telescope, she had experienced a reversal of this sensation, to her distress, and felt as though she had been wrenched up off the earth into the sky to be closer to the stars. It alarmed her greatly to find herself drawn so suddenly into the remote, black emptiness where she then found herself, but release was easily and instantly achievable: she had only to close her eyes, or take a step backwards, to bring her self down to earth again. And occasionally she felt very peculiar and uncomfortable indeed because she wondered if she was looking up through the telescope at the stars, or if they were looking down (or up) the instrument at her.

Later, when at school she had been given a better understanding of the scientific principles involved, she had felt foolish and been angry with her father for deceiving her about something so fundamental, but by that time he was not around to defend what must, at the time, have seemed to him to have been nothing more than a harmless and amusing fantasy.

Millie sighed and patted the top of the telescope affectionately as though it were a dozing pet. To keep the instrument out of the possibly harmful rays of glaring sunlight streaming into the room she pulled it further back from the window through which it had been aimed and, as she did so, noticed movement in the garden of the house next door. That, in itself, was highly unusual.

A large van was parked close to the front gate and a team of overalled men were unloading it. There was a great deal of activity, but it was hard to see exactly what was going on through the branches of the intervening trees. After a while myopic Millie pulled up a chair, took the cap of the lens off the telescope again, swung its barrel down and around, made a few further adjustments, and squinted through it with her right eye.

What she was then able to see kept her intrigued for hours, until it was time to prepare the evening meal.

Harriet placed her briefcase carefully in the centre of a table near the front door as soon as she got back from work, nodded to her sister, poured herself a neat but modest gin, and sat a while in silent contemplation of the day's events. Millie had no way of telling, from her expressionless face and closed eyes, if Harriet was pleased with herself and the way things had gone or not, and she knew better than to ask. Instead, she broke the silence with a statement of fact that she considered to be of significance to them both.

"Someone has moved in next door at last."

Harriet cocked an eye at her.

"A *man*," Millie added.

"Single?"

"There was no sign of a wife."

"What's he like?"

"Not like the Ruggles."

Mr and Mrs Ruggles had been their previous neighbours. They had thrown frequent, long, tumultuous parties, with live bands playing on their patio. Their children had run wild. The police had raided the house a number of times. In the end, Mrs Ruggles had died of a drug overdose and Mr Ruggles removed what was left of his large family to Spain. Their over-priced house had been empty for more than two years.

"Did you get a chance to meet him?" Harriet asked.

"I only saw him from the window, while men were unloading various vans."

"Is his furniture good?"

"Couldn't say. He didn't have much, and everything was in boxes."

"*Everything*?"

"In cardboard boxes. He must have bought new things straight from the shops."

"How peculiar."

"Oh, except for a huge mirror. Antique, I think, with an ornate gold frame. That was delivered last of all."

"Sounds as though he may be a bit – eccentric," Harriet said, with an edge of distaste.

"He was smartly dressed."

"Hmm." Harriet was unconvinced. "I suppose that's something. More than could have been said about the Ruggles. But what about the mirror? Sounds as though it might be valuable. You'd have thought he'd have taken more care to protect it. The sort of thing most likely to get damaged when you're moving house."

"True," Millie agreed, "but, as far as I could see, the delivery men treated it with *particular* care. Our new neighbour made sure of that." She glanced up as the fingers of the clock on the wall marked the hour. "Your meal's ready now, Harriet," she announced dutifully.

"And I'm ready for it," Harriet said, climbing eagerly out of her chair.

* * *

Next morning, Millie had little appetite for breakfast. It was one of her two Volunteering days, when she helped deliver lunch and comfort to housebound pensioners in the area and this prospect made her apprehensive. She had recently become a volunteer helper because she thought by doing so she might meet interesting people and perhaps make friends with them. It hadn't worked out like that. She had met people as lonely and isolated as herself, and had not felt at ease in their company. She persisted, however, and kept up the "good work" as Harriet called it, because she felt any company was better than none, and she feared that, otherwise, she would become a hermit, with her sister providing her only contact with the human race.

Fifteen years earlier, when they had been in their late teens, the two very different looking women presently ignoring each other across the breakfast table had often been mistaken for identical twins, though there was three years difference in their ages. Then, they had had similarly attractive, though not beautiful, and rather expressionless faces, elegant figures, and identical masses of fair, unruly hair. Emotionally, too, they had been very close. They had seemed, to outsiders, somehow to share a single life, and some who knew them at that time found the intensity of their mutual dependence downright disturbing. They were considered cool and unapproachable and, some said, selfish and arrogant. Hardly anyone who knew the sisters at that time was aware of the childhood traumas that had welded the two girls so closely together.

On Millie's ninth birthday, when Harriet had been just six, their father told them he could no longer stand the company of their increasingly mad mother, and left them for good. They never saw him again. One afternoon a month later their mother sat and drank half a bottle of whisky in front of them, kissed them both on the tops of their heads, then ran out into the garden and shut herself in the garage. The two girls, watching through the window, waited for her to return. Very soon there was a soft explosion, they saw smoke surging out from under the garage door, and the wooden building erupted into flames. Their mother had poured petrol over her head and flicked a lighter.

Millie and Harriet spent the rest of their childhood with foster parents – kindly people who loved and cared for them, but who never really understood how deeply they had been damaged, and who therefore never made any effort to render them whole and independent of each other.

Shortly after Millie was nineteen the sisters suffered a double bereavement when their foster parents drowned while on a boating holiday on the Norfolk Broads. Alone in the world again, the girls had to find some way to support themselves. In this, Harriet had been successful. She had the confidence and good fortune to get herself a job at an Estate Agency, and was swiftly promoted. At first Millie tried and failed to emulate her younger sister then, perhaps due to her total lack of success, became increasingly ill. Afflicted with various obscure complaints, she shrivelled and aged, while Harriet became plump and prosperous. Though they stayed together, in as much as they continued to live together, they drifted far apart in many other ways.

Millie was by far the oldest of the two in appearance. Already, in her mid thirties, she had some of the fragile, edgy manners of an old maid, while Harriet had the dapper air of a still quite young and rising executive.

"I'd like more coffee," Harriet announced quietly, without looking up from the documents on the table beside her empty breakfast plate. "And more toast."

Millie, the kept woman, promptly slid out of her chair. As she flitted about in the kitchen, filling her sister's order, half-remembered scraps from the edges of her dreams of the previous night flashed swiftly through her mind like subliminal messages – she caught glimpses of a man stepping back and forth, now making small but urgent motions with his upraised hand . . .

She turned on the radio to drive him away until the toast was done, and she could return to the company of her sister.

Harriet left for work at 8:35a.m. and, as always, Millie drifted from room to room obliterating the small signs of disorder left by her sister – used ashtrays, an out-of-place gin bottle and a couple of glasses, a clumsily folded copy of yesterday's newspaper – then cleared the remains of their meal and washed the dishes. All this took less than an hour, leaving her with twice that length of time to fill before she was to be collected and taken off on her do-gooding rounds.

She drifted upstairs to make the beds and took a disapproving look at the new neighbour's garden through her telescope. During the last two years it had become a chaotic wilderness. When the

Ruggles had been in residence they had at least kept their grounds in some kind of order. Since their departure everything had run wild.

At last, spurred on by the sight of this vegetative anarchy, Millie spent the rest of the empty period that morning mowing her own lawn; keenly shaving the short bright spears of newly sprouted emerald green grass down almost level with the soil.

Because two members of the team of volunteers were sick, Millie and her companion didn't finish their duties distributing food and encouragement to the old and infirm until after 4:00p.m. in the afternoon Normally, she was back home by 2:00p.m.

She was aware, as she walked up the front path to her house, of fresh and powerful scents in the air. New mown grass, of course, and other more pungent, sappy smells of cut wood and the darker aroma of recently turned soil. Following her nose, she crossed the lawn towards the tall hedge that divided and concealed her garden from her neighbour's, that had been such a blessing during the time of the Ruggles' occupancy. It had not kept the young members of the family out, and even some of the adult guests had broken through from time to time, but it had shielded her and Harriet from the worst scenes of depravity they were sure were being enacted in the Ruggles' grounds.

Because the Ruggles children had chosen a favourite place to break into the two sisters' garden, one bush in the hedge had been snapped off and finally uprooted, leaving a gap. Millie had replaced it with a new plant that had not prospered, so it was still possible to see into the garden next door through a narrow space in the hedge. She peered through it now, searching for the source of the rich scents, and saw, to her astonishment, that a large part of the newcomer's garden had been completely re-landscaped that day. During the comparatively brief period she had been absent, the place had been transformed. The garden had been given a completely new lay-out and planted with flowers, shrubs, and even trees. Whole areas of soil had been dug over, turf had been neatly laid, and crazy-paved pathways had been set down to connect the various plots. It looked slightly unreal, like an exhibition at a horticultural show. She looked up at the house beyond the metamorphosed garden and saw a figure standing in one of the uncurtained upper story windows. It was the new owner of the house, and he was watching her, she was sure. Embarrassed, she was about to move away when the man lifted one hand to his shoulder, in an imperious gesture that Millie assumed meant he wanted her to remain where she was. Then he stepped back and vanished.

Obligingly, Millie waited until he emerged from somewhere at the back of the house and made his way swiftly towards her round the edges of one of the newly planted flower beds. Millie's first impression was that, close up and in profile, he was an ugly man. He had a big, forward-thrusting chin, a high forehead with a receding hairline and a broken nose with a dent about an inch from its tip. When he swung round towards her she could see his broad mouth, square face, and dark, alarming eyes. Smiling rather fixedly, he strode the last few yards towards her.

"Eden H. Wychammer," he announced. "Pleased to meet you."

Wondering about the 'H' Millie accepted the offered hand. She felt her fingers gripped slightly, then discarded. When she didn't respond to his verbal advance at once he turned up the intensity of his smile a few notches and said, "And you are . . .?" increasing the confusion Millie always felt when confronted by someone new.

"Miss Malcolm," Millie squawked hastily, aware of her lack of suavity.

Eden H. Wychammer, who was the same height as Millie, tilted back his head and stared down his nose at her, as though this information was not enough. Millie saw that the line of his nose curved slightly to the left, but didn't look nearly as damaged as it did from the side. She noticed his lips were glossy and shiny, as though he had been eating oily food.

"*Millicent* Malcolm, that is," she said, over loudly, into the tight silence that had come between them. "I live here with my sister Harriet."

"I believe I saw your sister this morning, driving off in a blue Porsche."

"She works in the city."

"You are single women?"

"Yes."

"You both keep very busy"

"My sister has a full life, but I have no employment," Millie said primly. Had he been spying on them already?

It seemed he had.

"You don't seem to waste a moment of your time however," Wychammer protested. "I saw you at work in your garden earlier, then you were whisked off somewhere as soon as you'd finished." When he saw Millie's expression, he said, "I couldn't help noticing. I was looking out for the landscape designer's team, who were due here first thing to do my garden. There was a hold-up. They were late."

Glad of the opportunity to turn the conversation away from herself and her circumstances, Millie looked beyond her neighbour and said, "They've done a remarkable job. The place was a jungle. I wouldn't have thought it possible to do so much in so short a time."

Wychammer turned to admire his garden. "You get what you pay for."

"It's odd that I saw no sign of anyone at work," Millie said.

Wychammer gave Millie a look that she thought may have been slightly contemptuous and said, "They are very – discreet."

"Very," Millie agreed. "Anyway, the new plants look healthy."

"Hand picked from the best nurseries."

"It's impressive. It will look extremely beautiful when it matures."

"It's a start; nothing more," Wychammer said modestly, and his face took on a far-away, oddly tragic look.

Millie apologised for the state of the hedge between them, that on her side had grown spiky and unruly, and badly needed clipping. Wychammer offered to lend her his state-of-the-art trimmer, the use of which she accepted as a gesture of good neighbourliness, though she was nervous of machines. He went to the house to fetch the thing, returned, and demonstrated how simple it was to operate. The device, that made a sharp, silvery sound as it cut, was, Millie had to admit, efficient, safe, and easy to handle.

Millie was forced to make her excuses and leave Mr Wychammer. She had Harriet's evening meal to prepare, she explained.

"I look forward to meeting your sister," Wychammer said as they parted. "Perhaps the pair of you would like to call round sometime . . .?" He held his head back and peered down his nose at her again. Millie found herself looking into his flared nostrils.

She smiled inanely, then hurried away, holding the trimmer in her arms like a baby.

Wychammer watched her retreating figure for a few moments, nodded to himself once, then slid back through the gap into his own grounds.

"You mean you are quite happy to go there on your own?" Millie said.

Harriet, looking plump but elegant in her working clothes, crossed her legs, sat back in her chair, and sipped her gin. "Why not, if you won't come with me? He's not an ogre is he?"

"I shouldn't think so," Millie admitted.

"He didn't ogle your body with greedy, lustful eyes?"

"Not at all, no."

"Then I should be safe enough."

"I don't doubt your safety, Harriet," Millie said, "it isn't that. But I didn't find him an easy man to talk to."

"He was awkward?"

"The opposite. Very smooth. But rather distant. He made me feel uncomfortable."

"He sounds interesting, anyway. Is he good looking?"

"His appearance is striking, but not handsome."

"How old would you say he is?"

"Hard to say. Something makes me think he's older than he looks."

Harriet got up out of her seat and stretched. "And how old does he look?"

"Oh, about our age."

"I wonder what he does for a living."

"No idea. He *is* well off, though." Millie told Harriet about the miraculous metamorphosis of their neighbour's garden. "I saw no sign of gardeners and their equipment, or vans delivering plants. He said the workmen had been 'discreet' but they must have been more than that. More like invisible."

Harriet was not particularly impressed. "Transformations of that kind take place all the time nowadays," she said. "I see them frequently in my line of work, when clients buy new homes. The world's changing faster than you imagine, Mill."

Millie gave her sister a pale, unhappy smile.

"Well," Harriet said, "it was right and polite of him to ask us round, and I don't see why I shouldn't take up the invitation at once: go and introduce myself, and take a look at him. Sure you won't come?"

"I'll stay and watch TV, if you don't mind. I've had a hard day."

Harriet snorted at this, but made no further comment. Minutes later, Millie heard her leave the house.

Millie was not in the habit of waiting up for her sister, who occasionally sought evening entertainment in Sheffield, more than twenty miles away, and was sometimes back very late. That evening, however, she found herself starting to listen out for Harriet's return at around ten o'clock, just an hour and a half after she had set out to call on their neighbour. Millie turned the volume on the TV down low, the better to hear the sound of a key turning in the front door, then, a little later, she suddenly switched the set off in the middle of a programme she regularly watched, and sat for a long time, pensive and totally still, in the perfect silence of the house. Perhaps she dozed off, because when she next looked at the clock it read 23:45. This was not late for Harriet, but it was for Millie, who was normally in bed by eleven. She went to the kitchen, poured herself a glass of milk, then went upstairs and peered through her telescope at the house next door. She was surprised to see that lights were on in a number of rooms. None of the windows had been curtained yet, doors stood wide open, so Millie could penetrate deep into parts of the building. There was little obvious sign of occupancy, as all the rooms seemed empty, except for one on the ground floor at the front, where she could see dozens of the featureless boxes that had arrived with the house's new owner, stacked almost ceiling high over most of the floor. Harriet and Mr Wychammer were nowhere to be seen, and Millie detected no movement anywhere in the house.

At last, reluctantly, she went to bed, turned off the light, and prepared to sleep, but soon found she could not. When she shut her eyes, parts of Mr Wychammer's face hung on top of each other in her mind in alarming disorder. The man's nostrils, without the rest of his nose, were at the top of the heap, his eyes were at the bottom, and in between hung his oil-slicked lips, that seemed to be mouthing words she could not hear. At first, she made some effort to understand what was being said, but then thought better of it. She decided she didn't want to know. At this rejection, the topsy-turvy face began to fade and, at last, flicked out, leaving her with an empty, anxious feeling.

Her bedside clock showed 01:17 when she gave up trying to sleep, and made her way back down to the kitchen. As she passed the window she had looked through earlier, she noticed all the lights were still blazing in the house next door.

"Good God, Millie, what are you doing up at this time?"

Millie opened her eyes and saw her sister's face looming in front of her.

"I came down for something to eat." Millie indicated towards a half-eaten sandwich on a plate on the table beside her.

"That's most unlike you. I thought you were dead."

Millie felt caught out. "Sorry."

"You weren't waiting up for me, were you?"

"Of course not. I went to bed ages ago." Millie touched the top of her nightdress under her dressing gown, as though presenting it as evidence. Millie noticed, now she was fully awake, that her sister looked preoccupied. Her eyes were bright with some inner satisfaction. Elation, even.

As she made a pot of tea for them both, Millie asked Harriet for her impressions of their new neighbour.

"Remarkable person," Harriet said. "A one-off. Never met anyone remotely like him."

"You approve, then?"

"*Approve*? I don't know what you mean by that. He's very interesting. And I like his attitude. So positive, enthusiastic."

"He certainly did seem that," Millie concurred. "I suppose he's more your sort of person than mine."

"You didn't like him, did you?"

"Not really."

"I found him fascinating."

This was strong talk from Harriet. Millie wondered if her sister was in love. "And not at all *eccentric*?" she asked, emphasised the word Harriet had uttered with distaste during an earlier conversation on the subject.

Harriet gave her a sharp look, pursed her lips, and shook her head. "He is *unique*, if you like, but there's nothing wrong with that is there," she challenged. "After all, it wouldn't do for us all to be the same."

Millie dared to smile at the banality of this ancient wisdom, to her sister's annoyance. For a while, they sipped their tea in silence.

As they climbed the stairs together, Millie tried Harriet with another question. "Did you find out what he does?"

"From his conversation, he's an expert in a number of things. He's very wide ranging. The type all sorts of people would go to for help."

"Do you mean he's some kind of guru?"

"Not in the pejorative sense, no. But he has written a few guide books."

Millie stopped at the top of the stairs. "*Guide* books?"

"You know," Harriet said rather vaguely, as she moved towards her bedroom door. "Self help – personal development, that sort of thing."

It occurred to Millie that some kind of religious fanatic might have moved in next door.

It was almost three in the morning when Millie climbed into bed for the second time. Harriet had been with Mr Wychammer for nearly six hours! A lot could have gone on between them in that time.

This thought, and others associated with it, meant Millie had a restless time of it for the remainder of the night.

Next morning, using Wychammer's clippers, Millie cut the long hedge around her garden in a couple of hours, a task that normally took all day. She had no idea how the machine worked, but she was naturally incurious about such things and assumed that, if Wychammer was half as clever as Harriet thought he was, he may well have invented it himself. When she had gathered up the severed twigs and leaves into a heap for a future bonfire she considered returning the clippers to their owner, but found she was disinclined to confront the man again so soon. After a moment of indecision, she carried the tool indoors and stored it away in a safe place.

The remainder of the day she fidgeted about the house doing nothing of consequence. All that evening she expected Harriet, who was still palpably glowing with the heat of her new preoccupation, to make some excuse to revisit Wychammer, but she never actually got to the point of doing so. She didn't even mention his name, which was a frustration to Millie, because there were a number of questions she wanted to ask about the man, though she was reluctant to raise the subject herself. The matter that most intrigued her was that, as far as she could see (she'd taken a peep through her telescope as soon as it had grown dark), though he kept lights burning all night in almost every room, their neighbour had done nothing to furnish the place, and had not, as far as she could tell, even begun to unpack any of his boxes.

Harriet, obviously feeling the effects of the previous late night, went to bed earlier than usual, and Millie did likewise. As she closed her eyes, she had a vision of her sister tiptoeing out of the house in the small hours to some tryst with Wychammer, but dismissed the notion as preposterous.

"I'm just slipping out for a while," Harriet announced, in an exaggeratedly casual way, half way through the following evening. She had put on one of her most expensive and attractive dresses: not the sort of thing she would wear if she intended taking a crepuscular stroll down the local lanes.

"Will you be long?" Millie inquired.

"Not sure."

"I see."

"Don't wait up for me."

"Of *course* not," Millie protested, as if to do so would be to commit a crime.

Nevertheless, she lay awake a long time that night. Harriet had not returned when she fell asleep.

A horrible dream lingered on in Millie's mind long into the following day. In it, she had found herself in a vast ruined church-like building. She had spent some time trying to find a way out, but all the doors were held shut by heaps of broken masonry. Part of the roof, and much of the upper structure of the walls had fallen, and well established plants grew out of the many heaps of rubble. Millie, following her instinct for tidiness, began to trim back this wild growth with Mr Wychammer's clippers, that she discovered she had brought with her. She stuck to this task for some time, but seemed to have made little difference to the general appearance of the place, and was beginning to experience a familiar sense of failure, when she heard a sound above her head, and looked up.

A rope had been lowered through one of the many circular holes in the roof, and Wychammer himself was climbing nimbly down it. Behind him followed Harriet, and Millie saw at once that her sister was terrified. Millie knew the reason for this; Harriet was extremely afraid of heights. Also, Harriet was shivering, because she was wearing just her underclothing, one of the brief, exotic sets she wore for certain special occasions, and the atmosphere inside the ancient building had, during the last few moments, gone icy cold.

When Wychammer reached the ground he nodded politely towards Millie, stepped back, and shouted advice to Harriet, telling her where to put her feet and hands. Harriet was so scared, she could hardly move at all, and Millie witnessed her agonisingly slow descent with painful concern. When, after what seemed a very long time, Harriet had almost reached the ground, Wychammer reached up, took hold of her leg, and told her to drop into his arms.

Millie grew furious at this, and screamed at Wychammer to take his hands off her sister but, if he heard her, he ignored her. When he was more or less carrying Harriet, he stared back up the rope, and Millie, doing likewise, saw that someone else was descending through the gap in the roof. It had gone much darker and it was impossible to see exactly what manner of being had now come into the church. It was dressed in some long, loose garment that flapped around it like huge wings. It seemed to flow down and around the hanging rope in a violent, determined way – so much so that the lower few yards of the rope began to flick and crack around Wychammer and Harriet like a whip. To avoid this possible danger Wychammer began to carry Harriet towards one end of the building where, Millie realized, an altar had been prepared. When the person descending behind them detached itself from the ladder, he or she went in pursuit of them, and Millie followed after.

Some kind of ceremony took place then. It didn't look quite like a wedding, though it involved a ring. Someone, somewhere, began to chant. Millie, standing rooted to the spot behind the bulk of the third person to come down the rope, could make no sense of what was happening or being said. She called out to Harriet a number of times, but all three of the celebrants ignored her totally.

When the ring was produced, Harriet, her whole body shuddering with cold, shakily held out the middle finger of her left hand, and the person in front of Millie attempted to slip on the ring. It was obvious at once to Millie that it was too small, and she began thumping the back of the figure closest to her, protesting aloud that the ring would never fit. Nobody took any notice of her.

When Wychammer saw there was a problem with the ring, he took hold of it and began wrenching it down hard on Harriet's finger. The other person encouraged and assisted him.

Harriet cried out, but made no effort to remove her hand even when beads of blood began to appear on the tip of her finger. Wychammer and the other person pushed and tugged even harder at the ring. By the time they had forced it into place, they had stripped Harriet's finger of skin to the bottom of the middle joint.

Blood began to flow down Harriet's uplifted arm to her elbow, where it dripped to the floor. The figure that had been last down the rope reached for a little stone bottle chained round its neck, unstoppered it, and stooped to collect the falling blood. When the bottle was full it rose again, turned towards Millie for the first time, and held out its arms towards her.

As he moved his head up the hood fell back, but before she could see the person's face, Millie started running. She found she was heading towards a huge mirror lying flat on the floor, the surface of which rippled like water. Without hesitation she took a frantic dive into it, and moments later found herself thrashing around in the sticky-damp sheets of her sweat-soaked bed.

The impression made on Millie by the dream was so strong it still haunted her when she was preparing to set out to do her second session of voluntary work later that morning. She was eager to get out of the house and have something to do to occupy her mind. When the doorbell rang, she assumed the woman who picked her up and took her to work had come a little early, and hurried thankfully to the door.

Mr Wychammer was standing on the step, clutching a thick book to his chest. Millie did not step back to let him in, as he seemed to expect her to. After dryly wishing Millie a good morning Wychammer said, "Perhaps your sister told you to expect me?" in a way that suggested he realized Harriet had done nothing of the kind.

"No," Millie said, resisting an urge to close the door firmly in his face, to shut out the creature of her nightmare.

"I trust the instrument I lent you was of some use?" he said ingratiatingly.

"It was very effective, thank you."

"I have in my possession many other contraptions I could put at your disposal. Time and energy savers of various kinds to assist you in your daily work. You have only to ask."

Millie thought of the little catalogues that came unbidden through the letter box every few weeks, that offered dozens of unlikely and gimmicky household devices for sale by mail, and sniffed dismissively.

Wychammer looked uncomfortable holding the heavy book. "I told your sister I'd bring this round," he explained. "She must have forgotten to mention it."

"She doesn't read books."

"I assure you, Harriet expressed an interest in this one."

Not many people, Millie reflected, got on first name terms with her sister so quickly, in just a few days. She pointed to the table near the door, where Harriet placed her briefcase when she returned from work. "Put it there, please."

Wychammer edged past her, deposited the book, and looked around. He stepped forward to peer at a painting hanging on the wall. After stooping to give it a close inspection he gave a nod of approval, murmured, "Charming," and moved further down the hall to scrutinise another picture.

"He's in now," Millie thought. "How am I going to get him out?"

"You have nice things," Wychammer observed. "Are you a collector?"

"Everything is Harriet's. She owns the house and all it contains. I am totally dependent on her. I have no income. Never have had." Millie fancied she sounded sad and foolish.

"So I believe," Wychammer said.

Millie felt betrayed. Harriet had been talking to him about her. What else had she said?

The door bell rang again. Wychammer turned towards the source of the sound with a look of resentment, as though the mellow chime pained his ears.

"I'm afraid I must ask you to leave," Millie said with relief. "Someone's come to take me away."

Wychammer didn't bother to hide his dissatisfaction. "That's unfortunate. I was beginning to enjoy our talk. I must call round again, sometime."

Millie failed to encourage this suggestion as she let her friend into the house. Moments later the two women followed Wychammer down the garden path.

"Who's your friend," whispered Millie's companion.

"*Not* a friend, Jenny," Millie insisted. "A new neighbour."

"What a slimy looking sod," Jenny said.

"Is that how he strikes you?" Millie was delighted with her companion's acuity.

"I wouldn't want him living next to me. I'd move."

Millie found she wanted to laugh. "My sister seems to have become very fond of him."

"More fool her," Jenny said.

Millie went straight to Wychammer's book when she returned home that afternoon, opened it, and riffled through the pages. It was called *A Place for Everyone* and subtitled "And Everyone In Their Place": by "Professor E. H. Wychammer."

"Professor of what?" Millie asked herself.

The blurb on the inside flap of the dust-jacket was enthusiastic in the extreme. "Polymath Professor Wychammer's cornucopia of advice and information is indispensable to anyone wishing to rise and prosper in today's demanding and stressful world." it proclaimed, after listing the man's virtues at length. Much more pompous, portentous nonsense followed

A surge of irritation suffused Millie's mind. She felt furiously angry with the book and slammed it shut with both hands. The dull thump it made in the empty house reminded her briefly of the quiet explosion she had heard in the garage at the moment of her mother's self destruction, an event she recalled at least once every day.

Hastily, with an expression of sharp distaste distorting her features, she replaced the book and left it for Harriet to discover.

II

A week passed. The level of the gin in Harriet's bottle no longer sank at the rate of an inch a day, Millie noticed. Previously, for many years, measuring out her two or three evening tipples with clinical precision, as though they were fortifying medicine, Harriet had gotten through a bottle and a half of Gordon's in seven days. This abrupt adoption of abstinence was only the most obvious outward evidence of the changes in Harriet's life. For Millie, who knew her better than she knew herself, there were plenty of more subtle signs that her sister was going through some inner alteration. *Conversion*, was the word Millie found most fitting to describe, in her own mind, this metamorphosis.

The sight of Harriet sitting at the dinner table long after the evening meal was over, poring over Wychammer's wretched book, and scribbling notes in an note-pad she had brought specially for the purpose, drove Millie to despair. At first, Harriet had attempted to get her sister to share her enthusiasm for the man and his work, but Millie's instinctive and, to Harriet, unreasonable rejection of both, was total. They came to the point where Millie shuddered at the mere mention of Wychammer's name, and she begged her sister to talk of something else.

Millie no longer felt secure in Harriet's house. She was losing her interest in star-gazing and only used her telescope to spy on her next door neighbour. Worse still, she found she was becoming afraid of the dark, and subject to night fears. At first, she thought her dreams, most of which were visited by Wychammer in some guise or another, were the cause of this unease, even though she could only remember snatches of them. But in a couple of weeks she wasn't dreaming much because she was hardly sleeping, and she spent the nights twisting in her bed, listening for Harriet's footsteps on the stairs.

It was Millie's volunteering day again, and she had never been so glad to get out of the house. She decided to confront her sister about her relationship with Wychammer that evening: she would talk to Harriet, even if Harriet wouldn't talk to her.

When it came to it, however, she noticed, to her surprise, that Harriet appeared to be sickly and off-colour, and took pity on her. Like the coat of an out of condition cat, Harriet's dyed black hair looked dull and dank, and clung to her scalp. Her eyes had lost the extra brightness that had been noticeable recently, and she seemed awkward and out of sorts. Millie imagined her sister had even lost some weight.

By then, Millie was in the habit of scuttling upstairs at all times of the day to take a look at the property next door. Just before serving the evening meal she couldn't resist sneaking off again to her telescope. Through it, she was surprised to see a number of people in Wychammer's garden, wandering about casually, as though it were a public park. Some of them were even picnicking. The last rays of a lurid sunset were fading fast. Millie thought they would soon feel the chill, sitting there on the grass in the gathering dusk.

After dinner Harriet glanced sharply up from time to time and stared at the curtained windows. There seemed to be a lot of traffic on the normally quiet road outside the house, and car doors banged somewhere nearby. At each slam Harriet started and winced as though her nerves were frazzled. At last, driven by curiosity, Millie left her, went up again to the first floor, and again peered through the telescope.

There were lights shining all through Wychammer's house. Strings of multi-coloured coloured bulbs, like Christmas decorations, hung in the newly planted trees along the front drive and in various places in the garden. In their bright illumination it was possible to count twenty or more cars parked nose to tale on the drive. Many more stretched along the road beyond. Others were arriving all the time. Their drivers sneaked past slowly, searching for parking space. Two large coaches pulled up outside Harriet's house as Millie watched. Streams of people disembarked and followed each other through Wychammer's front door, which stood welcomingly open. None of the passengers had any kind of luggage, Millie noticed, so presumable they had come for a meeting of short duration or possibly some kind of party. The latter explanation of the presence seemed unlikely, as all Wychammer's guests were dressed rather formally, in dark, sombre clothes. Millie did not get the impression they had come to let their hair down: they looked a sober, serious lot. Once inside the house they made their way purposefully towards particular rooms where they stood waiting patiently, not drifting about like party-goers. They acted as though they were under instructions. Millie saw Wychammer enter a couple of rooms, address a few words to the crowds there assembled, then quickly leave. It was obvious he was completely in charge of whatever was taking place.

Noises from the floor below alerted Millie to the fact that Harriet was leaving the house. Moments later she saw her sister, a slightly hunched and ungainly figure, like someone escaping furtively from a long, uncomfortable confinement, almost running along the drive towards the neighbouring house. Millie could hear the crunch of her feet on the gravel. Harriet paused for a moment when she reached Wychammer's door step, straightened up, turned to take one glance behind her, as though to satisfy herself that she had not been followed, then marched deliberately into the building.

After a while Millie noticed that no more cars were arriving. Everything had gone still and quiet.

Then all the lights in the garden went out, and the front door of Wychammer's house slammed shut.

Millie was unable to witness what happened next, however, because the windows of the next door building gradually became opaque, as though the place was filling with steam. This phenomenon, more than anything else she had seen, greatly disturbed her. She shuddered and became afraid for her sister. And, she realized, for herself.

She remained where she was for a long time, gazing out but seeing nothing, her mind full of a multiplicity of apprehensions that demanded all her attention.

Next morning, Millie couldn't remember getting into bed. She had slept well, but too heavily. Her brain felt stodgy. She looked at the clock beside her and saw it was quite early, before seven.

She got up, looked out of the window, saw all the vehicles that had been parked outside the night before had gone, then went and tapped on her sister's bedroom door. After a few long seconds of silence a voice she hardly recognized as Harriet's called out, "What do you want?"

For a moment Millie was speechless, because her sister sounded so strange. Her voice was high and constricted, like a record played a little too fast, and heard through a damaged speaker. Millie wanted to open the door but dared not without being invited to do so. Harriet was fanatical about protecting her own private space.

At last, Millie found herself telling a lie. "I wondered if you had called out to me," she said. "Something must have woken me early, and I couldn't think what else it could have been."

"I didn't hear anything."

"I'm sorry if I disturbed you."

"Perhaps you had a bad dream."

Millie was grateful for this possibility. Briefly, she wondered if the events of the past couple of weeks, since the arrival of their new neighbour, had all been merely a bad dream, but the sound of her sister's voice when she spoken again was enough to shatter this hope.

"Millie," Harriet said, "I'm – hurt. Fetch the first-aid box and leave it outside my door."

"Hurt!" Millie yelped, appalled. "How?"

"It's not serious. But I need a bandage."

Millie almost grabbed the door handle to force an entry into the room, but restrained herself. "I'll call a doctor."

"No," Harriet snapped. "I can manage on my own," she added. "Just do as I say. *Please*." There was more than pain in her voice, Millie realized, there was a note of embarrassment, humiliation even. She was begging.

"I'll get what you want," Millie said, and ran down stairs.

At first she couldn't remember where the first aid box was stored. It took her a couple of minutes to locate it in the back of a little-used cupboard in the kitchen. In front of it on the shelf lay the hedge clipper that Wychammer had lent her, that she had also forgotten about, and should have returned. The shock of this discovery was almost sickening, as though she had come across something organic that had been left a long time to rot. The strange shining machine looked sinister as a human skull which, she realized, to some extent, it did resemble. She could not, at that moment, have brought herself to touch it. Avoiding even looking at it, she reached above it for the handle of the red box marked with a white cross, lifted it out, and ran with it to her sister's room. She knocked on the door and said, "I've got it."

"Leave it, Millie," Harriet said. "Go away. I'll bring it in myself."

"Harriet," Millie said, finding herself suddenly in tears. "What have you done? What's happened to you?"

"I don't want to talk about it." Harriet said.

Millie had always felt she was unable to do enough for her sister, who supported her with every material thing she needed in life, and was too independent to require much, except loyalty, in return. "But Harriet, I want to help you," she said miserably. "Please tell me what I can do."

"Go away," Harriet repeated.

Millie realized her sister was now standing close to her, just behind the door. The door opened a crack.

"Millie." Harriet's voice now had a wheedling tone. "You've done all you can. Thank you. Now leave me alone. Do what you normally do. Make breakfast."

Millie fled. Behind her, she heard Harriet step onto the landing and take the first-aid box into her room. When the door had closed behind Harriet, Millie stopped and looked back. Something glistened on the polished wooden floor. She retraced her steps and saw it was a little pool of blood, about an inch in diameter. She reached for some tissues in the pocket of her dressing-gown, stooped down, and blotted up the blood.

Inside her room Harriet cried out, presumably with pain.

Harriet came down for breakfast at the usual time and took her place at the table without speaking. Millie had her back to her when she entered the room, and found a number of unnecessary but time consuming things to do before she felt she could turn to face her sister. When they did finally confront each other, Millie was relieved to see that Harriet's features, at least, bore no signs of damage. Her expression was hard and tight, however, she looked ill, and the smile she attempted did not succeed. It was not until Harriet began to try to eat the food in front of her that Millie realized her sister only had the use of her right hand. The left one was resting on her lap, out of sight below the edge of the table. After disposing of her cereal in silence, Harriet came to a halt when she started to try to deal with bacon and eggs. She pushed the full plate away from her a little way, then drank some of her coffee slowly, with exaggerated calmness, as though nothing was amiss.

Millie said, "Did you find what you needed?"

"In the first-aid box? Yes. Everything was in place. It's hardly ever been used."

"And your wound? I take it you've hurt your other hand?"

Harriet nodded, and lifted her almost empty cup to her lips, perhaps in an attempt to avoid having to make any further comment.

Millie wasn't going to let her get away with that. "Did the – accident – happen at our neighbour's house?" she asked. "I saw you going in there. I happened to be looking out of a window . . ."

"Did I say anything about an accident?" Almost wearily, as though she was tired and her arm was heavy, Harriet lifted her left hand and placed it on the table beside her plate. Her fingers were bandaged inexpertly together. Only her thumb and the lower part of the back of her hand was visible.

"I assumed . . ." Millie's voice died on her.

Harriet shook her head. "Not an accident," she said.

Millie stared at the bandaged hand. Blood was seeping through the gauze at the tip of the fingers. She said, "Harriet, are you not going to tell me anything about what's happened?"

Harriet shook her head, got up, went into the hall, and picked up her briefcase.

Millie said, "Surely you are not going into work like that?"

"Why not?"

"You don't intend driving with your hand in that condition?"

For a moment Harriet looked nonplussed, as though the possible difficulty of doing this had not occurred to her. After a moment's deliberation, she dismissed the problems. "I'll manage," she said. "Don't worry."

As soon as Harriet had gone Millie went to the cupboard where she had found the first-aid box and pulled out Wychammer's clipping machine. She stood inspecting the peculiar object for some minutes, turning it over and over in her hands absentmindedly, as though her thoughts were on other things. Then she made up her mind, and left the house with the thing under her arm. She strode across the garden to the gap in the hedge that separated the grounds of the two houses and slipped through quickly. Becoming apprehensive as soon as her feet were on Wychammer's land, she forced herself forward through the recently planted shrubs and bushes, that were now thickly leaved and, in some cases, covered in blossom, as though they had been rooted there for years, then followed the mossy, seemingly ancient, but actually modern, crazy-paved pathway that wound round towards the side of the house. When she was within fifteen feet of the nearest window, Millie took advantage of the cover offered by a trellis of intertwined roses, and came to a halt. She peered round one end of the trellis so she could see through the window into the house. She was surprised to see the window's wooden frame was very rotten, with most of the paint peeled off. It was hard to believe the structure of the house had degenerated so much in two years since the Ruggles had left. The room beyond the window was, as far as she could see, empty. There was an emerald green carpet on the floor, but no furniture of any kind anywhere. She realized that if she walked a few yards to the far end of the trellis, she would get an even better view into another nearby window. She made her way towards it keeping her head well down.

This room was not empty. A large, gilt-framed mirror, some six feet high by eight wide, rested against the opposite wall. The floor was covered with midnight blue carpet, and on this carpet, danced Mr Wychammer. He was swooping backwards and forwards with his hands held out in front of him, working his fingers all the while, bending them into complex shapes, as though sending messages to his own image in elaborate sign language. The image in the mirror was darker than the reality it imperfectly copied and it took a few moments for Millie to realize that the reflection of Mr Wychammer in the mirror was not mimicking his actions in an exact reverse copy of his movements, but had a life of its own. It did its own, slightly different, more lethargic dance. And the two of them *were* communicating somehow: information of some kind was passing from one to the other. They were conversing.

Millie's hands, still clutching the machine, began to tremble. She realized Wychammer was not just a charismatic, powerful, dangerous, possibly evil man. She had underestimated him, he was much more than that.

The creature that was not quite a reflection wore clothes similar to Wychammer's, but its hands were hidden in long, wide sleeves and its head was partially covered by an antiquated looking headpiece that flopped down around its ears and over the upper part of its face like a cowl. Millie studied the half-concealed face and saw that it wasn't quite the same as Wychammer's because, as far as she could tell, the features were unmarked, the nose unbroken. It was more conventionally handsome, appealing even, and could have been Wychammer's younger brother.

With a final rather clumsy, windmilling gesture of its arms the figure in the mirror jerked to a halt and leaned sharply forward from the waist. Millie realized it was looking straight at her, that it could see her. Better, perhaps, than she could see it because, without realizing, in an attempt to get a better look at the creature, she had stepped out from concealment behind the trellis. The second "Wychammer" stretched out a hand towards her and she saw the tip of a pointing finger emerge from a sleeve and reach forward towards the surface of the glass. At this, Wychammer himself, who had had his back towards Millie, turned casually round and stared blankly at her. His arms, caught in mid gesture, held out beside him, could have expressed welcome or surprise, but in fact he seemed quite unperturbed to find Millie gazing back at him.

The second figure, that seemed more interested in her, stepped sluggishly forward until it was very close to the mirror. When he was standing just inches behind the glass, he opened his mouth and Millie saw he had many sharp little teeth. Crouching, giving her a slack jawed smile, he made movements that suggested to Millie that he was going to leap through the mirror and window towards her. She suspected he could do that; could pass through both sheets of glass without breaking either. She was about to turn and run when the thing made a sudden, possibly aggressive gesture towards her and, acting without thought of the consequences, she lifted Wychammer's machine above her head with both hands and flung it with all her strength towards the face of the grinning figure.

Then she ran. Behind her the window shattered: a noise that gave her a brief feeling of elation, and seemed to make running easier. She hurtled forward in a straight line towards the gap in the hedge, trampling through flower-beds, and kicking aside any plants that got in her way. She stumbled, but did not stop until she reached her own front door. Once there, as she searched for her key, she looked back the way she had come and saw she had not been followed.

* * *

Millie sat for some hours in her favourite chair, thinking a great deal but moving not at all, waiting for her sister. Harriet returned looking sicker than ever. She sneaked into the house at three in the afternoon and locked herself in her room without saying a word to Millie. Millie put food and drink outside her door, but this was a wasted gesture. Harriet did not respond in any way.

Millie left the door of her room open when she went to bed so she would hear if Harriet started to move about, but she was not disturbed: the house remained silent that night.

Nevertheless, Harriet was nowhere to be found next morning.

Millie searched the house, furiously cursing Wychammer as she did so, then went to the kitchen. She jerked open the cutlery drawer, pulled out a six inch knife with a pointed blade she used to prepare vegetables, and made it safe by wrapping it in a number of paper towels. Feeling ashamed and afraid, she hid the knife in the side pocket of her slacks. This almost certainly foolhardy action had slowed her down, and taken the edge off her anger. She now felt in better possession of herself. She marched out of the house and crossed the ground towards the house next door with determination and a sense of purpose, though in fact she had no idea what she was going to do or say to Wychammer if she could find him. She thought this time he might have gone, taking Harriet with him.

Wychammer must have seen her coming, because he was sauntering towards her as she slipped through the gap in the hedge. When she stood in front of him he held his head slightly up and back, as he had done during their first meeting. Again, he looked down his nose at her, giving the impression he was glaring down at her from a great height. Both remained still and silent for some moments. Millie was glad to find she was easily able to give him back as hard a stare as he gave her.

At last Millie said, "You know why I'm here. Take me to her".

Wychammer seemed to be expecting this instruction. He nodded and, without further comment, led her down an unfurnished, untidy hallway littered with discarded, screwed up scraps of paper that she guessed were discarded leaflets of some kind. Wychammer kicked at some off these and sent them bowling along ahead of him, as a happy, heedless child might have done. There was other rubbish strewn about and, in a number of places, stains on the floor that could have been vomit or dried blood. The interior of the house was in uniformly poor condition. The air was full of unpleasant and, to Millie, unidentifiable smells. They went through a number of rooms, some of them scattered with now-empty cardboard boxes, until they came to the one where Wychammer had been when she had spied on him from the garden. She knew this because the window she had smashed had been hastily boarded up with wooden slats, and the huge mirror still rested against one of the walls: otherwise, it was a featureless space, like all the others she had passed through in the house. As with those other rooms there was not a single item of furniture to be seen – not so much as a chair to sit on.

"What have you done with her?" Millie demanded, when Wychammer came to a halt close to the mirror. Her voice, echoing in the emptiness, sounded less confident now, and had a wheedling edge.

Wychammer said. "You'll soon see. I'll fetch her."

He walked towards the mirror, stooped down below the level of the top of the frame, which must have been a little less than six feet high, and stepped through the glass.

Millie gasped, and put her hand to her gaping mouth, but she had known what was about to happen as soon as Wychammer had turned away from her.

After some moments of trepidation, she went closer to the mirror and stared at the reflection of the room she was in. Her own image was not reproduced there. The only figure she could see was Wychammer, retreating towards the door through which they had entered together.

Less than a minute later Wychammer and Harriet appeared at the door in the reflection in the mirror and passed through it. Instinctively, Millie turned to glance behind her at the actual doorway, which was empty.

Somewhere, wherever he really was, Wychammer laughed softly.

Harriet looked pale, tired, wounded. She had lost much of the extra weight she had carried for years but this had not improved her appearance. She resembled a recuperating invalid; someone who had been half-starved and bed-ridden for weeks. Her hair was plastered flat against her skull and her chalky skin glistered with sweat. Without the fastidiously applied make-up she normally wore her face looked flat, her features undefined.

Millie spoke her sister's name querulously once, but found she had nothing else to say. The sight of Harriet horrified her into silence.

Wychammer stretched his arm across Harriet's back in a familiar gesture and hugged her close to him. Harriet allowed herself to be mauled in this way and continued to regard Millie with empty, unresponsive eyes.

"Your sister has been very concerned about your welfare, Harriet," Wychammer said at last. "Please say something to calm her fears."

Harriet's body jerked slightly. The sides of her almost white lips parted slightly. She made clicking sounds in her throat before she said, "Don't trouble yourself about me. I don't need you any more, Millie."

Harriet held up her right hand and unwound the bandage on her middle finger to reveal a bloody stump. The top joint had been severed.

Millie stared at the stump, then turned towards Wychammer, who nodded gravely.

"It was done at my request," he said, "but voluntarily."

"Why?"

"As a token of commitment."

"In return for what?"

"My patronage and protection," Wychammer said. "And a place by my side. Obviously."

"And are you happy with that bargain, Harriet?" Millie asked irritably. She was exasperated because she knew what the answer to the question would be.

"I want nothing else. There *is* nothing else for me now."

"You may have given yourself up," Millie said, "but what about me? How am I to live?"

At this, Wychammer let go of Harriet and said, "Other arrangements have been made for you."

He stepped through the mirror into the room where Millie was standing, leaving Harriet on the other side.

Millie heard his soft steps getting closer to her, and remembered that she was not altogether powerless. She turned to face him, sliding her hand into her pocket as she did so to grasp the handle of the knife she had armed herself with. Millie wondered if she was strong enough to thrust the knife deep into his chest to

reach his heart. She knew she could and would act. She longed for
the sight of the creature's blood. Only her physical frailty could
let her down. The way to do it, she decided, was to lunge upward
and force the blade in under his ribs.

Wychammer was watching her face curiously and with some
amusement. He had stopped three feet away from Millie, who
needed him closer. She had wrapped the blade of the knife too
well and found to withdraw it she would first have to partly
unravel its paper sheath. In doing so, fumbling in the tight space
of her pocket, she ran her fingers against the blade. At first, the
sensation was more alarming than painful, but even so, she was
unable to repress a yelp of distress that Wychammer misinter-
preted as a cry of despair. He started to speak, perhaps to offer
some kind of perverse consolation and stepped towards her, until
Millie judged he was close enough. She had the knife in her grasp
now.

The sight of Millie's clenched fist as it arced up towards him
was the first warning Wychammer had that he was being
attacked. He made no effort to avoid the blow but swung his
right hand round with such speed that, for a fraction of a second,
it was invisible, then grabbed Millie's wrist and twisted it once.
Millie shrieked, and dropped the knife. Wychammer stooped,
caught the weapon by the handle before it hit the ground, and
withdrew with it back into the mirror. Millie, driven to a fury
beyond reason by Wychammer's contemptuous treatment of her
and the pain he had inflicted, threw herself after him.

The man in the mirror had half turned back towards her as she
smashed against the silvered glass, that cracked from top to
bottom, but did not shatter. Millie, who had not doubted she
would be able to pass through as easily as her enemy had,
bounced back like a migrating bird that had flown full tilt against
a window pane, and collapsed on the floor. Stunned, she remained in that position until a slight sound alerted her to the
possibility of further danger, and she pulled herself up and looked
back at the mirror.

Wychammer was standing very close on the other side of the
glass, reaching up with both hands towards the back of the upper
section of the mirror's thick, heavy frame. His feet were wide
apart, his knees slightly bent, his chest thrust forwards. Millie
understood what he was straining so hard to achieve when the

top of the mirror began to dip towards her. As she tried to scuttle back away from it on her hands and knees she heard Wychammer give a wordless shout. Very soon after, the mirror smashed down on top of her.

The intensity of the subsequent pain mercifully drew her away into unconsciousness.

The sound of her own whimpering was the first thing Millie was able to identify when consciousness returned. She lay absolutely still for some time while she reconstructed the events that had led to her being where she now was. She realised she was lying face down on a filthy, stinking carpet covered with fragments of broken glass. She hauled herself up a little way from the ground and forced the top half of her body round into something like a sitting position. As she did so various sharp, agonising sensations below her knees made her gasp.

The room she was in was darker than it had been, but she was just able to see that she was situated in the centre of the frame of the shattered mirror. She lay down then, feeling exhausted and defeated. On her back, finding herself, perforce, gazing upwards, she saw there was a mark like an uneven black disk on the ceiling directly above her. Its outline wavered slightly, as though her eyes were unable to keep it in focus.

She stared harder, trying to give greater definition to the dark shape but, as she did so, it seemed to move smoothly up away from her. It sank into the ceiling and soon Millie found she was looking into a vertical tunnel about five feet in width that was stretching further and further away. The far end of it became increasingly dark. When, after perhaps ten minutes, this most remote part had become utterly black, one or two tiny dots of silvery light appeared, as though pin pricks had been made in its surface. Other light emerged in that vicinity, unevenly spaced, and shining with unequal brilliance. Millie watched this process in stunned wonder, realizing gradually that what she could see was a section of the sky, but not a part that she recognized.

Millie knew all about the stars. Her father had taught her to identify the major constellations and she had never forgotten those first lessons. She tried now to make sense of the circle of sky above her and fit it into what she knew of the layout of the universe, but was unable to do so. The spread of stars above shone in a different sky than the one she had studied in her childhood.

Awed and alarmed by this revelation, Millie forced herself to look away and tried to take stock of her immediate situation. What little light there was in the room seemed to be merely that of the stars that must have been shining down from a very remote part of the universe. She could just make out the outline of her hand when she held it, fingers outstretched, above her face. Some sensation, mostly of cold, had returned to her body that had been, for a while, insensate. She could hear nothing at all, not even the sound of her own breathing, but there was a curious taste in her mouth, and she was aware of a particularly foul smell in the air around her, that seemed somehow to be associated with the taste.

There was a tiny sound in the air above her, like the silky hissing of a snake. Up above her face something that had been descending slowly and unseen towards her came to a halt a foot or so away from her forehead. She reached up to touch it and realized that a thick rope was dangling down from the hole in the ceiling. She took hold of the rope with both hands and began to tug at it, passing hand over hand twice in order to pull herself partially upright. Hanging on to the rope like a drowning mariner who had been thrown a line she wondered if, were the rope to be withdrawn, she would have the strength to keep a hold of it while she was lifted up into the unfamiliar section of heaven above, and decided, with absolute certainly, that she had not. If she were borne up, she would fall off very soon, and perhaps increase her injuries when she tumbled back into the frame down on earth.

Millie leaned back, already exhausted, and was about to let go of the rope's end when it seemed to come alive in her hand and was twitched violently out of her grasp.

There was a pause then, while the rope hovered, quite still again, above her head, for what could have been seconds or hours – her perception of the passing of – time seemed to have deserted her, or become deranged, until, at last. Then the tip of the rope started moving again, swaying swiftly from side to side, like the tail of an impatient dog.

It was fascinating, hypnotic, snake-like, the rope.

Its movements captured all Millie's attention, absorbed her completely in her semiconscious state, and it was only very slowly and vaguely that the gesticulations of the rope became meaningful and significant. Gradually, however, she understood that someone was clambering towards her, climbing down from heaven. She could even, she fancied, make out, against the alien pattern of the stars, the outline of a fluidly mobile figure, dressed in some loose outfit, or in tattered rags, and still a long way above her, clinging to the rope.

After an unmeasurable expanse of time, she realized who was descending.

Who it had to be.

As she waited to receive him, to *welcome* him, now, she tried to move into a posture from which she could greet him and meet him face to face. To her great distress, as she forced herself to struggle from one cramped position to another, she was aware that the stink she had previously noticed in the air around her became stronger and more pungent until it became thick enough almost to encase her and hinder her movements.

Nevertheless, she continued to twist listlessly about until at last, overwhelmed by exhaustion that it was an exquisite pleasure to succumb to, she gave up all effort and became still.

The rope continued to snap and sway above her motionless head. And motionless Millie was to remain until someone came to claim her.

He dropped nimbly down from the rope's end and took a brief look down at what was left of Millie. Then, slowly, scrupulously missing nothing, he gathered together, bit by bit, all there was of her. He threw the pieces into a sack made of skin he always carried with him beneath his robes, tied it tight at the neck, and swung the sack over his shoulder.

After refreshing himself from a little bottle chained round his neck he carried Millie away to join her sister, who was waiting for her in the place they had both come from.

Where their mother still looked down at the petrol she had poured over her head and body.

Where their father still gazed up at the sky.

And where the stars look neither up nor down at anyone.

NICHOLAS ROYLE

Empty Stations

NICHOLAS ROYLE LIVES IN WEST LONDON with his wife and two children. He is the author of four novels – *Counterparts*, *Saxophone Dreams*, *The Matter of the Heart* and *The Director's Cut* – and more than a hundred short stories. He has edited eleven anthologies, including *Darklands*, *The Ex Files*, *A Book of Two Halves* and *The Time Out Book of London Short Stories Volume 2*. He is currently writing a new novel, a sequel to *The Director's Cut*, entitled *Straight to Video*.

"I'm drawn to lost things," reveals the author, "lost films, lost stations, lost minds – because of the mystery that springs up around anything that is lost, but also because they reflect the ephemerality of all things. This story spins off a narrative strand from my last novel, *The Director's Cut*. It stands alone, but reflects a growing interest in intertextuality, as well as a lasting affection for *Death Line* (aka *Raw Meat*), Gary Sherman's 1972 Tube cannibal movie."

G areth Sangster, freelance hack and sometime actor, was sitting in front of a computer screen in the office/spare bedroom of his Stoke Newington flat. He was staring just past the screen at the rear windows of the houses in the next street. He wasn't watching anything in particular, just passing the time, seeking distraction from an unfinished review. A press release lay on his desk next to the keyboard. He'd read it a dozen times. He'd seen the film he was trying to write about only the night before in a Wardour Street basement. But something about it resisted his attempts to get it down.

He knew what it was. It was the fact that he'd seen the film a hundred times before, and read the press kit as often. The studios went to the trouble of giving them different titles, but they were all the same movie. The script got a minor rewrite and the actors ghosted through ninety minutes without breaking a sweat.

The phone rang, shattering his reverie. He picked it up and listened.

"Where?" he asked. "When?"

He hung up and went back to looking out of the window. He was wondering if his life was about to change. Or if Ash had fired the starting pistol for another wild goose chase. You never knew with Ash. He could be right, he could be wrong. Most of the time he was wrong.

Gareth looked at the screen. He knew he should shut the machine down and go out to meet Ash, but a phrase had entered his tidy mind and he decided to write it down before he forgot it. The phrase proved to be the key to unlocking the piece and his review wrote itself in less than ten minutes. He e-mailed the review to his editor, then selected "Shut Down" and left the flat while the machine was still finishing up.

Most life-threatening situations that cannot be blamed on the random concurrence of unrelated events are reached as a direct result of people delving too deep into their own obsessions. When the alarm bells should no longer go ignored is when two people's crazy desires are indulged at the same time and one of them shows all the signs of being quietly mad.

The alarm bells would have been ringing to wake the dead and Gareth should have heard them, but for some reason he had his head stuck up his arse. He always had had where Ash was concerned.

He picked up a black cab on Church Street and allowed its fluid acceleration to propel him back in his seat as the gates to Abney Park Cemetery flickered past the window. Whenever he passed the great Victorian boneyard, a still image of its fabled subterranean catacombs would light up like a silent movie behind his eyes.

Gareth's obsession was with lost London films. He'd been in

one, of course, which was how the bug bit him. When he was doing stage acting, appearing in fringe productions and living hand-to-mouth in a squat in South Street, Mayfair, he'd agreed to take a part in Harry Foxx's *Nine South Street*. The conceit – that the film would feature a bunch of Mayfair squatters playing themselves – appealed to him. He liked the fact that the director wanted them to improvise around a basic thriller plot that was already in place. He also liked the director. It was Harry Foxx's first film, but the tyro seemed confident beyond his experience.

Since its initial, extremely limited release, *Nine South Street* had never been screened. While other British independent films of the same era, such as Richard Stanley's *Hardware* and Vadim Jean's *Leon the Pig Farmer*, would enjoy an occasional afterlife at the Watermans or the Riverside, *Nine South Street* simply disappeared. Its only scheduled network TV broadcast was postponed due to a live football match going into extra time, and it was never reprogrammed, so Gareth Sangster's only screen performance went unseen by most of the world, including its casting directors and independent producers.

Years later, when attempts were made to locate prints of the film for a revival at the NFT, none was unearthed. Even the negative had vanished. Ash, who had been Gareth's co-star in *Nine South Street*, was less concerned by the disappearance of the film, since he'd had no acting ambitions in the first place, despite being a talented mimic. Ash was squatting in South Street at the same time as Gareth and they had formed a relationship, in spite of personal incompatibility, based on their shared interest in film. They went to movies together, making the most of the Lumière, the Electric, the Scala, while they were still in business. Mostly they saw British films from the 1960s and '70s – Nicolas Roeg, Lindsay Anderson, John Schlesinger. They caught Skolimowski's rarely screened *Deep End* at the ICA, and *The Shout* at the Roxie. Gareth watched Malcolm McDowell and James Fox with the concentration of a counterfeiter staring at legal banknotes, then reproduced their tics and mannerisms in his fringe work.

"It's not the same as what you do," he explained to Ash. "It's not impersonation, but reinterpretation.

"Tell that to the judge," Ash replied in his best Bogart.

And, so, when Gareth and Ash encountered a tall, long-haired stranger prowling around the disused corridors of 9 South Street

– a forbidding ex-office building they squatted with a dozen or so others – they were only too happy to buy his story about scouting for locations for a low-budget film. The three of them shared a bottle of Stolly that Harry fetched from the off-licence in Shepherd Market and the idea for the film was born.

For Gareth it was the perfect opportunity to fulfil his dreams. Ash was less clear about what he wanted out of life. South Street was his first base in London and he'd only been there a couple of months, having moved south from the West Midlands, where, he claimed, he had been the drummer in a band. He'd quit before they'd got a recording deal and then, as soon as they started to acquire a cult following, had been written out of their past, he said, airbrushed out of rock history, but Gareth soon learned to treat whatever Ash told him with caution. The Midlander drank heavily and did a lot of drugs. When they had first met, Gareth had been slightly in awe of him. Despite being a year or two younger, Ash was astonishingly dissolute. He maintained his various expensive habits by stealing books and CDs, which he sold on to secondhand dealers. He never paid for a meal in a restaurant, and so never visited the same establishment twice. Later, when it became clear that unreliability was part of Ash's character, Gareth could never quite erase the power of those earliest memories.

Consequently, when Ash called to report a lead in the search for a lost London film, Gareth jumped.

The cab cut through the top end of Barnesbury and hit the Cally Road a few yards from the tube station that bore its name. As he paid the driver, Gareth spotted Ash peering up and down the street from just inside the station entrance.

"Are they after you again?" Gareth asked.

"It's no joke, man," Ash insisted. "Anyway, I don't think I was followed. On this occasion."

"Ash, who the fuck would follow you?"

Ash looked pale and unwell, fish out of water. "You might," he said.

Gareth shook his head in exasperation.

"Come on," Ash pressed him. "We haven't got much time."

They took the stairs and within moments were waiting on the westbound Piccadilly line. Gareth noticed, in the sickly gloom that prevailed on the tube platform, that Ash didn't look so pale.

He was also less tense than he seemed on the streets these days. Increasingly, it seemed, they hung out underground – travelling by tube to basement bars or preview theatres beneath Wardour Street. Getting from the tube to the venue was always something of a dash. It was one reason why Gareth didn't see as much of Ash as he used to.

It had started as an interest in the city beneath the city, London under London, like the book by Trench and Hillman, one of the few books Ash had stolen and not off-loaded the next day. The interest had gradually eclipsed any others, apart from film: he combined the two by being selective about which cinemas he went to. Out went the Gate and the Phoenix, in came the Lumiére, the Metro, the Renoir – cinemas where the auditoria were located below ground level.

Once on the train itself, Ash seemed to glow with vitality. He even started grinning at Gareth.

"Stop that. I don't like it," Gareth said. "Tell me where we're going. Is this a wind-up?"

Ash leaned forward. "You know how sometimes late at night," he said, "you're waiting on the tube platform and an empty train goes by without stopping? No lights on. It barely slows down, just passes through the station as if it weren't there."

Gareth nodded.

Instead of continuing, Ash sat back and crossed one leg over the other. He was grinning again. Gareth looked away. The train was pulling into King's Cross. He thought about getting off and leaving Ash to head off on his own, but then he remembered he felt the same impulse most times they saw each other and he never acted on it. When the doors closed and the train set off again, Ash crossed the carriage and sat next to Gareth. He had to shout to make himself heard over the din of the train's progress through the tunnels.

"Just as there are empty trains that go through 'our' stations – your stations and my stations, everybody's stations – without stopping, so there are other stations where these trains –" he pointed at the carriage floor for emphasis – "go through without stopping. Empty stations."

Gareth's nose was close to Ash's mouth, but for once he couldn't smell alcohol on the younger man's breath.

"Empty stations?" Gareth said, humouring him.

"Empty stations."

"You mean disused? Like York Way, British Museum, Wood Lane?"

"No. I mean empty. These stations have never been used. At least not by the likes of you and me. These stations are not on the network. They're off the map."

"I suppose you've found a way to get out at one of these stations?" Gareth couldn't keep the sarcasm out of his voice.

"You just have to get on the right train. You have to get on one of the trains that stops at those stations. Some of them stop at empty stations as well as normal stations. Some only stop at the empty ones." Ash indicated the rush of light that signalled their arrival in the next station.

"And you've done that, I suppose?" Gareth snapped.

"No, I haven't. But I know a guy who has. He lives in the tunnels."

"Yeah, right – and here we are at Russell Square. I've seen *Death Line*, Ash. Do us a favour and stop bullshitting me, OK? Just piss off!" Gareth jumped to his feet and stepped smartly between the closing doors, leaving Ash in his seat with a strange, sad little smile on his face.

Gareth marched off up the platform, angry with himself more than anything for allowing himself to get sucked into Ash's paranoid fantasies. The train accelerated past him. He looked up in time to catch a smeared glimpse of Ash's face through the last window, his features as blurry as those of a corpse behind heavy plastic.

Gareth watched as the train slid into the tunnel. Its red light burned until the first bend had been navigated.

He reached the end of the platform, glared at the unbroken wall and cursed. He'd been so wrapped up in his anger, he'd managed to miss the exit. He turned round and looked down the full length of platform. There was no exit sign, but that didn't mean anything, as half the stations on the network were falling apart. He started walking back down the platform, paying more attention to his surroundings. He must have got confused when he'd been talking to Ash, because this didn't look like Russell Square. In fact, he couldn't see the station's name anywhere. Half way down the platform, however, he found the exit. It was still unsigned, but it appeared to be a way out, so he took it.

The corridor led away from the platform and turned a corner. Faced with a flight of steps, Gareth climbed them rapidly. The dull echo of his footfalls disturbed him. He'd noticed a lack of posters on the walls – but then some stations were like that, in parts at least. There were no other people in evidence apart from himself. He moved faster. At the top of the steps, the corridor went left, then right – and then it stopped. It didn't run into a rough concrete wall or massive steel doors. It didn't end in barred gates, scraps of litter idling in desultory circles on the dusty, unattainable floor beyond. It ended in a perfectly ordinary, perfectly grouted, green-tiled wall. There was a subtle bevel where one wall joined the next, just as there would be if it was a proper wall, if it was supposed to be there. The effect was like that of an amputation on a living limb. It was a dead end.

Gareth touched his fingers to the cool tiled surface. He was aware of no particular sensation. But a strange feeling was growing inside him, in his stomach and creeping down into his legs. It was fear.

He walked back to the platform, forcing himself not to run, but he passed no other opening on the way. He checked up and down the platform, but there was no other exit as far as he could see.

Movement on the track caught his eye. Moving closer to the edge, he peered into the suicide pit, the space between the rails. He saw it again: a tiny fragment of darkness detaching itself from the background and scuttling away, a mouse.

Then Gareth felt the displacement of air on his face. He looked up but there was nothing to see. The rails began to whine and the turbulence increased. Suddenly, pushing air out of the tunnel ahead of it, a train burst into the empty station at speed. Gareth staggered back from the edge, waiting for the train to stop. But it didn't. It didn't even slow down. Once he had realized it wasn't going to, he started waving his arms in the air and shouting. Not a single passenger caught his eye or reacted in any way. They seemed to stare right through him. Almost as if they were staring at the dark rushing of the tunnel wall.

He watched the red light of the disappearing train with an emptiness growing inside him that felt like death.

Ash told the police that London was built not on clay, as most people believed, but on celluloid. Some of the deeper tube lines bore right through the stuff, he said. Key locations in significant films were not picked at random: location scouts went looking for spots where the material ran close enough to the surface to affect the atmosphere.

His witness statement was not worth the tape it was recorded on.

It had been me who had dragged him into the enquiry after Gareth's girlfriend had called me to say he was missing.

Gareth, he said, had gone looking for a copy of a lost London movie starring Terence Stamp and Theresa Russell. Ash was one of the few people who had seen it. Since it bore no credits, it was impossible to say who had directed it. The presence of Theresa Russell suggested Roeg, but the style was too laidback for him. Ash suspected the hand of Jerzy Skolimowski, although he couldn't say why, and in any case the police didn't give a fuck. They were going to charge him with wasting police time, but when they realized that they would have to get psychiatrists' reports and all that carry-on, they let it drop and Ash was a free man.

Gareth, however, was still missing. His girlfriend was unconsolable. Couldn't I do something, she wanted to know. I'd known Gareth almost as long as she had. Surely I had some idea where he might have gone, where he might have buried himself. I told her I'd do my best, but what did I have to go on? Not a great deal.

I checked out the big homeless areas. I rode the tube system – every line, each station. Once I thought I saw the back of his head at Archway, but I lost him in the crowd and later convinced myself I'd been mistaken. I didn't really know Gareth as well as his girlfriend thought I did. It was more a professional relationship, and a sporadic one at that. I commissioned film reviews off him and various longer pieces. But her need impressed itself upon me.

One night, in the early hours, the phone rang and it was Gareth. At least I thought it was Gareth. It was hard to be sure. His voice sounded a long way off, obscured by static and interference. He kept breaking up. But I managed to pick out the name of a tube station before the line went dead. Russell Square. I was down there at 5:00am, first customer through the gate. I prowled every corridor, bumped up and down in the old lifts. I peered into airshafts furred with years' worth of dead skin.

Nothing. If I'd been hoping to get, at the very least, a sense of Gareth's recently departed presence, I was disappointed there, too. Dejected and worn out, I slumped down on to one of the blue metal seats to wait for the next train. On the seat next to mine was an unlabelled, scuffed video cassette.

I took the tape home and played it. There was nothing on it but static. If I try really hard, after a dozen or so viewings, I imagine I can hear Terence Stamp's voice (the laconic London drawl of *The Hit*, rather than the forced cockney caricature of *The Limey*) struggling to make itself heard over the interference on the soundtrack. Or I convince myself that the snowy picture is about to resolve itself into a tasteful interior shot of Theresa Russell's naked back.

Times when I'm still stuck in front of the screen way into the quiet hours, the bottle on the floor beside me more or less empty, I kid myself the voice I think I can hear is Gareth's, but then I remember Ash's talent for mimicry and reach for the remote. Stop, rewind, play.

CHARLEE JACOB

Flesh of Leaves, Bones of Desire

CHARLEE JACOB HAS PUBLISHED ALMOST 400 poems and around 200 short stories, mostly in the small press. Her first novel, *This Symbiotic Fascination*, appeared in 1998 from Necro Publications. It was nominated for both Bram Stoker and International Horror Guild Awards in the First Novel category. It has recently been reprinted by Leisure Books, who will follow it with her second novel, *Soma*.

Jacob's short story collection, *Dread in the Beast*, was published by Necro in 1999 and the title novella was nominated for a Bram Stoker Award. It was followed by *Up, Out of Cities That Blow Hot and Cold*, released by Delirium Books and also nominated for a Stoker. She has another collection forthcoming from Delirium, *Guises*, and she is currently finishing a third novel, *Vestal*.

"I am one of those people who likes to go out for walks," explains the author, "trying to unkink from extended periods spent sitting at the computer. I use the time to consider various story aspects. One day I was trying to write a Halloween story but was stuck searching for a fresh idea. It was only a few days before October 31st. Strolling around the neighbourhood, I barely glanced at the Halloween decorations people had put out. I'd done quite a few at my own house: rubber bats, fanged rats, screaming skulls, etc.

"Out of the corner of my eye I saw something which startled

me, hung from a tree branch, not swinging for there was no wind. It was red and yellow-brown, slick-looking, like some *piñata* made in the shape of an adult man. Well, right after Halloween would be *El Dia de los Muertos*. It wasn't uncommon to see Day of the Dead decorations in Dallas. This particular object was uncanny, reminding me of a body comprised out of dead vegetation, like some twisted nature god.

"On closer inspection I discovered it was only a regular, life-sized, cut-out cardboard skeleton. But leaves falling from the big oak tree it was hung in were damp from a recent rain. They were stuck everywhere on the bones, between the ribs and through eye sockets. I had only seen it wrong. This was when I got the idea for skeletons of leaf people."

I t was the day which would eventually turn into the night of Halloween that the seller of skeletons came to our town. Obviously intended as decorations for the traditional celebration of good-natured horror, they were immediately more interesting than those plastic or cardboard types which the five-and-dimes sold. They weren't flat, for one thing, but had three dimensions, having been molded out from an intricate form of *papier-mâché* perhaps. The skulls in particular were startling, almost an origami of macabre beauty. These were nothing mass-produced in some far-off Oriental country, created by near-slave labor who didn't even know what Halloween was.

Simonville was not a big place and the foundling strings of bones soon found niches in front yard trees and on broad, covered porches. The mayor, who ran into the skeleton-seller outside of the luncheonette where he habitually went each noon-day, even bought twenty-six to be hung about the park – twenty-six being twice thirteen and somehow appropriate for the light-hearted festival of modern Samhain.

I lived in an apartment so there was no place where I might have put one up. But I noted the skeleton-seller as he took the wheelbarrow from his pickup truck and peddled his bones from place to place. I followed him when he had sold them all, curious as to where he would go. Did he have relatives in Simonville? Would he sleep in his truck that night or in the park where so many of his wares would be shaking in the branches?

He journeyed to the edge of town where the old surgical instrument factory used to be, before the recession and the popular advent of lasers overcoming more antique steel. The building had been empty for twenty years and the overall appearance of it used to cause embarrassed townfolk to insist on its demolition. One day soon, the city fathers kept promising. If the land sold that would be done. Eventually people just stopped complaining. Every window had been broken by children and the glass spiked like the fangs in deformed jack-o-lanterns. The roof sagged like a broken back and had gaping holes in places where the weather had free access to the rooms below. The grounds had grown up with weeds.

He parked his truck and got out and walked over to me. I was, of course, mortified that he'd noticed I was following. But I'd meant nothing unfriendly in it. I always had all day with nothing to do but walk the town, and there was only so much in such a small, unchanging place to keep me from boredom. I hadn't been able to work since the fire. If it hadn't been for the disability checks, what would I have done? I walked Simonville from one end to the other and had done so for years, for so long that nobody even stared at me anymore, having become as used to my scars as they were accustomed to the eyesore of the former instruments factory.

"Yes, this is where I will be staying the night," the skeleton-seller told me, as if answering a question I had never said aloud.

I noticed how incredible his complexion was, smooth and glowing with health. And yet he didn't seem to be a young man, and life out of a pickup truck purveying *faux-squelettes* couldn't have been easy. It made me squirm, standing there with the pocks and ripples of my own devastated skin. It made me envious.

"My year is up. Come see me tonight," he said, then turned away and walked into the dilapidated building.

I wondered what he could have meant by that yet I'd replied with nothing. I'd only swung around because this was the edge of Simonville. I began another predictable journey across the face of the town.

But it had piqued my interest and so I didn't return to my little rooms at day's end. Usually I would never be caught outside after dark on Halloween – not with the mask I always wore.

Instead I walked the streets, keeping to the shadows, a strong sense of impending phenomena keeping me more alert than usual. Children ran from house to house, doing their time-honored begging. The air was as still as it had been all day, suffocating with humidity and the cloying rot of fallen leaves. It was terribly hot for so late in the year, the temperature breaking the old record set back in the last century.

The skeletons hung wherever they had been placed, limp but strangely elegant – considering what they represented. They seemed like vessels waiting to be filled. Sweating in rivulets down the channels of ruined skin, I went up to several and examined them, touching them along the straight lengths of thigh bones, tracing with my fingertips the curves of ribs which slid into such pale hollows. I closed my eyes and imagined these were the bodies of lovers, cool and unblemished, never judging with their lips, never reflecting back cruel mirrors with their eyes.

If I'd believed something would happen when I caressed them, I was sorely disappointed.

The hour grew late and children went home. The adults came out to party, some with heavily-painted faces and a few even costumed for fright soirées hosted at the local bars. Drunken stragglers stumbled down the sidewalks. People who were just too hot indoors came out to walk through the park and look at the stars.

The wind came up sharply. The bones jangled in chimes which could be heard clear across Simonville. I watched as those in the park actually seemed to dance, suspended from the ground, limbs moving in graceful, hovering ballet. The leaves on raked piles on the ground rose up as if burst apart by lightning, then swirled about the skeletons, then clung. Whatever trees still had leaves were finally denuded of them in sudden downdrafts of wind that also blew them onto the skeletons.

I rubbed my eyes. What had been strings of bones were now covered with rustling red and gold skins. Crackling hands reached overhead to break the strings which tied them up. They let themselves down and before I could see where they were going, they'd slipped into the shadows and were gone.

I walked on a bit, leaving the park. On Main Street I spied a drunken man weaving past the shops, his face made up like a vampire. I was close enough I heard the whisper which stirred from the dark doorway of a drug store, medicines for sleep and pain advertised in the filmy windows.

"Trick or treat . . ."

He stopped, looking about him, and a figure stepped from the blackened rectangle. It was a burnished woman, all of sorrel and bronze limbs and breasts, the texture scratchy in the wind. Naked she glided up to him and put her arms around his neck. She lifted herself up, putting her legs around his hips, pressing the soft thatch of her crotch to his groin. For a moment they seemed to dance, turning in autumn tango, her face pressed to his and his breath soughing into her lips. If he resisted her sexual assault he didn't show it.

Then they collapsed to the sidewalk, she continuing to grind against him, his own pelvic thrusts seismic through his clothes. The wind howled, stray leaves skittering in miniature whirlwinds down the street. The drunk made the soft moaning noises of a wounded animal trapped beneath them and then he stopped moving altogether. The woman climbed back to her feet.

I marveled at the appearance of her flesh now, bright under the lamplight, no longer a beautiful-but-uneven patchwork of brittle rouges and aureolin. She had perfected herself and now walked away from the man she'd accosted.

I crept forward and found his suit full of odd, dessicated bones . . . and nothing else.

"Trick or treat," I heard murmured from between parked cars at the hospital. I saw one of the leaf men slide out and wrap himself around a nurse coming off her shift. Her white uniform had been spattered with blood as she exited the building, like the dappling on the leaves of some diseased elm.

His member stood out, a thick twig, forked and throbbing like a dowser's rod. He gently pushed her to the macadam and she didn't scream, didn't struggle. I could hear her sighing, heard it rendered sepulchral like an echo down a well as the leaf man swallowed it. Watched while she tore off her own underthings and guided his branch-flesh into herself. Observed as they undulated for minutes and then he got up from her bones, refined, whole, human – or reasonably so.

I went back into the park, saw two-times-thirteen foliage

bodies of harvest gold and seasonal blood red clasped about a party of revelers who'd left a midnight barbecue to come count meteors. The withered but brilliantly-colored skins rolled obscenely across these people, folks perhaps I even knew. The rustling limbs moved insatiably, carnal boughs which held the shapes of secret femurs and ulnas and clavicles.

I watched with sick fascination, too much heat in my own flesh. I wanted to lie down with them and be a part of what made them smooth and indefective. I wanted to experience that melting closeness of passion and desperation . . . for I could see one or two of the people squirm, hands flailing free from the orgiastic assemblage – as of victims left for dead beneath piles of leaves reaching out.

The appetite boiled, then grew chill in the hard wind. The skeletons were left in the disarray of their various garments. The new people rose and walked off in different directions into Simonville. I wondered where they were going, whose lives they were going to assume. If they would need to replenish themselves ever again and if someday all of the town would be made up of such creatures. I tried to guess what other places were filled either partially or entirely of these artificial folk.

The seller of skeletons had left his keys in his truck. I borrowed it and then drove it back to the old factory. I knocked lightly at the door which hung only by half its rusted hinges.

"Come in," I heard from inside. "I've been waiting for you."

The flawless man smiled as I entered the building. Here and there beneath the shadows and dust were glints of razor-sharp metal once used to make scalpels with. A rack of needles gleamed in a corner where moonlight stabbed through one of the rents in the roof. For a moment I almost mistook them for pine needles instead of the business ends of hypos.

"I've brought all the skeletons in the back of the truck," I told him.

I'd been amazed while doing so how light the bones were, how peculiar their substance. They hadn't seemed like human bones at all. The essence was neither dense nor porous and didn't appear to be anything associated with vertibrate beings. This seemed to indicate that something essential had been drained from them, metamorphosing into what more clearly resembled *papier-mâché*.

He nodded as if this was what he'd expected of me.

"It's . . . it's my turn, isn't it?" I asked, feeling a little humiliated because I knew my voice had a pleading quality to it. Oh, I was so afraid of being rejected.

"Yes, this will be your year," he replied. He stripped off his peddler's clothes, the glow of his polished skin almost so good it hurt my eyes.

I stripped and rushed forward to let him love me, to allow him to shrivel away in our erotic harvest. I felt his erection of smooth muscle come up between us and then fall away into a twig, semen a spurt of vegetation spore and then dust. The wet sponge of his tongue became a parched leaf against mine.

As for me, my bones rang with desire. I could sense a resonance all the way down to my marrow. I trembled giving my scars, hearing everything which descends in autumn shaking, brittle or reborn in the wind.

TIM LEBBON

The Repulsion

TIM LEBBON'S RECENT BOOKS INCLUDE *As The Sun Goes Down*, *Hush* (co-written with Gavin Williams), *The Nature of Balance* and the British Fantasy Award-winning *White* (about to be optioned by a London-based production company). Forthcoming titles include the novel *Face* from Night Shade Books; *Until She Sleeps*, a short novel from Cemetery Dance, and several more collections and novels.

His recent short fiction has appeared in *Best New Horror*, *The Year's Best Fantasy & Horror*, *October Dreams*, *Cemetery Dance* and online at *SciFi.com*. Lebbon also writes a regular horror column for *At the World's End* and is currently Vice-President of the Horror Writers Association.

"I wrote 'The Repulsion' whilst on holiday in Amalfi, Italy," recalls the author. "The whole place had a profound effect on me; it's so steeped in history that it almost oozes from the walls, you can taste the past and feel it in the breeze that flows along the alleyways. There really is a sign saying FOLLOW THE ANCIENT STEPS, and I did follow them, wondering just where they may take me. The sounds of tourism disappeared and for a while I was in Amalfi as it really was, and although the feeling was quite exhilarating it was also a relief when I emerged into the central square once more.

"That evening, sitting on my hotel balcony with a bottle of local red wine, I wrote the first draft of this story. I imagined how easy it must be to get so wrapped up in the feel of Amalfi that you lose yourself there. Lucky for me, I made it home."

A s they rounded a bend in the road and the whole majesty of Amalfi was laid out before them, Dean knew that it was over. He grabbed Maria's hand and she squeezed back in surprise.

It was their second attempt at loving each other. Dean had the feeling that trying to make it work again would be like buying a new version of a favourite shirt – the original would always be special, however much the second looked, smelled and felt like the first. They had been travelling for ten hours and each time he glanced sideways at Maria, he knew her less.

The minibus wound its way down the cliff road, the driver tooting at nothing, other horns blaring in response. Mopeds chased each other through the traffic like dogs in heat, their drivers cool in shades and shirtsleeves. Pedestrians took their lives in their hands and walked along the roads, bending sideways and holding in their stomachs to allow for wing mirrors.

"Busy place," Dean said. Maria glanced at him and smiled, but she did not reply. He caught a whiff of her perfume, mixed in with the stale scents of a dozen hours of travelling. Obsession. It gave him a headache.

When they had been on holiday before, the arrival at the resort and the discovery of the hotel was often something of a let-down, an anti-climax propagated by tiredness and dislocation. Today, however, it was not the same. Maria waltzed into the hotel ahead of him, her jaunty step raising a nostalgic desire rather than the real thing. When Dean reached her with their suitcases she was chatting to the woman at reception, laughing, joking, excluding him even more. The woman looked at Dean and smiled sadly, as if she could see through the charade.

"Please," she said, "leave your bags here. They will be brought up to you. We have a lovely room for you, sea view, balcony with a wonderful romantic view of the town and harbour."

Dean smiled at Maria, and she smiled back. "Okay?" he asked.

"Yep. Here at last. At last." She followed the woman.

Their room was big, sparsely furnished, floored with old marble and opening out onto a large balcony. The doors were already clipped open, outside table set for a meal as if the previous residents had only just left. Dean could smell them in the air: a hint of aftershave; the incongruous scent of pine shampoo. He tipped the receptionist and fell onto the bed, burying his face in the pillow, breathing in deeply. Old smells; soap powder; dead dreams

"Shall we go out, have a look around?" Maria asked.

Dean was tired and jaded and suddenly, for no apparent reason, he wanted to be back home. Hopelessness rumbled in his stomach, tingled his skin.

"Dean?"

He nodded. "Sure." He sensed her perfume again. It smelled like someone else had bought it for her, and he knew that they had already failed.

The road took them past the front of the hotel and down to the town square, where it sat facing the ocean; hundreds of people, tourists and locals alike, sat outside cafés and bars doing likewise. Waiters buzzed them like black and white bees, balancing impossibly large trays on unfeasibly splayed fingers.

Dean suggested a beer, but Maria wanted to get away from the tourist areas immediately. He followed her lead, wishing they could be walking side by side instead of in single file. As he was not holding her hand his own ached for something to do, so he lit up a cigarette.

"Thought you were going to give up on this holiday?" Maria said, glancing back at the sound of the match popping alight.

"Thought we were going to be together this holiday," Dean retorted. He tried on a smile to take the edge off his voice, but the damage was already done. Maria shrugged, turned and started towards an arched walkway between two shops.

As they strolled, the streets began to lose themselves in darkened alleyways. Washing overhung the paths like sleeping bats, dripping soapy saliva to the ground. Traffic argued at roundabouts, and the sea purred onto the beach, constantly, relentlessly. Between buildings they could see up to the cliff tops, where ruined churches or Saracen watchtowers commanded wise old views of the sea and town. The whole place oozed history, wallowing in its past; each slab in the path possessed a million untold stories. And it was hot. The sun splashed from whitewashed walls and twisted its way behind Dean's sunglasses.

They saw only locals, as if this were the real Amalfi and the chaos of the square was there only to appease marketing managers at package tour operators. Sometimes the people they passed would nod a curt greeting, other times Dean felt unseen. They walked for twenty minutes without emerging from the warren of alleys and paths. Steps led up and down again, and more than once Dean was certain that they had crossed their own path from a different direction.

It was strange how the wonder of the place touched them individually and distinctly, as if its magic sought to emphasise the bad air between them. Sometimes it was almost physical, an impenetrable barrier forcing them apart like similar magnetic poles. Amalfi had so much to offer; Dean and Maria took their fill of different things.

"I'm hungry," Dean said. "Airline meals don't do much to fill you up. Pizza?"

"If you like." Maria stopped and leant over a fountain, its outlet concealed in the groin of a five hundred year old stone boy. Damp circles had marked her blouse beneath her arms, and a haze of perspiration clung to the fine hairs on her top lip. She used to sweat like that when they were making love.

They turned around, and it seemed natural for Dean to lead the way back. At some point – he could not really tell when – the echoes of two sets of footsteps turned into one. When he looked over his shoulder Maria had vanished.

"Mi!" It seemed all right to use his familiar name for her now that she might not hear it. "You hiding?" He walked back up the path, glancing at closed doors. When he looked between buildings he could no longer see the cliffs; now, there was only sky. A flight of worn stairs curved down from higher up and he could hear hesitant footsteps descending, but their owner never arrived.

Street noises appeared from nowhere, and within a few strides he found himself back at the edge of the main square. He glanced back, confused, and then he saw Maria sitting on the steps of the huge cathedral. She stood when he approached and walked back towards their hotel, hardly acknowledging his presence. He was sure that if he were to stop and sit down for a drink, she would walk all the way back to their room without noticing.

"Maria," he called.

She waited for him, running her hands over strings of red chillies hanging outside a shop. When she looked up her eyes were hard and distant.

"Where did you get to?" Dean said. "I was worried."

"Why?"

"You vanished. One second you were there, the next I couldn't find you."

"I was behind you all the time," she sighed, turning and walking away. She had not even tried to hide the fact that she was lying.

By the end of that first afternoon, when they returned to their room to get ready for dinner, they were strangers. Maria went into the bathroom and closed the door to shower and change.

The food was fantastic. Throughout their several years together, Dean and Maria had always put good cuisine at the top of their list of priorities when choosing their holidays. If they wanted a beach, it would have to be near a good restaurant. A hotel, though it may have health suite, rooftop gardens and apartment-sized rooms, was only as good as its chef.

Dean ate without tasting. He was thinking of those few minutes earlier in the day when Maria had been lost to him, trying to analyze his emotions and convince himself that he had been scared, not quietly, selfishly pleased. They had come here to be together, but alone was much more comfortable. Even now Maria's mind was far beyond these four walls. Dean could see it every time he looked at her.

When a waiter trundled over with the sweet trolley Dean was subject to a sudden, weird moment of utter optimism, one of those rare flushes of rapture that strike all too seldom and are as difficult to keep a hold of as a lover's gasp. He smiled, tapped his fingers on the table, glad to be alive and confident that everything was going to turn out all right. He looked at Maria, grinning, and he was about to tell her how lovely she was when she spoke.

"Have you ever come face to face with yourself?" she said. "Ever really seen yourself from someone else's point of view? It's the most humbling thing I can ever imagine."

Dean felt the moment leave him, bleeding away like blood from a stuck pig. "Are we going to really try this week?" he said. "I mean, really? Look at this place, Maria. It's our perfect holiday. It's as if we were drawn here to . . . give it one last go. Are we?"

Maria shrugged, stared into her glass of red wine as if trying to define a truth in there. "Maybe some things are more important," she said.

"Where did you go today? Before I found you in the square?"

"I want to go to bed," she said suddenly, and Dean was shocked by her paleness. "Take me to bed." On any other occasion – weeks, maybe months ago – this plea would have stirred him in other ways. Now it merely made him afraid.

They went up in the rickety lift and Maria waited for Dean to unlock the door. She leant against the wall in the hallway, fingers splayed against the cold plaster as if reading its history. She did not even undress before flopping onto the bed and stretching her way into a deep sleep.

Dean opened the doors and went out onto the balcony. The thought of going inside and lying next to Maria, perhaps naked, perhaps with love in mind, now seemed alien and foolish. However much he tried to convince himself otherwise, their relationship was still a shadow of its former self, and coming here could have been a big mistake. If there had been some serious misdemeanour it would be simpler, but in reality it was simply a matter of things growing stale. Neither of them wanted to be the one finally to pull the plug.

He lit a cigarette, inhaled deeply and watched the smoke haze away in the dark, picked up briefly by the lights from the harbour. It was a noisy night in Amalfi, straining scooter motors underlying the aimless car horns that seemed to spring out of nowhere, and unknown conversations were shouted through the dark. He could sense rather than see bats jerking about in the night, dipping and weaving like points of black light thrown from a negative torch. From inside he heard the toilet gurgling its displeasure at someone flushing elsewhere in the hotel. Outside again, a splash as something fell into, or jumped out of the water down below, confident of safety under cover of night.

He stood to go to the loo. The cigarette had burned down and fused itself to his two fingers, but he felt no pain. In the bathroom Maria stood before the full length mirror, naked, a breast in each hand. Her nipples were pink and risen, as if recently pinched.

"Have you ever come face to face with yourself?" she asked, turning to look at him. Seconds later her reflection followed suit. Its eyes were not her eyes. They were eyes painted by a bad artist, unable to follow him around the room, shallow and soulless. "Am I asleep?" the reflection said. "I've pinched, but I don't wake up."

A pain in his fingers pinched Dean and jerked him from sleep, and for a couple of seconds he did not even know which country he was in. He dropped the cigarette butt and stomped it to death, hissing as he felt the blister already rising on his index finger. Shaking, he went in from the balcony and shut the doors, locking out the night. Maria was naked on the bed, covers screwed around her waist. Her nipples were soft and pink.

After running cool water over his fingers Dean stripped and climbed into bed next to Maria. There was no warmth to share with her; not because she was cold, but because he could not imagine cuddling as they once had.

The next day they were booked on a boat trip to Capri; Dean had thought that exploring together may encourage sparks from the dying embers of their love. Now, the most he could hope for was a smile for old times. And he realized, in a moment of shocking clarity, that he really didn't know Maria that well at all. He was unaware of her past, other than what she had chosen to tell him. If she had problems, maybe he had not even discovered them yet. If she had always wanted to come here, and she did not want him to know . . . then he never would.

Maria rose late and readied herself as if still half asleep. They had breakfast brought to their room but Dean ate it alone on the balcony. He kept glancing into the room at Maria, watching her move slowly across the marble floor as she searched both suitcases for some elusive item of clothing. She looked up, saw him staring and smiled, a vague twitching of the lips which was still better than he had had all day yesterday.

He went back to his strong coffee, unsettled by the notion that she had not been smiling *at* him at all, but *past* him.

They were already late when they left the room. Dean was a constant ten steps ahead on their walk down to the harbour. He glanced at his watch every few seconds, trying to will the minute hand back fifteen minutes to before the time when they were due to leave. Passing through the square they heard the hooting horn of a boat, and a huge catamaran turned gently away from the pier.

"Come on!" he shouted, hurrying towards the boat, knowing already that they had missed it. He slowed and stopped, aware that dozens of people watching him. "Have a good time," he muttered, then turned back to Maria.

She was standing with her back to him, facing into the square. She brushed hair back from her face, her short dress stretching around her hips as she did so. She was a beautiful woman, but now Dean felt only a nebulous anger, and a certainty that she had made them miss the boat on purpose.

"Well," he said as he approached her from behind, "looks like we're stuck here today. You could have just said you didn't want to go."

"I thought it was obvious," Maria said. "Besides, now we can explore the town in detail. We only scratched the surface yesterday."

"Didn't you want to see Capri?"

Maria shrugged. "Maybe. But we're here now. There's so much history here. Can't you feel it? Can't you breathe in the old times? I can almost see them . . . Come on, Deano. We can still make a day of it."

It was the first time she had used her nickname for him since they had left home yesterday morning, and it went some way to quashing his disappointment. But as she walked on ahead of him, heading for a shady corner of the square, he could not help scrutinizing how she had said it. The more he replayed it in his mind, the more he became sure that she had forced it to make him happy.

He felt used, manipulated, putty in the hands of an imaginative child. He wondered what shape she would twist him into next.

They came to an alley leading off from the square, so hidden beneath the old buildings of the town that it would never be touched by the sun. A sign screwed to the wall above said FOLLOW THE ANCIENT STEPS, the script gnarled-looking where decades of heat had chipped the paint. The path curved out of sight no more than a dozen paces in. Without looking back Maria walked on.

For an instant, Dean considered not going after her. He would go back into the square, buy a beer, sit down and light a cigarette, watching the world go by as he waited for Maria to return. Then the moment passed, and Maria was little more than a shadow moving away from him. He followed.

"It's a beautiful place," he said, not really believing himself. Maria mumbled an incoherent reply. "I wonder who lives back here?" He did not want to know, and again there was only a vague response from Maria. The walls were swallowing her words.

He was looking down at the path most of the time, making sure he did not trip over a loose stone or step in the occasional splash of dog mess. He should not have been surprised when he looked up to find Maria no longer there; should not have been, but was, because there was nowhere she could have gone.

He thought about going back, but feared he may be nearer the end of the path than the beginning.

Smells and sounds pulsed in and out, as if Dean were moving to and fro in reality. He guessed that it was some strange quality of the maze-like construction of this place, that even sound and scent would become momentarily lost between buildings. It became darker still and looking up he could see eaves reaching across the alley like long-lost lovers craving a final touch.

He turned a corner and suddenly found himself back with civilization. Soon he was among people again, standing at the edge of a one way street used by loud two way traffic, happy to hold back and watch the hustle while he gathered his thoughts. He had found no ancient steps. Indeed, there had been no steps in the alley at all.

No side-alleys, either.

No open doors.

Where had Maria gone?

He felt a rush of unreality blur his senses – a mixture of nausea, dizziness and the urge to giggle at the absurdities around him. He sat down at a table and barked a laugh when a menu was forced into his hands. There were three women chatting away at the next table, oblivious to the noise around them, and when he strained to hear what they were saying he could not identify their language. It could have been a new one. The waiter wafted by with a casual glare; Dean ordered a pizza for appearance sake, a beer for his throat and a red wine for Maria. Then he waited for her to come back to him.

He was finishing his unwanted meal when she scraped back a chair and sat down. She did not reach for her wine, but sat there staring through her fringe at the ground.

"Maria," he said, "where have you been? I've been worried."

"I doubt that," she said, but there was no reproach there. It was merely a statement of fact. Her mouth twitched, as if haunted by the memory of a smile.

The three women had been replaced by a short, athletic-looking American, sitting with her back to them, mobile phone pressed to her ear like a field dressing. "I'm concerned about what will happen if I come home right now," Dean heard her say. "I worry about the kids. I don't want to subject you to the strangeness I'm going through right now."

He turned back to Maria and stroked her arm, but it felt as alien as kissing a bus driver on the cheek. He withdrew his hand, embarrassed, sure that everyone in the street would see through the sham.

"Shall we go back to the hotel?" he said. "Or another walk. An ice cream?"

"All right," Maria said and, not knowing which suggestion she had agreed to, Dean followed her into the thronging street.

The American woman had left, apparently without paying. The waiter seemed unconcerned. Her table was already set for the next customer.

They spent the rest of the day by the pool, not talking, lying back and letting the sun slowly burn their skin. Dean tried to read but he could not concentrate. He kept glancing sideways at the woman he had used to love, watching her chest rise and fall with peaceful breaths, certain that behind her glasses her eyes were wide open. Her skin remained pale.

Maria had always been lively, inquisitive, sometimes too much so for Dean. He was happy to sit in and watch the television, open a bottle of wine, cook a nice meal. Maria would want to know who the director was, find out where the wine came from and search out an alternate recipe for whatever they were eating. He'd often tell her to sit back and enjoy, not worry about things. Loosen up.

She had loosened up now. She was so loose she was almost flapping in the wind. She was not the Maria he had used to know, but then that Maria had been leaving him for a long time, so that did not trouble him so much. What troubled him was that she was becoming a woman he had *never* known.

Later, at dinner, Dean tried to catch Maria's attention and smile, attempted to edge her into conversation, but all talk was one-sided.

They went straight to their room after the meal. Maria lay on the bed and seemed to fall asleep instantly. Dean bent over her and lowered himself to within kissing distance, trying to breathe in her scent, recall when they had used to kiss. But her breath was insipid and untainted, and as light as a sigh hitting his face. Her perfume only gave out a ten-hour staleness.

He stayed that way for a while, hoping she would look up at him, but there was no movement beneath her ivory eyelids.

Eventually he moved out onto the balcony and lit up a cigarette, closing his eyes and enjoying the light-headedness of wine and nicotine. He listened to the sounds from the town, trying but failing to pick out single voices.

Three cigarettes later, when he went back into the room, he was not surprised to find it empty. Maria had not even worn her shoes when she left; they lay on the floor next to the bed, looking as if they had never been owned.

Dean curled up on the bed. Maria had gone of her own accord, of that he was sure. He was also sure that he had let her go too easily.

He slept within minutes. A loud, insistent thump echoed its way into his dreams; a door opening and shutting deep inside the hotel, or perhaps a trapdoor. Voices mumbled in distant rooms, or from somewhere else entirely. Footsteps forever promised to suddenly increase their volume and darken the strip of light beneath the door. It was a night pregnant with the promise of something happening, but in the end potential was aborted. Dean slept long and deep, and when he woke up the sun was shining through the still-open balcony doors.

Guilt grabbed him and would not let go. Maria had not returned, her suitcase still lay open, its contents hauled out like luggage intestines. She could be anywhere, she could be in trouble.

She could be nowhere.

Have you ever come face to face with yourself?

Without changing or washing Dean hurried from the hotel, hardly sparing a glance for the surprised receptionist. He almost ran down the road, and he was glad that the bustle of the rush hour camouflaged his concern. The place felt even more impersonal than it had the previous day, but he put it down to being alone. Even though he and Maria had really had no hope at all, at least they had been in each other's company. Their time together may be doomed, but the past still held a charge. They would always have a history. There would always be a story to tell.

He found himself in the corner of the square without really thinking about where he was going. FOLLOW THE ANCIENT STEPS the sign said, and within thirty seconds of entering the alleyway, he had found them. They had not been there before, he was sure, but everything lately had been all a-tangle, and he could so easily have missed them the first time. They were dusty and cobwebbed with underuse, the shadows beneath their risers soupy with age. Dean started up them without hesitation, subconsciously sniffing at the air for Maria's perfume but knowing it had changed beyond his ken. Even if he did find her, it could mean nothing. She may be where she wanted to be.

He came face to face with himself. His double was as shocked as he, and they both raised their hands in fright. His opposite's eyes were sunken, full of a deep-set hopelessness, but then he realized that he was facing a mirrored door. He felt foolish, even though he was alone. Alone, but perhaps not unwatched.

The steps ended in a courtyard. The sun was almost directly overhead, but the area was still swathed in shadow. It was timeless, echoing with sighs uttered centuries ago, its walls bathed in history and stained by it. The graffiti of ages, chips and cracks and the words of eloquent vandals. Shuttered windows stared down like the closed eyes of the dead.

Maria was there . . . but she was not. Her perfume hung heavy in the air, fresh and vibrant. He knew what she was thinking, though he could not see her. He knew, suddenly, of the times before they had met: the hurried drug-taking in train station toilets; the bursts of temper at her parents, unreasonable but more intense because of that; kicking her pet dog when it had stained her carpet, kicking until it bled. He knew her mind in more detail than he ever had, and this made him sad. Now, of all times, he could try to love her fully. She had what she wanted, and he was glad, but it also made him sorrowful. It meant that they had failed. Their time together really was at an end.

He turned and fled, coolness stroking his back as he staggered down the dusty steps. It felt like fingernails of ice piercing his skin, leaving him an invisible scar to remind him of where he had been, and where Maria remained. He would always be troubled by this place but he hoped, selfishly, that in his dreams he would somehow lose his way.

He saw no mirrored doors.

And as he arrived back in the square, he knew that during the loneliest of nights he would find those steps once more.

DENNIS ETCHISON

The Detailer

DENNIS ETCHISON HAS BEEN CALLED "the most original living horror writer in America" (*The Viking-Penguin Encyclopedia of Horror and the Supernatural*) and "the finest writer of psychological horror this genre has produced" (Karl Edward Wagner in *The Year's Best Horror Stories*).

His stories have appeared in numerous periodicals and anthologies since 1961, and some of the best have been collected in *The Dark Country* (1982), *Red Dreams* (1984), *The Blood Kiss* (1987), *The Death Artist* (2000) and the forthcoming *Got to Kill Them All and Other Stories* and the e-collection *Fine Cuts*. *Talking in the Dark* (2001) is a retrospective volume marking the fortieth anniversary of his first professional sale.

He is also well-known as a novelist (*The Fog, Darkside, Shadowman, California Gothic* and *Double Edge*) and an editor (*Cutting Edge, Masters of Darkness I-III, MetaHorror*, the HWA anthology *The Museum of Horrors*, and *Gathering the Bones*, the latter co-edited with Ramsey Campbell and Jack Dann).

His other novels include *Halloween II, Halloween III* and *Videodrome*, all written under the pseudonym "Jack Martin". He has won two World Fantasy Awards and three British Fantasy Awards.

"I live in Los Angeles, where the automobile rules," explains Etchison. "Here car culture has influenced every aspect of human life – not only the construction of freeways and the roads and streets and highways that must feed them but the shape and geography of Southern California and the very existence of towns and cities, which seem to spring up, evolve and disappear from our maps to serve the needs of the internal combustion engine.

"I once wrote a science fiction story called 'The Machine Demands a Sacrifice', imagining L.A. in a state of permanent gridlock, a full-fledged nightmare in metal; but that future became passé long ago. The question remains, however: What has this way of life really done to us? Is the smog, the pollution something that can be washed away, or has it penetrated our skins more deeply than we realize? And if so, what if anything can be done about it?

"As always, I believe the answer begins with the individual, with what remains pure and incorruptible in a single human heart."

P aulino was whistling by the time he got to work.
     He could not remember the name of the song. It had started running through his head as soon as the alarm went off, and then he heard it in the shower and all through breakfast. When Rosalie asked him why he was so happy he told her he didn't know, but he kept on hearing the song until finally he began to whistle. He had to let it out, like steam.

On the way the streets were jammed and the air was so brown that the sun was only a pale, dirty glint. He kept his window rolled up and tried to think of the words but he could not get the first line.

Ruben was in the driveway of the Palm Vista Car Wash, setting out the *Yes, We're Ready for Your Dirt* sign. He had a blue towel in the pocket of his clean white jumpsuit and an expression on his face that would not give him away. Paulino rolled the window down.

"Little Paulie," said Ruben.

"O Rosalinda – she won, right?"

"Yeah, by a nose."

Paulino grinned and turned up the driveway. He parked his Ford Escort and hurried back to the building, whistling louder than ever. Ruben was inside at the snack machines.

"How much?"

"Twelve-to-one," said Ruben.

"All right!"

"I had forty . . ."

"And forty for me."

"But, see, I got there late. The race already started. They closed the window."

"*No la!*"

Ruben fumbled coins into the soda machine, missed the Pepsi button and hit Mr Pibb instead.

"I'll pay you back."

"You don't even have my forty?"

"My kids, they ate a lot of crap. Two-fifty for a hot dog. Plus nachos and Cokes. You know."

Paulino turned away, went to another machine and waited while a paper cup dropped and filled with coffee. He stirred in some creamer, breathing the steam while it cooled. Then he heard the water come on and the shammies start to move in the car wash tunnel. When he felt the rhythm through the thick soles of his shoes he thought of the song again. He could still make it out over the wet, grinding rhythm.

"Okay, *compá*," he said. "Friday for sure . . ."

But Ruben was already outside, guiding the first car onto the automated track. It was an Isuzu Rodeo so new it glistened before it got to the jets.

Paulino finished the coffee, punched his time card and put on his jumpsuit.

He saw the Rodeo disappear as the wall of shammies closed over the back end. Then foam spurted as the soap hit the rear tires. The sidewalls were black and gleaming and there was still a dealer card in the license plate holder. This one was not ready to be washed. The paint had not even set. It only needed a dusting to take off the pollution from the air.

But at Palm Vista the customer was king.

He looked around to see who owned it. Several people already had receipts from the glass office. He recognized a half-dozen regulars, businessmen and college students and mothers on their way back from the elementary school, ready to start the week off right.

There was Mrs McLintock, who took such good care of her old Pontiac that it shone even in the overcast. Jason, the kid with the Cabrio and the UCLA parking permit. And Cheryl, who had a smile to match her bright yellow Beetle. She spent a lot of time at the beach, he knew, because there was always sand in the floor mats. And Mr Travis, who had just traded up his Camry for an Audi A4. Paulino wondered how he liked it.

He would have to ask.

It cost nothing to make conversation with the customers, and besides, Mr Travis was his friend. They all were. They called him by name, telling him to be careful about the grocery bags in the back seat and could he make sure to get the rearview mirror because it fogged up last night on the way home and they almost had an accident. When he did these special things for them they tipped him extra, and when they forgot he would talk about something else till they remembered, and if they didn't have any small bills he would tell them to catch him next time and they usually did. It was only fair. He listened to their problems and did his best to make them happy and that was worth something. A clean car gave them another chance at life. They understood that and kept coming back. This morning the sedans and station wagons and sport utility vehicles were backed up into the alley. They could hardly wait.

A new customer was hanging around the tables, a salesman in a short-sleeved dress shirt and polyester tie with blue and white stripes. He kept checking his watch. That's the one with the Rodeo, Paulino thought. It has to be. He looks like he just started a new job and he's worried sick about making a good impression. Well, you can relax, *vato*. I'm ready to straighten your tie and wash behind your ears and polish your chrome before you go out into the world. Leave it to Paulie.

He picked up his detail kit and walked down to the other end of the tunnel to meet the Rodeo when it came out.

Ruben was inside with Manny and the others, sponging the hubcaps as the vehicle went by, wiping the grille and the door handles till they shone like liquid silver. The next car was moving up behind it, Cheryl's Beetle with the happy face front-end. Paulino watched the Rodeo pass under the hot-wax nozzles, then got into the front seat and steered it over the blacktop to the vacuum hoses.

He set the brake, suctioned the new floor mats and polished the mirror and instrument panel while he waited for the water to drain off the hood. He checked the ashtray, saw a few coins and a paperclip there and slid it back in without disturbing them, then sprayed silicone protectant over the dash and rubbed it to a deep luster. That was an extra. The salesman had only paid for a basic wash and hot wax, but Paulino knew he would appreciate it. Cheryl's car always got the same treatment. She never paid for detailing, either. But if he and Rosalie had a daughter he hoped she would grow up with a smile just like that.

He climbed out of the Rodeo and set to work on the rubber trim before the water spots burned in, and heard music again.

It was not the same song. This time there was a heavy, throbbing bass line, very close by. He glanced up, almost expecting to see a thunderhead on the horizon behind the marquee. The moveable letters spelled out this week's slogan, *No Job's Too Dirty for Us*. Beyond that he saw only the power lines and the signal lights at the corner and the hot disk of the sun about to break through the smog. The pressure in his ears grew stronger.

He looked out at the smear of cars on the street, locked bumper-to-bumper as the traffic inched past. A Buick Regal and a Crown Vic LTD pulled even at the red light, sub-woofers booming, shaking the hoods with each beat like two hearts at war. The radios drowned out the song in his mind. He turned his back on the street and hunkered down behind the Rodeo, sprayed Armor All on the molded bumper, and wondered why Rosalie never woke up with music in her head.

There was no time for that, she had said in the kitchen, especially not on a Monday. What was wrong with him? Did he think she liked spending all day cleaning other people's houses? The things they left for her were disgusting, things they wouldn't touch themselves, things she had never thought she'd have to touch when she came here, after he had promised her so much. Well, he said, maybe you should go home and visit your family for a week, two weeks, he didn't care, and that was what tore it. When she started crying he did not say anything else. She would not even let him kiss her when he dropped her off.

He finished wiping down the Rodeo.

Ruben was working on the yellow Beetle, Manny had the Audi and Craig was about to start on Mrs McLintock's cherry Pontiac. She was already opening her purse for a tip that could have been Paulino's. He hoped she and Mr Travis and Cheryl did not think he was avoiding them. If he had not spent so much time on the

Rodeo he would be ready. The line moved forward and two more cars from the alley were about to enter the tunnel.

The salesman checked his watch nervously and shifted his weight in tight brown shoes. Paulino ran his towel over the windows, brushed out the front seat, waved him over and handed him the keys.

The salesman got in without a word.

"Nice car," said Paulino.

The salesman inserted his key.

"You want to be careful with that clear-coat, though. It scratches real easy." Paulino closed the door in slow motion, holding onto it as long as he could. "You put on some sealer and glaze, you won't have to worry."

"It's a lease," said the salesman.

"Yeah, well, just the same, I'd get a full detail. Say every sixty to ninety days. You need it around here."

"Thanks for the advice."

"Hey, no problem. Just ask for Paulie."

The salesman got the message. He reached into his pocket and pulled out a dollar bill before he turned the key.

"I'll think about it."

"I only use Mother's Gold." Paulino winked and showed the man his teeth. "One-hundred-percent pure carnauba. Guaranteed."

The salesman started the engine and drove away.

Paulino saw Craig folding paper money into his pocket and thought, I should get some cards printed up. It wouldn't cost much. Plain white business cards, with my name, and underneath that *The Detailer*. And maybe my phone number, too, so I can make house calls on my day off. Why not?

He picked up his kit.

On the way to the glass office he asked Mrs McLintock how she was doing today. She beamed as if he were her favorite son. He said hello to Mr Travis, who told him the A4 was the best car he had ever owned. When he came up behind Cheryl she was digging out some loose change for Manny.

"How's the Vee-Dub?"

"Great! Hi, Paulie. I missed you!"

"You oughta let me get those wheels."

"Well . . ."

Paulino frowned. "See, they're alloy. All that nitrous from the diesels, it wrecks the aluminum. If you don't do nothing about it, you got a problem. I can put on some Wheel Brite . . ."

"I'm late for class. Will you be here, um, Thursday?"

"Sure. Any time."

"Cool. See you then!"

She grinned and gave a little wave with her fingers.

At the office he held his kit up so Linda the cashier could see the cans of wax and polish through the glass and shrugged at her. She pointed to the job board and shook her head. No one had signed up for detailing so far, just washes and spray wax.

It was going to be a slow morning.

He took a copy of the *Times* from the counter and went back to see who else was waiting. Mr Nolan was at the tables, sipping black coffee and eating a donut from the Winchell's on the corner. His Geo Metro had not been hand-waxed all year. Paulino was about to bring him the newspaper, when he spotted a metallic grey Lexus LX420 in the driveway. It had just moved forward from the alley and was next in line.

That would be Mrs Ellsworth.

He smiled and gave her the high sign.

When there was no response he went to the driveway and stood before the tinted windshield, motioning for her to get out so he could take it the rest of the way. 4SUZIE, said the license plate on the front bumper. He knew whose it was without looking. The vehicle came in once a week like clockwork.

The door opened and a man with dark glasses climbed down.

"Oh," said Paulino. "Morning, Mr Ellsworth. The usual?"

"Not this time."

"You don't want the wash and hot wax?"

"Give me the works."

Paulino was confused. "You mean a full detail?"

The man nodded and pushed his glasses farther up his nose so that no part of his eyes showed. "Get this baby clean, inside and out."

Paulino had given the Lexus a complete detail only last Monday, when Mrs Ellsworth brought it in right on schedule. A perfect layer of wax still showed through the mud spatters on the fenders. There was some dirt clinging to the sidewalls that would come off as soon as the spray hit them. But the customer was king.

"It'll take about an hour . . ."

"I'll wait."

Mr Ellsworth had never waited around for the detailing. When he first got the Lexus he used to drop it off on Mondays and his wife would drive him the rest of the way to his office in the LS400, but after a while he started taking the sedan so that she could use the sport utility. She brought the LX420 in every week for a wash and one Monday a month for a detail. It was her responsibility now, not his.

"Okay," said Paulino, to be sure he understood. "Wheels, trim, upholstery, hand-wax . . ."

"Forget the wax."

"Steam-clean the engine?"

Mr Ellsworth shook his head impatiently. "I don't give a damn. Just make everything look fresh as a daisy. Got it?"

"Yes, sir," said Paulino.

"You'll take care of it for me." The man slipped a hundred-dollar bill out of his wallet. "Won't you."

"Sure, Mr Ellsworth." Without the hand-wax and steam-clean, that was more than enough. A lot more. Paulino took the bill and started for the office. "I'll get your change."

"The car, first."

"No problem." It was too early for Paulino to break a large bill. He would take it in to Linda when he finished. "Did you have a nice vacation?"

"What?"

"Triangle Lake."

"How do you know about that?"

"Mrs Ellsworth . . ." Paulino faltered. "She said you were going on a trip. For the weekend."

"We didn't go anywhere."

"Oh, too bad. I hear it's really great up there. All those trees and everything. Some other time, huh?"

The man pushed his glasses up his nose again, so hard that his hand trembled.

"There was no trip."

"Yes, sir, Mr Ellsworth."

Paulino put his kit in the back seat and got behind the wheel. As he steered the car forward the front wheels made contact with the track and the strips of wet cloth began to sway from side to side. Then the rollers tripped the sensor and the first nozzles sprayed foam at the tires.

He saw the next line of flaps closing over the Metro ahead of him as the ceiling jets went on. The water was a falling black mist in the tunnel. He felt himself drawn into the darkness, heard the wet ratcheting of the machinery all around and checked to see that the windows were tightly closed, then remembered to get out now before it was too late. Otherwise he would have to ride it out to the end, trapped. This was not Paulino's job. He was the one who finished up after the heavy dirt had been washed away. Let the others take care of that. His work was to make things pretty again, at least the parts that showed. He opened the door and jumped down before the shammies touched the windshield.

He stepped around Manny, heading for the square of daylight at the end of the tunnel.

"Where's Suzie Q?"

"Mrs Ellsworth?"

"The Body!" said Manny. He had to shout over the hissing water. "The one with the headlights!"

"She didn't come in."

As the sport utility vehicle crept by, Ruben snapped his rag at a crust of dirt on the tailpipe. "Aw, I been waiting all week!"

"Maybe she's sick," said Paulie.

"Or she got a new boyfriend!"

"Too much dick last night!" said Craig.

They laughed.

Paulino made his way through the tunnel and waited for the sport utility to roll off the track. Then he started it up and drove a few feet to the hoses.

He did not like to hear them talk that way. Mrs Ellsworth had posed for some magazines a few years ago but it stopped when she got married. She was a nice person. She always stood around even in her high heels and talked to him while she waited. They had some good conversations. On the Mondays when he did the detailing he had a chance to learn all about her.

He removed the beads of water with a clean blue towel, then opened the doors and got started with the vacuum.

She probably told him too much. About her marriage, for example. Paulino knew it was not going great. That was easy to understand. Sometimes people want different things. They don't tell each other before they get married and by the time it comes out it's too late. Then they just have to do the best they can and hope everything gets better.

Paulino swiped the vacuum between the seats, heard a flapping sound and stopped. A lot of times candy wrappers got stuck there or pieces of paper too big for the hose. He reached down and caught something between his fingers.

It was a credit card receipt from a gas station.

He laid it on the dashboard and got on his knees so he could see if there were any more. He ran his hand under the springs but did not feel anything. When he got up he lifted the floormat and found a crushed dirt clod, some loose pine needles and another receipt under the edge. This one was a hotel bill. He set it on the dashboard, too.

Mr Ellsworth wanted a trophy wife, someone he could show off to his business friends. The rest of the time she was supposed to be happy with what she had, which was a lot. But she was a smart woman. She needed a life of her own. That was why they started growing apart. At least Mr Ellsworth had tried to do something about it. Paulino remembered how happy she was last Monday. She could not stop talking about the weekend getaway, just the two of them, like a second honeymoon. When he had to cancel she must have been sad.

Paulino saw the address at the top of the hotel bill.

It was from the Doubletree Lodge at Triangle Lake.

The other receipt was from a Union 76 station on Highway 5, just north of L.A.

That was on the way.

If they took the trip, after all, why didn't Mr Ellsworth want him to know?

Paulino tried to put it out of his mind. It was none of his business. He placed the receipts in the glovebox, then went around to the other side.

As he opened the passenger door he noticed some streaks on the inside of the window. He imagined Mrs Ellsworth falling asleep last night, on the way home from the lake, with her face against the glass. It looked like she had put her hand there, too, to support her head. He placed his fingers over the streaks.

Then he remembered that there had not been a trip.

That was what Mr Ellsworth said.

Paulino decided to roll the window down into the door before wiping it. That way the rubber seal would do some of the work for him, like a squeegee. He turned the key and hit the button. But when the window came back up one of her lacquered fingernails came with it, wedged halfway under the seal. And the streaks were worse, with a pink rainbow clinging to them, as if the gears inside the door were wet with strawberry soda.

A faint purple residue came off on his blue towel.

Something had spattered or spilled against the window, a soft drink, maybe. And she had tried to wipe it off and broken her nail. The litter bag under the glovebox held a few crumpled tissues. Paulino emptied it and saw stains on the tissues that had dried to a darker color, like dirty lipstick.

He probed under the seat with the vacuum.

As soon as he did that something hard started to rattle. It was not a piece of paper. This time there was a long, pointed object, rounded at one end, stuck between the floormat and the door. He plucked it from the nozzle and looked at it.

One of Mrs Ellsworth's high heels.

The rubber tip had cut a sharp black line into the mat. The line continued out of the passenger compartment and left a gouge in the paint, just inside the door, before the heel snapped off.

If she was asleep Mr Ellsworth must have carried her out of the car. But he had not lifted her legs. It was more like he had dragged her. The edge of the mat was curled where her shoe had snagged it.

He pulled on the mat, and the rubberized backing made a sucking sound as it peeled away. The carpet underneath was wet. He dropped the mat on the asphalt and looked at his fingers.

They were red.

Suddenly a breeze came up and blew through the open doors. He felt it in his chest and in his fingers as he waited for them to dry. He tried wiping them on the towel but they were still sticky.

Now there was an emptiness in his stomach, as if he had skipped breakfast and the coffee was ready to pass out of his body in a rush. He wished it were time for lunch but he had hours, long hours, ahead of him. He looked around at the car wash where he worked, where everything was made clean and spotless again and no one had to think about what happened in the world outside. He heard the grinding of the machinery and the hiss of the spray, saw the scum on the water as it ran down to the sewer and the steam rising into the polluted sky, and knew that even this place was not safe anymore.

The street was packed with cars, dirty inside and out, pumping so much filth into the air that the sky might never open again. It was too soon to pick up Rosalie, and if he tried to drive home in the morning rush he could lose his way and be trapped out there forever.

He saw the rest of the crew, wiping and polishing for tips, joking and staying busy so they would not have to look at what was on their towels, as the laundry barrel filled up until it would be too heavy to lift at the end of the day. He saw the customers, reading newspapers and making cel phone calls and staring at nothing, waiting to be born again, fresh and squeaky-clean. And he saw Mr Ellsworth, watching him.

The man came over and stood next to the mat with its sticky underside turned up.

"What do you want me to do with this?" said Paulino.

"Throw it away."

"Why?"

"I'll get new ones."

"But why?"

"Because they're ruined."

Paulino knew he should not say anything else but could not stop himself. "How's Mrs Ellsworth?"

The man squinted at him.

"She went away."

"Where?"

"To visit her relatives. She won't be back for a long time." He took out his wallet and handed over another hundred dollar bill. "Here. For the mats."

"We don't have any," said Paulino.

"Get some."

"You have to go to the dealer for that."

"You do it for me." He tried to give him fifty more. "Keep the change."

Paulino got out of the car.

"Where are you going? You're not finished . . ."

He went over to Ruben, who was working on a Sportage at the end of the ramp.

"I can pay you twenty today," Ruben said.

"Forget about it, *vato*." Paulino took the first hundred from his pocket and handed him both bills.

"What's this for?"

"The LX420."

"Huh?"

"If you don't want to do it, that's okay with me. Give some to Craig and Manny. And Linda. She works hard, too."

Paulie walked on to his Escort at the back of the lot. He took off his jumpsuit as he went, stepped out of it and left it on the asphalt without breaking stride. Then he got behind the wheel and turned the key.

He pulled into the alley and squeezed past the line of waiting cars, hoping to spot a sidestreet that was clear. On the way to find Rosalie he turned on his radio to block out the traffic noise. The first station he came to was playing power oldies. He raised the volume and began to sing along, not paying attention to the words. After a mile or so he realized it was the same tune he had heard when he woke up this morning, a love song that kept circling back on itself and starting again. *You make me feel so brand-new*, sang Al Green's high, soulful voice. *Let's stay together, whether times are good or bad or happy or sad . . .* The lyrics sounded so beautiful to Paulino that his eyes burned. He kept singing along even after the record was over. He did not want it to end.

MARK MORRIS

Coming Home

MARK MORRIS BECAME A FULL-TIME WRITER IN 1988 on the British government's Enterprise Allowance Scheme, and a year later saw the release of his first novel, *Toady*. To date he has had ten books published, and has contributed short fiction, articles and reviews to a variety of anthologies and magazines.

His latest novel, *Fiddleback*, (under the byline "J.M. Morris") is forthcoming from Pan Macmillan in the UK and Bantam in the US, before which he will have a new short story collection available from RazorBlade Press entitled *Long Shadows, Nightmare Light*.

About the following story, he recalls: "*The Big Issue* commissioned me to write a seasonal ghost story for their Christmas issue and then decided, late in the day, that they didn't have enough room for any fiction, after all. A few weeks later I happened to mention the story to Peter Crowther, who informed me that he had a tiny space left in the anthology he was then editing. I sent the story to Pete and happily he accepted it.

"If I may, I'd like to dedicate this story to the memory of R. Chetwynd-Hayes, whose stories – both those he has written and those he has selected for various anthologies in his role of editor – I read throughout my adolescent years, and whose spirit hopefully lives on in tales such as this one."

E ach time the baby kicked, Jane winced and recalled her mother gleefully telling her that she'd been a ten-pounder and that it ran in the family. It wasn't what she wanted to hear, but she knew Mum had just been trying to reassure her that her baby would be big and healthy.

Snow flurried outside, tapping slyly against the window, making the house seem cosy. Radiators breathed out heat; occasionally one burbled, and Jane hoped they wouldn't break down like last year, not when it was almost impossible to persuade plumbers to come all the way out here at Christmas. Sometimes she wished their nearest neighbour wasn't over a mile away, but mostly she didn't mind. If they still lived in London, they wouldn't be able to watch the sun setting spectacularly over the distant fields, wouldn't have badgers ambling through their garden at night, wouldn't be spending their lives accompanied by the soothing rush of the river which paralleled the narrow road that twisted for two miles before reaching the village of Brackley where Gerry had his estate agent's.

The baby kicked again, so hard that Jane, crossing the lounge, had to grip the back of a chair to steady herself. She decided to lie down in her studio, and once the baby had stopped kicking made her way not to the kitchen where she'd been heading to find something to nibble, but to the staircase, which she ascended slowly, stopping every few steps to gasp for breath.

As she sank on to the camp bed in the cluttered room which also contained her easel, her boxes of chalk pastels, a dusty bookcase stuffed with reference material, and dozens of stacked frames and half-finished pictures, she wondered whether she would go the full term. Today was the 21st, the baby was due on the 29th, but already she felt fit to pop. If she had it within the next couple of days she might still be home for Christmas. However, ideally she would prefer to get Christmas out of the way before the endless round of feeding and nappies and sleepless nights began.

She was just drifting off when she heard a sound coming from the landing directly outside her door. It sounded like breathing, though it was heavy and liquid, somehow *sludgy*. Jane imagined the man (she was sure it was a man) pressing his nose against the wood. She lay rigid until the stealthy ticking of snow against the window became a sudden flurry, making her jump. When the

flurry subsided, the breathing had gone. Jane lay and listened for
five minutes longer, but all she could hear was the river rushing
along outside.

When she told Gerry that evening he looked concerned, but
tried to come up with reasons why she must have been mistaken.

"If the house was empty and the doors locked then you must
have imagined it. Besides, why would a man break into the house
and then leave without . . . doing anything?"

"Perhaps he thought the house was empty and fled when he
realized it wasn't," she said, trying to convince herself. "Or
perhaps we've got a ghost."

"Don't be silly. I won't have you scaring yourself witless over
nothing, not in your condition."

"I'm not scaring *myself*, Gerry. I know what I heard."

Frowning, he said, "I could always drop you at Katy's before I
go to work."

"No. I won't be forced out of my own house. Don't worry, I
keep the mobile close by anyway in case of you know what." She
pointed at her belly.

Despite her tiredness, she was too uncomfortable to sleep that
night. She shifted with an effort from one position to another,
rearranging the cushions she had been using to support her
stomach and ease the ache in her back, but it was no use. In
the end she gave up and gazed for a while into the wavering
darkness, listening to Gerry's soft snoring, the river telling him to
hush, the distant cry of an owl.

At length, inevitably, the pricking of her bladder prodded her
from her cocoon. She shivered as she pushed the duvet aside, the
night's chill coaxing goosebumps from her flesh. She pulled on
her dressing gown and plodded to the toilet for the umpteenth
time that day, then decided that she couldn't face returning to
bed. With luck, if she made herself a hot drink downstairs and
stretched out on the settee with her book, she might end up dozing
off.

The lounge was still warm from the embers in the fire, whose
glow lapped the walls. She picked up her book from the sideboard, then immediately dropped it with a cry of disgust. The
cover was spongy and slimy, as if slugs had been crawling across
it all night.

As if touching the bloated paperback had prompted it, a smell suddenly touched Jane's nostrils. It was a damp, rotten, salty smell like decaying seaweed. She turned her head towards the kitchen door from behind which the smell seemed to be emanating, and heard a bumping, slithering sound, as if something large and soft and uncoordinated was moving about.

Though her instinct was to sink down into the shadows between the sideboard and the broken grandfather clock that Gerry was always tinkering with, she told herself firmly that she mustn't give in to her fear. She marched boldly across the hall, the tiles like ice beneath her bare feet, and pushing open the kitchen door to reveal a block of fetid and somehow bulging darkness, reached in and slapped the light switch.

Did something clammy, something disconcertingly like slug-flesh, briefly caress the back of her hand before the room was filled with light? Apparently not, for the kitchen was empty.

No, not quite empty. The dank smell was still there, though fading now, and there were patches of wet leading across the lino to the back door. Jane licked her lips, then also paced across the lino, taking care not to step in the puddles. She inspected the door. It was locked and bolted from the inside. Suddenly she felt queasy and faint; she needed to sit down. She hurried out of the kitchen, leaving the light on, and back into the lounge.

She sank on to the settee, curled her hands protectively around her belly and stared into the crumbling embers of the fire. Next thing she knew it was morning, the fire was nothing but grey ash and her feet were numb with cold. She tried to massage some life into them, then padded back across the hallway to the kitchen. The wet patches on the lino had dried, leaving no indication that they had ever been there.

Katy, Jane's elder sister, picked her up at noon that day and took her for lunch at The Leaping Hare, a pub five miles and two villages away that was on Egon Ronay's recommended list. Jane had not told Gerry about her experiences in the early hours because he had woken up irritable as if *he* was the one who'd had a night of broken sleep. Neither, she decided, would she tell Katy, for daylight had diminished the power of the experience and she knew that relating it in the Christmas cheer of a country pub would only make her sound silly. Nevertheless the experience preyed on her mind enough for Katy to comment on how quiet she was.

"I'm not getting much sleep," Jane said, and placed a hand on her stomach.

"Soon be over," said Katy who had two school-age boys of her own.

The food in the pub was better than good. The leaping flames in the grate at the far end of the room reminded Jane of muscles that the bellowing fire kept flexing. Once she thought the tree guarding the cigarette machine had grown hot enough to burn, but the flames she saw dancing in its branches were only reflections in the baubles that the tree wore. Barmaids sported silver tinsel scarves and Noddy Holder yelled, "It's Christmaaaasss!" from the juke box, all of which helped Jane relax.

Nevertheless she was frowning as she wafted at a thread of cigarette smoke, thinking of the baby, when the landlord shouted, "Phone call for Mrs Grainger."

As Jane reached the bar the landlord said cheerily, "Sounds like your man's got flu," and handed her the receiver.

"Hello," said Jane, pressing a hand to her exposed ear to block out Shakin' Stevens. She thought the connection had been broken until she realized it was not static she was listening to, but sludgy, tortured breathing.

"Who is this?" she demanded, sharply enough to earn several curious glances.

Did the breathing possess a voice that was attempting to form words? "Kaaaa," it seemed to be gurgling, "mirrrr."

Jane put the phone down. Though she was shaking, the pub suddenly seemed too stuffy. She stumbled back to her seat and plumped down, her breath coming in short gasps.

"Are you all right?" asked Katy, alarmed. "You look terrible."

Jane blurted out everything. She didn't care any more how silly Katy might think her. Her sister listened with pursed lips, then paid the bill and took her home.

Later, Jane was following a trail of dying fish up the stairs, their twitching silver bodies gleaming like Christmas decorations. Did the slow, squelching footsteps she could hear belong to her or to whoever had left the trail for her to follow? She inched open the bathroom door and caught a glimpse of the bloodless, slimy flesh of the figure in the bath as it turned its dripping ruin of a face towards her . . .

She woke with a cry, Katy sitting beside her. The late-afternoon darkness outside the window was hard and cold like black ice.

The next day was Saturday. As Gerry went to the supermarket and to pick up the tree they had ordered, Jane stayed in by the fire. She turned the radio up loud enough for the carol singers' voices to become distorted on the high notes. The sound she could hear in the pauses between hymns was not sludgy breathing but the gurgling of the river across the road from the house.

When the phone rang she almost left it, but eventually snatched it up and aggressively said, "Yes?" It was Katy, who seemed not to notice her tone, ringing to ask what time she should invade with her clan on Christmas Day. Soon afterwards Gerry arrived home, full of Christmas cheer and laden with goodies. They sipped wine as they dressed the tree, then settled down to watch *It's A Wonderful Life* as snow swirled around the house like a swarm of white flies looking for a way in. Gerry rested a hand on her stomach as the baby squirmed, and smiled soporifically.

"There'll be three of us next Christmas."

She kissed him on the nose. "There's still time for there to be three of us *this* Christmas."

Though she had only drunk two glasses, the wine helped her fall asleep quickly that night, but in the early hours she jolted awake as if someone had shaken her. Immediately she heard the sound of something rustling stealthily by the window. She looked in that direction and saw a figure with a pale, round head and rudimentary features. She sat up so suddenly that she wrenched her stomach, waking the baby, though even as the pain made her gasp she realized what she had really seen and heard: the glow of the moon through the curtains, the sound of snow settling on the window.

She was snuggling down again when she heard the screech of tyres from outside, followed by a thunderous splash. Instinct made her want to leap out of bed, though her aching stomach forced her to perform the manoeuvre with care. She hurried to the window and yanked back the curtains. Could she see car headlights sinking beneath the river or was it merely an odd reflection of the moon? Certainly there appeared to be something large and black just beneath the river's surface.

"Gerry, Gerry." Try as she might, Jane could not wake him. He had always been a heavy sleeper and had drunk far more wine than she had. Dragging on her dressing gown and a pair of

trainers she hurried downstairs and out of the house. It was
bitterly cold, though the snow's kisses were gentle on her face.
The river, its banks crusted with ice, flashed as if filled with
churning chunks of metal. Taking care not to slip, Jane craned
forward to peer into the water, but could see nothing.

Turning back towards the house she saw a figure standing by
the front door that she had left ajar. It was only a momentary
glimpse before a swirl of snow broke it up and carried it away,
but she was left with the impression of bloated white flesh and
dark clothes slick with water or slime. A pulse jumped in her
throat as she stalked back to the house, her nervousness making
her angry. Inside, she went straight to the phone and called the
police, who arrived twenty minutes later and spent almost an
hour searching the river, to no avail.

"Are you sure you'll be all right if I pop out for a couple of
hours?" Gerry asked her the next day. It was Christmas Eve and
his friend Graham, who he played five-a-side with, had invited
him for a pint with the lads.

"I'll be fine," Jane said, secretly relishing the chance to be on
her own for a while. Gerry had been bemused to find the police on
his doorstep at three in the morning and had spent the day
treating her with a kind of amused indulgence. When he said
something about pregnant women's hormones doing funny
things to their minds she had had to stop herself from thumping
him.

She was angry when he wasn't back by nine, but didn't really
start worrying until after eleven. By midnight her anxiety was a
hard lump at the base of her throat. She phoned Katy, who was
up late wrapping the boys' presents, and who came over immediately.

Jane had just decided to call the police when they arrived with a
swish of tyres on the snowy drive. Katy held her as the power of
her dread seemed to make them say the words she had been
expecting to hear. Coming back from the pub, Gerry had lost
control of the car which had plunged into the river. The accident
had happened several hours ago, but it had taken a while for
police divers to recover his body from the submerged vehicle.

After the police had gone, Jane sat and stared into space as Katy
wept and clung to her. Jane felt numb, unable to produce tears.
The Christmas tree twinkled in the corner like a joke in appal-

lingly bad taste. The baby that Gerry had been so looking forward to but which he would now never see, moved inside her, but Jane felt distanced from it and its imminent birth. Later, in a flat voice, she said, "He tried to warn me."

Katy, bleary with tears and exhaustion, said, "What?"

"Everything that's happened. Don't you see, it was Gerry coming back. Why didn't I listen to what he was trying to say?"

Katy looked at her for a moment, then said softly, "Jane, you don't know what you're saying. How can someone come back to you before they're even . . ." She choked on the last word.

Jane's face was expressionless, her voice eerily calm. "He wanted this baby so much, so he found some way . . ." Then suddenly, shockingly, her face twisted and she was wailing, almost screaming, the grief pouring out of her.

It was five o'clock on Christmas morning when the knock came on the front door. Katy was asleep in an armchair, so exhausted that she didn't even stir. Jane was still awake, quiet again now, shattered though unable to sleep, staring into the fire. She padded into the hallway and pulled the door open.

When she saw what was standing outside she remembered the phone call in the pub and all at once realized what the caller had been trying to say. Gerry had wanted her to know that nothing in this world or beyond would prevent him coming home for Christmas.

JOEL LANE

The Hunger of the Leaves

JOEL LANE LIVES IN BIRMINGHAM, ENGLAND. His short horror stories have appeared in *Best New Horror*, *Dark Terrors 4* and *5*, *Darklands*, *Little Deaths*, *The Mammoth Book of Dracula*, *The Ex Files*, *White of the Moon*, *The Third Alternative*, *Twists of the Tale* and elsewhere.

He is the author of a collection of short stories, *The Earth Wire*; a collection of poems, *The Edge of the Screen*, and a novel set in the world of post-punk rock music, *From Blue to Black*. His second novel, *Your Broken Face*, is nearing completion. He has also edited *Beneath the Ground*, an anthology of subterranean horror stories from The Alchemy Press.

As the author reveals: " 'The Hunger of the Leaves' originally appeared in Mike Chinn's anthology *Swords Against the Millennium* (also from Alchemy), a book of weird-heroic fantasies in the pulp tradition. My story was written as a tribute to Clark Ashton Smith, whose brooding, morbid tales of Zothique and other strange realms appeared in *Weird Tales* in the 1930s. It was also influenced by the Cure song 'A Forest'. To my taste, the best fantasy is always tinged with horror – such as *Beowulf*, which did my head in at an early age."

T he forest realm of Yhadli occupied many miles of unpopulated terrain within the central lowlands of Zothique, the last of Earth's continents. It was rumoured to include the barren remains of towns and garrisons, abbeys and cemeteries, which the forest had reclaimed. None knew its full extent, since there were no longer any maps. No man living had seen its infamous ruler, the aged sorcerer Niil; if he still lived, he and his subjects had no need of the outside world. Like Zothique itself, the forest realm lived in a silence bound by the shadows of the past.

The three men passing from the twilit fields to the deeper gloom of the forest canopy were possessed of no desire to escape into a bygone time. Nor had they rejected such convivial pleasures as the violent towns of Ultarn and Acoxgrun had to offer to embrace the austere life of a hermit. Passing through these towns, they had heard tales of the great wealth of the sorcerer Niil: a wealth that must have been hoarded, since it had never been spent. It was a permanent harvest, with gold for wheat and jewels for berries. That harvest had been gathered through deeds of blood and terror that were already the stuff of grim legend. They intended to reap some portion of it through kidnap, robbery or simple theft. All three were experienced villains, with an acquired lack of scruples and imagination. Their evil repute in the regions of Tasuun and Xylac had forced them to come to a place where they were unknown – and thus, one which was unknown to them.

The forest was as quiet and still as a vast underground vault. In places, the faint red light of the Earth's dying sun played on complex traceries of black twigs, jagged leaves and bark mottled with pale lichen and mould. Cobwebs hung everywhere, fine and translucent like shrouds; but no spiders could be seen. Nor could any bird or beast be discerned in the tangled branches or the shadowy, yielding undergrowth. The dead leaves beneath the robbers' feet were of an unfamiliar kind: clawlike, with three hooked points and hard, reddish veins. As the thieves continued, the shadows thickened; soft tatters of cobweb clung unpleasantly to their sleeves. Soon they were forced to light torches in order to see where they were going. The paths were twisted, overgrown and impossible to follow. The torchlight distorted the shapes of the overhanging branches, made them resemble the faces of starving creatures or the intertwined bodies of human lovers in the grip of desire.

After nightfall, they took their direction from the northern star (which an ancient myth told them was a world much like their own). The nocturnal life of the forest seemed oddly subdued. No owl cried in the darkness; no bat swooped overhead. Even the lonely baying of wild hounds, thin demons that preyed on their former masters, was absent. The only sound was a faint, dry rustling, like the sand on a desert shore, only just distinguishable from silence.

At length, they came upon a small clearing where they might pause for the night. Jharscain and Dimela cut some twigs and branches; while Medarch prepared a small fire. By its light, they saw that another traveller had reached this place. Hanging from the twisted branches of a squat black tree was the wide, hooded robe of a monk. It was full of dead leaves, from which the pale glimmer of bones indicated the presence of a long-decayed cadaver. No rope held the skeleton in place, and the cause of death was not evident. His skull was packed with leaves, like the black thoughts of a madman; leaves clung to his ribs and pelvis, and to the inner surface of his ample robe. Beneath the dangling bones of his feet lay the dull shards of a broken wine flagon.

More imaginative souls might have deemed such grisly company unwelcome; but the thieves had lit a fire, and were loth to delay their rest. They ate of their spiced provisions, and drank deeply from a flask of the thrice-distilled spirit of grain. Jharscain raised his cup in ironic salute to their silent companion: "Wilt thou not share a drink with us? Hath Mordiggian taken thy thirst along with they throat and belly? But know this: we too are of his realm. We are merely in that earlier phase of death which we please to call life. What thou seest tonight, we too shall see in the red light of morning."

They slept that night the deep sleep of drunkards, each man soaked the light of his own visions. Jharscain dreamed of finding the house of the sorcerer Niil untenanted, and of gaining access to the treasures of his wine-cellar: wines so rich and fragrant, spirits so fiery and evocative, that they would shame even the abbeys of Puthuum. The dreaming soul of Dimela visited not the cellars of Niil, but his comfortable bedchamber, where it was entertained by the seven young women of the sorcerer's harem on sheets of the finest black silk. The dreams of Medarch had less of actual theft about them: he saw himself beside the ageing sorcerer as a valued servant, entrusted with the patient torture and execution of his master's enemies. And among those dying in blind, limbless, voiceless ruin were Dimela and Jharscain, wearing bright skins of blood.

In the morning, all three men had the furtive and bloodshot eyes of villains who had not slept well. Under the vacant gaze of the monk, they partook of a hasty breakfast and continued on their way. The ebon trees and their harvest of pale cobwebs showed no sign of thinning out; every step of the way had to be forced through damp undergrowth and drifts of leaves as brittle as fired clay. Repeatedly they passed the hanging skeletons or withered corpses of men in the trees, their loose clothing snagged on branches, dead leaves clamped to their skulls like sleeping bats; and this convinced them that the house of the sorcerer Niil could not be far away.

It was a day of twilight, fatigue and silent horror. The three men forged onward, certain that the house of Niil must be surrounded by widespread farming and habitation. However, they found no occupied houses, fields or gardens. The black trees and their spectral veils of cobweb held dominion over all. Yet this region had once been tenanted. Crumbling walls and broken flagstones could be glimpsed through the undergrowth. And everywhere, human skulls stared whitely from hoods of dead leaves. A house stood with its roof and front wall in ruins, three skeletons sitting at a table covered with the smaller bones of rats. A temple of carven stone lay in fragments, the skeleton of a small child on a rust-stained altar bearing witness to the sacred rituals of the priests of Thasaidon. Among the surface roots of a great tree, two almost fleshless cadavers lay in a permanent embrace that was no longer restrained by the boundaries of skin; a fine layer of cobweb surrounded them, like the sheet of a marriage bed. Most strange of all was a great well, ringed with black stone and deeper than Medarch could discern, yet full almost to the brim with clean-picked human bones.

This domain, Medarch realized, was more than abandoned: it was the scene of some terrible annihilation, and had been preserved as a bleak reliquary of the human race. The hideous soul of a mad poet had created this roofless vault as a symbol of the Earth and its place in a blind cosmos. What the people of Zothique knew in their fearful hearts was here proven. Medarch thought this and smiled within himself, but said nothing. For his soul was deeper than those of his companions. He was a murderer, where they were merely thieves. His parents had lived and died on the

accursed isle of Uccastrog; and he had been delivered from his
mother's womb by the jaws of a hound.

When the haze of reddish light beyond the trees tuned to
illimitable blackness, clouds obscuring even the brightest stars,
the three men stopped to light a fire and rest once more. They ate
little, unsure of their destination; but drank deep of the spirit of
grain, since a certain unease had come upon them. Jharscain, who
was the most afraid, drank most deeply. They spoke little, but
stared thoughtfully into the heart of the fire, where the twigs and
branches were charred to a bonelike white. At length, they
stamped out the fire and gave themselves up to sleep.

Jharscain slept poorly, troubled by a thirst that his previous
intake had served only to intensify. The darkness itched at his eyes
like a coarse fabric. Silently, he reached for the bag containing the
vessel of grain liquor; with infinite care, he tilted it above his
gaping mouth. Only a few precious mouthfuls remained. He
fancied he could see the creeping denizens of the cobwebs,
spinning fine threads to reach him; when he shut his eyes, he
saw them still. A death-mask of perspiration covered his face.
Then he heard a voice close by: "Wilt thou not drink with us?"
When he opened his eyes, he saw lights flickering just beyond the
nearest trees.

As he staggered through the undergrowth toward the blurred
lights, Jharscain heard the faint sounds of some terrific revel; wine
was poured and gulped, voices were raised in drunken litany to
Thasaidon. The very air seemed hazy with the fumes of wine.
Around him, pale hands raised drinking-vessels and tipped them
into faces of mist. The leaves shifted underfoot, and he fell to his
knees. Dead leaves rose and drifted around him, their veins
swollen with sweet-scented wine. But when a leaf touched his
face, its thin flesh was dry as the driest paper. It stuck to his lips;
as he raised a hand to pull it away, more leaves settled on his face.
Where they touched him, his skin dried out; it shrivelled and
broke, as if burned by the cold flame of sobriety. However much
blood the leaves took from him, they remained as dry as bones in
the desert.

Later in the night, Dimela stirred from his uneasy slumber. Was
that a laugh he had heard: a sound bright with youthful vigour,
yet strangely curdled with desire? Perhaps a hanging cobweb had
fallen on him; it had felt as soft and clinging as a maiden's long

hair. He had last savoured the pleasures of carnal love three nights before, at a debauched inn of the town known as Acox-grun. Now loneliness rode on his back, and the darkness was faintly scented with the perfume of roses. A figure moved between the nearest trees, backlit by a distant fire: a silhouette whose contours were drawn by the hand of his needs. And now he could hear the crackling of the fire, and the voices of those who writhed and danced around it: whispering, pleading, laughing, sobbing, gasping. He could not see them clearly; yet he heard their message of joy and anguish. "Wilt thou not dance with us?"

Tearing at his clothes, Dimela stumbled towards the blood-red fire. Though it appeared close, his steps brought it no closer. Eventually he stopped, confused; and a cloud of dead leaves rose gently around him, evading his outstretched arms to drift like patches of lonely skin upon his body. So overwhelming were his sensations that the loss of blood went unnoticed. The leaves that floated before Dimela's fading gaze bore the reddened imprint of faces transfigured by the secret fire of ecstasy. As his flesh joined with theirs, the night exposed the keen nakedness of bone. And so it began over again.

Medarch slept like a child until dawn, twining about his thin fingers a cloth formerly used for strangling. The rumour of light that was sunrise in Zothique roused him and told him he was alone. His first thought was that the other two villains had abandoned him to continue their search for the house of Niil together. Then he saw that their shoulder-bags remained. Had they been taken by some wild beast of the nighted forest? But there was no sign of struggle, no blood on the dead leaves. Besides, what animal life had they seen in this crypt of shadows? Then a faint sound, as of choking breath or waterlogged footfalls, came from beyond the trees on the other side of the dead fire. Medarch gripped his dagger and crossed the ashes. Some cob-webs, he saw, had been torn aside; he stepped through the gap.

The body of Jharscain lay in a drift of leaves that half-covered him. The skin of his face was stretched like parchment over his skull, and was so dry that the corners of his mouth had torn into a hideous thin grimace. As Medarch watched, the cadaver's sere hands twitched mindlessly; and from the stretched parody of a mouth, a pale tongue emerged to lick the cracked and bloodless lips. A dead leaf moved on his throat with a horrible purpose, cutting into skin that was already as ravaged as that of a desiccated corpse in the deep catacombs of Naat. Despite his long and pleasurable experience of horror, Medarch felt a shiver pass through him. Raising his eyes, he saw a red blur through the veil of cobweb that linked two branches: a brighter red than that of the crepuscular daylight.

The body in the next glade was not recognizable as that of Dimela. It was a scattering crimson ruin, flayed and dismembered, at its centre a mound of leaves the size of a human head. A few items of clothing lay torn on the ground. Hands, eyes, lungs, bones and patches of skin crawled among the black leaves, somehow unable to die. They shuddered as if still infused by a common pulse. The three-pointed leaves clung to them in a terrible embrace, a slow dance that was truly the pleasure of the flesh. The odour of blood and decay was like a cloud in the chill air. Medarch was no innocent; but he was human, and this was an alien horror beyond his comprehension. Madness laughed and danced within his brain as he rushed on through the twilit forest, crashing through drifts of leaves and shrouds of tenantless cobweb, blind instinct driving him first in one direction and then in another. He no longer remembered what it was that he was searching for.

After hours of insane stumbling and circling, he came upon a part of the forest realm where the trees were bare and brittle like stone. The hanging cobwebs were corpse-grey, stained with the imprints of tormented faces. It was so cold here that Medarch's ragged breath formed tissue in the air. Memories floated before his eyes, random and meaningless: the dead and dying victims of his career. He had known many trades: mercenary in Tasuun, torturer in Naat, executioner in Cincor, jailer in Xylac. Among the scattered and frightened peoples of Zothique, warfare was vicious and perpetual. Crime and punishment were lucrative parallel trades, and the fate of prisoners was rarely a matter of public concern. It was not distressing for Medarch to recall the men, women and children he had mutilated; indeed, he kept a trunk full of dried souvenirs to help him remember his most cherished atrocities. Many times, when unable to torture within the law, he had found other means to procure young victims; and his knowledge of the ways of villains had opened many a secret and nighted door to him.

Yet, alone in the bleak forest realm of Yhadli, his sense of status deserted him; he could scarcely remember his own name. The ruined faces of his victims swam in a grey mist before him: nameless, voiceless, eyeless, hopeless. Their silence felt like mockery.

Eventually, sheer exhaustion brought the torturer to a standstill. His body was gashed and bruised from a thousand small injuries, and he had with him neither food nor water. The stark trees about him felt as cold as stone. The ground beneath his feet was slimy with leaf-mould and buried decay. Before him stood another ruined house, one different from the others they had passed: this one was made of wood, and had no windows. The black, dead twigs of the surrounding trees were woven into its dense roof. The walls were coated with layers of cobweb that glistened, rotting from within. He could discern no door in this unearthed tomb, until it opened.

The figure in the lightless doorway was like a monk, though thinner than any monk that Medarch had ever seen. He was clad in a black gown that clung to his bony frame. His hooded face was a shadow without features or skin; it was broken by countless fine cracks and wrinkles. It was a visage of dead leaves. Within it, two crimson eyes glowed with the cold distant fire of alien suns. Medarch felt those frozen eyes stare through him, dismissing him as if he were a ghost. A misshapen hand with three hooked fingers reached up to the door. And then the creature had gone, back into the darkness of its sealed house.

At once, Medarch knew that he had found the house of the sorcerer Niil, and that his offer of service had been rejected as of no value. A terrible breath of loneliness passed through him. At last, he understood why only the *dead* leaves were hungry. If Niil had ever been human, he was so no more. He was one with his realm of stillness and decay.

For a long time, the man who had dedicated his life to pain stood before the windowless abode of the creature for whom pain had no meaning. Then, as the weak sun bled into the western sky, Medarch set his face toward the distant towns of Ultarn and Acoxgrun. No longer running, but with steady and relentless steps, he made his way back to the abodes of men. The marks cut on his face by leaves and twigs bled freely, and decaying cobwebs tangled in his hair. It no longer mattered. Half-naked, filthy, bloody and red-eyed, Medarch strode forward to his destiny: to be the silent emissary of Niil throughout the continent of Zothique, and any other lands that might remain, until the legions of the dead lay scattered on the dying Earth like the fallen leaves of a splendid and fertile autumn.

GRAHAM JOYCE

Xenos Beach

FOUR-TIMES WINNER OF THE British Fantasy Society's August Derleth Award for Best Novel – for *Dark Sister* (1992), *Requiem* (1995), *The Tooth Fairy* (1996) and *Indigo* (1999) – Graham Joyce quit an executive job and went to the Greek island of Lesbos to live in a beach shack with a colony of scorpions (the setting for his 1993 novel *House of Lost Dreams*) and concentrate on his writing.

He sold his first novel, *Dreamside* (1991), while still in Greece and travelled in the Middle East on the proceeds. *The Storm-watcher* (1998) preceded *Indigo*, and he has since published a young adult science fiction novel, *Spiderbite* (1997), and the novella *Leningrad Nights* (1999). His latest novel, *Smoking Poppy*, is set on the mountain borders of Thailand and Myanmar.

"'Xenos Beach' was inspired by a magical but disturbing beach on which my wife and I slept when we were rootless and travelling around Greece," reveals the author. "It was on the island of Chios. The broken temple and the row of abandoned tents was a genuine feature of the beach. I couldn't help wondering about who they belonged to and why they'd been left there."

H e went to the island to get as far away as he could from the rowdy parties of Ios and the commercialism of Mykonos. He'd had enough. The tourist season was smoked out and the recommended cure for heartbreak hadn't worked. The word was

that this particular island had turned its back on tourists, that it
neither needed nor wanted them, and that if you were not lying to
yourself and you really did want to get away from it all, this was
the place to go.

Sunlight lancing off the brilliant white paint of the hull had him
squinting as he stepped off the inter-island ferry. Even in the
dazzle the tiny port exhibited a post-industrial, neglected character. The place wasn't designed to take tourists and backpackers,
and he had to step smartly around coils of rope and tarred
capstans. Disinclined to practise his Greek on one of the grizzled
old mariners languishing on the quayside, he dithered and
scratched his head. Other passengers hurried away or were
collected in rattletrap trucks. Only two minutes on the island
and the long tooth of loneliness was beginning to bite.

Centuries of spice trading hung in the air of the old port. Dank
warehouses of biscuit-coloured brick were crumbling into the
water. Empty, cobwebby bars of fretwork shadows dotted the
small waterfront, and the harbour slumbered under pearly, in-
spirational light.

He had a battered old *Giffords*, found on a Mykonos beach. As
a tour guide its yellowing pages were hopelessly out of date, but
he savoured the elegant Edwardian prose and its sniffy English
reserve. About the island the book had very little to say, except to
recommend that one should "quit the port at the earliest opportunity" and make for the west coast, where there were *mastic*
villages and deserted, thrilling beaches. The island was the richest
in Greece for *mastic*: the resin on the bushes crystallizes, har-
vested by the women, to be sold on for its aromatic properties.
And on one of the beaches, the guidebook indicated, lay strewn
the rubble of a marble temple to Aphrodite. The author claimed
to have spent a sleepless night there under the stars.

At mid-day he climbed aboard a sweltering bus, sharing a seat
with a crone in widow's black. Partially hooded by a dark cotton
headscarf, her tooled-leather face could have been a thousand
years old. On her lap rested a cardboard box, in which there was
something live, black and feathery. The old woman dipped in a
bag for seed, which she sucked in her toothless mouth, occasionally letting some of the seed fall into the box. At some point along
the journey she offered him a seed, which he accepted and tried to
nibble with good grace.

"*Pou pa?*" she asked energetically. "Where are you going?"

"Here." He pointed on his map.

She clucked at him. "Why? There are no bars. No tavernas. Nothing." She repeated the word for nothing with heavy emphasis. "Why go there?"

He wanted to explain a need for seclusion, but it was obvious she'd already decided he was a lunatic. The Greeks seemed to regard any solitary act, like hiking in the hills, as an expression of mental illness or depression; even in his own experience, a casual stroll would be quite likely to attract the desperate sympathy of an entire family who must then insist on keeping one company. Far better, he'd discovered, to lie about the purpose of your expedition and pretend to be going to see a man about a goat.

"Married?" she wanted to know. This familiarity was also normal for Greeks.

"Yes." He had no intention of going into detail about Alison. "Children?"

"Yes," he lied, not wanting to evoke the universal sympathy accorded to the childless.

She spent the next few moments engaging every other passenger on the bus in his business. His Greek let him down as the pitch of her voice grew animated, even agitated. Everyone else was leaning forward and regarding him with rather too much interest. He still had the book open at the map. She tapped it vigorously and spat. Then she smacked her gums together conclusively. He was relieved when, along with most of the other passengers, his new acquaintance disembarked at one of the *mastic* villages.

When he came to get off the bus, the driver shook his head before driving off, leaving him standing in a cloud of diesel-exhaust on a parched, volcanic hillside.

Below the blue Aegean darted with sodium light. Hoisting backpack and tent, he descended the baked-earth path. It was some hike. Huge boulders ticked with heat. The hum of millions of insects among the sticky-looking mountain vegetation was like the idling of a vast and invisible engine.

The climb down was almost two hours under a merciless sun. He thought about Alison. "There's only one solution to a woman who doesn't want you, and that's another woman." Peter had poured his advice like an after-dinner liqueur. "Go to Greece. Have some experiences. You'll get over her. Exhaust yourself on a romantic island with some beautiful French woman. Fall in love with a German goddess. Cry your eyes out over a Danish siren. Go to Greece. Visit the Gods."

He had swallowed Peter's prescription, hoping even that his classical studies in ancient Greek would help him get by. It didn't, but after making a fool of himself a few times he worked hard at the demotic. Four months had been spent island-hopping, camping, visiting the sights, the antiquities. Some days were lonely; some days were spent partying with people he didn't really want to be with. There *was* a dalliance with a beautiful Frenchwoman, and a night of shockingly rough passion with a Norwegian girl. Then towards the end of the season he woke, and not for the first time, with his face in the sand, his dry mouth tasting of aniseed, and decided the cure hadn't worked.

The worst night was when he found himself drunk and blubbering on a beach. A small dog, rib-thin and suffering from appalling mange trotted across and licked his hand in pity. He stopped feeling sorry for himself, brought the dog a meal and phoned home to see how things stood.

Alison answered the phone and told him that she and Pete had got together. He laughed. For the first time in four months, he actually laughed. He laughed for so long he woke with his face in the sand for the second morning running. Then he decided to come to the island and do some thinking.

Approaching the bay he saw not the promised temple, but a tiny whitewashed Byzantine church with red terracotta roof. Higher up the beach of fine volcanic grey sand a fringe of trees marked off an area of deciduous scrub, contrasting emerald green with the barren ochre rock of the hillside above. The leaves of the scrub were peculiarly luminous and verdant, and he suspected that somewhere there he might find the sweetwater spring promised in his copy of *Giffords*.

The church was built in the centre of the ruined temple. Fluted marble columns lay half-submerged in the sand, along with toppled capitals and broken plinths. Perhaps the Christian builders of the small church wanted to take advantage of the marble foundation; or maybe they sought to deactivate the power of the old gods. The tiny chapel itself had a dilapidated air as if it too were a relic of a broken culture. He tried the door. Unusually for an isolated Greek church, it was locked.

Deciding to pitch his tent under the shady protection of the trees, he moved further up the beach but was soon dismayed. It seemed he had company. Pitched between the trees at irregular intervals were six or seven other tents of differing shapes and sizes. All of the tents faced the sea, and in every case the original canvas or nylon colour had been bleached out by salt spray and harsh sunlight.

Passing by the tents, he tried to peek inside to see what kind of people were there, but the flaps were closed and there was no sound from within. Perhaps they were all in siesta, but there was no one swimming, and no other activity on the beach. After pitching his tent he went looking for the sweetwater spring, but couldn't locate it. He'd brought enough water for two or possibly three days if economical; but he had in mind staying a little longer. No one came out of the other tents, and no one returned to them either. Eventually the sunset turned the sea ember red, but after the sun had dipped under the water there was no moon and it quickly got cold. He cast about for wood to make a fire but he'd left it too late; so he climbed into his sleeping bag and read his *Giffords* by torchlight.

"A quite singular and beautiful cove," the *Giffords* reported, "but I do not care ever to return there."

Sometime in the night he was woken by a noise. He poked his head out of the tent. The sea, no more than twenty yards away, was calm, but there was still no moon. A light flickered, up at the other end of the beach, near the temple. The light hovered briefly, shifted, then it went out. He zipped up his tent and lay back, straining to listen for further sounds. Nothing. He opened his clasp knife and put it under his pillow.

In the morning he lay dozing in his sleeping bag, unable to surface. As the sun got up it became impossibly hot under the nylon and he wrenched himself awake. Tumbling out of the tent he walked like a somnambulist in an undeviating line to the sea. The water was chilly, effervescing on his skin. In the middle of snorting and splashing he suddenly remembered the other tents. There was still no sign of life. He'd hoped to be able to ask someone about water. Eventually he peeked inside the tent nearest to his own.

It was empty. So was the next. Examining them one by one he discovered the tents were all abandoned. No equipment had been left behind, nor any hint that their former occupants were about to return. Perhaps the local Greeks pitched them for convenient use at weekends or holiday times. It was October after all, and even though the days were still hot, the season was turning on the hinge of the Aegean autumn, and the nights could get very cold. No, he decided, he was alone, and with that realization a slight breeze picked up off the water. One of the tent-flaps fluttered in the airstream.

He went about naked. Eating only when hungry from the things he'd brought with him, he also went without cigarettes and alcohol for the first time in fifteen years. Much of the first day was spent searching for the fresh spring, without success. At the temple, on one of the marble blocks, he found the ugly carcass of a sea snake. Buzzing with flies, its razor-fine teeth were bared and its rotting scales gleamed magnificently. He found, under a stone, the key to the church.

Inside, a small icon hung on the wall above the altar, but the lamps were dust-covered and hadn't been lit for some time. A bottle of oil and matches stood on a small table. He lit a lamp and a breath of light seemed to sigh around the tiny chamber. The flame winked on the silver icon. The face enclosed in the silver frame, one of the patriarchs of Greek orthodoxy, seemed stirred to anger rather than to one of the tender emotions. He got out, but left the lamp burning.

Soon it was dusk and this time he had his fire assembled ready for the dark. He was just finishing up a meal of olives, bread and cheese when he saw a dark flag-like figure by the water's edge. Again the dying sun had turned the water the colour of live coals. The figure approached in silhouette, his back to the sun, see-mingly clothed in flapping black rags. A thrill of alarm passed through him with unnecessary force.

It was a Greek Orthodox priest. For some reason he didn't feel comforted. His skin flushed. The priest carried his stovepipe hat in his hand, his pace diminishing as he came closer. Finally he stood off by a good few yards.

"*Yia sas!*" he said to the priest, forcing a smile, "*Yia!*"

"*Yia sas,*" the priest echoed quietly, eyeing him suspiciously, peering round him at the tent. A single bead of sweat ran darkly between the priest's eyebrows.

Even though as a traveller he was the *xenos*, the stranger, he tried to offer the priest some of the food he'd been eating. This desperate parody of Greek courtesy irritated the priest, who declined with a gesture. "What are you doing?" he asked.

"Camping." He wanted to add something rude. He'd taken a huge and irrational dislike to the priest.

"It's not a good place for that."

"Why?"

The question was ignored. "What do you do here?"

"I swim. I fish." It was true; he'd brought a hand-line along and hoped to catch something.

"Dangerous to swim here. Very dangerous. There are currents out there that can take you out to sea. Very dangerous."

Not having noticed any currents while swimming in the bay earlier, he raised his eyebrows at the priest. "Can you show me where there is water?"

"Water?"

"Yes! Water! For drinking! My book says there's fresh water somewhere." The priest, startled by this sudden animation, was torn by how to respond and merely mopped his sweating brow. "For goodness sake, it's only water!"

The priest unaccountably turned his back and began to retrace his steps. He leapt to his feet and followed. "How long are you staying here?" the priest barked over his shoulder.

"Not long."

When they reached the temple, the priest led him behind the marble blocks and grudgingly pointed to a slab. "There. But it's brackish."

Watched by the priest he removed the slab to uncover a shallow well. With a cupped hand he drew out a few drops of water. It tasted fresh and cool and clear. The priest's nostrils began to twitch as if he was sniffing the air. "Have you been burning *mastic*?" he demanded angrily, mopping his brow with a handkerchief.

"Why would I do that?"

"Are you certain?"

"Of course I'm certain!"

He'd had enough of this priest who, scowling, went inside the church and closed the door. He retreated up the beach. Some time later when he returned to the church, it was locked and the priest had gone.

He lit a fire and pretty soon had a decent blaze going, though the piles of thin scrub flared too quickly. Crackling fiercely, it sent white sparks arcing across the fire before burning smokily. Very soon he realized what the priest had been talking about. The incense-rich smell of burning *mastic* was everywhere.

He'd unwittingly piled dead *mastic* bushes on his fire. The entire beach already smelled like a gargantuan temple. Flames writhed in the dark, flinging indigo shadows across the sand, and with the waves crowding nearer behind his back the fire assumed a sacramental quality. He sat with a blanket around his shoulders, hypnotized by the flames, drugged by perfumed smoke. He felt his forehead: his temperature was high.

When he awoke sweating in his tent the next morning he had no recollection of having gone to bed. Outside, his fire had burned out, and he stumbled across the sand and into the cold water, where he was shocked properly awake. While brushing his teeth in seawater he spotted activity at the other end of the beach.

Three or four figures, perhaps a family, were busy close to the temple. Conscious of his own nakedness, he splashed through the water and jogged back to his tent, where he pulled on some shorts. He sat in his tent, wondering what to do.

Of course, he didn't have to *do* anything. They were campers, just like him. Perhaps they would cook *souvlaki* on a barbecue, stay for an hour or two and go home. What difference could it make? Concerned to announce his presence, he hit on the solution of going to draw some water from the spring.

He carried his water bottle the length of the beach. Four figures were busy with something on the ground. Rather than occupying one of the available tents, they had rigged up a large but crude shelter, immediately adjacent to the temple. Advertising his presence by a noisy approach, he actually got quite close before one of them looked up. Then all four of them stopped what they were doing and gaped back at him, open-mouthed.

He had the uncanny sensation that he was himself a ghost.

The older of the two men rose very slowly and stared, his hands hanging loose at his sides.

"*Yia sas.*"

"*Yia sas,*" they replied, in precise and hasty concert.

"Where did you come from?" the older man said quickly, still in a state of astonishment. The accent was difficult, but just comprehensible. They were gypsies in all probability. When the tent at the far end of the beach was pointed out the man stepped forward, his eyes followed the line of the pointing finger. His manly perspiration was strong and blended with an overpowering scent of *mastic*. Then one of the women spoke rapidly. Only the word *philoxenia* stood out, like a bright pearl among flat stones, before the man gestured to a sharing of the meal they were preparing. They had been slicing some kind of offal on a marble slab. It looked less than appetising.

The older man went into the rough tent and came out proffering a pottery tumbler filled to the brim with blood-red wine. It was slightly salty, acidic and rather thick, but it was to be drunk. Reciprocation of Greek hospitality demanded so. It was after all entirely possible that they were entertaining one of the Gods unawares, and he should behave as if he believed that to be the case. He tipped back the wine and they immediately seemed to relax; except for the younger man, who seemed unable to do anything but stare.

It was difficult not to stare back. The family was distinctive from most Greeks. These were darker skinned, and yet with copper hair, totally unlike the blueblack of most island Greeks. But they were not of the Asiatic descent seen in the islands close to Turkey. Gypsies, surely. He had to make a conscious effort to avoid gazing at the younger of the two women. His eyes returned to her time and again as they ate slices of cooked heart and liver, during which the older couple plied him with questions about his former life.

"From England? England, you say?" It was as if he'd stipulated that he had recently arrived from the lost city of Atlantis. Meanwhile the younger man maintained a hostile silence.

He noticed that the locked door of the chapel had been kicked down. He could see the priest's hat and cloak and shoes strewn around the floor. It was while he took in this disturbing detail that he felt a hand lightly brush his shoulder. "Will you swim with me?" the younger woman asked, smiling.

She ran the same hand through her hair and the sun flaked fire around her. He felt a jab to the viscera. Her fingers playing with her hair were uncommonly long. Her white teeth flashed; the heavy lashes of her oval eyes blinked lazily.

"Swim! Swim!" said the father, waving towards the water.

"Will you swim with us?" he asked the younger man, trying to make some sort of point, but the fellow shook his head contemptuously, picked up a handline and jogged to the waters' edge.

The young woman set off up the beach. "It's better this way," she murmured. None of her group seemed inclined to follow, and the two of them clambered over some rocks, going out of view of the others. There she slipped off her rough costume and waded in, her shins swishing through the water.

He blinked at the naked girl. She had a large birthmark on her bottom. As he slipped off his own trunks and followed her she waited, her eyes unashamedly assessing his body. Unconsciously, or perhaps not, she moistened her lips with her tongue. When he drew abreast of her she turned in a smooth motion and made an elegant crawl stroke through the water. Following, he found it difficult to keep up, feeling the tug of a strong undertow. The priest hadn't been lying about the swift currents. Afraid, he swam back alone.

He sat on the shoreline panting hard, trying to spot her. Alarmed over her safety he considered calling the others, but at last he descried a tiny dot returning from far out. Eventually she fell down beside him, uncomfortably close. Hardly out of breath she said, "But you didn't come all the way!" A teasing note in her voice.

"Not me."

She squeezed water from her hair and it trickled down the ridge of her spine, where he wanted to brush his fingers. With her toes dipped in the water she wriggled her bottom deeper into the grey sand. A strong whiff of *mastic* incense came off the girl. Again his skin flushed, as it had in the presence of the priest, but differently this time. It was as if some warning chill came off her, some marine odour alerting him to a danger he had no capacity to understand. She locked eyes with him, and her breathing became shallower. He wanted to lean across and take the dark, erect berry of her nipple in his mouth. Too afraid, he asked her name.

"Alethea." She stepped back into her beach garb. An important moment had slipped.

But he was glad he hadn't chanced his arm, because seconds later the young man appeared. He paced by, scowling, suspicious. A fishing line trailed from his wrist, and swinging from the hook was a vicious looking sea-snake, jaw open, fangs bared, exactly

like the specimen rotting by the temple. A wave of hostility
emanated from the young man as he passed, and it occurred
to him that he'd made a mistake.

The situation was unclear. "Is that your brother?" he asked
Alethea.

"Of course."

So why, he wanted to ask, is he behaving like a jealous lover?
But after all, he was the *xenos* here, the one who didn't know the
rules. Perhaps her nudity was innocent. Perhaps only her brother
of all of them guessed the sensational effect she was having on an
outsider.

For the next two or three days he ate, drank and swam with the
family. They made fires in the evening and in the incense clouds
they talked little. He went on long walks with Alethea. Together
they explored nearby beaches, rock-pools and sea-caves, all of the
time their hands almost touching and he never once thought of
England or of Alison.

One afternoon, as they waded between rocks carpeted with
slippery, luminous green weed, both naked having been swimming, Alethea missed her footing and grabbed his arm. It was the
first time they had touched. Again he felt a visceral punch and a
white-hot flare in his brain before he pressed his mouth roughly to
hers, tasting salt-spray on her lips, scenting that strange mixture
of marine odour and incense. Her hand cupped around his
genitals. At that moment Alethea's brother chose to reveal
himself.

Leaping from behind a rock he ran at them, puce in the face,
screaming incomprehensible insults. But he failed to follow
through, and quickly stalked away.

"It was only a kiss!"

Alethea looked stung and betrayed.

He knew he was wrong. "No. It wasn't only a kiss," he said. "I
want to be with you."

"You can't," she said simply. "Let's go back."

They walked hand in hand along the sand, but she let go as they
approached her family. Her brother was still red-faced and angry.
Her mother too looked furious, but her father, scratching the
back of his leathery neck, looked sad. An impenetrable conversation began which he couldn't follow, though several times he
heard them refer to him in the usual way.

At last he said, "I want to be with your daughter. I'm prepared to do anything it takes."

"It's not that simple," her father said.

"What could be more simple?"

"You don't understand. You are a stranger. Even if you were one of the local Greeks from this island, it would still be impossible."

"Is it because you are gypsies?"

"Gypsies? Ha!"

"And anyway," the boy spat, "you are not worthy!"

A furious quarrel broke out between the family, bitter and vindictive. Alethea broke away and ran up the beach. He went to go after her, but her father held him by the arm. "Leave her. It's no good. It's no good *for you*."

He shrugged off the old man and took off after Alethea. She'd gone beyond the rocks on to the next bay. "What do they mean?" he asked when he caught up with her. "Why do they say these things?"

She shook her head. They sat on the sand holding each other, her staring out to sea at some invisible point on the horizon. At last she said, "I sometimes think they don't want me to have anyone."

"Has this happened before?"

She nodded sadly, and he felt profoundly disappointed to be a second-comer. "They won't allow us to put this beach behind us."

He nodded, trying to accommodate the Greek figure of speech.

"No, you don't understand at all. It isn't just a way of speaking. It means lovers must go on, to another beach." She pointed out to sea, to a rock barely discernible in the distance. "To that beach. But I don't think you can make it."

It dawned on him that she was being quite literal. Some kind of gypsy ritual perhaps, a rite-of-passage for a courting couple. "Swim? You mean swim to that rock? What are you saying?"

"We could get away. I would be at your side, swimming with you."

She was proposing an elopement! He slumped to the sand and sat with his head in his hands. "But that's out of the question!"

"Why?"

He had to think about it, but his head was on fire. She was

actually inviting him to elope, and he couldn't think of a single reason why they shouldn't. The gravity of the moment pounded the beach like a wave. She was still searching his eyes for an answer. It shocked him that he was being offered a truly spontaneous moment of decision, in which he could make something astonishing happen or lose her forever. He'd been granted a miraculous opportunity to redeem his life with a single passionate act.

And yet what she proposed was madness. It was heady and dangerous. He looked at the rock in the distance, trying to calculate the swim. Last time he'd tried something like that he'd turned back exhausted at far less than half the distance. He feared the currents. But that phrase haunted, the one about "putting the beach behind him". He thought of the uselessness and the sadness of his life back in England. He had nothing to return to there. He gave no thought to what happened once the rock was reached. He assumed at that point that the statement had been made, that they would cross a symbolic or ritual line beyond which no challenge could be made to them. Then they would swim back.

Drunk on the romance of the situation, and on the reckless inspiration of her youth, he took one last look round. In the few days he'd been camping on the beach the dye had been almost bleached from his tent. It only convinced him to leave it all with the row of other tattered tents abandoned under the fringe of trees.

"You don't have to do this," Alethea said.

He said nothing. She stripped off her costume and waded out into the water. Not until she was waist deep did she turn and beckon him to follow.

The water was buoyant and he felt strong. They swam for a long time. He even felt the sun shifting in the sky. Once out of a sense of anxiety, he tried to look back to the shore, but Alethea rebuked him. After swimming for almost two hours, the distant rock seemed no nearer.

He began to feel cold. Then he felt the undertow strike, and despite his efforts, began to sense he was failing to make progress. The distance between him and Alethea increased.

For the first time since they'd set out he took a lungful of water. Coughing and thrashing about, he had to rescue himself from a moment of panic. The distance between them widened, though he could hear her exhorting him to stay close. In a thrill of horror he wondered if she might abandon him; because he also sensed that if she didn't make the pace then they would both fail. The current was sweeping him to the side. He couldn't make progress and found it impossible to swim in her wake.

His muscles ached. While trying to lie on his back to snatch a moment's rest the current dragged and flipped him back on his stomach. He took another lungful of water. When he looked back he could barely discern the shore.

And when he turned, he heard the cry of a gull and Alethea was gone.

Calling her name and struggling against the current he lost all sense of direction. He swam desperately in the bearing he thought she had gone, his muscles turning to a fiery, unresolved slush and his feet cramping. The cold was penetrating and primal.

He despaired. Shouting her name again, in his panic and confusion he heard himself calling not for her, but for Alison. It was all too much; not just the swim, but everything that had driven him to this island, and to this pass. In his overwhelming tiredness he felt a tremendous desire to simply close his eyes. The possibility of surrender seemed at last sweet and comforting. He dropped his arms into the water, the better to accept the chilly sleep.

But anger sparked him awake again. Turning, he tried to swim. Still the current dragged. He took a lungful of air, and dived down, trying to swim under the surface tow, finding he could make better progress that way. He surfaced, breathed deep and dived again. He did this several times, until he had escaped the spiralling current. Catching sight of the headland, he made agonizing progress towards it.

Then the land was before him. It was not the distant rock: he'd returned to his starting point. The sun was setting, the sea was burning ember-red. Crawling out of the water on hands and knees, he collapsed, shuddering, weeping, clawing and biting at the sand with relief. The gritty particles of sand under his finger-nails were like grains of light, jewels of deliverance, shredded tokens of the life he had almost thrown away in this desperately stupid act.

When he woke it was dark. He got to his feet and staggered up the beach. He was alone. Desperate for water he cast around in the dark trying but failing to locate the spring. Returning to his tent he found a drop of water in a plastic bottle. Shivering uncontrollably he unrolled his sleeping bag and climbed inside.

When morning came around, his muscles were on fire. He lay sweating under the nylon, thinking about what he'd done. His head pounded. He got out of the tent and went to find water. There was neither spring nor the stone slab which had covered it. It was absurd: both himself and Alethea's family had been sustained by the spring over several days.

Alethea's family had made a tidy departure. There was no trace of them, not even an impression in the sand of where they'd been sheltered. Neither was there any sign of their campfire. The charred remains and blackened stones of his own fire were there, sure enough, further along the beach, but where was the evidence of the fire around which he'd spent those few happy evenings? The sun pulsed directly overhead. Sand gusted along the beach.

He decamped hurriedly. The bus which had delivered him there was due to pass again that afternoon. At the temple he saw what was perhaps the only evidence of the gypsy family's presence. A second decomposing sea snake lay on a broken plinth, next to the first one he'd seen, almost like an offering.

For the last time he glanced back at the row of tattered tents, and again he wondered to whom they belonged. Hoisting his pack he made the climb up the hillside. At the roadside he sat on his pack until the bus came, and flagged it to stop.

It was the same driver. He looked somewhat surprised, and when asked for water he produced a tin of Sprite from a coolbox. "Take it. Where have you been all these days?"

"Down on the beach."

"Alone?"

He started to explain that there had been other people, and that a priest had shown him where to find water, and that—

"Priest? There is no priest on this side of the island."

The driver stared blankly then crunched through his gears as the bus moved up the hill. After that he would only look at his passenger through the rear-view mirror.

"I wouldn't go to that beach," he said.

"Why not?"

He merely shook his head. As they travelled back across the island, stopping at the *mastic* villages with their singular, geometrically patterned houses, the stranger thought of the last few days, and of Alethea. He wondered where she was. He thought also of the row of tattered tents under the trees, and wondered if he had narrowly escaped something deeply dangerous; or if he had forfeited some experience transcendent and beautiful.

KATHE KOJA

At Eventide

KATHE KOJA WON THE BRAM STOKER AWARD for her 1991 debut novel, *The Cipher*. Since then she has published the novels *Bad Brains*, *Skin*, *Strange Angels* and *Famished*, with *Stray Dog* and *Buddha Boy* forthcoming from Farrar, Straus & Giroux.

Her short fiction was recently collected in *Extremities* and has appeared in such magazines and anthologies as *Omni*, *The Magazine of Fantasy & Science Fiction*, *Dark Voices 3, 5* and *6*, *Still Dead: Book of the Dead 2*, *A Whisper of Blood*, *Little Deaths*, *The Year's Best Horror Stories* and *Best New Horror 3, 5* and *10*.

As the author explains: "I was invited to participate in Thomas Roche and Nancy Kilpatrick's anthology *Graven Images*, which allowed me to examine the idea of idolatry, the mask upon the mask upon the heart. This story is the result."

W hat he carried to her he carried in a red string bag. Through its mesh could be seen the gleam and tangle of new wire, a package of wood screws, a green plastic soda bottle, a braided brown coil of human hair; a wig? It could have been a wig.

To get to her he had come a long way: from a very large city through smaller cities to Eventide, not a city at all or even a town, just the nearest outpost of video store and supermarket, gas and ice and cigarettes. The man at the Stop-N-Go had directions to her place, a map he had sketched himself; he spoke as if he had been there many times: "It's just a little place really, just a couple rooms, living room and a workshop, there used to be a garage out back but she had it knocked down."

The man pointed at the handmade map; there was something wrong with his voice, cancer maybe, a sound like bones in the throat; he did not look healthy. "It's just this feeder road, all the way down?"

"That's right. Takes about an hour, hour and ten, you can be there before dark if you—"

"Do you have a phone?"

"Oh, I don't have her number. And anyway you don't call first, you just drive on down there and—"

"A phone," the man said; he had not changed his tone, he had not raised his voice but the woman sorting stock at the back of the store half-rose, gripping like a brick a cigarette carton; the man behind the counter lost his smile and "Right over there," he said, pointing past the magazine rack bright with tabloids, with *Playboy* and *Nasty Girls* and *Juggs*; he lit a cigarette while the man made his phone call, checked with a wavering glance the old Remington 870 beneath the counter.

But the man finished his call, paid for his bottled water and sunglasses, and left in a late-model pick up, sober blue, a rental probably and "I thought," said the woman with the cigarette cartons, "that he was going to try something."

"So did I," said the man behind the counter. The glass doors opened to let in heat and light, a little boy and his tired mother, a tropical punch Slush Puppy and a loaf of Wonder bread.

Alison, the man said into the phone. *It's me.*

A pause: no sound at all, no breath, no sigh; he might have been talking to the desert itself. Then: Where are you? she said. What do you want?

I want one of those boxes, he said. The ones you make. I'll bring you everything you need.

Don't come out here, she said, but without rancor; he could imagine her face, its Goya coloring, the place where her eye had been. Don't bring me anything, I can't do anything for you.

See you in an hour, the man said. An hour and ten.

*   *   *

He drove the feeder road to the sounds of Mozart, 40s show tunes, flashy Tex-Mex pop; he drank bottled water; his throat hurt from the air conditioning, a flayed unchanging ache. Beside him sat the string bag, bulging loose and uneven, like a body with a tumor, many tumors; like strange fruit; like a bag of gold from a fairy tale. The hair in the bag was beautiful, a thick and living bronze like the pelt of an animal, a thoroughbred, a beast prized for its fur. He had braided it carefully, with skill and a certain love, and secured it at the bottom with a small blue plastic bow. The other items in the bag he had purchased at a hardware store, just like he used to; the soda bottle he had gotten at the airport, and emptied in the men's room sink.

There was not much scenery, unless you like the desert, its lunar space, its brutal endlessness; the man did not. He was a creature of cities, of pocket parks and dull anonymous bars; of waiting rooms and holding cells; of emergency clinics; of pain. In the beige plastic box beneath the truck's front seat there were no less than eight different pain medications, some in liquid form, some in pills, some in patches; on his right bicep, now, was the vague itch of a Fentanyl patch. The doctor had warned him about driving while wearing it: *There might be some confusion,* the doctor said, *along with the sedative effect. Maybe a headache, too.*

A headache, the man had repeated; he thought it was funny. *Don't worry, doctor. I'm not going anywhere.* Two hours later he was on a plane to New Mexico. Right now the Fentanyl was working, but only just; he had an assortment of patches in various amounts – 25, 50, 100 mgs – so he could mix and match them as needed, until he wouldn't need them anymore.

Now Glenn Gould played Bach, which was much better than Fentanyl. He turned down the air conditioning and turned the music up loud, dropping his hand to the bag on the seat, fingers worming slowly through the mesh to touch the hair.

They brought her what she needed, there in the workshop: they brought her her life. Plastic flowers, fraying T-shirts, rosaries made of shells and shiny gold; school pictures, wedding pictures, wedding rings, books; surprising how often there were books. Address books, diaries, romance novels, murder mysteries, Bibles; one man even brought a book he had written himself, a ruffled stack of printer paper tucked into a folding file.

Everything to do with the boxes she did herself: she bought the lumber, she had a lathe, a workbench, many kinds and colors of stain and varnish; it was important to her to do everything herself. The people did their part, by bringing the objects – the baby clothes and car keys, the whiskey bottles and Barbie dolls; the rest was up to her.

Afterwards they cried, some of them, deep tears strange and bright in the desert, like water from the rock; some of them thanked her, some cursed her, some said nothing at all but took their boxes away: to burn them, pray to them, set them on a shelf for everyone to see, set them in a closet where no one could see. One woman had sold hers to an art gallery, which had started no end of problems for her, out there in the workshop, the problems imported by those who wanted to visit her, interview her, question her about the boxes and her methods, and motives, for making them. Totems, they called them, or Rorschach boxes, called her a shaman of art, a priestess, a doctor with a hammer and an "uncanny eye." They excavated her background, old pains exposed like bones; they trampled her silence, disrupted her work and worst of all they sicked the world on her, a world of the sad and the needy, the desperate, the furious and lost. In a very short time it became more than she could handle, more than anyone could handle and she thought about leaving the country, about places past the border that no one could find but in the end settled for a period of hibernation, then moved to Eventide and points south, the older, smaller workshop, the bleached and decayed garage that a man with a bulldozer had kindly destroyed for her; she had made him a box about his granddaughter, a box he had cradled as if it were the child herself. He was a generous man, he wanted to do something to repay her although "no one," he said, petting the box, "could pay for this. There ain't no money in the world to pay for this."

She took no money for the boxes, for her work; she never had. Hardly anyone could understand that: the woman who had sold hers to the gallery had gotten a surprising price but money was so far beside the point there was no point in even discussing it, if you had to ask, and so on. She had money enough to live on, the damages had bought the house, and besides she was paid already, wasn't she? paid by the doing, in the doing, paid by peace and silence and the certain knowledge of help. The boxes helped them, always: sometimes the help of comfort, sometimes the turning knife but sometimes the knife was what they needed; she never judged, she only did the work.

Right now she was working on a new box, a clean steel frame to enclose the life inside: her life: she was making a box for herself. Why? and why now? but she didn't ask that, why was the one question she never asked, not of the ones who came to her, not now of herself. It was enough to do it, to gather the items, let her hand choose between this one and that: a hair clip shaped like a feather, a tube of desert dirt, a grimy nail saved from the wrecked garage; a photo of her mother, her own name in newsprint, a hospital bracelet snipped neatly in two. A life was a mosaic, a picture made from scraps: her boxes were only pictures of that picture and whatever else they might be or become – totems, altars, fetish objets – they were lives first, a human arc in miniature, a précis of pain and wonder made of homely odds and ends.

Her head ached from the smell of varnish, from squinting in the sawdust flume, from the heat; she didn't notice. From the fragments on the table before her, the box was coming into life.

He thought about her as he drove. The Fentanyl seemed to relax him, stretch his memories like taffy, warm and ropy, pull at his brain without tearing it, as the pain so often did. Sometimes the pain made him do strange things: once he had tried to drink boiling water, once he had flung himself out of a moving cab. Once he woke blinking on a restaurant floor, something hard jammed in his mouth, an EMS tech above him: *'Bout swallowed his tongue*, the tech said to the restaurant manager, who stood watching with sweat on his face. *People think that's just a figure of speech, you know, but they wrong.*

He had been wrong himself, a time or two: about his own stamina, the state of his health; about *her*, certainly. He had thought she would die easily; she had not died at all. He had thought she could not see him, but even with one eye she picked him out of a line-up, identified him in the courtroom, that long finger pointing, accusing, dismissing all in one gesture, wrist arched like a bullfighter's before he places the killing blade, like a dancer's *en pointe*, poised to force truth out of air and bone: with that finger she said who he was and everything he was not, *mene, mene, tekel, upharsin.* It was possible to admire such certainty.

And she spared herself nothing; he admired her for that, too. Every day in the courtroom, before the pictures the prosecutor displayed: terrible Polaroids, all gristle and ooze, police tape and matted hair but she looked, she listened carefully to everything that was said and when the foreman said *guilty* she listened to that, too; by then the rest of her hair had come in, just dark brown down at first but it grew back as lush as before. Beautiful hair . . . it was what he had noticed first about her, in the bar, the Blue Monkey filled with art school students and smoke, the smell of cheap lager, he had tried to buy her a drink but *No thanks*, she had said, and turned away. Not one of the students, one of his usual prey, she was there and not – there at the same time, just as she was in his workshop later, there to the wire and the scalping knife, not-there to the need in his eyes.

In the end he had gotten nothing from her; and he admired her for that, too.

When he saw the article in the magazine – pure chance, really, just a half – hour's numb distraction, *Bright Horizons* in the doctor's office, one of the doctors, he could no longer tell them apart – he felt in his heart an unaccustomed emotion: gratitude. Cleaved from him as the others had been, relegated to the jail of memory but there she was, alive and working in the desert, in a workshop filled with tools that – did she realize? – he himself might have used, working in silence and diligence on that which brought peace to herself and pure release to others; they were practically colleagues, though he knew she would have resisted the comparison, she was a good one for resisting. The one who got away.

He took the magazine home with him; the next day he bought a map of New Mexico and a new recording of Glenn Gould.

She would have been afraid if it were possible, but fear was not something she carried; it had been stripped from her, scalped from her, in that room with the stuttering overheads, the loud piano music and the wire. Once the worst has happened, you lose the place where the fear begins; what's left is only scar tissue, like old surgery, like the dead pink socket of her eye. She did not wait for him, check the roads anxiously for him, call the police on him;

the police had done her precious little good last time, they were only good for cleaning up and she could clean up on her own, now, here in the workshop, here where the light fell empty, hard and perfect, where she cut with her X-Acto knife a tiny scrolling segment from a brand-new Gideon Bible: blessed are the merciful, for they shall obtain mercy.

Her hand did not shake as she used the knife; the light made her brown hair glow.

The man at the Stop-N-Go gave good directions: already he could see the workshop building, the place where the garage had been. He wondered how many people had driven up this road as he did, heart high, carrying what they needed, what they wanted her to use; he wondered how many had been in pain as he was in pain; he wondered what she said to them, what she might say to him now. Again he felt that wash of gratitude, that odd embodied glee; then the pain stirred in him like a serpent, and he had to clench his teeth to hold the road.

When he had pulled up beside her workshop, he paused in the dust his car had raised to peel off the used patch and apply a fresh one; a small one, one of the 25 mgs. He did not want to be drowsy, or distracted; he did not want sedation to dilute what they would do.

He looked like her memories, the old bad dreams, yet he did not; in the end he could have been anyone, any aging tourist with false new sunglasses and a sick man's careful gait, come in hope and sorrow to her door; in his hand he held a red string bag, she could see some of what was inside. She stood in the doorway waiting, the X-Acto knife in her palm; she did not wish he would go away, or that he had not come, wishing was a vice she had abandoned long ago and anyway the light here could burn any wish to powder, it was one of the desert's greatest gifts. The other one was solitude; and now they were alone.

"Alison," he said. "You're looking good."

She said nothing. A dry breeze took the dust his car had conjured; the air was clear again. She said nothing.

"I brought some things," he said, raising the bag so she could see: the wires, the bottle, the hair; her hair. "For the box, I mean . . . I read about it in a magazine, about you, I mean."

Those magazines: like a breadcrumb trail, would he have found her without one? wanted to find her, made the effort on his own? Like the past to the present, one step leading always to another and the past rose in her now, another kind of cloud: she did not fight it but let it rise, knew it would settle again as the dust had settled; and it did. He was still watching her. He still had both his eyes, but other things were wrong with him, his voice for one, and the way he walked, as if stepping directly onto broken glass and "You don't ask me," he said, "how I got out."

"I don't care," she said. "You can't do anything to me."

"I don't want to. What I want," gesturing with the bag, his shadow reaching for her as he moved, "is for you to make a box for me. Like you do for other people. Make a box of my life, Alison."

No answer; she stood watching him as she had watched him in the courtroom. The breeze lifted her hair, as if in reassurance; he came closer; she did not move.

"I'm dying," he said. "I should have been dead already. I have to wear this," touching the patch on his arm, "to even stand here talking, you can't imagine the pain I'm in."

Yes I can, she thought.

"Make me a box," as he raised the bag to eye-level: fruit, tumor, sack of gold, she saw its weight in the way he held it, saw him start as she took the bag from him, red string damp with sweat from his grip and "I told you on the phone," she said. "I can't do anything for you." She set the bag on the ground; her voice was tired. "You'd better go away now. Go home, or wherever you live. Just go away."

"Remember my workshop?" he said; now there was glass in his voice, glass and the sound of the pain, whatever was in that patch wasn't working anymore: grotesque, that sound, like a gargoyle's voice, like the voice of whatever was eating him up. "Remember what I told you there? Because of me you can do this, Alison, because of what I did, what I gave you . . . Now it's your turn to give to me."

"I can't give you anything," she said. Behind her her workshop stood solid, door frame like a box frame, holding, enclosing her life: the life she had made, piece by piece, scrap by scrap, pain and love and wonder, the boxes, the desert and he before her now was just the bad – dream man, less real than a dream, than the shadow he made on the ground: he was nothing to her, nothing and "I can't make something from nothing," she said, "don't you get it? All you have is what you took from other people, you don't have anything I can *use*."

His mouth moved, jaw up and down like a ventriloquist dummy's: because he wanted to speak, but couldn't? because of the pain? which pain? and "Here," she said: not because she was merciful, not because she wanted to do good for him but because she was making a box, because it was her box she reached out with her long strong fingers, reached with the X-Acto knife and cut some threads from the bag, red string, thin and sinuous as veins and "I'll keep these," she said, and closed her hand around them, said nothing as he looked at her, kept looking through the sunglasses, he took the sunglasses off and "I'm *dying*," he said finally, his voice all glass now, a glass organ pressed to a shuddering chord but she was already turning, red threads in her palm, closing the door between them so he was left in the sun, the dying sun; night comes quickly in the desert; she wondered if he knew that.

He banged on the door, not long or fiercely; a little later she heard the truck start up again, saw its headlights, heard it leave but by then she had already called the state police: a sober courtesy, a good citizen's compunction because her mind was busy elsewhere, was on the table with the bracelet and the varnish, the Gideon Bible and the red strings from the bag. She worked until a trooper came out to question her, then worked again when he had gone: her fingers calm on the knife and the glue gun, on the strong steel frame of the box. When she slept that night she dreamed of the desert, of long roads and empty skies, her workshop in its center lit up like a burning jewel; as she dreamed her good eye roved beneath its lid, like a moon behind the clouds.

In the morning paper it explained how, and where, they had found him, and what had happened to him when they did, but she didn't see it, she was too far even from Eventide to get the paper anymore. The trooper stopped by that afternoon, to check on how she was doing; she told him she was doing fine.

"That man's dead," he said, "stone dead. You don't have to worry about him."

"Thank you," she said. "Thank you for coming." In the box the red strings stretched from top to bottom, from the bent garage nail to the hospital bracelet, the Bible verse to the Polaroid, like roads marked on a map to show the way.

STEVE RASNIC TEM

Pareidolia

STEVE RASNIC TEM'S LATEST SHORT STORY COLLECTION is *The Far Side of the Lake*, now available from Ash-Tree Press. His new collaboration with his wife, the writer Melanie Tem, is the high fantasy novel *Daughters*, currently available from Time-Warner's iPublish division. Early in 2002, Subterranean Press will be bringing out his experimental fantasy novel *The Book of Days* in a limited edition.

As the author explains: "Pareidolia is described as a condition in which a vague stimulus is perceived as something distinct. It is used to explain why a person might see the Virgin Mary in a rust stain or Bette Miller kissing Bill Clinton in a potato. It is used to explain away the visions of such artists as Van Gogh and William Blake.

"Blake's works (the words and the pictures) had a profound effect on me when I first read them in high school. To me, they crystallized much of what I felt about the importance of an invisible world which had heretofore defied expression. They also recalled a time when I was ten or eleven and I was seeing gods in the evening clouds and the face of the Devil in the rusted screen door of a neighbour's front porch (I would not pass that house for years). At a certain point I decided enough was enough and that I would not see such things again.

"At the time I made the decision I felt vaguely disappointed with myself – later I came to realize how very wise my childhood self had been. Now that I'm a writer and past fifty I can see the face of Leonard Bernstein in the first bite out of my afternoon apple without fear of repercussion."

If I lay my face in the dust,
The grave opens its mouth for me.
                    – William Blake,
                    The Couch of Death

Somewhere in the distance a baby was crying. Blake could not understand why they let it go on. Someone should pick the baby up. If he were there, and saw such a baby, he would pick it up, and hold it, kiss its eyes and tell it lies about how everything would turn out, turn out just fine.

He'd not been to many funerals in his lifetime. He didn't think this made him at all unusual. Guys he'd grown up with, now in their forties and fifties, they'd see their moms and dads buried, but usually no one else, not even when one of their own dropped a few years prematurely. Especially when it was one of their own.

He was just beginning to imagine what old age was going to be like – functions decreasing, capacities diminishing, the world spinning so fast with more and more of his life slipping off the edge, and him just sitting there with his eyes leaking, running out of ways to say goodbye. Every day like a funeral.

Blake had been out of state when his grandparents died; he'd waited until the last minute to tell the family he wasn't coming. A torrent of cries and recriminations from family members who'd loved the couple no more than he, but he hadn't been swayed. No one could make him come. It shamed him now that in idle moments he imagined the excuses he would use when one of his own parents died.

His last funeral might have been when he was ten or eleven. An aunt, looking white waxy in the coffin, her hands folded over daisies plucked from her front yard. That had bothered him: everybody in the family knew she'd hated daisies, thought of them as weeds and mowed them down whenever possible. Later on it came out that the daisies in her hands had been a gossipy neighbor's idea, someone who claimed to be her best friend, who – she said – knew all there was to know about the deceased.

This year he would be the age of his aunt when she'd died. Fifty-two. He told himself the number wasn't that high, and in the mirror he still managed to find most of his senior high school yearbook face. But pictures taken of him said otherwise. The last few years an old man had sneaked into the photographs, a pale face that seemed to float over the noticeably swollen torso, brown hair washed out into a sandy gray blending subtly into the background. He looked like one of those specters so popular in books of unexplained phenomena, photographed accidentally at a relative's birthday party, a smudge on the negative or a glare in the lens. The uncle who's always forgetting he's been dead for years.

In recent years Blake had insisted on himself taking all the pictures at the few family gatherings. His ex-wife had remarried and he felt uncomfortable around her new husband. The man was Blake's age yet he seemed so damned young, so self-assured. "Pleased to meet you, Blake!" Tom had beamed the first time Ellie had introduced them, huge square hand hovering in the air between them. When Blake didn't respond immediately the hand grabbed him, folded him up inside. "Like the poet, right?"

Blake enjoyed using that line himself, even though most people he met had never heard of William Blake, and never mind that among that group would have been his own parents, who'd named their only son after a newly dead uncle, a retired butcher.

Ye worms of death feasting upon your aged parents' flesh. That was from *Tiriell*. He'd done poorly in his English courses, but he'd made learning his Blake a priority. Not that he understood all of the poems; in fact he wasn't sure he really understood more than a few. But he appreciated the feeling of Blake's poetry, sympathized with its obsessive quality, and most of all understood that need to see beyond the simple lies of the everyday world.

Tom stood with his wife, *their* wife, on the other side of the funeral party. A strange phrase that, funeral party. Most of the attendees were wearing appropriate party clothes: somber suits, dark dresses, limp ties.

Bound these black shoes of death, and on my hands, death's iron gloves.

Today he wore a black T-shirt, black jeans, the closest thing he had to full funeral uniform. He could imagine what his wife might have to say about that – she always said he dressed like a kid, ate like a kid, so what kind of adult role model could he be? – but he knew she'd keep her mouth shut because the girls were there with them. She was good about that sort of thing. Earlier Amy had nodded from across the gravestones and smiled. He'd smiled back, knowing he'd get to talk to her later. Janice pretended not to see him – she'd be embarrassed by his clothes, but there was nothing he could have done to please her; he was chronically incapable of sparing his older daughter embarrassment. The last four or five visits she'd made herself invisible, and in his dreams she'd become the imaginary daughter, the one the men in their ghostly white coats would insist had never existed.

Somewhere a baby was crying again. A funeral was no place for a baby, he thought. He wasn't sure why he thought that, wasn't even sure it was true. A cemetery wasn't a nursery, or a playground. But then again, he could be wrong.

Slumped on a chair in the middle of the crowd was Charlie, his best friend and the reason Blake had broken his funeral non-attendance record. It was Charlie's wife who had died, crashed her car into a tree after an aneurysm. Quickly, he supposed, and with little pain, *yet death is terrible, tho' borne on angels' wings.* Charlie was one of the people Blake had lied to about the origins of his name. "After the poet, you know? My parents had great hopes for me." Lied for no particular reason, since Charlie was hardly the literary type. And it was that inconsequential lie and the lack of trust it betrayed which had always made Blake wonder if he was even capable of close friendships.

Charlie cried with his mouth slightly open, making no sound. He'd been doing that since Blake had arrived, which was why Blake hadn't yet said anything to him, or been able to touch him. Sad to say, Charlie's death wouldn't have been much of a surprise. He drank too much and ate too much and the worse he felt about it the more he indulged the excess. People said Charlie was hard to understand but Blake found no mystery there at all. *In forests of eternal death, shrieking in hollow trees.* It came from looking at things too long and too deeply. Thinking too much, his father would have said, his most common complaint about his son. The terror of seeing might make you a mystic or make you a drunk, depending on your temperament.

Young children and babies populated much of William Blake's illuminated poetry. *Songs of Innocence. Songs of Experience.* They usually had ethereal expressions, heavenly colorings, probably due to their recent contact with an invisible world. The baby's cries were inaudible now, but he could still feel them in the air, gathering, waiting.

Blake could hear Charlie's soundless shrieking coming out of the mouth hung open in that terrible way, slightly lopsided, the lip on one side thicker than the other, as if something were hiding there. And above that mouth the swollen cheeks, the alteration of the underlying bone, the evolution brought on by grief so profound that in any other context Blake would never have recognized Charlie. Blake had always known this, he supposed, but watching Charlie brought it into focus: those we loved so much lie buried in our faces.

An old man walked behind Charlie then, rested a fleshy hand on his shoulder, bent and whispered, but Charlie's expression did not alter, and the old man went on, threading himself through mourners still as stones.

Blake didn't recognize the man as anyone he'd ever seen before and yet he recognized everything about him. An old man with a washed-out face wandering practically unnoticed among strangers and family, *for he is the king of rotten wood and of the bones of death*.

When that other Blake – poet and renowned schizophrenic – was four years old, he'd seen God's face at his window. Once he'd found the prophet Ezekiel in the fields near his home. One afternoon in his tenth year, he'd gone out into the woods and discovered a tree full of angels. He'd seen the spirit of his brother Robert fly away immediately after his death. *I look through it and not with it*. Behind each object in the real world Blake had imagined a spirit of which the visible object was only the symbol.

When *this* Blake – equally ill-at-ease with the way the world is commonly presented – had been in college he used to stare at the bark of trees until he'd imagined he could see the vibration of individual cells, and the light that flowed up out of roots and finally circulated to individual buds and leaves. For a brief time the world had opened up like a Van Gogh painting, but eventually the experience had frightened him so much he'd stopped looking.

Now Blake turned his back on the assembled mourners and attempted to make his way to where he'd last seen the old man. It was good timing in that the minister had begun to speak of Charlie's wife in those general and ritualistic phrases reserved for dead strangers.

The baby had started up again, sounding more distressed than ever. Perhaps in that mysterious way babies seemed to have it knew something sad was happening, something highly emotional. Or, the baby might be lost, ill, or in some real danger. Blake should have been doing something about that, alerting others to the existence of this distressed infant, in the unlikely event they hadn't already noticed. But he didn't do anything. The baby probably had mom and dad close at hand, and if Blake didn't leave now, he'd never find that old man.

Blake wondered if Ellie had seen him leave and that in turn generated concern that she might think he was running away from Charlie when the man needed him most. And that unaccountably led to his imagining how he would feel if he were in Charlie's shoes and it was Ellie who had died in that terrible secret way which might take anyone, anytime.

He supposed for some people divorce permitted escape from that kind of grief, but he had never stopped loving Ellie. She just couldn't deal with the things he saw in the world and he certainly could accept that. *Has my soul fainted with these views of death . . .*

"Hey, wait up!" The old man paused within a small grove of trees under whose shelter lay a number of ancient white headstones splotched black and gray with mildew. They appeared to be collected here, the spacings too slight for grave markers.

"They've lost their graves – it happens," the old man said as if reading his mind. "Sometimes the old maps get misplaced, burial records destroyed, and these smaller stones are tempting for children to move. I don't suppose the administrators mind – it allows them to reuse the plots."

"Who the hell are you?" Blake's nerves seemed to have gone liquid, dripping down his arms and legs. Then he realized it had begun to sprinkle. He moved closer to the old man under the trees, although he still couldn't see his face. Rain mumbled in the leaves overhead.

"I'm just an old man who goes to a lot of funerals. I'm sure you've heard before about fellows like me: old men, and all these funerals. Gives you something to do, a way to pass the time. And of course it never stops."

The baby screamed, cries exploding with ragged breath. Blake gazed around in panic. He had to do something. Somebody had to do something.

The rain answered with increased intensity. Here and there it got through the leaves and struck the stones, darkening them with its touches. Blake turned around to find the party, wondering if he could trust Ellie to get his girls out of the weather, was immediately embarrassed by his doubt. They seemed still to be standing out there, however, their images broken by the downpour. "I'd best be getting back," he said, but made no movement. After all, there was nowhere to go just now, not with the rain, and this old man standing closer to him now, and Blake not knowing when the old man had moved, or why.

" 'Shadows of Eternal death sit in the leaden air,' " the old man whispered.

"What?" Blake turned, and saw movement in the other's face, and could not bring himself to look more closely, but followed the yellowing eyes to a sky lowered by thunderheads. "Oh, the sky. It's coming down pretty good now, isn't it? I hope Ellie . . ." He stopped.

"*The Four Zoas.* I trust I quoted the poet correctly?"

"Well, yes. Yes, you did." Something showed itself in the old man's right cheek. For a moment it was like gazing into rapidly changing clouds: an eye, a hand, a mouth silently shrieking.

The baby answered with cries of its own. *In forests of eternal death, shrieking in hollow trees.*

"I have to get back," Blake said, but did not move.

"We all say we have to get back, we must return. And yet most of us never leave – we are already there. The next day comes, and then the next, but it's all another yesterday. Nothing has changed. We cannot bring ourselves to move, to go on to the new day. Why is that, Blake?"

"I wouldn't know," he snapped, turning away quickly, for he was sure he saw an arm caught in the old man's face, reaching from just under the left side of the neck, rising up through the cheekbone and across the muscled forehead, rough fingers resting by the right ear.

In the rain-dimmed glow of the afternoon, leaves and bark had become discarded flesh seeking a body.

"No need to look if it troubles you," came the soft voice behind him.

"There's just . . . so much of it."

" 'How terrible then is the field of death.' Odd how he, too, seemed to see it everywhere, and yet seeing brought him so much pleasure. William Blake gloried in the seeing, didn't he?"

"Yes, he certainly did. But when I look around me . . ."

"Not around you. Inside . . . what do you see inside?"

"Food becomes painful to eat, as if some change has made everything a poison the acids from my gut have to burn away. And when I get up every morning these new, constant adjustments to gravity exhaust me. There's been blood in my stool for weeks, and every errant thought threatens a headache."

"Go see a doctor."

"I'm afraid."

"There's no cure for that. 'Talking with death, answering his hard demands!' You should have learned that much from your poet. It's a continuous conversation we all must have. There may be glories in the imagination, but it's still a rotting, vegetable universe where we perform all this dreaming."

But the rain had slackened, and in the distance through steam rising like smoke off the tombstones – and how many times had a glimpse of smoke reminded him of someone lost to memory? – Blake could see that the funeral had ended, the party breaking up, his beautiful girls with their mother, and he should have been there. The baby's cries had softened to a distant, choked sobbing, but he could hear them all the same. He imagined he would always hear them, whatever the circumstance.

He ran from under the trees and between stones through tides of wet, dissolving earth, permitting himself to see what had always been too terrible to allow: how the flesh of his own newborn babies just out of their mother's blood had reminded him so much of mud, their heads, their tiny brains just clumps of mud, and so temporary, so mortal, however profound the miracle of their sudden appearance in the world. How excrement in all its forms opened a door for him into the concentration camps, led by chains of teeth and arms and legbones, chains of intestine, chains of love for the shuffling Muselmanner forced to cannibalize, to eat their own waste, left behind to drown in the tides of history. How the cemeteries could not possibly hold all those who had died. How the hills and shallows of every battlefield had come to resemble the human form. How the ground was filling with bodies and heads with their endless hair and silent tongues. How *weeds of death have wrap'd around my limbs in the hoary deeps*. How *like a dark lamp, Eternal death haunts all my expectation*. How there were eggs and snakes and faces buried under each step he took from the day his parents snapped pictures of his early crawling until what would be his final faltering steps into his last bed. How he had no answer to what bound him to these dead bodies and this thriving earth, or who was left for him to kiss.

He fell to his knees at the gravesite among broken flowers and discarded prayers scribbled hastily on the backs of party napkins. A soft crying led him to folds of artificial turf laid out to disguise the freshly-turned ground. The baby who had been abandoned there wailed with eyes squeezed shut against the sky. Blake could not believe someone could have done such a thing. The baby's cries did not mask its perfection, and Blake thought it possessed much the same beauty as his own children when they'd come into the world. He scooped up the child, his arms throbbing with pain. "When the body loses its order so goes the world," he said softly.

The baby had skin as soft as mud. The baby had a head too large for its body and a mind too large for its head. The baby peeled back its translucent lids, and the world grew eyes to witness its own terror.

THOMAS LIGOTTI

I Have a Special Plan
for This World

THOMAS LIGOTTI'S HORROR FICTION HAS BEEN critically praised for its richly evocative prose style and its ability to suggest the nightmarish essence of existence itself.

In 1982 he won the award for Best Author of Horror/Weird Fiction from the Small Press Writers and Artists Organization, and in 1997 he received the Bram Stoker Award for superior achievement for his novella "The Red Tower" and both the Bram Stoker and British Fantasy Award for his short story collection, *The Nightmare Factory*.

His other books include *Songs of a Dead Dreamer*, *Grimscribe: His Lives and Works*, *Noctuary*, *The Agonizing Resurrection of Victor Frankenstein and Other Gothic Tales*, *In a Foreign Land In a Foreign Town* and *I Have a Special Plan for This World*.

"My stories often focus on those anomalous moments in which a character's perception of his world is shaken and he is forced to confront a frightening and essentially chaotic universe," explains the author.

"'I Have a Special Plan for This World' is included in a collection of three thematically linked works published by Mythos Books. The volume is titled *My Work Is Not Yet Done: An Odyssey of Corporate Horror* and features a previously unpublished novella."

I remember working in an office where the atmosphere of tension had become so severe and pervasive that one could barely see more than a few feet in any direction. This resulted in considerable difficulties for those of us who were trying to perform the tasks which our jobs required. For instance, if for some reason we needed to leave our desks and negotiate our way to another part of the building, it was not possible to see beyond a certain distance, which was at most a few feet. Outside of this limited perimeter – this "cocoon of clarity," as I thought of it – everything became obscured in a kind of quivering blur, an ambience of agitation within which the solid and dreary decor of the company offices appeared quite distorted.

People were constantly bumping into each other in the narrow aisleways and high-ceilinged hallways of the Blaine Company offices, so severe was this state of affairs in which the atmosphere of tension at that place had caused any object more than a few feet away to be lost in a jittering and filmy tableau. One might glimpse some indistinct shape nearby, perhaps something resembling a face, which at best would look like a rubber mask. Then suddenly you found yourself colliding with one of your fellow office workers. At that moment the image of the other person became grotesquely clarified in contrast to the otherwise blurry environment brought on by the severe tension, the incredible agitation that existed in the office and pervaded its every corner, even into the smallest storage room and the sub-basement of the old office building in which the Blaine Company was the only tenant.

After one of those collisions between co-workers, which occurred with great frequency during this time of tension, each of the persons involved would quickly mouth some words of pardon to the other. Of course I can only be sure about my own words – they were always polite expressions of self-pardoning, no matter how I actually felt at that precise moment of collision. As for the words that were spoken by the other person, I cannot attest, because these were invariably garbled or sometimes entirely lost in that same atmosphere of tension and agitation that obtained throughout the Blaine workplace. (Even in the closest quarters all exchanges of conversation carried only a few inches at most before they turned into a senseless babble or were lost altogether.) But whatever these words might have been was irrelevant, for very soon you had collected yourself and were rushing off once again into the blurred spaces before you in the Blaine offices, trying to put out of your mind that intensely clarified image you had witnessed, if only for a flashing moment – that microscopically detailed eyeball, that pair of super-defined lips (or just a single one of those lips), a nostril bristling with tiny hairs, a mountainous knuckle. Whatever you might have seen you wanted only to drive from your mind as soon as possible. Otherwise this image of some part of a human face or a human body would hook itself into your brain and become associated with the viciously tense and agitated state in which we all existed, thereby initiating a series of violent thoughts and fantasies concerning that eyeball or pair of lips, especially if you recognized the person to whom those parts were attached and could give a name to the object of your murderous rage.

To a certain extent the conditions I have described could be attributed to the management system under which the company was organized. It seemed evident that the various departmental supervisors, and even upper-level managers, operated according to a mandate that require them to create and maintain an environment of tension-filled conflict among the lower staff members of the company. Whether this practice was dictated by some trend in managing technique or was endemic to the Blaine Company was a matter of speculation. But there was another, and more significant, reason for this climate of tense agitation under which we labored, a situation that, after all, is common to working environments everywhere. The reason to which I refer is this: the city in which the Blaine Company offices were located – in fact had very recently *re*-located – had once been known, quite justly, as "Murder Town." Hence, it was not unreasonable to conclude that the atmosphere of tension, of agitation, that, at certain times, severely affected the spaces of the building in which the Blaine Company was the only tenant, had its counterpart in the streets of the city outside the building.

More often than not, this city which had once been known as Murder Town was permeated by a yellowish haze. This particular haze was usually so dense that the streetlights of the downtown section as well as the vast, decaying neighborhoods surrounding this area were in operation both day and night. Furthermore, there existed a direct correlation between the murders that took place in the city and the density of the yellowish haze which veiled its streets. Even though no one openly recognized this correspondence, it was a mensurable fact: the heavier this yellowish haze weighed upon the city, the more murders would need to be reported by the local news sources. It was as simple as that.

The actual number of murders could most accurately be traced only in a tabloid newspaper called the *Metro Herald*, which of course thrived on sensational stories and statistics. The other newspapers, those which purveyed a more dignified image of themselves, proved to be a far less reliable record of both the details of the murders that were occurring throughout the city and also the actual number of these murders. These latter newspapers also failed to indicate any link between the density of the yellowish haze and the city's murder count. True enough, neither did the *Metro Herald* draw direction attention to this link – it was simply a reality that was easier to follow in their pages than in those newspapers with a more dignified image, let alone the radio and television sources, which labored under the burden of delivering their information, respectively, by means of either a human voice or by a human head accompanied by a human voice, lending both of these media a greater immediacy and reality than their printed counterparts. The consequence of the heightened reality of the radio and television news sources was that they could not afford to report anything close to the true quantity or the full details of murders that were always happening. Because if they did offer such reports by means of a human voice, with or without the presence of a human head, they would make themselves intolerable to their listeners and viewers, and ultimately they would lose advertising revenue because their audiences would abandon them, leaving only these human voices and heads reporting one murder after another without anyone listening to them or watching them recite these crimes . . . whereas the newspapers with a dignified image were able to relegate a modicum of such murder stories to the depths of their ample pages, allowing their readers to take or leave these accounts as they wished, while the Metro Herald actually thrived upon disseminating such sensational news to a readership eager to consume dispatches on the bleakest, most bizarre, and most scandalous business of the world. Yet even the *Metro Herald* was forced to draw the line at some point when it came to making known to their readers the full quantity as well as the true nature of all of the murderous goings-on in the city to which the Blaine Company had relocated – the city that was once known as Murder Town.

Of course by the time of the company's relocation the epithet of Murder Town was longer in wide usage, having been eradicated by a sophisticated public relations campaign specifically designed to attract commercial entities like the Blaine Company. Thus, the place formerly known as Murder Town had now acquired an informal civic designation as the Golden City. As anyone might have observed, no specific rationale was ever advanced to justify the city's new persona – the quality of being "golden" was merely put forth as a given trait, a new identity which was bolstered in the most shameless manner in radio, television, and newspaper ads, not to mention billboards and brochures. It was something assumed to be so, as though "goldenness" – with all the associations attending this term – had always been a vital element of the city. Certainly there was never any reference made, as one might have assumed, to the meteorological phenomenon of the yellowish haze that was truly the preeminent distinction of the physical landscape of city, including the vast and decaying neighborhoods that surrounded it. In radio, television, and newspaper ads, across billboards, and in the glossy pages of brochures that were mailed out on a worldwide scale, the city was always depicted as a place with clear skies above and tidy metropolitan avenues below. This image, of course, could not have been more at odds with the city's crumbling and all-but-abandoned towers, beneath which were streets so choked with a yellowish haze that one was fortunate to be able to see more than a few yards in any direction.

I knew for a fact that a deal had been struck between the local bureaus of commerce and businesses like the Blaine Company, which could not, for the sake of appearances, relocate their offices to a place whose second name was Murder Town but could easily settle themselves in the Golden City. Nevertheless, it was this place – this haze-choked Murder Town – to which the Blaine Company had been attracted and which well suited, as I well knew, its purposes as a commercial entity.

Not long after the Blaine Company had relocated itself, a memorandum went out to all employees from the office of the founder and president of the company, U. G. Blaine, a person whom none of us, with the exception of some members of senior management, had ever seen and from whom we had never received a direct communication of any kind, at least not since I had been hired to work in its offices. The memo was brief and simply announced that a "company-wide restructuring" was imminent, although no dates or details, and no reasoning of any kind, were offered for this dramatic action. Within a few months of the announcement of this obscure "restructuring," the supervisors of the various departments within the Blaine Company, as well as a small number of upper-level management, were all murdered.

Perhaps I might allowed a moment to elaborate on the murders I have just mentioned, which were indeed unusual even for a city that had once been known as Murder Town. The most crucial datum which I should impart is that every one of the murders of persons holding management positions at the Blaine Company had taken place within the Golden City on days when the yellowish haze had been especially dense. This fact could have been corroborated by anyone who had taken the least interest in the matter, even if none of the local newspapers (nevermind the radio and television reports) ever indicated this connection. Nonetheless, it was quite conspicuous, if one only took the time to glance out the window on certain days when the streets outside were particularly hazy or particularly yellowish, what was in the works. Sometimes I would peek over the enclosure that surrounded my desk and look out into the streets thick with haze. On those occasions I would think to myself, "Another one of them will be murdered today." And without exception this would be the case: before the day was out, or sometime during the night, the body of another supervisor, and sometimes a member of upper-level management, would be found lying dead somewhere in the Golden City.

Most often the murders took place as the victims were walking from their cars on their way into work or walking back to their cars after the workday was over, while some of the crimes actually transpired when the victims were actually inside their cars. Less frequently was the body of a supervisor, or someone of even higher rank within the company, found dead in the evening hours or on weekends. The reason that far fewer of these murders occurred during the evening and on weekends was blatant, even if no one ever made an issue of it. As I have already pointed out, murders always took place in the Golden City, and even needed to take place there. However, very few of the supervisors, and certainly none of the members of upper-level management, resided within the city limits for the simple reason that they could afford to live in one of the outlying suburbs, where the yellowish haze was seldom as dense and quite often not even visible, or at least not visible to the unaided or unobservant eye. Consequently the victims had scant motivation to make an appearance in the Golden City after working hours or on weekends, for there was nothing, or very little, to attract anyone to this place – and many things that gave cause to avoid it – other than this happened to be the location where one was forced to come to work Yet these persons, who spent as little time as possible in the Golden City, were exclusively the ones, out of the large roster of those employed by the Blaine Company, to be viciously murdered there. Or so it was in the beginning.

On some days more than one supervisor's body would be discovered exhibiting the signs of the most violent physical attack, which often suggested the work of more than one assailant, although the crime scene otherwise suggested no evidence of a premeditated conspiracy or thoughtful planning. They all seemed, in fact, to be makeshift affairs. Sometimes they were crude assaults with whatever objects might have been close at hand (such as a fragment of crumbling sidewalk or a piece of broken window in a back alley). Often the cause of death was simply strangulation or even suffocation in which lice-ridden rags had been jammed deep into the victim's throat. Quite often it was just a beating unto death that left indications of more than one pair of pummeling fists and more than one kind of savagely kicking shoe. Frequently the corpses of these unfortunate supervisors, and the occasional member of upper-level management, were stripped of their clothing, as well as robbed of their money and other valuable effects. This was typical of so many of the murders in the Golden City, a fact that could be verified by the many detectives who interviewed almost everyone at the Blaine Company in the course of their investigations of these crimes, which, in the absence of any other peculiar facts of evidence, were attributed to the numerous derelicts who made their home in the city's streets.

There was, of course, the salient fact – which did not escape the investigating detectives but which, for some reason, they never saw as a relevant issue – that for quite some time all of the victims who worked at the Blaine Company offices had attained the level of supervisor, if not an even higher position in the company. I doubt that the detectives were even aware that it was in the nature of a supervisor's function at the company to foment exactly the kind of violent and even murderous sentiments that would lead low-level staff members to form images in their minds of doing away with these people, however we tried to cast such imagined scenes from our minds as soon as they began to form. And now that all of these supervisors had been murdered, we only had each other upon whom to exercise our violent thoughts and fantasies. This situation was aggravated by the tension that derived from our concern over the installation of an entirely new group of supervisors throughout the company.

As most of the lower staff employees realized, it was possible to become accustomed to the violent thoughts and fantasies inspired by a supervisor of longstanding, and for precisely this reason these supervisors would often be replaced in their position because they were no longer capable of inspiring fresh images of violence in the minds of those they were charged with supervising. With the arrival of a newly appointed supervisor there was inevitably a revival of just the sort of tension that developed into an office atmosphere in which you could barely see a few feet in any direction whenever you were required to move about the aisleways and hallways of the building to which the company had relocated not long before these events which I have chosen to document transpired. It was therefore welcome news to employees when it was made known, by means of a brief memo from one of the highest members of senior management, that none of the murdered supervisors would be replaced and that this position was to be permanently eliminated as part of the scheme for restructuring the company.

The relief experienced among the lower staff of the various departments and divisions of the Blaine Company that they would not have to face the prospect of newly appointed supervisors – or supervisors of any kind, since they had all been murdered – allowed the tension which had been so severe and pervasive to abate, thereby clearing the air around the offices from its previous condition of a blurry atmosphere of agitation and also clearing our minds of the violent thoughts and fantasies that we had come to direct so viciously at one another. However, this state of relative well-being was only temporary and was soon replaced by symptoms of acute apprehension and anxiety. This reversal occurred following a company-wide meeting held in the sub-basement of the building where the Blaine offices had been relocated.

While the senior officers who called for this meeting readily admitted that a sub-basement in an old and crumbling office building was perhaps not the ideal place to hold a company-wide meeting, it was nevertheless the only space large enough to accommodate the company's full staff of employees and was thought preferable to convening at a site elsewhere in the Golden City, since we would then be required to travel through the yellowish haze which lately had become far more consistently dense owing to "seasonal factors," according to the radio and television reports of local meteorologists. Thus we all came to be huddled in the dim and dirty realm of the building's sub-basement, where we were required to stand for lack of adequate seating and where the senior officers of the company addressed us from a crude platform constructed of thin wooden planks which creaked and moaned throughout this session of speeches and announcements, their words sounding throughout that sub-basement space as hollow and dreamlike echoes.

What we were told, in essence, was that the Blaine Company was positioning itself to become a "dominant presence in the world marketplace," in the rather vague words of an executive vice president. This declaration struck nearly everyone who stood crushed together in that sub-basement as a preposterous ambition, given that the company provided no major products or services to speak of, its principal commercial activity consisting almost wholly of what I would describe as *manipulating documents* of one sort or another, none of which had any great import or interest beyond a narrow and financially marginal base of customers, including such clients as a regional chain of dry cleaners, several far-flung restaurants that served inexpensive or at most moderately priced fare, some second-rate facilities featuring dog races that were in operation only part of a given year, and a few private individuals whose personal affairs were such that they required – or perhaps only persuaded themselves

out of vanity that they required – the type of document manipulation in which the Blaine Company almost exclusively specia-
lized. However, it was soon revealed to us that the company had
plans to become active in areas far beyond, and quite different
from, its former specialization in manipulating documents. This
announcement was delivered by an elderly man who was introduced to us as Henry Winston, the new Vice President of Development. Mr Winston spoke in a somewhat robotic tone as he
recited to us the radical transformations the company would need
to undergo in order to make, or remake, itself into a dominant
force in the world marketplace, although he never disclosed the
full nature that these transformations, or "restructurings," as they
were called, would take. Nor did Mr Winston specify the new
areas of commercial activity in which the company would be
engaged in the very near future.

During the course of Mr Winston's address, none of us could
help noticing that he seemed terribly out of place among the other
members of senior management who occupied that rickety wood-
en platform constructed especially for this meeting. His suit
appeared to have been tailored for a larger body rather than
the bony frame which now shifted beneath the high-priced
materials which hung upon the old man. And his thick white
hair was heavily greased and slicked back, yet as he spoke it
began to sprout up in places, as if his lengthy, and in some places
yellowed locks were not accustomed to the grooming now forced
upon them.

As murmurs began to arise among those of us pressed together
in that dim and dirty sub-basement, Mr Winston's mechanical
monologue was cut short by one of the the other senior officers,
who took the spotlight from the old man and proceeded to deliver
the final announcement of the meeting. Yet even before this final
announcement was made by a severe-looking woman with close-
cropped hair, many of those among the crowed huddled into the
confines of that sub-basement had already guessed or intuited its
message. From the moment we descended into that lowest level of
the building by way of the freight elevator, there was a feeling
expressed by several employees that an indefinable presence
inhabited that place, something that was observing us very closely
without ever presenting a lucid image of itself. Several people
from the lower staff even claimed to have glimpsed a peculiar

figure in the dark reaches of the sub-basement, a shape of some kind that seemed to maneuver about the edges of the congregation, a hazy human outline that drifted as slowly and silently as the yellowish haze in the streets of the Golden City and was seen to be of a similar hue.

So by the time the woman with the close-cropped hair made what might otherwise have been a striking revelation, most of the lower staff were beyond the point of receiving the news as any great surprise. "Therefore," continued the severe-looking woman, "the role of those supervisors who have been so tragically lost to our organization will now be taken over by none other than the founder and president of the Blaine Company – Mr U. G. Blaine. In an effort to facilitate the restructuring of our activities as a business, Mr Blaine will henceforth be taking a *direct hand* in every aspect of the company's day-to-day functions. Unfortunately, Mr Blaine could not be present today, but he extends his assurance that he looks forward to working with each and every one of you in the near future. So, if there are no questions" – and there were none – "this meeting is therefore concluded." And as we ascended in the freight elevator to return to our desks, nothing at all was said about the plans revealed to us for the company's future.

Later that day, however, I heard the voices of some of my co-workers in conversation nearby the enclosure that surrounded my desk. "It's perfectly insane what they're doing," whispered a woman whose voice I recognized as that of a longtime employee and a highly productive manipulator of documents. Others in this group more or less agreed with this woman's evaluation of the company's grandiose ambition of becoming a dominant force in the world marketplace. Finally someone said, "I'm thinking of giving my notice. For some time now I've been regretting that I ever followed the company to this filthy city." The person who spoke these words was someone known around the office as The Bow Tie Man, a name granted to him due to his penchant for sporting this eponymous item of apparel on a daily basis. He seemed to enjoy the distinction he gained by wearing a wide variety of bow ties rather than ordinary straight ties, or even no tie at all. Although there were possibly millions of men around the world who also wore bow ties as a signature of sartorial distinction, he was the only one in the Blaine Company offices to do so.

This practice of his allowed him to express a mode of personal identity, however trivial and illusory, as if such a thing could be achieved merely by adorning oneself with a particular item of apparel or even by displaying particular character traits such as a reserved manner or a high degree of intelligence, all and any of which qualities were shared by millions and millions of persons past and present and would continue to be exhibited by millions and millions of persons in the future, making the effort to perpetrate a distinctive sense of an identity apart from other persons or creatures, or even inanimate objects, no more than a ludicrous charade.

It was after I heard The Bow Tie Man proclaim that he was of a mind to "give his notice" that I stepped away from my desk and walked over to join the conversation being carried on by some of my co-workers. "And after you give your notice," I asked The Bow Tie Man, "then what? Where will you go? What other place could you find that would be any different?" Then the woman whose voice I had previously recognized as that of a longtime member of the company's staff spoke up, protesting that it was absolutely deranged for the company to imagine that it could ever become a dominant force in the world marketplace. "Do you really think so?" I replied. "Haven't you observed that there is a natural tendency, deranged or not, for all such entities as the Blaine Company, for any kind of business or government or even private individual, to extend themselves as far as possible – to force themselves on the world as much as they can, either by becoming a dominant commercial entity or merely by wearing bow ties everyday, thereby imposing themselves on the persons and things around them, imposing what they are or what they believe themselves to be without regard or respect for anything else aside from how far they can reach out into the world and put their seal upon it, even stretching out into other worlds, shouting commands at the stars themselves and claiming the universe as their own?"

By that point, I think my co-workers were taken aback, not as much by the words I had spoken as by the fact that I had spoken to them at all, something I had never done apart from the verbal exchanges required by our work as document manipulators. From their expressions I could see that my speaking to them in this way was somehow monstrous and wrong – a freak happening whose occurrence signified something they did not wish to name. Almost immediately afterward the group broke up, and we all returned to our desks. That afternoon the yellowish haze of the Golden City was especially dense and pushed itself heavily against the windows of the building where the Blaine Company had relocated itself. And on the very same day that upper-level management had announced to us that none of the murdered supervisors would be replaced and that U. G. Blaine himself was going to take a direct hand in the day-to-day operations of each department and division within the company, it seemed that his supervisory presence was already among us.

The most conspicuous early sign of what I will call the "Blaine presence" was the distinct yellowish tint which now permeated the company's office space. Less obvious was the sense, which a number of persons had previously experienced during the company-wide meeting, that we were at all times under the eye of something we could not see but which was intimately aware of our every word and action. Before the day was over, everyone in the office seemed to have gained a silent understanding of why we had relocated to the Golden City and why this place, which had once been known as Murder Town, was so well suited to the purposes of commercial entities like the Blaine Company . . . or were at least perceived to be so by the heads of such corporate bodies.

By the following business day there was no longer any talk around the office about the deranged strategy of the company to become a dominant force in the world marketplace. And no one commented on the absence of the man who wore bow ties each and every day. Perhaps the others actually believed that he had given his notice – a course of action he had suggested he might take – even though none of his personal items had been removed from his desk. Since the supervisor of our department had been murdered like all the others, there was no one whose duty it was to be concerned with the failure of The Bow Tie Man to show up at the office, just as there was no one who proffered any information about the meaning of his absence. After a few days had passed, his desk was occupied by a new employee, a man whom no one had ever seen working elsewhere in the company and who did not seem like the sort of person any company would hire to manipulate documents. His age was difficult to discern because his face was almost entirely obscured by shaggy strands of unwashed hair and an ample growth of untended beard, both of which were streaked with the discoloration which we noticed affected anything that was subject to longtime exposure to the peculiar atmospheric elements of the Golden City. As for the clothes worn by our new co-worker, they appeared to be very much in the same style as his predecessor who formerly inhabited that particular desk. However, due to the length of the new employee's beard, it was not possible to verify whether or not he was wearing a bow tie each and every day. And no one in the office desired to look close enough to find out if this was the case. Nevertheless, there was one woman whom I overheard telling another that she was going to check on The Bow Tie Man in order to establish what had become of him. Then she herself failed to show up for work the next day. Afterward no one else pursued the disappearance of either of these two employees, nor that of any of several other employees who on a fairly regular basis now began drop out of the ranks of the lower staff at the Blaine Company, which by this time was known to the world simply as "Blaine."

Needless to say, the degree of tension that now pervaded the offices at Blaine was once again at an extremely high level. Yet this tense environment, which had always served as a hothouse for the most violent thoughts and fantasies among the office personnel, no longer had an effect on the atmosphere of our workplace, such that you could not see more than a few feet in front of your face. Instead, the offices continued to be evenly permeated by a yellowish tint. While I have already identified this distinct yellowish coloration of the office atmosphere with what I have called the Blaine presence, others around me – and throughout the company – held the view that the haze which choked the streets of the Golden City had somehow seeped into the building where we spent each day manipulating documents. But it seemed to me that these differing explanations were in fact complementary. In my view there was a terrible equation between the Blaine presence, which now supervised every activity throughout the company, even the smallest manipulations of the the most insignificant documents, and the yellowish haze casting itself so densely over the Golden City – a place that seemed so well suited to the purposes of commercial entities like Blaine, which of course were merely extensions of the purposes of human entities like U. G. Blaine himself, specifically his seemingly preposterous ambition to turn his business into a dominant force in the world marketplace. All of this remained hypothetical for some time . . . until one day a certain turn of events allowed me to confirm my suspicions and at the same time – after so much patient restraint – enabled me to pursue my own purposes with respect to the relocation of the company.

This turning point came in the form of a summons to the office of the new Vice President of Development, Mr Henry Winston, who was located in a remote part of the building in which Blaine was the only tenant. Mr Winston's office, I noted when I first entered, was a sty. Judging by the stained mattress in a corner behind some rusted filing cabinets and the remnants of food and beverage containers scattered about the floor, Mr Winston had transformed the place into his personal hovel. The Vice President of Development himself was seated behind an old and heavily scarred wooden desk, his arms stretched across the desktop and his head lying sideways upon it in noisy slumber. When I closed the door behind me, Mr Winston slowly awakened and looked up at me, his hair and beard no longer groomed in the way they had been for the sub-basement meeting at which he spoke some months before. And what he had to say to me now still sounded as though he were reading from a script, although the quality of his voice was far less robotic than it had been at the company-wide meeting.

Mr Winston rubbed his eyes and ran his tongue around the inside of his mouth, catching the aftertaste of the sleep I had disturbed. Then, as if he were a busy man, he got right to the point. "He wants to have a conference with you. There's a . . ." Mr Winston paused a moment, apparently at a loss to recall or properly enunciate his next words. "A proposal. There's a proposal he has for you . . . a personal proposal."

Mr Winston then informed me of the time and place for this conference with U. G. Blaine – after the end of that working day, in a lavatory on one of the uppermost floors of the building. This seemed to be everything that the Vice President of Development was required to communicate to me, and I turned to leave his office. But before I was out the door he blurted out a few words that genuinely seemed to be his own.

"He should never have brought you here," said Mr Winston, which very well might have been his real name.

"You mean the relocation of the company to this city," I replied, attempting to clarify the issue.

"That's right. The re-lo-cation," he said, breaking into a little laugh and revealing an incomplete set of yellow teeth. But he stopped laughing when I looked over my shoulder back at him, focusing my eyes deep into his.

"Mr Blaine isn't entirely responsible," I said. "We both know how it is with this city."

After a brief pause Mr. Winston spoke. "I know you now," he said as if speaking softly in a dream. "You were here before . . . when the sky was clear. What did you do?"

I simply smiled at the Vice President of Development and then exited that squalid office, leaving the man inside with his sleep-polluted mouth hanging open in stupified wonder.

By this juncture in the company's progress, there were no longer many employees remaining who were not of a kind with Henry Winston. One by one all the regular staff stopped appearing for work, and their desks came to be occupied by new persons who always looked like fugitives from the great tribe of derelicts living in the Golden City, a shadow population that moved day and night through that yellowish haze. No doubt they too had made accommodations for themselves in the buildings, little havens similar to the one I saw in Henry Winston's office. I imagined that such accommodations and a modicum of food may have been offered to them by the company in lieu of a paycheck. This scheme for "cost-cutting" would alone account for the elevated profits that Blaine had realized in the past quarter. Of course this manner of fiscal growth could not continue much longer, and other measures would need to be taken if the company was truly to become a dominant force in the market-place of this world or any other. These measures, I assumed, would emerge as the chief topic of the conference U. G. Blaine had scheduled with me after the close of the working day in a lavatory on one of the uppermost floors of that crumbling building.

When the time came, I began ascending the shaft of stairways – the elevator having ceased to function by that time – in anticipation of my private meeting with the company's president and founder. As I made my way in nearly total darkness up these steps

I recalled the day that I came to interview for my position with what was then called the Blaine Company. That interview took place in another building in another city. In the reception area where I waited to be called for my interview there hung a portrait of U. G. Blaine. It was a flattering enough likeness of a middle-aged man in a business suit, but the effect of contemplating this portrait was such that I wanted to turn away and purge it from my mind before I started thinking thoughts that I did not want in my head. But I found it impossible to turn away. Fortunately, someone came along and called me to my interview before my thoughts reached a pitch of intolerable tension and agitation.

The person who interviewed me asked, among other things, what single personal quality I believed I might possess that would distinguish me for consideration as an employee of the Blaine Company. I hesitated for some time, and even thought it might be best if I gave no reply at all, or a very feeble and conventional response. Instead I spoke some words that I was sure the interviewer wanted to hear and that, in fact, were true. "My quality," I said, "my personal quality is the capacity to drive myself and those around me to the uttermost limits of our potential – to affect persons, and even places, in a way that brings their unsuspected possibilities and purposes out of hiding and into the full light of realization. That is my personal quality."

As oddly phrased and vehement as this statement might sound to other individuals, it was, I knew, exactly what my interviewer wanted to hear. On the spot I was offered the position for which I had applied at the Blaine Company – that of a manipulator of documents. When I entered the company's old offices to be interviewed my only purpose was to lose myself in the manipulation of documents, to bury as deeply as I could this passionate personal quality of mine, which had always resulted in the most unfortunate and twisted consequences for those involved, whether it was an individual person or a group of persons or a commercial entity like the Blaine Company. Because my personal quality, as stated to my interviewer at the Blaine Company, was more than a figure of speech or an exaggerated claim for the purposes of self-promotion, even if I have been at a lifelong loss to account for the full force of this extraordinary quality. For years my only purpose had been to suppress this quality, to crush it as best I could. However, after contemplating that portrait of U. G.

Blaine – after seeing written upon that face what I might describe as a "profoundly baseless sense of purpose in the world" – everything changed inside my head, which I could no longer keep from filling up with strange and violent thoughts and fantasies. "This company will soon need to relocate," I thought as I walked away from my interview that day. "In order to satisfy its sense of purpose as a commercial entity, and the baseless sense of purpose of its founder and president, this company will need to relocate to another place." And I knew precisely the place that was well suited to the company's purposes . . . and to my own. Thus, when I finally located and entered the small lavatory where U. G. Blaine wished to confer with me, I was incited to the point of derangement by the grim drama which was now coming to a climax.

"Opportunity awaits you in the Golden City," I shouted, my voice resounding against the tile walls and floor, the metal doors and porcelain fixtures of the antiquated lavatory surrounding me. "Opportunity awaits you in the Golden City," I repeated, mocking the slogan that a public relations company had used to transform the image of the city once known as Murder Town. It was this preposterous dream of changing its public image that made the Golden City ideal for the purposes of Blaine (the company), which held the deranged and preposterous idea that it could ever become a dominant force in the world marketplace, even though its only commercial activity was that of manipulating documents for small-time businesses and a few private individuals. Only in this atmosphere of a crumbling city surrounded by vast, decaying neighborhoods, its streets filled with hordes of wandering derelicts and permeated by a yellowish haze that no meteorologist or scientist or any kind had ever successfully accounted for . . . only in this Murder Town could I manage to drive Mr U. G. Blaine to the uttermost limit of his potential – just as I had driven this city itself, whose streets I inhabited for a time, to the vile and devious limit of its potential, leaving behind an inexplicable yellowish haze, a mere side effect of the things that I had done there, things that I was born to do as a freak of this world (or perhaps another world altogether, so unknown am I to myself), things that my freakish nature learned to do over many years, and things that made me seek my own burial in an occupation where I could forget my freakish self and everything

I knew about this world where I did not belong. Only here could Blaine be made to realize his unsuspected possibilities and purposes, especially that baseless sense of purpose which I could not escape seeing in that portrait of a middle-aged man in a business suit.

Of course it was not a man in a business suit who awaited my arrival in that small lavatory – it was the Blaine presence, as I called it, that pervaded the bright little room with its yellow tint. "Your restructuring of the company has been a great success," I said to the Blaine presence, which now quivered and curled about the room in trembling, yellow-tinted waves. "Soon it will be just you and your derelicts in this building. You will be the dominant force in the marketplace of the Golden City, manipulating all the documents in town. But you will never go further than that. This is where you belong. This is where you will stay. And there's nothing either of us can do to change that. You think that I can assist you in extending your power and influence, your market-place dominance, but I came to tell you that no such thing will ever happen. This place is your uttermost limit."

The Blaine presence was now becoming extremely agitated, its yellow tint swirling about the room and batting itself against the walls. "There's no use in blaming me for what you are," I screamed. "You're the creator of a marketplace for violent thoughts and fantasies. I saw that in the portrait of the mid-dle-aged man in a business suit, and I can feel it in the presence you have now made of yourself. That's all there can ever be for you in this world."

At that point I picked up a wastepaper container that stood by the lavatory sink and was shaped like a bullet with a rounded point. Across the room was a small window with panes of frosted glass. I smashed those glass panes by ramming the rounded top of the wastepaper container into it with all the violent force within me. Through the smashed panes of that window in a lavatory on one of the uppermost floors of the building you could see out over the city, the moon shining down through the yellowish haze. "There," I shouted while pointing out the broken window. "Go out into your world of haze. That's your element now. And you can't survive beyond its limits. The limits of the Golden City."

I felt a powerful, almost cyclonic gust sweep past me on all sides, even moving through me as it soared out the broken window and blended into the yellowish haze beyond, leaving behind it a room charged with the residue of vicious and violent impulses.

After that night, the Golden City was rechristened as Murder Town. Early the next morning, the streetlights still shining through the yellowish haze, brutally mauled bodies were discovered lying in every street of the city and far into the vast, decaying neighborhoods surrounding it. For a time news reports broadcast by radio and television and printed in newspapers with a dignified image as well as tabloid rags like the *Metro Herald* – where I once worked as a reporter myself – were concerned with nothing but these murders, which they called "Murders of Mystery" or "Mysterious Mass Murders."

However, it was not long before serious consideration was given to the possibility that these were not murders at all but the consequences of what the *Metro Herald* designed as the "Yellow Plague," because the bodies of the victims all displayed jaundiced blotches that overworked hospital personnel, police investigators, and morgue attendants had at first assumed to be bruises caused by violent attacks. For a day or so city officials had the opportunity to present the cause of these astonishingly lurid and numerous deaths as, quite possibly, an instance of a mysterious disease rather than of mysterious murder. With the cooperation of local law enforcement and medical officials, along with the services of a sophisticated public relations campaign, the issue of how such an incredible number of corpses might have been produced during a single night could have been confused long enough for the city to waver between its old reputation as a place of murder and an entirely new identity as a place of disease. Of course, given the alternative of henceforth being known to the world as the "City of the Yellow Plague," on the one hand, or as "Murder Town," on the other, the latter appellative seemed the preferable choice.

Apparently unrelated to the Mystery Murders, according to news reports disseminated by all the local media, was the discovery of the body of a middle-aged man dressed in a worn business suit in a suburb just outside the city limits. Eventually identified as U. G. Blaine, the corpse was found lying in the parking lot of a small outdoor shopping center. Investigators uncovered no signs that might have connected Blaine's death to those which took place the night before in Murder Town. To all appearances the man had simply collapsed and died in a place where the yellowish haze of what was once known as the Golden City dissolved altogether, giving way to the lucid atmosphere of an upper-class suburb contiguous with the city's outlying neighborhoods.

On that same morning that Blaine's body was found, I walked through the deserted streets of a city where others were still afraid to walk, strolling calmly through the stillness and the yellowish haze. For a moment I felt that I had finally driven myself to my limit, and I was content as errant pages from local newspapers flapped idiotically along the sidewalk and streetlights glared down upon me.

But before the morning had passed I was ready to move on – to relocate once more. My purpose, for a time, had exhausted itself. But now I could see there were other cities, other people and places. I could see all the world as if it loomed only a few feet in front of me – its every aspect so clear to my eyes that I would never be able to drive it from my mind until the last of my violent thoughts and fantasies had been fulfilled. Even though I knew in the depths of myself that it was all just another preposterous entity, a false front propped up by baseless purposes and dreams, I could not help thinking to myself – "I have a special plan for this world."

May this document, unmanipulated, stand as my declaration of purpose.

MICHAEL MARSHALL SMITH

The Handover

MICHAEL MARSHALL SMITH IS A NOVELIST AND SCREENWRITER
who lives in London. His first novel, *Only Forward*, won the August
Derleth Award and, following its belated publication in America,
was presented with the Philip K. Dick Memorial Award in 2001.

Spares was optioned by Steven Spielberg's DreamWorks SKG
and translated in seventeen countries around the world; *One of
Us* is under option by Warner Brothers; and his latest novel, *The
Straw Men*, is forthcoming from HarperCollins. His short fiction
has appeared in various anthologies and magazines and has been
collected in *What You Make It*.

"In terms of the story itself," Smith reveals, "there's not much
to say except that I got the idea during a fantastic three-week
drive from one side of the United States to the other; that, and a
love of the deserted and the ruined so acute that in the end I was
actively banned from saying 'Oh, look – a fallen-down barn' even
just one more time . . ."

Nobody moved much when he came into the bar. From the
way Jack shut the door behind him – quietly, like the door
of a cupboard containing old things seldom needed but neatly
stored – we could tell he didn't have any news that we'd be in a
hurry to hear. There were three guys sipping beer up at the

counter. One of them glanced up, gave him a brief nod. That was it.

It was nine thirty by then. There were five other men in the place, each sitting at a different table, nobody talking. Some had books in front of them, but I hadn't heard a page turn in a while. I was sitting near the fire and working steadily through a bowl of chilli, mitigating it with plenty of crackers. I'd like to say Maggie's chilli is the best in the West, but, to be frank, it isn't. It's probably not even the best in town: even this town, even now. I wasn't even very hungry, merely eating for something to do. Only alternative would have been drinking, but just a couple will go to my head these days, and I didn't want to be drunk. Being drunk has a tendency to make everything run into one long dirge, like being stoned, or living in Iowa. I haven't ever taken a drink on important days, on Thanksgiving, anniversaries or my birthday. Not a one. This evening wasn't any kind of celebration, not by a long chalk, but I didn't want to be drunk on it either.

Jack walked up to the bar, water dripping from his coat and onto the floor. He wasn't moving fast, and he looked old and cold and worn through. It was bitter outside, and the afternoon had brought a fresh fall of snow. Only a couple of inches, but it was beginning to mount up. Maggie poured a cup of coffee without being asked, and set it in front of him. Her coffee isn't too bad, once you've grown accustomed to it. Jack methodically poured about five spoons of sugar into the brew, which is one of the ways of getting accustomed to it, then stirred it slowly. The skin on his hand looked delicate and thin, like blue-white tissue paper that had been scrunched into a ball and absently flattened out again. Sixty-eight isn't so old, not these days, not in the general scheme of things. But some nights it can seem ancient, if you're living inside it. Some nights it can feel as if you're still trying to run long after the race is finished. At sixty-four, and the second youngest in the place, I personally felt older than God.

Jack stood for a moment, looking around the place as if memorizing it. The counter itself was battered with generations of use, as was the rest of the room. The edges of chairs and tables were worn smooth, the pictures on the walls so varnished with smoke you'd had to have known them for forty years to guess what they showed. We all knew what they showed. The bulbs in the wall fixings were weak and dusty, giving the room a dark and gloomy cast. The one area of brightness was in the corner, where the jukebox sat. Was a big thing when Pete, my old friend and Maggie's late husband, bought it. But only the lights work these days, and not all of them, and none of us are too bothered. Nobody comes into the bar who wouldn't rather sit in peace than hear someone else's choice of music, played much too loud. I guess that comes with age, and anyway the 45s in the machine are too old to evoke much more than sadness. The floor was clean, and the bar only smelt slightly of old beer. You want it to smell that way a little, otherwise it would be like drinking in a church.

Maggie waited until Jack had caught his breath, then asked. Someone had to, I guess, and it was always going to be her. She said: "No change?"

Jack raised his head, looked at her. "Course there's a change," he muttered. "No-one said she weren't going to change."

He picked up his coffee and came to sit on the other side of my table. But he didn't catch my eye, so I let him be, and cleared up the rest of my food, rejecting the raw onion garnish in deference to my innards. They won't stand for that kind of thing any more. It wasn't going to be long before a cost-benefit analysis of the chilli itself consigned it to history alongside them.

When I was done I pushed the bowl to one side, burped as quietly as I could, and lit up a Camel. I left the pack on the table, so Jack could take one if he had a mind to. He would, sooner or later. The rest of the world may have decided that cigarettes are more dangerous than a nuclear war, but in Eldorado, Montana, a man's still allowed to smoke after his meal if he wants to. What are they going to do: come and bust us? The people who make the rules live a long ways from here, and the folk in this town have never been much for caring what State ordinances say.

One of the guys at the bar finished his beer, asked for another. Maggie gave him one, but didn't wait for any money. Outside, the wind picked up a little, and a door started banging, the sound like an unwelcome visitor knocking to be let out of the cellar. But it was a ways up the street, and you stopped noticing it after a while. It's not an uncommon sound in Eldorado.

Other than that, everyone just held their positions, and eventually Jack reached forward and helped himself to a cigarette. I struck a match for him, as his fingers still seemed numb and awkward. He still hadn't taken his coat off, though with the fire it was pretty warm in the room.

Once he was lit, and he'd stopped coughing, he nodded at me through the smoke. "How's the chilli?"

"Filthy," I confirmed. "But warm. Most of it."

He smiled. He rested his hands on the table, palms down, and looked at them for a while. Liver spots and the shadow of old veins, like a fading map of territories once more uncharted. "She's getting worse," he said. "Going to be tonight. Maybe already."

I'd guessed as much, but hearing it said still made me feel tired and sad. He hadn't spoken loudly, but everybody else heard too. It got even quieter, and the tension settled deeper, like a dentist's waiting room where everyone's visiting for the first time in years and has their suspicions about what they're going to hear. Maybe "tension" isn't the right word. That suggests someone might have felt there was something they could do, that some virile force was being held in abeyance, ready for the sign, the right time. There wasn't going to be any sign. This night had been a while in coming, but it had come, like a phone call in the night. We knew there wasn't anything to be done.

Maggie pottered around, put on a fresh jug of coffee. I started to stand up, meaning to get me a cup, but Jack put his hand on my arm. I sat back, waited for him to speak.

"Wondered if you'd walk with me," he said.

I looked back at him, feeling a dull twinge of dread. "Already?"

"Only really came down here to fetch you, if you had a mind to go."

I realized in a kind of way that I was honoured. I took the heavy coat from the back of my chair and put it on. A couple of heads raised to watch us leave, but most people turned away. Every one of them knew where we were going, the job we were going to do. Maybe you'd expect something to be said, the occasion to be marked in some way: but in all my life, of all the things I heard that were worth saying, none of them were actually said in words. And I ask you: what could anyone have said

Outside it was even colder than I expected, and I stuffed my hands deep in my pockets and pulled my neck down into my scarf like a turtle. The snow was six inches deep in the street, and I was glad I had my thick boots on. The moon was full above, snow clouds hidden away someplace around a corner, recuperating and getting ready for more. There would be more, no doubt of that. The winters just keep getting colder and deeper around here, or so my body tells me. The winters are coming into their prime.

Jack started walking up the street, and I fell in beside him. Within seconds my long bones felt like they were being slowly twisted, and the skin on my face like it was made of lead. We walked past the old fronts, all of them dark now. The hardware store, the pharmacy, the old tea rooms. Even in light of day the painted signs are too faded to read, and the boardwalk which used to run the length of the street has rotted away to nothing. It happened like a series of paintings. One year it looked fine; then another it was tatty; then finally it was broken down and there was no reason to put it back. Sometimes, when I'd walked up the street in recent years, I would catch myself recalling the way things had once been, working my memory like a tongue worrying the site where a tooth had once sat. I could remember standing or sitting outside certain stores, the people who'd owned them, the faces of the people I'd spied from across the way. The times all tended to blend into one, and I could be the young boy running to the drug store, or the youth mooning over the younger of two sisters, or a man buying whiskey to blur the night away: switching back and forth in a blink, like one man looking out of three sets of eyes. It was like hearing a piece of music you grew up to, some tune you had in your head day after day until it was as much a part of your life as breathing. It was also a kind of time travel, and for a moment I'd feel as I once had, young and empty of darkness, ready to learn and experience and do. Eager to be shown what the world had in store for me, to conquer and make mistakes. To love, and lose, and love again. Amen.

Eldorado was founded in 1850 by two miners, Joseph and Ezekial Clarke: boys who came all the way from New Hampshire with nothing but a pair of horses and a dream. Sounds funny now, calling it a dream, probably even corny. People don't think of money that way any more. These days they think it's a right, and they don't go looking for it. They stay where they are, and try to make it come to them, instead of going off to find it for themselves. The brothers came in search of gold, like so many others. They were late on the trail, and worked through the foothills, finding nothing or stakes that had already been worked dry, and then climbed higher and higher into the mountains. They panned a local river, and found nothing once more, but then one afternoon came upon the seam – just as they were about to give up and move on, maybe head over to Oregon or California and see if it was paradise like everyone said. It must have seemed like magic. They found gold. When we were young we all heard the story. A kind of Genesis tale. A little glade, hidden up amidst the mountains at over three thousand feet: and there for the taking, a seam of money, a pocket of dreams.

The brothers stayed, and built themselves a cabin out of the good wood that grew all around. But news travelled fast, even in those days, and it wasn't long before they had company. A lot of company. The old mine workings have gone to ruin now, but it was a big old construction, I can tell you that. Was a few years when Eldorado was home to over four thousand people, and produced five million dollars a year in gold. The town had saloons and boarding houses, a post office and a fistful of gambling rooms, even a grand hotel. Almost all have fallen down now, though until ten years ago people still used the hotel to board their animals in, when it got real cold. Two walls are still more or less there, hidden amongst the trees, though I wouldn't want to stand underneath them for long. I once showed them to a couple of tourists who came up all this way in a rental car, having seen the town sign down the road. They seemed a little disappointed to find there was still people living here, and were soon on their way again.

That was near ten years ago, and no one's come up to look since, though the town sign's still there. It says "Eldorado, 15 miles", and stands on a turn of the local road from Giles to Covent Fort, though lately I swear the trees around it have been growing faster. Neither Giles nor Covent are much themselves these days, and the road between them isn't often used. If it weren't for that town sign, there would be no way of knowing we were up here at all.

When the gold ran out there was zinc for a while, and a little copper. The gold fever died away, but Eldorado continued to prosper for a while. There was a Masonic lodge built, and two banks, and a school house with a clock and a bell – the fanciest building in town, a symbol that there was a community here, and that we were living well. I can't even remember where the lodge was now, the banks are gone, and the school closed in 1957. I went to that school, learned most of what I know. Everybody did. It was the place where you turned into a grown-up, one year at a time, back when a year was as long as anyone could imagine, when two seemed like infinity. Probably that was why, for a long time, folks would stop by the abandoned school every now and then, by themselves and on the quiet, and do a little patching up. Wasn't any sense in it, because it wasn't going to re-open, not least because there were no new children – but I know I did it, and Jack did, and Pete before he died. Had to be that others did too, otherwise it would have fallen down a lot earlier than it did.

Now it's gone, and even on the brightest spring day that patch of the mountain seems awful quiet. I guess you could say that no one here has learned anything since then. Certainly what you see on television doesn't seem to have much application to us. I stopped watching a long time ago, and I know I'm not the only one. TVs don't last forever, and there ain't no-one around here knows how to fix them. And anyway it just showed a world that isn't ours, and things that we can't buy and wouldn't want to, so what use was it anyway. We've got a few books, spread amongst us.

Eventually the copper ran out, and though people looked hard and long, there wasn't anything else useful to be found. The gambling dens moved on, in search of people who still had riches to throw away. The boarding houses closed soon afterwards, as those who hadn't made Eldorado their home moved on. Plenty people stayed, for a while. My folks did, in the 1920s. Never got to the bottom of why. But anyhow they came, and they stayed, and I followed in their footsteps, I guess, by staying here too. So did some others. But not enough. And nobody new.

Halfway down to the end of Main, Jack and I turned off the road and made our way as best we could up what used to be Fourth Street. I guess it still is, but you'd be hard pressed to find the first three, or the other eight, unless you'd once walked them, and gone visiting on them, or grown up in a house that used to stand on one. Now they've gone to trees and grass, just a few piles of lumber dotted around, like forgotten games of giant pick-up-sticks. You'd think people might have made an effort to keep the houses standing, even after people stopped living in them. But it's not the kind of thing that occurs to you until far too late, and then there doesn't seem a great deal of point. Spilt milk, stable door, all of those.

The grade has always been kind of steep on Fourth, and Jack and I both found the going hard. Jack had already made the trip once that night, and I let him go in front, following his footprints in the snow. There was another way of getting up to the house, a little less steep, but that involved going past the town's first cemetery, now overgrown, and the notion wasn't even discussed. Ahead of us, a single light shone in one of the upper windows of the Buckley house, which sits alone right at the end, a last stand against the oncoming trees. I felt sick to my stomach, remembering times I'd made the walk before, towards that grand old house hunkered beneath the wall of the mountain. Hundreds of times, but a handful of times in particular. My life often seems that way to me now. So much of it was just landscape I passed through, like a long open plain with little to distinguish the miles. Then there's like a little bag inside me, which I keep the real things in. A few smells, and sounds, touches like a faint summer breeze. Some evenings, a couple afternoons, and a handful of dawns, when I woke up somewhere I was happy to be, coddled warm with someone and protected from the bright light of day and tomorrow. But it's nights I remember most. Some bad, some good. You fall in love at night, and that's also when people die. Even if their last breath is drawn in daylight, by the time you've understood what's happened, the darkness has come to claim the event as its own. Nights last the longest, without doubt, both at the time and afterwards. They contain multitudes, and don't fade as easily as the sun. They're there, in my bag, and I'll take them with me when I go.

When we got to the house we stomped the snow off our boots on the porch, and then let ourselves in. Over the last few weeks of visiting I had gotten used to the dust, how it overlaid the way the house had used to be. She'd kept it up as well as she could over the years, but now you could almost hear it running down, like the wind dropping after a storm. The downstairs was empty but for Naomi's cat, who was sitting in the middle of the hall, looking at the wall. It glanced up at us as we started on the stairs, then walked slowly away into the darkness of the kitchen.

I knew then that it was already over.

When we reached the upper landing, we hesitated outside the doorway to the bedroom, as if feeling we had to be invited in. The interior was lit by candles, with an old kerosene lamp by the window. The Doc was sitting on a blanket box at the end of the bed, elbows on his knees. He looked like an old man, very tired, waiting for a train to take him home. Not much like someone who'd once been the second-fastest runner in town, after me, a boy who could run like the wind. He'd gone away, many years ago. Left town, got trained up, spent some years out there in the other places. Half the books in town were his, brought with him when he came back to Eldorado. He looked up, beckoned us in with an upward nod of the head. We approached like a pair of children, with short steps and hands down by our sides. I kept my eyes straight ahead, knowing there'd be a time to look after the words had been said.

Jack rested a hand on the Doc's shoulder. "She wake at all?"

He shook his head. "Just died. That's all she did."

"So that's it," I said.

The three of us sighed then, all together. Nothing long, or melodramatic. Just an exhalation, letting out what had once been inside us.

The Doc started to speak, faltered. Then tried again. "Maybe it's not going to happen," he said, trying for a considered tone, but coming out querulous and afraid. "After all, how do we know?"

Jack and I shook our heads. Wasn't any use in this line of thought. Nobody knew how we knew. But we knew. We'd known since the children stopped coming.

We walked around on separate sides of the bed, and looked down. I don't know what Jack was looking at, but I can tell you what I saw. An old woman, face lined, though less so than when I'd seen her in the afternoon of the previous day. Death had levelled the foothills of her suffering, filled in the dried stream beds of age. The coverlet was pulled up to just under her chin, so she looked tucked up nice and warm. The shape beneath the blankets was so thin it barely seemed to be there at all: it could have been just a runkle in the sheets, covering nothing more than cooling air. Most of all she looked still, like a mountain range seen from the sky.

Wasn't the first time I'd seen someone dead, not nearly. I saw my own parents laid out, inexplicably cold and quiet, and my wife, and many of my friends. There's been a lot of dying hereabouts over the last few years, every passing marked and mourned. But Naomi looked different.

It's funny how, when you first know someone, it will be the face you notice most of all. The eyes, the mouth, the way they have their hair. Everybody has the same number of limbs, but their face is their own. Then, over the years, it's as if this part of them leaves their body and goes into your head, crystallizes there. You hardly notice what the years are doing, the way people's real faces thicken and dim and change. Every now and then something brings you up short, and makes you see the way things have become. Then you lose it again, almost as quick as it came, and you just see the continuity, the essence behind the face. The person as they were.

I saw Naomi as she and her sister had once been, the two brightest sparks in Eldorado, the girls most likely to make you lose your stride and catch your breath – whether you were fifteen, same as them, or so old that your balls barely still had their wits about them. I saw her as the little lady who could shout loudest in the playground, who could give you a Chinese burn you'd remember for days. I saw her as I had when Pete and I used to hike up Fourth with flowers in our hands and our hearts in our throats, when Pete was cautiously dating Naomi, and I was going with her sister Sarah, who was two years younger and much prettier, or so I thought back then.

It's that year that many of the nights I keep in my bag came from, that brings faint memories of music to my head. Sarah and I came to a parting of the ways before Thanksgiving, and she eventually married Jack, had no children but generally seemed content, and died in 1984. Pete and Naomi lasted a couple more months than we had, and then Pete met Maggie and things changed. Five years later, both on rebounds from different people altogether, gloriously grouchy and full of cheap liquor, Naomi and I spent a night walking together through the woods which used to stop on the edge of town. We looked for the stream where the Clarkes first panned, and maybe even found it, and we didn't do anything more than kiss, but that was exciting enough. Then the morning came, and brought its light, and everything was burned away. We'd never have been right for each other anyhow, that was clear, and it wasn't the way it was supposed to be. Of course a decade or two later, when I first started to look back upon my life and read it properly, like a book I should have paid more attention to the first time, I realized that this might have been wrong. When I thought back, it was always Naomi's face that was clearest in my mind, though she'd been Pete's and I'd been Sarah's and anyhow both futures were long in the past and dead and buried half a lifetime ago. By then Naomi was married, and when we met we were polite. Almost as if that current which can pass between any two people, the spark of possibility, however small, had been used up all in that night in the woods, underused and thrown away, and now we could be nothing but friends. Naomi never had children either, nor Maggie. None of us did.

Even now, when the forest has started to march its way right up Main Street, I can remember that night with her as if I'm still wearing the same clothes and haven't had time to change. Remember also the way the sisters always seemed to glow, all of their lives, as if they were running on more powerful batteries than the rest of us, as if whoever had stirred their bodies into being had been more practised at the art than whoever did the rest of us. I loved my wife a great deal, and we had many good years together, but as I get older it's like those middle years were a long game we all played, a long and complex game of indeterminate rules. Those seasons fade, and we return to the playground like tired ghosts coming home after a long walk, and it's how we were then that seems most important. I can't remember much of what happened last year, but I can still picture those girls when we were young. On the boardwalk, in the big old house their father built, around the soda fountain when they were still little girls and we were all sparkling and young and blessed, a crop of new flowers bursting into life in a field which would always be there.

Almost all of those people are dead now. Distributed amongst the two cemeteries, biding their time, like broken panes in the windows of an old building. A few of the windows are still intact, like me and Jack and Maggie and all, but you have to wonder why. There's nothing to see through us now.

When Jack and I had looked down on Naomi a while, and nothing had changed, we turned away from the bed. The Doc had quietly gotten his things together, but didn't look ready to leave just yet.

"There's something me and Bill have to do," Jack said. "Only stopped by for the truck. And, well, you know."

The Doc nodded, not really looking at us. He knew what we were going to do. "I'll stay a while," he said. Back in '72 there'd been something going on between him and Naomi. He probably didn't realise that we knew. But everybody did. Then after her husband died in '85 oftentimes the Doc had taken his evening meal at the Buckley table. I'd always wondered if it might be me who did that. Didn't work out that way.

"What are we going to do about her cat?" I asked.

"What can anyone do about a cat?" the Doc said, with the ghost of a smile. "Reckon it'll do pretty much what it wants. I'll feed it, though."

We shook his hand, not really knowing why, and left the house.

Jack's truck was parked around the side. It wasn't going to be a picnic getting down the hill, but it was too far to walk. We got it started after only a couple of tries, and Jack nosed her carefully out into the ruts of the street. Fate was kind to us, and we got down to main without much more than a spot of grief. Turned right, away from the bar, away from what's left of the town.

When we drew level with the other cemetery, Jack slowed to a halt and turned the engine off.

We sat with the windows down for a while, smoking and listening. It was mighty cold. Wasn't anything to hear apart from wind up in the mountains, and the rustle of trees bending our way. Beyond the fence the stones and wooden crosses marched away in ranks into the night. Friends, parents, lovers, children, in their hundreds. A field full of the way things might have been, or had been once, and could never be again. Folks are dead for an awfully long time. The numbers mount up.

Jack turned, looked at me. "We're sure, aren't we?"

"Yes," I said. "We've been outnumbered for a long, long while. After Naomi, there's only fifteen of us left."

It felt funny, Jack turning to me, wanting to be reassured. I still remembered him as one of the big kids, someone I hoped I might be like one day. I did grow up to be like him, then older'n he'd once been, and then just old, exactly like him. Everything seemed so different back then, everyone so distinct from one another. Just your haircut can make you a different colour, when everyone's only got ten years of experience to count on. Then you get older, and everyone seems the same. Everybody gets whittled away at about the same rate. Like the '50s, and '60s, and '70s and '80s, times that once seemed so different to each other, but are now just stuff that happened to us once and then went away; like good weather or a stomach ache.

Jack stared straight out the windshield for a while. "I don't hear anything."

"May not happen for hours," I said. "No way of telling. May not even happen tonight."

He laughed quietly. "You think so?"

"No," I admitted. "It'll happen tonight. It's time."

I thought then that I might have heard something, out there in the darkness, the first stirring beyond the fence. But if I did, it was quiet, and nothing came of it right then. It was only midnight. There was plenty of darkness left.

Jack nodded slowly. "Then I guess we might as well get it over with."

We smiled at each other, briefly, like two boys passing in the school yard. Boys who grew to like each other, and who could never have realized that they'd be sharing such a task, on a far-away night such as this.

Later we'd drive back up into town, park outside Maggie's bar, and sit inside with the others and wait. She was staying open for good that night. But first we went down the hill, down a rough track to an old road hardly anyone drove any more.

We got out the truck and stood a while, looking down the mountain at a land as big as Heaven, and then together we took down the town sign.

KIM NEWMAN

The Other
Side of Midnight

" 'CASTLE IN THE DESERT' AND THIS STORY are part of an ongoing
series which will eventually add up to a novel, *Johnny Alucard*,"
explains Kim Newman. "The story so far consists of 'Coppola's
Dracula', from *The Mammoth Book of Dracula* (also in *Best
New Horror* a few years back), and 'Andy Warhol's Dracula',
published as a chapbook (and now available in softcover back-to-
back with Michael Marshall Smith's 'The Vaccinator' as *Binary
2*).

" 'The Other Side of Midnight' was written for Marvin Kaye's
Vampire Sextette, and then I did 'Castle in the Desert' for Ellen
Datlow's *SciFi.com* website; like the earlier stories – and 'You Are
the Wind Beneath My Wings', published by Paula Guran in
Horror Garage – these pieces are designed to stand alone, but
probably gain if you've been following the series, which began
with the novels *Anno Dracula*, *The Bloody Red Baron: Anno
Dracula 1918* and *Dracula Cha Cha Cha: Anno Dracula 1959*
(aka *Judgment of Tears*).

"The two slices of the story in this volume should be considered
as the first and last episodes of a 1970s TV series along the lines of
The Rockford Files. Part of the fun (or the irritation for non-fans)
of the *Anno Dracula* series is identifying the borrowed characters,
so I won't over-explain here – though I'd like to extend thanks to
Raymond Chandler and Dennis Etchison for their explorations of
Los Angeles. Don't be too surprised if one of the fictional films

mentioned in 'The Other Side of Midnight' gets made in the near future.

"The big climax of the Johnny Alucard series will come in 'A Concert for Transylvania'."

Anno Dracula 1981

I

At midnight, 1980 flew away across the Pacific and 1981 crept in from the East. A muted cheer rose from the pretty folk around the barbecue pit, barely an echo of the raucous welcome to a new decade that erupted at the height of the last Paradise Cove New Year party.

Of this company, only Geneviève clung to the old – the proper – manner of reckoning decades, centuries and (when they came) millennia. The passing of time was important to her; born in 1416, she'd let more time pass than most. Even among vampires, she was an elder. Five minutes ago – last year, last decade – she'd started to explain her position to a greying California boy, an ex-activist they called "the Dude". His eyes glazed over with more than the weed he'd been toking throughout the party, indeed since Jefferson Airplane went Starship. She quite liked the Dude's eyes, in any condition.

"It's as simple as this," she reiterated, hearing the French in her accent ("eet's", "seemple", "ziss") that only came out when she was tipsy ("teep-see") or trying for effect. "Since there was no Year Nothing, the first decade ended with the end of Year Ten AD; the first century with the end of 100 AD; the first millennium with the end of 1000 AD. Now, at this moment, a new decade is to begin. 1981 is the first year of the 1980s, as 1990 will be the last."

Momentarily, the Dude looked as if he understood, but he was just concentrating to make out her accented words. She saw insight spark in his mind, a vertiginous leap that made him want to back away from her. He held out his twisted, tufted joint. It might have been the one he'd rolled and started in 1968, replenished on and off ever since.

"Man, if you start questioning time," he said, "what have you got left? Physical matter? Maybe you question that next, and the mojo won't work any more. You'll think holes between molecules and sink through the surface of the Earth. Drawn by gravity. Heavy things should be left alone. Fundamental things, like the ground you walk on, the air you breathe. You do breathe, don't you, man? Suddenly, it hits me I don't know if you do."

"Yes, I breathe," she said. "When I turned, I didn't die. That's not common."

She proved her ability to inhale by taking a toke from the joint. She didn't get a high like his; for that, she'd have to sample his blood as it channelled the intoxicants from his alveoli to his brain. She had the mellow buzz of him, from saliva on the roach as much as from the dope smoke. It made her thirsty.

Because it was just after midnight on New Year's Eve, she kissed him. He enjoyed it, non-committally. Tasting straggles of tobacco in his beard and the film of a cocktail – white Russian – on his teeth and tongue, she sampled the ease of him, the defiant crusade of his back-burnered life. She understood now precisely what the expression "ex-activist" meant. If she let herself drink, his blood would be relaxing.

Breaking the kiss, she saw more sparks in his eyes, where her face was not reflected. Her lips were sometimes like razors, even more than her fang-teeth. She'd cut him slightly, just for a taste, not even thinking, and left some of herself on his tongue. She swallowed: mostly spit, but with tiny ribbons of blood from his gums.

French kissing was the kindest form of vampirism. From the minute exchange of fluid, she could draw a surprising sustenance. For her, just now, it was enough. It took the edge off her red thirst.

"Keep on breathing, man," said the Dude, reclaiming his joint, smiling broadly, drifting back towards the rest of the party, enjoying the unreeling connection between them. "And don't question time. Let it pass."

Licking her lips daintily, she watched him amble. He wasn't convinced 1980 had been the last year of the old decade and not the first of the new. Rather, he wasn't convinced that it mattered. Like a lot of Southern Californians, he'd settled on a time that suited him and stayed in it. Many vampires did the same thing, though Geneviève thought it a waste of longevity. In her more pompous moments, she felt the whole point was to embrace change while carrying on what was of value from the past.

When she was born and when she was turned, time was reckoned by the Julian Calendar, with its annual error of eleven minutes and fourteen seconds. Thinking of it, she still regretted the ten days – the fifth to the fourteenth of October, 1582 – Pope Gregory XIII had stolen from her, from the world, to make his sums add up. England and Scotland, ten days behind Rome, held out against the Gregorian Calendar until 1752. Other countries stubbornly stuck with Julian dating until well into the twentieth Century; Russia had not chimed in until 1918, Greece until 1923. Before the modern era, those ten-day shifts made diary-keeping a complex business for a necessarily much-travelled creature. In his 1885 journal, maintained while travelling on the continent and later excerpted by Bram Stoker, Jonathan Harker refers to May the 4th as the eve of St George's Day, which would have been April the 22nd back home in England. The leap-frogged weeks had been far much more jarring than the time-zone-hopping she sometimes went through as an air passenger.

The Paradise Cove Trailer Park Colony had been her home for all of four years, an eyeblink which made her a senior resident among the constitutionally impermanent peoples of Malibu. Here, ancient history was Sonny and Cher and *Leave It to Beaver*, anything on the "golden oldies" station or in off-prime time re-run.

Geneviève – fully, Geneviève Sandrine de l'Isle Dieudonné, though she went by Gené Dee for convenience – remembered with a hazy vividity that she had once looked at the Atlantic and *not known* what lay between France and China. She was older than the name "America"; had she not turned, she'd probably have been dead before Columbus brought back the news. In all those years, ten days shouldn't matter, but supposedly significant dates made her aware of that fold in time, that wrench which pulled the future hungrily closer, which had swallowed one of her birthdays. By her internal calendar, the decade would not fully turn for nearly two weeks. This was a limbo between unarguable decades. She should have been used to limbos by now. For her, Paradise Cove was the latest of a long string of pockets out of time and space, cosy coffins shallowly buried away from the rush of the world.

She was the only one of her kind at the party; if she took "her kind" to mean vampires – there were others in her current profession, private investigation, even other in-comers from far enough out of state to be considered foreign parts. Born in Northern France under the rule of an English king, she'd seen enough history to recognize the irrelevance of nationality. To be Breton in 1416 was to be neither French nor English, or both at the same time. Much later, during the Revolution, France had scrapped the calendar again, ducking out of the 1790s, even renaming the months. In the long term, the experiment was not a success. That was the last time she – Citizen Dieudonné – had really lived in her native land; the gory business soured her not only on her own nationality, but humanity in general. Too many eras earned names like "the Terror". Vampires were supposed to be obscenely bloodthirsty and she wasn't blind to the excesses of her kind, but the warm drank just as deeply from open wounds and usually made more of a mess of it.

From the sandy patio beside her chrome-finished airstream trailer, she looked beyond the gaggle of folks about the pit, joking over franks impaled on skewers. The Dude was mixing a pitcher of White Russians with his bowling buddies, resuming a months-long argument over the precise wording of the opening narration/ song of *Branded*. An eight-track in an open-top car played "Hotel California", The Eagles' upbeat but ominous song about a vampire and her victims. Some were dancing on the sand, shoes in a pile that would be hard to sort out later. White rolls of surf crashed on the breakers, waves edged delicately up to the beach.

Out there was the Pacific Ocean and the curve of the Earth, and beyond the blue horizon, as another shivery song went, was a rising sun. Dawn didn't worry her; at her age, as long as she dressed carefully – sunglasses, a floppy hat, long sleeves – she wouldn't even catch a severe tan, let alone frazzle up into dust and essential salts like some *nosferatu* of the Dracula bloodline. She had grown out of the dark. To her owl eyes, it was no place to hide, which meant she had to be careful where she looked on party nights like this. She liked living by the sea: its depths were still impenetrable to her, still a mystery.

"Hey, Gidget," came a rough voice, "need a nip?"

It was one of the surfers, a shaggy bear of a man she had never heard called anything but Moondoggie. He wore frayed shorts, flip-flops and an old blue shirt, and probably had done so since the 1950s. He was a legendary veteran of tubes and pipes and waves long gone. He seemed young to her, though his friends called him an old man.

His offer was generous. She had fed off him before, when the need was strong. With his blood came a salt rush, the sense of being enclosed by a curl of wave as his board torpedoed across the surface of the water.

Just now, she didn't need it. She still had the taste of the Dude. Smiling, she waved him away. As an elder, she didn't have the red thirst so badly. Since Charles, she had fed much less. That wasn't how it was with many vampires, especially those of the Dracula line. Some *nosferatu* got thirstier and thirstier with passing ages, and were finally consumed by their own raging red needs. Those were the ones who got to be called monsters. Beside them, she was a minnow.

Moondoggie tugged at his open collar, scratching below his salt-and-pepper beard. The LAPD had wanted to hang a murder rap on him two years ago, when a runaway turned up dead in his beach hut. She had investigated the situation, clearing his name. He would always be grateful to his "Gidget", which she learned was a contraction of "Girl Midget". Never tall, she had turned – frozen – at sixteen. Recently, after centuries of being treated almost as a child, she was most often taken for a woman in her twenties. That was: by people who didn't know she wasn't warm, wasn't entirely living. She'd have examined her face for the beginnings of lines, but looking glasses were no use to her.

Shots were fired, in the distance. She looked at the rise of the cliffs and saw the big houses, decks lit by fairy light UFO constellations, seeming to float above the beach, heavy with heavy hitters. Firing up into the sky was a Malibu New Year tradition among the rich. Reputedly started by the film director John Milius, a famous surf and gun nut, it was a stupid, dangerous thing to do. Gravity and momentum meant bullets came down somewhere, and not always into the water. In the light of New Year's Day, she found spent shells in the sand, or pocked holes in driftwood. One year, someone's head would be under a slug. Milius had made her cry with *Big Wednesday*, though. Movies with coming-of-age, end-of-an-era romanticism crawled inside her heart and melted her. She would have to tell Milius it got worse and worse with centuries.

So, the Nineteen-Eighties?

Some thought her overly formal for always using the full form, but she'd lived through decades called "the eighties" before. For the past hundred years, "the eighties" had meant the Anni Draculae, the 1880s, when the Transylvanian Count came to London and changed the world. Among other things, the founding of his brief Empire had drawn her out of the shadow of eternal evening into something approaching the light. That brought her together with Charles, the warm man with whom she had spent seventy-five years, until his death in 1959, the warm man who had shown her that she, a vampire, could still love, that she had turned without dying inside.

She wasn't unique, but she was rare. Most vampires lost more than they gained when they turned; they died and came back as different people, caricatures of their former selves, compelled by an inner drive to be extreme. Creatures like that were one of the reasons why she was here, at the far Western edge of a continent where "her kind" were still comparatively rare.

Other vampires had nests in the Greater Los Angeles area: Don Drago Robles, a landowner before the incorporation of the State into the Union, had quietly waited for the city to close around his *hacienda*, and was rising as a political figure with a growing constituency, a Californian answer to Baron Meinster's European Transylvania Movement; and a few long-lived movie or music people, the sort with reflections in silver and voices that registered on recording equipment, had Spanish-style castles along Sunset Boulevard, like eternal child rock God Timmy Valentine or silent movie star David Henry Reid. More, small sharks mostly, swam through Angelino sprawl, battening on marginal people to leech them dry of dreams as much as blood, or – in that ghastly new thing – selling squirts of their own blood ("drac") to sad addicts ("dhampires") who wanted to be a vampire for the night but didn't have the heart to turn all the way.

She should be grateful to the rogues; much of her business came from people who got mixed up with bad egg vampires. Her reputation for extricating victims from predators was like gold with distressed parents or cast-aside partners. Sometimes, she worked as a deprogrammer, helping kids out of all manner of cults. They grew beliefs stranger than Catholicism, or even vampirism, out here among the orange groves: the Moonies, the Esoteric Order of Dagon, Immortology, Psychoplasmics.

Another snatch of song: *the Voice said Daddy there's a million pigeons, waiting to be hooked on new religions.*

As always, she stuck it out until the party died. All the hours of the night rolled away and the rim of the horizon turned from navy blue to lovely turquoise. January cold gathered, driving those warmer folks who were still sensible from their barbecues and beach-towels to their beds.

Marty Burns, sometime sit-com star and current inhabitant of a major career slump, was passed out face down on the chilling sands in front of her trailer space. She found a blanket to throw over him. He murmured in liquor-and-pills lassitude, and she tucked the blanket comfortably around his neck. Marty was hilarious in person, even when completely off his face, but *Salt & Pepper*, the star-making show he was squandering residuals from, was puzzlingly free of actual humour. The dead people on the laugh-track audibly split sides at jokes deader than they were. The year was begun with a moderate good deed, though purging the kid's system and dragging him to A-A might have been a more lasting solution to whatever was inside him, chewing away.

She would sleep later, in the morning, locked in her sleek trailer, a big metal coffin equipped with everything she needed. Of all her homes over the years, this was the one she cherished the most. The trailer was chromed everywhere it could be, and customized with steel shutters that bolted over the windows and the never-used sun roof. Economy of space had forced her to limit her possessions – so few after so long – to those that really meant the most to her: ugly jewelry from her mediaeval girlhood, some of Charles' books and letters, a Dansette gramophone with an eclectic collection of sides, her beloved answering machine, a tacky Mexican crucifix with light-up eyes that she kept on show just to prove she wasn't one of *those* vampires, a rubber duck with a story attached, two decent formal dresses and four pairs of Victorian shoes (custom-cobbled for her tiny feet) which had outlasted everything made this century and would do for decades more. On the road, she could kink herself double and rest in the trunk of her automobile, a pillar-box red 1958 Plymouth Fury, but the trailer was more comfortable.

She wandered towards the sea-line, across the disturbed sands of the beach. There had been dancing earlier, grown-ups who had been in Frankie and Annette movies trying to fit their old moves to current music. *Le freak, c'est chic.*

She trod on a hot pebble that turned out to be a bullet, and saluted Big John up on his A-list Hollywood deck. Milius had written *Dracula* for Francis Ford Coppola, from the Bram Stoker novel she was left out of. Not wanting to have the Count brought back to mind, she'd avoided the movie, though her vampire journalist friend Kate Reed, also not mentioned in Stoker's fiction, had worked on it as technical advisor. She hadn't heard from Kate in too long; Geneviève believed she was behind the Iron Curtain, on the trail of the Transylvania Movement, that odd faction of the Baron Meinster's which wanted Dracula's estates as a homeland for vampires. God, if that ever happened, she would get round to re-applying for American citizenship; they were accepting *nosferatu* now, which they hadn't been in 1922 when she last looked into it. Meinster was one of those Dracula wannabes who couldn't quite carry off the opera cloak and ruffle shirt, with his prissy little fangs and his naked need to be the new King of the Cats.

Wavelets lapped at her bare toes. Her nails sparkled under water.

1970s music hadn't been much, not after the 1960s. Glam rock. The Bee Gees. The Carpenters. She had liked Robert Altman's films and *Close Encounters*, but didn't see what all the fuss was about *Star Wars*. Watergate. An oil crisis. The Bicentennial Summer. The Iran hostage crisis. No Woodstock. No Swinging London. No one like Kennedy. Nothing like the Moon Landing.

If she were to fill a diary page for every decade, the 1970s would have to be heavily padded. She'd been to some parties and helped some people, settled into the slow, pastel, dusty ice-cream world of Southern California, a little to one side of the swift stream of human history. She wasn't even much bothered by memories, the curse of the long-lived.

Not bad, not good, not anything.

She wasn't over Charles, never would be really. He was a constant, silent presence in her heart, an ache and a support and a joy. He was a memory she would never let slip. And Dracula, finally destroyed soon after Charles' death, still cast a long cloak-shadow over her life. Like Bram Stoker, she wondered what her life, what the world, would have been like if Vlad Tepes had never turned or been defeated before his rise to power.

Might-have-beens and the dead. Bad company.

John Lennon was truly dead, too. Less than a month ago, in New York, he had taken a silver bullet through the heart, a cruel full stop for the 1970s, for what was left of the 1960s. Annie Wilkes, Lennon's killer, said she was the musician's biggest fan, but that he had to die for breaking up the Beatles. Geneviève didn't know how long Lennon had been a vampire, but she sadly recognized in the dirge "Imagine" that copy-of-a-copy voidish-ness characteristic of creatives who turned to prolong their artistic lives but found the essential thing that made them who they were, that powered their talent, gone and that the best they could hope for was a kind of rarefied self-plagiarism. Mad Annie might have done John a favour, making him immortal again. Currently the most famous vampire-slayer in the world, she was a heroine to the bedrock strata of warm America that would never accept *nosfer-atu* as even kissing cousins to humanity.

What, she wondered as the sun touched the sky, would this new decade bring?

II

COUNT DRACULA

a screenplay

by Herman J. Mankiewicz and Orson Welles

based on the novel by Bram Stoker

Nov 30, 1939

Fade In

1. Ext. Transylvania – Faint Dawn – 1885

Window, very small in the distance, illuminated. All around this an almost totally black screen. Now, as the camera moves slowly towards this window, which is almost a postage stamp in the frame, other forms appear; spiked battlements, vast granite walls, and now, looming up against the still-nighted sky, enormous iron grillwork.

Camera travels up what is now shown to be a gateway of gigantic proportions and holds on the top of it – a huge initial "D" showing darker and darker against the dawn sky. Through this and beyond we see the Gothic-tale mountaintop of Dracula's estate, the great castle a silhouette at its summit, the little window a distant accent in the darkness.

Dissolve

(A series of setups, each closer to the great window, all telling something of:)

2. The Literally Incredible Domain of Vlad, Count Dracula

Its right flank resting for forty miles along the Borgo Pass, the estate truly extends in all directions farther than the eye can see. An ocean of sharp tree-tops, with occasionally a deep rift where there is a chasm. Here and there are silver threads where the rivers wind in deep gorges through the forests. Designed by nature to be almost completely vertical and jagged – it was, as will develop, primordial forested mountain when Dracula acquired and changed its face – it is now broken and shorn, with its fair share of carved peaks and winding paths, all man-made.

Castle Dracula itself – an enormous pile, compounded of several demolished and rebuilt structures, of varying architecture, with broken battlements and many towers – dominates the scene, from the very peak of the mountain. It sits on the edge of a very terrible precipice.

Dissolve

3. The Village

In the shadows, literally the shadows, of the mountain. As we move by, we see that the peasant doors and windows are shuttered and locked, with crucifixes and obscene clusters of garlic as further protection and sealing. Eyes peep out, timid, at us. The camera moves like a band of men, purposeful, cautious, intrepid, curious.

Dissolve

4. Forest of Stakes

Past which we move. The sward is wild with mountain weeds, the stakes tilted at a variety of Dutch angles, the execution field unused and not seriously tended for a long time.

Dissolve

5. What Was Once a Good-Sized Prison Stockade

All that now remains, with one exception, are the individual plots, surrounded by thorn fences, on which the hostages were kept, free and yet safe from each other and the landscape at large. (Bones in several of the plots indicate that here there were once human cattle, kept for blood.)

Dissolve

6. A Wolf Pit

In the f.g., a great shaggy dire wolf, bound by a silver chain, is outlined against the fawn murk. He raises himself slowly, with more thought than an animal should display, and looks out across the estates of Count Dracula, to the distant light glowing in the castle on the mountain. The wolf howls, a child of the night, making sweet music.

Dissolve

7. A Trench Below the Walls

A slow-scuttling armadillo. A crawling giant beetle. Reflected in the muddy water – the lighted window.

Dissolve

8. The Moat

Angled spears sag. An old notebook floats on the surface of the water – its pages covered in shorthand scribble. As it moves across the frame, it discloses again the reflection of the window in the castle, closer than before.

Dissolve

9. A Drawbridge

Over the wide moat, now stagnant and choked with weeds. We move across it and through a huge rounded archway into a formal courtyard, perhaps thirty feet wide and one hundred yards deep, which extends right up to the very wall of the castle. Let's see Toland keep all of it in focus. The landscaping surrounding it has been sloppy and casual for centuries, but this particular courtyard has been kept up in perfect shape. As the camera makes its way through it, towards the lighted window of the castle, there are revealed rare and exotic blooms of all kinds: *mariphasa lupino lumino*, strange orchid, *audriensis junior, triffidus celestus*. The dominating note is one of almost exaggerated wildness, sprouting sharp and desperate – rot, rot, rot. The Hall of the Mountain King, the night the last troll died. Some of the plants lash out, defensively.

Dissolve

10. The Window

Camera moves in until the frame of the window fills the frame of the screen. Suddenly the light within goes out. This stops the action of the camera and cuts the music (Bernard Herrmann) which has been accompanying the sequence. In the glass panes of the window we see reflected the stark, dreary mountainscape of the Dracula estate behind and the dawn sky.

Dissolve

11. Int. Corridor in Castle Dracula – Faint Dawn – 1885

Ornate mirrors line both walls of the corridor, reflecting arches into infinity. A bulky shadow figure – Dracula – proceeds slowly, heavy with years, through the corridor. He pauses to look into the mirror, and has no reflection, no reflections, to infinity. It seems at last that he is simply not there.

Dissolve

12. Int. Dracula's Crypt – Faint Dawn – 1885

A very long shot of Dracula's enormous catafalque, silhouetted against the enormous window.

Dissolve

13. Int. Dracula's Crypt – Faint Dawn – 1885

An eye. An incredible one. Big impossible drops of bloody tears, the reflections of figures coming closer, cutting implements raised. The jingling of sleigh bells in the musical score now makes an ironic reference to Indian temple bells – the music freezes—

DRACULA'S OLD VOICE
Rose's blood!

The camera pulls back to show the eye in the face of the old Dracula, bloated with blood but his stolen youth lost again, grey skin parchmented like a mummy, fissures cracking open in the wrinkles around his eyes, fangteeth too large for his mouth, pouching his cheeks and stretching his lips, the nose an improbable bulb. A flash – the descent of a guillotine-like kukri knife, which has been raised above Dracula's neck – across the screen. The head rolls off the neck and bounds down two carpeted steps leading to the catafalque, the camera following. The head falls off the last step onto the marble floor where it cracks, snaky tendrils of blood glittering in the first ray of the morning sun. This ray cuts an angular pattern across the floor, suddenly crossed with a thousand cruciform bars of light as a dusty curtain is wrested from the window.

14. The Foot of Dracula's Catafalque

The camera very close. Outlined against the uncurtained window we can see a form – the form of a man, as he raises a bowie knife over his head. The camera moves down along the catafalque as the knife descends into Dracula's heart, and rests on the severed head. Its lips are still moving. The voice, a whisper from the grave

DRACULA'S OLD VOICE
Rose's blood!

In the sunlight, a harsh shadow cross falling upon it, the head lap-dissolves into a fanged, eyeless skull.

Fade Out

III

Count Dracula Cast and Credits, as of January, 1940.

Production Company: Mercury Productions. Distributor: RKO Radio Pictures. Executive Producer: George J. Schaefer. Producer: Orson Welles. Director: Orson Welles. Script: Herman J. Mankiewicz, Orson Welles. From the novel by Bram Stoker. Director of Photography: Gregg Toland. Editors: Mark Robson, Robert Wise. Art Director: Van Nest Polglase. Special Effects: Vernon L. Walker. Music/Musical Director: Bernard Herrmann.

Orson Welles (Dracula), Joseph Cotten (Jedediah Renfield), Everett Sloane (Van Helsing), Dorothy Comingore (Mina Murray), Robert Coote (Artie Holmwood), William Alland (Jon Harker), Agnes Moorehead (Mrs Westenra), Lucille Ball (Lucy), George Couloris (Dr Walter Parkes Seward), Paul Stewart (Raymond, Asylum Attendant), Alan Ladd (Quincey P. Morris), Fortunio Bonanova (Inn-Keeper at Bistritz), Vladimir Sokoloff (Szgany Chieftain), Dolores Del Rio, Ruth Warrick, Rita Cansino (Vampire Brides), Gus Schilling (Skipper of the *Demeter*).

IV

"Mademoiselle Dieudonné," intoned the voice on her answering machine, halfway between a growl and a purr, "this is Orson Welles."

The voice was deeper even than in the 1930s, when he was a radio star. Geneviève had been in America over Halloween, 1938, when Welles and the Mercury Theatre of the Air broadcast their you-are-there dramatisation of H.G. Wells' "The Flowering of the Strange Orchid" and convinced half the Eastern seaboard that the country was disappearing under a writhing plague of vampire blossoms. She remembered also the whisper of "who *knows* what evil *lurks* in the hearts of *men*?", followed by the triumphant declaration "the *Shadow* knows!" and the low chuckle which rose by terrifying lurches to a fiendish, maniacal shriek of insane laughter.

When she had first met the man himself, in Rome in 1959, the voice hadn't disappointed. Now, even on cheap tape and through the tinny, tiny amplifier, it was a call to the soul. Even hawking brandy or frozen peas, the voice was a powerful instrument. That Welles had to compete with Welles imitators for gigs as a commercial pitchman was one of the tragedies of the modern age. Then again, she suspected he drew a deal of sly enjoyment from his long-running role as a ruined titan. As an actor, his greatest role was always himself. Even leaving a message on a machine, he invested phrases with the weight – a quality he had more than a sufficiency of – of a Shakespearean deathbed speech.

"There is a small matter upon which I should like your opinion, in your capacities as a private detective and a member of the undead community. If you would call on me, I should be most grateful."

She thought about it. Welles was as famous for being broke as for living well. It was quite likely he wouldn't even come through with her modest rate of a hundred dollars a day, let alone expenses. And gifts of rare wine or Cuban cigars weren't much use to her, though she supposed she could redeem them for cash.

Still, she was mildly bored with finding lost children or bail-jumpers. And no one ever accused Welles of being boring. He had left the message while she was resting through the hours of the day. This was the first of the ten or so days between the Gregorian

1980s and the Julian 1980s. She could afford to give a flawed genius – his own expression – that much time.

She would do it.

In leaving a message, Welles had given her a pause to think. She heard heavy breaths as he let the tape run on, his big man's lungs working. Then, confident that he had won her over, he cut in with address details, somewhere in Beverly Hills.

"I do so look forward to seeing you again. Until then, remember . . . *the weed of crime bears bitter fruit*!"

It was one of his old radio catch-phrases.

He did the laugh, the King Laugh, the Shadow Laugh. It properly chilled her bones, but made her giggle too.

V

She discovered Orson Welles at the centre of attention, on the cracked bottom of a drained pool behind a rented bungalow. Three nude vampire girls waved objects – a luminous skull, a Macbethian blooded dagger, a fully-articulated monster bat puppet – at him, darting swiftly about his bulky figure, nipping at his head with their Halloween props. The former Boy Wonder was on his knees, enormous Russian shirt open to the waist, enormous (and putty) nose glistening under the lights, enormous spade-beard flecked with red syrup. A man with a hand-held camera, the sort of thing she'd seen used to make home movies, circled the odd quartet, not minding if the vampires got between him and his director-star.

A few other people were around the pool, holding up lights. No sound equipment, though: this was being shot silent. Geneviève hung back, by the bungalow, keeping out of the way of the work. She had been on film sets before, at Cinecittà and in Hollywood, and knew this crew would be deemed skeletal for a student short. If anyone else were directing, she'd have supposed he was shooting make-up tests or a rehearsal. But with Welles, she knew that this was the real film. It might end up with the dialogue out of sync, but it would be extraordinary.

Welles was rumbling through a soliloquy.

It took her a moment to realise what the undead girls were doing, then she had to swallow astonished laughter. They were nude not for the titillation of an eventual audience, for they wouldn't be seen. Non-reflecting *nosferatu* would be completely invisible when the footage was processed. The girls were naked because clothes would show up on film, though some elders – Dracula had been one – so violated the laws of optics that they robbed any costume they wore of its reflection also, sucking even that into their black hearts. In the final film, Welles would seem to be persecuted by malignly animated objects – the skull, the dagger and the bat. Now, he tore at his garments and hair like Lear, careful to leave his nose alone, and called out to the angry heavens. The girls flitted, slender and deathly white, not feeling the cold, faces blank, hands busy.

This was the cheapest special effect imaginable.

Welles fell forward on his face, lay still for a couple of beats and hefted himself upright, out of character, calling "cut". His nose was mashed.

A dark woman with a clipboard emerged from shadows to confer with the master. She wore a white fur coat and a matching hat. The vampire girls put the props down and stood back, nakedness unnoticed by the crew members. One took a cloak-like robe from a chair and settled it over her slim shoulders. She climbed out of the pool.

Geneviève had not announced herself. The vampire girl fixed her eye. She radiated a sense of being fed up with the supposed glamour of show business.

"Turning was supposed to help my career," she said. "I was going to stay pretty forever and be a star. Instead, I lost my image. I had good credits. I was up for the last season of *Charlie's Angels*. I'd have been the blonde."

"There's always the theatre," Geneviève suggested.

"That's not being a star," the girl said.

She was obviously a new-born, impatient with an eternity she didn't yet understand. She wanted all her presents *now*, and no nonsense about paying dues or waiting her turn. She had cropped blonde hair, very pale, almost translucent skin stretched over bird-delicate bones and a tight, hard, cute little face, with sharp angles and glinting teeth, small reddish eyes. Her upper arm was marked by parallel claw-marks, not yet healed, like sergeant's stripes. Geneviève stored away the detail.

"Who's that up there, Nico?" shouted one of the other girls.

Nico? Not the famous one, Geneviève supposed.

"Who?" the girl asked, out loud. "Famous?"

Nico – indeed, not the famous one – had picked the thought out of Geneviève's mind. That was a common elder talent, but unusual in a new-born. If she lasted, this girl might do well. She'd have to pick a new name though, to avoid confusion with the singer of "All Tomorrow's Parties".

"Another one of us," the starlet said, to the girl in the pool. "An invisible."

"I'm not here for a part," Geneviève explained. "I'm here to see Mr Welles."

Nico looked at her askew. Why would a vampire who wasn't an actress be here? Tumblers worked in the new-born's mind. It worked both ways: Nico could pick words up, but she also sent them out. The girls in the pool were named Mink and Vampi (please!), and often hung with Nico.

"You're old, aren't you?"

Geneviève nodded. Nico's transparent face showed eagerness.

"Does it come back? Your face in the mirror?"

"Mine hasn't."

Her face fell, a long way. She was a loss to the profession. Her feelings were all on the surface, projected to the back stalls.

"Different bloodlines have different qualities," Geneviève said, trying to be encouraging.

"So I heard."

Nico wasn't interested in faint hopes. She wanted instant cures.

"Is that Mademoiselle Dieudonné?" roared the familiar voice.

"Yes, Orson, it's me," she said.

Nico reacted, calculating. She was thinking that Geneviève might be an important person.

"Then that's a wrap for the evening. Thank you, people. Submit your expenses to Oja, and be back here tomorrow night, at midnight sharp. You were all stupendous."

Oja was the woman with the clipboard: Oja Kodar, Welles's companion and collaborator. She was from Yugoslavia, another refugee washed up on this California shore.

Welles seemed to float out of the swimming pool, easily hauling his enormous girth up the ladder by the strength of his own meaty arms. She was surprised at how light he was on his feet.

He pulled off his putty nose and hugged her.

"Geneviève, Geneviève, you are welcome."

The rest of the crew came up, one by one, carrying bits of equipment.

"I thought I'd get Van Helsing's mad scene in the can," explained Welles.

"Neat trick with the girls."

The twinkle in his eye was almost Santa Clausian. He gestured hypnotically.

"Elementary movie magic," he said. "Georges Méliès could have managed it in 1897."

"Has it ever been done before? I don't recall seeing a film with the device."

"As a matter of fact, I think it's an invention of my own. There are still tricks to be teased out of the cinema. Even after so many years – a single breath for you, my dear – the talkies are not quite perfected. My little vampires may have careers as puppeteers, animators. You'd never see their hands. I should shoot a short film, for children."

"You've been working on this for a long time?"

"I had the idea at about seven o'clock this evening," he said, with a modest chuckle. "This is Hollywood, my dear, and you can get anything with a phone call. I got my vampires by ordering out, like pizza."

Geneviève guessed the invisible girls were hookers, a traditional career option for those who couldn't make a showing in the movies. Some studio execs paid good money to be roughed up by girls they'd pass over with contempt at cattle calls. And vampires, properly trained, could venture into areas of pain and pleasure a warm girl would find uncomfortable, unappetizing or unhealthy.

She noticed Nico had latched on to a young, male assistant and was alternately flirting with him and wheedling at him for some favour. Welles was right: she could have a career as a puppet-mistress.

"Come through into the house, Geneviève," said Welles. "We must talk."

The crew and the girls bundled together. Oja, as production manager, arranged for them to pool up in several cars and be returned to their homes or – in the case of Nico, Mink and Vampi – to a new club where there were hours to be spent before the dawn. Gary, the cameraman, wanted to get the film to the lab and hurried off on his own to an all-night facility. Many movie people kept vampire hours without being undead.

There was an after-buzz in the air. Geneviève wondered if it was genius, or had some of the crew been sniffing drac to keep going. She had heard it was better than speed. She assumed she would be immune to it; even as a blood-drinker – like all of her kind, she had turned by drinking vampire blood – she found the idea of dosing her system with another vampire's powdered blood, diluted with the Devil knew what, disgusting.

Welles went ahead of her, into the nondescript bungalow, turning on lights as he went. She looked back for a moment at the cast-off nose by the pool.

Van Helsing's mad scene?

She knew the subject of Welles' current project. He had mentioned to her that had always wanted to make *Dracula*. Now, it seemed, he was acting on the impulse. It shouldn't have, but it frightened her a little. She was in two minds about how often that story should be told.

VI

Orson Welles arrived in Hollywood in 1939, having negotiated a two-picture deal as producer-director-writer-actor with George Schaefer of RKO Pictures. Drawing on an entourage of colleagues from the New York theatre and radio, he established Mercury Productions as a filmmaking entity. Before embarking on *Citizen Kane* (1941) and *The Magnificent Ambersons* (1942), Welles developed other properties: Nicholas Blake's just-published anti-fascist thriller *The Smiler With a Knife* (1939), Conrad's *Heart of Darkness* (1902) and Stoker's *Dracula* (1897). Like the Conrad, *Dracula* was a novel Welles had already done for the *Mercury Theatre on the Air* radio series (July 11, 1938). A script was prepared (by Welles, Herman Mankiewicz and, uncredited, John Houseman), sets were designed, the film cast, and "tests" – the extent of which have never been revealed – shot, but the project was dropped.

The reasons for the abandonment of *Count Dracula* remain obscure. It has been speculated that RKO were nervous about Welles's stated intention to film most of the story with a first-person camera, adopting the viewpoints of the various characters as Stoker does in his might-have-been fictional history. House-man, in his memoir *Run-Through* (1972), alleges that Welles' enthusiasm for this device was at least partly due to the fact that it would keep the fearless vampire slayers – Harker, Van Helsing, Quincey, Holmwood – mostly off screen, while Dracula, object of their attention, would always be in view. Houseman, long es-tranged from Welles at the time of writing, needlessly adds that Welles would have played Dracula. He toyed with the idea of playing Harker as well, before deciding William Alland could do it if kept to the shadows and occasionally dubbed by Welles. The rapidly-changing political situation in Europe, already forcing the Roosevelt administration to reassess its policies about vampirism and the very real Count Dracula, may have prompted certain factions to bring pressure to bear on RKO that such a film was "inadvisable" for 1940.

In an interview with Peter Bogdanovich, published in *This is Orson Welles* (1992) but held well before Francis Ford Coppola's controversial *Dracula* (1979), Welles said: "*Dracula* would make a marvellous movie. In fact, nobody has ever made it; they've never paid any attention to the book, which is the most hair-raising, marvellous book in the world. It's told by four people, and must be done with four narrations, as we did on the radio. There's one scene in London where he throws a heavy bag into the corner of a cellar and it's full of screaming babies! They can go that far out now."

Jonathan Gates, "Welles' Lost Draculas",
Video Watchdog No. 23 May–July 1994

VII

Welles did not so much live in the bungalow as occupy it. She recognized the signs of high-end, temporary tenancy. Pieces of extremely valuable antique furniture, imported from Spain, stood among ugly, functional, modern sticks that had come with the let. The den, largest space in the building, was made aesthetically bearable by a hanging she put at sixteenth century, nailed up over the open fireplace like a curtain. The tapestry depicted a knight trotting in full armour through forest greenery, with black-faced, red-eyed-and-tongued devils peeping from behind tall, straight trees. The piece was marred by a bad burn that had caught at one corner and spread evil fingers upwards. All around were stacks of books, square-bound antique volumes and bright modern paperbacks, and rickety towers of film cans.

Geneviève wondered why Welles would have cases of good sherry and boxes of potato chips stacked together in a corner, then realized he must have been part-paid in goods for his commercial work. He offered her sherry and she surprised him by accepting.

"I do sometimes drink wine, Orson. Dracula wasn't speaking for us all."

He arched an eyebrow and made a flourish of pouring sherry into a paper cup.

"My glassware hasn't arrived from Madrid," he apologized.

She sipped the stuff, which she couldn't really taste, and sat on a straight-backed Gothic chair. It gave her a memory-flash, of hours spent in churches when she was a warm girl. She wanted to fidget.

Welles plumped himself down with a Falstaffian rumble and strain on a low couch that had a velvet curtain draped over it. He was broad enough in the beam to make it seem like a throne.

Oja joined them and silently hovered. Her hair was covered by a bright headscarf.

A pause.

Welles grinned, expansively. Geneviève realized he was protracting the moment, relishing a role. She even knew who he was doing, Sydney Greenstreet in *The Maltese Falcon*. The ambiguous mastermind enjoying himself by matching wits with the perplexed private eye. If Hollywood ever remade *Falcon*, which would be a sacrilege, Welles would be in the ring for Gutman. Too many of his acting jobs were like that, replacing another big personality in an inferior retread of something already got right.

"I'll be wondering why you asked me here tonight," she prompted.

"Yes," he said, amused.

"It'll be a long story."

"I'm rather afraid so."

"There are hours before dawn."

"Indeed."

Welles was comfortable now. She understood he had been switching off from the shoot, coming down not only from his on-screen character but from his position as backyard God.

"You know I've been playing with Dracula for years? I wanted to make it at RKO in '40, did a script, designed sets, cast everybody. Then it was dropped."

She nodded.

"We even shot some scenes. I'd love to steal in some night and rescue the footage from the vaults. Maybe for use in the current project. But the studio has the rights. Imagine if paintings belonged to whoever mixed the paints and wove the canvas. I'll have to abase myself, as usual. The children who inherited RKO after Hughes ran it aground barely know who I am, but they'll enjoy the spectacle of my contrition, my pleading, my total dejection. I may even get my way in the end."

"Hasn't *Dracula* been made? I understand that Francis . . ."

"I haven't seen that. It doesn't matter to me or the world. I didn't do the first stage productions of *Macbeth* or *Caesar*, merely the best. The same goes for the Stoker. A marvellous piece, you know."

"Funnily enough, I have read it," she put in.

"Of course you have."

"And I met Dracula."

Welles raised his eyes, as if that were news to him. Was this all about picking her brains? She had spent all of fifteen minutes in the Royal Presence, nearly a hundred years ago, but was quizzed about that (admittedly dramatic) occasion more than the entire rest of her five hundred and sixty-five years. She'd seen the Count again, after his true death – as had Welles, she remembered – and been at his last funeral, seen his ashes scattered. She supposed she had wanted to be sure he was really finally dead.

"I've started *Dracula* several times. It seems like a cursed property. This time, maybe, I'll finish it. I believe it has to be done."

Oja laid hands on his shoulders and squeezed. There was an almost imperial quality to Welles, but he was an emperor in exile, booted off his throne and cast out, retaining only the most loyal and long-suffering of his attendants.

"Does the name Alucard mean anything to you?" he asked. "John Alucard?"

"This may come as a shock to you, Orson, but 'Alucard' is 'Dracula' spelled backwards."

He gave out a good-humoured version of his Shadow laugh.

"I had noticed. He is a vampire, of course."

"Central and Eastern European *nosferatu* love anagrams as much as they love changing their names," she explained. "It's a real quirk. My late friend Carmilla Karnstein ran through at least half a dozen scramblings of her name before running out. Mill-arca, Marcilla, Allimarc . . ."

"My name used to be Olga Palinkas," put in Oja. "Until Orson thought up 'Oja Kodar' for me, to sound Hungarian."

"The promising sculptor 'Vladimir Zagdrov' is my darling Oja too. You are right about the undead predilection for *noms des plumes*, alter egos, secret identities, anagrams and palindromes and acrostics. Just like actors. A hold-over from the Byzantine mindset, I believe. It says something about the way the creatures think. Tricky but obvious, as it were. The back-spelling might also be a compensation: a reflection on parchment for those who have none in the glass."

"This Alucard? Who is he?"

"That's the exact question I'd like answered," said Welles. "And you, my dear Mademoiselle Dieudonné, are the person I should like to provide that answer."

"Alucard says he's an independent producer," said Oja. "With deals all over town."

"But no credits," said Welles.

Geneviève could imagine.

"He has money, though," said Welles. "No credits, but a line of credit. Cold cash and the Yankee Dollar banish all doubt. That seems unarguable."

"Seems?"

"Sharp little word, isn't it. Seems and is, syllables on either side of a chasm of meaning. This Mr Alucard, a *nosferatu*, wishes to finance my *Dracula*. He has offered me a deal the likes of which I haven't had since RKO and *Kane*. An unlimited budget, major studio facilities, right of final cut, control over everything from casting to publicity. The only condition he imposes is that I must make this subject. He wants not my *Don Quixote* or my *Around the World in 80 Days*, but my *Dracula* only."

"The Coppola," – a glare from Welles made her rephrase – "that other film, with Brando as the Count? That broke even in the end, didn't it? Made back its budget. *Dracula* is a box office subject. There's probably room for another version. Not to mention sequels, a spin-off TV series and imitations. Your Mr Alucard makes sense. Especially if he has deep pockets and no credits. Being attached to a good, to a *great*, film would do him no harm. Perhaps he wants the acclaim?"

Welles rolled the idea around his head.

"No," he concluded, almost sadly. "Gené, I have never been accused of lack of ego. My largeness of spirit, my sense of self-worth, is part of my act, as it were. The armour I must needs haul on to do my daily battles. But I am not blind to my situation. No producer in his right mind would bankroll me to such an extent, would offer me such a deal. Not even these kids, this Spielberg and that Lucas, could get such a sweetheart deal. I am as responsible for that as anyone. The studios of today may be owned by oil companies and hotel magnates, but there's a race memory of that contract I signed when I was twenty-four and of how it all went wrong, for me and for everyone. When I was kicked off the lot in 1943, RKO took out ads in the trades announcing their new motto, 'showmanship, not genius'! Hollywood doesn't want to have me around. I remind the town of its mistakes, its crimes."

"Alucard is an independent producer, you say. Perhaps he's a fan?"

"I don't think he's seen any of my pictures."

"Do you think this is a cruel prank?"

Welles shrugged, raising huge hands. Oja was more guarded, more worried. Geneviève wondered whether she was the one who had insisted on calling in an investigator.

"The first cheques have cleared," said Welles. "The rent is paid on this place."

"You are familiar with the expression . . ."

"The one about equine dentistry? Yes."

"But it bothers you? The mystery?"

"The Mystery of Mr Alucard. That is so. If it blows up in my face, I can stand that. I've come to that pass before and I shall venture there again. But I should like some presentiment, either way. I want you to make some discreet inquiries about our Mr Alucard. At the very least, I'd like to know his real name and where he comes from. He seems very American at the moment, but I don't think that was always the case. Most of all, I want to know what he is up to. Can you help me, Mademoiselle Dieu-donné?"

VIII

"You know, Gené," said Jack Martin wistfully, contemplating the melting ice in his empty glass through the wisps of cigarette smoke that always haloed his head, "none of this matters. It's not important. Writing. It's a trivial pursuit, hardly worth the effort, inconsequential on any cosmic level. It's just blood and sweat and guts and bone hauled out of our bodies and fed through a typewriter to slosh all over the platen. It's just the sick soul of America turning sour in the sunshine. Nobody really reads what I've written. In this town, they don't know Flannery O'Connor or Ray Bradbury, let alone Jack Martin. Nothing will be remembered. We'll all die and it'll be over. The sands will close over our civilization and the sun will turn into a huge red fireball and burn even you from the face of the earth."

"That's several million years away, Jack," she reminded him.

He didn't seem convinced. Martin was a writer. In high school, he'd won a national competition for an essay entitled "It's Great to Be Alive". Now in his grumbling forties, the sensitive but creepy short stories that were his most personal work were published in small science fiction and men's magazines, and put out in expensive limited editions by fan publishers who went out of business owing him money. He had made a living as a screenwriter for ten years without ever seeing anything written under his own name get made. He had a problem with happy endings.

However, he knew what was going on in "the Industry" and was her first port of call when a case got her mixed up with the movies. He lived in a tar-paper shack on Beverly Glen Boulevard, wedged between multi-million dollar estates, and told everybody that at least it was earthquake-proof.

Martin rattled the ice. She ordered him another Coca-Cola. He stubbed out one cigarette and lit another.

The girl behind the hotel bar, dressed as a magician, sloshed ice into another glass and reached for a small chromed hose. She squirted coke into the glass, covering the ice.

Martin held up his original glass.

"Wouldn't it be wonderful if you could slip the girl a buck and have her fill up *this* glass, not go through all the fuss of getting a fresh one and charging you all over again. There should be infinite refills. Imagine that, a utopian dream, Gené. It's what America needs. A *bottomless* coke!"

"It's not policy, sir," said the girl. With the coke came a quilted paper napkin, an unhappy edge of lemon and a plastic stirrer.

Martin looked at the bar-girl's legs. She was wearing black fishnets, high-heeled pumps, a tight white waistcoat, a tail coat and top-hat.

The writer sampled his new, bottomed, coke. The girl went to cope with other morning customers.

"I'll bet she's an actress," he said. "I think she does porno."

Geneviève raised an eyebrow.

"Most X-rated films are better directed than the slop that comes out of the majors," Martin insisted. "I could show you a reel of something by Gerard Damiano or Jack Horner that you'd swear was Bergman or Don Siegel. Except for the screwing."

Martin wrote "scripts" for adult movies, under well-guarded pseudonyms to protect his Writer's Guild membership. The Guild didn't have any moral position on porno, but members weren't supposed to take jobs which involved turning out a full-length feature script in two afternoons for three hundred dollars. Martin claimed to have invented Jamie Gillis's catch-phrase, "suck it, bitch!"

"What can you tell me about John Alucard?"

"The name is . . ."

"Besides that his name is 'Dracula' written backwards."

"He's from New York. Well, that's where he was last. I heard he ran with that art crowd. You know, Warhol and Jack Smith. He's got a first-look deal at United Artists, and something cooking with Fox. There's going to be a story in the trades that he's set up an independent production company with Griffin Mill, Julia Phillips and Don Simpson."

"But he's never made a movie?"

"The word is that he's never *seen* a movie. That doesn't stop him calling himself a producer. Say, are you working for him? If you could mention that I was available. Mention my rewrite on *Can't Stop the Music*. No, don't. Say about that TV thing that didn't happen. I can get you sample scripts by sun-down."

Martin was gripping her upper arm.

"I've never met Alucard, Jack. I'm checking into him for a client."

"Still, if you get the chance, Gené. You know what it would mean to me. I'm fending off bill-collectors and Sharkko Press still hasn't come through for the *Tenebrous Twilight* limiteds. A development deal, even a rewrite or a polish, could get me through winter and spring. Buy me time to get down to Ensenada and finish some stories."

She would have to promise. She had learned more than the bare facts. The light in Jack Martin's eyes told her something about John Alucard. He had some sort of magic effect, but she didn't know whether he was a conjurer or a wizard.

Now, she would have to build on that.

IX

Short of forcing her way into Alucard's office and asking outright whether he was planning on leaving Orson Welles in the lurch, there wasn't much more she could do. After Martin, she made a few phone calls to industry contacts, looked over recent back numbers of *Variety* and the *Hollywood Reporter* and hit a couple of showbiz watering holes, hoping to soak up gossip.

Now, Geneviève was driving back along the Pacific Coast Highway to Paradise Cove. The sun was down and a heavy, unstarred darkness hung over the sea. The Plymouth, which she sometimes suspected of having a mind of its own, handled gently, taking the blind curves at speed. She twiddled the radio past a lot of disco, and found a station pumping out two-tone. That was good, that was new, that was a culture still alive.

". . . *mirror in the bathroom, recompense
all my crimes of self-defence* . . ."

She wondered about what she had learned.

It wasn't like the old days, when the studios were tight little fiefdoms and a stringer for Louella Parsons would know everything going on in town and all the current scandal. Most movies weren't even made in Hollywood any more, and the studios were way down on the lists of interests owned by multi-national corporations with other primary concerns. The buzz was that

United Artists might well be changing its name to TransAmerica Pictures.

General word confirmed most of what Martin had told her, and turned up surprisingly few extra details. Besides the Welles deal, financed off his own line of credit with no studio production coin as yet involved, John Alucard had projects in development all over town, with high-end talent attached. He was supposed to be in bed with Michael Cimino, still hot off *The Deer Hunter*, on *The Lincoln County Wars*, a Western about the vampire outlaw Billy the Kid and a massacre of settlers in Roswell, New Mexico, in the 1870s. With the Mill–Simpson–Phillips set-up, he was helping the long in-development Anne Rice project, *Interview With the Mummy*, which Elaine May was supposed to be making with Cher and Ryan O'Neal, unless it was Nancy Walker, with Diana Ross and Mark Spitz.

In an interview in the, *Reporter* Alucard said, "The pursuit of making money is the only reason to make movies. We have no obligation to make history. We have no obligation to make art. We have no obligation to make a statement. Our obligation is to make money." A lot of execs, and not a few directors and writers, found his a refreshing and invigorating stance, though Geneviève had the impression Alucard was parroting someone else's grand theory. If he truly believed what he said, and was not just laying down something the studios' corporate owners wanted to hear, then John Alucard did not sound like someone who would happily want to be in business with Orson Welles. Apart from anything else, his manifesto was a 1980s rewrite, at five times the length with in-built repetition to get through to the admass morons at the back of the hall, of "showmanship, not genius".

The only thing she couldn't find out was what his projects really were. Besides Welles's *Dracula*, which wasn't mentioned by anyone she had talked with, and the long-gestating shows he was working with senior production partners, he had half a dozen other irons in the fire. Directors and stars were attached, budgets set, start dates announced, but no titles ever got mentioned, and the descriptions in the trades – "intense drama", "romantic comedy" – were hardly helpful. That was interesting and unusual. John Alucard was making a splash, waves radiating outwards, but surely he would have eventually to say what the pictures were. Or had that become the least important part of the package? An agent at CAA told her that for men like Alucard, the art was in the deal not on the screen.

That did worry her.

Could it be that there wasn't actually a pot of gold at the end of this rainbow? The man was a vampire, but was he also a phantom? No photographs existed, of course. Everyone had a second-hand description, always couched as a casting suggestion: a young Louis Jourdan, a smart Jack Palance, a rough trade David Niven. It was agreed that the man was European, a long time ago. No one had any idea how long he had been a vampire, even. He could be a new-born fresh-killed and risen last year, or a centuried elder who had changed his face a dozen times. His name always drew the same reaction: excitement, enthusiasm, fear. There was a sense that John Alucard was getting things on the road, and that it'd be a smart career move to get close, to be ready to haul out of the station with him.

She cruised across sandy tarmac into the trailer park. The sea-food restaurant was doing a little New Year's Day business. She would be thirsty soon.

Someone sat on the stairs of her trailer, leaning back against her door, hands loose in his lap, legs in chinos, cowboy boots.

Someone dead.

X

Throughout Welles' career, *Dracula* remained an *idée fixée*. The Welles–Mankiewicz script was RKO property and the studio resisted Welles' offer to buy it back. They set their asking price at the notional but substantial sum accountants reckoned had been lost on the double debacle of *Ambersons* and the unfinished South American project, *It's All True*.

When Schaefer, Welles' patron, was removed from his position as Vice-President in Charge of Production and replaced by Charles Koerner, there was serious talk of putting the script into production through producer Val Lewton's unit, which had established a reputation for low-budget supernatural dramas with *Cat People* (1942). Lewton got as far as having DeWitt Bodeen and then Curt Siodmak take runs at further drafts, scaling the script down to fit a strait-jacket budget. Jacques Tourneur was attached to direct, though editor Mark Robson was considered when Tourneur was promoted to A pictures. Stock players were assigned supporting roles: Tom Conway (Dr Seward), Kent Smith (Jonathan Harker), Henry Daniell (Van Helsing), Jean Brooks (Lucy), Alan Napier (Arthur Holmwood), Skelton Knaggs (Renfield), Elizabeth Russell (Countess Marya Dolingen), Sir Lancelot (a calypso-singing coachman). Simone Simon, star of *Cat People*, was set for Mina, very much the focus of Lewton's take on the story, but the project fell through because RKO were unable to secure their first and only choice of star, Boris Karloff, who was committed to *Arsenic and Old Lace* on Broadway.

In 1944, RKO sold the Welles–Mankiewicz script, along with a parcel of set designs, to Twentieth Century-Fox. Studio head Darryl F. Zanuck offered Welles the *role* of Dracula, promising Joan Fontaine and Olivia de Havilland for Mina and Lucy, suggesting Tyrone Power (Jonathan), George Sanders (Arthur), John Carradine (Quincey) and Laird Cregar (Van Helsing). This *Dracula* would have been a follow-up to Fox's successful Welles–Fontaine *Jane Eyre* (1943) and Welles might have committed if Zanuck had again assigned weak-willed Robert Stevenson, allowing Welles to direct in everything but credit. However, on a project this "important", Zanuck would consider only two directors; John Ford had no interest – sparing us John Wayne, Victor McLaglen, Ward Bond and John Agar as brawling, boozing fearless vampire slayers – so it inevitably fell to Henry King, a specialist in molasses-slow historical subjects like *Lloyd's of London* (1936) and *Brigham Young* (1940). King, a plodder who had a brief flash of genius in a few later films with Gregory Peck, had his own, highly-developed, chocolate box style and gravitas, and was not a congenial director for Welles, whose mercurial temperament was unsuited to methods he considered conservative and dreary. The film still might have been made, since Welles was as ever in need of money, but Zanuck went cold on *Dracula* at the end of the War when the Count was moving into his Italian exile.

Fox wound up backing *Prince of Foxes* (1949), directed by King, with Power and Welles topping the cast, shot on location in Europe. A lavish bore, enlivened briefly by Welles' committed Cesare Borgia, this suggests what the Zanuck *Dracula* might have been like. Welles used much of his earnings from the long shoot to pour into film projects made in bits and pieces over several years: the completed *Othello* (1952), the unfinished Don Quixote (begun 1955) and, rarely mentioned until now, yet another *Dracula*. *El conde Dràcula*, a French-Italian-Mexican-American-Irish-Liechtensteinian-British-Yugoslav-Moroccan-Iranian co-production, was shot in snippets, the earliest dating from 1949, the latest from 1972.

Each major part was taken by several actors, or single actors over a span of years. In the controversial edit supervised by the Spaniard Jesus Franco – a second-unit director on Welles' *Chimes at Midnight* (1966) – and premiered at Cannes in 1997, the cast is as follows: Akim Tamiroff (Van Helsing), Micheál MacLiammóir (Jonathan), Paola Mori (Mina), Michael Redgrave (Arthur), Patty McCormick (Lucy), Hilton Edwards (Dr Seward), Mischa Auer (Renfield). The vampire brides are played by Jeanne Moreau, Suzanne Cloutier and Katina Paxinou, shot in different years on different continents. There is no sight of Francisco Reiguera, Welles' Quixote, cast as a skeletal Dracula, and the Count is present only as a substantial shadow voiced (as are several other characters) by Welles himself. Much of the film runs silent, and a crucial framing story, explaining the multi-narrator device, was either never filmed or shot and lost. Jonathan's panicky exploration of his castle prison, filled with steam like the Turkish bath in *Othello*, is the most remarkable, purely Expressionist scene Welles ever shot. But the final ascent to Castle Dracula, with Tamiroff dodging patently *papier-mâché* falling boulders and wobbly zooms into and out of stray details hardly seems the work of anyone other than a fumbling amateur.

In no sense "a real film", *El conde Dràcula* is a scrapbook of images from the novel and Welles' imagination. He told Henry Jaglom that he considered the project a private exercise, to keep the subject in his mind, a series of sketches for a painting he would execute later. As Francis Coppola would in 1977, while his multi-million-dollar *Dracula* was bogged down in production problems in Romania, Welles often made comparisons with the Sistine Chapel. While Coppola invoked Michelangelo with some desperation as the vast machine of his movie seemed to be collapsing around him, Welles always resorted playfully to the metaphor, daring the interviewer with a wave and a wink and a deep chuckle to suggest the Pope probably did turn up every day wanting to know when the great artist would be finished and how much it was going to cost.

In 1973, Welles assembled some *El conde Dràcula* footage, along with documentary material about the real Count Dracula and the scandals that followed his true death in 1959: the alleged, much-disputed will that deeded much of his vast fortune to English housewife Vivian Nicholson, who claimed she had encountered Dracula while on a school holiday in the early '50s; the autobiography Clifford Irving sold for a record-breaking advance in 1971, only to have the book exposed as an arrant fake written by Irving in collaboration with Fred Saberhagen; the squabbles among sundry vampire elders, notably Baron Meinster and Princess Asa Vajda, as to who should claim the Count's unofficial title as ruler of their kind, King of the Cats. Welles called this playful, essay-like film – constructed around the skeleton of footage shot by Calvin Floyd for his own documentary, *In Search of Dracula* (1971) – *When Are You Going to Finish El conde Dràcula?*, though it was exhibited in most territories as *D is for Dracula*. On the evening Premier Ceausescu withdrew the Romanian Cavalry needed for Coppola's assault on Castle Dracula in order to pursue the vampire banditti of the Transylvania Movement in the next valley, Francis Ford Coppola held a private screening of *D is for Dracula* and cabled Welles that there was a curse on anyone who dared invoke the dread name.

Gates, ibid.

XI

The someone on her steps was *truly* dead. In his left chest, over his punctured heart, a star-shaped blotch was black in the moonlight.

Geneviève felt no residue. The intangible thing – immortal soul, psychic energy, battery power – which kept mind and body together, in *nosferatu* or the warm, was gone.

Broken is the golden bowl, the spirit flown forever.

She found she was crying. She touched her cheek and looked at the thick, salt, red tears, then smeared them away on her handkerchief.

It was Moondoggie. In repose, his face looked old, the lines his smile had made appealing turned to slack wrinkles.

She took a moment with him, remembering the taste of the

living man, that he was the only one who called her "Gidget", his inability to put in words what it was about surfing that made him devote his life to it (he'd been in pre-med once, long, long ago – when there was a crack-up or a near-drowning, the doctor he might have been would surface and take over), and the rush of the seas that came with his blood.

That man was gone. Besides sorrow at the waste, she was angry. And afraid.

It was easy to see how it had happened. The killer had come close, face to face, and stuck Moondoggie through the heart. The wound was round, not a slit. The weapon was probably a wooden stake or a sharpened metal pole. The angle of the wound was upwards, so the killer was shorter than the rangy surfer. Stuck through, Moondoggie had been carefully propped up on her doorstep. She was being sent a message.

Moondoggie was a warm man, but he'd been killed as if he were like her, a vampire.

He was not cold yet. The killing was recent.

Geneviève turned in a half-circle, looking out across the beach. Like most vampires, she had above average night vision for a human being – without sun glare bleaching everything bone-white, she saw better than by day – but no hawklike power of distinguishing far-off tiny objects or magical X-ray sight.

It was likely that the assassin was nearby, watching to see that the message was received. Counting on the popular belief that vampires did have unnatural eyesight, she moved slowly enough that anyone in concealment might think she was looking directly at them, that they had been seen.

A movement.

The trick worked. A couple of hundred yards off, beyond the trailer park, out on the beach, something – someone – moved, clambering upright from a hollow depression in the dry sand.

As the probable murderer stood, Geneviève saw a blonde pony-tail whipping. It was a girl, mid-to-late teens, in halter-top and denim shorts, with a wispy gauze neckscarf and – suggestive detail – running shoes and knee-pads. She was undersized but athletic. Another girl midget: no wonder she'd been able to get close enough to Moondoggie, genial connoisseur of young bodies, to stab him in the heart.

She assumed the girl would bolt. Geneviève was fast enough to run her down, but the killer ought to panic. In California, what people knew about vampires was scrambled with fantasy and science fiction.

For once, Geneviève was tempted to live up to her image. She wanted to rip out the silly girl's throat.

(and drink)

She took a few long steps, flashing forwards across the beach.

The girl stood her ground, waiting.

Geneviève paused. The stake wasn't in the dead man's chest. The girl still had it. Her right hand was out of sight, behind her back.

Closer, she saw the killer's face in the moonlight. Doll-pretty, with an upturned nose and the faintest fading traces of freckles. She was frowning with concentration now, but probably had a winning smile, perfect teeth. She should be a cheerleader, not an assassin.

This wasn't a vampire, but Geneviève knew she was no warm creampuff, either. She had killed a strong man twice her weight with a single thrust and was prepared for a charging *nosferatu*.

Geneviève stood still, twenty yards from the girl.

The killer produced her stake. It was stained.

"Meet Simon Sharp," she said. She had a clear, casual voice. Geneviève found her flippancy terrifying.

"You killed a man," Geneviève said, trying to get through to her, past the madness.

"Not a man, a viper. One of you, undead vermin."

"He was alive."

"You'd snacked on him, Frenchie. He would have turned."

"It doesn't work like that."

"That's not what I hear, not what I *know*."

From her icy eyes, this teenager was a fanatic. There could be no reasoning with her.

Geneviève would have to take her down, hold her until the police got here.

Whose side would the cops take? A vampire or a prom queen? Geneviève had fairly good relations with the local law, who were more uneasy about her as a private detective than as a vampire, but this might stretch things.

The girl smiled. She did look awfully cute.

Geneviève knew the mad bitch could probably get away with it.

At least once. She had the whole Tuesday Weld thing going for her, pretty poison.

"You've been warned, not spared," said the girl. "My A plan was to skewer you on sight, but the Overlooker thinks this is better strategy. It's some English kick, like cricket. Go figure."

The Overlooker?

"It'd be peachiest all around if you left the state, Frenchie. The country, even. Preferably, the planet. Next time we meet, it won't be a warning. You'll get a formal introduction to the delightful Simon. *Capisce*?"

"Who are you?"

"The Slayer," said the girl, gesturing with her stake. "Barbie, the Vampire Slayer."

Despite herself, despite everything, Geneviève had to laugh.

That annoyed Barbie.

Geneviève reminded herself that this silly girl, playing dress-up-and-be-a-heroine, was a real live murderess.

She laughed more calculatedly.

Barbie wanted to kill her, but made no move. Whoever this Overlooker – bloody silly title – was, his or her creature didn't want to exceed the brief given her.

(Some English kick, like cricket.)

Geneviève darted at the girl, nails out. Barbie had good reactions. She pivoted to one side and launched a kick. A cleated shoe just missed Geneviève's midriff but raked her side, painfully. She jammed her palm-heel at Barbie's chin, and caught her solidly, shutting her mouth with a click.

Simon Sharp went flying. That made Geneviève less inhibited about close fighting.

Barbie was strong, trained and smart. She might have the brain of a flea, but her instincts were panther-like and she went all out for a kill. But Geneviève was still alive after five hundred and fifty years as a vampire.

Barbie tried the oldest move in girly martial arts and yanked her opponent's hair, cutting her hand open. Geneviève's hair was fine but stronger and sharper than it looked, like pampas grass. The burst of hot blood was a distraction, sparking lizardy synapses in Geneviève's brain, momentarily blurring her thoughts. She threw Barbie away, skittering her across the sand on her can in an undignified tangle.

Mistake.

Barbie pulled out something that looked like a mace spray and squirted at Geneviève's face.

Geneviève backed away from the cloud, but got a whiff of the mist. Garlic, holy water and silver salts. Garlic and holy water didn't bother her – more mumbo-jumbo, ineffective against someone not of Dracula's bloodline – but silver was deadly to all *nosferatu*. This spray might not kill her, but it could scar her for a couple of centuries, or even life. It was vanity, she supposed, but she had got used to people telling her she was pretty.

She scuttled away, backwards, across the sand. The cloud dissipated in the air. She saw the droplets, shining under the moon, falling with exaggerated slowness, pattering onto the beach.

When the spray was gone, so was Barbie the Vampire Slayer.

XII

". . . and, uh, this is exactly where you found Mr Griffin, miss?" asked the LAPD homicide detective.

Geneviève was distracted. Even just after dawn, the sun was fatiguing her. In early daylight, on a gurney, Moondoggie – whose name turned out to have been Jeff Griffin – looked colder and emptier, another of the numberless dead stranded in her past while she went on and on and on.

"Miss Dew-dun-ee?"

"Dieudonné," she corrected, absent-mindedly.

"Ah yes, Dieudonné. Accent *grave* over the e. That's French, isn't it? I have a French car. My wife says . . ."

"Yes, this is where I found the body," she answered, catching up.

"Ah. There's just one thing I don't understand."

She paid attention to the crumpled little man. He had curly hair, a gravel voice and a raincoat. He was working on the first cigar of the day. One of his eyes was glass, and aimed off to the side.

"And what might that be, Lieutenant?"

"This girl you mentioned, this . . ." he consulted his note-book, or pretended to, "this 'Barbie'. Why would she hang around after

the murder? Why did she have to make sure you found the
body?"

"She implied that she was under orders, working for this
Overlooker."

The detective touched his eyebrow as if to tuck his smelly cigar
behind his ear like a pen, and made great play of thinking hard,
trying to work through the story he had been told. He was
obviously used to people lying to him, and equally obviously
unused to dealing with vampires. He stood between her and the
sun, as she inched into the shrinking shadow of her trailer.

She wanted to get a hat and dark glasses but police tape still
barred her door.

"'Overlooker', yes. I've got a note of that, miss. Funny expression, isn't it. Gives the impression the 'Overlooker' is supposed *not* to see something, that the whole job is about, ah,
overlooking. Not like my profession, miss. Or yours either, I
figure. You're a PI, like on TV?"

"With fewer car chases and shoot-outs."

The detective laughed. He was a funny little duck. She realized
he used his likability as a psychological weapon, to get close to
people he wanted to nail. She couldn't mistake the situation: she
was in the ring for the killing, and her story about Barbie the
Slayer didn't sound straight in daylight. What sane professional
assassin gives a name, even a partial name, to a witness?

"A vampire private eye?" the detective scratched his head.

"It makes sense. I don't mind staying up all night. And I've got
a wealth of varied experience."

"Have you solved any big cases? Really big ones?"

Without thinking, she told a truth. "In 1888, I half-way found
out who Jack the Ripper was."

The detective was impressed.

"I thought no-one knew how that panned out. Scotland Yard
still have it open. What with you folk living longer and longer, it's
not safe to close unsolved files. The guy who took the rap died,
didn't he? These days, the theorists say it couldn't have been
him."

"I said I half-way found out."

She had a discomfiting memory flash, of her and Charles in an
office in Whitechapel in 1888, stumbling over the last clue, all the
pieces falling into place. The problem was that solving the

mystery hadn't meant sorting everything out, and the case had
continued to spiral out of control. There was a message there.

"That wouldn't be good enough for my captain, I'm afraid,
miss. He has to answer to Police Chief Exley, and Chief Exley
insists on a clearance and conviction rate. I can't just catch them, I
have to prove they did it. I have to go to the courts. You'd be
surprised how many guilty parties walk free. Especially the rich
ones, with fancy lawyers. In this town, it's hard to get a conviction
against a rich man."

"This girl looked like a high-school kid."

"Even worse, miss. Probably has rich folks."

"I've no idea about that."

"And pretty is as good as being rich. Better. Juries like pretty
girls as much as lawyers like rich men."

There was a shout from the beach. One of the uniformed cops
who had been combing the sand held up a plastic evidence bag.
Inside was Barbie's bloody stake.

"Simon Sharp," Geneviève said. The detective's eyebrows rose.
"That's what she called it. What kind of person gives a pet-name
to a murder weapon?"

"You think you've heard everything in this business and then
something else comes along and knocks you flat. Miss, if you
don't mind me asking, I know it's awkward for some women, but,
um, well, how old are you?"

"I was born in 1416," she said.

"That's five hundred and, um, sixty-five."

"Thereabouts."

The detective shook his head again and whistled.

"Tell me, does it get easier? Everything?"

"Sadly, no."

"You said you had – uh, how did you put it? – 'a wealth of
varied experience'. Is that like getting cleverer every year? Knowing more and more of the answers?"

"Would that it did, Lieutenant. Sometimes I think it just means
having more and more questions."

He chuckled. "Ain't that the truth."

"Can I get into my trailer now?" she asked, indicating the
climbing sun.

"We were keeping you out?" he asked, knowing perfectly well
he was. "That's dreadful, with your condition and everything. Of

course you can go inside, miss. We'll be able to find you here, if there are any more questions that come up? It's a trailer, isn't it? You're not planning on hitching it up to your car and driving off, say, out of state?"

"No, Lieutenant."

"That's good to know."

He gallantly tore the police tape from her door. She had her keys out. Her skin tingled, and the glare off the sea turned everything into blobby, indistinct shapes.

"Just one more thing," said the detective, hand on her door.

The keys were hot in her fingers.

"Yes," she said, a little sharply.

"You're on a case, aren't you? Like on TV?"

"I'm working on several investigations. May I make a bet with you, Lieutenant? For a dime?"

The detective was surprised by that. But he fished around in his raincoat pocket and, after examining several tissues and a book of matches, came up with a coin and a smile.

"I bet I know what you're going to ask me next," she said. "You're going to ask me who I'm working for?"

He was theatrically astonished.

"That's just incredible, miss. Is it some kind of vampire mind-reading power? Or are you like Sherlock Holmes, picking up tiny hints from little clues, like the stains on the cigar-band or the dog not howling in the night?"

"Just a lucky guess," she said. Her cheeks were really burning, now.

"Well, see if I can luckily guess your answer. Client confidentiality privilege, like a lawyer or a doctor, eh?"

"See. You have hidden powers too, Lieutenant."

"Well, Miss Dieudonné, I do what I can, I do what I can. Any idea what I'm going to say next?"

"No."

His smile froze slightly and she saw ice in his real eye.

"Don't leave town, miss."

XIII

On rising, she found Jack Martin had left a message on her machine. He had something for her on "Mr A". Geneviève listened to the brief message twice, thinking it over.

She had spent only a few hours asking about John Alucard, and someone had got killed. A connection? It would be weird if there wasn't. Then again, as the detective reminded her, she'd been around for a long time. In her years, she'd ticked off a great many people, not a few as long-lived as she was herself. Also, this was Southern California, La-La Land, where the nuts came from: folk didn't necessarily need a reason to take against you, or to have you killed.

Could this Overlooker be another Manson? Crazy Charlie was a vampire-hater too, and used teenage girls as assassins. Everyone remembered the death of Sharon Tate, but the Manson Family had also destroyed a vampire elder, Count von Krolock, up on La Cienaga Drive, and painted bat-symbols on the walls with his old blood. Barbie the Slayer was cutie-pie where the Family chicks had been skaggy, but that could be a 1980s thing as opposed to a 1960s one.

Geneviève knew she could take care of herself, but the people who talked to her might be in danger. She must mention it to Martin, who wasn't long on survival skills. He could at least scurry down to Mexico for a couple of months. In the meantime, she was still trying to earn her fifty dollars a day, so she returned Martin's call. The number he had left was (typically) a bar, and the growling man who picked up had a message for her, giving an address in the valley where she could find Martin.

This late in the afternoon, the sun low in the sky. She loved the long winter nights.

In a twist-tied plastic bag buried among the cleaning products and rags under her sink unit was a gun, a ladylike palm-sized automatic. She considered fishing it out and transferring it to the Plymouth Fury, but resisted the impulse. No sense in escalating. As yet, even the Overlooker didn't want her dead.

That was not quite a comfort.

XIV

The address was an anonymous house in an anonymous neighbourhood out in the diaspora-like sprawl of ranchos and villas and vistas, but there were more cars and vans outside than a single family would need. Either there was a party on or this was a suburban commune. She parked on the street and watched for a moment. The lights from the windows and the patio were a few candles brighter than they needed to be. Cables snaked out of a side-door and round to the backyard.

She got out of the Plymouth and followed the hose-thick cables, passing through a cultivated arbour into a typical yard-space, with an oval pool, currently covered by a heavy canvas sheet that was damp where it rested on water, and a white wooden gazebo, made up with strands of dead ivy and at the centre of several beams of light. There were a lot of people around but this was no party. She should have guessed: it was another film set. She saw lights on stands and a camera crew, plus the usual assortment of hangers-on, gophers, rubberneckers, fluffers, runners and extras.

This was more like a "proper" movie set than the scene she had found at Welles' bungalow, but she knew from the naked people in the gazebo that this was a far less proper movie. Again, she should have guessed. This was a Jack Martin lead, after all.

"Are you here for 'Vampire Bitch, Number Three'?"

The long-haired, chubby kid addressing her wore a tie-dyed T-shirt and a fisherman's waistcoat, pockets stuffed with goodies. He carried a clipboard.

Geneviève shook her head. She didn't know whether to be flattered or offended. Then again, in this town, everyone thought everyone else was an actor or actress. They were usually more or less right.

She didn't like the sound of the part. If she had a reflection that caught on film and were going to prostitute herself for a skinflick, she would at least hold out for "Vampire Bitch, Number One".

"The part's taken, I'm afraid," said the kid, not exactly dashing her dreams of stardom. "We got Seka at the last minute."

He nodded towards the gazebo, where three warm girls in pancake make-up hissed at a hairy young man, undoing his Victorian cravat and waistcoat.

"I'm here to see Jack Martin?" she said.

"Who?"

"The writer?"

She remembered Martin used pseudonyms for this kind of work, and spun off a description: "Salt and pepper beard, *Midnight Cowboy* jacket with the fringes cut off, smokes a lot, doesn't believe in positive thinking."

The kid knew who she meant. "That's 'Mr Stroker'. Come this way. He's in the kitchen, doing rewrites. Are you sure you're not here for a part? You'd make a groovy vampire chick."

She thanked him for the compliment, and followed his lead through a mess of equipment to the kitchen, torn between staring at what was going on between the three girls and one guy in the gazebo and keeping her eyes clear. About half the crew were of the madly ogling variety, while the others were jaded enough to stick to their jobs and look at their watches as the shoot edged towards golden time.

"Vampire Bitch Number Two, put more tongue in it," shouted an intense bearded man whose megaphone and beret marked him as the director. "I want to see fangs, Samantha. You've got a jones for that throbbing vein, you've got a real lust for blood. Don't slobber. That's in bad taste. Just nip nicely. That's it. That's colossal. That's the cream."

"What is the name of this picture?" Geneviève asked.

"*Debbie Does Dracula*," said the kid. "It's going to be a four-boner classic. Best thing Boris Adrian has ever shot. He goes for production values, not just screwing. It's got real crossover potential, as a 'couples' movie. Uh oh, there's a gusher."

"Spurt higher, Ronny," shouted the director, Boris Adrian. "I need the arc to be highlit. Thank you, that's perfect. Seka, Samantha, Désirée, you can writhe in it if you like. That's outstanding. Now, collapse in exhaustion, Ronny. That's perfect. Cut, and print."

The guy in the gazebo collapsed in real exhaustion, and the girls called for assistants to wipe them off. Some of the crew applauded and congratulated the actors on their performances, which she supposed was fair enough. One of the "Vampire Bitches" had trouble with her false fang-teeth.

The director got off his shooting-stick and sat with his actors, talking motivation.

The kid held a screen door open and showed her into the kitchen. Martin sat at a tiny table, cigarette in his mouth, hammering away at a manual typewriter. Another clipboard kid, a wide girl with a frizz of hair and Smiley badges fastening her overall straps, stood over him.

"Gené, excuse me," said Martin. "I'll be through in a moment."

Martin tore through three pages, working the carriage return like a gunslinger fanning a Colt, and passed them up to the girl, who couldn't read as fast as he wrote.

"There's your Carfax Abbey scene," Martin said, delivering the last page.

The girl kissed his forehead and left the kitchen.

"She's in love with me."

"The assistant?"

"She's the producer, actually. Debbie W. Griffith. Had a monster hit distributing *Throat Sprockets* in Europe. You should see that. It's the first real adult film for the vampire market. Plays at midnight matinees."

"She's 'D.W. Griffith', and you're . . . ?"

Martin grinned, "Meet 'Bram Stroker'."

"And why am I here?"

Martin looked around, to make sure he wasn't overheard, and whispered "This is it, this is his. Debbie's a front. This is *un film de* John Alucard."

"It's not Orson Welles."

"But it's a start."

A dark girl, kimono loose, walked through the kitchen, carrying a couple of live white rats in one hand, muttering to herself about "the Master". Martin tried to say hello, but she breezed past, deeply into her role, eyes drifting. She lingered a moment on Geneviève, but wafted out onto the patio and was given a mildly sarcastic round of applause.

"That's Kelly Nicholls," said Martin. "She plays Renfield. In this version, it's not *flies* she eats, not in the usual sense. This picture has a great cast: Dirk Diggler as Dracula, Annette Haven as Mina, Holly Body as Lucy, John Leslie as Van Helsing."

"Why didn't you tell me about this yesterday?"

"I didn't know then."

"But you're the screenwriter. You can't have been hired and written the whole thing to be shot this afternoon."

"I'm the rewriter. Even for the adult industry, their first pass at the script blew dead cats. It was called *Dracula Sucks*, and boy did it ever. They couldn't lick it, as it were. It's the subject, *Dracula*. You know what they say about the curse, the way it struck down Coppola in Romania. I've spent the day doing a page one rewrite."

Someone shouted "quiet on set," and Martin motioned Geneviève to come outside with him, to watch the shooting.

"The next scene is Dracula's entrance. He hauls the three vampire bitches – pardon the expression – off Jonathan and, ah, well, you can imagine, satiates them, before tossing them baby in a bag."

"I was just offered a role in the scene. I passed."

Martin harrumphed. Unsure about this whole thing, she began to follow.

A movement in an alcove distracted her. A pleasant-faced warm young man sat in there, hunched over a sideboard. He wore evening dress trousers and a bat-winged black cloak but nothing else. His hair was black and smoothed back, with a prominent widow's peak painted on his forehead. For a supposed vampire, he had a decent tan.

He had a rolled up ten-dollar bill stuck in his nose.

A line of red dust was on the sideboard. He bent over and snuffed it up. She had heard of drac, but never seen it.

The effect on the young man was instant. His eyes shone like bloodied marbles. Fang-teeth shot out like switchblades.

"Yeah, that's it," he said. "Instant vamp!"

He flowed upright, unbending from the alcove, and slid across the floor on bare feet. He wasn't warm, wasn't a vampire, but something in between – a dhampire – that wouldn't last more than an hour.

"Where's Dracula?" shouted Boris Adrian. "Has he got the fangs-on yet?"

"I am Dracula," intoned the youth, as much to himself, convincing himself. "I *am* Dracula!"

As he pushed past her, Geneviève noticed the actor's trousers were held together at the fly and down the sides by strips of Velcro. She could imagine why.

She felt obscurely threatened. Drac – manufactured from vampire blood – was extremely expensive and highly addictive. In her own veins flowed the raw material of many a valuable fangs-on instant vamp fugue. In New York, where the craze came from, vampires had been kidnapped and slowly bled empty to make the foul stuff.

Geneviève followed the dhampire star. He reached out his arms like a wingspread, cloak billowing, and walked across the covered swimming pool, almost flying, as if weightless, skipping over sagging puddles and, without toppling or using his hands, made it over the far edge. He stood at poolside and let the cloak settle on his shoulders.

"I'm ready," he hissed through fangs.

The three fake vampire girls in the gazebo huddled together, a little afraid. They weren't looking at Dracula's face, his hypnotic eyes and fierce fangs, but at his trousers. Geneviève realized there were other properties of drac that she hadn't read about in the newspapers.

The long-haired kid who had spoken to her was working a pulley. A shiny cardboard full-moon rose above the gazebo. Other assistants held bats on fishing lines. Boris Adrian nodded approval at the atmosphere.

"Well, Count, go to it," the director ordered. "Action."

The camera began to roll as Dracula strode up to the gazebo, cloak rippling. The girls writhed over the prone guy, Jonathan Harker, and awaited the coming of their dark prince.

"This man is mine," said Dracula, in a Californian drawl that owed nothing to Transylvania. "As you all are mine, you vampire bitches, you horny vampire bitches."

Martin silently recited the lines along with the actor, eyes alight with innocent glee.

"You never love," said the least-fanged of the girls, who had short blonde hair, "you yourself have never loved."

"That is not true, as you know well and as I shall prove to all three of you. In succession, and together. Now."

The rip of Velcro preceded a gasp from the whole crew. Dirk Diggler's famous organ was blood-red and angry. She wondered if he could stab a person with it and suck their blood, or was that just a rumour like the Tijuana werewolf show Martin spent his vacations trying to track down.

The "vampire bitches" huddled in apparently real terror.

"Whatever he's taking, I want some of it," breathed Martin.

XV

Later, in an empty all-night diner, Martin was still excited about *Debbie Does Dracula*. Not really sexually, though she didn't underestimate his prurience, but mostly high on having his words read out, caught on film. Even as "Bram Stroker", he had pride in his work.

"It's a stopgap till the real projects come through," he said, waving a deadly cigarette. "But it's cash in hand, Gené. Cash in hand. I don't have to hock the typewriter. Debbie wants me for the sequel they're making next week, *Taste the Cum of Dracula*, with Vanessa Del Rio as Marya Zaleska. But I may pass. I've got something set up at Universal, near as damn it. A remake of *Buck Privates*, with Belushi and Dan Aykroyd. It's between me and this one other guy, Lionel Fenn, and Fenn's a drac-head from the East with a burn-out date stamped on his forehead. I tell you, Gené, it's adios to 'Bram Stroker' and 'William Forkner' and 'Charles Dickings'. You'll be my date for the premiere, won't you? You pretty-up good, don't you? When the name Jack Martin means something in this town, I want to direct."

He was tripping on dreams. She brought him down again.

"Why would John Alucard be in bed with Boris Adrian?" she asked.

"And Debbie Griffith," he said. "I don't know. There's an invisible barrier between adult and legit. It's like a parallel world. The adult industry has its own stars and genres and awards shows. No one ever crosses. Oh, some of the girls do bit-parts. Kelly was in *The Toolbox Murders*, with Cameron Mitchell."

"I missed that one."

"I didn't. She was the chickie in the bath, who gets it with a nail-gun. Anyway, that was a fluke. You hear stories that Stallone made a skinflick once, and that some on-the-skids directors take paying gigs under pseudonyms."

"Like 'Bram Stroker'?"

Martin nodded, in his flow. "But it's not an apprenticeship, not really. Coppola shot nudies, but that was different. Just skin, no sex. Tame now. Nostalgia bait. You've got to trust me, Gené, don't tell anyone, and I mean not anyone, that I'm 'Bram Stroker'. It's a crucial time for me, a knife-edge between the big ring and the wash-out ward. I really need this *Buck Privates* deal. If it comes to it, I want to hire you to scare off Fenn. You do hauntings, don't you?"

She waved away his panic, her fingers drifting through his nicotine cloud.

"Maybe Alucard wants to raise cash quickly?" she suggested.

"Could be. Though the way Debbie tells it, he isn't just a sleeping partner. He originated the whole idea, got her and Boris together, borrowed Dirk from Jack Horner, even – and I didn't tell you this – supplied the bloody nose candy that gave Dracula's performance the added *frisson*."

It was sounding familiar.

"Did he write the script?" she asked. "The first script?"

"Certainly, no writer did. It might be Mr A. There was no name on the title page."

"It's not a porno movie he wants, not primarily," she said. "It's a Dracula movie. Another one. Yet another one."

Martin called for a coffee refill. The ancient, slightly mouldy character who was the sole staff of the Nighthawks Diner shambled over, coffee sloshing in the glass jug.

"Look at this guy," Martin said. "You'd swear he was a god-damned reanimated corpse. No offence, Gené, but you know what I mean. Maybe he's a dhamp. I hear they zombie out after a while, after they've burned their bat-cells."

Deaf to the discussion, the shambler sloshed coffee in Martin's mug. Here, in Jack Martin Heaven, there were infinite refills. He exhaled contented plumes of smoke.

"Jack, I have to warn you. This case might be getting danger-ous. A friend of mine was killed yesterday night, as a warning. And the police like me for it. I can't prove anything, but it might be that asking about Alucard isn't good for your health. Still, keep your ears open. I know about two John Alucard productions now, and I'd like to collect the set. I have a feeling he's a one-note musician, but I want that confirmed."

"You think he only makes Dracula movies?"

"I think he only makes Dracula."

She didn't know what she meant by that, but it sounded horribly right.

XVI

There was night enough left after Martin had peeled off home to check in with the client. Geneviève knew Welles would still be holding court at four in the morning.

He was running footage.

"Come in, come in," he boomed.

Most of the crew she had met the night before were strewn on cushions or rugs in the den, along with a few new-comers, movie brats and law professors and a very old, very grave black man in a bright orange dashiki. Gary, the cameraman, was working the projector.

They were screening the scene she had seen shot, projecting the picture onto the tapestry over the fireplace. Van Helsing tormented by vampire symbols. It was strange to see Welles' huge, bearded face, the luminous skull, the flapping bat and the dripping dagger slide across the stiff, formal image of the mediaeval forest scene.

Clearly, Welles was in mid-performance, almost holding a dialogue with his screen self, and wouldn't detach himself from the show so she could report her preliminary findings to him.

She found herself drifting into the yard. There were people there, too. Nico, the vampire starlet, had just finished feeding, and lay on her back, looking up at the stars, licking blood from her lips and chin. She was a messy eater. A too-pretty young man staggered upright, shaking his head to dispel dizziness. His clothes were Rodeo Drive, but last year's in a town where last week was another era. She didn't have to sample Nico's broadcast thoughts to put him down as a rich kid who had found a new craze to blow his trust fund money on, and her crawling skin told her it wasn't a sports car.

"Your turn," he said to Nico, nagging.

She kept to the shadows. Nico had seen her but her partner was too preoccupied to notice anyone. The smear on his neck gave Geneviève a little prick of thirst.

Nico sat up with great weariness, the moment of repletion spoiled. She took a tiny paring knife from her clutch-purse. It glinted, silvered. The boy sat eagerly beside her and rolled up the left sleeve of her loose muslin blouse, exposing her upper arm. Geneviève saw the row of striped scars she had noticed last night. Carefully, the vampire girl opened a scar and let her blood trickle. The boy fixed his mouth over the wound. She held his hair in her fist.

"Remember, lick," she said. "Don't suck. You won't be able to take a full fangs-on."

His throat pulsed, as he swallowed.

With a roar, the boy let the girl go. He had the eyes and the fangs, even more than Dirk Diggler's Dracula. He moved fast, a temporary new-born high on all the extra senses and the sheer sense of power.

The dhampire put on wraparound mirror shades, ran razor-nailed hands through his gelled hair and stalked off to haunt the La-La night. Within a couple of hours, he would be a real live boy again. By that time, he could have got himself into all manner of scrapes.

Nico squeezed shut her wound. Geneviève caught her pain. The silver knife would be dangerous if it flaked in the cut. For a vampire, silver rot was like bad gangrene.

"It's not my place to say anything," began Geneviève.

"Then don't," said Nico, though she clearly received what Geneviève was thinking. "You're an elder. You can't know what it's like."

She had a flash that this new-born would never be old. What a pity.

"It's a simple exchange," said the girl. "Blood for blood. A gallon for a scratch. The economy is in our favour. Just like the President says."

Geneviève joined Nico at the edge of the property.

"This vampire trip really isn't working for me," said Nico. "That boy, Julian, will be warm again in the morning, mortal and with a reflection. And when he wants to, he'll be a vampire. If I'm not here, there are others. You can score drac on Hollywood Boulevard for twenty-five dollars a suck. Vile stuff, powdered, not from the tap, but it works."

Geneviève tidied Nico's hair. The girl lay on her lap, sobbing silently. She hadn't just lost blood.

This happened when you became an elder. You were mother and sister to the whole world of the undead.

The girl's despair passed. Her eyes were bright, with Julian's blood.

"Let's hunt, elder, like you did in Transylvania."

"I'm from France. I've never even been to Romania."

Now she mentioned it, that was odd. She'd been almost everywhere else. Without consciously thinking of it, she must have been avoiding the supposed homeland of the *nosferatu*. Kate Reed had told her she wasn't missing much, unless you enjoyed political corruption and paprika.

"There are human cattle out there," said Nico. "I know all the clubs. X is playing at the Roxy, if you like West Coast punk. And the doorman at After Hours always lets us in, vampire girls. There are so few of us. We go to the head of the line. Powers of fascination."

"Human cattle" was a real new-born expression. This close to dawn, Geneviève was thinking of her cosy trailer and shutting out the sun, but Nico was a race-the-sun girl, staying out until it was practically light, bleeding her last as the red circle rose in the sky.

She wondered if she should stick close to the girl, keep her out of trouble. Why? She couldn't protect everyone. She barely knew Nico, probably had nothing in common with her.

She remembered Moondoggie. And all the other dead, the ones she hadn't been able to help, hadn't tried to help, hadn't known about in time. The old gumshoe had told her she should get into her current business because there were girls like this, vampire girls, that only she could understand.

This girl really was none of her business.

"What's that?" said Nico, head darting. There was a noise from beyond the fence at the end of the garden.

Dominating the next property was a three-storey wooden mansion, California cheesecake. Nico might have called it old. Now Geneviève's attention was drawn to it, her night-eyes saw how strange the place was. A rusted-out pickup truck was on cinderblocks in the yard, with a pile of ragged auto tires next to it. The windshield was smashed out, and dried streaks – which any vampire would have scented as human blood, even after ten years – marked the hood.

"Who lives there?" Geneviève asked.

"In-bred backwoods brood," said Nico. "Orson says they struck it rich down in Texas, and moved to Beverly Hills. You know, swimming pools, movie stars . . ."

"Oil?"

"Chilli sauce recipe. Have you heard of Sawyer's Sauce?" Geneviève hadn't. "I guess not. I've not taken solid foods since I turned, though if I don't feed for a night or two I get this terrible phantom craving for those really shitty White Castle burgers. I suppose that if you don't get to the market, you don't know the brand-names."

"The Sawyers brought Texas style with them," Geneviève observed. "That truck's a period piece."

The back-porch was hung with mobiles of bones and nail-impaled alarm clocks. She saw a napping chicken, stuffed inside a canary cage.

"What's that noise?" Nico asked.

There was a wasplike buzzing, muted. Geneviève scented burning gas. Her teeth were on edge.

"Power tool," she said. "Funny time of the night for warm folks to be doing carpentry."

"I don't think they're all entirely warm. I saw some gross Grand-paw peeping out the other night, face like dried leather, licking livery lips. If he isn't undead, he's certainly nothing like alive."

There was a stench in the air. Spoiled meat.

"Come on, let's snoop around," said Nico, springing up. She vaulted over the low fence dividing the properties and crept across the yard like a four-legged crab.

Geneviève thought that was unwise, but followed, standing upright and keeping to shadows.

This really was none of her business.

Nico was on the porch now, looking at the mobiles. Geneviève wasn't sure whether it was primitive art or voodoo. Some of the stick-and-bone dangles were roughly man-shaped.

"Come away," she said.

"Not just yet."

Nico examined the back door. It hung open, an impenetrable dark beyond. The buzzing was still coming from inside the ramshackle house.

Geneviève *knew* sudden death was near, walking like a man. She called to Nico, more urgently.

Something small and fast came, not from inside the house but from the flatbed of the abandoned truck. The shape cartwheeled across the yard to the porch and collided purposefully with Nico. A length of wood pierced the vampire girl's thin chest. A look, more of surprise than pain or horror, froze on her face.

Geneviève felt the thrust in her own heart, then the silence in her mind. Nico was gone, in an instant.

"How do you like your stake, ma'am?"

It was Barbie. Only someone truly witless would think stake puns the height of repartee.

This time, Geneviève wouldn't let her get away.

"Just the time of night for a little viper-on-a-spit," said the Slayer, lifting Nico's deadweight so that her legs dangled. "This really should be you, Frenchie. By the way, I don't think you've met Simon's brother, Sidney. Frenchie, Sidney. Sidney, hellbitch creature of the night fit only to be impaled and left to rot in the light of the sun. That's the formalities out of the way."

She threw Nico away, sliding the dead girl off Sidney the Stake. The new-born, mould already on her startled face, flopped off the porch and fell to the yard.

Geneviève was still shocked by the passing, almost turned to ice. Nico had been in her mind, just barely and with tiny fingers, and her death was a wrench. She thought her skull might be leaking.

"They don't cotton much to trespassers down Texas way," said Barbie, in a bad cowboy accent. "Nor in Beverly Hills, neither."

Geneviève doubted the Sawyers knew Barbie was here.

"Next time, the Overlooker says I can do you too. I'm wishing and hoping and praying you ignore the warning. You'd look so fine on the end of a pole, Frenchie."

An engine revved, like a signal. Barbie was bounding away, with deerlike elegance.

Geneviève followed.

She rounded the corner of the Sawyer house and saw Barbie climbing into a sleek black Jaguar. In the driver's seat was a man wearing a tweed hunting jacket with matching bondage hood. He glanced backwards as he drove off.

The sports car had vanity plates. OVRLKER1.

Gravel flew as the car sped off down the drive.

"What's all this consarned ruckus?" shouted someone, from the house.

Geneviève turned and saw an American Gothic family group on the porch. Blotch-faced teenage boy, bosomy but slack-eyed girl in a polka-dot dress, stern patriarch in a dusty black suit, and hulking elder son in a stained apron and crude leather mask. Only the elder generation was missing, and Geneviève was sure they were up in rocking chairs on the third storey, peeking through the slatted blinds.

"That a dead'n?" asked the patriarch, nodding at Nico.

She conceded that it was.

"*True* dead'n?"

"Yes," she said, throat catching.

"What a shame and a waste," said Mr Sawyer, in a tone that made Geneviève think he wasn't referring to a life but to flesh and blood that was highly saleable.

"Shall I call the Sheriff, Paw?" asked the girl.

Mr Sawyer nodded, gravely.

Geneviève knew what was coming next.

XVII

". . . there's just one thing I don't understand, miss."

"Lieutenant, if there were 'just one thing' I didn't understand, I'd be a very happy old lady. At the moment, I can't think of 'just one thing' I do understand."

The detective smiled craggily.

"You're a vampire, miss. Like this dead girl, this, ah, Nico. That's right, isn't it?"

She admitted it. Orson Welles had lent her a crow-black umbrella which she was using as a parasol.

"And this Barbie, who again nobody else saw, was, ah, a living person?"

"Warm."

"Warm, yes. That's the expression. That's what you call us."

"It's not offensive."

"That's not how I take it, miss. No, what I'm wondering is: aren't vampires supposed to be faster than a warm person, harder to catch hold of in a tussle?"

"Nico was a new-born, and weakened. She'd lost some blood."

"That's one for the books."

"Not any more."

The detective scratched his head, lit cigar-end dangerously near his hair. "So I hear. It's called 'drac' on the streets. I have friends on the Narco Squad. They say it's worse than heroin, and it's not illegal yet."

"Where is this going, Lieutenant?"

He shut his notebook and pinned her with his eye.

"You could have, ah, *taken* Miss Nico? If you got into a fight with her?"

"I didn't."

"But you could have."

"I could have killed the Kennedys and Sanford White, but I didn't."

"Those are closed cases, as far as I'm concerned. This is open."

"I gave you the numberplate."

"Yes, miss. OVRLKER1. A Jaguar."

"Even if it's a fake plate, there can't be that many English sports cars in Los Angeles."

"There are, ah, one thousand, seven hundred and twenty-two registered Jaguars. Luxury vehicles are popular in this city, in some parts of it. Not all the same model."

"I don't know the model. I don't follow cars. I just know it was a Jaguar. It had the cat on the bonnet, the hood."

"Bonnet? That's the English expression, isn't it?"

"I lived in England for a long time."

With an Englishman. The detective's sharpness reminded her of Charles, with a witness or a suspect.

Suspect.

He had rattled the number of Jaguars in Greater Los Angeles off the top of his head, with no glance at the prop notebook. Gears were turning in his head.

"It was a black car," she said. "That should make it easier to find."

"Most automobiles look black at night. Even red ones."

"Not to me, Lieutenant."

Uniforms were off, grilling the Sawyers. Someone was even talking with Welles, who had let slip that Geneviève was working for him. Since the client had himself blown confidentiality, she was in an awkward position; Welles still didn't want it known what exactly she was doing for him.

"I think we can let you go now, miss," said the detective.

She had been on the point of presenting him her wrists for the cuffs.

"There isn't 'just one more thing' you want to ask?"

"No. I'm done. Unless there's anything you want to say."

She didn't think so.

"Then you can go. Thank you, miss."

She turned away, knowing it would come, like a hand on her shoulder or around her heart.

"There is one thing, though. Not a question. More like a

circumstance, something that has to be raised. I'm afraid I owe you an apology."

She turned back.

"It's just that I had to check you out, you know. Run you through the books. As a witness, yesterday. Purely routine."

Her umbrella seemed heavier.

"I may have got you in trouble with the state licensing board. They had all your details correctly, but it seems that every time anyone looked at your licence renewal application, they misread the date. As a European, you don't write an open four. It's easy to mistake a four for a nine. They thought you were born in 1916. Wondered when you'd be retiring, in fact. Had you down as a game old girl."

"Lieutenant, I am a game old girl."

"They didn't pull your licence, exactly. This is really embarrassing and I'm truly sorry to have been the cause of it, but they want to, ah, review your circumstances. There aren't any other vampires licensed as private investigators in the State of California, and there's no decision on whether a legally dead person can hold a licence."

"I never died. I'm not legally dead."

"They're trying to get your paperwork from, ah, France."

She looked up at the sky, momentarily hoping to burn out her eyes. Even if her original records existed, they'd be so old as to be protected historical documents. Photostats would not be coming over the wire from her homeland.

"Again, miss, I'm truly sorry."

She just wanted to get inside her trailer and sleep the day away.

"Do you have your licence with you?"

"In the car," she said, dully.

"I'm afraid I'm going to have to ask you to surrender it," said the detective. "And that until the legalities are settled, you cease to operate as a private investigator in the State of California."

XVIII

At sunset, she woke to another limbo, with one of her rare headaches. She was used to knowing what she was doing tonight, and the next night, if not specifically then at least generally. Now, she wasn't sure what she *could* do.

Geneviève wasn't a detective any more, not legally. Welles had not paid her off, but if she continued working on John Alucard for him she'd be breaking the law. Not a particularly important one, in her opinion . . . but vampires lived in such a twilight world that it was best to pay taxes on time and not park in towaway zones. After all, this was what happened when she drew attention to herself.

She had two other ongoing investigations, neither promising. She should make contact with her clients, a law firm and an Orange County mother, and explain the situation. In both cases, she hadn't turned up any results and so would not in all conscience be able to charge a fee. She didn't even have that much Welles could use.

Money would start to be a problem around Valentine's Day. The licensing board might have sorted it out by then.

(in some alternate universe)

She should call Beth Davenport, her lawyer, to start filing appeals and lodging complaints. That would cost, but anything else was just giving up.

Two people were truly dead. That bothered her too.

She sat at her tiny desk, by a slatted window, considering her telephone. She had forgotten to switch her answering machine on before turning in, and any calls that might have come today were lost. She had never done that before.

Should she re-record her outgoing message, stating that she was (temporarily?) out of business? The longer she was off the bus, the harder it would be to get back.

On TV, suspended cops, disbarred private eyes and innocent men on the run never dropped the case. And this was Southern California, where the TV came from.

She decided to compromise. She wouldn't work Alucard, which was what Welles had been paying her for. But, as a concerned – indeed, involved – citizen, no law said she couldn't use her talents unpaid to go after the slayer.

Since this was a police case, word of her status should have filtered down to her LAPD contacts but might not yet have reached outlying agencies. She called Officer Baker, a contact in the Highway Patrol, and wheedled a little to get him to run a licence plate for her.

OVRLKER1.

The call-back came within minutes, excellent service she admitted was well worth a supper and cocktails one of these nights. Baker teased her a while about that, then came over.

Amazingly, the plate *was* for a Jaguar. The car was registered in the name of Ernest Ralph Gorse, to an address in a town up the coast, Shadow Bay. The only other forthcoming details were that Gorse was a British subject – not citizen, of course – and held down a job as a high school librarian.

The Overlooker? A school librarian and a cheerleader might seem different species, but they swam in the same tank.

She thanked Baker and rang off.

If it was that easy, she could let the cops handle it. The Lieutenant was certainly sharp enough to run a Gorse down and scout around to see if a Barbie popped up. Even if the detective hadn't believed her, he would have been obliged to run the plate, to puncture her story. Now, he was obliged to check it out.

But wasn't it all too easy?

Since when did librarians drive Jaguars?

It had the air of a trap.

She was where the Lieutenant must have been seven hours ago. She wouldn't put the crumpled detective on her list of favourite people, but didn't want to hear he'd run into another of the Sharp Brothers. Apart from the loss of a fine public servant who was doubtless also an exemplary husband, it was quite likely that if the cop sizing her up for two murders showed up dead she would be even more suitable for framing.

Shadow Bay wasn't more than an hour away.

XIX

Welles' final Dracula project came together in 1981, just as the movies were gripped by a big vampire craze. Controversial and slow-building, and shut out of all but technical Oscars, Coppola's *Dracula* proved there was a substantial audience for vampire subjects. The next half-decade would see Werner Herzog's *Renfield, Jeder fur Sich und die Vampir Gegen Alle*, a retelling of the story from the point of the fly-eating lunatic (Klaus Kinski); of Tony Scott's *The Hunger*, with Catherine Deneuve and David Bowie as New York art patrons Miriam and John Blaylock, at the centre of a famous murder case defended by Alan Dershowitz (Ron Silver); of John Landis's *Scream, Blacula, Scream*, with Eddie Murphy as Dracula's African get Prince Mamuwalde, searching for his lost bride (Vanity) in New York – best remembered for a plagiarism lawsuit by screenwriter Pat Hobby that forced Paramount to open its books to the auditors; of Richard Attenborough's bloated, mammoth, Oscar-scooping B*Varney*, with Anthony Hopkins as Sir Francis Varney, the vampire Viceroy overthrown by the Second Indian Mutiny; of Brian De Palma's remake of *Scarface*, an explicit attack on the Transylvania Movement, with Al Pacino as Tony Sylvana, a Ceausescu cast-out rising in the booming drac trade and finally taken down by a Vatican army led by James Woods.

Slightly ahead of all this activity, Welles began shooting quietly, without publicity, working at his own pace, underwritten by the last of his many mysterious benefactors. His final script combined elements from Stoker's fiction with historical fact made public by the researches of Raymond McNally and Radu Florescu – associates as far back as *D is for Dracula* – and concentrated on the last days of the Count, abandoned in his castle, awaiting his executioners, remembering the betrayals and crimes of his lengthy, weighty life. This was the project Welles called *The Other Side of Midnight*. From sequences filmed as early as 1972, the director culled footage of Peter Bogdanovich as Renfield, while he opted to play not the stick insect vampire but the corpulent slayer, finally gifting the world with his definitive Professor Van Helsing. If asked by the trade press, he made great play of having offered the role of Dracula to Warren Beatty, Steve McQueen or Robert De Niro, but this was a conjurer's distraction, for he had fixed on his Count for some years and was now finally able to fit him for his cape and fangs. Welles' final Dracula was to be John Huston.

Gates, ibid

XX

She parked on the street but took the trouble to check out the Shadow Bay High teachers' parking lot. Two cars: a black Jaguar (OVERLKR1) and a beat-up silver Peugeot ("I have a French car"). Geneviève checked the Peugeot and found LAPD ID on display. The interior was a mess. She caught the after-whiff of cigars.

The school was as unexceptional as the town, with that faintly unreal movie-set feel that came from newness. The oldest building in sight was put up in 1965. To her, places like this felt temporary.

A helpful map by the front steps of the main building told her where the library was, across a grassy quadrangle. The school grounds were dark. The kids wouldn't be back from their Christmas vacation. And no evening classes. She had checked Gorse's address first, and found no one home.

A single light was on in the library, like the cover of a Gothic romance paperback.

Cautious, she crossed the quad. Slumped in the doorway of the library was a raincoated bundle. Her heart plunging, she knelt and found the Lieutenant insensible but still alive. He had been bitten badly and bled. The ragged tear in his throat showed he'd been taken the old-fashioned way – a strong grip from behind, a rending fang-bite, then sucking and swallowing. Non-consensual vampirism, a felony in anyone's books, without the exercise of powers of fascination to cloud the issue. It was hard to mesmerize someone with one eye, though some vampires worked with whispers and could even put the fluence on a blind person.

There was another vampire in Shadow Bay. By the look of the leavings, one of the bad 'uns. Perhaps that explained Barbie's prejudice. It was always a mistake to extrapolate a general rule from a test sample of one.

She clamped a hand over the wound, feeling the weak pulse, pressing the edges together. Whoever had bitten the detective hadn't even had the consideration to shut off the faucet after glutting themselves. The smears of blood on his coat and shirt collar over-rode her civilized impulses: her mouth became sharp-fanged and full of saliva. That was a good thing. A physical adaption of her turning was that her spittle had antiseptic properties. Vampires of her bloodline were evolved for gentle, repeated feedings. After biting and drinking, a full-tongued lick sealed the wound.

Angling her mouth awkwardly and holding up the Lieutenant's lolling head to expose his neck, she stuck out her tongue and slathered saliva over the long tear. She tried to ignore the euphoric if cigar-flavoured buzz of his blood. She had a connection to his clear, canny mind.

He had never thought her guilty. Until now.

"Makes a pretty picture, Frenchie," said a familiar girlish voice. "Classic Bloodsucker 101, viper and victim. Didn't your father-in-darkness warn you about snacking between meals? You won't be able to get into your party dresses if you bloat up. Where's the fun in that?"

Geneviève knew Barbie wasn't going to accept her explanation. For once, she understood why.

The wound had been left open for her.

"I've been framed," she said, around bloody fangs.

Barbie giggled, a teen vision in a red ra-ra skirt, white ankle socks, mutton-chop short-sleeved top and *faux* metallic choker. She had sparkle glitter on her cheeks and an alice band with artificial antennae that ended in bobbling stars.

She held up her stake and said "Scissors cut paper."

Geneviève took out her gun and pointed it. "Stone blunts scissors."

"Hey, no fair," whined Barbie.

Geneviève set the wounded man aside as carefully as possible and stood up. She kept the gun trained on the slayer's heart.

"Where does it say vampires have to do kung fu fighting? Everyone else in this country carries a gun, why not me?"

For a moment, she almost felt sorry for Barbie the Slayer. Her forehead crinkled into a frown, her lower lip jutted like a sulky five-year-old's and tears of frustration started in her eyes. She had a lot to learn about life. If Geneviève got her wish, the girl would complete her education in Tehachapi Women's Prison.

A silver knife slipped close to her neck.

"Paper wraps stone," suaved a British voice.

XXI

"Barbie doesn't know, does she? That you're *nosferatu*?"

Ernest Ralph Gorse, high school librarian, was the epitome of tweedy middle-aged stuffiness, so stage English that he made Alistair Cooke sound like a Dead End Kid. He arched an elegant eyebrow, made an elaborate business of cleaning his granny glasses with his top-pocket hankie, and gave out a little I'm-so-wicked moué that let his curly fangs peep out of beneath his stiff upper lip.

"No, 'fraid not. Lovely to look at, delightful to know but frightfully thick, that's our little Barbara."

The Overlooker – "yes," he had admitted, "bloody silly name, means nothing, just sounds 'cool' if you're a twit" – had sent Barbie the Slayer off with the drained detective, to call at the hospital ER and the Sheriff's office. Geneviève was left in the library, in the custody of Gorse. He had made her sit in a chair, and kept well beyond her arms' length.

"You bit the Lieutenant?" she stated.

Gorse raised a finger to his lips and tutted.

"Shush now, old thing, mustn't tell, don't speak it aloud. Jolly bad show to give away the game and all that rot. Would you care for some instant coffee? Ghastly muck, but I'm mildly addicted to it. It's what comes of being cast up on these heathen shores."

The Overlooker pottered around his desk, which was piled high with unread and probably unreadable books. He poured water from an electric kettle into an oversized green ceramic apple. She declined his offer with a headshake. He quaffed from his apple-for-the-teacher mug, and let out an exaggerated ahh of satisfaction.

"That takes the edge off. Washes down *cop au nicotin* very nicely."

"Why hasn't she noticed?"

Gorse chuckled. "Everything poor Barbara knows about the tribes of *nosferatu* comes from me. Of course, a lot of it I made up. I'm very creative, you know. It's always been one of my skills. Charm and persuasion, that's the ticket. The lovely featherhead hangs on my every word. She thinks all vampires are gruesome creatures of the night, demons beyond hope of redemption, frothing beasts fit only to be put down like mad dogs. I'm well aware of the irony, old thing. Some cold evenings, the hilarity becomes almost too much to handle. Oh, the stories I've spun for her, the wild things she'll believe. I've told her she's the Chosen One, the only girl in the world who can shoulder the burden of the crusade against the forces of Evil. Teenage girls adore that I'm-a-secret-Princess twaddle, you know. Especially the Yanks. I copped a lot of it from *Star Wars*. Bloody awful film, but very revealing about the state of the national mind."

Gorse was enjoying the chance to explain things. Bottling up his cleverness had been a trial for him. She thought it was the only reason she was still alive for this performance.

"But what's the point?"

"Originally, expedience. I've been 'passing' since I came to America. I'm not like you, sadly. I can't flutter my lashes and have pretty girls offer their necks for the taking. I really am one of those hunt-and-kill, rend-and-drain sort of *nosferatu*. I tried the other way, but courtship dances just bored me rigid and I thought, well, why not? Why not just rip open the odd throat. So, after a few months here in picturesque Shadow Bay, empties were piling up like junk mail. Then the stroke of genius came to me. I could hide behind a Vampire Slayer and since there were none in sight I made one up. I checked the academic records to find the dimmest dolly bird in school, and recruited her for the Cause. I killed her lunk of a boyfriend – captain of football team, would you believe it? – and a selection of snack-size teenagers. Then, I revealed to Barbara that her destiny was to be the Slayer. Together, we tracked and destroyed that first dread fiend – the school secretary who was nagging me about getting my employment records from Jolly Old England, as it happens – and staked the bloodlusting bitch. However, it seems she spawned before we got to her, and ever since we've been doing away with her murderous brood. You'll be glad to know I've managed to rid this town almost completely of real estate agents. When the roll is called up yonder, that must count in the plus column, though it's my long-term plan not to be there."

Actually, Gorse was worse than the vampires he had made up. He'd had a choice, and *decided* to be Evil. He worked hard on fussy geniality, modelling his accent and speech patterns on *Masterpiece Theatre*, but there was ice inside him, a complete vacuum.

"So, you have things working your way in Shadow Bay?" she said. "You have your little puppet theatre to play with. Why come after me?"

Gorse was wondering whether to tell her more. He pulled a half-hunter watch from his waistcoat pocket and pondered. She wondered if she could work her trick of fascination on him. Clearly, he loved to talk, was bored with dissimulation, had a real need to be appreciated. The sensible thing would have been to get this over with, but Gorse had to tell her how brilliant he was. Everything up to now had been his own story; now, there was more important stuff and he was wary of going on.

"Still time for one more story," he said. "One more *ghost* story."

Click. She had him.

He was an instinctive killer, probably a sociopath from birth, but she was his elder. The silver-bladed letter-opener was never far from his fingers. She would have to judge when to jump.

"It's a lonely life, isn't it? Ours, I mean. Wandering through the years, wearing out your clothes, lost in a world you never made? There was a golden age for us once, in London when Dracula was on the throne. 1888 and all that. You, famous girl, did your best to put a stop to it, turned us all back into nomads and parasites when we might have been masters of the universe. Some of us want it that way again, my darling. We've been getting together lately, sort of a pressure group. Not like those Transylvania fools who want to go back to the castles and the mountains, but like Him, battening onto a new, vital world, making a place for ourselves. An exalted place. He's still our inspiration, old thing. Let's say I did it for Dracula."

That wasn't enough, but it was all she was going to get now. People were outside, coming in.

"Time flies, old thing. I'll have to make this quick."

Gorse took his silver pig-sticker and stood over her. He thrust.

Faster than any eye could catch, her hands locked around his wrist.

"Swift filly, eh?"

She concentrated. He was strong but she was old. The knife-point dimpled her blouse. He tipped back her chair and put a knee on her stomach, pinning her down.

The silver touch was white hot.

She turned his arm and forced it upwards. The knife slid under his spectacles and the point stuck in his left eye.

Gorse screamed and she was free of him. He raged and roared, fangs erupting from his mouth, two-inch barbs bursting from his fingertips. Bony spars, the beginnings of wings, sprouted through his jacket around the collar and pierced his leather elbow-patches.

The doors opened and people came in. Barbie and two crucifix-waving Sheriff's Deputies.

The Slayer saw
(and recognized?)
the vampire and rushed across the room, stake out. Gorse

caught the girl and snapped her neck, then dropped her in a dead tangle.

"Look what you made me do!" he said to Geneviève, voice distorted by the teeth but echoing from the cavern that was his reshaped mouth. "She's *broken* now. It'll take ages to make another. I hadn't even got to the full initiation rites. There would have been bleeding and I was making up something about tantric sex. It would have been a real giggle, and you've spoiled it."

His eye congealed, frothing grey deadness in his face.

She motioned for the deputies to stay back. They wisely kept their distance.

"Just remember," said Gorse, directly to her. "You can't stop Him. He's coming back. And then, oh my best beloved, you will be as sorry a girl as ever drew a sorry breath. He is not one for forgiveness, if you get my drift."

Gorse's jacket shredded and wings unfurled. He flapped into the air, rising above the first tier of bookshelves, hovering at the mezzanine level. His old school tie dangled like a dead snake.

The deputies tried shooting at him. She supposed she would have too.

He crashed through a tall set of windows and flew off, vast shadow blotting out the moon and falling on the bay.

The deputies holstered their guns and looked at her. She wondered for about two minutes whether she should stick with her honesty policy.

Letting a bird flutter in her voice, she said, "that man . . . The was a v-v-vampire."

Then she did a pretty fair imitation of a silly girl fainting. One deputy checked her heartbeat while she was "out", and was satisfied that she was warm. The other went to call for back-up.

Through a crack in her eyelids, she studied "her" deputy. His hands might have lingered a little too long on her chest for strict medical purposes. The thought that he was the type to cop a feel from a helpless girl just about made it all right to get him into trouble by slipping silently out of the library while he was checking out the dead slayer.

She made it undetected back to her car.

XXII

In her trailer, after another day of lassitude, she watched the early evening bulletin on Channel 6. Anchor-persons Karen White and Lew Landers had details of the vampire killing in Shadow Bay. Because the primary victim was a cute teenage girl, it was top story. The wounding of a decorated LAPD veteran – the Lieutenant was still alive, but off the case – also rated a flagged mention. The newscast split-screened a toothpaste commercial photograph of "Barbara Dahl Winters", smiling under a prom queen tiara, and an "artist's impression" of Gorse in giant bat-form, with blood tastefully dripping from his fangs. Ernest "Gory" Gorse turned out to be a fugitive from Scotland Yard, with a record of petty convictions before he turned and a couple of likely murders since. Considering a mug shot from his warm days, Karen said the killer looked like such a nice fellow, even scowling over numbers, and Lew commented that you couldn't judge a book by its cover.

Geneviève continued paying attention, well into the next item – about a scary candlelight vigil by hooded supporters of Annie Wilkes – and only turned the sound on her portable TV set down when she was sure her name was not going to come up in connection with the Shadow Bay story.

Gorse implied she was targeted because of her well-known involvement in the overthrow of Count Dracula, nearly a century ago. But that didn't explain why he had waited until now to give her a hard time. She also gathered from what he had let slip in flirtatious hints that he wasn't the top of the totem pole, that he was working with or perhaps for someone else.

Gorse had said: "You can't stop Him. He's coming back."

Him? He?

Only one vampire inspired that sort of *quondam rex que futurus* talk. Before he finally died, put out of his misery, Count Dracula had used himself up completely. Geneviève was sure of that. He had outlived his era, several times over, and been confronted with his own irrelevance. His true death was just a formality.

And He was not coming back.

A woodcut image of Dracula appeared on television. She turned the sound up.

The newscast had reached the entertainment round-up, which in this town came before major wars on other continents. A fluffy-haired woman in front of the Hollywood sign was talking about the latest studio craze, Dracula pictures. A race was on between Universal and Paramount to get their biopics of the Count to the screens. At Universal, director Joel Schumacher and writer-producer Jane Wagner had cast John Travolta and Lily Tomlin in *St George's Fire*; at MGM, producer Steven Spielberg and director Tobe Hooper had Peter Coyote and Karen Allen in *Vampirgeist*. There was no mention of Orson Welles – or, unsurprisingly, Boris Adrian – but another familiar name came up.

John Alucard.

"Hollywood dealmakers have often been characterised as bloodsuckers," said the reporter, "but John Alucard is the first actually to be one. Uniquely, this vampire executive is involved in *both* these competing projects, as a packager of the Universal production and as associate producer of the MGM film. Clearly, in a field where there are too few experts to go around, John Alucard is in demand. Unfortunately, Mr A – as Steven Spielberg calls him – is unable because of his image impairment to grant interviews for broadcast media, but he has issued a statement to the effect that he feels there is room for far more than two versions of the story he characterizes as 'the most important of the last two centuries'. He goes on to say 'there can be no definitive Dracula, but we hope we shall be able to conjure a different Dracula for every person'. For decades, Hollywood stayed away from this hot subject but, with the Francis Coppola epic of a few years ago cropping up on Best of All Time lists, it seems we are due, like the Londoners of 1885, for a veritable *invasion* of Draculas. This is Kimberley Wells, for Channel 6 KDHB *Update News*, at the Hollywood sign."

She switched the television off. The whole world, and Orson Welles, knew now what John Alucard was doing, but the other part of her original commission – who he was and where he came from – was still a mystery. He had come from the East, with a long line of credit. A source had told her he had skipped New York ahead of an investigation into insider-trading or junk bonds, but she might choose to put that down to typical Los Angeles cattiness. Another whisper had him living another life up in Silicon Valley as a consultant on something hush-hush President Reagan's people were calling the Strategic Defense Initiative, supposedly Buck Rogers stuff. Alucard could also be a Romanian shoe salesman with a line in great patter who had quit his dull job and changed his name the night he learned his turning vampire wasn't going to take in the long run and set out to become the new Irving Thalberg before he rotted away to dirt.

There must be a connection between the movie-making mystery man and the high school librarian. Alucard and Gorse. Two vampires in California. She had started asking around about one of them, and the other had sent a puppet to warn her off.

John Alucard could not *be* Count Dracula.

Not yet, at least.

XXIII

On her way up into the Hollywood Hills, to consult the only real magician she knew, she decided to call on Jack Martin, to see if he wanted to come along on the trip. The movie mage would interest him.

The door of Martin's shack hung open.

Her heart skipped. Loose manuscript pages were drifting out of Martin's home, catching on the breeze, and scuttling along Beverly Glen Boulevard, sticking on the manicured hedges of the million-dollar estates, brushing across the white-painted faces of lawn jockeys who had been coal-black until Sidney Poitier made a fuss.

She knocked on the door, which popped a hinge and hung free.

"Jack?"

Had Gorse got to him?

She ventured inside, prepared to find walls dripping red and a ruined corpse lying in a nest of torn-up screenplays.

Martin lay on a beat-up sofa, mouth open, snoring slightly. He was no more battered than usual. A Mexican wrestling magazine was open on his round tummy.

"Jack?"

He came awake, blearily.

"It's you," he said, cold.

His tone was like a silver knife.

"What's the matter?"

"As if you didn't know. You're not good to be around, Gené. Not good at all. You don't see it, but you're a wrecker."

She backed away.

"Someone tipped off the Writers' Guild about the porno. My ticket got yanked, my dues were not accepted. I'm off the list. I'm off all the lists. All possible lists. I didn't get *Buck Privates*. They went with Lionel Fenn."

"There'll be other projects," she said.

"I'll be lucky to get *Buck's Privates*."

Martin had been drinking, but didn't need to get drunk to be in this despair hole. It was where he went sometimes, a mental space like Ensenada, where he slunk to wallow, to soak up the misery he turned into prose. This time, she had an idea he wasn't coming back; he was going lower than ever, and would end up a beachcomber on a nighted seashore, picking broken skulls out of bloody seaweed, trailing bare feet through ink-black surf, becoming the exile king of his own dark country.

"It just took a phone call, Gené. To smash everything. To smash me. I wasn't even worth killing. That hurts. You, they'll kill. I don't want you to be near me when it happens."

"Does this mean our premiere date is off?"

She shouldn't have said that. Martin began crying, softly. It was a shocking scene, upsetting to her on a level she had thought she had escaped from. He wasn't just depressed, he was scared.

"Go away, Gené," he said.

XXIV

This was not a jaunt any more. Jack Martin was as lost to her as Moondoggie, as her licence.

How could things change so fast? It wasn't the second week of January, wasn't the Julian 1980s, but everything that had seemed certain last year, last decade, was up for debate or thrown away.

There was a cruelty at work. Beyond Gorse.

She parked the Plymouth and walked across a lawn to a ranch-style bungalow. A cabalist firmament of star-signs decorated the mail-box.

The mage was a trim, fiftyish man, handsome but small, less a fallen angel than a fallen cherub. He wore ceremonial robes to receive her into his *sanctum sanctorum*, an arrangement of literal shrines to movie stars of the 1920s and '30s: Theda Bara, Norma Desmond, Clara Bow, Lina Lamont, Jean Harlow, Blanche

Hudson, Myrna Loy. His all-seeing amulet contained a long-lashed black and white eye, taken from a still of Rudolph Valentino. His boots were black leather motorcycle gear, with polished chrome buckles and studs.

As a boy, the mage – Kenneth Anger to mortals of this plane – had appeared as the Prince in the 1935 Max Reinhardt film of *A Midsummer Night's Dream*. In later life, he had become a film-maker, but for himself not the studios (his "underground" trilogy consisted of *Scorpio Rising, Lucifer Rising* and *Dracula Rising*), and achieved a certain notoriety for compiling Hollywood Babylon, a collection of scurrilous but not necessarily true stories about the seamy private lives of the glamour gods and goddesses of the screen. A disciple of Aleister Crowley and Adrian Marcato, he was a genuine movie magician.

He was working on a sequel to *Hollywood Babylon*, which had been forthcoming for some years. It was called *Transylvania Babylon*, and contained all the gossip, scandal and lurid factoid specula-tion that had ever circulated about the elder members of the vampire community. Nine months ago, the manuscript and all his research material had been stolen by a couple of acid-heads in the employ of a pair of New Orleans-based vampire elders who were the focus of several fascinating, enlightening and perversely amusing chapters. Geneviève had recovered the materials, though the book was still not published, as Anger had to negotiate his way through a maze of injunctions and magical threats before he could get the thing in print.

She hesitated on the steps that led down to his slightly sunken *sanctum*. Incense burned before the framed pictures, swirling up to the low stucco ceiling.

"Do you have to be invited?" he asked. "Enter freely, spirit of dark."

"I was just being polite," she admitted.

The mage was a little disappointed. He arranged himself on a pile of harem cushions and indicated a patch of Turkish carpet where she might sit.

There was a very old bloodstain on the weave.

"Don't mind that," he said. "It's from a thirteen-year-old movie extra deflowered by Charlie Chaplin at the very height of the Roaring Twenties."

She decided not to tell him it wasn't hymenal blood (though it was human).

"I have cast spells of protection, as a precaution. It was respectful of you to warn me this interview might have consequences."

Over the centuries, Geneviève had grown out of thinking of herself as a supernatural creature, and was always a little surprised to run into people who still saw her that way. It wasn't that they might not be right, it was just unusual and unfashionable. The world had monsters, but she still didn't know if there was magic.

"One man who helped me says his career has been ruined because of it," she said, the wound still fresh. "Another, who was just my friend, died."

"My career is beyond ruination," said the mage. "And death means nothing. As you know, it's a passing thing. The lead-up, however, can be highly unpleasant, I understand. I think I'd opt to skip that experience, if at all possible."

She didn't blame him.

"I've seen some of your films and looked at your writings," she said. "It seems to me that you believe motion pictures are rituals."

"Well put. Yes, all real films are invocations, summonings. Most are made by people who don't realize that. But I do. When I call a film Invocation of My Demon Brother, I mean it exactly as it sounds. It's not enough to plop a camera in front of a ceremony. Then you only get religious television, God help you. It's in the lighting, the cutting, the music. Reality must be banished, channels opened to the Beyond. At screenings, there are always manifestations. Audiences might not realize on a conscious level what is happening, but they always know. Always. The amount of ectoplasm poured into the auditorium by drag queens alone at a West Hollywood revival of a Joan Crawford picture would be enough to embody a minor djinn in the shape of the Bitch Goddess, with a turban and razor cheekbones and shoulderpads out to here."

She found the image appealing, but also frightening.

"If you were to make a dozen films about, say, the Devil, would the Prince of Darkness appear?"

The mage was amused. "What an improbable notion. But it has some substance. If you made twelve ordinary films about the Devil, he might seem more real to people, become more of a figure in the culture, get talked about and put on magazine covers. But, let's face it, the same thing happens if you make one ordinary film about a shark. It's the thirteenth film that makes the difference, that might work the trick."

"That would be your film? The one made by a director who understands the ritual?"

"Sadly, no. A great tragedy of magick is that the most effective must be worked without conscious thought, without intent. To become a master mage, you must pass beyond the mathematics and become a dreamer. My film, of the Devil you say, would be but a tentative summoning, attracting the notice of a spirit of the beyond. Fully to call His Satanic Majesty to Earth would require a work of surpassing genius, mounted by a director with no other intention but to make a wonderful illusion, a von Sternberg or a Frank Borzage. That thirteenth film, a *Shanghai Gesture* or a *History is Made at Night*, would be the perfect ritual. And its goaty hero could leave his cloven hoofprint in the cement outside Grauman's Chinese."

XXV

In January 1981, Welles began filming BI;The Other Side of Midnight on the old Miracle Pictures lot, his first studio-shot – though independently-financed – picture since *Touch of Evil* in 1958, and his first "right of final cut" contract since *Citizen Kane*. The ins and outs of the deal have been assessed in entire books by Peter Bart and David J. Skal, but it seems that Welles, after a career of searching, had found a genuine "angel", a backer with the financial muscle to give him the budget and crew he needed to make a film that was truly his vision but also the self-effacing trust to let him have total artistic control of the result.

There were nay-saying voices and the industry was already beginning to wonder whether still in-progress runaway budget auteur movies like Michael Cimino's *The Lincoln County Wars* or Coppola's *Dracula* follow-up *One from the Heart* were such a great idea, but Welles himself denounced those runaways as examples of fuzzy thinking. As with his very first Dracula movie script and *Kane*, *The Other Side of Midnight* was meticulously pre-planned and pre-costed. Forty years on from Kane, Welles must have known this would be his last serious chance. A Boy Wonder no longer, the pressure was on him to produce a "mature masterpiece", a career book-end to the work that had topped so many Best of All Time lists and eclipsed all his other achievements. He must certainly have been aware of the legion of cineastes whose expectations of a film that would eclipse the flashy brilliance of the Coppola version were sky-rocketing. It may be that so many of Welles' other projects were left unfinished deliberately, because their creator knew they could never compete with the imagined masterpieces that were expected of him. With *Midnight*, he had to show all his cards and take the consequences.

The Other Side of Midnight occupied an unprecedented three adjacent sound-stages, where Ken Adam's sets for Bistritz and Borgo Pass and the exteriors and interiors of Castle Dracula were constructed. John Huston shaved his beard and let his moustache sprout, preparing for the acting role of his career, cast apparently because Welles admired him as the Los Angeles predator-patriarch Noah Cross (*Chinatown*, 1974). It has been rumoured that the seventy-four-year-old Huston went so far as to have transfusions of vampire blood and took to hunting the Hollywood night with packs of new-born vampire brats, piqued because he couldn't display trophies of his "kills". Other casting was announced, a canny mix of A-list stars who would have worked for scale just to be in a Welles film, long-time associates who couldn't bear to be left out of the adventure and fresh talent. Besides Welles (Van Helsing), the film would star Jack Nicholson (Jonathan Harker), Richard Gere (Arthur Holmwood), Shelley Duvall (Mina), Susan Sarandon (Lucy), Cameron Mitchell (Renfield), Dennis Hopper (Quincey), Jason Robards (Dr Seward), Joseph Cotten (Mr Hawkins), George Couloris (Mr Swales) and Jeanne Moreau (Peasant Woman). The three vampire brides were Anjelica Huston, Marie-France Pisier and then-unknown Kathleen Turner. John Williams was writing the score, Gary Graver remained Welles' preferred cinematographer, Rick Baker promised astounding and innovative special make-up effects and George Lucas's ILM contracted for the optical effects.

There were other vampire movies in pre-production, other *Dracula* movies, but Hollywood was really only interested in the Welles version.

Finally, it would happen.

Gates, ibid

XXVI

Geneviève parked the Plymouth near Bronson Caverns, in sight of the Hollywood Sign, and looked out over Los Angeles, transformed by distance into a carpet of Christmas lights. MGM used to boast "more stars than there were in the Heavens", and there they were, twinkling individually, a fallen constellation. Carlights on the freeways were like glowing platelets flowing through neon veins. From up here, you couldn't see the hookers on Hollywood Boulevard, the endless limbo motels and real estate developments, the lost, lonely and desperate. You couldn't hear the laugh track, or the screams.

It came down to magic. And whether she believed in it.

Clearly, Kenneth Anger did. He had devoted his life to rituals. A great many of them, she had to admit, had worked. And so did John Alucard and Ernest Gorse, vampires who thought themselves magical beings. Dracula had been another of the breed, thanking Satan for eternal night-life.

She just didn't know.

Maybe she was still undecided because she had never slipped into the blackness of death. Kate Reed, her Victorian friend, had done the proper thing. Kate's father-in-darkness, Harris, had drunk her blood and given of his own, then let her die and come back, turned. Chandagnac, Geneviève's mediaeval father-in-darkness, had worked on her for months. She had transformed slowly, coming alive by night, shaking off the warm girl she had been.

In the last century, since Dracula came out of his castle, there had been a lot of work done on the subject. It was no longer possible to disbelieve in vampires. With the *nosferatu* in the open, vampirism had to be incorporated into the prevalent belief systems and this was a scientific age. These days, everyone generally accepted the "explanation" that the condition was a blood-borne mutation, an evolutionary quirk adapting a strain of humankind for survival. But, as geneticists probed ever further, mysteries deepened: vampires retained the DNA pattern they were born with as warm humans, and yet they were *different* creatures. And, despite a lot of cracked theorizing, no one had ever convincingly adjusted the laws of optics to account for the business with mirrors.

If there were vampires, there could be magic.

And Alucard's ritual – the mage's thirteen movies – might work. He could come back, worse than ever.

Dracula.

She looked up, from the city-lights to the stars.

Was the Count out there, on some intangible plane, waiting to be summoned? Reinvigorated by a spell in the beyond, thirsting for blood, vengeance, power? What might he have learned in Hell, that he could bring to the Earth?

She hated to think.

XXVII

She drove through the studio gates shortly before dawn, waved on by the uniformed guard. She was accepted as a part of Orson's army, somehow granted an invisible arm-band by her association with the genius.

The Miracle Pictures lot was alive again. "If it's a good picture, it's a Miracle!" had run the self-mocking, double-edged slogan, all the more apt as the so-called fifth-wheel major declined from mounting Technicolor spectacles like the 1939 version of *The Duelling Cavalier*, with Errol Flynn and Fedora, to financing drive-in dodos like *Machete Maidens of Mora Tau*, with nobody and her uncle. In recent years, the fifty-year-old sound stages had mostly gone unused as Miracle shot their product in the Philippines or Canada. The standing sets seen in so many vintage movies had been torn down to make way for bland office buildings where scripts were "developed" rather than shot. There wasn't even a studio tour.

Now, it was different.

Orson Welles was in power and legions swarmed at his command, occupying every department, beavering away in the service of his vision. They were everywhere: gaffers, extras, carpenters, managers, accountants, make-up men, effects technicians, grips, key grips, boys, best boys, designers, draughtsmen, teamsters, caterers, guards, advisors, actors, writers, planners, plotters, doers, movers, shakers.

Once Welles had said this was the best train-set a boy could have. It was very different from three naked girls in an empty swimming pool.

She found herself on Stage 1, the Transylvanian village set. Faces she recognized were on the crew: Jack Nicholson, tearing through his lines with exaggerated expressions; Oja Kodar, handing down decisions from above; Debbie W. Griffith (in another life, she presumed), behind the craft services table; Dennis Hopper, in a cowboy hat and sunglasses.

The stage was crowded with on-lookers. Among the movie critics and TV reporters were other directors – she spotted Spielberg, De Palma and a shifty Coppola – intent on kibbitzing on the master, demonstrating support for the abused genius or suppressing poisonous envy. Burt Reynolds, Gene Hackman and Jane Fonda were dressed up as villagers, rendered unrecognizable by make-up, so desperate to be in this movie that they were willing to be unbilled extras.

Somewhere up there, in a platform under the roof, sat the big baby. The visionary who would give birth to his Dracula. The unwitting magician who might, this time, conjure more than even he had bargained for.

She scanned the rafters, a hundred feet or more above the studio floor. Riggers crawled like pirates among the lights. Someone abseiled down into the village square.

She was sorry Martin wasn't here. This was his dream.

A dangerous dream.

XXVIII

THE OTHER SIDE OF MIDNIGHT

a script by Orson Welles

based on *Dracula*, by Bram Stoker

revised final, January 6, 1981

1: An ominous chord introduces an extreme CU of a crucifix, held in a knotted fist. It is sunset, we hear sounds of village life. We see only the midsection of the VILLAGE WOMAN holding the crucifix. She pulls tight the rosary-like string from which the cross hangs, as if it were a strangling chord. A scream is heard off camera, coming from some distance. The WOMAN whirls around abruptly to the left, in the direction of the sound. Almost at once the camera pans in this direction too, and we follow a line of PEASANT CHILDREN, strung out hand in hand and dancing, towards the INN, of the Transylvanian Village of Bistritz. We close on a leaded window and pass through – the set opening up to let in the camera – to find JONATHAN HARKER, a young Englishman with a tigerish smile, in the centre of a tableau Breughel interior, surrounded by peasant activity, children, animals, etc. He is framed by dangling bulbs of garlic, and the VILLAGE WOMAN's crucifix is echoed by one that hangs on the wall. Everyone, including the animals, is frozen, shocked. The scream is still echoing from the low wooden beams.

HARKER: What did I say?

The INN-KEEPER crosses himself. The peasants mutter.

HARKER: Was it the place? Was it [relishing each syllable] Castle Dra-cu-la?

More muttering and crossing. HARKER shrugs and continues with his meal. Without a cut, the camera pans around the cramped interior, to find MINA, HARKER's new wife, in the doorway. She is huge-eyed and tremulous, more impressed by "native superstitions" than her husband, but with an inner steel core which will become apparent as JONATHAN's outward bluff crumbles. Zither and fiddle music conveys the bustle of this border community.

MINA: Jonathan dear, come on. The coach.

JONATHAN flashes a smile, showing teeth that wouldn't shame a vampire. MINA doesn't see the beginnings of his viperish second face, but smiles indulgently, hesitant. JONATHAN pushes away his plate and stands, displacing children and animals. He joins MINA and they leave, followed by our snake-like camera, which almost jostles them as they emerge into the twilight. Some of the crowd hold aloft flaming torches, which make shadow-featured flickering masks of the worn peasant faces. JONATHAN, hefting a heavy bag, and MINA, fluttering at

every distraction, walk across the village square to a waiting
COACH. Standing in their path, a crow-black figure centre-
frame, is the VILLAGE WOMAN, eyes wet with fear, crucifix
shining. She bars the HARKERS' way, like the Ancient Mariner,
and extends the crucifix.

VILLAGE WOMAN: If you must go, wear this. Wear it for your
mother's sake. It will protect you.

JONATHAN bristles, but MINA defuses the situation by taking
the cross.

MINA: Thank you. Thank you very much.

The WOMAN crosses herself, kisses MINA's cheek, and departs.
JONATHAN gives an eyebrows-raised grimace, and MINA
shrugs, placatory.

COACHMAN: All aboard for Borgo Pass, Visaria and Klausen-
burg.

We get into the coach with the HARKERS, who displace a fat
MERCHANT and his "secretary" ZITA, and the camera gets
comfortable opposite them. They exchange looks, and MINA holds
JONATHAN's hand. The coach lurches and moves off – it is vital
that the camera remain fixed on the HARKERS to cover the progress
from one sound stage to the next, with the illusion of travel
maintained by the projection of reflected Transylvanian mountain
road scenery onto the window. We have time to notice that the
MERCHANT and ZITA are wary of the HARKERS; he is middle-
aged and balding, and she is a flashy blonde. The coach stops.

COACHMAN (v.o.): Borgo Pass.

JONATHAN: Mina, here's our stop.

MERCHANT: Here?

MINA (proud): A carriage is meeting us here, at midnight. A
nobleman's.

MERCHANT: Whose carriage?

JONATHAN: Count Dracula's.

JONATHAN, who knows the effect it will have, says the name with defiance and mad eyes. The MERCHANT is terror-struck, and ZITA hisses like a cat, shrinking against him. The HARKERS, and the camera, get out of the coach, which hurries off, the COACHMAN whipping the horses to make a quick getaway. We are alone in a mountain pass, high above the Carpathians. Nightsounds: wolves, the wind, bats. The full moon seems for a moment to have eyes, DRACULA's hooded eyes.

JONATHAN (pointing): You can see the castle.

MINA: It looks so . . . desolate, lonely.

JONATHAN: No wonder the Count wants to move to London. He must be raging with cabin fever, probably ready to tear his family apart and chew their bones. Like Sawney Beane.

MINA: The Count has a family?

JONATHAN (delighted): Three wives. Like a Sultan. Imagine how that'll go down in Piccadilly.

Silently, with no hoof or wheel-sounds, a carriage appears, the DRIVER a black, faceless shape. The HARKERS climb in, but this time the camera rises to the top of the coach, where the DRIVER has vanished. We hover as the carriage moves off, a LARGE BAT flapping purposefully over the lead horses, and trundles along a narrow, vertiginous mountain road towards the castle. We swoop ahead of the carriage, becoming the eyes of the BAT, and take a flying detour from the road, allowing us a false perspective view of the miniature landscape to either side of the full-size road and carriage, passing beyond the thick rows of pines to a whited scrape in the hillside that the HARKERS do not see, an apparent chalk quarry which we realize consists of a strew of complete human skeletons, in agonized postures, skulls and ribcages broken, the remains of thousands and thousands of murdered men, women, children and babies. Here and there, skeletons of armoured horses and creatures between wolf or lion and man. This gruesome landscape passes under us and we close on CASTLE DRACULA, a miniature constructed to allow our nimble camera to close on the highest tower and pass down a stone spiral stairway that affords covert access to the next stage . . .

. . . and the resting chamber of DRACULA and his BRIDES. We stalk through a curtain of cobweb, which parts unharmed, and observe as the three shroud-clad BRIDES rise from their boxes, flitting about before us. Two are dark and feral, one is blonde and waif-like. We have become DRACULA and stalk through the corridors of his castle, brassbound oaken doors opening before us. Footsteps do not echo and we pass mirrors that reveal nothing – reversed sets under glass, so as not to catch our crew – but a spindle-fingered, almost animate shadow is cast, impossibly long arms reaching out, pointed head with bat-flared ears momentarily sharp against a tapestry. We move faster and faster through the CASTLE, coming out into the great HALLWAY at the very top of a wide staircase. Very small, at the bottom of the steps, stand JONATHAN and MINA, beside their luggage. Sedately, we fix on them and move downwards, our cloaked shadow contracting. As we near the couple, we see their faces: JONATHAN awestruck, almost in love at first sight, ready to become our slave; MINA horrified, afraid for her husband, but almost on the point of pity. The music, which has passed from lusty human strings to ethereal theremin themes, swells, conveying the ancient, corrupt, magical soul of DRACULA. We pause on the steps, six feet above the HARKERS, then leap forwards as MINA holds up the crucifix, whose blinding light fills the frame. The music climaxes, a sacred choral theme battling the eerie theremin.

2: CU on the ancient face, points of red in the eyes, hair and moustaches shocks of pure white, pulling back to show the whole stick-thin frame wrapped in unrelieved black.

THE COUNT: I . . . am . . . Dracula.

XXIX

Welles had rewritten the first scenes – the first shot – of the film to make full use of a new gadget called a Louma crane, which gave the camera enormous mobility and suppleness. Combined with breakaway sets and dark passages between stages, the device meant that he could open *The Other Side of Midnight* with a single tracking shot longer and more elaborate than the one he had pulled off in *Touch of Evil*.

Geneviève found Welles and his cinematographer on the road to Borgo Pass, a full-sized mock-up dirt track complete with wheelruts and milestones. The night-black carriage, as yet not equipped with a team of horses, stood on its marks, the crest of Dracula on its polished doors. To either side were forests, the nearest trees half life-size and those beyond getting smaller and smaller as they stretched out to the studio back-drop of a Carpathian night. Up ahead was Dracula's castle, a nine-foot-tall edifice, currently being sprayed by a technician who looked like a colossal man, griming and fogging the battlements.

The two men were debating a potentially thorny moment in the shot, when the camera would be detached from the coach and picked up by an aerial rig. Hanging from the ceiling was a contraption that looked like a Wright Brothers–Georges Méliès collaboration, a man-shaped flying frame with a camera hooked onto it, and a dauntless operator inside.

She hated to think what all this was costing.

Welles saw her, and grinned broadly.

"Gené, Gené," he welcomed. "You must look at this cunning bit of business. Even if I do say so myself, it's an absolute stroke of genius. A simple solution to a complex problem. When *Midnight* comes out, they'll all wonder how I did it."

He chuckled.

"Orson," she said, "we have to talk. I've found some things out. As you asked. About Mr Alucard."

He took that aboard. He must have a thousand and one mammoth and tiny matters to see to, but one more could be accommodated. That was part of his skill as a director, being a master strategist as well as a visionary artist.

She almost hated to tell him.

"Where can we talk in private?" she asked.

"In the coach," he said, standing aside to let her step up.

XXX

The prop coach, as detailed inside as out, creaked a lot as Welles shifted his weight. She wondered if the springs could take it.

She had laid out the whole thing.

She still didn't know who John Alucard was, though she supposed him some self-styled last disciple of the King Vampire, but she told Welles what she thought he was up to.

"He doesn't want a conjurer," Welles concluded, "but a sorcerer, a magician."

Geneviève remembered Welles had played Faustus on stage.

"Alucard needs a genius, Orson," she said, trying to be a comfort.

Welles' great brows were knit in a frown that made his nose seem like a baby's button. This was too great a thing to get even his mind around.

He asked the forty thousand dollar question: "And do you believe it will work? This conjuring of Dracula?"

She dodged it. "John Alucard does."

"Of that I have no doubt, no doubt at all," rumbled Welles. "The colossal conceit of it, the enormity of the conception, boggles belief. All this, after so long, all this can be mine, a real chance to, as the young people so aptly say, do my thing. And it's part of a Black Mass. A film to raise the Devil Himself. No mere charlatan could devise such a warped, intricate scheme."

With that, she had to agree.

"If Alucard is wrong, if magic doesn't work, then there's no harm in taking his money and making my movie. That would truly be beating the Devil."

"But if he's right . . ."

"Then I, Orson Welles, would not merely be Faustus, nor even Prometheus, I would be Pandora, unloosing all the ills of the world to reign anew. I would be the father-in-darkness of a veritable Bright Lucifer."

"It could be worse. You could be cloning Hitler."

Welles shook his head.

"And it's my decision," he said, wearily. Then he laughed, so loud that the interior of the prop carriage shook as with a thunderbolt from Zeus.

She didn't envy the genius his choice. After such great beginnings, no artist of the twentieth century had been thwarted so consistently and so often. Everything he had made, even *Kane*, was compromised as soon as it left his mind and ventured into the marketplace. Dozens of unfinished or unmade films, unstaged theatrical productions, projects stolen away and botched by lesser talents, often with Welles still around as a cameo player to see the potential squandered. And here, at the end of his career, was the chance to claw everything back, to make good on his promise, to be a Boy Wonder again, to prove at last that he was the King of his World.

And against that, a touch of brimstone. Something she didn't even necessarily believe.

Great tears emerged from Welles' clear eyes and trickled into his beard. Tears of laughter.

There was a tap at the coach door.

"All ready on the set now, Mr Welles," said an assistant.

"This shot, Gené," said Welles, ruminating, "will be a marvel, one for the books. And it'll come in under budget. A whole reel, a quarter of an hour, will be in the can by the end of the day. Months of planning, construction, drafting and setting up. Everything I've learned about the movies since 1939. It'll all be there."

Had she the heart to plead with him to stop?

"Mr Welles," prompted the assistant.

Suddenly firm, decided, Welles said, "We take the shot."

XXXI

On the first take, the sliding walls of the Bistritz Inn jammed, after only twenty seconds of exposure. The next take went perfectly, snaking through three stages, with over a hundred performers in addition to the principals and twice that many technicians focusing on fulfilling the vision of one great man. After lunch, at the pleading of Jack Nicholson – who thought he could do better – Welles put the whole show on again. This time, there were wobbles as the flying camera went momentarily out of control, plunging towards the toy forest, before the operator (pilot?) regained balance and completed the stunt with a remarkable save.

Two good takes. The spontaneous chaos might even work for the shot.

Geneviève had spent the day just watching, in awe.

If it came to a choice between a world without this film and a world with Dracula, she didn't know which way she would vote. Welles, in action, was a much younger man, a charmer and a tyrant, a cheerleader and a patriarch. He was everywhere, flirting in French with Jeanne Moreau, the peasant woman, and hauling ropes with the effects men. Dracula wasn't in the shot, except as a subjective camera and a shadow-puppet, but John Huston was on stage for every moment, when he could have been resting in his trailer, just amazed by what Welles was doing, a veteran as impressed as parvenus like Spielberg and De Palma, who were taking notes like trainspotters in locomotive heaven.

Still unsure about the outcome of it all, she left without talking to Welles.

Driving up to Malibu, she came down from the excitement.

In a few days, it would be the Julian 1980s. And she should start working to get her licence back. Considering everything, she should angle to get paid by Welles, who must have enough of John Alucard's money to settle her bill.

When she pulled into Paradise Cove, it was full dark. She took a moment after parking the car to listen to the surf, an eternal sound, pre- and post-human.

She got out of the car and walked towards her trailer. As she fished around in her bag for her keys, she sensed something that made quills of her hair.

As if in slow motion, her trailer exploded.

A burst of flame in the sleeping section, spurted through the shutters, tearing them off their frames, and then a second, larger fireball expanded from the inside as the gas cylinders in the kitchen caught, rending the chromed walls apart, wrecking the integrity of the vessel.

The light hit her a split-second before the noise.

Then the blast lifted her off her feet and threw her back, across the sandy lot.

Everything she owned rained around her in flames.

XXXII

After a single day's shooting, Orson Welles abandoned *The Other Side of Midnight*. Between 1981 and his death in 1985, he made no further films and did no more work on such protracted projects as *Don Quixote*. He made no public statement about the reasons for his walking away from the film, which was abandoned after John Huston, Steven Spielberg and Brian De Palma in succession refused to take over the direction.

Most biographers have interpreted this wilful scuppering of what seemed to be an ideal, indeed impossibly perfect, set-up as a final symptom of the insecure, self-destructive streak that had always co-existed with genius in the heart of Orson Welles. Those closest to him, notably Oja Kodar, have argued vehemently against this interpretation and maintained that there were pressing reasons for Welles' actions, albeit reasons which have yet to come to light or even be tentatively suggested.

As for the exposed film, two full reels of one extended shot, it has never been developed and, due to a financing quirk, remains sealed up, inaccessible, in the vaults of a bank in Timisoara, Romania. More than one cineaste has expressed a willingness to part happily with his immortal soul for a single screening of those reels. Until those reels, like Rosebud itself, can be discovered and understood, the mystery of Orson Welles's last, lost *Dracula* will remain.

Gates, ibid

XXXIII

"Do you know what's the funny side of the whole kit and kaboodle?" said Ernest Gorse. "I didn't even think it would work. Johnny Alucard has big ideas and he is certainly making something of himself on the coast, but this Elvis Lives nonsense is potty. Then again, you never know with the dear old Count. He's been dead before."

She was too wrung out to try to get up yet.

Gorse, in a tweed ulster and fisherman's hat, leaned on her car, scratching the finish with the claws of his left hand. His face was demonized by the firelight.

Everything she owned.

That's what it had cost her.

"And, who knows, maybe Fatty wasn't the genius?" suggested Gorse. "Maybe it was Boris Adrian. Alucard backed all those Dracula pictures equally. Perhaps you haven't thwarted him after all. Perhaps He really is coming back."

All the fight was out of her. Gorse must be enjoying this.

"You should leave the city, maybe the state," he said. "There is nothing here for you, old thing. Be thankful we've left you the motor. Nice roadboat, by the way, but it's not a Jag, is it? Consider the long lines, all the chrome, the ostentatious muscle. D'you think the Yanks are trying to prove something? Don't trouble yourself to answer. It was a rhetorical question."

She pushed herself up on her knees.

Gorse had a gun. "Paper wraps stone," he said. "With silver foil."

She got to her feet, not brushing the sand from her clothes. There was ash in her hair. People had come out of the other trailers, fascinated and horrified. Her trailer was a burning shell.

That annoyed her, gave her a spark.

With a swiftness Gorse couldn't match, she took his gun away from him. She broke his wrist and tore off his hat too. He was surprised in a heart-dead British sort of way, raising his eyebrows as far as they would go. His quizzical, ironic expression begged to be scraped off his face, but it would just grow back crooked.

"Jolly well done," he said, going limp. "Really super little move. Didn't see it coming at all."

She could have thrown him into the fire, but just gave his gun to one of the on-lookers, the Dude, with instructions that he was to be turned over to the police when they showed up.

"Watch him, he's a murderer," she said. Gorse looked hurt. "A common murderer," she elaborated.

The Dude understood and held the gun properly. People gathered around the shrinking vampire, holding him fast. He was no threat any more: he was cut, wrapped and blunted.

There were sirens. In situations like this, there were always sirens.

She kissed the Dude goodbye, got into the Plymouth, and drove North, away from Hollywood, along the winding coast road, without a look back. She wasn't sure whether she was lost or free.

STEPHEN JONES & KIM NEWMAN

Necrology: 2000

As THE TWENTIETH CENTURY PASSES INTO MEMORY, so too have many of those writers, artists, performers and technicians who, during their lifetimes, made significant contributions to the horror, science fiction and fantasy genres (or left their mark on popular culture and music in other, often fascinating, ways) . . .

AUTHORS/ARTISTS

Best known for his descriptive sound effects, *Mad* cartoonist **Don Martin** died of cancer on January 6th, aged 68. He also worked for *Galaxy* and *Cracked*, and his license plate apparently read "Shtoink!"

76-year-old **March "Marsh" Laumer**, the older brother of the late SF author Keith Laumer, died on January 12th in Sweden, after a short illness. He self-published a number of pseudonymous non-fiction books, and edited, translated and wrote several *Oz* books.

British children's novelist and historical biographer **Meriol Trevor** died the same day, aged 80. Her books for younger readers include *Merlin's Ring* and *The Other Side of the Moon* (both 1957).

Illustrator and film-maker **Pat Boyette** died of cancer of the oesophagus on January 14th, aged 77. As an artist he worked on such titles as *Creepy*, *Blackhawk* and *Turok Dinosaur Hunter*, while in the early 1960s he produced and directed the low budget horror movies *The Weird Ones* and *Dungeon of Horror*.

Finnish-born American pulp author **Oliver E. Saari**, died on January 25th, aged 81. Between 1936 and 1954 he sold stories to *Astounding*, *Super Science Stories*, *The Magazine of Fantasy & Science Fiction* and other magazines, and in 1940 was an organiser of the Minneapolis Fantasy Society, working alongside director Clifford D. Simak.

Canadian-born Golden Age SF author **A. (Alfred) E. (Elton) van Vogt** died on January 26th of complications from pneumonia. He was 87 and had suffered from Alzheimer's disease for most of the past decade. After selling true confession stories and radio plays, he began writing science fiction in the late 1930s for John W. Campbell's pulp *Astounding*, and his more than sixty-five books include *Slan* (published by Arkham House), *The Weapon Makers*, *The World of Null-A*, *The Voyage of the Space Beagle*, *The Weapon Shops of Isher* and *Empire of the Atom*. Some of his best fantasy stories were collected in *Out of the Unknown* (aka *The Sea Thing and Other Stories*) and *Monsters*. He became involved with L. Ron Hubbard's Dianetics in 1950 and was head of the California Dianetics movement until the 1980s. In 1980 Twentieth Century-Fox paid the author $50,000 as a quit claim settlement over similarities between the 1979 movie *Alien* and his 1939 story "Discord in Scarlet".

Screenwriter **Jeffrey Boam**, died of heart failure caused by a rare lung disease the same day, aged 53. He scripted Stephen King's *The Dead Zone*, *The Lost Boys*, *Innerspace*, *Indiana Jones and the Last Crusade* and *The Phantom* (1996), and co-created the TV series *The Adventures of Brisco County, Jr.* (1993) starring Bruce Campbell. Steven Spielberg and George Lucas still plan to produce Boam's screenplay for a fourth Indiana Jones adventure.

Latvian-born, self-taught comic book artist **Gil Kane** (Eli Katz) died of cancer in Miami on January 31st, aged 73. Best known for his "Silver Age" versions of such DC Comics characters as Green Lantern, Atom and The Flash during the 1950s and '60s, he eventually freelanced for several comics publishers (including Marvel) and also designed stage sets. In 1990 he illustrated a version of Wagner's *The Ring* by writer Roy Thomas.

Journalist and author **Stewart Farrar**, who wrote a number of occult novels, died on February 7th, aged 83. A disciple of self-styled "King of the Witches" Alex Sanders and a practising Wiccan with his own coven, Farrar's books include *The Twelve Maidens: A Novel of Witchcraft* (1974), *The Serpent of Lilith*, *The Sword of Orley* and *The Dance of Blood*. With his wife Janet he also wrote a number of non-fiction volumes about witchcraft, most of them published by Robert Hale in the 1980s and '90s.

A former editor and prolific genre author, 57-year-old **Laurence [William] James** died of a heart attack on February 10th, following several years of major health problems. While an editor at New English Library during the early 1970s, where he published such authors as Bob Shaw, M. John Harrison and Christopher Priest, he began writing space operas. After becoming a full-time author, he wrote the erotic horror series *The Witches* as "James Darke", the post-holocaust *Deathlands* series as "James Axler", and *The Farm* was the first in a monster pigs trilogy under the pseudonym "Richard Haigh". He reportedly wrote one or two novels a month for twenty years, and his other pseudonyms include "Charles C. Garrett", "John J. McLaglen" and "James W. Marvin".

Italian screenwriter **Bernardino Zapponi** died of a heart attack in Rome on February 11th, aged 73. His credits include *Fellini Satyricon*, the "Toby Dammit" episode from *Histoires Extraordinaires/Spirits of the Dead*, Dario Argento's *Deep Red* (aka *Profundo Rosso*), *Fellini Roma*, *Casanova* and *City of Women*.

Charles M. Schulz, the creator of the popular *Peanuts* comic strip, worth an estimated $1.1 billion per year, died in his sleep of a heart attack on February 12th, aged 77. He had been suffering from colon cancer and his final cartoon strip, heralding his planned retirement, was published the following day. More than 2,500 people turned up for his memorial service.

African-American comic book artist **Steven Hughes** died of cancer on February 17th. He was best known for his work on the *Evil Ernie* and *Lady Death* titles from Chaos!.

Prolific British author **Roger Erskine Longrigg**, who wrote horror fiction under the pseudonym "Domini Taylor" died on February 26th, aged 70.

American music director, composer and former jazz trumpeter **George Duning** died of cardiovascular disease on February 27th, aged 92. Nominated five times for an Oscar, his credits include *You'll Find Out* (with Boris Karloff, Peter Lorre and Bela Lugosi), *The Corpse Came COD*, *The Werewolf*, *Earth vs. the Flying Saucers*, *The Giant Claw*, *20 Million Miles to Earth*, *Bell Book and Candle*, *Terror in the Wax Museum*, *Arnold* and the TV movie *Goliath Awaits*.

Pulp author **Don Wilcox** (Cleo Eldon Wilcox) died on March 9th, aged 94. He wrote nearly 100 SF and fantasy stories, most of which appeared under his own name and various pseudonyms in *Amazing Stories* and *Fantastic Adventures* during the 1940s. He also wrote several scripts for the *Captain Video* TV series.

Satirical American SF and mystery writer **John** [Thomas] **Sladek** died in Minnesota of an hereditary chronic lung ailment on March 10th, aged 62. A member of the British "New Wave" movement in London during the 1960s, he collaborated with Thomas M. Disch on the novels *The House That Fear Built* and *Black Alice*, while his solo books include the spoof Gothic, *The Castle and the Key* (by "Cassandra Knye"), *The Reproductive System*, *The Müller-Fokker Effect*, *Tik-Tok*, *Bugs* and two novels about the guileless robot *Roderick*. *The New Apocrypha* was a non-fiction guide to unusual science and occult beliefs, while *Arachne Arising* (under the pseudonym "James Vogh") revealed the secrets of the (entirely fictitious) thirteenth sign of the zodiac.

Popular Canadian children's author **Martyn Godfrey** died the same day, aged 51, after falling into a coma three days earlier. He had been suffering from a liver disease for more than a year. Several of his books were SF.

Scriptwriter and voice actor **Stanley Ralph Ross** died of cancer on March 16th, aged 64. He scripted such TV movies as *The New Original Wonder Woman* and *Gold of the Amazon Women* as well as episodes of *Batman* and *The Man from U.N.C.L.E.* He was the voice of Perry White in the cartoon *Superman* series and appeared in Woody Allen's *Sleeper*.

Screenwriter **Jim Cash**, whose scripts include *Top Gun*, *Dick Tracy* (1990) and *Anaconda*, died of an intestinal ailment on March 24th, aged 59.

Dutch-born SF, fantasy and horror artist **Karel** (Carolus Adrianus Maria) **Thole** died at his home in Italy on March 26th, aged 86. From the 1950s to 1986 (when failing eyesight forced him to retire) his often surreal paintings graced the covers of many books in the UK, USA, Italy, Germany and Spain, and his work was collected in a number of volumes.

The same day saw the death after a series of strokes of 80-year-old British sexologist **Dr Alex Comfort**, who will be remembered for his 1972 bestseller *The Joy of Sex*, from which he earned an estimated $3 million. He also wrote several SF and historical novels and books of poetry and criticism.

American book editor and author **Jean [Edna] Karl**, who founded the young adult imprint Atheneum Argo, died on March 30th, aged 72. Along with several fantasy and SF books, she wrote the critical study *From Childhood to Childhood: Children's Books and Their Creators*.

The same day saw the death of **Major Norman Kark**, who edited and published *London Mystery Magazine* from 1949 to 1982 (132 issues). He was 102.

Catherine [Adelaide] Crook de Camp, wife, business partner and sometime-collaborator with her husband, author L. Sprague de Camp, died on April 9th, aged 92. The couple had recently celebrated their sixtieth wedding anniversary. Despite also suffering from Alzheimer's disease, she had undergone abdominal surgery three months earlier for cancer and appeared to be recovering. Editor of the young adult anthology *Creatures of the Cosmos*, she collaborated with her husband on a number of novels, anthologies and non-fiction titles as well as the 1983 Robert E. Howard biography *Dark Valley Destiny*.

Phillip W. Katz, the designer of the PKZip compression software for computers, was found dead from alcoholism on April 14th, aged 37.

Described by one magazine as "a pen-and-ink Poe", weird and wonderful writer/illustrator **Edward [St John] Gorey** died in Massachusetts on April 15th, aged 75, three days after suffering a heart attack and less than a month before he was due to receive the Horror Writer's Association Life Achievement Award. The winner of two World Fantasy Awards for Best Artist, his distinctive artwork appeared on book jackets and in his more than 100 strange little books of horror and pornography, many originally self-published. Some of his best-known titles include *The Double Guest*, *The Object Lesson*, *The Gashlycrumb Tinies*, *The Evil Garden*, *The Disrespectful Summons*, *The Haunted Tea-Cosy* and the collections *Amphigorey*, *Amphigorey Too* and

Amphigorey Also. Gorey's 1959 anthology *The Haunted Looking Glass* contained his twelve favourite ghost stories. He won a Tony Award for his costume designs for the 1978 Broadway adaptation of *Dracula*, and his scenic designs for the show were also nominated. More recently, Gorey designed the animated credits of the PBS TV series *Mystery!*. Hundreds of unpublished stories and sketches were found in his Cape Cod home after his death, while most of his estate was left to a charitable trust for animals, including bats and insects.

Hollywood film composer **Arthur Morton** died the same day, aged 91. His numerous credits as an arranger and orchestrator include *Night Life of the Gods*, *Mark of the Gorilla*, *Planet of the Apes* (1967), *Escape from the Planet of the Apes*, *Logan's Run*, *The Omen*, *Star Wars*, *The Boys from Brazil*, *Magic*, *Superman*, *Psycho II*, *Poltergeist*, *Poltergeist II The Other Side* and *The Shadow* (1994).

Canadian-born film composer **Louis Applebaum** died in Toronto of cancer on April 20th, aged 82. His credits include the 1961 3-D movie *The Mask* (aka *Eyes of Hell*).

Booker Prize-winning novelist **Penelope Fitzgerald** (Penelope Mary Knox) died in London on April 28th, aged 83. The daughter of *Punch* editor E.V. Knox, her work includes "The Axe" (published in *The Times Anthology of Ghost Stories*), *The Bookshop* (a novella featuring an angry poltergeist) and the 1990 novel *The Gate of Angels* (which included a thinly-disguised M.R. James).

British publisher **James Matthew Barrie**, the great-nephew, godson and legal ward of playwright Sir J.M. Barrie, died on May 2nd, aged 86. Having set up his own imprint, James Barrie Books (later Barrie & Jenkins) in 1947, he published L.P. Hartley's *The Travelling Grave*, *What Dreams May Come* by Lady Cynthia Asquith (his great-uncle's former secretary), and continued Asquith's long-dormant anthology series with *The Second Ghost Book* (aka *A Book of Modern Ghosts*) and *The Third Ghost Book*. He retired in 1979.

Author **Frances Wellman** (aka Frances Garfield), the widow of pulp giant Manly Wade Wellman, died in Chapel Hill, North Carolina, on May 7th, aged 91. After publishing a few stories in *Weird Tales* in the late 1930s and early '40s, she returned to the genre in the 1980s with fiction in *Fantasy Tales*, *Whispers*, *The Year's Best Horror Stories* and *The Mammoth Book of Vampires*.

Comic book artist **Dick Sprang**, best known for his work on the 1950s *Batman*, died on May 10th, aged 85.

Horror novelist **Patricia Graversen** (Patricia Ann Spears) died after a long illness in New Jersey on May 17th, aged 65. Founder of the Garden State Horror Writers organization, her fifteen novels include *Stones*, *Dollies*, *Sweet Blood*, *The Fagin*, *Black Ice*, *Precious Blood*, *Graythings* and *Ghost Train*, the latter a collaboration with her son, Paul Erik Graversen.

Comic strip and film historian, scriptwriter and journalist **Denis Gifford** died on May 18th, aged 72. A former illustrator for *The Beano* and *Marvelman*, he had a collection of 20,000 comics and was the author of more than fifty books, including *Movie Monsters*, *Karloff The Man The Monster The Movies*, *A Pictorial History of Horror Movies*, *The International Book of Comics*, *Encyclopedia of Comic Characters*, *American Comic Book Catalogue* and the definitive *British Film Catalogue 1895-1985*. Co-founder of Britain's Society of Strip Illustration, he also wrote an unproduced script for a *Carry On* movie.

Eccentric romance novelist **Barbara Cartland**, named the world's best-selling living novelist by *Guinness Book of World Records*, died in her sleep on May 21st, just two months before her 99th birthday. Cartland, who was Princess Diana's step-grandmother, wrote 723 books and claimed sales of one billion copies in thirty-six different languages. Despite that, she apparently left nothing in her will.

Playwright and screenwriter **Samuel Taylor**, whose credits include co-scripting Alfred Hitchcock's *Vertigo*, died of heart failure on May 25th, aged 87.

Ray Gibberd, who had been with Birmingham's Andromeda Bookshop for more than twenty years, died on May 28th, aged 52. He had undergone two operations during a long struggle with brain tumours.

74-year-old science fiction author and poet **David R. (Roosevelt) Bunch** died of an apparent heart attack on May 29th while recovering from a series of strokes. His first SF story appeared in *If* in 1957, and his fiction is collected in *Moderan* and *Bunch!*

Actor, editor and writer **Nils Hardin**, who published the fanzine *Xenophile* in the late 1970s, also died in May of prostate cancer, aged around 65.

Pulitzer Prize-winning cartoonist **Jeff MacNelly**, best known for his political cartoons and the *Shoe* strip, died on June 8th, aged 52.

58-year-old fanzine cartoonist, writer and mainstay of the Washington SF Association, **Joe** (Joseph) [Thomas] **Mayhew** died of Creuzfeldt-Jakob Disease (CJD) on June 10th following a month's hospitalization. His SF cartoons also appeared in *Asimov's* and *Analog*, and he won the Fan Artist Hugo in both 1998 and 2000. He apparently still managed to attend the 58th World Science Fiction Convention in August in a jar.

Newsweek editor and critic **Jack Kroll** died June 8th, aged 74.

Shirley Kassler Ulmer, the widow of film director Edgar G. Ulmer (who died in 1972), died on July 6th, aged 86. The couple met when she worked as script supervisor on Ulmer's *The Black Cat* (1934). At the time she was married to the nephew of Carl Laemmle, head of Universal Studios, and her relationship with the director resulted in Ulmer being blacklisted in Hollywood by "Uncle Carl". She worked on all her husband's subsequent scripts (*Daughter of Dr. Jekyll*, *The Amazing Transparent Man*, *Beyond the Time Barrier*, etc), including his projects for PRC, but only received credit on those from 1934–1940. As "Shirley Castle" she also worked as a script supervisor for a number of other directors, and contributed to such TV series as *The Lone Ranger* and *Batman*. She was director of the Edgar G. Ulmer Preservation Corporation.

Artist **Eyvind Earle**, who worked on the backgrounds for such Walt Disney features as *Sleeping Beauty*, *Lady and the Tramp* and *Peter Pan*, died of oesophageal cancer on July 20th, aged 84. He designed the Oscar-winning short *Toot, Whistle, Plunk and Bloom* and was just twenty-three when he sold his first painting to New York's Metropolitan Museum of Art. He also produced more than 800 top-selling Christmas cards.

British scriptwriter **Terence Feely** died on August 13th, aged 72. Besides writing for such TV shows as *The Avengers*, *The Prisoner*, *Space: 1999* and *The New Avengers*, he also scripted the 1971 film *Quest for Love*, based on a story by John Wyndham.

A. (Albert) **Reynolds Morse**, who owned the largest private collection of M.P. Shiel material, died of Alzheimer's disease in Florida on August 15th, aged 85. He compiled the 1948 bibliography *The Works of M.P. Shiel*, later expanded and updated into a four-volume set.

Weird Tales author and poet **Emil Petaja** died at his San Francisco home on August 17th, aged 85. A member of California SF fandom since the late 1930s, Petaja befriended upcoming author Ray Bradbury, Clark Ashton Smith, Forrest J. Ackerman, Henry Kuttner, Fritz Leiber, E. Hoffman Price, Henry Hasse and artist Hannes Bok and corresponded with H.P. Lovecraft, Robert E. Howard and August Derleth, amongst others. The author of more than fifteen books and 150 short stories (some under the byline "Theodore Pine"), his first story "The Two Doors" was published in *Unusual Stories* (1935), and his books of poetry, *Brief Candle* (1935) and *As Dream and Shadow* (1972) were illustrated by Bok. As founder of the Bokanalia Foundation, he also published the biography, *And Flights of Angels* (1968), and a commemorative volume of the artist's work, *The Hannes Bok Memorial Showcase of Fantasy Art* (1974), after Bok's death.

Walt Disney writer, animator and artist **Carl Barks**, most famous for creating Scrooge McDuck and developing his nephew Donald, died of leukaemia on August 25th, aged 99. He also created Donald's three young nephews, Huey, Dewey and Louie, as well as working on *Snow White and the Seven Dwarfs*, *Bambi* and *Fantasia*. After producing the comic book *Donald Duck Finds Pirate Gold* with Jack Hannah in 1942, Barks left films to script and illustrate Walt Disney Comics' Donald Duck titles full time for the next twenty-four years. Following his retirement, he was granted unprecedented permission by Disney to paint Donald Duck characters in oils, which he sold for up to six-figure sums.

The same day saw the death from cardiac arrest, brought on by a recurring bronchial infection, of 63-year-old record producer, performer and film composer **Jack [Bernard Alfred] Nitzsche**. He worked with Elvis Presley, Doris Day, The Rolling Stones, The Monkees, Captain Beefheart, Neil Young, Graham Parker, Mink DeVille and Marianne Faithfull, and as an arranger with Phil Spector from 1962–66 created such hits as "He's a Rebel" and "River Deep, Mountain High". His film scores include Bert I. Gordon's *Village of the Giants*, *Performance*, *The Exorcist* (as arranger), *Stand By Me*, *The Jewel of the Nile*, *Starman* and *The*

Seventh Sign, and he won an Oscar for co-writing the song "Up Where We Belong" for *An Officer and a Gentleman* with his second wife, Buffy Sainte-Marie. He was arrested in 1979 for pistol-whipping his then-girlfriend, actress Carrie Snodgress, and his drug problems and frequent run-ins with the law led to him appearing on the TV show *Cops*.

Linda Grey, the former editor-in-chief of Dell Books and president and publisher of Bantam Books and Ballantine Books, died of lung cancer on August 30th, aged 54.

Lucille Fletcher, the former wife of composer Bernard Herrmann, died on August 31st, aged 88. She scripted *Sorry Wrong Number* and various other radio dramas, including the ghost story *Hitchhiker* starring Orson Welles.

German-born writer and director **Curt** (Kurt) **Siodmak** died on September 2nd, aged 98. The younger brother of director Robert Siodmak (who died in 1973), he began his long career as an extra in Fritz Lang's 1926 *Metropolis* (Siodmak was working on a sequel at the time of his death). His 1931 novel *FP1 Antwortet Nicht* was filmed the following year as *Secrets of F.P.1*, and he co-scripted the British production *The Tunnel* (1935). Fleeing the Nazis in 1937, Siodmak arrived in Hollywood the following year. Hired to script *The Wolf Man* (1940), he created a memorable new monster in lycanthrope Larry Talbot (Lon Chaney, Jr). A joke made by Siodmak in the Universal commissary resulted in *Frankenstein Meets the Wolf Man*, and he came up with the initial concept for *House of Frankenstein*. His other film credits include *Her Jungle Love*, *The Invisible Man Returns*, *The Ape* (with Karloff), *Black Friday* (co-starring Karloff and Lugosi), *The Invisible Woman*, *The Invisible Agent*, *London Blackout Murders*, *Son of Dracula* (directed by his brother, who had him fired), *I Walked With a Zombie*, *The Climax*, *The Beast With Five Fingers*, *Tarzan's Magic Fountain*, *Bride of the Gorilla*, *Riders to the Stars*, *The Magnetic Monster*, *Creature With the Atom Brain*, *Earth vs. the Flying Saucers*, *Curucu Beast of the Amazon*, *Love Slaves of the Amazon* and *Sherlock Holmes and the Deadly Necklace* (with Christopher Lee as Holmes). He also directed the half-hour pilot for Hammer's unsold TV series *Tales of Frankenstein* (1958) and several episodes of the Swedish series *No.13 Demon Street* (1959), hosted by Chaney, Jr. In 1926 his story "The Eggs from Lake Tanganyika" appeared in the third issue of *Amazing Stories*, and his influential 1942 novel *Donovan's Brain* has been filmed many times and was adapted for the radio show *Suspense* in 1944 starring Orson Welles. Among Siodmak's other novels are *Skyport*, *Hauser's Memory* (filmed for TV), *The Third Ear*, *Gabriel's Body*, *City in the Sky* and *The Witch of Paris*. His autobiography *Wolf Man's Maker: Memoir of a Hollywood Writer* was published two months after his death.

Academy Award-winning screenwriter and film producer **Edward Anhalt** died of multiple myeloma in Los Angeles on September 3rd, aged 86. With his first wife Edna (with whom he collaborated on short fiction for the pulps under the name "Andrew Holt") he won the original story Oscar for *Panic in the Streets* starring Jack Palance, and his other credits include *Bulldog Drummond Strikes Back*, *The Crime Doctor's Diary*, *The Sniper*, *Girls! Girls! Girls!* (with Elvis Presley), *The Satan Bug*, *Hour of the Gun* and *The Boston Strangler*.

Mary Poppins illustrator **Mary Shepard** died on September 4th, aged 90. Her father was Winnie-the-Pooh illustrator E.H. Shepard.

Nancy Tucker Shaw (Nancy Ellen Jung), the second wife of SF author Bob Shaw (who died in 1996), died on September 17th, aged 72. She had been in poor health since suffering a stroke in 1998.

Armenian-born screenwriter and novelist **R. (Robert) Wright Campbell**, whose credits include such Roger Corman films as *Five Guns West*, *Machine Gun Kelly*, *Teenage Caveman*, *Dementia 13*, *The Secret Invasion* and *The Masque of the Red Death* (with Charles Beaumont) died of cancer on September 21st, aged 73. The brother of actor William Campbelll, he wrote twenty-seven novels and fourteen screenplays (including the Oscar-nominated 1957 Lon Chaney, Sr biopic *Man of a Thousand Faces*) and *Captain Nemo and the Underwater City*, and was a winner of the Mystery Writers of America Edgar and Allan Poe award.

Theatre organist **Lee Erwin** died the same day, aged 92. He composed the music scores for more than seventy silent films, including Lon Chaney, Sr's 1923 *The Hunchback of Notre Dame*.

Bryan E. (Edwin) Smith, who found notoriety as the man who hit and nearly killed Stephen King with his 1985 blue Dodge Caravan on June 19th 1999 while the author was taking a walk along a rural highway in western Maine, was found dead in his trailer home by his deputy sheriff brother on September 22nd. The former construction worker had suffered from a number of health problems, including arthritis brought on by an old back injury, carpal tunnel syndrome and depression. An empty bottle of painkillers was found near the body and, according to the medical examiner, toxicology reports indicated that Smith died of an accidental overdose of painkiller Fentanyl. "I was very sorry to hear of the passing of Bryan Smith," King told the media. "The death of a forty-three-year-old man can only be termed untimely. I would wish better for anyone. Our lives came together in a strange way. I'm grateful I didn't die. I'm sorry he's gone."

Lyricist **Carl Sigman**, who wrote the theme songs for the 1950s *Robin Hood* TV series and *Love Story*, plus the Glenn Miller hit "Pennsylvania 6-5000", died on September 26th, aged 91.

Sometimes difficult and unpredictable British SF writer and illustrator **Keith [John Kingston] Roberts** died of complications from pneumonia and bronchitis on September 27th, aged 65. He had been ill with multiple sclerosis and its side-effects since 1990 and had been hospitalized for a chest infection. He began publishing in 1964, and his best-known novels include the 1968 alternate history *Pavane*, *The Furies*, *The Chalk Giants*, *Molly Zero*, *Kiteworld*, *Gráinne* and *The Road to Paradise*. Some of his more than 100 short stories have been collected in *Machines and Me*, *The Passing of the Dragons*, *Ladies from Hell*, *Kaeti & Company*, *Winterwood and Other Hauntings* and *Kaeti on Tour*, and his illustrations appeared in such magazines as *Science Fantasy/SF Impulse* (for which he worked as associate editor/editor, respectively) and *New Worlds* during the 1960s. He is the only person to ever win the British Science Fiction Award in the Novel, Short Fiction and Artwork categories.

Italian screenwriter **Rodolfo Sonego**, whose credits include Tinto Brass' *The Flying Saucer* and *Fellini Satyricon*, died of complications following a fall on October 15th, aged 79.

The New York Times film critic **Vincent Canby** died the same day, aged 76.

51-year-old **Frederick S. Clarke**, creator, editor and designer of the premier genre movie magazine *Cinefantastique*, and publisher of *Femme Fatales*, *Imagi-Movies* and *AnimeFantastique*, killed himself by carbon monoxide poisoning on October 17th. He had apparently been depressed and suicidal for years and had been undergoing therapy. While a Freshman at Chicago's University of Illinois (1967–70) he published five issues of a mimeographed fantasy film fanzine entitled *Cinefantastique*. In his Senior year he revived the title as a glossy magazine and it grew from an initial circulation of 1,000 in 1970 to a current readership of 30,000. During its history, the magazine was blacklisted by a number of studios and major industry figures, including Steven Spielberg, George Lucas, Joe Dante and Warner Bros.

85-year-old screenwriter, novelist and two-time Oscar winner **Ring** (Ringgold) [Wilmer] **Lardner, Jr.**, the last surviving member of the blacklisted "Hollywood Ten", died of cancer in New York City on October 31st.

Young adult author **Robert Cormier**, whose 1988 novel *Fade* was nominated for a World Fantasy Award, died of complications from a blood clot on November 2nd, aged 75.

Science fiction and fantasy author and editor **L.** (Lyon) **Sprague de Camp** died after suffering a major stroke on November 6th in his home town of Plano, Texas, less than a month before his 93rd birthday. His wife of sixty years, Catherine, died almost exactly seven months earlier at the same age. Their ashes were interred together in Arlington National Cemetery in Washington, D.C. Following his debut in *Astounding Science Fiction* in 1937, de Camp went on to contribute many fine stories to the fantasy magazine *Unknown* and elsewhere, and his more than 100 books include *The Incomplete Enchanter*, *The Castle of Iron*, *Land of Unreason*, *The Carnelian Cube* and *Wall of Serpents* (all with Fletcher Pratt), *Lest Darkness Fall*, *Rogue Queen*, *The Glory That Was*, *The Goblin Tower*, *The Hand of Zei* and *The Tower of Zanid*. He also edited and completed a number of Robert E. Howard's Conan stories before adding his own contributions to the series (including the novelization of the 1982 movie, co-written with Lin Carter and his wife Catherine), and he was the author of a controversial 1975 biography of H.P. Lovecraft. De Camp's 1996 autobiography, *Time & Chance*, won the Hugo Award for Best Non-Fiction.

British publisher **Rayner** [Stephens] **Unwin C.B.E.** died of cancer on November 23rd, aged 74. In 1936 he wrote a favourable report of J.R.R. Tolkien's *The Hobbit* for a shilling which convinced his father, Sir Stanley Unwin, to publish it the following year under the family's George Allen & Unwin imprint. In 1952 he advised Tolkien to break *The Lord of the Rings* into three separate volumes.

Scriptwriter and producer **George Wells** died on November 27th, aged 91. Born in New York City, he began his career in radio, scripting such acclaimed series as *Lux Radio Theatre* (he was the show's principal writer for nine years) and *Suspense*. After moving to Hollywood, he worked as a contract writer at MGM for more than twenty years, scripting mostly musicals and comedies. He won an Academy Award for his story and screenplay for *Designing Women* (1957) and his other credits include *Angels in the Outfield* and *Jupiter's Darling*.

78-year-old Hanna-Barbera music composer **Hoyt Curtin**, who wrote the theme tunes for such cartoon favourites as *The Flintstones, The Jetsons, Jonny Quest, The Godzilla Power Hour* and *Scooby Doo Where Are You!* died on December 3rd after a long illness. His film credits include the awful score for *Mesa of Lost Women*, reused the following year in Ed Wood's *Jailbait*.

Argentinean author **Enrique Anderson Imbert** died on December 6th, aged 90. Some of his best supernatural stories were collected in *El Grimorio*.

The co-founder of DC Comics (with Harry Donenfeld), Ukraine-born **Jack S. Liebowitz** died on December 11th, aged 100.

James Allen, president of the Virginia Kidd Literary Agency, died suddenly of kidney failure on December 12th, three days after being diagnosed with a form of leukaemia.

Randolph Apperson Hearst, the last surviving son of William Randolph Hearst, died in New York on December 18th, aged 85. Heir to the newspaper magnate's £1.8 billion publishing fortune, his daughter Patty was kidnapped by the Symbionese Liberation Army in 1974.

American composer **Richard P. Hazard**, whose career encompassed *Bela Lugosi Meets a Brooklyn Gorilla* and *The Color Purple*, died on December 20th, aged 79. His other credits include *Some Call it Loving, Xanadu, Looker* and *Airplane II The Sequel*.

Phyllis White (Phyllis May Price), the widow of author/editor Anthony Parker White (aka Anthony Boucher), died on December 22nd, aged 85. During the late 1940s and early 1950s she read the slush pile and did the uncredited office work for *The Magazine of Fantasy & Science Fiction*, co-founded by her husband (who died in 1968).

British romantic novelist and short story writer **Mary Williams** (Winifred Mary Harvey) died of a viral infection in Cornwall on December 26th, aged 97. She had more than 200 genteel ghost stories collected into seventeen volumes (mostly for William Kimber or Robert Hale): *The Dark Land, Chill Company, Where Phantoms Stir, They Walk at Twilight, Unseen Footsteps, Where No Birds Sing, The Haunted Valley, Whisper in the Night, The Dark God, Ghostly Carnival, The Haunted Garden, Haunted Waters, Ravenscarne, Creeping Fingers, Trembling Shadows, Time After Time* and *The Secret Pool*.

Academy Award-winning screenwriter and producer **Julius J. Epstein** died on December 30th, aged 91. His more than fifty screen credits include the classic horror comedy *Arsenic and Old Lace* (1944). About *Casablanca* (written with his twin brother Philip, who died in 1952), he once said: "We were not making art, we were making a living."

ACTORS/ACTRESSES

American actress **Marguerite Churchill**, who appeared in *Charlie Chan Carries On, The Walking Dead* (with Boris Karloff), *Dracula's Daughter* and *Legion of Terror*, died on January 9th, aged 89.

Actor and director **John Newland** died of a stroke on January 10th, aged 82. Best remembered as "Algy" in the *Bulldog Drummond* movies (1948–49) and the host and director of all ninety-four episodes of *Alcoa Presents One Step Beyond* (1959–61), he also appeared as Dr Victor Frankenstein in the 1952 episode of *Tales of Tomorrow* with Lon Chaney, Jr as the Monster, and directed the TV movie *Don't Be Afraid of the Dark, The Spy With My Face, Crawlspace* (1972), the 1974 adaptation of Manly Wade Wellman's stories *The Legend of Hillbilly John* and episodes of *Thriller, Alfred Hitchcock Presents, Night Gallery, The Sixth Sense, Harry O* and *Wonder Woman*. He returned to TV to host *The Next Step Beyond*, which lasted for one season in 1978–79.

American leading lady and former model **Helena Carter** (Helen

Rickerts), whose credits include the 1953 *Invaders from Mars*, died on January 11th, aged 76.

Louisiana-born bass singer **Will** (William) **Jones**, who performed with both The Cadets and The Coasters, died on January 16th, aged 71. During the 1950s and '60s he sang the distinctive hook lines on such hits as "Yakety Yak" ("Don't talk back"), "Charlie Brown", "Along Came Jones" and "Poison Ivy" before becoming a minister.

Former nightclub dancer and Hollywood leading lady **Frances Drake** (Frances Dean) died on January 17th, aged 91. She is best remembered as the object of Peter Lorre's obsession in MGM's *Mad Love* (1935), director Karl Freund's reworking of *The Hands of Orlac*. She also appeared opposite Karloff and Lugosi in Universal's *The Invisible Ray*, *Prevue Murder Mystery* and *The Lone Wolf in Paris* before marrying Cecil John Howard, the son of the 19th Earl of Suffolk, and retiring from the screen in 1940.

Black vaudeville actor **Jester Hairston**, who appeared in both the radio and TV versions of *Amos 'n' Andy*, died on January 18th, aged 98. He worked in movies from *Cabin in the Sky* through *Tarzan's Hidden Jungle* to *Being John Malkovich*, and appeared in the title role of the *Thriller* episode "Papa Benjamin". Also a well-known singer and composer, for more than twenty years Hairston was the musical arranger for Dmitri Tiomkin, starting with *Lost Horizon* (1937).

Austrian-born actress **Hedy Lamarr** (Hedwig Eva Maria Kiesler) died in her sleep on January 19th, aged 86. A personal pupil of Max Reinhardt, she moved to Hollywood and a MGM contract in 1937 after the notoriety of her nude scene in the 1933 Czech film *Extase*. She turned down *Casablanca* and *Gaslight*, but her credits include *The Trunks of Mr. O* with Peter Lorre, *Samson and Delilah* (1949), *My Favorite Spy* with Bob Hope, and *The Story of Mankind* (as Joan of Arc). During World War II she helped invent the concept that is now at the heart of cellular telephone and Internet technology. With her acting career over by the late 1950s, she was arrested but not convicted for shoplifting in 1966 and 1991, and sued Warner Bros. for the use of the name "Hedley Lamarr" in Mel Brooks' *Blazing Saddles*. A virtual recluse in later life, she was married six times and left £51,000 in her will to a police officer who ran occasional errands for her.

K.N. Singh, a villain in more than 200 Indian films, died on January 31st, aged 91.

Doris Coley (Doris Kenner-Jackson, aka Doris Kenner), one of the four original members of 1950s girl group The Shirelles, died of breast cancer on February 4th, aged 58. Their first million-seller was "Tonight's the Night", followed by such hits as "Will You Love Me Tomorrow", "Baby It's You" and "Dedicated to the One I Love" (on which Coley sung lead).

Todd Karns, who portrayed George Bailey's brother Harry in the 1946 Christmas classic *It's a Wonderful Life*, died of cancer on February 5th, aged 75. He also appeared in *Invaders from Mars* (1953) and acted with his father Roscoe Karns on the *Rocky King, Detective* TV series (1950–54).

Canadian-born illusionist **Doug Henning** died of liver cancer in Los Angeles on February 7th, aged 53. Inspired by the tricks of Harry Houdini, he appeared on Broadway in such musicals as *The Magic Show* and *Merlin*. His hands were insured for $3 million by Lloyds of London, and in 1992 he bizarrely campaigned for the Blackpool South seat in Britain's general election on behalf of Maharishi Mahesh Yogi's Natural Law Party.

698-pound Latino rap star **Big Pun(isher)** (Christopher Rios) collapsed and died of extreme obesity on February 7th, the same day the 28-year-old was due to see a doctor so that he could start a slimming programme. A coffin had to be especially constructed to fit his body.

Ernest Goes to Heaven: Kentuckian comedy actor **Jim Varney**, who portrayed the dumb Ernest P. Worrell in a series of children's films for Disney's Touchstone and other studios, died of lung cancer on February 10th, aged 50. After appearing as the character in around 4,000 local TV commercials, he starred in such movies as *Ernest Saves Christmas* (1988), *Ernest Scared Stupid* (1991), *Ernest Rides Again* (1993) and *Ernest Goes to School* (1994). Following surgery for the disease in September 1998, Varney continued to make films up until his death.

Outrageous American blues singer and pianist **Screamin' Jay Hawkins** (Jalacy Hawkins), whose best-known hit was a 1956 version of "I Put a Spell on You", died of multiple organ failure in Paris on February 12th, aged 70. He appeared in the films *American Hot Wax*, *Mystery Train*, *A Rage in Harlem* and *Dance With the Devil*. Early in his career he would be carried on stage in a coffin, dressed in a Dracula-style cloak. He was reportedly married nine times and claimed to have sired fifty-seven illegitimate children.

The same day saw the death from cancer of 54-year-old pop singer **William Oliver Swofford** whose hits include "Good Morning Starshine" and "Jean".

Russian-born actress **Lila Kedrova**, who won an Academy Award for her role as a doomed French prostitute in *Zorba the Greek*, died on February 16th, aged around 81. She won a Tony award twenty years later for the same role in the Broadway hit *Zorba*. Her other films include Hitchcock's *Torn Curtain*, *The Tenant*, *Sword of the Valiant* and *Blood Tide*.

Silent actress **Marceline Day** who co-starred with Lon Chaney, Sr. in the lost vampire movie *London After Midnight* (1927), died on February 16th, aged 91. She retired from the screen after appearing in a number of 1930s Westerns.

Radio announcer **Bob Hite, Sr.** died on February 19th, aged 86. Starting out at Detroit's WXYZ in the 1930s, he voiced the memorable introduction to *The Lone Ranger* ("From out of the past . . .") and was also in *The Green Hornet* radio show.

Mexican actress **Begona Palacios**, the widow of film director Sam Peckinpah, died of a liver ailment in Mexico City on March 1st, aged 58. She appeared in several *Santo* films and *The Bloody Vampire*.

30-year-old French porn star, singer and television presenter **Lolo Ferrari** (Eve Valois) died from an overdose of various medicines on March 5th. She was famous for her enormous, silicone breasts – according to *Guinness Book of World Records* the largest in the world at a size 54G. She underwent twenty-five operations to recreate her body and a flight to Britain was nearly cancelled when it was thought her breasts might explode in a pressurized cabin. In 1996, Italian motor giant Ferrari successfully lodged a trademark complaint against her using the name on a fashion label.

Canadian actor **John Colicos**, best remembered as the evil Count Baltar in TV's *Battlestar Galactica* series (1978–79), died of a series of heart attacks on March 6th, aged 71. His films include *Phobia*, *King Solomon's Treasure* (as Allan Quatermain) and *The Changeling*, and he also appeared in episodes of *Star Trek*, *Night Gallery*, *Wonder Woman*, *War of the Worlds*,

Beyond Reality and *Alfred Hitchcock Presents* (as *both* Inspector Lestrade and Professor Moriarty). On the daytime soap opera *General Hospital* he played mad scientist Dr Cassadine in the "Voyage of the Ice Princess" science fiction episodes, and he reprised his role as the original Klingon, Kor, on several *Star Trek: Deep Space Nine* episodes.

Suave British character actor **Charles Gray** (Donald Marshall Gray) died in London on March 7th, aged 71. Best known for his role as Ernst Stavro Blofeld in the 1971 James Bond spectacular *Diamonds Are Forever* and as the diabolical Satanist Mocata in Hammer's *The Devil Rides Out* (aka *The Devil's Bride*), he also appeared in *The Night of the Generals*, *You Only Live Twice*, *The Beast Must Die*, *The Seven-Per-Cent Solution* (as Mycroft Holmes, a role he repeated in the TV series starring Jeremy Brett), *The Legacy*, *Shock Treatment*, and as the narrator in *The Rocky Horror Picture Show*. "It's just a jump to the left!"

Veteran stuntman and actor **Wally Rose** died of cancer on March 15th, aged 89. His sixty year career included such films as *Hawk of the Wilderness*, *Dick Tracy vs. Crime Inc.* and *Alien Nation*.

Dance instructor **Fred Kelly**, who taught his brother Gene to tap-dance, died the same day, aged 83.

African-American actress **Helen Martin** died of a heart attack on March 25th, aged 90. Best known for her TV appearances, including the mini-series *Roots*, her film credits include *Repo Man*, *Beverly Hills Cop III* and *Kiss the Girls*.

After a long battle against colon cancer, British singer, composer and occasional character actor **Ian Dury** died on March 27th, aged 57. Leader of the rock bands Kilburn & The High Roads and The Blockheads, and best known for such hits as "Reasons to be Cheerful", "Hit Me With Your Rhythm Stick" and "Sex and Drugs and Rock and Roll", he also appeared in such films as *Number One*, *Pirates*, *The Cook The Thief His Wife & Her Lover*, *Split Second*, *Judge Dredd*, *The Raggedy Rawney* and *The Crow 2 City of Angels*.

Norwegian-born actress **Greta Gynt** (Greta Woxholt), who co-starred with Bela Lugosi in *Dark Eyes of London* (aka *The Human Monster*), died in London on April 2nd, aged 83. Her other credits include *The Arsenal Stadium Mystery* and *Bluebeard's Ten Honeymoons*.

Hollywood character actress **Claire Trevor** (Claire Wemlinger), who won a Best Supporting Actress Oscar for *Key Largo*, died on April 8th, aged 91. Her many films include the 1935 version of *Dante's Inferno*, John Ford's *Stagecoach*, *Dead End* and *Murder My Sweet*.

German-born **Heinz Burt**, who as the dyed platinum blond bass guitarist with the Tornados took "Telstar" to the top of the music charts in 1962, died after a long battle with motor neurone disease on the same day, aged 57. Under just his first name he also had a solo hit with "Just Like Eddie". His mentor/producer Joe Meek shot himself with Heinz's gun in 1967.

Character actor **Larry Linville**, best remembered for his role as the slimy Maj. Frank Burns in the TV series *M*A*S*H* (1972–77), died of complications of pneumonia on April 10th, aged 60. After suffering from cancer, he had a lung removed in 1998. His films include *School Spirit*, *Earth Girls Are Easy* and *Chud II Bud the Chud*, and he appeared in such TV series as *Night Gallery*, *Kolchak: The Night Stalker*, *The Sixth Sense*, *Fantasy Island* and *Lois and Clark*.

The same day saw the death of 79-year-old British character actor and comedian **Peter Jones**. Best remembered for playing the voice of "The Book" in both the radio and TV versions of *The Hitch-Hiker's Guide to the Galaxy*, he also appeared in *Dead of Night* (1945), *Vice Versa* (1948), *Whoops Apocalypse* and TV's *The Avengers*.

Soviet film star **Alla Larionova** died of heart failure in Moscow on April 25th, aged 69. She appeared in *The Magic Voyage of Sinbad* (aka *Sadko*), *The Witches* and *The Forbidden Zone*.

Muscleman actor and former Mr World and Mr Universe **Steve Reeves** died unexpectedly in hospital of complications from lymphoma cancer on May 1st, aged 74. After appearing in Ed Wood's *Jailbait* (1953), most of his films were made in Europe and include *Hercules* (1957), *Hercules Unchained*, *Last Days of Pompeii* (1960), *The Giant of Marathon*, *Thief of Baghdad* (1960) and *Duel of the Titans*. He retired from films in 1969 and raised pure-bred horses on a ranch in California.

Veteran Hollywood swashbuckler **Douglas Fairbanks, Jr**, the son of the silent screen star, died in New York City on May 7th, aged 90. His many films include *Outward Bound* (1930), *The Prisoner of Zenda* (1937), *Sinbad the Sailor*, *Mr. Drake's Duck* and the 1981 adaptation of Peter Straub's *Ghost Story*. He received an honorary knighthood in 1949 from King George VI for furthering Anglo-American unity. Once married to Joan Crawford, he also left behind a legacy of sex scandals, including affairs with Marlene Dietrich and Gertrude Lawrence, and was later identified as "the headless man" in a sexually explicit photograph with married aristocrat Margaret, Duchess of Argyll, which led to a scandal that rocked the British Government in 1963. His body was placed inside a crypt alongside his father at the Hollywood Forever Cemetery in Los Angeles.

American leading man **Craig Stevens** (Gail Shikles, Jr) died of cancer on May 10th, aged 81. Best known for his portrayal as the eponymous suave private eye in the TV series *Peter Gunn* (1958–61) and as Walter Carlson on *The Invisible Man* (1975–76), he also appeared in such films as *The Body Disappears*, *The Hidden Hand*, *Night Unto Night*, *Abbott and Costello Meet Dr. Jekyll and Mr. Hyde* (with Boris Karloff), *The Deadly Mantis* and *The Killer Bees*. He was married to actress Alexis Smith from 1944 until her death in 1993.

Actor, writer and director **Paul Bartel** died on May 13th, aged 61. He had undergone eight hours of surgery two weeks earlier for cancer of the liver. Trained as an animator, he directed such black comedies as *Private Parts*, *Death Race 2000* and *Eating Raoul* (in which he co-starred with Mary Woronov), and appeared in around forty movies, including *Piranha* (1978), *Heartbeeps*, *Hollywood Boulevard*, *Trick or Treats*, *Frankenweenie*, *Chopping Mall*, *Killer Party*, *Munchies*, *Amazon Women on the Moon*, *Mortuary Academy*, *Out of the Dark*, *Gremlins 2 The New Batch*, *Soulmates*, *Escape from L.A.*, *Liquid Dreams* and *The Usual Suspects*.

Macaulay Culkin's long-lost half-sister, 29-year-old **Jennifer Adamson**, died of an accidental heroin overdose on May 20th, just days before she was due to meet the *Home Alone* star for the first time.

Distinguished classical stage performer and movie character actor **Sir [Arthur] John Gielgud**, died at his home near Aylesbury on May 21st, aged 96. The grandnephew of celebrated theatrical actress Ellen Terry, he was knighted in 1953. His numerous film and TV appearances include Hitchcock's *Secret Agent*, *Hamlet* (1963), *The Loved One*, *The Shoes of the Fisherman*, *Probe*, *Lost*

Horizon (1973), *Frankenstein: The True Story*, *Providence*, *Murder By Decree*, *The Elephant Man*, *Sphinx*, *Caligula*, *The Hunchback*, *Frankenstein* (1984), *The Canterville Ghost* (1986), *Arthur 2: On the Rocks*, *Prospero's Books*, James Herbert's *Haunted*, and the TV mini-series *Gulliver's Travels* and *Merlin*. Theatres in London's West End dimmed their lights for a minute as a mark of respect.

Czechoslovakian-born Hollywood star **Francis** (Frantisek) **Lederer** died in Palm Springs on May 25th, aged 100. He had appeared in G.W. Pabst's *Pandora's Box* (1929) with Louise Brooks before making his American movie debut in 1934. Later in his career his portrayed the suburban "Count Bellac" in *The Return of Dracula* (aka *The Fantastic Disappearing Man*), and his last film was *Terror is a Man*, a 1959 Filipino reworking of H.G. Wells' *The Island of Doctor Moreau*. He played Dracula again in the 1971 episode of TV's *Rod Serling's Night Gallery*, "The Devil is Not Mocked", based on the story by Manly Wade Wellman.

Salsa king **Tito Puente** died on May 31st, aged 77. Best known for his hit "Oyo Coma Va (Mi Vida)", he was a suspect in the shooting of Mr. Burns on TV's *The Simpsons*.

Burly British character actor and controversial Labour MP (1966–97) **Andrew Faulds** died at a nursing home on May 31st, aged 77. He portrayed SF hero Jet Morgan in BBC Radio's three *Journey Into Space* series (1954–60) and appeared in such films as *Blood of the Vampire*, *The Trollenberg Terror* (aka *The Crawling Eye*), *The Flesh and the Fiends* (aka *Mania*), *The Hellfire Club*, *Jason and The Argonauts* (1963), *The Devils* and *Lisztomania*.

86-year-old stuntman and actor **Chester Hayes**, who played Tabanga, the radioactive walking tree monster in the 1957 *From Hell it Came*, died in a fire at his Hollywood home on June 9th. A former professional wrestler, he also appeared in *Veils of Bagdad* and *Valley of the Dragons*.

52-year-old stunt co-ordinator **Terry Forrestal** was killed while attempting a parachute jump from a cliff in Norway on June 10th. His many credits include *Flash Gordon* (1980), *An American Werewolf in London*, *Indiana Jones and the Temple of Doom*, *Greystoke*, *Brazil*, *Lifeforce*, *Batman*, *Titanic* (1997) and several James Bond films.

British character actor **David Tomlinson** died in his sleep in hospital on June 24th, aged 83. He had suffered a series of strokes over the previous few months. A spitfire pilot in World War II, he starred in such films as *Miranda*, *Castles in the Air*, *Mary Poppins*, *City Under the Sea* (with Vincent Price), *The Love Bug*, *Bedknobs and Broomsticks*, *Dominique*, *The Water Babies* (aka *Slip Slide Adventures*), *Wombling Free* and *The Fiendish Plot of Dr. Fu Manchu*, before retiring from the screen twenty years ago.

Dependable British character actor [George] **Michael Ripper** died after a brief illness on June 28th, aged 88. In movies since the mid-1930s and a staple of Hammer Films for more than a decade playing body-snatchers, innkeepers and policemen, his numerous credits include Laurence Olivier's *Richard III* (1955), *Quatermass 2*, *X The Unknown*, *The Revenge of Frankenstein*, *The Ugly Duckling*, *The Mummy* (1959), *The Man Who Could Cheat Death*, *The Anatomist*, *The Brides of Dracula*, *The Curse of the Werewolf*, *The Phantom of the Opera* (1962), *The Curse of the Mummy's Tomb*, *The Plague of the Zombies*, *The Reptile*, *The Mummy's Shroud*, *The Deadly Bees*, *Dracula Has Risen from the Grave*, *The Lost Continent*, *Taste the Blood of Dracula*, *Mumsy Nanny Sonny and Girly*, *Scars of Dracula*, *The Creeping Flesh*, *Legend of the Werewolf* and *The Revenge of Billy the Kid*.

Italian actor **Vittorio Gassman** died on June 29th, aged 77. His numerous credits include *Il Sogno di Zorro* (1951), *Ghosts in Rome*, *Ghosts Italian Style*, *Quintet*, *The Nude Bomb* and *The 1001 Nights*. He was briefly married to Shelley Winters.

Following a serious fall in April, in which he fractured his spine, Oscar-winning Hollywood star **Walter Matthau** (Walter Matuschanskavasky) died of a heart attack in Santa Monica on July 1st, aged 79. After appearing as a villain in such films as *The Kentuckian* (his debut), *King Creole* (with Elvis Presley) and *Charade*, he starred in a number of light comedies (often teamed with Jack Lemmon), *Fail Safe*, *Candy*, *Pirates*, *JFK*, and used his real name for a cameo role in *Earthquake*.

Actress **Meredith MacRae**, the daughter of Hollywood singing star Gordon MacRae, died of brain cancer on July 14th, aged 56. Best known for her role as Billie Jo Bradley in the TV series *Petticoat Junction* (1966–70), she also co-hosted the Los Angeles TV talk show *Mid-Morning L.A.* in the mid-1980s. Her film credits include *Beach Party* (1963), *Bikini Beach*, *The Werewolf* *of Woodstock*, *My Friends Need Killing*, *Sketches of a Strangler*, *Earthbound* and *Vultures*.

Singer **Paul Young**, a member of such groups as Sad Cafe and Mike and the Mechanics, died of a suspected heart attack on July 15th, aged 53. His hits include "All I Need is a Miracle".

47-year-old **Jerome Smith**, the former rhythm guitarist for KC and the Sunshine Band ("Get Down Tonight", "That's the Way Ah-Hah I Like It"), was crushed to death after falling off a bulldozer on July 28th. He went into the building trade after the hits dried up.

Actor and composer **Max Showalter** (aka Casey Adams) died of cancer on July 30th, aged 83. He appeared in *The Indestructible Man* and *The Monster That Challenged the World*.

36-year-old adult film actress **Leslie Glass**, who also appeared in the softcore *Vampire Vixens of Venus*, died of colon cancer on August 4th.

Oscar-winning British stage and screen star **Sir Alec Guinness** (Alec Guinness de Cuffe) died of cancer on August 5th, aged 86. After touring with John Gielgud's acting company during the 1930s, Guinness appeared in such films as *Great Expectations* (1946), *Oliver Twist* (1948, as Fagin), *Kind Hearts and Coronets* (in which he portrayed eight different murder victims), *The Ladykillers*, *The Man in the White Suit*, *Scrooge* (1970, as Marley's ghost), *Murder by Death*, *Raise the Titanic*, *Mute Witness* and *Kafka*. As the Jedi master Obi-Wan Kenobi, he appeared in *Star Wars* and its sequels, *The Empire Strikes Back* and *Return of the Jedi*. Although he hated the role, it earned him millions of dollars because George Lucas gave him a reported two per cent of the profits.

Australian actor **Max Phipps** died of cancer on August 6th, aged 60. He appeared in *The Cars That Ate Paris*, *Thirst*, *Nightmares*, *Mad Max 2* (aka *Road Warrior*) and *Dark Age*.

73-year-old British stuntman **Eddie Powell** died on August 11th. Long associated with Hammer, he doubled for Christopher Lee's Count in *Dracula Prince of Darkness* and *Dracula Has Risen from the Grave*, and he portrayed the living mummy Prem in *The Mummy's Shroud*. His many other credits include *The Mummy* (1959), *She* (1965), *Daleks' Invasion Earth 2150 A.D.*, *The Devil Rides Out* (as the Satanic Goat of Mendes), *The Lost Continent*, *Dracula* (1973), *The Omen*, *To the Devil a Daughter*,

Dracula (1979), *Flash Gordon* (1980), *Krull*, *The Keep*, *Howling II Stirba – Werewolf Bitch*, *Legend* and *Batman*. He also appeared uncredited as the titular creature in *Alien* and *Aliens*.

Oscar-winning Hollywood leading lady **Loretta Young** (Gretchen Michaela Young) died in Los Angeles on August 12th, aged 87. She had battled against ovarian cancer for several months and recently returned home following surgery. She made her movie debut at the age of four, and starred alongside Lon Chaney, Sr in *Laugh Clown Laugh* (1928), Boris Karloff in *The House of Rothschild*, Ronald Coleman in *Bulldog Drummond Strikes Back*, Gale Sondergaard in *A Night to Remember*, and Cary Grant and David Niven in *The Bishop's Wife* (1947). She retired from the screen in 1953 to host a weekly anthology show for NBC-TV, *Letters to Loretta/The Loretta Young Show* (1953–61), which earned three Emmy Awards. After eloping in the early 1930s with actor Grant Withers, which ended in an annulment after eight months, she had a secret affair with Clark Gable that in 1936 resulted in the birth of a daughter who she later "adopted".

Russian ballerina of the 1930s, **Tatiana Riabouchinska,** who served as the model for the dancing hippo in Walt Disney's *Fantasia*, died of heart failure in Los Angeles on August 24th, aged 83.

Hollywood actress **Rose Hobart** (Rose Keefer) died on August 29th, aged 94. She made her stage debut at the age of fifteen in a touring production of *Liliom*, and won her Hollywood contract eight years later for her performance as Grazia in Alberto Casella's play *Death Takes a Holiday*. She appeared as the fiancée in *Dr. Jekyll and Mr. Hyde* (1932), and her other film credits include *Liliom* (1930), *East of Borneo*, *The Shadow Laughs*, *Tower of London* (1939, with Karloff and Basil Rathbone), *The Crime Doctor's Strangest Case*, *The Mad Ghoul*, *The Soul of a Monster*, *The Brighton Strangler*, *The Cat Creeps*, *Conflict* (as the apparition of Humphrey Bogart's murdered wife) and *Bride of Vengeance*. She was blacklisted as a communist in 1949 by the House of Un-American Activities Committee for her attempts to gain better working conditions for actors.

British stage, film and TV actress **Shelagh Fraser** died the same day, aged 79. She appeared in Hammer's *The Witches* (aka *The Devil's Own*), *The Body Stealers*, *Nothing But the Night*, *Doomwatch*, and played Luke Skywalker's Aunt Beru in *Star Wars*.

American actor **David Haskell**, who starred in the stage and film versions of *Godspell* as Jesus, died of brain cancer on August 30th, aged 52. His other film credits include Brian De Palma's *Body Double*.

Canadian-born leading lady **Patricia Owens**, best known for her role in the 1958 *The Fly*, died on August 31st, aged 75. She also appeared in *Panic at Madame Tussaud's*, *Ghost Ship* and *The Destructors*.

Tony McCoy, who co-produced Ed Wood's *Bride of the Monster* with his father and starred as Lieutenant Craig opposite Bela Lugosi's mad Dr Varoff, also died in August.

British character actor **Gary Olsen** died of cancer in Australia on September 12th, aged 42. Best known for his starring role in the popular BBC-TV sitcom *2 Point 4 Children*, he also appeared in such films as *Outland*, *The Sender*, *Pink Floyd's The Wall* and *Underworld* (scripted by Clive Barker). His other credits include the 1981 TV series *The Day of the Triffids* and a stage production of *The Rocky Horror Show*.

Emmy Award-winning African-American actress **Beah Richards** died after a long battle with emphysema on September 14th, aged 80. One of her final film appearances was in *Beloved*.

40-year-old British TV presenter **Paula Yates** apparently committed suicide with a cocktail of heroin, vodka and pills at her Notting Hill home on September 17th. The former wife of Bob Geldof and mother of four daughters (Fifi Trixibelle, Peaches, Pixie and Heavenly Hiraani Tiger Lily!) reportedly never got over the death of her lover, INXS singer Michael Hutchence, in 1997. Earlier DNA testing had revealed her as the daughter of TV presenter Hughie Green (*Opportunity Knocks*) not Jess Yates (*Stars on Sunday*).

Veteran American character actress **Ann Doran** died on September 19th after suffering a series of strokes. She was 89. In an eight decade career spanning more than 500 movies, her credits include *Charlie Chan in London*, *Night Life of the Gods*, *The Shadow* (1937), *The Man They Could Not Hang* (with Karloff), *The Green Hornet* (1939 serial), *Fear in the Night* (1947), *The Snake Pit*, *Them!*, *The Man Who Turned to Stone*, *It! The Terror from Beyond Space*, *The Brass Bottle*, *The Werewolf of Woodstock* and *Dead of Night* (1976).

B-movie star **Gloria Talbott** died on September 19th, aged 69.

Her best-known films include *Daughter of Dr Jekyll*, *The Cyclops* (with Lon Chaney, Jr.), *I Married a Monster from Outer Space*, *The Leech Woman* plus the 1985 *Attack of the B-Movie Monsters*.

Honolulu-born professional wrestler and sometimes character actor **Professor Toru Tanaka** (Charles Kalani) died of a heart attack on August 22nd, aged 70. Best remembered for his role as Subzero in the 1987 adaptation of Stephen King's *The Running Man*, his other credits include *Pee-wee's Big Adventure*, *Dead Heat*, *Alligator II The Mutation*, *Darkman* and *The Last Action Hero*.

67-year-old stage, TV and movie character actor **Richard Mulligan**, the younger brother of director Robert Mulligan, died of colon cancer on September 26th at his home in Los Angeles. The star of such series as *Empty Nest* (1988–95) and the increasingly bizarre *Soap* (1977–81), for both of which he won Emmy awards, his credits also include *Little Big Man* (as Custer), *Trail of the Pink Panther*, *Meatballs Part 2*, *Oliver & Company*, *The Heavenly Kid*, *Babes in Toyland* (1986), *The Big Bus* and TV's *Most Deadly Game* and *Harvey* (1972). His five wives included the late actress Joan Hackett and, in 1992, he was briefly married to 32-year-old porn actress Serina Robinson (aka Rachel Ryan/Penny Morgan).

London East End gangster **Reggie Kray** died of bladder cancer on October 1st, aged 66. After serving more than thirty years for murder, he was released from prison on compassionate grounds two months earlier. During the 1960s, Reggie and his twin brother Ronnie (who died in 1995) ran a string of protection rackets controlled through gang violence. They also rubbed shoulders with such celebrities as Judy Garland, Diana Dors and George Raft, and their life story was filmed in 1990 starring Gary and Martin Kemp.

American character actor and former stuntman **Richard Farnsworth** shot himself to death with a .38 revolver at his ranch house in Albuquerque, New Mexico, on October 6th. The 80-year-old had secretly been battling prostate and bone cancer for a long time. In 1961 he co-founded the Stuntman's Association, and his films include *The Adventures of Marco Polo* (1938), *Mighty Joe Young*, *Cult of the Cobra*, *The Ten Commandments*, *Spartacus* (in which he doubled Kirk Douglas), *Chamber of Horrors*, *The*

Ωmega Man, The Soul of Nigger Charlie, High Plains Drifter, Strange New World, Resurrection, The Natural, Space Rage, Misery and *Highway to Hell*. He received his second Oscar nomination for his starring role in David Lynch's *The Straight Story* (1999) and was the oldest actor ever nominated in the Academy's Best Actor category.

55-year-old American actor **David Dukes**, who starred in the 1986 adaptation of Clive Barker's *Rawhead Rex* and also appeared in *A Fire in the Sky, The First Deadly Sin, Space, The Handmaid's Tale, Date With an Angel* and *Gods and Monsters*, died suddenly on the set of the Stephen King mini-series *Rose Red* in Lakewood, Washington, on October 9th. Doctors believe he suffered a massive heart attack. He also played Dracula on Broadway.

Rick Jason, who starred as Lt. Gil Hanley in the television series *Combat!* (1962–67), was found dead in his California home from a self-inflicted gunshot wound on October 16th. The 74-year-old film and TV actor, who also appeared in the syndicated TV series *The Case of the Dangerous Robin* (1960) and the 1976 movie *The Witch Who Came from the Sea*, had apparently been despondent over unspecified personal matters.

74-year-old American singer and actress **Julie London** (Julie Peck) died of a cardiac arrest on October 18th due to complications from a stroke she suffered five years earlier. Although her scenes in Universal's *Jungle Woman* (1944) were cut prior to release, she got to co-star opposite another gorilla (and Buster Crabbe) in PRC's *Nabonga* the same year. Her other films include *The Red House* and *Tap Roots* (with Boris Karloff). She was married to actor/producer Jack Webb from 1947–53, and her biggest hit was her first single, "Cry Me a River", in 1955. Her second husband Bobby Troup (who composed the song "Route 66") had died a year-and-a-half earlier.

Four-time Tony Award-winning Broadway dancer and film actress **Gwen** (Gwyneth) [Evelyn] **Verdon** died in her sleep the same day, aged 75. Billed as "the world's fastest tapper", for her second husband Bob Fosse she starred as Lola in the stage musical *Damn Yankees* (1955) and repeated her performance in the 1958 movie. Her other screen appearances include *David and Bathsheba, Cocoon, Cocoon The Return* and Woody Allen's *Alice*. The lights of Broadway were dimmed for a minute in her memory.

73-year-old **Ivan Owen**, who created (and also voiced) British TV's popular glove-puppet fox Basil Brush with Peter Firmin in 1963, also died on October 18th after a long battle with cancer. He made it a policy never to be photographed or interviewed.

Czechoslovakian-born film actress **Lida Baarová** (Ludmila Babkova) was found dead in her Salzburg flat on October 27th, aged 86. Living in Berlin and married to *Metropolis* star Gustav Fröhlich during the 1930s, she was romantically pursued by both Adolf Hitler and his propaganda minister Josef Goebbels, becoming the latter's mistress. After World War II she was accused of being a Nazi collaborator and briefly imprisoned.

39-year-old black character actor **Anthony** [Dwain] **Lee**, whose film credits include *Liar Liar*, was shot dead in the early hours of October 28th by a LAPD police officer responding to a noise complaint at a Beverly Hills Halloween party. Police said that Lee, who was wearing a devil costume, pointed a fake gun at two officers who were outside the rented house. He was shot nine times in the back. Attorney Johnnie Cochran subsequently filed a claim on behalf of the family of Lee, suing the Los Angeles Police Department for $100 million.

American comedian, writer and television and radio personality **Steve Allen** (Stephen Valentine Patrick William Allen) died of a heart attack on October 30th, aged 78. As the first host (1953–56) of NBC's *The Tonight Show*, he is credited as the creator of the TV talk show format. He also wrote fifty-three books, recorded nearly fifty albums, appeared in such films as *The Benny Goodman Story*, *A Man Called Dagger*, *Amazon Women on the Moon* and *The Player*, and is listed in the *Guinness Book of World Records* as the most prolific modern song writer, with more than 4,000 songs published, including "This Could Be the Start of Something Big" and the lyrics to the theme of *Bell, Book and Candle*. Allen also wrote a musical TV adaptation of *Alice in Wonderland* (1985) and portrayed Scrooge in his musical stage version of *A Christmas Carol*. He was married to actress Jayne Meadows.

British stage and TV actress **Elizabeth Bradley** died the same day, also aged 78. Her film appearances include *The Flesh and Blood Show*, *Four Dimensions of Greta*, *An American Werewolf in London* and *Brimstone and Treacle*.

50-year-old British stage singer and actress **Stephanie Lawrence** apparently committed suicide on November 4th at her home in London. She appeared in O Lucky Man! and the 1989 The Phantom of the Opera with Robert Englund.

American TV actress **Mary Sinclair**, who co-starred with Hurd Hatfield in Robert Montgomery Presents: The Hunchback of Notre Dame (1954) and Michael Rennie in Climax!: Dr. Jekyll and Mr. Hyde, died on November 5th, aged 78.

British radio, stage and screen actor **Hugh Paddick** died on November 9th, aged 85. Best remembered for his double-act with Kenneth Williams in the 1960s BBC radio series Round the Horne, he also starred in the 1972 children's TV series Pardon My Genie.

Diminutive rapper **Joe C** (Joseph Calleja) died of a chronic intestinal disorder on November 16th, aged 26. The three-feet, nine-inch performer appeared with Kid Rock since 1998. He performed a solo track on the South Park Bigger, Longer and Uncut soundtrack, and appeared as himself in an episode of The Simpsons.

Britain's answer to Liberace, 75-year-old pianist **Russ Conway**, died in an Eastbourne hospital the same day of cancer. Known as the "Prince Charming of Pop", he appeared in Hammer's A Weekend With Lulu.

German actor **Harald Leipnitz**, whose credits include the Edgar Wallace krimis The Sinister Monk and Creature With the Blue Hand, died of lung cancer on November 21st, aged 74. He was also in Brides of Fu Manchu.

French leading man **Christian Marquand**, who also directed Candy (1968), died of Alzheimer's disease on November 22nd, aged 73. He was in La Belle et La Bête (1946), but his role in Apocalypse Now was deleted.

American leading man **Lewis Wilson**, best remembered as the star of the 1943 serial Batman, reportedly died in the autumn, aged 80. His son, Michael G. Wilson, is executive producer of the James Bond movies.

German-American character actor **Werner Klemperer** died after a two-year battle with cancer on December 5th, aged 80. Best known for his Emmy Award-winning performance as Colonel Wilhelm Klink in the TV show Hogan's Heroes (1965–71), he also appeared in the 1965 sleeper Dark Intruder, The Cabinet *of Dr. Ramirez, Macmillan & Wife:* 'The Devil You Say' and voiced the role of a guardian angel on *The Simpsons*.

Former beauty queen and artist's model **Christabel Leighton-Porter** (Christabel Jane Drewry), who was the real-life model for Norman Pett's cartoon pin-up Jane in the *Daily Mirror* newspaper from the 1930s until the late '50s, died on December 6th, aged 87. As the scatty *ingénue* who always ended up semi-naked, Leighton-Porter also toured the UK until 1964 in a striptease act, *Jane of the Daily Mirror*, and she starred in the 1948 film *The Adventures of Jane*.

British-born 1961 Miss World **Rosemarie Frankland**, who claimed to be Bob Hope's mistress, committed suicide in Marina Del Rey, California. The 57-year-old was found naked on December 8th after apparently taking a lethal mix of prescription pills and tequila almost a week earlier. She appeared in the Beatles' *A Hard Day's Night* and the 1965 Hope comedy *I'll Take Sweden*.

Hollywood film and radio actress **Marie Windsor** (Emily Marie Bertelsen) died on December 10th, aged 80. A former Miss Utah who studied acting with Maria Ouspenskaya, she appeared in *Song of the Thin Man*, *The Three Musketeers* (1948), *Cat Women of the Moon*, *Abbott and Costello Meet the Mummy*, Stanley Kubrick's *The Killing*, Roger Corman's *Swamp Women*, *The Story of Mankind*, *The Day Mars Invaded Earth*, *Chamber of Horrors*, *Freaky Friday* and the Stephen King TV mini-series *Salem's Lot*.

Actor-comedian **Lewis Arquette**, the father of actors Rosanna, Richmond, Patricia, Alexis and David, died of congestive heart failure the same day, aged 65. His films include *Johnny Got His Gun*, *The Horror Show*, *Chopper Chicks in Zombie Town*, *Syngenor*, *Attack of the 50ft Woman* (1993), *Scream 2* and *Little Nicky*.

Writer and producer **Don Devlin**, the father of producer Dean Devlin, died of cancer on December 11th, aged 70. A former actor, he appeared in *Blood of Dracula* and *Anatomy of a Psycho* (which he also scripted), and he executive produced *The Witches of Eastwick*.

Gloria Somborn Daly, the daughter of actress Gloria Swanson and for years operator of the landmark Brown Derby restaurant in Los Angeles, died of brain cancer the same day, aged 80.

Veteran character actor **David Lewis** also died on December 11th, aged 84. Best remembered for his TV roles as Lieutenant Cromwell on *Captain Video and His Video Rangers* and Warden Crichton on the 1960s *Batman* series, he also appeared in episodes of *Lights Out, One Step Beyond* and *Voyage to the Bottom of the Sea*.

Former boxer and stuntman turned Hollywood leading actor **George Montgomery** [Letz] died of heart failure on December 12th, aged 84. Best known for his Westerns, he made one of his early screen appearances in the 1938 Republic serial *The Lone Ranger*. In a career that spanned nearly 100 movies he also appeared in *Hawk of the Wilderness, The Brasher Doubloon* (as Philip Marlowe), *Sword of Monte Cristo, Hallucination Generation* and *Marlowe*. He was married to singer Dinah Shore for nineteen years, until they divorced in 1963.

Mexican wrestler and actor **Alejandro Cruz**, better known as the masked Blue Demon, died of a heart attack on December 16th, aged 78. He appeared in numerous low budget SF and horror films during the 1960s and '70s, often teaming up with his silver-masked rival Santo for such titles as *Santo y Blue Demon contra Los Monstruos, Santo y Blue Demon contra Dracula y el Hombre Lobo* and *Santo y Blue Demon contra el Dr. Frankenstein*.

Silent film star **Pauline Curley** [Peach] died of pneumonia the same day, aged 97. She appeared in the very first Frankenstein movie, *Life Without a Soul* (1915), plus *The Veiled Mystery, The Valley of Tomorrow, The Invisible Hand, The Fall of the Roman Empire* (1917) and King Vidor's first movie as a director, *The Turn in the Road* (1919). She retired from the screen in 1929.

Actor and dancer **Nick "Nicodemus" Stewart**, the voice of Br'er Bear in Disney's *Song of the South* (1946), also died on December 16th aged 90. He appeared in such films as *Cabin in the Sky, Gildersleeve's Ghost, Down to Earth, Killer Ape, Tarzan's Fight for Life* and *Carmen Jones*, and had a recurring role as Lightnin" in the TV series *Amos 'n' Andy* before becoming a black activist and founder of the prestigious Los Angeles Ebony Showcase Theater with his wife Edna.

British singer and songwriter **Kirsty MacColl** was killed during a boating accident in Mexico on December 19th, aged 41. The daughter of the late folk singer Ewan MacColl, her biggest hits were "They Don't Know" and the Christmas favourite "Fairytale of New York" with Shane McGowan and the Pogues in 1987.

Three-foot, ten-inch actor and "Little People" activist **Billy Barty** (William John Bertanzetti) died on December 23rd of heart failure, aged 76. In films since 1927, his more than 200 credits include *Roman Scandals*, *Alice in Wonderland* (1933), *Gold Diggers of 1933*, *A Midsummer Night's Dream* (1935), *Bride of Frankenstein* (as the baby in a jar), *Pygmy Island*, *The Undead*, *Day of the Locust*, *Pufnstuf*, *Lord of the Rings* (1978), *Legend*, *Rumpelstiltskin* (1987), *Snow White* (1987), *Masters of the Universe*, *Willow*, *Lobster Man from Mars* and *The Rescuers Down Under*. Although he was in *Under the Rainbow*, he wasn't in *The Wizard of Oz*.

78-year-old American stage and screen actor **Jason** [Nelson] **Robards, Jr.**, the son of Hollywood character actor Jason Robards, died in a Connecticut hospital on December 26th after a long battle with cancer. A two-time Oscar winner, his films include *Fools*, *Murders in the Rue Morgue* (1971), *A Boy and His Dog*, *Mr. Sycamore*, *Johnny Got His Gun*, *Raise the Titanic*, *The Legend of the Lone Ranger*, *The Day After*, *Something Wicked This Way Comes*, *Black Rainbow*, *Dream a Little Dream*, *Magnolia* and Dan Curtis' aborted 1967 TV production of *The Strange Case of Dr. Jekyll and Mr. Hyde*. He was married four times, once to actress Lauren Bacall.

Tough-guy character actor turned screenwriter **Leo V. Gordon**, died after a short illness the same day, aged 78. A former convict who served four years during the late 1940s in San Quentin, his numerous credits include Hitchcock's *The Man Who Knew Too Much* (1956), Roger Corman's *The Terror* (with Boris Karloff), *The Haunted Palace* (with Vincent Price) and *The St. Valentine's Day Massacre* (1967, with Jason Robards), *The Lucifer Complex*, *Bog*, *Big Top Pee Wee*, *Saturday the 14th Strikes Back* and *Alienator*. He also scripted Corman's *The Wasp Woman*, *Attack of the Giant Leeches*, *The Tower of London* (1962) and *The Terror*.

Stage actor and director **Stuart Lancaster**, whose grandfather was Charles Ringling of The Ringling Brothers Circus, died on December 29th, aged 80. During the 1960s he appeared in six of Russ Meyer's soft porn movies, including the 1966 cult classic

Faster Pussycat! Kill! Kill!, and narrated *Beneath the Valley of the Ultravixens*. More recently, director Tim Burton cast him in *Edward Scissorhands* and *Batman Returns*.

Spanish-Italian dancer **José Greco**, who toured America in 1978 playing the Count in the stage production *The Passion of Dracula*, died on December 31st, aged 81.

FILM/TV TECHNICIANS

Veteran Walt Disney animator **Marc Davis**, whose credits include *Snow White and the Seven Dwarfs* and *Bambi*, died on January 12th, aged 86. Famous for his female characters, he designed Alice in *Alice in Wonderland*, Tinker Bell in *Peter Pan*, Briar Rose and Maleficent in *Sleeping Beauty* and Cruella De Vil in *101 Dalmations*. He later designed characters and scenes for the Disneyland rides Pirates of the Caribbean, The Enchanted Tiki Room, It's a Small World and The Jungle Cruise.

Cartoon animator **Michael Webster** died of pneumonia on January 15th, aged 60. His credits include TV's *Ducktales*, *Darkwing Duck*, *Aladdin*, *Little Mermaid* and *The Flintstones*.

Former vice-president in charge of programming at NBC-TV, **David Levy** died on January 25th, aged 87. Although credited with bringing the "Movie of the Week" format to the network, he is best remembered as the creator of the classic ABC-TV show *The Addams Family* (1964–66), based on Charles Addams' cartoon characters. When the first feature film appeared in 1991, Levy sued the makers for stealing his concept.

Norman Thomson, co-founder of Orson Welles' Mercury Theatre, died of congestive heart failure on February 3rd, aged 84. He took part in Welles' infamous *War of the Worlds* broadcast.

Scottish-born film and TV director **Sidney Hayers** died in Spain of cancer on February 8th, aged 78. Best remembered for his 1961 film *Night of the Eagle* (aka *Burn Witch Burn*), based on Fritz Leiber's novel *Conjure Wife*, his other credits include *Circus of Horrors* (featuring his wife Erika Remberg), *Revenge* (aka *Terror from Under the House*), and episodes of TV's *The Avengers*, *Galactica 1980*, *Manimal* and *Werewolf*.

72-year-old French writer and director **Roger Vadim** (Roger Vladimir Plemiannikov), best known for his marriages to Brigitte

Bardot (when she was just eighteen), Annette Stroyberg and Jane Fonda and his love affair with Catherine Deneuve, died of cancer in Paris on February 11th. His 1960 adaptation of J. Sheridan Le Fanu's "Carmilla", *Blood and Roses*, starred his second wife, Stroyberg, while Fonda starred in his "Metzengerstein" episode of the Edgar Allan Poe omnibus *Spirits of the Dead* and *Barbarella*. His other credits include the psychological thrillers *Pretty Maids All in a Row* and *Night Games*.

Director and producer **Newt** (Newton) **Arnold**, whose credits include *Hands of a Stranger*, *Blood Thirst* and *Bloodsport* (1988), died of leukaemia on February 12th, aged 72. He was better known as a first assistant director on such films as *The Towering Inferno*, *Blade Runner*, *The Abyss* and *The Guardian*.

French film director and later a controversial neo-fascist member of the European parliament, **Claude Autant-Lara** died the same day, aged 96. A former assistant to René Clair, his films include *Sylvie et la Fantôme*, a comedy-romance that introduced Jacques Tati as a ghost; *The Red Inn*, which starred Fernandel and was banned by the British censor for six years; and *Marguerite de la Nuit*, an updating of the Faust legend to the 1920s.

Jim Kearley, co-founder of London's Gothique Film Society, died of Alzheimer's disease on March 4th, aged 77.

86-year-old British film director and producer **Anthony Gilkison**, who made six episodes of *Algernon Blackwood Stories* for the cinema in 1949, all introduced by the author himself, died on March 13th.

American cinematographer and 3-D expert **Lothrop Worth** died on March 15th, aged 96. His many credits include *Bwana Devil*, *House of Wax*, *I Was a Teenage Frankenstein*, *Gog*, *Jesse James Meets Frankenstein's Daughter*, *Billy the Kid vs. Dracula* and the *I Dream of Jeannie* TV series (1965–70).

Canadian writer and director **Lew Lehman** died of a heart attack in Toronto on March 25th, aged 66. He scripted the 1980 horror film *Phobia* and directed *The Pit* (1981).

Film producer **Sy Weintraub** died of pancreatic cancer on April 4th, aged 77. His credits include *Tarzan's Greatest Adventure*, *Tarzan the Magnificent*, *Tarzan Goes to India*, *Tarzan's Three Challenges*, *Tarzan and the Valley of Gold*, *Tarzan and the Great River*, *Tarzan and the Jungle Boy* and the TV movies *Hound of* *the Baskervilles* and *The Sign of the Four*, both featuring Ian Richardson as Sherlock Holmes.

Oscar-winning art director **Carmen Dillon**, whose credits include *Hamlet* (1948), *Carry on Constable* and *The Omen*, died in London on April 12th, aged 91.

British-born Hollywood director **Lewis Allen** died on May 3rd in Santa Monica, aged 94. His many films include the classic ghost story *The Uninvited*, its less successful follow-up *The Unseen*, *So Evil My Love* and *Suddenly* with Frank Sinatra. Before moving to America he was Raymond Massey's theatrical manager.

Veteran television producer **Al Simon** died of Alzheimer's disease on May 18th, aged 88. Credited with helping to develop the three-camera technique for shooting sitcoms, as the president of Filmways Productions his credits include the talking horse series *Mr. Ed* (1961–65).

Prolific B-movie director **Edward L. Bernds** died on May 20th, aged 94. A pioneer sound recordist and mixer for Frank Capra, Howard Hawks and others, he is best remembered for directing twenty-five *Three Stooges* shorts and the 1960s features *The Three Stooges Meet Hercules* and *The Three Stooges in Orbit*. His numerous other credits include *The Bowery Boys Meet the Monsters*, *Bowery in Baghdad*, *World Without End*, *Reform School Girl*, *Space Master X-7*, *Queen of Outer Space* with Zsa Zsa Gabor, *Return of the Fly* with Vincent Price, and *Valley of the Dragons*. He retired in 1965 and his autobiography was published in 1999.

Stage and screen producer **Robert Fryer**, whose film credits include *The Boston Strangler*, *Myra Breckinridge*, Stanley Kubrick's *The Shining* and *The Boys from Brazil*, died of Parkinson's Disease on May 28th, aged 79. He also staged *Sweeney Todd* on Broadway.

Oscar-winning costume designer **Bill Thomas**, whose credits include *Logan's Run*, died on May 30th, aged 79. He had recently undergone bypass surgery. At Universal from 1949–59, he was Academy Award-nominated for his work on such films as *Babes in Toyland* and *Bedknobs and Broomsticks*, and won for *Spartacus*.

Italian writer and director **Franco Rossi** died of a stroke in Rome on June 5th, aged 81. His credits include an episode of *The*

Witches (1965) and TV productions of *The Odyssey* (1968), *A Boy Named Jesus* and *The Aenid*.

74-year-old television producer **Laurel Vlock** died on July 8th of injuries from an automobile accident. Following a television interview with Holocaust survivor Jerzy Kosinski in 1978, she founded the Holocaust Survivors Film Project the following year, with the resulting testimonies archived at Yale University. In 1981 she won an Emmy Award for her documentary *Forever Yesterday*.

Costume designer **Wes Jefferies**, whose credits include *Bela Lugosi Meets a Brooklyn Gorilla*, *Tarzan and the She-Devil*, *Pharaoh's Curse*, *The Black Sleep*, *Voodoo Island* and *The Manchurian Candidate*, died on July 12th, aged 93.

American director **James B. Clark** died on July 19th, aged 92. A former editor, his many credits include *Charlie Chan at the Wax Museum*.

Film and TV director **Don Weis** died on July 25th, aged 78. After entering the film industry as a messenger boy for Warner Bros., he made his directing debut in 1951. His films include *The Adventures of Hadji Baba*, *Pajama Party* and *The Ghost in the Invisible Bikini* (with Boris Karloff and Basil Rathbone). For TV he directed *The Munsters Revenge* plus episodes of *The Twilight Zone* ("Steel"), *Alfred Hitchcock Presents*, *Fantasy Island* and the pilot for *Planet of the Apes*, and won six Directors Guild of America Awards as the year's best television director for his work on *M*A*S*H* in the 1970s.

Children's book illustrator and former Walt Disney animator **Warren Schloat** died on July 30th, aged 86. His film credits include *Snow White and the Seven Dwarfs* and *Dumbo*.

Former nudist film-maker **Edward Craven Walker** (aka Michael Keatering) died in London of cancer on August 15th, aged 82. He used the money he made from the 1959 film *Travelling Light* – a nude underwater "ballet" – to perfect and manufacture the Astro Lamp in 1963, now better known as the Lava Lamp. He once said, "If you buy my lamp, you won't need drugs."

American film editor **Robert Swink**, whose credits include *Captain Sinbad*, *Sphinx* and *The Boys from Brazil* (for which he earned an Oscar nomination), died the same day, aged 82.

American former editor and film director **Lee Sholem**, whose credits include *Tarzan's Magic Fountain*, *Tarzan and the Slave*

STEPHEN JONES & KIM NEWMAN

Girl, Superman and the Mole Men, Tobor the Great, Pharaoh's Curse, The Doomsday Machine and a couple of *Jungle Jim* films, died on August 19th, aged 99.

TV director **John Florea** died on August 25th in Las Vegas, aged 84. During the 1960s he worked as a writer, producer and director for Ivan Tors Productions, co-scripting/directing *Island of the Lost* with Ricou Browning in 1967. He also directed *Invisible Strangler*. As a World War II correspondent and staff photographer for *Life* magazine, he was the only photographer present at both the VE Day and VJ Day peace treaty signings.

Disney animator **Wathel Rogers** died the same day, aged 80. He worked on *Pinocchio, Cinderella, Peter Pan, Bambi, Sleeping Beauty* and various *Donald Duck* shorts. He also helped create the Disneyland rides Pirates of the Caribbean, The Enchanted Tiki Room and The Jungle Cruise.

Jacques Wellington Rupp, who designed the Tinker Bell titles for TV's *The Wonderful World of Disney*, died on August 22nd, aged 79.

David Bellamy who, as an assistant to Harvard Medical School's Professor Carl Walter co-invented the blood bag, died of brain cancer on August 29th. He was 74.

Cult Hollywood B-movie director **Joseph H. Lewis** died on August 30th, aged 93. He joined MGM as a camera loader in the early 1920s, before becoming an editor on such serials as *Undersea Kingdom* (1936). He made his directing debut the following year, and his more than forty films include *The Ghost Creeps, Invisible Ghost* (with Bela Lugosi), *The Mad Doctor of Market Street* (with Lionel Atwill), *The Falcon in San Francisco, My Name is Julia Ross, So Dark the Night, Terror in a Texas Town* and his *noir* gems *Gun Crazy* (1949) and *The Big Combo*. In the late 1950s he moved to television, where he worked until his retirement.

Yasuyoshi Tokuma, president of Japanese film company Daiei, died in Tokyo on September 20th, aged 78. Amongst the films he produced were *Gamera Super Monster, Gamera 3: Revenge of Iris* and the animated *Princess Mononoke*.

British film producer **Antony Darnborough** died on September 24th, aged 86. During the late 1940s and early '50s he produced three episodic films based on stories by Somerset Maugham, and with Terence Fisher he co-directed *The Astonished Heart* and *So Long At the Fair*.

Polish film director **Wojciech Has** died of complications from diabetes following intestinal surgery on October 3rd, aged 75. His films include the fantastical *The Saragossa Manuscript* (1964), based on the 1813 novel by Count Jan Potocki.

Mexican-born set decorator **Emile Kuri**, who won his second Academy Award plaque for Disney's *20000 Leagues Under the Sea* (1954), died on October 10th, aged 93. His other film credits include *Topper* (1937), *It's a Wonderful Life*, Hitchcock's *Spellbound* and *Rope*, *War of the Worlds*, *The Absent-Minded Professor*, *Mary Poppins* and *Bedknobs and Broomsticks*. He was also among the major "imagineers" who created Disneyland and Walt Disney World.

UK independent film distributor **Stanley Hart**, who worked with Antony Balch, Russ Meyer etc., died of kidney failure the same day, aged 70.

Film editor and director **Sam O'Steen** died of a heart attack on October 11th, aged 76. He edited such movies as *Rosemary's Baby*, *The Day of the Dolphin*, *Amytiville II: The Possession* and *Wolf*, and directed the 1976 TV film *Look What's Happened to Rosemary's Baby*.

American animator **William T. Hurtz** died on October 14th, aged 81. Dismissed by Disney after proposing the 1941 animators strike, which lasted several months, Hurtz was one of the founders of UPA, where he directed *A Unicorn in the Garden* (1953), based on a story by James Thurber. After directing such Saul Bass-designed title sequences as *Around the World in 80 Days* (1956) and *Psycho* (1960), Hurtz joined Jay Ward Productions, where he supervised the TV series *Rocky and His Friends* (1959) and *George of the Jungle* (1967). In 1992 he co-directed the feature cartoon *Little Nemo Adventures in Slumberland*, conceived for the screen by Ray Bradbury and based on Winsor McCay's comic strip.

American-born **Walter Shenson**, the producer of the Beatles films *A Hard Day's Night* and *Help!* died of complications from a stroke after a long illness on October 17th, aged 81. His other credits include *Inner Sanctum* (1948), *The Mouse That Roared*, *The Mouse on the Moon* and *Digby the Biggest Dog in the World*.

American B-movie director and former child stage star **Sidney**

Salkow died on October 18th, aged 89. Born to Hungarian parents in New York, his numerous credits include *The Lone Wolf Strikes*, *Bulldog Drummond at Bay*, *Sword of the Avenger*, and *Twice Told Tales* and *The Last Man on Earth* (both with Vincent Price).

Film and television producer **Mort Briskin**, whose credits include *You'll Like My Mother*, *Willard* and its sequel *Ben*, died on October 21st, aged 87.

Broadway director **Mary Hunter Wolf**, whose credits include *Peter Pan* with Mary Martin, died on November 3rd, aged 95.

37-year-old German film producer and distributor **Werner Koenig** was killed in an avalanche while scouting locations in Switzerland on November 12th. He produced the animated sequel *Heavy Metal 2000*.

Douglas Benton, who produced such TV shows as Boris Karloff's *Thriller* and *The Girl from U.N.C.L.E.*, plus the 1971 TV movie *A Howling in the Woods*, died of cancer on November 16th, aged 75.

American-born director **Bernard Vorhaus**, whose films include *The Ghost Camera* (1933) and *The Spiritualist* (aka *The Amazing Mr. X*), died in London on November 23rd, aged 95. Named as a communist by directors Edward Dmytryk and Frank Tuttle during the House of UnAmerican Activities Committee witch-hunts, he moved to Britain with his Welsh-born wife in the early 1950s and eventually became a British citizen.

BBC-TV's first film-buyer, **Gordon Smith** (Gordon Sidery-Smith), died on November 26th, aged 88. Along with Leslie Halliwell at ITV, he was instrumental in beating the film indus-try's ban on showing feature films on British television in the late 1950s and early '60s.

Canadian producer/director **Julian Roffman** also died in No-vember, aged 84. He directed the 1961 3-D movie *The Mask* (aka *Eyes of Hell*) and produced *Spy in Your Eye*, *The Pyx* and *The Glove* (which he also scripted).

Japanese film director **Jun Fukuda** died of cancer in Tokyo on December 3rd, aged 76. Born in occupied Korea, his many films include *Secret of the Telegian*, *Ebirah Horror of the Deep*, *Son of Godzilla*, *Godzilla vs. Gigan* (aka *War of the Monsters/Godzilla on Monster Island*), *Godzilla vs. Megalon* and *Godzilla vs. The Bionic Monster* (aka *Godzilla vs. The Cosmic Monster*).

Barney McNulty, who invented the cue card while working as an usher at CBS-TV in 1949 for *The Ed Wynn Show,* died on December 18th, aged 77. McNulty went on to become Hollywood's best-known cue card man, providing lines for Fred Astaire, Lucille Ball, Milton Berle, George Burns, Jimmy Durante, Bob Hope, Groucho Marx, Frank Sinatra, John Wayne and Orson Welles, amongst many others.

USEFUL ADDRESSES

T HE FOLLOWING LISTING OF ORGANIZATIONS, publications, dealers and individuals is designed to present readers with further avenues to explore. Although I can personally recommend all those listed on the following pages, neither myself nor the publisher can take any responsibility for the services they offer. Please also note that all the information below is subject to change without notice.

ORGANIZATIONS

The British Fantasy Society <www.britishfantasysociety.com> began in 1971 and publishes the bi-monthly *Prism UK: The British Fantasy Newsletter*, produces other special booklets, and organizes the annual British FantasyCon and semi-regular meetings in London. Yearly membership is £25.00 (UK), £30.00 (Europe) and £35.00 (USA and the rest of the world) made payable in sterling to "The British Fantasy Society" and sent to The BFS Secretary, c/o 201 Reddish Road, South Reddish, Stockport SK5 7HR, UK. E-mail: <syrinx.2112@btinternet.com>.

Horror Writers Association <www.horror.org/> was formed in the 1980s and is open to anyone seeking Active, Affiliate or Associate membership. The HWA publishes a regular *Newsletter* and organizes the annual Bram Stoker Awards ceremony. Standard membership is $55.00 (USA), £45.00/ $65.00 (overseas); Corporate membership is $100.00 (USA), £74.00/$120.00 (overseas), and Family Membership is $75.00 (USA), £52.00/$85.00 (overseas). Send to "HWA", PO Box 50577 Palo Alto, CA 94303, USA. If paying by sterling cheque send to "HWA", c/o 24 Pearl Road, London E17 4QZ, UK.

World Fantasy Convention <www.worldfantasy.org/> is an annual convention held in a different (usually American) city each year.

MAGAZINES

Now published by Celeste C. Clarke and edited by Dan Persons, **Cinefantastique** <http://www.cfq.com> is a bi-monthly SF/fantasy/horror movie magazine with a "Sense of Wonder". Cover price is $5.95/Cdn$9.50/£4.30 and a 12-issue subscription is $48.00 (USA) or $55.00 (Canada and overseas) to PO Box 270, Oak Park, IL 60303, USA. E-mail: <mail@cfq.com>.

Interzone is Britain's leading magazine of science fiction and fantasy. Single copies are available for £3.50 (UK) or £4.00/$6.00 (overseas) or a 12-issue subscription is £34.00 (UK), $60.00 (USA) or £40.00 (overseas) payable by cheque or International Money Order. Payments can also be made by MasterCard, Visa or Eurocard to "Interzone", 217 Preston Drove, Brighton, BN1 6FL, UK.

Locus <www.Locusmag.com> is the monthly newspaper of the SF/fantasy/horror field. $4.95 a copy, a 12-issue subscription is $46.00 (USA), $52.00 (Canada), $85.00 (International Air Mail) to "Locus Publications", PO Box 13305, Oakland, CA 94661, USA. Dollar or Stirling cheques only can be sent to Fantast (Medway) Ltd, PO Box 23, Upwell Wisbech, Cambs PE14 9BU, UK. E-mail: <Locus@Locusmag.com>.

The Magazine of Fantasy & Science Fiction <www.fsfmag.com> has been publishing some of the best imaginative fiction for more than fifty years, now under the capable editorship of new owner Gordon Van Gelder. Single copies are $3.50 (US) or $3.95 (Canada) and an annual subscription (which includes the double October/November anniversary issue) is $29.97 (US) and $39.97 (rest of the world). US cheques or credit card information to "Fantasy & Science Fiction", PO Box 3447, Hoboken, NJ 07030, USA, or subscribe online.

Science Fiction Chronicle <www.dnapublications.com> is a monthly newsmagazine that covers the SF/fantasy/horror field with news, interviews, columns, markets, letters, calendar and extensive reviews. A one-year subscription is $45.00 (USA), $56.00 (Canada) and $125.00 (rest of the world, airmail). Make cheques payable to "DNA Publications" and send to PO Box 2988, Radford, VA 24143-2988, USA. E-mail: Warren Lapine, publisher <WarrenLapine@dnapublications.com>. News editor: Andrew I. Porter, <sfchronicle@dnapublications.com>. British correspondent: Paul Kincaid, <paul@appomattox.demon.co.uk>.

Shivers <www.visimag.com/shivers> is a monthly magazine of horror entertainment. Cover price is £3.25 (UK), $5.99 (USA), Cdn$7.95 (Canada). Yearly subscriptions comprise 12 issues at £36.00 (UK), $68.00 (USA), £46.00 (Europe airmail and rest of the world surface) or £50.00 (rest of the world airmail) to "Visual Imagination Limited", Shivers Subscription, PO Box 371, London SW14 8JL, UK, or PMB#469, PO Box 6061, Sherman Oaks, CA 91413, USA. E-mail: <mailorder@visimag.com>.

The Third Alternative <www.tta-press.freewire.co.uk> is a quarterly magazine of new horror fiction, interviews, artwork, articles and reviews. Cover price is £3.75/$7.00, and a six-issue subscription is £18.00 (UK), £21.00 (Europe), $28.00 (USA) or £24.00 (rest of the world) to "TTA Press", 5 Martins Lane, Witcham, Ely, Cambs CB6 2LB, UK. US orders can be sent to "TTA Press", PO Box 219, Olyphant, PA 18447, USA. You can also subscribe by credit card via the secure website. E-mail: <ttapress@aol.com>.

Video Watchdog <www.cinemaweb.com/videowd> is a monthly magazine described as "the Perfectionist's Guide to Fantastic Video". $6.50 a copy, an annual 12-issue subscription is $48.00 bulk/$70.00 first class (USA), $66.00 surface/$88.00 airmail (overseas). US funds only or VISA/MasterCard to "Video Watchdog", PO Box 5283, Cincinnati, OH 45205-0283, USA. E-mail: <Videowd@aol.com>.

BOOK DEALERS

Cold Tonnage Books offers excellent mail order new and used SF/fantasy/horror, art, reference, limited editions etc. with regular catalogues. Write to Andy & Angela Richards, Cold Tonnage Books, 22 Kings Lane, Windlesham, Surrey GU20 6JQ, UK.

Credit cards accepted. Tel: +44 (0)1276-475388. E-mail: <andy@coldtonnage.demon.co.uk>.

Ken Cowley offers mostly used SF/fantasy/horror/crime/ supernatural, collectibles, pulps, videos etc. by mail order with 2–3 catalogues per year. Write to Trinity Cottage, 153 Old Church Road, Clevedon, North Somerset, BS21 7TU, UK. Tel: +44 (0)1275-872247. E-mail: <kencowley@excite.co.uk>.

Richard Dalby issues semi-regular mail order lists of used ghost and supernatural volumes at very reasonable prices. Write to 4 Westbourne Park, Scarborough, North Yorkshire YO12 4AT, UK. Tel: +44 (0)1723 377049.

Dark Delicacies <www.darkdel.com> is a friendly Burbank, California, store specialising in horror books, vampire merchandize and signings. They also do mail order and run money-saving book club and membership discount deals. 4213 West Burbank Blvd., Burbank, CA 91505, USA. Tel: (818) 556-6660. Credit cards accepted. E-mail: <darkdel@darkdel.com>.

DreamHaven Books & Comics <www.dreamhavenbooks.com> store and mail order offers new and used SF/fantasy/ horror/art and illustrated etc. with regular catalogues. Write to 912 West Lake Street, Minneapolis, MN 55408, USA. Credit cards accepted. Tel: (612) 823-6070. E-mail: <dream@dreamhavenbooks.com>.

Fantastic Literature <www.fantasticliterature.com> mail order offers new and used SF/fantasy/horror etc. with regular catalogues. Write to Simon and Laraine Gosden, Fantastic Literature, 35 The Ramparts, Rayleigh, Essex SS6 8PY, UK. Credit cards accepted. Tel: +44 (0)1268-747564. E-mail: <sgosden@netcomuk.co.uk>.

Fantasy Centre <www.fantasycentre.demon.co.uk> shop and mail order has mostly used SF/fantasy/horror, art, reference, pulps etc. at reasonable prices with regular bi-monthly catalogues. Write to 157 Holloway Road, London N7 8LX, UK. Credit cards accepted. Tel/Fax: +44 (0)20-7607 9433. E-mail: <books@fantasycentre.demon.co.uk>.

House of Monsters <www.visionvortex/houseofmonsters> is a small treasure-trove of a store only open at weekends from noon that specializes in horror movie memorabilia, toys, posters, videos, books and magazines. 1579 N. Milwaukee Avenue, Gallery 218, Chicago, IL 60614, USA. Credit cards accepted. Tel: (773) 292-0980. E-mail: <Homonsters@aol.com>.

Mythos Books <www.abebooks.com/home/mythosbooks/> mail order presents books and curiosities for the Lovecraftian scholar and collectors of horror, weird and supernatural fiction with regular e-mail updates. Write to 351 Lake Ridge Road, Poplar Bluff, MO 63901-2160, USA. Credit cards accepted. Tel/Fax: (573) 785-7710. E-mail: <dwynn@LDD.net>.

Porcupine Books offers extensive mail order lists of used fantasy/horror/SF titles via e-mail <brian@porcupine.demon.co.uk> or write to 37 Coventry Road, Ilford, Essex IG1 4QR, UK. Tel: +44 (0)20 8554-3799.

Bob and Julie Wardzinski's **The Talking Dead** offers reasonably priced paperbacks, pulps and hardcovers, with catalogues issued regularly. They accept wants lists and are also the exclusive supplier of back issues of *Interzone*. Credit cards accepted. Contact them at 12 Rosamund Avenue, Merley, Wimborne, Dorset BH21 1TE, UK. Tel: +44 (0)1202 849212. E-mail: <talking.dead@tesco.net>.

Kirk Ruebotham <www.abebooks.com/home/kirk61/> sells out of print and used horror/SF/fantasy/crime and related non-fiction, with regular catalogues. Write to 16 Beaconsfield Road, Runcorn, Cheshire WA7 4BX, UK. Tel: +44 (0)1928 560540 (10:00a.m.-8:00p.m.). E-mail: <kirk@ruebotham.freeserve.co.uk>.

Weinberg Books at The Stars Our Destination <www.sfbooks.com> is a monthly mail order service from the friendly Chicago bookstore offering the latest horror, fantasy, science fiction and art books with regular catalogues featuring cover illustrations by Randy Broecker. Visit them at 705 Main Street, Evanston, IL 60202, USA. Credit cards accepted. Tel: (847) 570-5919. Fax: (847) 570-5927. E-mail: <stars@sfbooks.com> or <weinberg@sfbooks.com>.

MARKET INFORMATION AND NEWS

The Fix <tta-press.freewire.co.uk> features in-depth reviews of all SF/fantasy/horror magazines publishing short fiction; interviews with editors, publishers and writers; stories; news and comment columns; artwork and much more. Six-issue subscriptions are £12.00 (UK), £15.00 (Europe), $24.00 (USA/Canada) and £18.00 (rest of the world). Payable to "TTA Press", 5 Martins Lane, Witcham, Ely, Cambs CB6 2LB, UK.

US orders can be sent to "TTA Press", PO Box 219, Olyphant, PA 18447, USA. E-mail: <ttapress@aol.com>. Try before you buy: to sign up for the free e-Fix e-mail Trevor Mendham on <trevor@fnapf.demon.co.uk>.

The Gila Queen's Guide to Markets <www.gilaqueen.com> is a regular publication detailing markets for SF/fantasy/horror plus other genres, along with publishing news, contests, dead markets, anthologies, updates, etc. A sample copy is $6.00 and subscriptions are $45.00 (USA), $49.00 (Canada) and $60.00 (overseas). Back issues are also available. Cheques or money orders should be in US funds only and sent to "The Gila Queen's Guide to Markets", PO Box 97, Newton, NJ 07860-0097, USA. E-mail: <GilaQueen@worldnet.att.net>. In the UK *The Gila Queen* is distributed by: BBB Distribution <www.bbr-online.com>. Contact Chris Reed, PO Box 625, Sheffield, S1 3GY UK. E-mail: <c.s.reed@bbr-online.com>.

Hellnotes <www.hellnotes.com> is described as "Your Insider's Guide to the Horror Field". This weekly Newsletter is available in an e-mail edition for $21.00 per year or hardcopy subscriptions are available for $50 per year. To subscribe by credit card, go to: <www.hellnotes.com/subscrib.htm>. To subscribe by mail, send US cheques or money order to: "Hellnotes", 27780 Donkey Mine Road, Oak Run, CA 96069, USA. Tel/Fax: (916) 472-1050. E-mail: <dbsilva@hellnotes.com> or <pfolson@bresnanlink.net>. The Hellnotes Bookstore can be found at <www.hellnotes.com/book_store>.

Brian Keene's **Jobs in Hell!** is a weekly Internet guide to horror markets for professional horror writers and artists. A one-year, 52-issue subscription costs $20.00. E-mail: <jobsinhell@hotmail.com> for a complimentary issue.

Scavenger's Newsletter <www.jlgiftsshop.com/scav/index.html> is a monthly newsletter for SF/fantasy/horror writers with an interest in the small press. News of markets, along with articles, letters and reviews. A sample copy is $2.50 (USA/Canada) and $3.00 (overseas). An annual subscription is $24.00 by first class mail (USA), $23.00 (Canada) and $29.00 (overseas). *Scavenger's Scrapbook* is a twice yearly round-up, available for $5.00 (USA/Canada) and $6.00 (overseas). A year's subscription to the *Scrapbook* is $9.00 (USA/Canada) and $11.00 (overseas), payable to "Janet Fox" and send to 833 Main, Osage City, KS 66523-1241, USA. Canadian/foreign orders sent to the US address should be in a bank draft on a US bank in US funds. E-mail: <foxscav1@jc.net>. In the UK contact Chris Reed, BBR Distribution, PO Box 625, Sheffield S1 3GY, UK. <www.bbr-online.com>. E-mail: <c.s.reed@bbr-online.com>.